TELLING
STORIES

An Anthology for Writers

TELLING STORIES

An Anthology for Writers

edited and with introductions by
Joyce Carol Oates

W. W. NORTON & COMPANY • NEW YORK • LONDON

Since this page cannot legibly accommodate all of the copyright notices, pp. 723–29
constitute an extension of the copyright page.

The text of this book is composed in Perpetua
with the display set in Nofret Medium
Composition by ComCom
Manufacturing by Haddon Craftsmen
Book design by Joanne Metsch
Cover illustration: Grant Wood, American (1892–1942). *Death on the Ridge Road,*
1935. Oil on masonite, frame height 39 in., frame width 46¹⁄₁₆ in. Williams College
Museum of Art, Gift of Cole Porter, 47.1.3. © 1998 Estate of Grant Wood/Licensed
by VAGA, New York, NY.
Author photo: © Mary Cross.

Library of Congress Cataloging-in-Publication Data
Telling stories: an anthology for writers/edited and with
    introductions by Joyce Carol Oates.
        p.   cm.
    Includes index.

    ISBN 978-0-393-97176-7

    1. College readers.   2. English language–Rhetoric.   3. Narration
(Rhetoric)   4. Creative writing.   I. Oates, Joyce Carol, 1938–   .
PE1417.T44   1997
808'.0427—dc21   97–22548

W. W. Norton & Company, Inc., 500 Fifth Avenue, New York, N.Y. 10110
http://www.wwnorton.com

W. W. Norton & Company Ltd., Castle House, 75/76 Wells Street, London W1T 3QT

13 14 15 16 17 18 19

*This book is for the many wonderful writing students
with whom I've worked over the years at
the University of Windsor and at Princeton University;
and with special thanks to my inspired,
and inspiring, editor, Peter Simon.*

Contents

Why We Write,
Why We Read

**Art is not something you can take or leave, it is a necessity
of life.**

—Oscar Wilde

What is "art" but the effort of giving permanent form—in language, in painting, sculpture, music—to those elemental forces in our lives, those passions, hurts, triumphs, and mysteries that have no permanence otherwise, and so require art to be known at all? Our lives, especially at their happiest moments, fly past as quickly as a mountain stream rushing along its rocky course, throwing up frothy, sparkling spray; the effort of art is to slow the rapid motion, to bring it to a halt so that it can be *seen, known*. All artists know either consciously or instinctively that the secret intention of their life's work is to rescue from the plunge of time something of beauty, permanence, significance in another's eyes.

I have a story to tell. Help me tell my story!

Suddenly there began arriving in the mail, a few months ago, lengthy, handwritten, emotional letters from a former high school classmate of mine whom I hadn't seen in many years. He'd become a successful surgeon, having attended an Ivy League university and medical school after graduating from our high school; he had a large family, owned extensive property in New England. Yet how yearning, how rapturous his letters, filled with reminiscence for our high school years in Williamsville, New York, a suburb of gritty Buffalo. At Williamsville High School, he'd been an excellent student in English and history, as well as science and math; he'd published fiction in our student magazine, wanted to be a writer, and would have become a writer if his undergraduate professors hadn't discouraged him, suggesting he was better qualified to be a doctor. So he entered medical school instead, where he excelled, and entirely gave up writing and even reading the literary works he'd always loved; and twenty years passed, and more; and suddenly, out of a growing dissatisfaction with his own success, he was swept by the desire to return again imaginatively to his adolescence, to a time when he hadn't yet made his decision to reject a writing life. I was puzzled and touched by this man's letters, so passionately handwritten on his medical center stationery; I tried to match them with the boy I'd known years ago, but could not. We hadn't been so close in high school as he seemed now to be remembering, though we'd shared a strong interest in writing and were founding members of a student literary society quaintly called Quill and Scroll. Through the years of adulthood, of professional success, my ex-classmate's love of writing and storytelling had lain dormant in him, unexercised; now it came sweeping forth, and seemed to be transforming his emotional life. Over the months he sent me, along with his handwritten letters, which were marvels of lyricism and sharp, witty analyses of our high school past, many photocopied pages from our yearbook, heavily annotated. His intention was to stimulate me to write "the Great American Novel" of our high school years: he would supply all the information I needed, I would do the writing.

A romantic prospect, unfortunately unlikely.

Such letters suggest how powerful the instinct is to tell a story, to have one's story told, to be somehow transformed by the story of one's life told by another, and published, and read; how deep the yearning is to interpret one's life as, not mainly accident, as most lives are, but as a coherent narrative, with a supporting cast, set in a real, vividly recalled time and place. This instinct to memorialize is at the heart of writing, and the complex of bittersweet sensations we call homesickness is the predominant emotion.

To be yearning for—what? Something impossible to name? Not exactly the rooms of our first, childhood houses, nor the backyards, streets and alleys and landscapes of childhood, our long-ago parents, our long-ago relatives, friends, classmates, our long-ago pets; but rather the emotion these memories stimulate, which can be as powerful, as devastating, and as mysterious as romantic love, which it closely resembles. Even a young writer, who in theory hasn't as much to remember as my middle-aged ex-classmate, will find that his or her most compelling work is probably memory-based; the writing with which others identify most readily is usually stimulated by something "real" and its ideal mode of expression is first-person narration: "I."

Since I'd begun writing in my twenties I've received letters like those from my ex-classmate, though never before any quite so engaging and richly detailed. Most of the letters I receive are from complete strangers, and many of these make the plea *I have a story to tell, help me tell my story!* To amplify their requests these strangers send me news clippings, photocopies of legal documents and of private papers, snapshots, old diaries; one astonishing "gift" was a massive, not very legible journal kept by someone's grandmother in the early decades of the century. *This is a fantastic story, it will make a fantastic novel.*

Why we write, and why we read; why we so need "stories"—it's a mystery. A young man with a hope of becoming famous, well-to-do, talked-of, envied in his small Mississippi town, a young man of not much perceptible talent, and comical egocentricity—who can explain how William Faulkner began to write, in his late twenties, prose works of surpassing beauty, power, and genius? Another young man with outsized ambitions, aggressively egocentric, exploitative of both women and men, crude in his behavior and in his letters, and, at the outset of his career, a frankly derivative writer—how did Ernest Hemingway discipline himself to write, in his early twenties, prose works that would in time redefine American literature? It is as if seemingly callow motives, of seemingly callow men, are only the surface reasons for writing; other, deeper reasons compel the work, of which the writer himself may not be conscious. These writers are like those who claim their only motive for effort is money but who become yet more demanding of themselves with time, more compulsively perfectionist and competitive, as they have accumulated millions of dollars. "Trust the writing, not the writer," D. H. Lawrence has said, for the writer as an individual is likely to be a bloody liar; or, in any case, not to know the simplest truth about his or her deepest self—a truth any attentive reader might easily discern from reading the work.

For the writer, reading is part of the process of writing. Even before we know we will be writers, our reading is a part of our preparation for writing. Conversely, our writing might be defined as the preparation for our reading of that writing unique to ourselves—the writing no one else except us can do. Every book, every story, every sentence we read is a part of our preparation for our own writing, so it's wise to choose our reading carefully, as an athlete trains carefully, as a musician practices at his or her instrument for hours and for years in pursuit of excellence, of fully realizing a talent. The love of storytelling—to hear stories, and to tell them—is universal in our species. Those with an apparent talent for writing, which is to say a talent for using language as painters use paint, as musicians use their instruments, are not of a special breed but simply mirror the common human desire. If like my former high school classmate you have a natural talent for writing, and a love of the imagination, you risk a lifelong deprivation if you fail to cultivate it as vigorously as you can. Write your own "great American novel," I advised my ex-classmate; you're talented, you're intelligent, you have the driving passion, and you know as much as anyone about American life. Your story belongs uniquely to you.

There are art works that bide their time in us, which we don't fully understand, or perhaps we misunderstand, at the time we first encounter them. The
reason is that they provide answers to questions we don't yet know to ask.
We aren't yet old enough, or subtle enough, or deep enough. To reencounter
such work, years later, is to reencounter a supposition grown into a truth.
"For the question often arrives," as Oscar Wilde has said, "a terribly long time
after the answer."

The book of my early childhood I most loved was Lewis Carroll's *Alice
in Wonderland* and *Through the Looking-Glass,* which I read, reread, and partly
memorized when I was eight years old. I identified both with the wondrously
resilient, inquisitive, and courageous Alice and with the effort, mysterious to
a child, of making a "book"—a small portable object with pages, many of them
illustrated, and with illustrated covers. How children love to imitate! For what
is imitation but the sincerest form of love? Soon I was making my own "books"
out of tablet paper with construction paper covers; my miniature novels were
earnestly handwritten and illustrated, and seem to have been about, as my parents recall, talking cats and chickens. (We lived on a small farm in upstate New
York.) All children invent stories; all children love stories; children's self-
evolved stories are invariably fantasies of invisible playmates, some of them
animals; children can spin out of their imaginations, like the fairy-tale miller's
daughter spinning gold out of mere straw, remarkable creations, of a fanciful
beauty and significance startling in the very young. So in our deepest selves
writers are still children; the child-self is a sort of flame that continues to burn
throughout our lives, to which the writer or artist is by nature more attentive than other adults. We look to stories, our own and others', as we look
into mirrors: that which is locked inside of us can be released by the magic
of another's art, or maybe our own. This is the continual revelation of art,
and accounts for our enormous hunger for it.

Telling Stories represents to me a highly personal gathering of stories and
prose pieces; yet it isn't a private gathering, for most of the writers included
here are of unquestioned merit, and all have written exemplary works. Many
of these have been presented in my writing workshops at Princeton University, where I've taught since 1978. Students have been stimulated to write,
and to write well, by models of prose as divergent as Williams's minimalist
masterpiece "The Use of Force" and John Updike's domestic, conversational
"Friends from Philadelphia"; they've been excited by the formal possibilities
of very short stories, "miniature narratives" like those by Katherine Mansfield,
William Carlos Williams, Italo Calvino, and American contemporaries like
Stuart Dybek and Elizabeth Tallent; they've been encouraged to practice
"creative revision" by studying the texts of James Joyce's early story "The Sis-

ters"; they've been encouraged to write dramatic monologue/performance pieces; they've discovered the possibilities for the dramatic employment of "ordinary" life experiences by reading William Heyen's "Any Sport," Gish Jen's "In the American Society," Grace Paley's "Anxiety," Gary Soto's poems, and others; they've been challenged by the possibilities of reimagining classic tales and of reshaping "genre" for their own purposes and by discovering, in forms of prose like the journal/diary, the germ of narrative.

Within each section, arrangement is generally chronologically by authors' birthdates rather than the publication dates of work; in the final section, composed predominantly of our American contemporaries, arrangement is less strictly chronological and more thematic, with like-minded stories grouped together. Anthologies, too, tell stories; the underlying story of *Telling Stories* may be the development and expansion of the art of storytelling itself, from its roots in a firmly Anglo-Saxon mode of psychological realism to one of spirited diversity and inventiveness in which "genre" itself becomes fluid, no longer confining but liberating.

—*Joyce Carol Oates*

MINIATURE NARRATIVES

MINIATURE
NARRATIVES

Not that the story need be long, but it will take a long
while to make it short.

—*Henry David Thoreau*

"Miniature" narratives come first for obvious reasons: like the dramatic monologue (to follow), they present beginning writers with a form far more accessible and navigable than the traditional story of greater length and complexity. In fact, it is not advised that beginning writers attempt to write
conventionally structured stories with "characters," "dialogue," "exposition,"
"description," and other elements of a fully realized narrative until they have
experimented with the shorter form.

A "miniature narrative" is, of course, a very short story: a radical distil-
lation of a story that might in different circumstances have been considerably
expanded. These dramatically tight, spare, yet subtle and often poetically
evocative narratives are brilliantly composed; they are like the ideal lyric
poem, in Robert Frost's definition, that rides on its own momentum "like ice
melting on a hot stove."

The miniature form allows the writer immense freedom. A story can
be as short as a single paragraph, a single sentence; it can encompass
decades, or transcribe mere moments. Most obviously, a miniature narrative can be written, rewritten, and again rewritten in variants that allow
the writer to choose among them. Fairy tales are miniature narratives that
typically begin *Once upon a time* and swiftly, sometimes bluntly summarize
entire lives within a few paragraphs; the Hebrew Bible and the New Testament are composed of such miniature narratives, including miniature epics.
In such traditional works, "characterization" as we know it scarcely exists;

3

there is little dialogue, and a tale's significance is likely to be moral and historic. There are persons, but no personalities.

Consider the remarkable fluidity of the vernacular voice in William Carlos Williams's classic "The Use of Force"—a story as much admired for its poetically dramatic structure as for its disturbing insight into the nature of adult, authoritarian "force." Katherine Mansfield's "The Wind Blows" (set in New Zealand in the early 1900s) and Nadine Gordimer's "Is There Nowhere Else Where We Can Meet?" (set in South Africa in the 1960s, well before the dismantling of apartheid) are stories of a traditional structure, yet so quickly realized in terms of setting, action, and character that they pass by as convincing as dazzling landscapes seen from the window of a speeding vehicle. Traditional, too, in conception but cinematically concise and mysterious in what they leave out, which the reader must infer, are Alberto Moravia's "The House of the Crime" and Elizabeth Tallent's "No One's a Mystery"; Anton Chekhov's "The Student" is a quintessentially Chekhovian tale of the power of an individual to profoundly affect another and in so doing affect himself: "The past is linked to the present by an unbroken chain of happenings, each flowing from the other." The force of this insight is made the more compelling to the reader because the story is so short; very little time elapses between its outset and its denouement. In a longer story, the dramatic effect would be less demonstrable.

Since, in a miniature narrative, there is no time for the development of character, we are free of psychological detail, historic and cultural background, exposition—the tissue that comprises most of the substance of longer works of fiction. A story like Tadeusz Borowski's ironic and horrifying "The Supper" is a miniature only in the sense that it is short; to be understood, it requires on the reader's part a sense of European history in the first half of the twentieth century. Yet, because we know virtually nothing of the characters, we are able to identify with them in ways often not possible in longer fiction.

The miniature narrative is often most effective when boundaries between "real" and "surreal" are dissolved. A story is told that convinces us with its evocation of strong, seemingly intimate emotion, as in Bruno Schulz's "Father's Last Escape" (the final chapter of the dreamlike *Sanatorium under the Sign of the Hourglass*) and in Jean Rhys's "I Used to Live Here Once." Even more radically distilled as narratives are the surreal prose pieces by Franz Kafka, Peter Carey, Alan Lightman, Italo Calvino, Lydia Davis, and Stuart Dybek, which select aspects of narrative to emphasize; those by Daniel Halpern, James Wright, James Tate, Ron Padgett, and Phyllis Koestenbaum can be defined as "prose poems"—of all genres the most ambiguous. In such tightly wrought, dramatically compact works of prose, often generated by a single dominant image, each word is valuable as a gold coin.

One way of approaching the miniature narrative is to read it backward, for the final line is everything. And one helpful way of composing the miniature narrative is to write the final line first, and see how swiftly and gracefully one can move to it.

Anton Chekhov

THE STUDENT

The weather was fine and calm at first. Thrushes were singing, and in the nearby swamps some creature droned piteously as if blowing into an empty bottle. A woodcock flew over and a shot reverberated merrily in the spring air. But when darkness fell on the wood an unwelcome, piercing cold wind blew up from the east and everything grew silent. Ice needles formed on the puddles and the wood seemed inhospitable, abandoned, empty. It smelt of winter.

Ivan Velikopolsky, a student at a theological college and a sexton's son, was returning home along the path through the water meadow after a day's shooting. His fingers were numb, his face burned in the wind. This sudden onset of cold seemed to have destroyed the order and harmony of things, striking dread into Nature herself and causing the shades of night to thicken faster than was needful. Everything was so abandoned, so very gloomy, somehow. Only in the widows' allotments near the river did a light gleam. But far around, where the village stood about three miles away, everything drowned in the dense evening mist. The student remembered that, when he had left the house, his mother had been sitting barefoot on the lobby floor cleaning the samovar, while his father lay coughing on the stove. There was no cooking at home because today was Good Friday, and he felt famished. Cringing in the cold, he reflected that just such a wind had blown in the days of Ryurik, Ivan the Terrible, and Peter the Great. Their times had known just such ferocious poverty and hunger. There had been the same thatched roofs with the holes in them, the same ignorance and misery, the same desolation on all sides, the same gloom and sense of oppression. All these horrors had been, still were, and would continue to be, and the passing of another thousand years would make things no better. He did not feel like going home.

The allotments were called widows' because they were kept by two widows, a mother and daughter. A bonfire was burning briskly—crackling, lighting up the plow-land far around. Widow Vasilisa, a tall, plump old woman in a man's fur jacket, stood gazing pensively at the fire. Her short, pock-marked, stupid-looking daughter Lukerya sat on the ground washing a cooking pot and some spoons. They had just had supper, obviously. Men's voices were heard, some local laborers watering their horses by the river.

"So winter's come back," said the student, approaching the fire. "Good evening."

Vasilisa shuddered, but then saw who it was and smiled a welcome.

"Goodness me, I didn't recognize you," she said. "That means you'll be rich one day."

They talked. Vasilisa, a woman of some experience—having been wet nurse to gentlefolk and then a nanny—spoke delicately, always smiling a gentle, dignified smile. But her daughter Lukerya, a peasant whose husband had beaten her, only screwed up her eyes at the student, saying nothing and wearing an odd look as if she was deaf and dumb.

"On a cold night like this the Apostle Peter warmed himself by a fire." The student held out his hands toward the flames. "So it must have been cold then. What a frightening night that was, Granny, what a very sorrowful, what a very long night."

He looked at the darkness around and abruptly jerked his head. "Were you in church yesterday for the Twelve Gospel Readings?"

"Yes," Vasilisa answered.

"At the Last Supper, you'll remember, Peter said to Jesus, 'Lord, I am ready to go with Thee, both into prison, and to death.' And the Lord said, 'I say unto thee, Peter, before the cock crow twice, thou shalt deny me thrice.' After supper Jesus prayed in mortal agony in the garden, while poor Peter was weary in spirit, and enfeebled. His eyes were heavy, he couldn't fight off sleep, and he slept. Then, as you have heard, Judas that night kissed Jesus and betrayed Him to the torturers. They bound Him, they took Him to the high priest, they smote Him, while Peter—worn, tormented, anguished, perturbed, you understand, not having slept properly, foreseeing some fearful happening on this earth—went after them. He loved Jesus passionately, to distraction, and now, afar, he saw Him being buffeted."

Lukerya put down the spoons and stared at the student.

"They went to the high priest," he continued. "They put Jesus to the question, and meanwhile the workmen had kindled a fire in the midst of the hall, as it was cold, and were warming themselves. Peter stood with them near the fire—also warming himself, as I am now. A certain maid beheld him, and said, 'This man was also with Jesus.' In other words she was saying that he, too, should be taken for questioning. All the workmen round the fire must have looked at him suspiciously and sternly because he was confused and said, 'I know him not.' A little later someone recognized him as one of Jesus' disciples and said, 'Thou also wast with him.' But he denied it again. And for the third time someone addressed him. 'Did I not see thee in the garden with Him this day?' He denied Him for the third time. And after that the cock straightway crowed, and Peter, looking at Jesus from afar, remembered the words which He had said to him at supper. He remembered, his eyes were opened, and he went out of the hall and shed bitter tears. The Gospel says, 'And he went out, and wept bitterly.' I can imagine it was a very quiet, very dark garden and his hollow sobs could hardly be heard in the silence."

The student sighed, plunged deep in thought. Still smiling, Vasilisa suddenly sobbed and tears, large and profuse, flowed down her cheeks. She shielded her face from the fire with her sleeve as if ashamed of the tears, while Lukerya, staring at the student, blushed, and her expression became distressed and tense as if she was holding back a terrible pain.

The workmen returned from the river. One of them, on horseback, was already near, and the light from the fire quivered on him. The student said good night to the widows and moved on. Again darkness came upon him, and his hands began to freeze. A cruel wind blew, it was real winter weather again, and it did not seem as if Easter Sunday could be only the day after tomorrow.

The student thought of Vasilisa. Her weeping meant that all that had happened to Peter on that terrible night had a particular meaning for her.

He looked back. The lonely fire quietly flickered in the darkness, no one could be seen near it. Again the student reflected that, if Vasilisa had wept and her daughter had been moved, then obviously what he had just told them about happenings nineteen centuries ago—it had a meaning for the present, for both women, and also probably for this godforsaken village, for himself, for all people. It had not been his gift for poignant narrative that had made the old woman weep. It was because Peter was near to her, because she was bound up heart and soul with his innermost feelings.

Joy suddenly stirred within him. He even stopped for a moment to catch his breath.

"The past," thought he, "is linked to the present by an unbroken chain of happenings, each flowing from the other."

He felt as if he had just seen both ends of that chain. When he touched one end the other vibrated.

Crossing the river by ferry, and then climbing the hill, he looked at his home village and at the narrow strip of cold crimson sunset shining in the west. And he brooded on truth and beauty—how they had guided human life there in the garden and the high priest's palace, how they had continued without a break till the present day, always as the most important element in man's life and in earthly life in general. A sensation of youth, health, strength—he was only twenty-two years old—together with an anticipation, ineffably sweet, of happiness, strange, mysterious happiness, gradually came over him. And life seemed enchanting, miraculous, imbued with exalted significance.

Translated by Avraham Yarmolinsky

THE SIRENS

These are the seductive voices of the night; the Sirens, too, sang that way. It would be doing them an injustice to think that they wanted to seduce; they knew they had claws and sterile wombs, and they lamented this aloud. They could not help it if their laments sounded so beautiful.

Translated by Clement Greenberg

THE USE OF FORCE

They were new patients to me, all I had was the name, Olson. Please come down as soon as you can, my daughter is very sick. When I arrived I was met by the mother, a big startled looking woman, very clean and apologetic who merely said, Is this the doctor? and let me in. In the back, she added. You must excuse us, doctor, we have her in the kitchen where it is warm. It is very damp here sometimes.

The child was fully dressed and sitting on her father's lap near the kitchen table. He tried to get up, but I motioned for him not to bother, took off my overcoat and started to look things over. I could see that they were all very nervous, eyeing me up and down distrustfully. As often, in such cases, they weren't telling me more than they had to, it was up to me to tell them; that's why they were spending three dollars on me.

The child was fairly eating me up with her cold, steady eyes, and no expression to her face whatever. She did not move and seemed, inwardly, quiet; an unusually attractive little thing, and as strong as a heifer in appearance. But her face was flushed, she was breathing rapidly, and I realized that she had a high fever. She had magnificent blonde hair, in profusion. One of those picture children often reproduced in advertising leaflets and the photogravure sections of the Sunday papers.

She's had a fever for three days, began the father and we don't know what it comes from. My wife has given her things, you know, like people do, but it don't do no good. And there's been a lot of sickness around. So we tho't you'd better look her over and tell us what is the matter.

As doctors often do I took a trial shot at it as a point of departure. Has she had a sore throat?

Both parents answered me together, No . . . No, she says her throat don't hurt her.

Does your throat hurt you? added the mother to the child. But the little girl's expression didn't change nor did she move her eyes from my face.

Have you looked?

I tried to, said the mother, but I couldn't see.

As it happens we had been having a number of cases of diphtheria in the school to which this child went during that month and we were all, quite apparently, thinking of that, though no one had as yet spoken of the thing.

Well, I said, suppose we take a look at the throat first. I smiled in my best professional manner and asking for the child's first name I said, come on, Mathilda, open your mouth and let's take a look at your throat.

Nothing doing.

Aw, come on, I coaxed, just open your mouth wide and let me take a look. Look, I said opening both hands wide, I haven't anything in my hands. Just open up and let me see.

Such a nice man, put in the mother. Look how kind he is to you. Come on, do what he tells you to. He won't hurt you.

At that I ground my teeth in disgust. If only they wouldn't use the word "hurt" I might be able to get somewhere. But I did not allow myself to be hurried or disturbed but speaking quietly and slowly I approached the child again.

As I moved my chair a little nearer suddenly with one catlike movement both her hands clawed instinctively for my eyes and she almost reached them too. In fact she knocked my glasses flying and they fell, though unbroken, several feet away from me on the kitchen floor.

Both the mother and father almost turned themselves inside out in embarrassment and apology. You bad girl, said the mother, taking her and shaking her by one arm. Look what you've done. The nice man . . .

For heaven's sake, I broke in. Don't call me a nice man to her. I'm here to look at her throat on the chance that she might have diphtheria and possibly die of it. But that's nothing to her. Look here, I said to the child, we're going to look at your throat. You're old enough to understand what I'm saying. Will you open it now by yourself or shall we have to open it for you?

Not a move. Even her expression hadn't changed. Her breaths however were coming faster and faster. Then the battle began. I had to do it. I had to have a throat culture for her own protection. But first I told the parents that it was entirely up to them. I explained the danger but said that I would not insist on a throat examination so long as they would take the responsibility.

If you don't do what the doctor says you'll have to go to the hospital, the mother admonished her severely.

Oh yeah? I had to smile to myself. After all, I had already fallen in love with the savage brat, the parents were contemptible to me. In the ensuing struggle they grew more and more abject, crushed, exhausted while she surely rose to magnificent heights of insane fury of effort bred of her terror of me.

The father tried his best, and he was a big man but the fact that she was his daughter, his shame at her behavior and his dread of hurting her made him release her just at the critical times when I had almost achieved success, till I wanted to kill him. But his dread also that she might have diphtheria made him tell me to go on, go on though he himself was almost fainting, while the mother moved back and forth behind us raising and lowering her hands in an agony of apprehension.

Put her in front of you on your lap, I ordered, and hold both her wrists.

But as soon as he did the child let out a scream. Don't, you're hurting me. Let go of my hands. Let them go I tell you. Then she shrieked terrifyingly, hysterically. Stop it! Stop it! You're killing me!

Do you think she can stand it, doctor! said the mother.

You get out, said the husband to his wife. Do you want her to die of diphtheria?

Come on now, hold her, I said.

Then I grasped the child's head with my left hand and tried to get the wooden tongue depressor between her teeth. She fought, with clenched teeth, desperately! But now I also had grown furious—at a child. I tried to hold myself down but I couldn't. I know how to expose a throat for inspection. And I did my best. When finally I got the wooden spatula behind the last teeth and just the point of it into the mouth cavity, she opened up for an instant but before I could see anything she came down again and gripped the wooden blade between her molars she reduced it to splinters before I could get it out again.

Aren't you ashamed, the mother yelled at her. Aren't you ashamed to act like that in front of the doctor?

Get me a smooth-handled spoon of some sort, I told the mother. We're going through with this. The child's mouth was already bleeding. Her tongue was cut and she was screaming in wild hysterical shrieks. Perhaps I should have desisted and come back in an hour or more. No doubt it would have been better. But I have seen at least two children lying dead in bed of neglect in such cases, and feeling that I must get a diagnosis now or never I went at it again. But the worst of it was that I too had got beyond reason. I could have torn the child apart in my own fury and enjoyed it. It was a pleasure to attack her. My face was burning with it.

The damned little brat must be protected against her own idiocy, one says to one's self at such times. Others must be protected against her. It is a social necessity. And all these things are true. But a blind fury, a feeling of adult shame, bred of a longing for muscular release are the operatives. One goes on to the end.

In the final unreasoning assault I overpowered the child's neck and jaws. I forced the heavy silver spoon back of her teeth and down her throat till she gagged. And there it was—both tonsils covered with membrane. She had fought valiantly to keep me from knowing her secret. She had been hiding that sore throat for three days at least and lying to her parents in order to escape just such an outcome as this.

Now truly she was furious. She had been on the defensive before but now she attacked. Tried to get off her father's lap and fly at me while tears of defeat blinded her eyes.

THE WIND BLOWS

Suddenly—dreadfully—she wakes up. What has happened? Something dreadful has happened. No—nothing has happened. It is only the wind shaking the house, rattling the windows, banging a piece of iron on the roof and making her bed tremble. Leaves flutter past the window, up and away; down in the avenue a whole newspaper wags in the air like a lost kite and falls, spiked on a pine tree. It is cold. Summer is over—it is autumn—everything is ugly. The carts rattle by, swinging from side to side; two Chinamen lollop along under their wooden yokes with the straining vegetable baskets—their pigtails and blue blouses fly out in the wind. A white dog on three legs yelps past the gate. It is all over! What is? Oh, everything! And she begins to plait her hair with shaking fingers, not daring to look in the glass. Mother is talking to grandmother in the hall.

"A perfect idiot! Imagine leaving anything out on the line in weather like this. . . . Now my best little Teneriffe-work teacloth is simply in ribbons. *What* is that extraordinary smell? It's the porridge burning. Oh, heavens—this wind!"

She has a music lesson at ten o'clock. At the thought the minor movement of the Beethoven begins to play in her head, the trills long and terrible like little rolling drums. . . . Marie Swainson runs into the garden next door to pick the "chrysanths" before they are ruined. Her skirt flies up above her waist; she tries to beat it down, to tuck it between her legs while she stoops, but it is no use—up it flies. All the trees and bushes beat about her. She picks as quickly as she can, but she is quite distracted. She doesn't mind what she does—she pulls the plants up by the roots and bends and twists them, stamping her foot and swearing.

"For heaven's sake keep the front door shut! Go round to the back," shouts someone. And then she hears Bogey:

"Mother, you're wanted on the telephone. Telephone, Mother. It's the butcher."

How hideous life is—revolting, simply revolting. . . . And now her hat-elastic's snapped. Of course it would. She'll wear her old tam and slip out the back way. But Mother has seen.

"Matilda. Matilda. Come back im-me-diately! What on earth have you got on your head? It looks like a tea cosy. And why have you got that mane of hair on your forehead."

"I can't come back, Mother. I'll be late for my lesson."

"Come back immediately!"

She won't. She won't. She hates Mother. "Go to hell," she shouts, running down the road.

In waves, in clouds, in big round whirls the dust comes stinging, and with it little bits of straw and chaff and manure. There is a loud roaring sound from the trees in the gardens, and standing at the bottom of the road outside Mr. Bullen's gate she can hear the sea sob: "Ah! . . . Ah! . . . Ah-h!" But Mr. Bullen's drawing-room is as quiet as a cave. The windows are closed, the blinds half pulled, and she is not late. The-girl-before-her has just started playing MacDowell's "To an Iceberg." Mr. Bullen looks over at her and half smiles.

"Sit down," he says. "Sit over there in the sofa corner, little lady."

How funny he is. He doesn't exactly laugh at you . . . but there is just something. . . . Oh, how peaceful it is here. She likes this room. It smells of art serge and stale smoke and chrysanthemums . . . there is a big vase of them on the mantelpiece behind the pale photograph of Rubinstein . . . *à mon ami Robert Bullen.* . . . Over the black glittering piano hangs "Solitude"—a dark tragic woman draped in white, sitting on a rock, her knees crossed, her chin on her hands.

"No, no!" says Mr. Bullen, and he leans over the other girl, puts his arms over her shoulders and plays the passage for her. The stupid—she's blushing! How ridiculous!

Now the-girl-before-her has gone; the front door slams. Mr. Bullen comes back and walks up and down, very softly, waiting for her. What an extraordinary thing. Her fingers tremble so that she can't undo the knot in the music satchel. It's the wind. . . . And her heart beats so hard she feels it must lift her blouse up and down. Mr. Bullen does not say a word. The shabby red piano seat is long enough for two people to sit side by side. Mr. Bullen sits down by her.

"Shall I begin with scales," she asks, squeezing her hands together. "I had some arpeggios, too."

But he does not answer. She doesn't believe he even hears . . . and then suddenly his fresh hand with the ring on it reaches over and opens Beethoven.

"Let's have a little of the old master," he says.

But why does he speak so kindly—so awfully kindly—and as though they had known each other for years and years and knew everything about each other.

He turns the page slowly. She watches his hand—it is a very nice hand and always looks as though it had just been washed.

"Here we are," says Mr. Bullen.

Oh, that kind voice—Oh, that minor movement. Here come the little drums. . . .

"Shall I take the repeat?"

"Yes, dear child."

His voice is far, far too kind. The crotchets and quavers are dancing up and down the stave like little black boys on a fence. Why is he so . . . She will not cry—she has nothing to cry about. . . .

"What is it, dear child?"

Mr. Bullen takes her hands. His shoulder is there—just by her head. She leans on it ever so little, her cheek against the springy tweed.

"Life is so dreadful," she murmurs, but she does not feel it's dreadful at all. He says something about "waiting" and "marking time" and "that rare thing, a woman," but she does not hear. It is so comfortable . . . for ever . . .

Suddenly the door opens and in pops Marie Swainson, hours before her time.

"Take the allegretto a little faster," says Mr. Bullen, and gets up and begins to walk up and down again.

"Sit in the sofa corner, little lady," he says to Marie.

The wind, the wind. It's frightening to be here in her room by herself. The bed, the mirror, the white jug and basin gleam like the sky outside. It's the bed that is frightening. There it lies, sound asleep. . . . Does Mother imagine for one moment that she is going to darn all those stockings knotted up on the quilt like a coil of snakes? She's not. No, Mother. I do not see why I should. . . . The wind—the wind! There's a funny smell of soot blowing down the chimney. Hasn't anyone written poems to the wind? . . . "I bring fresh flowers to the leaves and showers." . . . What nonsense.

"Is that you, Bogey?"

"Come for a walk round the esplanade, Matilda. I can't stand this any longer."

"Right-o. I'll put on my ulster. Isn't it an awful day!" Bogey's ulster is just like hers. Hooking the collar she looks at herself in the glass. Her face is white, they have the same excited eyes and hot lips. Ah, they know those two in the glass. Good-bye, dears; we shall be back soon.

"This is better, isn't it?"

"Hook on," says Bogey.

They cannot walk fast enough. Their heads bent, their legs just touching, they stride like one eager person through the town, down the asphalt zigzag where the fennel grows wild and on to the esplanade. It is dusky—just getting dusky. The wind is so strong that they have to fight their way through it, rocking like two old drunkards. All the poor little pahutukawas on the esplanade are bent to the ground.

"Come on! Come on! Let's get near."

Over by the breakwater the sea is very high. They pull off their hats and her hair blows across her mouth, tasting of salt. The sea is so high that the waves do not break at all; they thump against the rough stone wall and suck up the weedy, dripping steps. A fine spray skims from the water right across the esplanade. They are covered with drops; the inside of her mouth tastes wet and cold.

Bogey's voice is breaking. When he speaks he rushes up and down the scale. It's funny—it makes you laugh—and yet it just suits the day. The wind carries their voices—away fly the sentences like little narrow ribbons.

"Quicker! Quicker!"

It is getting very dark. In the harbour the coal hulks show two lights—one high on a mast, and one from the stern.

"Look, Bogey. Look over there."

A big black steamer with a long loop of smoke streaming, with the portholes lighted, with lights everywhere, is putting out to sea. The wind does not stop her; she cuts through the waves, making for the open gate between the pointed rocks that leads to . . . It's the light that makes her look so awfully beautiful and mysterious. . . . *They* are on board leaning over the rail arm in arm.

". . . Who are they?"

". . . Brother and sister."

"Look, Bogey, there's the town. Doesn't it look small? There's the post office clock chiming for the last time. There's the esplanade where we walked that windy day. Do you remember? I cried at my music lesson that day—how many years ago! Good-bye, little island, good-bye. . . ."

Now the dark stretches a wing over the tumbling water. They can't see those two any more. Good-bye, good-bye. Don't forget. . . . But the ship is gone, now.

The wind—the wind.

Bruno Schulz

FATHER'S LAST ESCAPE

from *Sanatorium under the Sign of the Hourglass*

It happened in the late and forlorn period of complete disruption, at the time of the liquidation of our business. The signboard had been removed from over our shop, the shutters were halfway down, and inside the shop my mother was conducting an unauthorized trade in remnants. Adela had gone to America, and it was said that the boat on which she had sailed had sunk and that all the passengers had lost their lives. We were unable to verify this rumor, but all trace of the girl was lost and we never heard of her again.

A new age began—empty, sober, and joyless, like a sheet of white paper. A new servant girl, Genya, anemic, pale, and boneless, mooned about the rooms. When one patted her on the back, she wriggled, stretched like a snake, or purred like a cat. She had a dull white complexion, and even the insides of her eyelids were white. She was so absent-minded that she sometimes made a white sauce from old letters and invoices: it was sickly and inedible.

At that time, my father was definitely dead. He had been dying a number of times, always with some reservations that forced us to revise our attitude toward the fact of his death. This had its advantages. By dividing his death into installments, Father had familiarized us with his demise. We became gradually indifferent to his returns—each one shorter, each one more pitiful. His features were already dispersed throughout the room in which he had lived, and were sprouting in it, creating at some points strange knots of likeness that were most expressive. The wallpaper began in certain places to imitate his habitual nervous tic; the flower designs arranged themselves into the doleful elements of his smile, symmetrical as the fossilized imprint of a trilobite. For a time, we gave a wide berth to his fur coat lined with polecat skins. The fur coat breathed. The panic of small animals sewn together and biting into one another passed through it in helpless currents and lost itself in the folds of the fur. Putting one's ear against it, one could hear the melodious purring unison of the animals' sleep. In this well-tanned form, amid the faint smell of pole-cat, murder, and nighttime matings, my father might have lasted for many years. But he did not last.

One day, Mother returned home from town with a preoccupied face. "Look, Joseph," she said, "what a lucky coincidence. I caught him on the stairs, jumping from step to step"——and she lifted a handkerchief that covered something on a plate. I recognized him at once. The resemblance was strik-ing, although now he was a crab or a large scorpion. Mother and I exchanged looks: in spite of the metamorphosis, the resemblance was incredible.

"Is he alive?" I asked.

"Of course. I can hardly hold him," Mother said. "Shall I place him on the floor?"

She put the plate down, and leaning over him, we observed him closely. There was a hollow place between his numerous curved legs, which he was moving slightly. His uplifted pincers and feelers seemed to be listening. I tipped the plate, and Father moved cautiously and with a certain hesitation onto the floor. Upon touching the flat surface under him, he gave a sudden start with all of his legs, while his hard arthropod joints made a clacking sound. I barred his way. He hesitated, investigated the obstacle with his feelers, then lifted his pincers and turned aside. We let him run in his chosen direction, where there was no furniture to give him shelter. Running in wavy jerks on his many legs, he reached the wall and, before we could stop him, ran lightly up it, not paus-ing anywhere. I shuddered with instinctive revulsion as I watched his progress up the wallpaper. Meanwhile, Father reached a small built-in kitchen cup-board, hung for a moment on its edge, testing the terrain with his pincers, and then crawled into it.

He was discovering the apartment afresh from the new point of view of a crab; evidently, he perceived all objects by his sense of smell, for, in spite of careful checking, I could not find on him any organ of sight. He seemed to consider carefully the objects he encountered in his path, stopping and feel-ing them with his antennae, then embracing them with his pincers, as if to test them and make their acquaintance; after a time, he left them and con-tinued on his run, pulling his abdomen behind him, lifted slightly from the floor. He acted the same way with the pieces of bread and meat that we threw on the floor for him, hoping he would eat them. He gave them a perfunctory examination and ran on, not recognizing that they were edible.

Watching these patient surveys of the room, one could assume that he was obstinately and indefatigably looking for something. From time to time, he ran to a corner of the kitchen, crept under a barrel of water that was leak-ing, and, upon reaching the puddle, seemed to drink.

Sometimes he disappeared for days on end. He seemed to manage perfectly well without food, but this did not seem to affect his vitality. With mixed feelings of shame and repugnance, we concealed by day our secret fear that he might visit us in bed during the night. But this never occurred, although in the daytime he would wander all over the furniture. He particularly liked to stay in the spaces between the wardrobes and the wall.

We could not discount certain manifestations of reason and even a sense of humor. For instance, Father never failed to appear in the dining room during mealtimes, although his participation in them was purely symbolic. If the dining-room door was by chance closed during dinner and he had been left in the next room, he scratched at the bottom of the door, running up and down along the crack, until we opened it for him. In time, he learned how to insert his pincers and legs under the door, and after some elaborate maneuvers he finally succeeded in insinuating his body through it sideways into the dining room. This seemed to give him pleasure. He would then stop under the table, lying quite still, his abdomen slightly pulsating. What the meaning of these rhythmic pulsations was, we could not imagine. They seemed obscene and malicious, but at the same time expressed a rather gross and lustful satisfaction. Our dog, Nimrod, would approach him slowly and, without conviction, sniff at him cautiously, sneeze, and turn away indifferently, not having reached any conclusions.

Meanwhile, the demoralization in our household was increasing. Genya slept all day long, her slim body bonelessly undulating with her deep breaths. We often found in the soup reels of cotton, which she had thrown in unthinkingly with the vegetables. Our shop was open nonstop, day and night. A continuous sale took place amid complicated bargainings and discussions. To crown it all, Uncle Charles came to stay.

He was strangely depressed and silent. He declared with a sigh that after his recent unfortunate experiences he had decided to change his way of life and devote himself to the study of languages. He never went out but remained locked in the most remote room—from which Genya had removed all the carpets and curtains, as she did not approve of our visitor. There he spent his time, reading old price lists. Several times he tried viciously to step on Father. Screaming with horror, we told him to stop it. Afterward he only smiled wryly to himself, while Father, not realizing the danger he had been in, hung around and studied some spots on the floor.

My father, quick and mobile as long as he was on his feet, shared with all crustaceans the characteristic that when turned on his back he became largely immobile. It was sad and pitiful to see him desperately moving all his limbs and rotating helplessly around his own axis. We could hardly force ourselves to look at the conspicuous, almost shameless mechanism of his anatomy, completely exposed under the bare articulated belly. At such moments, Uncle Charles could hardly restrain himself from stamping on Father. We ran to his rescue with some object at hand, which he caught tightly with his pincers, quickly regaining his normal position; then at once he started a lightning, zigzag run at double speed, as if wanting to obliterate the memory of his unsightly fall.

I must force myself to report truthfully the unbelievable deed, from which my memory recoils even now. To this day I cannot understand how we became the conscious perpetrators of it. A strange fatality must have been driving us to it; for fate does not evade consciousness or will but engulfs them in its mechanism, so that we are able to admit and accept, as in a hypnotic trance, things that under normal circumstances would fill us with horror.

Shaken badly, I asked my mother in despair, again and again, "How could you have done it? If it were Genya who had done it—but you yourself?" Mother cried, wrung her hands, and could find no answer. Had she thought that Father would be better off? Had she seen in that act the only solution to a hopeless situation, or did she do it out of inconceivable thoughtlessness and frivolity? Fate has a thousand wiles when it chooses to impose on us its incomprehensible whims. A temporary blackout, a moment of inattention or blindness, is enough to insinuate an act between the Scylla and Charybdis of decision. Afterward, with hindsight, we may endlessly ponder that act, explain our motives, try to discover our true intentions; but the act remains irrevocable.

When Father was brought in on a dish, we came to our senses and understood fully what had happened. He lay large and swollen from the boiling, pale gray and jellified. We sat in silence, dumbfounded. Only Uncle Charles lifted his fork toward the dish, but at once he put it down uncertainly, looking at us askance. Mother ordered it to be taken to the sitting room. It stood there afterward on a table covered with a velvet cloth, next to the album of family photographs and a musical cigarette box. Avoided by us all, it just stood there.

But my father's earthly wanderings were not yet at an end, and the next installment—the extension of the story beyond permissible limits—is the most painful of all. Why didn't he give up, why didn't he admit that he was beaten when there was every reason to do so and when even Fate could go no farther in utterly confounding him? After several weeks of immobility in the sitting room, he somehow rallied and seemed to be slowly recovering. One morning, we found the plate empty. One leg lay on the edge of the dish, in some congealed tomato sauce and aspic that bore the traces of his escape. Although boiled and shedding his legs on the way, with his remaining strength he had dragged himself somewhere to begin a homeless wandering, and we never saw him again.

Translated by Celina Wieniewska

I USED TO
LIVE HERE ONCE

She was standing by the river looking at the stepping stones and remembering each one. There was the round unsteady stone, the pointed one, the flat one in the middle—the safe stone where you could stand and look round. The next wasn't so safe for when the river was full the water flowed over it and even when it showed dry it was slippery. But after that it was easy and soon she was standing on the other side.

The road was much wider than it used to be but the work had been done carelessly. The felled trees had not been cleared away and the bushes looked trampled. Yet it was the same road and she walked along feeling extraordinarily happy.

It was a fine day, a blue day. The only thing was that the sky had a glassy look that she didn't remember. That was the only word she could think of. Glassy. She turned the corner, saw that what had been the old *pavé* had been taken up, and there too the road was much wider, but it had the same unfinished look.

She came to the worn stone steps that led up to the house and her heart began to beat. The screw pine was gone, so was the mock summer house called the *ajoupa,* but the clove tree was still there and at the top of the steps the rough lawn stretched away, just as she remembered it. She stopped and looked towards the house that had been added to and painted white. It was strange to see a car standing in front of it.

There were two children under the big mango tree, a boy and a little girl, and she waved to them and called 'Hello' but they didn't answer her or turn their heads. Very fair children, as Europeans born in the West Indies so often are: as if the white blood is asserting itself against all odds.

The grass was yellow in the hot sunlight as she walked towards them. When she was quite close she called again shyly: 'Hello.' Then, 'I used to live here once,' she said.

Still they didn't answer. When she said for the third time 'Hello' she was quite near them. Her arms went out instinctively with the longing to touch them.

It was the boy who turned. His grey eyes looked straight into hers. His expression didn't change. He said: 'Hasn't it gone cold all of a sudden. D'you notice? Let's go in.' 'Yes let's,' said the girl.

Her arms fell to her sides as she watched them running across the grass to the house. That was the first time she knew.

THE HOUSE OF
THE CRIME

As they drove along a road glassy with rain, under a grey, wet sky, Tommaso observed his companion. She might have been a little over thirty; her smooth, flowing black hair hung down on either side of a pale, lean face, with an acquiline nose and brilliant black eyes. Lipstick of a very bright red gave her large, curving mouth the appearance of a wound. He looked down and noticed that, below her green skirt, she was wearing glossy black Wellington boots that came half-way up her legs. Finally he asked: "Is it much further?"

"No, it's not far now."

"What ever made you think of building a villa in such a solitary place? I could understand if it was near the sea. But it isn't."

"We built it there because the land was ours."

"And when was it built?"

"About 1930, over thirty years ago."

"In all those years, have you lived there all the time?"

"No, we used to go there until 1933, I think. Then we built the villa at Ansedonia and didn't go there any more."

"Abandoned for twenty-seven years! But why?"

"Oh, I don't know. I suppose we didn't like it."

"And what is the price? The agent told me, but I've seen so many villas recently that I've forgotten it."

"Fifteen million lire."

"Ah, yes. From what I understand, it's a very big villa."

"Yes, it's big, but there aren't many rooms. A living-room and four other rooms."

"According to the agent, it would be a good bargain."

"Yes, I think it is."

"Does the villa belong to you?"

"No, it belongs to my brother, my sister and myself."

"But you have no parents?"

"No, they're dead."

"Are your brother and sister married?"

"Yes."

"Do they live with you in Rome?"

"No, they live abroad."

"And you, are you married?"

"No."

"You live alone?"

"No. But, Signor Lantieri . . ."

"Yes?"

"Excuse me. I have to show you the villa, but I don't consider that I have to talk to you about my private life."

"You're perfectly right. Forgive me."

Silence followed. But, strange to say, Tommaso realized that the girl's brusque reply had neither mortified nor surprised him. He wondered what the reason could be for this serenity on his part, and finally understood: both the price of the villa, which was very low considering the size of the building, and, in general, the girl's curiously disinterested and distant attitude, had about them something mysterious which excused, if not actually justified, his indiscretion. He looked at her mouth and was struck by the brightness of her lipstick, which looked like blood. From her face, white as paper, his eyes travelled to the road, which ran, grey and shining, towards the grey, steaming landscape, and then he noticed that, like the red of her lips, other colours too stood out in an unusual, brilliant way from the greyness of the autumn day—the golden yellow of the leaves of a climbing plant on the front of a cottage, the wet blackness of the trunks of certain trees, the almost blue green of cabbages in vegetable gardens, the red of the clusters of berries in the hedges. It was a cloudy, rainy day, he thought, but it was also an extremely beautiful day in which colours stood out and were resonant as voices in a great silence. He enquired of the girl: "Is there any land round the villa?"

"The price includes two thousand square metres of garden. But the land all round belongs to us, and if you like you can buy more."

"At what price?"

"A thousand lire a square metre, I think."

Tommaso noticed once again that the price was lower than the rate usually quoted in that district; but this time he said nothing. The girl changed gear and, leaving the Via Aurelia, turned the car into a country road, between two antique pillars. "This is where our property begins," she said.

"Then this is the approach to the villa?"

"Yes, there is no other road."

The road wound along the bottom of a valley, between round, green, treeless hills on the top of which could be seen white farmhouses with green windows and red roofs, one on each hill. "Are all these farms yours?" asked Tommaso.

"Yes, they're ours."

Between one hill and another there were deep, narrow valleys, some of them cultivated, some left to scrub or woodland. Tommaso counted, on the left of the road, four hills and as many valleys; then the car turned sharply and proceeded along a small side road towards one of these valleys, at the far end of which could be distinguished, among the trees, the vague, grey outline of a building. "The villa's not on the sea," said the girl, with an absentminded, careless air, "but it's very near the sea. Five minutes in a car and you're at the beach, on the other side of the Via Aurelia."

They crossed a little bridge over a deep ditch and then the lane plunged into the scrub, which seemed to become steadily higher and thicker as they went on. All of a sudden the girl stopped the car in front of a wooden gate with a chain and a big padlock on it, both of them rusty. Beyond the gate, only part of the façade of the villa could be seen because of the trees. Tommaso noted with surprise that this façade had nothing attractive and rustic about it, as might have been expected in such a place; on the contrary, it was a gloomy, square structure, grey-cement-coloured, rather like a neo-classical temple, but of the type of neo-classicism which, round about 1930, had been known as the "twentieth-century style": a plain pediment, a peristyle with square pillars, brutal and squat and having neither capital nor base, a square stone door like that of an Egyptian tomb. The girl, in the meantime, had got out of the car and was fumbling with the padlock on the gate which, in the end, opened. "Why, is it the first time you've been here?" Tommaso asked.

"Almost. I haven't been here for years."

The eucalyptus-trees lining the short approach to the house opened out in front of a paved forecourt, on the far side of which, fully visible now, stood the enormous, gloomy cube of the villa. Behind and all round the villa there were many trees, and behind the trees rose the slopes of the hills. Tommaso noticed an odd fact: in spite of its having been deserted for twenty-seven years, nature had kept at a distance from the villa: the walls were bare, with patches and seepages of damp but no creepers; no green moss had invaded the cracked and crumbling steps that led up to the door; no grass had grown in the meandering fissures that had opened in the paving of the forecourt. It might have been thought, he said to himself, that nature had found the villa repugnant. A noise made him start: the girl had gone into the house and was now pulling up one of the big roller-blinds that hung on each side of the door. So he too went in.

He found himself faced by the living-room, which was spacious and remarkably lofty, and of the same gloomy, grey colour as the façade. The floor appeared to be covered with minute pieces of rubble and dirt upon which the dust had fallen softly like a shower of snow; at the end of the room there was a huge brick fireplace, black and lifeless, and, in front of the fireplace, a large sofa; no other furniture was to be seen. Tommaso walked over to the sofa and then discovered, between it and the fireplace, a little low table upon which stood two glasses and a whisky bottle, uncorked and with the cork beside it. The sofa was covered with a material of a colour now unrecognizable, possibly brown, possibly mauve, all split and ragged and with the stuffing sticking out of the crevices. Tommaso took up the bottle: it was empty but looked as though it had dried up over the years, and the label was spotted with yellow; and on the table, grey with dust, there was now a clean circle. "This is the living-room," said the girl.

Tommaso had noticed that one of the walls had a fresco painted on it, and he went over to look at it. In a style characteristic of the period, it represented a social scene—a group of bathers on a beach. You could see the sea, and the sand, and a big striped umbrella. Round the umbrella, in varying poses, were grouped a number of men and women in bathing-costumes. The men were all muscular and athletic, with broad shoulders and small heads, and some of them wore monocles; the women were very buxom, with rotundities which seemed to be bursting out of their scanty costumes. The faces of both men and women were haughty, handsome, immobile. In the midst of these prosperous, naked people the puny figure of a manservant stood out prominently; he was dressed to look like a performing monkey, in a little short white jacket and black trousers, and he was handing round a tray of drinks. There was nothing indecent about this fresco; but Tommaso nevertheless had the feeling that he was looking at a pornographic illustration. Behind him, the girl said: "They're comic, aren't they? Those were our fathers and mothers."

Tommaso wanted to reply: "You mean *your* father and *your* mother," but he restrained himself in time. There was something now, on the edge of his memory—just as one says sometimes that a word is on the tip of one's tongue. He seemed to recollect that the name of the girl's family was connected with a crime that had happened many years before, at about the time when the villa had been built. It was an old story now, and he had been a boy when it had happened; possibly he had heard it spoken of later. But if a crime had really taken place in the villa, that explained the modesty of the price and the strange, embarrassed off-handedness of the girl. Trying vainly to retrace in memory the name of the principle figure in the crime, Tommaso followed the girl, who now led him along a passage and showed him, one by one, the other rooms.

These rooms contained furniture in the same brutal, stark, "twentieth-century" style in which the villa had been built—wardrobes, cabinets and bed-side cupboards in the form of cubes, armchairs like boxes without lids, beds with enormous feet and square backs. All this furniture was in dark walnut—not solid walnut, however, but veneered; and the polish which had once disguised the fragility of these pieces that looked so massive had all vanished, and the veneer had an opaque look, was spotted with black stains, peeling off and in some places blistered and cracked. On a bed in one of these rooms there was still a sheet, thrown back and crumpled and with a large stain in the middle of it, of a faded, indeterminate colour somewhere between iodine yellow and greyish buff. On the bedside table was a small box. Tommaso read out the name of a laxative from the lid of the box, and then said: "You might at least have made somebody sweep out the house, seeing that you want to sell it."

"It's *I* who want to sell it," answered the girl, meeting his look of disgust with an air of defiance. "My brother and sister don't know anything about it. And I haven't had the time to get the place cleaned up. I put the advertisement in the paper, and you're the first potential buyer." She uttered these words in a tone of insulting haughtiness; then she went to the door of the bathroom and threw it open. "This is the bathroom."

Tommaso walked over and looked in, leaning cautiously forward. It was a normal bathroom; the white tiles were incrusted with dust and the taps green and lustreless. In the lavatory-bowl Tommaso saw something black sticking to the porcelain surface and, without a word, pointed it out to the girl. Disdainfully she turned her back upon him, went out of the room and opened a door in the passage. "This is supposed to be the maid's room," she said. Immediately something dark ran quickly away between their feet, there was a piercing scream, and for a moment Tommaso had the girl in his arms; she kept repeating, "A rat, a rat," and was trembling all over and digging her sharp nails into his neck. Tommaso said gently: "Keep calm, it was only a rat."

"Yes, I know, but I'm so terrified of rats."

"Never mind, it's gone."

"Thank you; I'm sorry."

They went back into the living-room. At the moment when the girl had let forth her despairing cry, Tommaso, with a sudden enlightenment, had remembered the name of the family connected with the crime. It was not the girl's name; moreover the situation of the villa did not correspond. No crime, therefore, had been committed in the villa, although appearances certainly seemed to suggest it. All of a sudden the girl said nervously: "Well, that's the villa, there's nothing more to see. You must admit that fifteen million is not a high price."

"No, it's not a high price. But it's not the kind of villa I was looking for."

"You don't like it?"

"No, it's built in a style I don't like at all."

"We have a proposal to make it into a school or something like that. In the end I daresay we shall accept."

"I think that would be a good solution."

They left the villa and walked across the forecourt in a thin, stinging rain. "What's the villa called?" asked Tommaso, just for something to say.

"It hasn't any name," replied the girl, "but the peasants have given it one which I can tell you now, since you're not going to buy it. They call it the house of the crime."

Translated by Angus Davidson

THE SUPPER

We waited patiently for the darkness to fall. The sun had already slipped far beyond the hills. Deepening shadows, permeated with the evening mist, lay over the freshly ploughed hillsides and valleys, still covered with occasional patches of dirty snow; but here and there, along the sagging underbelly of the sky, heavy with rain clouds, you could still see a few rose-coloured streaks of sunlight.

A dark, gusty wind, heavy with the smells of the thawing, sour earth, tossed the clouds about and cut through your body like a blade of ice. A solitary piece of tar-board, torn by a stronger gust, rattled monotonously on a rooftop; a dry but penetrating chill was moving in from the fields. In the valley below, wheels clattered against rails and locomotives whined mournfully. Dusk was falling; our hunger was growing more and more terrible; the traffic along the highway had died down almost completely, only now and then the wind would waft a fragment of conversation, a coachman's call, or the occasional rumble of a cow-drawn cart; the cows dragged their hooves lazily along the gravel. The clatter of wooden sandals on the pavement and the guttural laughter of the peasant girls hurrying to a Saturday night dance at the village were slowly fading in the distance.

The darkness thickened at last and a soft rain began to fall. Several bluish lamps, swaying to and fro on top of high lamp-posts, threw a dim light over the black, tangled tree branches reaching out over the road, the shiny sentry-shack roofs, and the empty pavement that glistened like a wet leather strap. The soldiers marched under the circle of lights and then disappeared again in the dark. The sound of their footsteps on the road were coming nearer.

And then the camp Kommandant's driver threw a searchlight beam on a passage between two blockhouses. Twenty Russian soldiers in camp stripes, their arms tied with barbed-wire behind their backs, were being led out of the washroom and driven down the embankment. The Block Elders lined them up along the pavement facing the crowd that had been standing there for many silent hours, motionless, bareheaded, hungry. In the strong glare, the Russians' bodies stood out incredibly clearly. Every fold, bulge or wrinkle in their clothing; the cracked soles in their worn-out boots; the dry lumps of brown clay stuck to the edges of their trousers; the thick seams along their crotches; the white thread showing on the blue stripe of their prison suits; their sagging buttocks; their stiff hands and bloodless fingers twisted in pain, with drops of dry blood at the joints; their swollen wrists where the skin had started turning blue from the rusty wire cutting into the flesh; their naked elbows, pulled back unnaturally and tied with another piece of wire—all this emerged out of the surrounding blackness as if carved in ice. The elongated shadows of the men fell across the road and the barbed-wire fences glittering with tiny drops of water, and were lost on the hillside covered with dry, rustling grasses.

The Kommandant, a greying, sunburned man, who had come from the village especially for the occasion, crossed the lighted area with a tired but firm step and, stopping at the edge of the darkness, decided that the two rows of Russians were indeed a proper distance apart. From then on matters proceeded quickly, though maybe not quite quickly enough for the freezing body and the empty stomach that had been waiting seventeen hours for a pint of soup, still kept hot perhaps in the kettles at the barracks. 'This is a serious matter!' cried a very young Camp Elder, stepping out from behind the Kommandant. He had one hand under the lapel of his 'Custom made', fitted black jacket, and in the other hand he was holding a willow crop which he kept tapping rhythmically against the top of his high boots.

'These men—they are criminals! I reckon I don't have to explain . . . They are Communists! Herr Kommandant says to tell you that they are going to be punished properly, and what the Herr Kommandant says . . . Well boys, I tell you, you too had better be careful, eh?'

'Los, los, we have no time to waste,' interrupted the Kommandant, turning to an officer in an unbuttoned top-coat. He was leaning against the fender of his small Skoda automobile and slowly removing his gloves.

'This certainly shouldn't take long,' said the officer in the unbuttoned top-coat. He snapped his fingers, a smile at the corner of his mouth.

'Ja, and tonight the entire camp again will go without dinner!' shouted the young Camp Elder. 'The Block Elders will carry the soup back to the kitchen and . . . if even one cup is missing, you'll have to answer to me. Understand, boys?'

A long, deep sigh went through the crowd. Slowly, slowly, the rear rows began pushing forward; the crowd near the road grew denser and a pleasant warmth spread along your back from the breath of the men pressing behind you, preparing to jump forward.

The Kommandant gave a signal and out of the darkness emerged a long line of S.S. men with rifles in their hands. They placed themselves neatly behind the Russians, each behind one man. You could no longer tell that they had returned from the labour Kommandos with us. They had had time to eat, to change to fresh, gala uniforms, and even to have a manicure. Their fingers were clenched tightly around their rifle butts and their fingernails looked neat and pink; apparently they were planning to join the local girls at the village dance. They cocked their rifles sharply, leaned the rifle butts on their hips and pressed the muzzles up against the clean-shaven napes of the Russians.

'*Achtung! Bereit, Feuer!*'[1] said the Kommandant without raising his voice. The rifles barked, the soldiers jumped back a step to keep from being splattered by the shattered heads. The Russians seemed to quiver on their feet for an instant and then fell to the ground like heavy sacks, splashing the pavement with blood and scattered chunks of brain. Throwing their rifles over their shoulders, the soldiers marched off quickly. The corpses were dragged temporarily under the fence. The Kommandant and his retinue got into the Skoda; it backed up to the gate, snorting loudly.

No sooner was the greying, sunburned Kommandant out of sight than the silent crowd, pressing forward more and more persistently, burst into a shrieking roar, and fell in an avalanche on the blood-spattered pavement, swarming over it noisily. Then, dispersed by the Block Elders and the barracks chiefs called in for help from the camp, they scattered and disappeared one by one inside the blocks. I had been standing some distance away from the place of execution so I could not reach the road. But the following day, when we were again driven out to work, a 'Muslimized'[2] Jew from Estonia who was helping me haul steel bars tried to convince me all day that human brains are, in fact, so tender you can eat them absolutely raw.

Translated by Michael Kandel

---

1. "Attention! Aim, Fire!" (German).
2. Depressed, defeated (slang).

CITIES &
THE DEAD

Never in all my travels had I ventured as far as Adelma. It was dusk when I landed there. On the dock the sailor who caught the rope and tied it to the bollard resembled a man who had soldiered with me and was dead. It was the hour of the wholesale fish market. An old man was loading a basket of sea urchins on a cart; I thought I recognized him; when I turned, he had disappeared down an alley, but I realized that he looked like a fisherman who, already old when I was a child, could no longer be among the living. I was upset by the sight of a fever victim huddled on the ground, a blanket over his head: my father a few days before his death had yellow eyes and a growth of beard like this man. I turned my gaze aside; I no longer dared look anyone in the face.

I thought: "If Adelma is a city I am seeing in a dream, where you encounter only the dead, the dream frightens me. If Adelma is a real city, inhabited by living people, I need only continue looking at them and the resemblances will dissolve, alien faces will appear, bearing anguish. In either case it is best for me not to insist on staring at them."

A vegetable vendor was weighing a cabbage on a scales and put it in a basket dangling on a string a girl lowered from a balcony. The girl was identical with one in my village who had gone mad for love and killed herself. The vegetable vendor raised her face: she was my grandmother.

I thought: "You reach a moment in life when, among the people you have known, the dead outnumber the living. And the mind refuses to accept more faces, more expressions: on every new face you encounter, it prints the old forms, for each one it finds the most suitable mask."

The stevedores climbed the steps in a line, bent beneath demijohns and barrels; their faces were hidden by sackcloth hoods; "Now they will straighten up and I will recognize them," I thought, with impatience and fear. But I could not take my eyes off them; if I turned my gaze just a little toward the crowd that crammed those narrow streets, I was assailed by unexpected faces, reappearing from far away, staring at me as if demanding recognition, as if to recognize me, as if they had already recognized me. Perhaps, for each of them, I also resembled someone who was dead. I had barely arrived at Adelma and I was already one of them, I had gone over to their side, absorbed in that kaleidoscope of eyes, wrinkles, grimaces.

I thought: "Perhaps Adelma is the city where you arrive dying and where each finds again the people he has known. This means I, too, am dead." And I also thought: "This means the beyond is not happy."

Translated by William Weaver

Italo Calvino

CONTINUOUS
CITIES

The city of Leonia refashions itself every day: every morning the people wake between fresh sheets, wash with just-unwrapped cakes of soap, wear brand-new clothing, take from the latest model refrigerator still unopened tins, listening to the last-minute jingles from the most up-to-date radio.

On the sidewalks, encased in spotless plastic bags, the remains of yesterday's Leonia await the garbage truck. Not only squeezed tubes of toothpaste, blown-out light bulbs, newspapers, containers, wrappings, but also boilers, encyclopedias, pianos, porcelain dinner services. It is not so much by the things that each day are manufactured, sold, bought that you can measure Leonia's opulence, but rather by the things that each day are thrown out to make room for the new. So you begin to wonder if Leonia's true passion is really, as they say, the enjoyment of new and different things, and not, instead, the joy of expelling, discarding, cleansing itself of a recurrent impurity. The fact is that street cleaners are welcomed like angels, and their task of removing the residue of yesterday's existence is surrounded by a respectful silence, like a ritual that inspires devotion, perhaps only because once things have been cast off nobody wants to have to think about them further.

Nobody wonders where, each day, they carry their load of refuse. Outside the city, surely; but each year the city expands, and the street cleaners have to fall farther back. The bulk of the outflow increases and the piles rise higher, become stratified, extend over a wider perimeter. Besides, the more Leonia's talent for making new materials excels, the more the rubbish improves in quality, resists time, the elements, fermentations, combustions. A fortress of indestructible leftovers surrounds Leonia, dominating it on every side, like a chain of mountains.

This is the result: the more Leonia expels goods, the more it accumulates them; the scales of its past are soldered into a cuirass that cannot be removed. As the city is renewed each day, it preserves all of itself in its only definitive form: yesterday's sweepings piled up on the sweepings of the day before yesterday and of all its days and years and decades.

Leonia's rubbish little by little would invade the world, if, from beyond the final crest of its boundless rubbish heap, the street cleaners of other cities were not pressing, also pushing mountains of refuse in front of themselves. Perhaps the whole world, beyond Leonia's boundaries, is covered by craters of rubbish, each surrounding a metropolis in constant eruption. The boundaries between the alien, hostile cities are infected ramparts where the detritus of both support each other, overlap, mingle.

The greater its height grows, the more the danger of a landslide looms: a tin can, an old tire, an unraveled wine flask, if it rolls toward Leonia, is enough to bring with it an avalanche of unmated shoes, calendars of bygone years, withered flowers, submerging the city in its own past, which it had tried in vain to reject, mingling with the past of the neighboring cities, finally clean. A cataclysm will flatten the sordid mountain range, canceling every trace of the metropolis always dressed in new clothes. In the nearby cities they are all ready, waiting with bulldozers to flatten the terrain, to push into the new territory, expand, and drive the new street cleaners still farther out.

Translated by William Weaver

Nadine Gordimer

IS THERE NOWHERE ELSE
WHERE WE CAN MEET?

It was a cool grey morning and the air was like smoke. In that reversal of the elements that sometimes takes place, the grey, soft, muffled sky moved like the sea on a silent day.

The coat collar pressed rough against her neck and her cheeks were softly cold as if they had been washed in ice-water. She breathed gently with the air; on the left a strip of veld fire curled silently, flameless. Overhead a dove purred. She went on over the flat straw grass, following the trees, now on, now off the path. Away ahead, over the scribble of twigs, the sloping lines of black and platinum grass—all merging, tones but no colour, like an etching—was the horizon, the shore at which cloud lapped.

Damp burnt grass puffed black, faint dust from beneath her feet. She could hear herself swallow.

A long way off she saw a figure with something red on its head, and she drew from it the sense of balance she had felt at the particular placing of the dot of a figure in a picture. She was here; someone was over there . . . Then the red dot was gone, lost in the curve of the trees. She changed her bag and parcel from one arm to the other and felt the morning, palpable, deeply cold and clinging against her eyes.

She came to the end of a direct stretch of path and turned with it round a dark-fringed pine and a shrub, now delicately boned, that she remembered hung with bunches of white flowers like crystals in the summer. There was a native in a red woollen cap standing at the next clump of trees, where the path crossed a ditch and was bordered by white-splashed stones. She had pulled a little sheath of pine needles, three in a twist of thin brown tissue, and as she walked she ran them against her thumb. Down; smooth and stiff. Up; catching in gentle resistance as the minute serrations snagged at the skin. He was standing with his back towards her, looking along the way he had come; she pricked the ball of her thumb with the needle-ends. His one trouser leg was torn off above the knee, and the back of the naked leg and half-turned heel showed the peculiarly dead, powdery black of cold. She was nearer to him now, but she knew he did not hear her coming over the damp dust of the path. She was level with him, passing him; and he turned slowly and looked beyond her, without a flicker of interest as a cow sees you go.

The eyes were red, as if he had not slept for a long time, and the strong smell of old sweat burned at her nostrils. Once past, she wanted to cough, but a pang of guilt at the red weary eyes stopped her. And he had only a filthy rag—part of an old shirt?—without sleeves and frayed away into a great gap from underarm to waist. It lifted in the currents of cold as she passed. She had dropped the neat trio of pine needles somewhere, she did not know at what moment, so now, remembering something from childhood, she lifted her hand to her face and sniffed: yes, it was as she remembered, not as chemists pretend it in the bath salts, but a dusty green scent, vegetable rather than flower. It was clean, unhuman. Slightly sticky too; tacky on her fingers. She must wash them as soon as she got there. Unless her hands were quite clean, she could not lose consciousness of them, they obtruded upon her.

She felt a thudding through the ground like the sound of a hare running in fear and she was going to turn around and then he was there in front of her, so startling, so utterly unexpected, panting right into her face. He stood dead still and she stood dead still. Every vestige of control, of sense, of thought, went out of her as a room plunges into dark at the failure of power and she found herself whimpering like an idiot or a child. Animal sounds came out of her throat. She gibbered. For a moment it was Fear itself that had her by the arms, the legs, the throat; not fear of the man, of any single menace he might present, but Fear, absolute, abstract. If the earth had opened up in fire at her feet, if a wild beast had opened its terrible mouth to receive her, she could not have been reduced to less than she was now.

There was a chest heaving through the tear in front of her; a face panting; beneath the red hairy woollen cap the yellowish-red eyes holding her in distrust. One foot, cracked from exposure until it looked like broken wood, moved, only to restore balance in the dizziness that follows running, but any move seemed towards her and she tried to scream and the awfulness of dreams came true and nothing would come out. She wanted to throw the handbag and the parcel at him, and as she fumbled crazily for them she heard him draw a deep, hoarse breath and he grabbed out at her and—ah! It came. His hand clutched her shoulder.

Now she fought with him and she trembled with strength as they struggled. The dust puffed round her shoes and his scuffling toes. The smell of him choked her—It was an old pyjama jacket, not a shirt—His face was sullen and there was a pink place where the skin had been grazed off. He sniffed desperately, out of breath. Her teeth chattered, wildly she battered him with her head, broke away, but he snatched at the skirt of her coat and jerked her back. Her face swung up and she saw the waves of a grey sky and a crane breasting them, beautiful as the figurehead of a ship. She staggered for balance and the handbag and parcel fell. At once he was upon them, and she wheeled about; but as she was about to fall on her knees to get there first, a sudden relief, like a rush of tears, came to her and, instead, she ran. She ran and ran, stumbling wildly off through the stalks of dead grass, turning over her heels against hard winter tussocks, blundering through trees and bushes. The young mimosas closed in, lowering a thicket of twigs right to the ground, but she tore herself through, feeling the dust in her eyes and the scaly twigs hooking at her hair. There was a ditch, knee-high in blackjacks; like pins responding to a magnet they fastened along her legs, but on the other side there was a fence and then the road . . . She clawed at the fence—her hands were capable of nothing—and tried to drag herself between the wires, but her coat got caught on a barb, and she was imprisoned there, bent in half, while waves of terror swept over her in heat and trembling. At last the wire tore through its hold on the cloth; wobbling, frantic, she climbed over the fence.

And she was out. She was out on the road. A little way on there were houses, with gardens, postboxes, a child's swing. A small dog sat at a gate. She could hear a faint hum, as of life, of talk somewhere, or perhaps telephone wires.

She was trembling so that she could not stand. She had to keep on walking, quickly, down the road. It was quiet and grey, like the morning. And cool. Now she could feel the cold air round her mouth and between her brows, where the skin stood out in sweat. And in the cold wetness that soaked down beneath her armpits and between her buttocks. Her heart thumped slowly and stiffly. Yes, the wind was cold; she was suddenly cold, damp-cold, all through. She raised her hand, still fluttering uncontrollably, and smoothed her hair; it was wet at the hairline. She guided her hand into her pocket and found a handkerchief to blow her nose.

There was the gate of the first house, before her.

She thought of the woman coming to the door, of the explanations, of the woman's face, and the police. Why did I fight, she thought suddenly. What did I fight for? Why didn't I give him the money and let him go? His red eyes, and the smell and those cracks in his feet, fissures, erosion. She shuddered. The cold of the morning flowed into her.

She turned away from the gate and went down the road slowly, like an invalid, beginning to pick the blackjacks from her stockings.

THE TURTLE OVERNIGHT

I remember him last twilight in his comeliness. When it began to rain, he appeared in his accustomed place and emerged from his shell as far as he could reach—feet, legs, tail, head. He seemed to enjoy the rain, the sweet-tasting rain that blew all the way across lake water to him from the mountains, the Alto Adige. It was as near as I've ever come to seeing a turtle take a pleasant bath in his natural altogether. All the legendary faces of broken old age disappeared from my mind, the thickened muscles under the chins, the nostrils brutal with hatred, the murdering eyes. He filled my mind with a sweet-tasting mountain rain, his youthfulness, his modesty as he washed himself all alone, his religious face.

For a long time now this morning, I have been sitting at this window and watching the grass below me. A moment ago there was no one there. But now his brindle shell sighs slowly up and down in the midst of the green sunlight. A black watchdog snuffles asleep just beyond him, but I trust that neither is afraid of the other. I can see him lifting his face. It is a raising of eyebrows toward the light, an almost imperceptible turning of the chin, an ancient pleasure, an eagerness.

Along his throat there are small folds, dark yellow as pollen shaken across a field of camomile. The lines on his face suggest only a relaxation, a delicacy in the understanding of the grass, like the careful tenderness I saw once on the face of a hobo in Ohio as he waved greeting to an empty wheat field from the flat-car of a freight train.

But now the train is gone, and the turtle has left his circle of empty grass. I look a long time where he was, and I can't find a footprint in the empty grass. So much air left, so much sunlight, and still he is gone.

REGRET FOR A
SPIDER WEB

Laying the foundations of community, she labors all alone. Whether or not God made a creature as deliberately green as this spider, I am not the one to say. If not, then He tossed a star of green dust into one of my lashes. A moment ago, there was no spider there. I must have been thinking about something else, maybe the twenty-mile meadows along the slopes of the far-off mountain I was trying to name, or the huge snows clinging up there in summer, with their rivulets exploding into roots of ice when the night comes down. But now all the long distances are gone. Not quite three inches from my left eyelash, the air is forming itself into avenues, back alleys, boulevards, paths, gardens, fields, and one frail towpath shimmering as it leads away into the sky.

Where is she?

I can't find her.

Oh: resting beneath my thumbnail, pausing, wondering how long she can make use of me, how long I will have sense enough to hold still.

She will never know or care how sorry I am that my lungs are not huge magnificent frozen snows, and that my fingers are not firmly rooted in earth like the tall cypresses. But I have been holding my breath now for one minute and sixteen seconds. I wish I could tower beside her forever, and be one mountain she can depend upon. But my lungs have their own cities to build. I have to move, or die.

Phyllis Koestenbaum

HARRIET FEIGENBAUM
IS A SCULPTOR

She is building a model of a concentration camp complex. She has not been to a camp but has seen an aerial model. What she noticed: the symmetry, the exactness. As maids place pillows (these are Harriet Feigenbaum's ideas, images), so was the concentration camp complex: orderly, but not in relation to a plan. The commandant's house with its kitchen was in the center—surrounded, then, by the ovens, gas chambers. In high school, several of my teachers' wives were in mental hospitals (asylums). No one said why, but it was understood they had started menopause and gone mad. One felt pity for these men, still devoted to their crazy, absent wives. I am post-menopausal. My doctor, Chinese, finds it difficult to examine my heavy breasts for lumps. The obgyn I went to for an abortion when I was pregnant, at forty, vigorously palpated my breasts for milk, maybe (to give him the benefit of the doubt) to see how far along I was. He hurt me. My Uncle Nat Lemler was a prison guard. My Aunt Jeannie was the least attractive of all my mother's sisters. Not that they were beauties, but she had absolutely no beauty, almost as if she deserved the terrible man she was married to, who would divorce her, the first divorce in the family. I felt terrible seeing Aunt Jeannie, who lived in poverty, as the ugly duckling of my mother's large family. The Vietnam War Memorial was created by an artist who was not a veteran. Reconnecting with a man I loved forty years ago, the chance for a new start and new loss. Terrible dreams too disgusting to write.

James Tate

DISTANCE FROM LOVED ONES

After her husband died, Zita decided to get the face-lift she had always wanted. Half-way through the operation her blood pressure started to drop, and they had to stop. When Zita tried to fasten her seat-belt for her sad drive home, she threw out her shoulder. Back at the hospital the doctor examined her and found cancer run rampant throughout her shoulder and arm and elsewhere. Radiation followed. And, now, Zita just sits there in her beauty parlor, bald, crying and crying.

My mother tells me all this on the phone, and I say: Mother, who is Zita?

And my mother says, I am Zita. All my life I have been Zita, bald and crying. And you, my son, who should have known me best, thought I was nothing but your mother.

But, Mother, I say, I am dying. . . .

COCKROACHES IN AUTUMN

On the white painted bolt of a door that is never opened, a thick line of tiny black grains—the dung of cockroaches.

They nest in the coffee filters, in the woven wicker shelves, and in the crack at the top of a door, where by flashlight you see the forest of moving legs.

Boats were scattered over the water near Dover Harbor at odd angles, like the cockroaches surprised in the kitchen at night before they move.

The youngest are so bright, so spirited, so willing.

He sees the hand coming down and runs the other way. There is too far to go, or he is not fast enough. At the same time we admire such a will to live.

I am alert to small moving things, and spin around toward a floating dust mote. I am alert to darker spots against a lighter background, but these are only the roses on my pillowcase.

A new autumn stillness, in the evening. The windows of the neighborhood are shut. A chill sifts into the room from the panes of glass. Behind a cupboard door, they squat inside a long box eating spaghetti.

The stillness of death. When the small creature does not move away from the lowering hand.

We feel respect for such nimble rascals, such quick movers, such clever thieves.

From inside a white paper bag comes the sound of a creature scratching—one creature, I think. But when I empty the bag, a crowd of them scatter from the heel of rye bread, like rye seeds across the counter, like raisins.

Fat, half grown, with a glossy dark back, he stops short in his headlong rush and tries a few other moves almost simultaneously, a bumper-car jolting in place on the white drainboard.

Daniel Halpern

COFFEE

There was a little coffee house in the mid-Sixties, placed halfway through Laurel Canyon, in Los Angeles. There was a woman who lived in the canyon with her small girl. I can't remember their names, twenty-five years ago, but it occurs to me that little girl is now thirty, perhaps with a child of her own. Quickly it's possible to look back and find yourself out far enough the land you so recently left is no longer in sight. The room where we slept that summer was screened-in, a porch really, set on the edge of woods. In the morning the little girl joined us until her mother got up to make coffee. She was the first woman I knew in that way with a child. We drove everywhere, the three of us, one family just driving—on our way. What she taught me during the long nights that summer, screened-in with the low whimper of wind floating down through the canyon, the casual closeness of that time, the mornings following, is just part of everything else. Sometimes, after she'd fall asleep, I'd walk to the cafe with a book in my pocket and some change for coffee. And then I'd walk home, late, the air hollow, flower-filled, the thought of her asleep enough. It wasn't possible. Coffee is the drink of the office, of insomniacs and lovers. She is so far removed now that I'm thinking of her. It was an easy passion, brief, thoughtful, even *passionate*. A few years ago I drove by the cafe, a garage now, and where I remembered her house to be. I parked the car and walked up the long ladder of stairs to the gate I painted dark brown one early day in mid-August. There was no one home, but I wouldn't have rung the bell anyway—that little girl would have been her mother's age the last time I saw her. The house bore small resemblance to my memory—it had grown ornate, the gate repainted white, shutters added and painted a cheerful teal, the garden gouged out of the earth behind the room that was once screened-in, now part of a two-story addition. Why should anything have remained? And my last thought before turning back down the steps was our last meal together. We ate in bed, a curried chicken she taught me to make, rice and a little date chutney she'd made for house gifts. And before I left we made love with considerable nostalgia, as if this last act were itself an act of memory recalled late in the dead of some night years and an age later, the book put aside, the cups of coffee cooling, just out of reach.

ADVICE TO YOUNG WRITERS

One of the things I've repeated to writing
students is that they should write when they don't
feel like writing, just sit down and start,
and when it doesn't go very well, to press on then,
to get to that one thing you'd otherwise
never find. What I forgot to mention was
that this is just a writing technique, that
you could also be out mowing the lawn, where,
if you bring your mind to it, you'll also eventually
come to something unexpected ("The robin he
hunts and pecks"), or watching the FARM NEWS
on which a large man is referring to the "Greater
Massachusetts area." It's alright, students, not
to write. Do whatever you want. As long as you find
that unexpected something, or even if you don't.

THE LAST DAYS
OF A FAMOUS MIME

1.

The Mime arrived on Alitalia with very little luggage: a brown paper parcel and what looked like a woman's handbag.

Asked the contents of the brown paper parcel he said, "String."

Asked what the string was for he replied: "Tying up bigger parcels."

It had not been intended as a joke, but the Mime was pleased when the reporters laughed. Inducing laughter was not his forte. He was famous for terror.

Although his state of despair was famous throughout Europe, few guessed at his hope for the future. "The string," he explained, "is a prayer that I am always praying."

Reluctantly he untied his parcel and showed them the string. It was blue and when extended measured exactly fifty-three meters.

The Mime and the string appeared on the front pages of the evening papers.

2.

The first audiences panicked easily. They had not been prepared for his ability to mime terror. They fled their seats continually. Only to return again.

Like snorkel divers they appeared at the doors outside the concert hall with red faces and were puzzled to find the world as they had left it.

3.

Books had been written about him. He was the subject of an award-winning film. But in his first morning in a provincial town he was distressed to find that his performance had not been liked by the one newspaper's one critic.

"I cannot see," the critic wrote, "the use of invoking terror in an audience."

The Mime sat on his bed, pondering ways to make his performance more light-hearted.

4.

As usual he attracted women who wished to still the raging storms of his heart.

They attended his bed like highly paid surgeons operating on a difficult case. They were both passionate and intelligent. They did not suffer defeat lightly.

5.

Wrongly accused of merely miming love in his private life he was somewhat surprised to be confronted with hatred.

"Surely," he said, "if you now hate me, it was you who were imitating love, not I."

"You always were a slimy bastard," she said. "What's in that parcel?"

"I told you before," he said helplessly, "string."

"You're a liar," she said.

But later when he untied the parcel he found that she had opened it to check on his story. Her understanding of the string had been perfect. She had cut it into small pieces like spaghetti in a lousy restaurant.

6.

Against the advice of the tour organizers he devoted two concerts entirely to love and laughter. They were disasters. It was felt that love and laughter were not, in his case, as instructive as terror.

The next performance was quickly announced.

TWO HOURS OF REGRET

Tickets sold quickly. He began with a brief interpretation of love using it merely as a prelude to regret which he elaborated on in a complex and moving performance which left the audience pale and shaken. In a final flourish he passed from regret to loneliness to terror. The audience devoured the terror like brave tourists eating the hottest curry in an Indian restaurant.

7.

"What you are doing," she said, "is capitalizing on your neuroses. Personally I find it disgusting, like someone exhibiting their clubfoot, or Turkish beggars with strange deformities."

He said nothing. He was mildly annoyed at her presumption: that he had not thought this many, many times before.

With perfect misunderstanding she interpreted his passivity as disdain.

Wishing to hurt him, she slapped his face.

Wishing to hurt her, he smiled brilliantly.

8.

The story of the blue string touched the public imagination. Small brown paper packages were sold at the door of his concert.

Standing on stage he could hear the packages being noisily unwrapped. He thought of American matrons buying Muslim prayer rugs.

9.

Exhausted and weakened by the heavy schedule he fell prey to the doubts that had pricked at him insistently for years. He lost all sense of direction and spent many listless hours by himself, sitting in a motel room listening to the air conditioner.

He had lost confidence in the social uses of controlled terror. He no longer understood the audience's need to experience the very things he so desperately wished to escape from.

He emptied the ashtrays fastidiously.

He opened his brown paper parcel and threw the small pieces of string down the cistern. When the torrent of white water subsided they remained floating there like flotsam from a disaster at sea.

10.

The Mime called a press conference to announce that there would be no more concerts. He seemed small and foreign and smelt of garlic. The press regarded him without enthusiasm. He watched their hovering pens anxiously, unsuccessfully willing them to write down his words.

Briefly he announced that he wished to throw his talent open to broader influences. His skills would be at the disposal of the people, who would be free to request his services for any purpose at any time.

His skin seemed sallow but his eyes seemed as bright as those on a nodding fur mascot on the back window ledge of an American car.

11.

Asked to describe death he busied himself taking Polaroid photographs of his questioners.

12.

Asked to describe marriage he handed out small cheap mirrors with MADE IN TUNISIA written on the back.

13.

His popularity declined. It was felt that he had become obscure and beyond the understanding of ordinary people. In response he requested easier questions. He held back nothing of himself in his effort to please his audience.

14.

Asked to describe an airplane he flew three times around the city, only injuring himself slightly on landing.

15.

Asked to describe a river, he drowned himself.

16.

It is unfortunate that this, his last and least typical performance, is the only one which has been recorded on film.

There is a small crowd by the riverbank, no more than thirty people. A small, neat man dressed in a gray suit picks his way through some children who seem more interested in the large plastic toy dog they are playing with.

He steps into the river, which, at the bank, is already quite deep. His head is only visible above the water for a second or two. And then he is gone.

A policeman looks expectantly over the edge, as if waiting for him to reappear. Then the film stops.

Watching this last performance it is difficult to imagine how this man stirred such emotions in the hearts of those who saw him.

NO ONE'S A
MYSTERY

For my eighteenth birthday Jack gave me a five-year diary with a latch and a little key, light as a dime. I was sitting beside him scratching at the lock, which didn't seem to want to work, when he thought he saw his wife's Cadillac in the distance, coming toward us. He pushed me down onto the dirty floor of the pickup and kept one hand on my head while I inhaled the musk of his cigarettes in the dashboard ashtray and sang along with Rosanne Cash on the tape deck. We'd been drinking tequila and the bottle was between his legs, resting up against his crotch, where the seam of his Levi's was bleached linen-white, though the Levi's were nearly new. I don't know why his Levi's always bleached like that, along the seams and at the knees. In a curve of cloth his zipper glinted, gold.

"It's her," he said. "She keeps the lights on in the daytime. I can't think of a single habit in a woman that irritates me more than that." When he saw that I was going to stay still he took his hand from my head and ran it through his own dark hair.

"Why does she?" I said.

"She thinks it's safer. Why does she need to be safer? She's driving exactly fifty-five miles an hour. She believes in those signs: 'Speed Monitored by Aircraft.' It doesn't matter that you can look up and see that the sky is empty."

"She'll see your lips move, Jack. She'll know you're talking to someone."

"She'll think I'm singing along with the radio."

He didn't lift his hand, just raised the fingers in salute while the pressure of his palm steadied the wheel, and I heard the Cadillac honk twice, musically; he was driving easily eighty miles an hour. I studied his boots. The elk heads stitched into the leather were bearded with frayed thread, the toes were scuffed, and there was a compact wedge of muddy manure between the heel and the sole—the same boots he'd been wearing for the two years I'd known him. On the tape deck Rosanne Cash sang, "Nobody's into me, no one's a mystery."

"Do you think she's getting famous because of who her daddy is or for herself?" Jack said.

"There are about a hundred pop tops on the floor, did you know that? Some little kid could cut a bare foot on one of these, Jack."

"No little kids get into this truck except for you."

"How come you let it get so dirty?"

" 'How come,' " he mocked. "You even sound like a kid. You can get back into the seat now, if you want. She's not going to look over her shoulder and see you."

"How do you know?"

"I just know," he said. "Like I know I'm going to get meat loaf for supper. It's in the air. Like I know what you'll be writing in that diary."

"What will I be writing?" I knelt on my side of the seat and craned around to look at the butterfly of dust printed on my jeans. Outside the window Wyoming was dazzling in the heat. The wheat was fawn and yellow and parted smoothly by the thin dirt road. I could smell the water in the irrigation ditches hidden in the wheat.

"Tonight you'll write, 'I love Jack. This is my birthday present from him. I can't imagine anybody loving anybody more than I love Jack.' "

"I can't."

"In a year you'll write, 'I wonder what I ever really saw in Jack. I wonder why I spent so many days just riding around in his pickup. It's true he taught me something about sex. It's true there wasn't ever much else to do in Cheyenne.' "

"I won't write that."

"In two years you'll write, 'I wonder what that old guy's name was, the one with the curly hair and the filthy dirty pickup truck and time on his hands.' "

"I won't write that."

"No?"

"Tonight I'll write, 'I love Jack. This is my birthday present from him. I can't imagine anybody loving anybody more than I love Jack.' "

"No, you can't," he said. "You can't imagine it."

"In a year I'll write, 'Jack should be home any minute now. The table's set—my grandmother's linen and her old silver and the yellow candles left over from the wedding—but I don't know if I can wait until after the trout à la Navarra to make love to him.' "

"It must have been a fast divorce."

"In two years I'll write, 'Jack should be home by now. Little Jack is hungry for his supper. He said his first word today besides "Mama" and "Papa." He said "kaka." ' "

Jack laughed. "He was probably trying to finger-paint with kaka on the bathroom wall when you heard him say it."

"In three years I'll write, 'My nipples are a little sore from nursing Eliza Rosamund.' "

"Rosamund. Every little girl should have a middle name she hates."

" 'Her breath smells like vanilla and her eyes are just Jack's color of blue.' "

"That's nice," Jack said.

"So, which one do you like?"

"I like yours," he said. "But I believe mine."

"It doesn't matter. I believe mine."

"Not in your heart of hearts, you don't."

"You're wrong."

"I'm not wrong," he said. "And her breath would smell like your milk, and it's kind of a bittersweet smell, if you want to know the truth."

DEATH OF
THE RIGHT FIELDER

After too many balls went out and never came back we went out to check. It was a long walk—he always played deep. Finally we saw him, from the distance resembling the towel we sometimes threw down for second base.

It was hard to tell how long he'd been lying there, sprawled on his face. Had he been playing infield, his presence, or lack of it, would, of course, have been noticed immediately. The infield demands communication—the constant, reassuring chatter of team play. But he was remote, clearly an outfielder (the temptation is to say out*sider*). The infield is for wisecrackers, pepper-pots, gum-poppers; the outfield is for loners, onlookers, brooders who would rather study clover and swat gnats than holler. People could pretty much be divided between infielders and outfielders. Not that one always has a choice. He didn't necessarily choose right field so much as accept it.

There were several theories as to what killed him. From the start the most popular was that he'd been shot. Perhaps from a passing car, possibly by that gang calling themselves the Jokers, who played sixteen-inch softball on the concrete diamond with painted bases in the center of the housing project, or by the Latin Lords, who didn't play sports, period. Or maybe some pervert with a telescopic sight from a bedroom window, or a mad sniper from a water tower, or a terrorist with a silencer from the expressway overpass, or maybe it was an accident, a stray slug from a robbery, or shoot-out, or assassination attempt miles away.

No matter who pulled the trigger it seemed more plausible to ascribe his death to a bullet than to natural causes like, say, a heart attack. Young deaths are never natural; they're all violent. Not that kids don't die of heart attacks. But he never seemed the type. Sure, he was quiet, but not the quiet of someone always listening for the heart murmur his family repeatedly warned him about since he was old enough to play. Nor could it have been leukemia. He

57

wasn't a talented enough athlete to die of that. He'd have been playing center, not right, if leukemia was going to get him.

The shooting theory was better, even though there wasn't a mark on him. Couldn't it have been, as some argued, a high-powered bullet traveling with such velocity that its hole fuses behind it? Still, not everyone was satisfied. Other theories were formulated, rumors became legends over the years: he'd had an allergic reaction to a bee sting, been struck by a single bolt of lightning from a freak, instantaneous electrical storm, ingested too strong a dose of insecticide from the grass blades he chewed on, sonic waves, radiation, pollution, etc. And a few of us liked to think it was simply that chasing a sinking liner, diving to make a shoestring catch, he broke his neck.

There *was* a ball in the webbing of his mitt when we turned him over. His mitt had been pinned under his body and was coated with an almost luminescent gray film. There was the same gray on his black, high-top gym shoes, as if he'd been running through lime, and along the bill of his baseball cap—the blue felt one with the red *C* which he always denied stood for the Chicago Cubs. He may have been a loner, but he didn't want to be identified with a loser. He lacked the sense of humor for that, lacked the perverse pride that sticking for losers season after season breeds, and the love. He was just an ordinary guy, .250 at the plate, and we stood above him not knowing what to do next. By then the guys from the other outfield positions had trotted over. Someone, the shortstop probably, suggested team prayer. But no one could think of a team prayer. So we all just stood there silently bowing our heads, pretending to pray while the shadows moved darkly across the outfield grass. After a while the entire diamond was swallowed and the field lights came on.

In the bluish squint of those lights he didn't look like someone we'd once known—nothing looked quite right—and we hurriedly scratched a shallow grave, covered him over, and stamped it down as much as possible so that the next right fielder, whoever he'd be, wouldn't trip. It could be just such a juvenile, seemingly trivial stumble that would ruin a great career before it had begun, or hamper it years later the way Mantle's was hampered by bum knees. One can never be sure the kid beside him isn't another Roberto Clemente; and who can ever know how many potential Great Ones have gone down in the obscurity of their neighborhoods? And so, in the catcher's phrase, we "buried the grave" rather than contribute to any further tragedy. In all likelihood the next right fielder, whoever he'd be, would be clumsy too, and if there was a mound to trip over he'd find it and break *his* neck, and soon right field would get the reputation as haunted, a kind of sandlot Bermuda Triangle, inhabited by phantoms calling for ghostly fly balls, where no one but the most desperate outcasts, already on the verge of suicide, would be willing to play.

Still, despite our efforts, we couldn't totally disguise it. A fresh grave is stubborn. Its outline remained visible—a scuffed bald spot that might have been confused for an aberrant pitcher's mound except for the bat jammed in the earth with the mitt and blue cap fit over it. Perhaps we didn't want to eradicate it completely—a part of us was resting there. Perhaps we wanted the new right fielder, whoever he'd be, to notice and wonder about who played there before him, realizing he was now the only link between past and future that mattered. A monument, epitaph, flowers, wouldn't be necessary.

As for us, we walked back, but by then it was too late—getting on to supper, getting on to the end of summer vacation, time for other things, college, careers, settling down and raising a family. Past thirty-five the talk starts about being over the hill, about a graying Phil Niekro in his forties still fanning them with the knuckler as if it's some kind of miracle, about Pete Rose still going in headfirst at forty, beating the odds. And maybe the talk is right. One remembers Willie Mays, forty-two years old and a Met, dropping that can-of-corn fly in the '73 Series, all that grace stripped away and with it the conviction, leaving a man confused and apologetic about the boy in him. It's sad to admit it ends so soon, but everyone knows those are the lucky ones. Most guys are washed up by seventeen.

Alan Lightman

from *Einstein's Dreams*

14 May 1905

There is a place where time stands still. Raindrops hang motionless in air. Pendulums of clocks float mid-swing. Dogs raise their muzzles in silent howls. Pedestrians are frozen on the dusty streets, their legs cocked as if held by strings. The aromas of dates, mangoes, coriander, cumin are suspended in space.

As a traveler approaches this place from any direction, he moves more and more slowly. His heartbeats grow farther apart, his breathing slackens, his temperature drops, his thoughts diminish, until he reaches dead center and stops. For this is the center of time. From this place, time travels outward in concentric circles—at rest at the center, slowly picking up speed at greater diameters.

Who would make pilgrimage to the center of time? Parents with children, and lovers.

And so, at the place where time stands still, one sees parents clutching their children, in a frozen embrace that will never let go. The beautiful young daughter with blue eyes and blond hair will never stop smiling the smile she smiles now, will never lose this soft pink glow on her cheeks, will never grow wrinkled or tired, will never get injured, will never unlearn what her parents have taught her, will never think thoughts that her parents don't know, will never know evil, will never tell her parents that she does not love them, will never leave her room with the view of the ocean, will never stop touching her parents as she does now.

And at the place where time stands still, one sees lovers kissing in the shadows of buildings, in a frozen embrace that will never let go. The loved one will never take his arms from where they are now, will never give back the bracelet of memories, will never journey far from his lover, will never place himself in danger in self-sacrifice, will never fail to show his love, will never become jealous, will never fall in love with someone else, will never lose the passion of this instant in time.

One must consider that these statues are illuminated by only the most feeble red light, for light is diminished almost to nothing at the center of time, its vibrations slowed to echoes in vast canyons, its intensity reduced to the faint glow of fireflies.

Those not quite at dead center do indeed move, but at the pace of glaciers. A brush of the hair might take a year, a kiss might take a thousand. While a smile is returned, seasons pass in the outer world. While a child is hugged, bridges rise. While a good-bye is said, cities crumble and are forgotten.

And those who return to the outer world . . . Children grow rapidly, forget the centuries-long embrace from their parents, which to them lasted but seconds. Children become adults, live far from their parents, live in their own houses, learn ways of their own, suffer pain, grow old. Children curse their parents for trying to hold them forever, curse time for their own wrinkled skin and hoarse voices. These now old children also want to stop time, but at another time. They want to freeze their own children at the center of time.

Lovers who return find their friends are long gone. After all, lifetimes have passed. They move in a world they do not recognize. Lovers who return still embrace in the shadows of buildings, but now their embraces seem empty and alone. Soon they forget the centuries-long promises, which to them lasted only seconds. They become jealous even among strangers, say hateful things to each other, lose passion, drift apart, grow old and alone in a world they do not know.

Some say it is best not to go near the center of time. Life is a vessel of sadness, but it is noble to live life, and without time there is no life. Others disagree. They would rather have an eternity of contentment, even if that eternity were fixed and frozen, like a butterfly mounted in a case.

15 May 1905

Imagine a world in which there is no time. Only images.

A child at the seashore, spellbound by her first glimpse of the ocean. A woman standing on a balcony at dawn, her hair down, her loose sleeping silks, her bare feet, her lips. The curved arch of the arcade near the Zähringer Fountain on Kramgasse, sandstone and iron. A man sitting in the quiet of his study, holding the photograph of a woman, a pained look on his face. An osprey framed in the sky, its wings outstretched, the sun rays piercing between feathers. A young boy sitting in an empty auditorium, his heart racing as if he were on stage. Footprints in snow on a winter island. A boat on the water at night, its lights dim in the distance, like a small red star in the black sky. A locked cabinet of pills. A leaf on the ground in autumn, red and gold and brown, delicate. A woman crouching in the bushes, waiting by the house of her estranged husband, whom she must talk to. A soft rain on a spring day, on a walk that is the last walk a young man will take in the place that he loves. Dust on a windowsill. A stall of peppers on Marktgasse, the yellow and green and red. Matterhorn, the jagged peak of white pushing into the solid blue sky, the green valley and the log cabins. The eye of a needle. Dew on leaves, crystal, opalescent. A mother on her bed, weeping, the smell of basil in the air. A child on a bicycle in the Kleine Schanze, smiling the smile of a lifetime. A tower of prayer, tall and octagonal, open balcony, solemn, surrounded by arms. Steam rising from a lake in early morning. An open drawer. Two friends at a café, the lamplight illuminating one friend's face, the other in shadow. A cat watching a bug on the window. A young woman on a bench, reading a letter, tears of joy in her green eyes. A great field, lined with cedar and spruce. Sunlight, in long angles through the window in late afternoon. A massive tree fallen, roots sprawling in air, bark, limbs still green. The white of a sailboat, with the wind behind it, sails billowed like wings of a giant white bird. A father and son alone at a restaurant, the father sad and staring down at the tablecloth. An oval window, looking out on fields of hay, a wooden cart, cows, green and purple in the afternoon light. A broken bottle on the floor, brown liquid in the crevices, a woman with red eyes. An old man in the kitchen, cooking breakfast for his grandson, the boy gazing out the window at a white painted bench. A worn book lying on a table beside a dim lamp. The white on water as a wave breaks, blown by wind. A woman lying on her couch with wet hair, holding the hand of a man she will never see again. A train with red cars, on a great stone bridge with graceful arches, a river underneath, tiny dots that are houses in the distance. Dust motes floating in sunlight through a window. The thin skin in the middle of a neck, thin enough to see the pulse of blood underneath. A man and woman naked, wrapped around each other. The blue shadows of trees in a full moon. The top of a mountain with a strong steady wind, the valley falling away on all sides, sandwiches of beef and cheese. A child wincing from his father's slap, the father's lips twisted in anger, the child not understanding. A strange face in the mirror, gray at the temples. A young man holding a telephone, startled at what he is hearing. A family photograph, the parents young and relaxed, the children in ties and dresses and smiling. A tiny light, far through a thicket of trees. The red at sunset. An eggshell, white, fragile, unbroken. A blue hat washed up on shore. Roses cut and adrift on the river beneath the bridge, with a château rising. Red hair of a lover, wild, mischievous, promising. The purple petals of an iris, held by a young woman. A room of four walls, two windows, two beds, a table, a lamp, two people with red faces, tears. The first kiss. Planets caught in space, oceans, silence. A bead of water on the window. A coiled rope. A yellow brush.

LA CORTADA

All those memoirs that begin with the author's recollections of life at age three, I never trust them. Never. What baloney, I think to myself, who is the author fooling, for heaven's sakes?

Sometimes I wonder if I had a childhood. My mother tells me I was a very happy child. Especially in Cuba. I was born in Havana. I lived there until I was nearly five. But I can't recall a thing. It's as if I sprang to life when we arrived in New York—for that is my earliest memory, the moment of arriving, of docking. If only I could remember the early years of my life, my mother says, I would know for myself how happy I was in Cuba. I wouldn't have to take her word for it.

So many of my Cuban friends, who left the island around the same age as I, recall perfectly the trauma of their departure, the sense of expulsion from paradise. But I don't recall leaving Cuba, either.

There's a term for my condition. I am *cortada*. Call me *La Cortada*. I grew up hearing that term as a description of my Aunt Silvia, my mother's older sister. When my mother would talk to her friends about my aunt's shyness, she would explain, *Es que se siente cortada. Cortar* means to cut, and to feel *cortada* is to feel cut short, at a loss. You freeze when you need to speak; you can't get out what you need to say because something holds you back, something makes you feel you would have to shout beyond the capacity of your own voice in order to be heard. It is as if you have forgotten how to speak, or why speaking is even necessary.

When I was in college I had such trouble speaking in class I became convinced I was suffering from aphasia. I spent days at the library reading the psychology manuals, trying to figure out which region of my brain might be impaired. Afraid to grow dumber if I left school, I never let myself out for recess, I became a professor. Now the shy, quiet girl in the back of the room sits in the front playing teacher. I am thankful for the talkative students, who save me from having to lecture. I avoid the gaze of the shy, quiet students. The mirror of their silence terrifies me.

At a Lego Fair at my son Gabriel's school, I run into the mother of one of his friends. Her arm is in a sling. She's broken her elbow cross-country skiing. The doctors, she tells me, needed for her to be awake while they set her arm, so they injected her with a drug that would induce amnesia, selectively, in her brain. That way she'd just forget the pain, the blood, the doctors' faces. She'd never remember what it felt like to have her arm set.

Who injected me? Who cut me short? Why did I forget?

I embark upon a series of return trips to Cuba. Over and over again I go. I keep returning to the same places, I keep retracing my steps, looking for a memory. I want to find the girl who used to chatter happily, the girl who was not yet *cortada,* and especially the girl who rode around in taxicabs by herself at age three, four. You see, my mother always told me it was so safe in the old days in Cuba that she'd send me by taxi from our apartment in El Vedado to my Aunt Zoila's house in Miramar. Alone? I would ask, amazed. Yes, she'd say, alone. There were never any problems. In our sad, brick apartment in New York, sitting by the picture window staring at the moon, I grew up enamored of the image of the precocious bourgeois girl in her party dress riding around in taxicabs, passing the sea on her way from El Vedado to Miramar.

And now, years later, in the course of my return journeys to Cuba, I have become close again to Caro, the black woman who took care of me as a child. She retains a crystal sharp image of my young girlhood, such a sharp image that I think she still sees little white Rutie in her wind-puffed party dress when she looks at me.

One day she says, "I ran into the taxi driver again."

I have no idea what she is talking about. "What taxi driver?"

"You don't remember?"

I shake my head mournfully. "No. Caro, please tell me. I don't remember anything from my childhood here."

She looks at me with curiosity. "I wouldn't tell him," she says. "And he still wanted to know. Would you believe that after thirty-five years he still wanted to know?"

"Know what?"

"Why you wouldn't ride in the taxicab with him."

And finally Caro tells me: When I was a little girl I told her the man pinched my thighs and I didn't like that. He'd pinch them all the way to my Aunt Zoila's house and back. That's why I wouldn't get into his car again, no matter what my mother or anyone said.

After Caro tells me this story, I realize that for me leaving Cuba was like crossing the river Lethe. I entered the otherworld. I was stripped of memory, stripped of speech, *cortada,* cut to the quick. I forgot all the happiness, but also all the sadness. I forgot all the things I failed to understand, like why the taxi driver wanted to pinch my thighs and why I told Caro but not my mother.

But I am learning that memories don't disappear. They leave traces. They make their way back to this world in subtle, yet insistent ways. For example, I have a horrible sense of direction. I cannot read a map to save my life. I find it a chore to have to distinguish between north and south. And now, after numerous return trips, I still just barely know my way around the city of Havana. The only method I have for learning my way around a city is to use intuition, to wander, to get lost. But I am afraid to get too lost in Havana. So I never take long walks there by myself. I am always walking with someone. Or being driven around by someone. I have many fears, but none is more terrible than my fear of getting too lost in the city of my birth and never being heard from again.

DRAMATIC MONOLOGUES

DRAMATIC
MONOLOGUES

Why do human beings like to "act"? Why is there such pleasure in "performance"?—in performing, and in witnessing performances? Are there countless undiscovered, buried selves in all of us, awaiting expression?

The monologue, the basic unit of drama, is the most direct, the most forceful, and for beginning writers the most accessible mode of writing. Not "easy," perhaps, but natural seeming, unpretentious. A form of ventriloquism—"throwing one's voice." A mode that can be wonderfully elastic and experimental: confessional, comic, terrifying, a means of truth telling that cuts through the trappings of traditional narrative, exposition, background, description, and the setting of a "mood." Here, an individual simply stands before us, usually on a bare stage, and speaks.

The form is ancient, yet any monologue has the air of the improvised and contemporary. Monologues are made to be performed; at the least, the writer should always recite the work out loud to test its effectiveness. My theory, which student-writers have confirmed in their practice, is that when we read our work out loud, redundant phrases, contrivances, falsely ringing language will be evident to the ear, as often they aren't to the eye in merely silent reading.

(Specific suggestions for monologues are included in "The Practice of Writing," the final chapter in this anthology.)

LETHAL

I just want to touch you a little. That delicate blue vein at your temple, the soft down of your neck. I just want to caress you a little. I just want to kiss you a little—your lips, your throat, your breasts. I just want to embrace you a little. I just want to comfort you a little. I just want to hold you tight!—like this. I just want to measure your skeleton with my arms. These are strong healthy arms, aren't they. I just want to poke my tongue in your ear. Don't giggle! Don't squirm! This is serious! This is the real thing! I just want to suck a little. I just want to press into you a little. I just want to penetrate you a little. I just want to ejaculate into you a little. It won't hurt if you don't scream but you'll be hurt if you keep straining away like that, if you exaggerate. Thank you, I just want to squeeze you a little. I just want to feel my weight against your bones a little. I just want to bite a little. I just want a taste of it. Your saliva, your blood. Just a taste. A little. You've got plenty to spare. You're being selfish. You're being ridiculous. You're being cruel. You're being unfair. You're hysterical. You're hyperventilating. You're provoking me. You're laughing at me. You want to humiliate me. You want to make a fool of me. You want to gut me like a chicken. You want to castrate me. You want to make me fight for my life, is that it?

You want to make *me* fight for my life, is that it?

Jane Martin

TWIRLER

[*A young woman stands center stage. She is dressed in a spangled, one-piece swimsuit, the kind for baton twirlers. She holds a shining silver baton in her hand.*]

I started when I was six. Momma sawed off a broom handle, and Uncle Carbo slapped some sort of silver paint, well, gray, really, on it and I went down in the basement and twirled. Later on Momma hit the daily double on horses named Spin Dry and Silver Revolver and she said that was a sign so she gave me lessons at the Dainty Deb Dance Studio, where the lady, Miss Aurelia, taught some twirling on the side.

I won the Ohio Juniors title when I was six and the Midwest Young Adult Division three years later, and then in high school I finished fourth in the nationals. Momma and I wore look-alike Statue of Liberty costumes that she had to send clear to Nebraska to get, and Daddy was there in a T-shirt with my name, April—my first name is April and my last name is March. There were four thousand people there, and when they yelled my name golden balloons fell out of the ceiling. Nobody, not even Charlene Ann Morrison, ever finished fourth at my age.

Oh, I've flown high and known tragedy, both. My daddy says it's put spirit in my soul and steel in my heart. My left hand was crushed in a riding accident by a horse named Big Blood Red, and though I came back to twirl, I couldn't do it at the highest level. That was denied me by Big Blood Red, who clipped my wings. You mustn't pitty me, though. Oh, by no means! Being denied showed me the way, showed me the glory that sits inside life where you can't see it.

People think you're a twit if you twirl. It's a prejudice of the unknowing. Twirlers are the niggers of a white university. Yes, they are. One time I was doing fire batons at a night game, and all of a sudden I see this guy walk out of the stands. I was doing triples and he walks right out past the half-time marshals, comes up to me—he had this blue bead headband, I can still see it. Walks right up, and when I come front after a back reverse he spits in my face. That's the only, single time I ever dropped a baton. Dropped 'em both in front of sixty thousand people, and he smiles, see, and he says this thing I won't repeat. He called me a bodily part in front of half of Ohio. It was like being raped. It shows that beauty inspires hate and that hating beauty is Satan.

You haven't twirled, have you? I can see that by your hands. Would you like to hold my silver baton? Here, hold it.

You can't imagine what it feels like to have that baton up in the air. I used to twirl with that baton up in the air. I used to twirl with this girl who called it blue-collar Zen. The 'tons catch the sun when they're up, and when they go up, you go up, too. You can't twirl if you're not *inside* the 'ton. When you've got 'em up over twenty feet, it's like flying or gliding. Your hands are still down, but your insides spin and rise and leave the ground. Only a twirler knows that, so we're not niggers.

The secret for a twirler is the light. You live or die with the light. It's your fate. The best is a February sky clouded right over in the late afternoon. It's all background then, and what happens is that the 'tons leave tracks, traces, they etch the air, and if you're hot, if your hands have it, you can draw on the sky.

God, Charlene Ann Morrison. God, Charlene Ann! She was inspired by something beyond man. She won the nationals nine years in a row. Unparalleled and unrepeatable. The last two years she had leukemia and at the end you could see through her hands when she twirled. Charlene Ann died with a 'ton thirty feet up, her momma swears on that. I roomed with Charlene at a regional in Fargo, and she may have been fibbin', but she said there was a day when her 'tons erased while they turned. Like the sky was a sheet of rain and the 'tons were car wipers and when she had erased this certain part of the sky you could see the face of the Lord God Jesus, and his hair was all rhinestones and he was doing this incredible singing like the sound of a piccolo. The people who said that Charlene was crazy probably never twirled a day in their life.

Twirling is the physical parallel of revelation. You can't know that. Twirling is the throwing of yourself up to God. It's a pure gift, hidden from Satan because it is wrapped and disguised in the midst of football. It is God-throwing, spirit fire, and very few come to it. You have to grow eyes in your heart to understand its message, and when it opens to you it becomes your path to suffer ridicule, to be crucified by misunderstanding, and to be spit upon. I need my baton now.

There is one twirling no one sees. At the winter solstice we go to a meadow God showed us just outside of Green Bay. The God throwers come there on December twenty-first. There's snow, sometimes deep snow, and our clothes fall away, and we stand unprotected while acolytes bring the 'tons. They are ebony 'tons with razors set all along the shaft. They are three feet long. One by one the twirlers throw, two 'tons each, thirty feet up, and as they fall back they cut your hands. The razors arch into the air and find God and then fly down to take your blood in a crucifixion, and the red drops draw God on the ground, and if you are up with the batons you can look down and see Him revealed. Red on white. Red on white. You can't imagine. You can't imagine how wonderful that is.

I started twirling when I was six, but I never really twirled until my hand was crushed by the horse named Big Blood Red. I have seen God's face from thirty feet up in the air, and I know Him.

Listen. I will leave my silver baton here for you. Lying here as if I forgot it. And when the people file out you can wait back and pick it up, it can be yours, it can be your burden. It is the eye of the needle. I leave it for you.

[*The lights fade.*]

August Wilson

TESTIMONIES

FOUR MONOLOGUES

HOLLOWAY

It ain't that he don't want to work. He don't want to haul no bricks on a construction site for three dollars a hour. That ain't gonna help him. What's he gonna do with twenty-five dollars a day. He can make two or three hundred dollars a day gambling . . . if he get lucky. If he don't, somebody else will get it. That's all you got around here is niggers with somebody else's money in their pocket. And they don't do nothing but trade it off on each other. I got it today and you got it tomorrow. Until sooner or later as sure as the sun shine . . . somebody gonna take it and give it to the white man. The money go from you to me to you and then . . . bingo, it's gone. From him to you to me, then . . . bingo, it's gone. You give it to the white man. Pay your rent, pay your telephone, buy your groceries, see the doctor . . . bingo. It's gone. Just circulate it around till it find that hole then . . . bingo. Like trying to haul sand in a bucket with a hole in it. Time you get where you going the bucket empty. That's why that twenty-five dollars a day ain't gonna do him no good. A nigger with five hundred dollars in his pocket around here is a big man. But you go out there where they at . . . you go out to Squirrel Hill, they walking around there with five thousand dollars in their pocket trying to figure out how to make it into five hundred thousand.

People kill me talking about niggers is lazy. Niggers is the most hardworking people in the world. Worked three hundred years for free. And didn't take no lunch hour. Now all of a sudden niggers is lazy. Don't know how to work. All of a sudden when they got to pay niggers, ain't no work for him to do. If it wasn't for you the white man would be poor. Every little bit he got he got standing on top of you. That's why he could reach so high. He give you three dollars a hour for six months and he got him a railroad for the next hundred years. All you got is six months' worth of three dollars an hour.

It's simple mathematics. Ain't no money in niggers working. Look out there on the street. If there was some money in it . . . if the white man could figure out a way to make some money by putting niggers to work, we'd all be working. He ain't building no more railroads. He got them. He ain't building no more highways. Somebody done already stuck the telephone poles in the ground. That's been done already.

The white man ain't stacking no more niggers. You know what I'm talking about stacking niggers, don't you? Well, here's how that go. If you ain't got nothing . . . you can go out here and get you a nigger. Then you got something, see. You got one nigger. If that one nigger get out there and plant something . . . get something out the ground . . . even if it ain't nothing but a bushel of potatoes . . . then you got one nigger and a bushel of potatoes. Then you take that bushel of potatoes and go get you another nigger. Then you got two niggers. Put them to work and you got two niggers and two bushels of potatoes. See, now you can go buy two more niggers. That's how you stack a nigger on top of a nigger. White folks got to stacking . . . and I'm talking about they stacked up some niggers! Stacked up close to fifty million niggers. If you stacked them on top of one another they make six or seven circles around the moon.

I always said I was gonna get me a dart board and put Eli Whitney's picture on one side and the boll weevil on the other. Eli Whitney invented the cotton gin and put niggers to work and the boll weevil come along and put them out of work. Eli Whitney and the boll weevil the cause of all the problems the colored man is having now. Man invented the cotton gin and they went over to Africa and couldn't find enough niggers. It's lucky the boat didn't sink with all them niggers they had stacked up there. It take them two extra months to get here cause it ride so low in the water. They couldn't find you enough work back then. Now that they got to pay you they can't find you none. If this was a different time wouldn't be nobody out there on the street. They'd all be in the cotton fields.

HOLLOWAY

West's wife been dead twenty years. Died right after the war. Two or three years after that. He buried her himself. Say he didn't want nobody touching her when she was living . . . he didn't want nobody else touching her when she was dead. She died and he ain't had nothing else to live for. He married Joe Westray's daughter. People say they was cousins. I don't know the truth of that but I know he ain't been the same since his wife died. See, I know West. I know him from way back. West used to be a gangster. West wasn't above breaking the law. He wasn't always Johnny B. Goode. This is way back in the thirties I'm talking about. This before you come up here. I been here since twenty-seven. I know West before he got to be an undertaker. West used to gamble, chase women, bootleg, and everything else. He always kept him four or five hundred dollars in his pocket. West used to carry a gun. See, Wolf don't know this . . . but West used to run numbers for the Alberts. Him and Big Dave used to run around together. Big Dave got killed holding up that insurance company and West went in the undertaking business. Opened that funeral home there down on Centre. Had four or five viewing rooms and tried to keep somebody in all of them. I remember one time he had two niggers laid out in the hallway and one on the back porch. Most of them had welfare caskets but West didn't care cause the government pay on time. He might have to worry his money out of some of them other niggers but the government pay quicker than the insurance companies. Come time to bury them, West would tell John D. to carry them niggers out there and dump them out and bring the casket on back. This is what John D. told me. Say West went out there and took the suits off the corpse. Bring them back to bury somebody else in. West was burying niggers so fast you couldn't keep up with him. Every nigger in Pittsburgh at some time or another was walking up handing West some money. He done buried their cousin . . . their uncle. Their mother. Started out with two cars and ended up with seven. Every year he'd buy him seven new Cadillacs—wear them out—and buy him seven more the next year. You could have fed everybody in the neighborhood on the checks West was getting from the government. Man worked twenty hours a day. Up at four and to bed at midnight. It got so every nigger looked alike to him. He couldn't tell one from the other. West got tired of seeing niggers. Niggers dying from pneumonia. Niggers dying from tuberculosis. Niggers getting shot. Niggers getting stabbed to death with ice picks. Babies dying. Old ladies dying. His wife dying. That's the only thing West ever loved. His wife. That's the only thing he understood. The rest of life baffled him.

MEMPHIS

That's what half the problem is . . . these black-power niggers. They got people confused. They don't know what they doing themselves. These niggers talking about freedom, justice, and equality and don't know what it mean. You born free. It's up to you to maintain it. You born with dignity and everything else. These niggers talking about freedom. But what you gonna do with it? Freedom is heavy. You got to put your shoulder to freedom. Put your shoulder to it and hope your back hold up. And if you around here looking for justice, you got a long wait. Ain't no justice. That's why they got that statue of her and got her blindfolded. Common sense would tell you anybody need to see she do. There ain't no justice. Jesus Christ didn't get justice. What makes you think you gonna get it? That's just the nature of the world. These niggers talking about they want freedom, justice, and equality. Equal to what? Hell, I might be a better man than you. What I look like going around here talking about I want to be equal to you? I don't know how these niggers think sometimes. Talking about black power with their hands and their pockets empty. You can't do nothing without a gun. Not in this day and time. That's the only kind of power the white man understand. They think they gonna talk their way up on it. In order to talk your way you got to have something under the table. These niggers don't understand that. If I tell you to get out my yard and leave my apples alone, I can't talk you out. You sit up in the tree and laugh at me. But if you know I might come out with a shotgun . . . that be something different. You'd have to think twice about whether you wanted some apples.

You could take it to the round table if you had one. Sit down and talk it out. But the white man and the black man ain't got no round table. Ain't never had none. The white man don't want you to have the chairs if you did have a table. You can't sit down with him. You always standing up in front of him. And he shaking his finger at you. You ain't got no right to sit down at the table with him. That's what the problem is. If you take it to the round table, you might be able to work something out. But he ain't gonna sit down with you as long as he got you under control. He sit and shake his finger at you and tell you what you better do.

These niggers around here talking about they black and beautiful. I been black all my life. And gonna be black till I die. You can't change that. If you live to be a hundred years you can't change that. I was black the day I was born. I didn't get black yesterday. These niggers crazy. Talking about they black and beautiful. Sound like they trying to convince themselves. When I was coming along, we knew that white people ran the world, but that didn't make us ugly. We was just the low man on the pole. Why you got to go around telling everybody you beautiful? That's some kind of trick the white man done put these people in. He got them thinking like they do. Every nigger they see is uglier than the next. Everything was alright till the white man got to separating the niggers like separating the wheat from the chaff telling them, "It ain't how you look, it's how you do. You do ugly. If you change the way you do, you won't be ugly. If you change, we'll let you be like us. Otherwise you stay over there and suffer." That's when niggers got to thinking they was ugly. You got to think you ugly to run around shouting you beautiful. You don't hear me say that. Hell, I know I look nice. Got good manners and everything.

MEMPHIS

I don't know how much they was gonna give me cause we didn't get that far. I didn't wait to find out when they started out like that. I told them I got a clause too. They ain't the only one got a clause. My clause say they got to give me what I want for it. It's my building. If they wanna buy it they got to meet my price. That's just common sense. I raised so much hell the judge postponed it . . . told me talk to my lawyer. The lawyer looked at the deed and told me that they was right. I told him, I don't need you no more. Fired him on the spot. He supposed to be on my side. They left it like that till I could get me another lawyer. He ain't even looked at the paper good . . . talking about they right. I don't care what the paper say. He supposed to fix it so they meet my price. I left out of there and called me one of them white lawyers, which is what I should have done in the first place. Fellow named Joseph Bartoromo.

I'll be glad to get rid of this old place. I can't make no money. At one time you couldn't get a seat in here. Had the jukebox working and everything. Time somebody get up somebody sit down before they could get out the door. People coming from everywhere. Everybody got to eat and everybody got to sleep. Some people don't have stoves. Some people don't have nobody to cook for them. Men whose wives done died and left them. Cook for them thirty years and lay down and die. Who's gonna cook for them now? Somebody's got to do it. I order four cases of chicken on Friday and Sunday it's gone. Fry it up. Make a stew. Boil it. Add some dumplings. You couldn't charge more than a dollar. But then you didn't have to. It didn't cost you but a quarter. I done seen everything. Patchneck Red sat right there. He sat right down there and ate a bowl of beans. I seen him here and I seen him over there across the street. I seen him both places. Mr. Samuels, the blind man . . . he sat right over there. He could find that table in his sleep. I seen him both places, too. People come from all over. The man used to come twice a week to collect the jukebox. He making more money than I am. He pay seventy-five cents for the record and he make two hundred dollars off of it. If it's a big hit, he's liable to make four hundred. The record will take all the quarters you can give it. It don't never wear out. The chicken be gone by Sunday.

People come in crying . . . you didn't have to ask what it was about. West right across the street. They come here for awhile and go back over there. I done seen that a lot. People arguing about who's gonna bury who . . . arguing over the insurance money. And I done seen a lot of love. People caring for and caring about each other. Touching each other. Right there in that booth I have seen grown men cry. And after they cry I seen them laugh and order another bowl of beans. It ain't nothing like that now. I'll be glad when they

tear it down. But they gonna meet my price. See, they don't know. The half
ain't never been told. I'm ready to walk through fire. I don't bother nobody.
The last person I bothered is dead. My mama died in fifty-four. I said then I
wasn't going for no more draws. They don't know I feel just like I did when
my mama died. She got old and grey and sat by the window till she died. She
must have done that cause she ain't had nothing else to do. I was gone. My
brother was gone. Sister gone. Everybody gone. My daddy was gone. She sat
there till she died. I was staying down on Logan Street. Got the letter one day
and telegram the next. They usually fall on top of one another . . . but not
that close. I got the letter say, if you wanna see your mother you better come
home. Before I could get out the door the telegram came saying it's too late
. . . your mother gone. I was trying to borrow some money. Called the train
station and found out the schedule and I'm trying to borrow some money. I
can't go down there broke. I don't know how long I got to be there. I ain't
even got the train fare. I got $2.63 cents.

I got the telegram and sat down and cried like a baby. I could beat any
new born baby in the world crying. I cried till the tears all run down in my
ears. Got up and went out the door and everything looked different. Everything had changed. I felt like I had been cut loose. All them years something
had a hold of me and I didn't know it. I didn't find out till it cut me loose. I
walked out the door and everything had different colors to it. I felt great. I
didn't owe nobody nothing. The last person I owed anything to was gone. I
borrowed fifty dollars from West and went on down to her funeral. I come
back and said everybody better get out my way. You couldn't hold me down.
It look like then I had somewhere to go fast. I didn't know where but I damn
sure was going there. That's the way I feel now. If there's an Aunt Ester I'm
going up there to see her. See if she can straighten this out . . . cause they don't
know I got a clause of my own. I'll get up off the canvas if I have to. They can
carry me out feet first . . . but my clause say, I ain't going for no more draws.

Emily Mann

STILL LIFE

Set in 1978 and based upon actual interviews, "Still Life" examines three people who have, in one way or another, been deeply affected by the Vietnam War.

Mark, an ex-Marine and Vietnam vet in his thirties, describes the process that made him into a killer.

MARK:

I don't think you understand.
Sure, I was pissed off at myself that I let myself go.
Deep down inside I knew I could have stopped it.
I could have just said:
I won't do it.
Go back in the rear, just not go out,
let them put me in jail.
I could have said:
"I got a tooth-ache," gotten out of it.
They couldn't have forced me.
But it was this duty thing.
It was like:
YOU'RE UNDER ORDERS.
You have your orders, you have your job,
you've got to DO it.

Well, it was like crazy.
At night, you could do anything . . .
It was free fire zones. It was dark. Then

All of a sudden, everything would just burn loose.
It was beautiful . . .
You were given all this power to work outside the law.
We all dug it.

But I don't make any excuses for it.
I may even be trying to do that now.
I could have got out.
Everybody could've.
If EVERYBODY had said *no,*
it couldn't have happened.
There were times we'd say:
let's pack up and go, let's quit.
But jokingly.
We knew we were there.
But I think I knew then
we could have got out of it.

See, there was a point, definitely,
when I was genuinely interested in trying to win the war.
It was my own area.
I wanted to do the best I could.
I mean I could have played it really low-key.
I could have avoided things,
I could have made sure we didn't move where we could have contacts.

And I watched the younger guys.
Maybe for six weeks there was nothing.
I'd drift in space wondering what he'd do under fire.
It only takes once.
That's all it takes . . .
and then—you dig it.

It's shooting fireworks off, the fourth of July.

           ▩   ▩   ▩

MARK:
    I . . . I killed three children, a mother and father in cold blood. *(Crying.)*

[CHERYL: Don't.]

MARK:
> I killed three children, a mother and father. . . . *(Long pause.)*

[NADINE:Mark.]

MARK:
> I killed them with a pistol in front of a lot of people.
>
> I demanded something from the parents and then
>   systematically destroyed them.
> And that's . . .
> that's the heaviest part of what I'm carrying around.
> You know about it now, a few other people know about it,
> my wife knows about it,
> and nobody else knows about it.
> For the rest of my life . . .
>
> I have a son . . .
> He's going to die for what I've done.
> This is what I'm carrying around.
> That's what this logic is about with my children.
>
> A friend hit a booby-trap.
> And these people knew about it.
> I knew they knew.
> I knew that they were working with the VC infra-structure.
> I demanded that they tell me.
> They wouldn't say anything.
> I just wanted them to confess before I killed them.
> And they wouldn't.
> So I killed their children
> and then I killed them.
>
> I was angry.
> I was angry with all the power I had.
> I couldn't beat them.
> They beat me. *(Crying.)*
>
> I lost friends in my unit. . . .
> I did wrong.
> People in the unit watched me kill them.
> Some of them tried to stop me.

I don't know.
I can't. . . . Oh, God. . . .

A certain amount of stink went all the way back to the rear.
I almost got into a certain amount of trouble.

It was all rationalized,
that there was a logic behind it.
But they knew.
And everybody who knew had a part in it.
There was enough evidence,
but it wasn't a very good image to put out in terms of . . .
the Marine's overseas,

I have a child . . .
a child who passed through the age
that the little child was.
My son . . . my son
wouldn't know the difference between a VC and a Marine.

The children were so little.
I suppose I could find a rationalization.

All that a person can do is try and find words
to try and excuse me,
but I know it's the same damn thing
as lining Jews up.
It's no different
than what the Nazis did.
It's the same thing.

I know that I'm not alone.
I know that other people did it, too.
More people went through more hell than I did . . .
but they didn't do this.

I don't know . . .
I don't know . . .
if it's a terrible flaw of *mine,*
then I guess deep down I'm just everything that's bad.

I guess there's a rationale that says
anyone who wants to live that bad and gets in that
situation. . . .
(Long pause.)
but I should have done better.
I mean, I really strove to be good.
I had a whole set of values.
I had 'em and I didn't.
I don't know.

I want to come to the point
where I tell myself that I've punished myself enough.
In spite of it all,
I don't want to punish myself anymore,
I knew I would want to censor myself for you.
I didn't want you to say:
what kind of a nut, what kind of a bad person is he?
And yet, it's all right.
I'm not gonna lie.
My wife tries to censor me . . .
from people, from certain things.
I can't watch war shows.
I can't drive.
Certain things I can't deal with.
She has to deal with the situation,
us sitting around, a car backfires,
and I hit the deck.

She knows about the graveyards, and RJ and the woman.
She lives with all this still hanging.
I'm shell-shocked.

III

EARLY
STORIES

EARLY
STORIES

Along with James Joyce's "The Sisters," included in the next section of this anthology, these ten stories are first-published stories, or stories published early in the writer's career. The writer youngest at the time of first publication is apparently Carson McCullers, whose appropriately titled "Wunderkind" ("wonder-child," prodigy) was written when the author was seventeen or eighteen years old, and published in 1936 in *Story* when she was nineteen. Like the other stories, "Wunderkind" repays numerous readings not for the mere fact that its author was precociously young at the time of publication, but for the story's being so skillfully and so movingly executed, so mature in its vision.

Franz Kafka's "A Judgment" (sometimes translated "The Verdict") is generally considered Kafka's first complete story, published in 1912 when the writer was twenty-nine years old; Kafka had published prose fragments and surrealist sketches, among them "The Aeroplanes at Brescia," as early as 1909, while he was still in law school. In the diary in which Kafka recorded his most intimate, candid thoughts, he notes for 21 June 1912:

> The tremendous world I have in my head! But how can I release it and release myself without tearing myself apart? And it is a thousand times better to tear myself apart than to keep it in check or buried in me. That is what I am here for, of that I am quite clear.

And again on 22–23 September, at the time of the composition of "A Judgment," which was written in one session through the night: "This is the only way to write, only a coherence like this, with such a complete flinging open of body and soul." Franz Kafka was one fated for literature, which was for him the soul's deepest expression: its defense, however precarious and impermanent, against the overwhelming seductions and dangers of the external world. "A Judgment" is a young man's story, cruel—startling in its abrupt reversal, a dream gone bad, veering out of the dreamer's control. It is a presentiment of the more meticulously imagined symbolist dream-parables to come that would constitute Kafka's great work: "The Metamorphosis," "A Hunger Artist," "In the Penal Colony" and the enigmatic, incomplete novels *The Trial, The Castle,* and *Amerika.*

Ernest Hemingway's "Indian Camp" was written when the young, already expatriated American was twenty-four years old, and published as the first story of *In Our Time* (1925), Hemingway's first, widely acclaimed book. "My Old Man," a Sherwood Anderson–inspired short story, and the blunt, crudely effective "Up in Michigan" predate "Indian Camp"; all three are youthful but accomplished works of fiction, suggesting those themes of disillusionment, estrangement, and irony that would characterize Hemingway's mature work. In "Indian Camp," a story of Nick Adams's childhood, the quintessential Hemingway chord is struck: short, simple declarative sentences; little background explanation or description; a swift, minimally delineated action; terse, stylized dialogue employed as a means of advancing the story; a final thematic statement, couched in irony.

Dylan Thomas's "The Burning Baby" is as brashly unpredictable and as powerfully imagined as any of Thomas's prose fictions. Both John Cheever's "Goodbye, My Brother" and John Updike's "Friends from Philadelphia" are wonderfully realized, and of the high quality of the writers' more mature work. ("More mature" seems an odd term when we are speaking of prolific, frequently published writers already much admired in literary circles before they reached thirty. See the prefatory note to Updike's "Friends from Philadelphia.") Updike would go on to compose more subtly modulated, more complex and challenging works of fiction; Cheever's "Goodbye, My Brother" not only strikes a dominant Cheeveresque chord—that of irrevocably estranged brothers, in a setting suffused with natural beauty and awash in alcohol—but is as strong as anything Cheever would ever write, including his several novels.

Lorrie Moore's early story "Amahl and the Night Visitors: A Guide to the Tenor of Love," from her first collection *Self-Help,* exhibits those qualities of wit, pathos, and stylistic dexterity for which the author has become well known; Madison Smartt Bell's "The Naked Lady," from his first collection *Zero db,* allows the versatile young writer to speak in a voice not his own, yet so very engagingly, and convincingly. Both Pinckney Benedict's "The Sutton Pie Safe," which won for its twenty-year-old author first prize in the Nelson Algren Story Competition sponsored by the *Chicago Tribune,* and Jonathan Ames's spare, mordant "A Portrait of a Father" began as outstanding undergraduate workshop stories; they were subsequently revised and refined after the writers graduated, to appear in, respectively, Benedict's first story collection, *Town Smokes,* and Ames's first novel, *I Pass Like Night.*

Is it significant that these stories, like James Joyce's "The Sisters," were all written when the authors were just beginning their careers? Or is this fact somehow incidental, coincidental? Biographical context, like historic context, can "explain" a work of art only to a very limited degree. We would like to think that any distinguished work transcends its historic, personal context to exist in a timeless region of pure achievement; yet it is unlikely that, for instance, "Indian Camp," despite its stark effectiveness, would be read today if the ambitious twenty-four-year-old writer, experimenting in a new, minimalist-realist mode of fiction, had not gone on to become "Ernest Hemingway." The artist, through his or her career, is at once creating new work and re-creating older work, recasting, in a sense, the terms in which the older work will be read and valued.

It has always seemed to me crucial that beginning writers, of whatever age—young, older, experienced in life or otherwise—understand that established writers, men and women of recognized "genius," were not always so; especially to themselves, they were not so; but rather they were doubtful, groping, aspiring, uncertain, and above all *undefined.* They were all, to put it sentimentally, young at one time, with their futures wholly unforeseen. We are fascinated by our sense, in reading such early work, of a writer setting out to explore by way of fiction the pathways, mysterious and unknowable as a dream, by which an enduring career—and life—might be forged.

Franz Kafka

THE JUDGMENT

It was a Sunday morning in the very height of spring. Georg Bendemann, a young merchant, was sitting in his own room on the first floor of one of a long row of small, ramshackle houses stretching beside the river which were scarcely distinguishable from each other in height and coloring. He had just finished a letter to an old friend of his who was now living abroad, had put it into its envelope in a slow and dreamy fashion, and with his elbows propped on the writing table was gazing out of the window at the river, the bridge, and the hills on the farther bank with their tender green.

He was thinking about his friend, who had actually run away to Russia some years before, being dissatisfied with his prospects at home. Now he was carrying on a business in St. Petersburg, which had flourished to begin with but had long been going downhill, as he always complained on his increasingly rare visits. So he was wearing himself out to no purpose in a foreign country, the unfamiliar full beard he wore did not quite conceal the face Georg had known so well since childhood, and his skin was growing so yellow as to indicate some latent disease. By his own account he had no regular connection with the colony of his fellow countrymen out there and almost no social intercourse with Russian families, so that he was resigning himself to becoming a permanent bachelor.

What could one write to such a man, who had obviously run off the rails, a man one could be sorry for but could not help. Should one advise him to come home, to transplant himself and take up his old friendships again—there was nothing to hinder him—and in general to rely on the help of his friends? But that was as good as telling him, and the more kindly the more offensively, that all his efforts hitherto had miscarried, that he should finally give up, come back home, and be gaped at by everyone as a returned prodigal, that only his friends knew what was what and that he himself was just a big child who should do what his successful and home-keeping friends prescribed. And was it certain, besides, that all the pain one would have to inflict on him would achieve its object? Perhaps it would not even be possible to get him to come home at all—he said himself that he was now out of touch with commerce in his native country—and then he would still be left an alien in a foreign land embittered by his friends' advice and more than ever estranged from them. But if he did follow their advice and then didn't fit in at home—not out of malice, of course, but through force of circumstances—couldn't get on with his friends or without them, felt humiliated, couldn't be said to have either friends or a country of his own any longer, wouldn't it have been better for him to stay abroad just as he was? Taking all this into account, how could one be sure that he would make a success of life at home?

For such reasons, supposing one wanted to keep up correspondence with him, one could not send him any real news such as could frankly be told to the most distant acquaintance. It was more than three years since his last visit, and for this he offered the lame excuse that the political situation in Russia was too uncertain, which apparently would not permit even the briefest absence of a small businessman while it allowed hundreds of thousands of Russians to travel peacefully abroad. But during these three years Georg's own position in life had changed a lot. Two years ago his mother had died, since when he and his father had shared the household together, and his friend had of course been informed of that and had expressed his sympathy in a letter phrased so dryly that the grief caused by such an event, one had to conclude, could not be realized in a distant country. Since that time, however, Georg had applied himself with greater determination to the business as well as to everything else.

Perhaps during his mother's lifetime his father's insistence on having everything his own way in the business had hindered him from developing any real activity of his own, perhaps since her death his father had become less aggressive, although he was still active in the business, perhaps it was mostly due to an accidental run of good fortune—which was very probable indeed—but at any rate during those two years the business had developed in a most unexpected way, the staff had had to be doubled, the turnover was five times as great; no doubt about it, further progress lay just ahead.

But Georg's friend had no inkling of this improvement. In earlier years, perhaps for the last time in that letter of condolence, he had tried to persuade Georg to emigrate to Russia and had enlarged upon the prospects of success for precisely Georg's branch of trade. The figures quoted were microscopic by comparison with the range of Georg's present operations. Yet he shrank from letting his friend know about his business success, and if he were to do it now retrospectively that certainly would look peculiar.

So Georg confined himself to giving his friend unimportant items of gossip such as rise at random in the memory when one is idly thinking things over on a quiet Sunday. All he desired was to leave undisturbed the idea of the home town which his friend must have built up to his own content during the long interval. And so it happened to Georg that three times in three fairly widely separated letters he had told his friend about the engagement of an unimportant man to an equally unimportant girl, until indeed, quite contrary to his intentions, his friend began to show some interest in this notable event.

Yet Georg preferred to write about things like these rather than to confess that he himself had got engaged a month ago to a Fräulein Frieda Brandenfeld, a girl from a well-to-do family. He often discussed this friend of his with his fiancée and the peculiar relationship that had developed between them in their correspondence. "So he won't be coming to our wedding," said she, "and yet I have a right to get to know all your friends." "I don't want to trouble him," answered Georg, "don't misunderstand me, he would probably come, at least I think so, but he would feel that his hand had been forced and he would be hurt, perhaps he would envy me and certainly he'd be discontented and without being able to do anything about his discontent he'd have to go away again alone. Alone—do you know what that means?" "Yes, but may he not hear about our wedding in some other fashion?" "I can't prevent that, of course, but it's unlikely, considering the way he lives." "Since your friends are like that, Georg, you shouldn't ever have got engaged at all." "Well, we're both to blame for that; but I wouldn't have it any other way now." And when, breathing quickly under his kisses, she still brought out: "All the same, I do feel upset," he thought it could not really involve him in trouble were he to send the news to his friend. "That's the kind of man I am and he'll just have to take me as I am," he said to himself, "I can't cut myself to another pattern that might make a more suitable friend for him."

And in fact he did inform his friend, in the long letter he had been writing that Sunday morning, about his engagement, with these words: "I have saved my best news to the end. I have got engaged to a Fräulein Frieda Brandenfeld, a girl from a well-to-do family, who only came to live here a long time after you went away, so that you're hardly likely to know her. There will be time to tell you more about her later, for today let me just say that I am very happy and as between you and me the only difference in our relationship is that instead of a quite ordinary kind of friend you will now have in me a happy friend. Besides that, you will acquire in my fiancée, who sends her warm greetings and will soon write you herself, a genuine friend of the opposite sex, which is not without importance to a bachelor. I know that there are many reasons why you can't come to see us, but would not my wedding be precisely the right occasion for giving all obstacles the go-by? Still, however that may be, do just as seems good to you without regarding any interests but your own."

With this letter in his hand Georg had been sitting a long time at the writing table, his face turned toward the window. He had barely acknowledged, with an absent smile, a greeting waved to him from the street by a passing acquaintance.

At last he put the letter in his pocket and went out of his room across a small lobby into his father's room, which he had not entered for months. There was in fact no need for him to enter it, since he saw his father daily at business and they took their midday meal together at an eating house; in the evening, it was true, each did as he pleased, yet even then, unless Georg—as mostly happened—went out with friends or, more recently, visited his fiancée, they always sat for a while, each with his newspaper, in their common sitting room.

It surprised Georg how dark his father's room was even on this sunny morning. So it was overshadowed as much as that by the high wall on the other side of the narrow courtyard. His father was sitting by the window in a corner hung with various mementoes of Georg's dead mother, reading a newspaper which he held to one side before his eyes in an attempt to overcome a defect of vision. On the table stood the remains of his breakfast, not much of which seemed to have been eaten.

"Ah, Georg," said his father, rising at once to meet him. His heavy dressing gown swung open as he walked and the skirts of it fluttered around him.—"My father is still a giant of a man," said Georg to himself.

"It's unbearably dark here," he said aloud.

"Yes, it's dark enough," answered his father.

"And you've shut the window, too?"

"I prefer it like that."

"Well, it's quite warm outside," said Georg, as if continuing his previous remark, and sat down.

His father cleared away the breakfast dishes and set them on a chest.

"I really only wanted to tell you," went on Georg, who had been vacantly following the old man's movements, "that I am now sending the news of my engagement to St. Petersburg." He drew the letter a little way from his pocket and let it drop back again.

"To St. Petersburg?" asked his father.

"To my friend there," said Georg, trying to meet his father's eye.—In business hours he's quite different, he was thinking, how solidly he sits here with his arms crossed.

"Oh yes. To your friend," said his father, with peculiar emphasis.

"Well, you know, Father, that I wanted not to tell him about my engagement at first. Out of consideration for him, that was the only reason. You know yourself he's a difficult man. I said to myself that someone else might tell him about my engagement, although he's such a solitary creature that that was hardly likely—I couldn't prevent that—but I wasn't ever going to tell him myself."

"And now you've changed your mind?" asked his father, laying his enormous newspaper on the window sill and on top of it his spectacles, which he covered with one hand.

"Yes, I've been thinking it over. If he's a good friend of mine, I said to myself, my being happily engaged should make him happy too. And so I wouldn't put off telling him any longer. But before I posted the letter I wanted to let you know."

"Georg," said his father, lengthening his toothless mouth, "listen to me! You've come to me about this business, to talk it over with me. No doubt that does you honor. But it's nothing, it's worse than nothing, if you don't tell me the whole truth. I don't want to stir up matters that shouldn't be mentioned here. Since the death of our dear mother certain things have been done that aren't right. Maybe the time will come for mentioning them, and maybe sooner than we think. There's many a thing in the business I'm not aware of, maybe it's not done behind my back—I'm not going to say that it's done behind my back—I'm not equal to things any longer, my memory's failing, I haven't an eye for so many things any longer. That's the course of nature in the first place, and in the second place the death of our dear mother hit me harder than it did you.—But since we're talking about it, about this letter, I beg you, Georg, don't deceive me. It's a trivial affair, it's hardly worth mentioning, so don't deceive me. Do you really have this friend in St. Petersburg?"

Georg rose in embarrassment. "Never mind my friends. A thousand friends wouldn't make up to me for my father. Do you know what I think? You're not taking enough care of yourself. But old age must be taken care of. I can't do without you in the business, you know that very well, but if the business is going to undermine your health, I'm ready to close it down tomorrow forever. And that won't do. We'll have to make a change in your way of living. But a radical change. You sit here in the dark, and in the sitting room you would have plenty of light. You just take a bite of breakfast instead of properly keeping up your strength. You sit by a closed window, and the air would be so good for you. No, Father! I'll get the doctor to come, and we'll follow his orders. We'll change your room, you can move into the front room and I'll move in here. You won't notice the change, all your things will be moved with you. But there's time for all that later, I'll put you to bed now for a little, I'm sure you need to rest. Come, I'll help you to take off your things, you'll see I can do it. Or if you would rather go into the front room at once, you can lie down in my bed for the present. That would be the most sensible thing."

Georg stood close beside his father, who had let his head with its unkempt white hair sink on his chest.

"Georg," said his father in a low voice, without moving.

Georg knelt down at once beside his father, in the old man's weary face he saw the pupils, overlarge, fixedly looking at him from the corners of the eyes.

"You have no friend in St. Petersburg. You've always been a leg-puller and you haven't even shrunk from pulling my leg. How could you have a friend out there! I can't believe it."

"Just think back a bit, Father," said Georg, lifting his father from the chair and slipping off his dressing gown as he stood feebly enough, "it'll soon be three years since my friend came to see us last. I remember that you used not to like him very much. At least twice I kept you from seeing him, although he was actually sitting with me in my room. I could quite well understand your dislike of him, my friend has his peculiarities. But then, later, you got on with him very well. I was proud because you listened to him and nodded and asked him questions. If you think back you're bound to remember. He used to tell us the most incredible stories of the Russian Revolution. For instance, when he was on a business trip to Kiev and ran into a riot, and saw a priest on a balcony who cut a broad cross in blood on the palm of his hand and held the hand up and appealed to the mob. You've told that story yourself once or twice since."

Meanwhile Georg had succeeded in lowering his father down again and carefully taking off the woolen drawers he wore over his linen underpants and his socks. The not particularly clean appearance of his underwear made him reproach himself for having been neglectful. It should have certainly been his duty to see that his father had clean changes of underwear. He had not yet explicitly discussed with his bride-to-be what arrangements should be made for his father in the future, for they had both of them silently taken it for granted that the old man would go on living alone in the old house. But now he made a quick, firm decision to take him into his own future establishment. It almost looked, on closer inspection, as if the care he meant to lavish there on his father might come too late.

He carried his father to bed in his arms. It gave him a dreadful feeling to notice that while he took the few steps toward the bed the old man on his breast was playing with his watch chain. He could not lay him down on the bed for a moment, so firmly did he hang on to the watch chain.

But as soon as he was laid in bed, all seemed well. He covered himself up and even drew the blankets farther than usual over his shoulders. He looked up at Georg with a not unfriendly eye.

"You begin to remember my friend, don't you?" asked Georg, giving him an encouraging nod.

"Am I well covered up now?" asked his father, as if he were not able to see whether his feet were properly tucked in or not.

"So you find it snug in bed already," said Georg, and tucked the blankets more closely around him.

"Am I well covered up?" asked the father once more, seeming to be strangely intent upon the answer.

"Don't worry, you're well covered up."

"No!" cried his father, cutting short the answer, threw the blankets off with a strength that sent them all flying in a moment and sprang erect in bed. Only one hand lightly touched the ceiling to steady him.

"You wanted to cover me up, I know, my young sprig, but I'm far from being covered up yet. And even if this is the last strength I have, it's enough for you, too much for you. Of course I know your friend. He would have been a son after my own heart. That's why you've been playing him false all these years. Why else? Do you think I haven't been sorry for him? And that's why you had to lock yourself up in your office—the Chief is busy, mustn't be disturbed—just so that you could write your lying little letters to Russia. But thank goodness a father doesn't need to be taught how to see through his son. And now that you thought you'd got him down, so far down that you could set your bottom on him and sit on him and he wouldn't move, then my fine son makes up his mind to get married!"

Georg stared at the bogey conjured up by his father. His friend in St. Petersburg, whom his father suddenly knew too well, touched his imagination as never before. Lost in the vastness of Russia he saw him. At the door of an empty, plundered warehouse he saw him. Among the wreckage of his showcases, the slashed remnants of his wares, the falling gas brackets, he was just standing up. Why did he have to go so far away!

"But attend to me!" cried his father, and Georg, almost distracted, ran toward the bed to take everything in, yet came to a stop halfway.

"Because she lifted up her skirts," his father began to flute, "because she lifted her skirts like this, the nasty creature," and mimicking her he lifted his shirt so high that one could see the scar on his thigh from his war wound, "because she lifted her skirts like this and this you made up to her, and in order to make free with her undisturbed you have disgraced your mother's memory, betrayed your friend, and stuck your father into bed so that he can't move. But he can move, or can't he?"

And he stood up quite unsupported and kicked his legs out. His insight made him radiant.

Georg shrank into a corner, as far away from his father as possible. A long time ago he had firmly made up his mind to watch closely every least movement so that he should not be surprised by any indirect attack, a pounce from behind or above. At this moment he recalled this long-forgotten resolve and forgot it again, like a man drawing a short thread through the eye of a needle.

"But your friend hasn't been betrayed after all!" cried his father, emphasizing the point with stabs of his forefinger. "I've been representing him here on the spot."

"You comedian!" Georg could not resist the retort, realized at once the harm done and, his eyes starting in his head, bit his tongue back, only too late, till the pain made his knees give.

"Yes, of course I've been playing a comedy! A comedy! That's a good expression! What other comfort was left to a poor old widower? Tell me—and while you're answering me be you still my living son—what else was left to me, in my back room, plagued by a disloyal staff, old to the marrow of my bones? And my son strutting through the world, finishing off deals that I had prepared for him, bursting with triumphant glee, and stalking away from his father with the closed face of a respectable businessman! Do you think I didn't love you, I, from whom you are sprung?"

Now he'll lean forward, thought Georg, what if he topples and smashes himself! These words went hissing through his mind.

His father leaned forward but did not topple. Since Georg did not come any nearer, as he had expected, he straightened himself again.

"Stay where you are, I don't need you! You think you have strength enough to come over here and that you're only hanging back of your own accord. Don't be too sure! I am still much the stronger of us two. All by myself I might have had to give way, but your mother has given me so much of her strength that I've established a fine connection with your friend and I have your customers here in my pocket!"

"He has pockets even in his shirt!" said Georg to himself, and believed that with this remark he could make him an impossible figure for all the world. Only for a moment did he think so, since he kept on forgetting everything.

"Just take your bride on your arm and try getting in my way! I'll sweep her from your very side, you don't know how!"

Georg made a grimace of disbelief. His father only nodded, confirming the truth of his words, toward Georg's corner.

"How you amused me today, coming to ask me if you should tell your friend about your engagement. He knows it already, you stupid boy, he knows it all! I've been writing to him, for you forgot to take my writing things away from me. That's why he hasn't been here for years, he knows everything a hundred times better than you do yourself, in his left hand he crumples your letters unopened while in his right hand he holds up my letters to read through!"

In his enthusiasm he waved his arm over his head. "He knows everything a thousand times better!" he cried.

"Ten thousand times!" said Georg, to make fun of his father, but in his very mouth the words turned into deadly earnest.

"For years I've been waiting for you to come with some such question! Do you think I concern myself with anything else? Do you think I read my newspapers? Look!" and he threw Georg a newspaper sheet which he had somehow taken to bed with him. An old newspaper, with a name entirely unknown to Georg.

"How long a time you've taken to grow up! Your mother had to die, she couldn't see the happy day, your friend is going to pieces in Russia, even three years ago he was yellow enough to be thrown away, and as for me, you see what condition I'm in. You have eyes in your head for that!"

"So you've been lying in wait for me!" cried Georg.

His father said pityingly, in an offhand manner: "I suppose you wanted to say that sooner. But now it doesn't matter." And in a louder voice: "So now you know what else there was in the world besides yourself, till now you've known only about yourself! An innocent child, yes, that you were, truly, but still more truly have you been a devilish human being!——And therefore take note: I sentence you now to death by drowning!"

Georg felt himself urged from the room, the crash with which his father fell on the bed behind him was still in his ears as he fled. On the staircase, which he rushed down as if its steps were an inclined plane, he ran into his charwoman on her way up to do the morning cleaning of the room. "Jesus!" she cried, and covered her face with her apron, but he was already gone. Out of the front door he rushed, across the roadway, driven toward the water. Already he was grasping at the railings as a starving man clutches food. He swung himself over, like the distinguished gymnast he had once been in his youth, to his parents' pride. With weakening grip he was still holding on when he spied between the railings a motor-bus coming which would easily cover the noise of his fall, called in a low voice: "Dear parents, I have always loved you, all the same," and let himself drop.

At this moment an unending stream of traffic was just going over the bridge.

Translated by Willa and Edwin Muir

INDIAN CAMP

At the lake shore there was another rowboat drawn up. The two Indians stood waiting.

Nick and his father got in the stern of the boat and the Indians shoved it off and one of them got in to row. Uncle George sat in the stern of the camp rowboat. The young Indian shoved the camp boat off and got in to row Uncle George.

The two boats started off in the dark. Nick heard the oarlocks of the other boat quite a way ahead of them in the mist. The Indians rowed with quick choppy strokes. Nick lay back with his father's arm around him. It was cold on the water. The Indian who was rowing them was working very hard, but the other boat moved further ahead in the mist all the time.

"Where are we going, Dad?" Nick asked.

"Over to the Indian camp. There is an Indian lady very sick."

"Oh," said Nick.

Across the bay they found the other boat beached. Uncle George was smoking a cigar in the dark. The young Indian pulled the boat way up on the beach. Uncle George gave both the Indians cigars.

They walked up from the beach through a meadow that was soaking wet with dew, following the young Indian who carried a lantern. Then they went into the woods and followed a trail that led to the logging road that ran back into the hills. It was much lighter on the logging road as the timber was cut away on both sides. The young Indian stopped and blew out his lantern and they all walked on along the road.

They came around a bend and a dog came out barking. Ahead were the lights of the shanties where the Indian bark-peelers lived. More dogs rushed out at them. The two Indians sent them back to the shanties. In the shanty nearest the road there was a light in the window. An old woman stood in the doorway holding a lamp.

Inside on a wooden bunk lay a young Indian woman. She had been trying to have her baby for two days. All the old women in the camp had been helping her. The men had moved off up the road to sit in the dark and smoke out of range of the noise she made. She screamed just as Nick and the two Indians followed his father and Uncle George into the shanty. She lay in the lower bunk, very big under a quilt. Her head was turned to one side. In the upper bunk was her husband. He had cut his foot very badly with an ax three days before. He was smoking a pipe. The room smelled very bad.

Nick's father ordered some water to be put on the stove, and while it was heating he spoke to Nick.

"This lady is going to have a baby, Nick," he said.

"I know," said Nick.

"You don't know," said his father. "Listen to me. What she is going through is called being in labor. The baby wants to be born and she wants it to be born. All her muscles are trying to get the baby born. That is what is happening when she screams."

"I see," Nick said.

Just then the woman cried out.

"Oh, Daddy, can't you give her something to make her stop screaming?" asked Nick.

"No. I haven't any anæsthetic," his father said. "But her screams are not important. I don't hear them because they are not important."

The husband in the upper bunk rolled over against the wall.

The woman in the kitchen motioned to the doctor that the water was hot. Nick's father went into the kitchen and poured about half of the water out of the big kettle into a basin. Into the water left in the kettle he put several things he unwrapped from a handkerchief.

"Those must boil," he said, and began to scrub his hands in the basin of hot water with a cake of soap he had brought from the camp. Nick watched his father's hands scrubbing each other with the soap. While his father washed his hands very carefully and thoroughly, he talked.

"You see, Nick, babies are supposed to be born head first but sometimes they're not. When they're not they make a lot of trouble for everybody. Maybe I'll have to operate on this lady. We'll know in a little while."

When he was satisfied with his hands he went in and went to work.

"Pull back that quilt, will you, George?" he said. "I'd rather not touch it."

Later when he started to operate Uncle George and three Indian men held the woman still. She bit Uncle George on the arm and Uncle George said, "Damn squaw bitch!" and the young Indian who had rowed Uncle George over laughed at him. Nick held the basin for his father. It all took a long time. His father picked the baby up and slapped it to make it breathe and handed it to the old woman.

"See, it's a boy, Nick," he said. "How do you like being an interne?"

Nick said, "All right." He was looking away so as not to see what his father was doing.

"There. That gets it," said his father and put something into the basin. Nick didn't look at it.

"Now," his father said, "there's some stitches to put in. You can watch this or not, Nick, just as you like. I'm going to sew up the incision I made."

Nick did not watch. His curiosity had been gone for a long time.

His father finished and stood up. Uncle George and the three Indian men stood up. Nick put the basin out in the kitchen.

Uncle George looked at his arm. The young Indian smiled reminiscently.

"I'll put some peroxide on that, George," the doctor said. He bent over the Indian woman. She was quiet now and her eyes were closed. She looked very pale. She did not know what had become of the baby or anything.

"I'll be back in the morning," the doctor said, standing up. "The nurse should be here from St. Ignace by noon and she'll bring everything we need."

He was feeling exalted and talkative as football players are in the dressing room after a game.

"That's one for the medical journal, George," he said. "Doing a Cæsarian with a jack-knife and sewing it up with nine-foot, tapered gut leaders."

Uncle George was standing against the wall, looking at his arm.

"Oh, you're a great man, all right," he said.

"Ought to have a look at the proud father. They're usually the worst sufferers in these little affairs," the doctor said. "I must say he took it all pretty quietly."

He pulled back the blanket from the Indian's head. His hand came away wet. He mounted on the edge of the lower bunk with the lamp in one hand and looked in. The Indian lay with his face toward the wall. His throat had been cut from ear to ear. The blood had flowed down into a pool where his body sagged the bunk. His head rested on his left arm. The open razor lay, edge up, in the blankets.

"Take Nick out of the shanty, George," the doctor said.

There was no need of that. Nick, standing in the door of the kitchen, had a good view of the upper bunk when his father, the lamp in one hand, tipped the Indian's head back.

It was just beginning to be daylight when they walked along the logging road back toward the lake.

"I'm terribly sorry I brought you along, Nickie," said his father, all his post-operative exhilaration gone. "It was an awful mess to put you through."

"Do ladies always have such a hard time having babies?" Nick asked.

"No, that was very, very exceptional."

"Why did he kill himself, Daddy?"

"I don't know, Nick. He couldn't stand things, I guess."

"Do many men kill themselves, Daddy?"

"Not very many, Nick."

"Do many women?"

"Hardly ever."

"Don't they ever?"

"Oh, yes. They do sometimes."

"Daddy?"

"Yes."

"Where did Uncle George go?"

"He'll turn up all right."

"Is dying hard, Daddy?"

"No, I think it's pretty easy, Nick. It all depends."

They were seated in the boat, Nick in the stern, his father rowing. The sun was coming up over the hills. A bass jumped, making a circle in the water. Nick trailed his hand in the water. It felt warm in the sharp chill of the morning.

In the early morning on the lake sitting in the stern of the boat with his father rowing, he felt quite sure that he would never die.

THE BURNING BABY

They said that Rhys was burning his baby when a gorse bush broke into fire on the summit of the hill. The bush, burning merrily, assumed to them the sad white features and the rickety limbs of the vicar's burning baby. What the wind had not blown away of the baby's ashes, Rhys Rhys had sealed in a stone jar. With his own dust lay the baby's dust, and near him the dust of his daughter in a coffin of white wood.

They heard his son howl in the wind. They saw him walking over the hill, holding a dead animal up to the light of the stars. They saw him in the valley shadows as he moved, with the motion of a man cutting wheat, over the brows of the fields. In a sanatorium he coughed his lung into a basin, stirring his fingers delightedly in the blood. What moved with invisible scythe through the valley was a shadow and a handful of shadows cast by the grave sun.

The bush burned out, and the face of the baby fell away with the smoking leaves.

It was, they said, on a fine sabbath morning in the middle of the summer that Rhys Rhys fell in love with his daughter. The gorse that morning had burst into flames. Rhys Rhys, in clerical black, had seen the flames shoot up to the sky, and the bush on the edge of the hill burn red as God among the paler burning of the grass. He took his daughter's hand as she lay in the garden hammock, and told her that he loved her. He told her that she was more beautiful than her dead mother. Her hair smelt of mice, her teeth came over her lip, and the lids of her eyes were red and wet. He saw her beauty come out of her like a stream of sap. The folds of her dress could not hide from him the shabby nakedness of her body. It was not her bone, nor her flesh, nor her hair that he found suddenly beautiful. The poor soil shudders under the sun, he said. He moved his hand up and down her arm. Only the awkward and the ugly, only the barren bring forth fruit. The flesh of her arm was red with the smoothing of his hand. He touched her breast. From the touch of her breast he knew each inch of flesh upon her. Why do you touch me there? she said.

In the church that morning he spoke of the beauty of the harvest, of the promise of the standing corn and the promise in the sharp edge of the scythe as it brings the corn low and whistles through the air before it cuts into the ripeness. Through the open windows at the end of the aisles, he saw the yellow fields upon the hillside and the smudge of heather on the meadow borders. The world was ripe.

The world is ripe for the second coming of the son of man, he said aloud.

But it was not the ripeness of God that glistened from the hill. It was the promise and the ripeness of the flesh, the good flesh, the mean flesh, flesh of his daughter, flesh, flesh, the flesh of the voice of thunder howling before the death of man.

That night he preached of the sins of the flesh. O God in the image of our flesh, he prayed.

His daughter sat in the front pew, and stroked her arm. She would have touched her breast where he had touched it, but the eyes of the congregation were upon her.

Flesh, flesh, flesh, said the vicar.

His son, scouting in the fields for a mole's hill or the signs of a red fox, whistling to the birds and patting the calves as they stood untimid at their mother's sides, came upon a dead rabbit sprawling on a stone. The rabbit's head was riddled with pellets, the dogs had torn open its belly, and the marks of a ferret's teeth were upon its throat. He lifted it gently up, tickling it behind the ears. The blood from its head dropped on his hand. Through the rip in the belly, its intestines had dropped out and coiled on the stone. He held the little body close to his jacket, and ran home through the fields, the rabbit dancing against his waistcoat. As he reached the gate of the vicarage, the worshippers dribbled out of church. They shook hands and raised their hats, smiling at the poor boy with his long green hair, his ass's ears, and death buttoned under his jacket. He was always the poor boy to them.

Rhys Rhys sat in his study, the stem of his pipe stuck between his flybuttons, the bible unopened upon his knees. The day of God was over, and the sun, like another sabbath, went down behind the hills. He lit the lamp, but his own oil burned brighter. He drew the curtains, shutting out the unwelcome night. But he opened his own heart up, and the bald pulse that beat there was a welcome stranger. He had not felt love like this since the woman who scratched him, seeing the woman witch in his male eyes, had fallen into his arms and kissed him, and whispered Welsh words as he took her. She had been the mother of his daughter and had died in her pains, stealing, when she was dead, the son of his second love, and leaving the greenhaired changeling in its place. Merry with desire, Rhys Rhys cast the bible on the floor. He reached for another book, and read, in the lamplit darkness, of the old woman who had deceived the devil. The devil is poor flesh, said Rhys Rhys.

His son came in, bearing the rabbit in his arms. The lank, redcoated boy was a flesh out of the past. The skin of the unburied dead patched to his bones, the smile of the changeling on his mouth, and the hair of the sea rising from his scalp, he stood before Rhys Rhys. A ghost of his mother, he held the rabbit gently to his breast, rocking it to and fro. Cunningly, from under halfclosed lids, he saw his father shrink away from the vision of death. Be off with you, said Rhys Rhys. Who was this green stranger to carry in death and rock it, like a baby under a warm shawl of fur, before him? For a minute the flesh of the world lay still; the old terror set in; the waters of the breast dried up; the nipples grew through the sand. Then he drew his hand over his eyes, and only the rabbit remained, a little sack of flesh, half empty, swaying in the arms of his son. Be off, he said. The boy held the rabbit close, and rocked it, and tickled it again.

Changeling, said Rhys Rhys. He is mine, said the boy, I'll peel him and keep the skull. His room in the attic was crowded with skulls and dried pelts, and little bones in bottles.

Give it to me.

He is mine.

Rhys Rhys tore the rabbit away, and stuffed it deep in the pocket of his smoking coat. When his daughter came in, dressed and ready for bed, with a candle in her hand, Rhys Rhys had death in his pocket.

She was timid, for his touch still ached on her arm and breast but she bent unblushing over him. Saying good-night, she kissed him, and he blew her candle out. She was smiling as he lowered the wick of the lamp.

Step out of your shift, said he. Shiftless, she stepped towards his arms.

I want the little skull, said a voice in the dark.

From his room at the top of the house, through the webs on the windows, and over the furs and the bottles, the boy saw a mile of green hill running away into the darkness of the first dawn. Summer storm in the heat of the rain, flooring the grassy mile, had left some new morning brightness, out of the dead night, in each reaching root.

Death took hold of his sister's legs as she walked through the calf-deep heather up the hill. He saw the high grass at her thighs. And the blades of the upgrowing wind, out of the four windsmells of the manuring dead, might drive through the soles of her feet, up the veins of the legs and stomach, into her womb and her pulsing heart. He watched her climb. She stood, gasping for breath, on a hill of the wider hill, tapping the wall of her bladder, fondling her matted chest (for the hair grew on her as on a grown man), feeling the heart in her wrist, loving her coveted thinness. She was to him as ugly as the sowfaced woman Llareggub who had taught him the terrors of the flesh. He remembered the advances of that unlovely woman. She blew out his candle as he stepped towards her on the night the great hail had fallen and he had hidden in her rotting house from the cruelty of the weather. Now half a mile off his sister stood in the morning, and the vermin of the hill might spring upon her as she stood, uncaring, rounding the angles of her ugliness. He smiled at the thought of the devouring rats, and looked around the room for a bottle to hold her heart. Her skull, fixed by a socket to the nail above his bed, would be a smiling welcome to the first pains of waking.

But he saw Rhys Rhys stride up the hill, and the bowl of his sister's head, fixed invisibly above his sheets, crumbled away. Standing straight by the side of a dewy tree, his sister beckoned. Up went Rhys Rhys through the calfdeep heather, the death in the grass, over the boulders and up through the reaching ferns, to where she stood. He took her hand. The two shadows linked hands, and climbed together to the top of the hill. The boy saw them go, and turned his face to the wall as they vanished, in one dull shadow, over the edge, and down to the dingle at the west foot of the lovers' alley.

Later, he remembered the rabbit. He ran downstairs and found it in the pocket of the smoking coat. He held death against him, tasting a cough of blood upon his tongue as he climbed, contented, back to the bright bottles and the wall of heads.

In the first dew of light he saw his father clamber for her white hand. She who was his sister walked with a swollen belly over the hill. She touched him between the legs, and he sighed and sprang at her. But the nerves of her face mixed with the quiver in his thighs, and she shot from him. Rhys Rhys, over the bouldered rim, led her to terror. He sighed and sprang at her. She mixed with him in the fourth and the fifth terrors of the flesh. Said Rhys Rhys, Your mother's eyes. It was not her eyes that saw him proud before her, nor the eyes in her thumb. The lashes of her fingers lifted. He saw the ball under the nail.

It was, they said, on a fine sabbath morning in the early spring that she bore him a male child. Brought to bed of her father, she screamed for an anaesthetic as the knocking head burst through. In her gown of blood she slept until twilight, and a star burst bloody through each ear. With a scissors and rag, Rhys Rhys attended her, and, gazing on the shrivelled features and the hands like the hands of a mole, he gently took the child away, and his daughter's breast cried out and ran into the mouth of the surrounding shadow. The shadow pouted for the milk and the binding cottons. The child spat in his arms, the noise of the running air was blind in its ears, and the deaf light died from its eyes.

Rhys Rhys, with the dead child held against him, stepped into the night, hearing the mother moan in her sleep and the deadly shadow, filled sick with milk, flowing around the house. He turned his face towards the hills. A shadow walked close to him and, silent in the shadow of a full tree, the changeling waited. He made an image for the moon, and the flesh of the moon fell away, leaving a star-eyed skull. Then with a smile he ran back over the lawns and into the crying house. Half way up the stairs, he heard his sister die. Rhys Rhys climbed on.

On the top of the hill he laid the baby down, and propped it against the heather. Death propped the dark flowers. The baby stiffened in the rigor of the moon. Poor flesh, said Rhys Rhys as he pulled at the dead heather and furze. Poor angel, he said to the listening mouth of the baby. The fruit of the flesh falls with the worm from the tree. Conceiving the worm, the bark crumbles. There lay the poor star of flesh that had dropped, like the bead of a woman's milk through the nipples of a wormy tree.

He stacked the torn heathers in the midst of the circle where the stones still howled on the sabbaths. On the head of the purple stack, he piled the dead grass. A stack of death, the heather grew as tall as he, and loomed at last over his windy hair.

Behind a boulder moved the accompanying shadow, and the shadow of the boy was printed under the fiery flank of a tree. The shadow marked the boy, and the boy marked the bones of the naked baby under their chilly cover, and how the grass scraped on the bald skull, and where his father picked out a path in the cancerous growths of the silent circle. He saw Rhys Rhys pick up the baby and place it on the top of the stack, saw the head of a burning match, and heard the crackle of the bush, breaking like a baby's arm.

The stack burst into flame. Rhys Rhys, before the red eye of the creeping fire, stretched out his arms and beckoned the shadow from the stones. Surrounded by shadows, he prayed before the flaming stack, and the sparks of the heather blew past his smile. Burn, child, poor flesh, mean flesh, flesh, flesh, sick sorry flesh, flesh of the foul womb, burn back to dust, he prayed.

And the baby caught fire. The flames curled around its mouth and blew upon the shrinking gums. Flame round its red cord lapped its little belly till the raw flesh fell upon the heather.

A flame touched its tongue. Eeeeeh, cried the burning baby, and the illuminated hill replied.

Carson McCullers

WUNDERKIND

She came into the living room, her music satchel plopping against her winter-stockinged legs and her other arm weighted down with school books, and stood for a moment listening to the sounds from the studio. A soft procession of piano chords and the tuning of a violin. Then Mister Bilderbach called out to her in his chunky, guttural tones:

"That you, Bienchen?"

As she jerked off her mittens she saw that her fingers were twitching to the motions of the fugue she had practiced that morning. "Yes," she answered. "It's me."

"I," the voice corrected. "Just a moment."

She could hear Mister Lafkowitz talking—his words spun out in a silky, unintelligible hum. A voice almost like a woman's, she thought, compared to Mister Bilderbach's. Restlessness scattered her attention. She fumbled with her geometry book and "Le Voyage de Monsieur Perrichon" before putting them on the table. She sat down on the sofa and began to take her music from the satchel. Again she saw her hands—the quivering tendons that stretched down from her knuckles, the sore finger tip capped with curled, dingy tape. The sight sharpened the fear that had begun to torment her for the past few months.

Noiselessly she mumbled a few phrases of encouragement to herself. A good lesson—a good lesson—like it used to be—Her lips closed as she heard the stolid sound of Mister Bilderbach's footsteps across the floor of the studio and the creaking of the door as it slid open.

For a moment she had the peculiar feeling that during most of the fifteen years of her life she had been looking at the face and shoulders that jutted from behind the door, in a silence disturbed only by the muted, blank plucking of a violin string. Mister Bilderbach. Her teacher, Mister Bilderbach.

The quick eyes behind the horn-rimmed glasses; the light, thin hair and the narrow face beneath; the lips full and loose shut and the lower one pink and shining from the bites of his teeth; the forked veins in his temples throbbing plainly enough to be observed across the room.

"Aren't you a little early?" he asked, glancing at the clock on the mantelpiece that had pointed to five minutes of twelve for a month. "Josef's in here. We're running over a little sonatina by someone he knows."

"Good," she said, trying to smile. "I'll listen." She could see her fingers sinking powerless into a blur of piano keys. She felt tired—felt that if he looked at her much longer her hands might tremble.

He stood uncertain, halfway in the room. Sharply his teeth pushed down on his bright, swollen lip. "Hungry, Bienchen?" he asked. "There's some apple cake Anna made, and milk."

"I'll wait till afterward," she said. "Thanks."

"After you finish with a very fine lesson—eh?" His smile seemed to crumble at the corners.

There was a sound from behind him in the studio and Mister Lafkowitz pushed at the other panel of the door and stood beside him.

"Frances?" he said, smiling. "And how is the work coming now?"

Without meaning to, Mister Lafkowitz always made her feel clumsy and overgrown. He was such a small man himself, with a weary look when he was not holding his violin. His eyebrows curved high above his sallow, Jewish face as though asking a question, but the lids of his eyes drowsed languorous and indifferent. Today he seemed distracted. She watched him come into the room for no apparent purpose, holding his pearl-tipped bow in his still fingers, slowly gliding the white horse hair through a chalky piece of rosin. His eyes were sharp bright slits today and the linen handkerchief that flowed down from his collar darkened the shadows beneath them.

"I gather you're doing a lot now," smiled Mister Lafkowitz, although she had not yet answered the question.

She looked at Mister Bilderbach. He turned away. His heavy shoulders pushed the door open wide so that the late afternoon sun came through the window of the studio and shafted yellow over the dusty living room. Behind her teacher she could see the squat long piano, the window, and the bust of Brahms.

"No," she said to Mister Lafkowitz, "I'm doing terribly." Her thin fingers flipped at the pages of her music. "I don't know what's the matter," she said, looking at Mister Bilderbach's stooped muscular back that stood tense and listening.

Mister Lafkowitz smiled. "There are times, I suppose, when one—"

A harsh chord sounded from the piano. "Don't you think we'd better get on with this?" asked Mister Bilderbach.

"Immediately," said Mister Lafkowitz, giving the bow one more scrape before starting toward the door. She could see him pick up his violin from the top of the piano. He caught her eye and lowered the instrument. "You've seen the picture of Heime?"

Her fingers curled tight over the sharp corner of the satchel. "What picture?"

"One of Heime in the *Musical Courier* there on the table. Inside the top cover."

The sonatina began. Discordant yet somehow simple. Empty but with a sharp cut style of its own. She reached for the magazine and opened it.

There Heime was—in the left hand corner. Holding his violin with his fingers hooked down over the strings for a pizzicato. With his dark serge knickers strapped neatly beneath his knees, a sweater and rolled collar. It was a bad picture. Although it was snapped in profile his eyes were cut around toward the photographer and his finger looked as though it would pluck the wrong string. He seemed suffering to turn around toward the picture-taking apparatus. He was thinner—his stomach did not poke out—but he hadn't changed much in six months.

Heime Israelsky, talented young violinist, snapped while at work in his teacher's studio on Riverside Drive. Young Master Israelsky, who will soon celebrate his fifteenth birthday, has been invited to play the Beethoven Concerto with—

That morning, after she had practiced from six until eight, her Dad had made her sit down at the table with the family for breakfast. She hated breakfast; it gave her a sick feeling afterward. She would rather wait and get four chocolate bars with her twenty cents lunch money and munch them during school—bringing up little morsels from her pocket under cover of her handkerchief, stopping dead when the silver paper rattled. But this morning her Dad had put a fried egg on her plate and she had known that if it burst—so that the slimy yellow oozed over the white—she would cry. And that had happened. The same feeling was upon her now. Gingerly she laid the magazine back on the table and closed her eyes.

The music in the studio seemed to be urging violently and clumsily for something that was not to be had. After a moment her thoughts drew back from Heime and the concerto and the picture—and hovered around the lessons once more. She slid over on the sofa until she could see plainly into the studio—the two of them playing, peering at the notations on the piano, lustfully drawing out all that was there.

She could not forget the memory of Mister Bilderbach's face as he had stared at her a moment ago. Her hands, still twitching unconsciously to the motions of the fugue, closed over her bony knees. Tired, she was. And with a circling, sinking away feeling like the one that often came to her just before she dropped off to sleep on the nights when she had over-practiced. Like those weary half dreams that buzzed and carried her out into their own whirling space.

A *Wunderkind*—a *Wunderkind*. The syllables would come rolling in the deep German way, roar against her ears and then fall to a murmur. Along with the faces circling, swelling out in distortion, diminishing to pale blobs—Mister Bilderbach, Mrs. Bilderbach, Heime, Mister Lafkowitz. Around and around in a circle revolving to the guttural *Wunderkind*. Mister Bilderbach looming large in the middle of the circle, his face urging—with the others around him.

Phrases of music seesawing crazily. Notes she had been practicing falling over each other like a handful of marbles dropped downstairs. Bach, Debussy, Prokofieff, Brahms—timed grotesquely to the far off throb of her tired body and the buzzing circle.

Sometimes—when she had not worked more than three hours or had stayed out from high school—the dreams were not so confused. The music soared clearly in her mind and quick, precise little memories would come back—clear as the sissy "Age of Innocence" picture Heime had given her after their joint concert was over.

A *Wunderkind*—a *Wunderkind*. That was what Mister Bilderbach had called her when, at twelve, she first came to him. Older pupils had repeated the word.

Not that he had ever said the word to her. "Bienchen—" (She had a plain American name but he never used it except when her mistakes were enormous). "Bienchen," he would say, "I know it must be terrible. Carrying around all the time a head that thick. Poor Bienchen—"

Mister Bilderbach's father had been a Dutch violinist. His mother was from Prague. He had been born in this country and had spent his youth in Germany. So many times she wished she had not been born and brought up in just Cincinnati. How do you say *cheese* in German? Mister Bilderbach, what is Dutch for *I don't understand you?*

The first day she came to the studio. After she played the whole Second Hungarian Rhapsody from memory. The room graying with twilight. His face as he leaned over the piano.

"Now we begin all over," he said that first day. "It—playing music—is more than cleverness. If a twelve-year-old girl's fingers cover so many keys to a second—that means nothing."

He tapped his broad chest and his forehead with his stubby hand. "Here and here. You are old enough to understand that." He lighted a cigarette and gently blew the first exhalation above her head. "And work—work—work. We will start now with these Bach Inventions and these little Schumann pieces." His hands moved again—this time to jerk the cord of the lamp behind her and point to the music. "I will show you how I wish this practiced. Listen carefully now."

She had been at the piano for almost three hours and was very tired. His deep voice sounded as though it had been straying inside her for a long time. She wanted to reach out and touch his muscle-flexed finger that pointed out the phrases, wanted to feel the gleaming gold band ring and the strong hairy back of his hand.

She had lessons Tuesday after school and on Saturday afternoons. Often she stayed, when the Saturday lesson was finished, for dinner, and then spent the night and took the street car home the next morning. Mrs. Bilderbach liked her in her calm, almost dumb way. She was much different from her husband. She was quiet and fat and slow. When she wasn't in the kitchen, cooking the rich dishes that both of them loved, she seemed to spend all her time in their bed upstairs, reading magazines or just looking with a half smile at nothing. When they had married in Germany she had been a *lieder* singer. She didn't sing anymore (she said it was her throat). When he would call her in from the kitchen to listen to a pupil she would always smile and say that it was *gut,* very *gut.*

When Frances was thirteen it came to her one day that the Bilderbachs had no children. It seemed strange. Once she had been back in the kitchen with Mrs. Bilderbach when he had come striding in from the studio, tense with anger at some pupil who had annoyed him. His wife stood stirring the thick soup until his hand groped out and rested on her shoulder. Then she turned—stood placid—while he folded his arms about her and buried his sharp face in the white, nerveless flesh of her neck. They stood that way without moving. And then his face jerked back suddenly, the anger diminished to a quiet inexpressiveness, and he had returned to the studio.

After she had started with Mister Bilderbach and didn't have time to see anything of the people at high school, Heime had been the only friend of her own age. He was Mister Lafkowitz's pupil and would come with him to Mister Bilderbach's on evenings when she would be there. They would listen to their teachers' playing. And often they themselves went over chamber music together—Mozart sonatas or Bloch.

A *Wunderkind*—a *Wunderkind.*

Heime was a *Wunderkind.* He and she, then.

Heime had been playing the violin since he was four. He didn't have to go to school; Mister Lafkowitz's brother, who was crippled, used to teach him geometry and European history and French verbs in the afternoon. When he was thirteen he had as fine a technique as any violinist in Cincinnati—everyone said so. But playing the violin must be easier than the piano. She knew it must be.

Heime always seemed to smell of corduroy pants and the food he had eaten and rosin. Half the time, too, his hands were dirty around the knuckles and the cuffs of his shirts peeped out dingily from the sleeves of his sweater. She always watched his hands when he played—thin only at the joints with the hard little blobs of flesh bulging over the short cut nails and the babyish looking crease that showed so plainly in his bowing wrist.

In the dreams, as when she was awake, she could remember the concert only in a blur. She had not known it was unsuccessful for her until months after. True, the papers had praised Heime more than her. But he was much shorter than she. When they stood together on the stage he came only to her shoulders. And that made a difference with people, she knew. Also, there was the matter of the sonata they played together. The Bloch.

"No, no—I don't think that would be appropriate," Mister Bilderbach had said when the Bloch was suggested to end the programme. "Now that John Powell thing—the Sonate Virginianesque."

She hadn't understood then; she wanted it to be the Bloch as much as Mister Lafkowitz and Heime.

Mister Bilderbach had given in. Later, after the reviews had said she lacked the temperament for that type of music, after they called her playing thin and lacking in feeling, she felt cheated.

"That oie oie stuff," said Mister Bilderbach, crackling the newspapers at her. "Not for you, Bienchen. Leave all that to the Heimes and vitses and skys."

A *Wunderkind.* No matter what the papers said, that was what he had called her.

Why was it Heime had done so much better at the concert than she? At school sometimes, when she was supposed to be watching someone do a geometry problem on the blackboard, the question would twist knife-like inside her. She would worry about it in bed, and even sometimes when she was supposed to be concentrating at the piano. It wasn't just the Bloch and her not being Jewish—not entirely. It wasn't that Heime didn't have to go to school and had begun his training so early, either. It was—?

Once she thought she knew.

"Play the Fantasia and Fugue," Mister Bilderbach had demanded one evening a year ago—after he and Mister Lafkowitz had finished reading some music together.

The Bach, as she played, seemed to her well done. From the tail of her eye she could see the calm, pleased expression on Mister Bilderbach's face, see his hands rise climactically from the chair arms and then sink down loose and satisfied when the high points of the phrases had been passed successfully. She stood up from the piano when it was over, swallowing to loosen the bands that the music seemed to have drawn around her throat and chest. But—

"Frances——" Mister Lafkowitz had said then, suddenly, looking at her with his thin mouth curved and his eyes almost covered by their delicate lids. "Do you know how many children Bach had?"

She turned to him, puzzled. "A good many. Twenty some odd."

"Well, then——" The corners of his smile etched themselves gently in his pale face. "He could not have been so cold—then."

Mister Bilderbach was not pleased; his guttural effulgence of German words had *Kind* in it somewhere. Mister Lafkowitz raised his eyebrows. She had caught the point easily enough, but she felt no deception in keeping her face blank and immature because that was the way Mister Bilderbach wanted her to look.

Yet such things had nothing to do with it. Nothing very much, at least, for she would grow older. Mister Bilderbach understood that, and even Mister Lafkowitz had not meant just what he said.

In the dreams Mister Bilderbach's face loomed out and contracted in the center of the whirling circle. The lips surging softly, the veins in his temples insisting.

But sometimes, before she slept, there were such clear memories; as when she pulled a hole in the heel of her stocking down, so that her shoe would hide it. "Bienchen, Bienchen!" And bringing Mrs. Bilderbach's work basket in and showing her how it should be darned and not gathered together in a lumpy heap.

And the time she graduated from Junior High:

"What you wear?" asked Mrs. Bilderbach the Sunday morning at breakfast when she told them how they had practiced to march into the auditorium.

"An evening dress my cousin had last year."

"Ah—Bienchen!" he said, circling his warm coffee cup with his heavy hands, looking up at her with wrinkles around his laughing eyes. "I bet I know what Bienchen wants——"

He insisted. He would not believe her when she explained that she honestly didn't care at all.

"Like this, Anna," he said, pushing his napkin across the table and mincing to the other side of the room, swishing his hips, rolling up his eyes behind his horn-rimmed glasses.

The next Saturday afternoon, after her lesson, he took her to the department stores downtown. His thick fingers smoothed over the filmy nets and crackling taffetas that the saleswomen unwound from their bolts. He held colors to her face, cocking his head to one side, and selected pink. Shoes, he remembered too. He liked best some white kid pumps. They seemed a little like old ladies' shoes to her and the Red Cross label in the instep had a charity look. But it really didn't matter at all. When Mrs. Bilderbach began to cut out the dress and fit it to her with pins, he interrupted his lessons to stand by and suggest ruffles around the hips and neck and a fancy rosette on the shoulder. The music was coming along nicely then. Dresses and commencement and such made no difference.

Nothing mattered much except playing the music as it must be played, bringing out the thing that must be in her, practicing, practicing, playing so that Mister Bilderbach's face lost some of its urging look. Putting the thing into her music that Myra Hess had, and Yehudi Menuhin—even Heime!

What had begun to happen to her four months ago? The notes began springing out with a glib, dead intonation. Adolescence, she thought. Some kids played with promise—and worked and worked until, like her, the least little thing would start them crying, and worn out with trying to get the thing across—the longing thing they felt—something queer began to happen—But not she! She was like Heime. She had to be. She—

Once it was there for sure. And you didn't lose things like that. A *Wunderkind.* . . . A *Wunderkind.* . . . Of her he said it, rolling the words in the sure, deep German way. And in the dreams even deeper, more certain than ever. With his face looming out at her, and the longing phrases of music mixed in with the zooming, circling round, round, round—A *Wunderkind.* A *Wunderkind.* . . .

This afternoon Mister Bilderbach did not show Mister Lafkowitz to the front door, as he usually did. He stayed at the piano, softly pressing a solitary note. Listening, Frances watched the violinist wind his scarf about his pale throat.

"A good picture of Heime," she said, picking up her music. "I got a letter from him a couple of months ago—telling about hearing Schnabel and Huberman and about Carnegie Hall and things to eat at the Russian Tea Room."

To put off going into the studio a moment longer she waited until Mister Lafkowitz was ready to leave and then stood behind him as he opened the door. The frosty cold outside cut into the room. It was growing late and the air was seeped with the pale yellow of winter twilight. When the door swung to on its hinges, the house seemed darker and more silent than ever before she had known it to be.

As she went into the studio Mister Bilderbach got up from the piano and silently watched her settle herself at the keyboard.

"Well, Bienchen," he said, "this afternoon we are going to begin all over. Start from scratch. Forget the last few months."

He looked as though he were trying to act a part in a movie. His solid body swayed from toe to heel, he rubbed his hands together, and even smiled in a satisfied, movie way. Then suddenly he thrust this manner brusquely aside. His heavy shoulders slouched and he began to run through the stack of music she had brought in. "The Bach—no, not yet," he murmured. "The Beethoven? Yes, the Variation Sonata. Opus 26."

The keys of the piano hemmed her in—stiff and white and dead-seeming.

"Wait a minute," he said. He stood in the curve of the piano, elbows propped, and looked at her. "Today I expect something from you. Now this sonata—it's the first Beethoven sonata you ever worked on. Every note is under control—technically—you have nothing to cope with but the music. Only music now. That's all you think about."

He rustled through the pages of her volume until he found the place. Then he pulled his teaching chair half way across the room, turned it around and seated himself, straddling the back with his legs.

For some reason, she knew, this position of his usually had a good effect on her performance. But today she felt that she would notice him from the corner of her eye and be disturbed. His back was stiffly tilted, his legs looked tense. The heavy volume before him seemed to balance dangerously on the chair back. "Now we begin," he said with a peremptory dart of his eyes in her direction.

Her hands rounded over the keys and then sank down. The first notes were too loud, the other phrases followed dryly.

Arrestingly his hand rose up from the score. "Wait! Think a minute what you're playing. How is this beginning marked?"

"*An-andante.*"

"All right. Don't drag it into an *adagio* then. And play deeply into the keys. Don't snatch it off shallowly that way. A graceful, deep-toned *andante*—"

She tried again. Her hands seemed separate from the music that was in her.

"Listen," he interrupted. "Which of these variations dominates the whole?"

"The dirge," she answered.

"Then prepare for that. This is an *andante*—but it's not salon stuff as you just played it. Start out softly, *piano,* and make it swell out just before the arpeggio. Make it warm and dramatic. And down here—where it's marked *dolce* make the counter melody sing out. You know all that. We've gone over all that side of it before. Now play it. Feel it as Beethoven wrote it down. Feel that tragedy and restraint."

She could not stop looking at his hands. They seemed to rest tentatively on the music, ready to fly up as a stop signal as soon as she would begin, the gleaming flash of his ring calling her to halt. "Mister Bilderbach—maybe if I—if you let me play on through the first variation without stopping I could do better."

"I won't interrupt," he said.

Her pale face leaned over too close to the keys. She played through the first part, and, obeying a nod from him, began the second. There were no flaws that jarred on her, but the phrases shaped from her fingers before she had put into them the meaning that she felt.

When she had finished he looked up from the music and began to speak with dull bluntness: "I hardly heard those harmonic fillings in the right hand. And incidentally, this part was supposed to take on intensity, develop the foreshadowings that were supposed to be inherent in the first part. Go on with the next one, though."

She wanted to start it with subdued viciousness and progress to a feeling of deep, swollen sorrow. Her mind told her that. But her hands seemed to gum in the keys like limp macaroni and she could not imagine the music as it should be.

When the last note had stopped vibrating, he closed the book and deliberately got up from the chair. He was moving his lower jaw from side to side—and between his open lips she could glimpse the pink healthy lane to his throat and his strong, smoke-yellowed teeth. He laid the Beethoven gingerly on top of the rest of the music and propped his elbows on the smooth, black top once more. "No," he said simply, looking at her.

Her mouth began to quiver. "I can't help it. I—"

Suddenly he strained his lips to smile. "Listen, Bienchen," he began in a new, forced voice. "You still play the Harmonious Blacksmith, don't you? I told you not to drop it from your repertoire."

"Yes," she said. "I practice it now and then."

His voice was the one he used for children. "It was among the first things we worked on together—remember. So strongly you used to play it—like a real blacksmith's daughter. You see, Bienchen, I know you so well—as if you were my own girl. I know what you have—I've heard you play so many things beautifully. You used to—"

He stopped in confusion and inhaled from his pulpy stub of cigarette. The smoke drowsed out from his pink lips and clung in a gray mist around her lank hair and childish forehead.

"Make it happy and simple," he said, switching on the lamp behind her and stepping back from the piano.

For a moment he stood just inside the bright circle the light made. Then impulsively he squatted down on the floor. "Vigorous," he said.

She could not stop looking at him, sitting on one heel with the other foot resting squarely before him for balance, the muscles of his strong thighs straining under the cloth of his trousers, his back straight, his elbows staunchly propped on his knees. "Simply now," he repeated with a gesture of his fleshy hands. "Think of the blacksmith—working out in the sunshine all day. Working easily and undisturbed."

She could not look down at the piano. The lights brightened the hairs on the backs of his outspread hands, made the lenses of his glasses glitter.

"All of it," he urged. "Now!"

She felt that the marrows of her bones were hollow and there was no blood left in her. Her heart that had been springing against her chest all afternoon felt suddenly dead. She saw it gray and limp and shrivelled at the edges like an oyster.

His face seemed to throb out in space before her, come closer with the lurching motion in the veins of his temples. In retreat, she looked down at the piano. Her lips shook like jelly and a surge of noiseless tears made the white keys blur in a watery line. "I can't," she whispered. "I don't know why, but I just can't—can't any more."

His tense body slackened and holding his hand to his side, he pulled himself up. She clutched the music and hurried past him.

Her coat. The mittens and galoshes. The school books and the satchel he had given her on her birthday. All from the silent room that was hers. Quickly—before he would have to speak.

As she passed through the vestibule she could not help but see his hands—held out from his body that leaned against the studio door, relaxed and purposeless. The door shut so firmly. Dragging her books and satchel she stumbled down the stone steps, turned in the wrong direction, and hurried down the street that had become confused with noise and bicycles and the games of other children.

GOODBYE,
MY BROTHER

We are a family that has always been very close in spirit. Our father was drowned in a sailing accident when we were young, and our mother has always stressed the fact that our familial relationships have a kind of permanence that we will never meet with again. I don't think about the family much, but when I remember its members and the coast where they lived and the sea salt that I think is in our blood, I am happy to recall that I am a Pommeroy—that I have the nose, the coloring, and the promise of longevity—and that while we are not a distinguished family, we enjoy the illusion, when we are together, that the Pommeroys are unique. I don't say any of this because I'm interested in family history or because this sense of uniqueness is deep or important to me but in order to advance the point that we are loyal to one another in spite of our differences, and that any rupture in this loyalty is a source of confusion and pain.

We are four children; there is my sister Diana and the three men—Chaddy, Lawrence, and myself. Like most families in which the children are out of their twenties, we have been separated by business, marriage, and war. Helen and I live on Long Island now, with our four children. I teach in a secondary school, and I am past the age where I expect to be made headmaster—or principal, as we say—but I respect the work. Chaddy, who has done better than the rest of us, lives in Manhattan, with Odette and their children. Mother lives in Philadelphia, and Diana, since her divorce, has been living in France, but she comes back to the States in the summer to spend a month at Laud's Head. Laud's Head is a summer place on the shore of one of the Massachusetts islands. We used to have a cottage there, and in the twenties our father built the big house. It stands on a cliff above the sea and, excepting St. Tropez and some of the Apennine villages, it is my favorite place in the world. We each have an equity in the place and we contribute some money to help keep it going.

Our youngest brother, Lawrence, who is a lawyer, got a job with a Cleveland firm after the war, and none of us saw him for four years. When he decided to leave Cleveland and go to work for a firm in Albany, he wrote Mother that he would, between jobs, spend ten days at Laud's Head, with his wife and their two children. This was when I had planned to take my vacation—I had been teaching summer school—and Helen and Chaddy and Odette and Diana were all going to be there, so the family would be together. Lawrence is the member of the family with whom the rest of us have least in common. We have never seen a great deal of him, and I suppose that's why we still call him Tifty—a nickname he was given when he was a child, because when he came down the hall toward the dining room for breakfast, his slippers made a noise that sounded like "Tifty, tifty, tifty." That's what Father called him, and so did everyone else. When he grew older, Diana sometimes used to call him Little Jesus, and Mother often called him the Croaker. We had disliked Lawrence, but we looked forward to his return with a mixture of apprehension and loyalty, and with some of the joy and delight of reclaiming a brother.

Lawrence crossed over from the mainland on the four-o'clock boat one afternoon late in the summer, and Chaddy and I went down to meet him. The arrivals and departures of the summer ferry have all the outward signs that suggest a voyage—whistles, bells, hand trucks, reunions, and the smell of brine—but it is a voyage of no import, and when I watched the boat come into the blue harbor that afternoon and thought that it was completing a voyage of no import, I realized that I had hit on exactly the kind of observation that Lawrence would have made. We looked for his face behind the windshields as the cars drove off the boat, and we had no trouble in recognizing him. And we ran over and shook his hand and clumsily kissed his wife and the children. "Tifty!" Chaddy shouted. "Tifty!" It is difficult to judge changes in the appearance of a brother, but both Chaddy and I agreed, as we drove back to Laud's Head, that Lawrence still looked very young. He got to the house first, and we took the suitcases out of his car. When I came in, he was standing in the living room, talking with Mother and Diana. They were in their best clothes and all their jewelry, and they were welcoming him extravagantly, but even then, when everyone was endeavoring to seem most affectionate and at a time when these endeavors come easiest, I was aware of a faint tension in the room. Thinking about this as I carried Lawrence's heavy suitcases up the stairs, I realized that our dislikes are as deeply ingrained as our better passions, and I remembered that once, twenty-five years ago, when I had hit Lawrence on the head with a rock, he had picked himself up and gone directly to our father to complain.

I carried the suitcases up to the third floor, where Ruth, Lawrence's wife, had begun to settle her family. She is a thin girl, and she seemed very tired from the journey, but when I asked her if she didn't want me to bring a drink upstairs to her, she said she didn't think she did.

When I got downstairs, Lawrence wasn't around, but the others were all ready for cocktails, and we decided to go ahead. Lawrence is the only member of the family who has never enjoyed drinking. We took our cocktails onto the terrace, so that we could see the bluffs and the sea and the islands in the east, and the return of Lawrence and his wife, their presence in the house, seemed to refresh our responses to the familiar view; it was as if the pleasure they would take in the sweep and the color of that coast, after such a long absence, had been imparted to us. While we were there, Lawrence came up the path from the beach.

"Isn't the beach fabulous, Tifty?" Mother asked. "Isn't it fabulous to be back? Will you have a Martini?"

"I don't care," Lawrence said. "Whiskey, gin—I don't care what I drink. Give me a little rum."

"We don't have any *rum*," Mother said. It was the first note of asperity. She had taught us never to be indecisive, never to reply as Lawrence had. Beyond this, she is deeply concerned with the propriety of her house, and anything irregular by her standards, like drinking straight rum or bringing a beer can to the dinner table, excites in her a conflict that she cannot, even with her capacious sense of humor, surmount. She sensed the asperity and worked to repair it. "Would you like some Irish, Tifty dear?" she said. "Isn't Irish what you've always liked? There's some Irish on the sideboard. Why don't you get yourself some Irish?" Lawrence said that he didn't care. He poured himself a Martini, and then Ruth came down and we went in to dinner.

In spite of the fact that we had, through waiting for Lawrence, drunk too much before dinner, we were all anxious to put our best foot forward and to enjoy a peaceful time. Mother is a small woman whose face is still a striking reminder of how pretty she must have been, and whose conversation is unusually light, but she talked that evening about a soil-reclamation project that is going on up-island. Diana is as pretty as Mother must have been; she is an animated and lovely woman who likes to talk about the dissolute friends that she has made in France, but she talked that night about the school in Switzerland where she had left her two children. I could see that the dinner had been planned to please Lawrence. It was not too rich, and there was nothing to make him worry about extravagance.

After supper, when we went back onto the terrace, the clouds held that kind of light that looks like blood, and I was glad that Lawrence had such a lurid sunset for his homecoming. When we had been out there a few minutes, a man

named Edward Chester came to get Diana. She had met him in France, or on
the boat home, and he was staying for ten days at the inn in the village. He was
introduced to Lawrence and Ruth, and then he and Diana left.

"Is that the one she's sleeping with now?" Lawrence asked.

"What a horrid thing to say!" Helen said.

"You ought to apologize for that, Tifty," Chaddy said.

"I don't know," Mother said tiredly. "I don't know, Tifty. Diana is in a
position to do whatever she wants, and I don't ask sordid questions. She's my
only daughter. I don't see her often."

"Is she going back to France?"

"She's going back the week after next."

Lawrence and Ruth were sitting at the edge of the terrace, not in the
chairs, not in the circle of chairs. With his mouth set, my brother looked to
me then like a Puritan cleric. Sometimes, when I try to understand his frame
of mind, I think of the beginnings of our family in this country, and his dis-
approval of Diana and her lover reminded me of this. The branch of the Pommeroys to which we belong was founded by a minister who was eulogized by
Cotton Mather for his untiring abjuration of the Devil. The Pommeroys were
ministers until the middle of the nineteenth century, and the harshness of their
thought—man is full of misery, and all earthly beauty is lustful and corrupt—has been preserved in books and sermons. The temper of our family
changed somewhat and became more lighthearted, but when I was of school
age, I can remember a cousinage of old men and women who seemed to hark
back to the dark days of the ministry and to be animated by perpetual guilt
and the deification of the scourge. If you are raised in this atmosphere—and
in a sense we were—I think it is a trial of the spirit to reject its habits of guilt,
self-denial, taciturnity, and penitence, and it seemed to me to have been a trial
of the spirit in which Lawrence had succumbed.

"Is that Cassiopeia?" Odette asked.

"No, dear," Chaddy said. "That isn't Cassiopeia."

"Who was Cassiopeia?" Odette said.

"She was the wife of Cepheus and the mother of Andromeda," I said.

"The cook is a Giants fan," Chaddy said. "She'll give you even money
that they win the pennant."

It had grown so dark that we could see the passage of light through the
sky from the lighthouse at Cape Heron. In the dark below the cliff, the continual detonations of the surf sounded. And then, as she often does when it
is getting dark and she has drunk too much before dinner, Mother began to
talk about the improvements and additions that would someday be made on
the house, the wings and bathrooms and gardens.

"This house will be in the sea in five years," Lawrence said.

"Tifty the Croaker," Chaddy said.

"Don't call me Tifty," Lawrence said.

"Little Jesus," Chaddy said.

"The sea wall is badly cracked," Lawrence said. "I looked at it this afternoon. You had it repaired four years ago, and it cost eight thousand dollars. You can't do that every four years."

"Please, Tifty," Mother said.

"Facts are facts," Lawrence said, "and it's a damned-fool idea to build a house at the edge of the cliff on a sinking coastline. In my lifetime, half the garden has washed away and there's four feet of water where we used to have a bathhouse."

"Let's have a very *general* conversation," Mother said bitterly. "Let's talk about politics or the boat-club dance."

"As a matter of fact," Lawrence said, "the house is probably in some danger now. If you had an unusually high sea, a hurricane sea, the wall would crumble and the house would go. We could all be drowned."

"I can't *bear* it," Mother said. She went into the pantry and came back with a full glass of gin.

I have grown too old now to think that I can judge the sentiments of others, but I was conscious of the tension between Lawrence and Mother, and I knew some of the history of it. Lawrence couldn't have been more than sixteen years old when he decided that Mother was frivolous, mischievous, destructive, and overly strong. When he had determined this, he decided to separate himself from her. He was at boarding school then, and I remember that he did not come home for Christmas. He spent Christmas with a friend. He came home very seldom after he had made his unfavorable judgment on Mother, and when he did come home, he always tried, in his conversation, to remind her of his estrangement. When he married Ruth, he did not tell Mother. He did not tell her when his children were born. But in spite of these principled and lengthy exertions he seemed, unlike the rest of us, never to have enjoyed any separation, and when they are together, you feel at once a tension, an unclearness.

And it was unfortunate, in a way, that Mother should have picked that night to get drunk. It's her privilege, and she doesn't get drunk often, and fortunately she wasn't bellicose, but we were all conscious of what was happening. As she quietly drank her gin, she seemed sadly to be parting from us; she seemed to be in the throes of travel. Then her mood changed from travel to injury, and the few remarks she made were petulant and irrelevant. When her glass was nearly empty, she stared angrily at the dark air in front of her nose, moving her head a little, like a fighter. I knew that there was not room in her mind then for all the injuries that were crowding into it. Her children were stupid, her husband was drowned, her servants were thieves, and the chair she sat in was uncomfortable. Suddenly she put down her empty glass and interrupted Chaddy, who was talking about baseball. "I know one *thing*," she said hoarsely. "I know that if there is an afterlife, I'm going to have a very different kind of family. I'm going to have nothing but fabulously rich, witty, and enchanting children." She got up and, starting for the door, nearly fell. Chaddy caught her and helped her up the stairs. I could hear their tender goodnights, and then Chaddy came back. I thought that Lawrence by now would be tired from his journey and his return, but he remained on the terrace, as if he were waiting to see the final malfeasance, and the rest of us left him there and went swimming in the dark.

When I woke the next morning, or half woke, I could hear the sound of someone rolling the tennis court. It is a fainter and a deeper sound than the iron buoy bells off the point—an unrhythmic iron chiming—that belongs in my mind to the beginnings of a summer day, a good portent. When I went downstairs, Lawrence's two kids were in the living room, dressed in ornate cowboy suits. They are frightened and skinny children. They told me their father was rolling the tennis court but that they did not want to go out because they had seen a snake under the doorstep. I explained to them that their cousins—all the other children—ate breakfast in the kitchen and that they'd better run along in there. At this announcement, the boy began to cry. Then his sister joined him. They cried as if to go in the kitchen and eat would destroy their most precious rights. I told them to sit down with me. Lawrence came in, and I asked him if he wanted to play some tennis. He said no, thanks, although he thought he might play some singles with Chaddy. He was in the right here, because both he and Chaddy play better tennis than I, and he did play some singles with Chaddy after breakfast, but later on, when the others came down to play family doubles, Lawrence disappeared. This made me cross—unreasonably so, I suppose—but we play darned interesting family doubles and he could have played in a set for the sake of courtesy.

Late in the morning, when I came up from the court alone, I saw Tifty on the terrace, prying up a shingle from the wall with his jackknife. "What's the matter, Lawrence?" I said. "Termites?" There are termites in the wood and they've given us a lot of trouble.

He pointed out to me, at the base of each row of shingles, a faint blue line of carpenter's chalk. "This house is about twenty-two years old," he said. "These shingles are about two hundred years old. Dad must have bought shingles from all the farms around here when he built the place, to make it look venerable. You can still see the carpenter's chalk put down where these antiques were nailed into place."

It was true about the shingles, although I had forgotten it. When the house was built, our father, or his architect, had ordered it covered with lichened and weather-beaten shingles. I didn't follow Lawrence's reasons for thinking that this was scandalous.

"And look at these doors," Lawrence said. "Look at these doors and window frames." I followed him over to a big Dutch door that opens onto the terrace and looked at it. It was a relatively new door, but someone had worked hard to conceal its newness. The surface had been deeply scored with some metal implement, and white paint had been rubbed into the incisions to imitate brine, lichen, and weather rot. "Imagine spending thousands of dollars to make a sound house look like a wreck," Lawrence said. "Imagine the frame of mind this implies. Imagine wanting to live so much in the past that you'll pay men carpenters' wages to disfigure your front door." Then I remembered Lawrence's sensitivity to time and his sentiments and opinions about our feelings for the past. I had heard him say, years ago, that we and our friends and our part of the nation, finding ourselves unable to cope with the problems of the present, had, like a wretched adult, turned back to what we supposed was a happier and a simpler time, and that our taste for reconstruction and candlelight was a measure of this irremediable failure. The faint blue line of chalk had reminded him of these ideas, the scarified door had reinforced them, and now clue after clue presented itself to him—the stern light at the door, the bulk of the chimney, the width of the floorboards and the pieces set into them to resemble pegs. While Lawrence was lecturing me on these frailties, the others came up from the court. As soon as Mother saw Lawrence, she responded, and I saw that there was little hope of any rapport between the matriarch and the changeling. She took Chaddy's arm. "Let's go swimming and have Martinis on the beach," she said. "Let's have a *fabulous* morning."

The sea that morning was a solid color, like verd stone. Everyone went to the beach but Tifty and Ruth. "I don't mind *him,*" Mother said. She was excited, and she tipped her glass and spilled some gin into the sand. "I don't mind *him.* It doesn't matter to me how *rude* and *horrid* and *gloomy* he is, but what I can't bear are the faces of his wretched little children, those fabulously unhappy little children." With the height of the cliff between us, everyone talked wrathfully about Lawrence; about how he had grown worse instead of better, how unlike the rest of us he was, how he endeavored to spoil every pleasure. We drank our gin; the abuse seemed to reach a crescendo, and then, one by one, we went swimming in the solid green water. But when we came out no one mentioned Lawrence unkindly; the line of abusive conversation had been cut, as if swimming had the cleansing force claimed for baptism. We dried our hands and lighted cigarettes, and if Lawrence was mentioned, it was only to suggest, kindly, something that might please him. Wouldn't he like to sail to Barin's cove, or go fishing?

And now I remember that while Lawrence was visiting us, we went swimming oftener than we usually do, and I think there was a reason for this. When the irritability that accumulated as a result of his company began to lessen our patience, not only with Lawrence but with one another, we would all go swimming and shed our animus in the cold water. I can see the family now, smarting from Lawrence's rebukes as they sat on the sand, and I can see them wading and diving and surface-diving and hear in their voices the restoration of patience and the rediscovery of inexhaustible good will. If Lawrence noticed this change—this illusion of purification—I suppose that he would have found in the vocabulary of psychiatry, or the mythology of the Atlantic, some circumspect name for it, but I don't think he noticed the change. He neglected to name the curative powers of the open sea, but it was one of the few chances for diminution that he missed.

The cook we had that year was a Polish woman named Anna Ostrovick, a summer cook. She was first-rate—a big, fat, hearty, industrious woman who took her work seriously. She liked to cook and to have the food she cooked appreciated and eaten, and whenever we saw her, she always urged us to eat. She cooked hot bread—crescents and brioches—for breakfast two or three times a week, and she would bring these into the dining room herself and say, "Eat, eat, eat!" When the maid took the serving dishes back into the pantry, we could sometimes hear Anna, who was standing there, say, "Good! They eat." She fed the garbage man, the milkman, and the gardener. "Eat!" she told them. "Eat, eat!" On Thursday afternoons, she went to the movies with the maid, but she didn't enjoy the movies, because the actors were all so thin. She would sit in the dark theatre for an hour and a half watching the screen anxiously for the appearance of someone who had enjoyed his food. Bette Davis merely left with Anna the impression of a woman who has not eaten well. "They are all so skinny," she would say when she left the movies. In the evenings, after she had gorged all of us, and washed the pots and pans, she would collect the table scraps and go out to feed the creation. We had a few chickens that year, and although they would have roosted by then, she would dump food into their troughs and urge the sleeping fowl to eat. She fed the songbirds in the orchard and the 128 chipmunks in the yard. Her appearance at the edge of the garden and her urgent voice—we could hear her calling "Eat, eat, eat"—had become, like the sunset gun at the boat club and the passage of light from Cape Heron, attached to that hour. "Eat, eat, eat," we could hear Anna say. "Eat, eat . . ." Then it would be dark.

When Lawrence had been there three days, Anna called me into the kitchen. "You tell your mother," she said, "that *he* doesn't come into my kitchen. If *he* comes into my kitchen all the time, I go. *He* is always coming into my kitchen to tell me what a sad woman I am. He is always telling me that I work too hard and that I don't get paid enough and that I should belong to a union with vacations. Ha! He is so skinny but he is always coming into my kitchen when I am busy to pity me, but I am as good as him, I am as good as *anybody,* and I do not have to have people like that getting into my way all the time and feeling sorry for me. I am a famous and a wonderful cook and I have jobs everywhere and the only reason I come here to work this summer is because I was never before on an island, but I can have other jobs tomorrow, and if he is always coming into my kitchen to pity me, you tell your mother I am going. I am as good as *anybody* and I do not have to have that skinny all the time telling how poor I am."

I was pleased to find that the cook was on our side, but I felt that the situation was delicate. If Mother asked Lawrence to stay out of the kitchen, he would make a grievance out of the request. He could make a grievance out of anything, and it sometimes seemed that as he sat darkly at the dinner table, every word of disparagement, wherever it was aimed, came home to him. I didn't mention the cook's complaint to anyone, but somehow there wasn't any more trouble from that quarter.

The next cause for contention that I had from Lawrence came over our backgammon games.

When we are at Laud's Head, we play a lot of backgammon. At eight o'clock, after we have drunk our coffee, we usually get out the board. In a way, it is one of our pleasantest hours. The lamps in the room are still unlighted, Anna can be seen in the dark garden, and in the sky above her head there are continents of shadow and fire. Mother turns on the light and rattles the dice as a signal. We usually play three games apiece, each with the others. We play for money, and you can win or lose a hundred dollars on a game, but the stakes are usually much lower. I think that Lawrence used to play—I can't remember—but he doesn't play any more. He doesn't gamble. This is not because he is poor or because he has any principles about gambling but because he thinks the game is foolish and a waste of time. He was ready enough, however, to waste his time watching the rest of us play. Night after night, when the game began, he pulled a chair up beside the board, and watched the checkers and the dice. His expression was scornful, and yet he watched carefully. I wondered why he watched us night after night, and, through watching his face, I think that I may have found out.

Lawrence doesn't gamble, so he can't understand the excitement of winning and losing money. He has forgotten how to play the game, I think, so that its complex odds can't interest him. His observations were bound to include the facts that backgammon is an idle game and a game of chance, and that the board, marked with points, was a symbol of our worthlessness. And since he doesn't understand gambling or the odds of the game, I thought that what interested him must be the members of his family. One night when I was playing with Odette—I had won thirty-seven dollars from Mother and Chaddy—I think I saw what was going on in his mind.

Odette has black hair and black eyes. She is careful never to expose her white skin to the sun for long, so the striking contrast of blackness and pallor is not changed in the summer. She needs and deserves admiration—it is the element that contents her—and she will flirt, unseriously, with any man. Her shoulders were bare that night, her dress was cut to show the division of her breasts and to show her breasts when she leaned over the board to play. She kept losing and flirting and making her losses seem like a part of the flirtation. Chaddy was in the other room. She lost three games, and when the third game ended, she fell back on the sofa and, looking at me squarely, said something about going out on the dunes to settle the score. Lawrence heard her. I looked at Lawrence. He seemed shocked and gratified at the same time, as if he had suspected all along that we were not playing for anything so insubstantial as money. I may be wrong, of course, but I think that Lawrence felt that in watching our backgammon he was observing the progress of a mordant tragedy in which the money we won and lost served as a symbol for more vital forfeits. It is like Lawrence to try to read significance and finality into every gesture that we make, and it is certain of Lawrence that when he finds the inner logic to our conduct, it will be sordid.

Chaddy came in to play with me. Chaddy and I have never liked to lose to each other. When we were younger, we used to be forbidden to play games together, because they always ended in a fight. We think we know each other's mettle intimately. I think he is prudent; he thinks I am foolish. There is always bad blood when we play anything—tennis or backgammon or softball or bridge—and it does seem at times as if we were playing for the possession of each other's liberties. When I lose to Chaddy, I can't sleep. All this is only half the truth of our competitive relationship, but it was the half-truth that would be discernible to Lawrence, and his presence at the table made me so self-conscious that I lost two games. I tried not to seem angry when I got up from the board. Lawrence was watching me. I went out onto the terrace to suffer there in the dark the anger I always feel when I lose to Chaddy.

When I came back into the room, Chaddy and Mother were playing. Lawrence was still watching. By his lights, Odette had lost her virtue to me, I had lost my self-esteem to Chaddy, and now I wondered what he saw in the present match. He watched raptly, as if the opaque checkers and the marked board served for an exchange of critical power. How dramatic the board, in its ring of light, and the quiet players and the crash of the sea outside must have seemed to him! Here was spiritual cannibalism made visible; here, under his nose, were the symbols of the rapacious use human beings make of one another.

Mother plays a shrewd, an ardent, and an interfering game. She always has her hands in her opponent's board. When she plays with Chaddy, who is her favorite, she plays intently. Lawrence would have noticed this. Mother is a sentimental woman. Her heart is good and easily moved by tears and frailty, a characteristic that, like her handsome nose, has not been changed at all by age. Grief in another provokes her deeply, and she seems at times to be trying to divine in Chaddy some grief, some loss, that she can succor and redress, and so re-establish the relationship that she enjoyed with him when he was sickly and young. She loves defending the weak and the childlike, and now that we are old, she misses it. The world of debts and business, men and war, hunting and fishing has on her an exacerbating effect. (When Father drowned, she threw away his fly rods and his guns.) She has lectured us all endlessly on self-reliance, but when we come back to her for comfort and for help—particularly Chaddy—she seems to feel most like herself. I suppose Lawrence thought that the old woman and her son were playing for each other's soul.

She lost. "Oh *dear,*" she said. She looked stricken and bereaved, as she always does when she loses. "Get me my glasses, get me my checkbook, get me something to drink." Lawrence got up at last and stretched his legs. He looked at us all bleakly. The wind and the sea had risen, and I thought that if he heard the waves, he must hear them only as a dark answer to all his dark questions; that he would think that the tide had expunged the embers of our picnic fires. The company of a lie is unbearable, and he seemed like the embodiment of a lie. I couldn't explain to him the simple and intense pleasures of playing for money, and it seemed to me hideously wrong that he should have sat at the edge of the board and concluded that we were playing for one another's soul. He walked restlessly around the room two or three times and then, as usual, gave us a parting shot. "I should think you'd go crazy," he said, "cooped up with one another like this, night after night. Come on, Ruth. I'm going to bed."

That night, I dreamed about Lawrence. I saw his plain face magnified into ugliness, and when I woke in the morning, I felt sick, as if I had suffered a great spiritual loss while I slept, like the loss of courage and heart. It was foolish to let myself be troubled by my brother. I needed a vacation. I needed to relax. At school, we live in one of the dormitories, we eat at the house table, and we never get away. I not only teach English winter and summer but I work in the principal's office and fire the pistol at track meets. I needed to get away from this and from every other form of anxiety, and I decided to avoid my brother. Early that day, I took Helen and the children sailing, and we stayed out until suppertime. The next day, we went on a picnic. Then I had to go to New York for a day, and when I got back, there was the costume dance at the boat club. Lawrence wasn't going to this, and it's a party where I always have a wonderful time.

The invitations that year said to come as you wish you were. After several conversations, Helen and I had decided what to wear. The thing she most wanted to be again, she said, was a bride, and so she decided to wear her wedding dress. I thought this was a good choice—sincere, lighthearted, and inexpensive. Her choice influenced mine, and I decided to wear an old football uniform. Mother decided to go as Jenny Lind, because there was an old Jenny Lind costume in the attic. The others decided to rent costumes, and when I went to New York, I got the clothes. Lawrence and Ruth didn't enter into any of this.

Helen was on the dance committee, and she spent most of Friday decorating the club. Diana and Chaddy and I went sailing. Most of the sailing that I do these days is in Manhasset, and I am used to setting a homeward course by the gasoline barge and the tin roofs of the boat shed, and it was a pleasure that afternoon, as we returned, to keep the bow on a white church spire in the village and to find even the inshore water green and clear. At the end of our sail, we stopped at the club to get Helen. The committee had been trying to give a submarine appearance to the ballroom, and the fact that they had nearly succeeded in accomplishing this illusion made Helen very happy. We drove back to Laud's Head. It had been a brilliant afternoon, but on the way home we could smell the east wind—the dark wind, as Lawrence would have said—coming in from the sea.

My wife, Helen, is thirty-eight, and her hair would be gray, I guess, if it were not dyed, but it is dyed an unobtrusive yellow—a faded color—and I think it becomes her. I mixed cocktails that night while she was dressing, and when I took a glass upstairs to her, I saw her for the first time since our marriage in her wedding dress. There would be no point in saying that she looked to me more beautiful than she did on our wedding day, but because I have grown older and have, I think, a greater depth of feeling, and because I could see in her face that night both youth and age, both her devotion to the young woman that she had been and the positions that she had yielded graciously to time, I think I have never been so deeply moved. I had already put on the football uniform, and the weight of it, the heaviness of the pants and the shoulder guards, had worked a change in me, as if in putting on these old clothes I had put off the reasonable anxieties and troubles of my life. It felt as if we had both returned to the years before our marriage, the years before the war.

The Collards had a big dinner party before the dance, and our family—excepting Lawrence and Ruth—went to this. We drove over to the club, through the fog, at about half past nine. The orchestra was playing a waltz. While I was checking my raincoat, someone hit me on the back. It was Chucky Ewing, and the funny thing was that Chucky had on a football uniform. This seemed comical as hell to both of us. We were laughing when we went down the hall to the dance floor. I stopped at the door to look at the party, and it was beautiful. The committee had hung fish nets around the sides and over the high ceiling. The nets on the ceiling were filled with colored balloons. The light was soft and uneven, and the people—our friends and neighbors—dancing in the soft light to "Three O'Clock in the Morning" made a pretty picture. Then I noticed the number of women dressed in white, and I realized that they, like Helen, were wearing wedding dresses. Patsy Hewitt and Mrs. Gear and the Lackland girl waltzed by, dressed as brides. Then Pep Talcott came over to where Chucky and I were standing. He was dressed to be Henry VIII, but he told us that the Auerbach twins and Henry Barrett and Dwight MacGregor were all wearing football uniforms, and that by the last count there were ten brides on the floor.

This coincidence, this funny coincidence, kept everybody laughing, and made this one of the most lighthearted parties we've ever had at the club. At first I thought that the women had planned with one another to wear wedding dresses, but the ones that I danced with said it was a coincidence and I'm sure that Helen had made her decision alone. Everything went smoothly for me until a little before midnight. I saw Ruth standing at the edge of the floor. She was wearing a long red dress. It was all wrong. It wasn't the spirit of the party at all. I danced with her, but no one cut in, and I was darned if I'd spend the rest of the night dancing with her and I asked her where Lawrence was. She said he was out on the dock, and I took her over to the bar and left her and went out to get Lawrence.

The east fog was thick and wet, and he was alone on the dock. He was not in costume. He had not even bothered to get himself up as a fisherman or a sailor. He looked particularly saturnine. The fog blew around us like a cold smoke. I wished that it had been a clear night, because the easterly fog seemed to play into my misanthropic brother's hands. And I knew that the buoys—the groaners and bells that we could hear then—would sound to him like half-human, half-drowned cries, although every sailor knows that buoys are necessary and reliable fixtures, and I knew that the foghorn at the lighthouse would mean wanderings and losses to him and that he could misconstrue the vivacity of the dance music. "Come on in, Tifty," I said, "and dance with your wife or get her some partners."

"Why should I?" he said. "Why should I?" And he walked to the window and looked in at the party. "Look at it," he said. "Look at that . . ."

Chucky Ewing had got hold of a balloon and was trying to organize a scrimmage line in the middle of the floor. The others were dancing a samba. And I knew that Lawrence was looking bleakly at the party as he had looked at the weather-beaten shingles on our house, as if he saw here an abuse and a distortion of time; as if in wanting to be brides and football players we exposed the fact that, the lights of youth having been put out in us, we had been unable to find other lights to go by and, destitute of faith and principle, had become foolish and sad. And that he was thinking this about so many kind and happy and generous people made me angry, made me feel for him such an unnatural abhorrence that I was ashamed, for he is my brother and a Pommeroy. I put my arm around his shoulders and tried to force him to come in, but he wouldn't.

I got back in time for the Grand March, and after the prizes had been given out for the best costumes, they let the balloons down. The room was hot, and someone opened the big doors onto the dock, and the easterly wind circled the room and went out, carrying across the dock and out onto the water most of the balloons. Chucky Ewing went running out after the balloons, and when he saw them pass the dock and settle on the water, he took off his football uniform and dove in. Then Eric Auerbach dove in and Lew Phillips dove in and I dove in, and you know how it is at a party after midnight when people start jumping into the water. We recovered most of the balloons and dried off and went on dancing, and we didn't get home until morning.

The next day was the day of the flower show. Mother and Helen and Odette all had entries. We had a pickup lunch, and Chaddy drove the women and children over to the show. I took a nap, and in the middle of the afternoon I got some trunks and a towel and, on leaving the house, passed Ruth in the laundry. She was washing clothes. I don't know why she should seem to have so much more work to do than anyone else, but she is always washing or ironing or mending clothes. She may have been taught, when she was young, to spend her time like this, or she may be at the mercy of an expiatory passion. She seems to scrub and iron with a penitential fervor, although I can't imagine what it is that she thinks she's done wrong. Her children were with her in the laundry. I offered to take them to the beach, but they didn't want to go.

It was late in August, and the wild grapes that grow profusely all over the island made the land wind smell of wine. There is a little grove of holly at the end of the path, and then you climb the dunes, where nothing grows but that coarse grass. I could hear the sea, and I remember thinking how Chaddy and I used to talk mystically about the sea. When we were young, we had decided that we could never live in the West because we would miss the sea. "It is very nice here," we used to say politely when we visited people in the mountains, "but we miss the Atlantic." We used to look down our noses at people from Iowa and Colorado who had been denied this revelation, and we scorned the Pacific. Now I could hear the waves, whose heaviness sounded like a reverberation, like a tumult, and it pleased me as it had pleased me when I was young, and it seemed to have a purgative force, as if it had cleared my memory of, among other things, the penitential image of Ruth in the laundry.

But Lawrence was on the beach. There he sat. I went in without speaking. The water was cold, and when I came out, I put on a shirt. I told him that I was going to walk up to Tanners Point, and he said that he would come with me. I tried to walk beside him. His legs are no longer than mine, but he always likes to stay a little ahead of his companion. Walking along behind him, looking at his bent head and his shoulders, I wondered what he could make of that landscape.

There were the dunes and cliffs, and then, where they declined, there were some fields that had begun to turn from green to brown and yellow. The fields were used for pasturing sheep, and I guess Lawrence would have noticed that the soil was eroded and that the sheep would accelerate this decay. Beyond the fields there are a few coastal farms, with square and pleasant buildings, but Lawrence could have pointed out the hard lot of an island farmer. The sea, at our other side, was the open sea. We always tell guests that there, to the east, lies the coast of Portugal, and for Lawrence it would be an easy step from the coast of Portugal to the tyranny in Spain. The waves broke with a noise like a "hurrah, hurrah, hurrah," but to Lawrence they would say *"Vale, vale."*[1] I suppose it would have occurred to his baleful and incisive mind that the coast was terminal moraine, the edge of the prehistoric world, and it must have occurred to him that we walked along the edge of the known world in spirit as much as in fact. If he should otherwise have overlooked this, there were some Navy planes bombing an uninhabited island to remind him.

That beach is a vast and preternaturally clean and simple landscape. It is like a piece of the moon. The surf had pounded the floor solid, so it was easy walking, and everything left on the sand had been twice changed by the waves. There was the spine of a shell, a broomstick, part of a bottle and part of a brick, both of them milled and broken until they were nearly unrecognizable, and I suppose Lawrence's sad frame of mind—for he kept his head

---

1. Farewell (Latin).

down——went from one broken thing to another. The company of his pessimism began to infuriate me, and I caught up with him and put a hand on his shoulder. "It's only a summer day, Tifty," I said. "It's only a summer day. What's the matter? Don't you like it here?"

"I don't like it here," he said blandly, without raising his eyes. "I'm going to sell my equity in the house to Chaddy. I didn't expect to have a good time. The only reason I came back was to say goodbye."

I let him get ahead again and I walked behind him, looking at his shoulders and thinking of all the goodbyes he had made. When Father drowned, he went to church and said goodbye to Father. It was only three years later that he concluded that Mother was frivolous and said goodbye to her. In his freshman year at college, he had been very good friends with his roommate, but the man drank too much, and at the beginning of the spring term Lawrence changed roommates and said goodbye to his friend. When he had been in college for two years, he concluded that the atmosphere was too sequestered and he said goodbye to Yale. He enrolled at Columbia and got his law degree there, but he found his first employer dishonest, and at the end of six months he said goodbye to a good job. He married Ruth in City Hall and said goodbye to the Protestant Episcopal Church; they went to live on a back street in Tuckahoe and said goodbye to the middle class. In 1938, he went to Washington to work as a government lawyer, saying goodbye to private enterprise, but after eight months in Washington he concluded that the Roosevelt administration was sentimental and he said goodbye to it. They left Washington for a suburb of Chicago, where he said goodbye to his neighbors, one by one, on counts of drunkenness, boorishness, and stupidity. He said goodbye to Chicago and went to Kansas; he said goodbye to Kansas and went to Cleveland. Now he had said goodbye to Cleveland and come East again, stopping at Laud's Head long enough to say goodbye to the sea.

It was elegiac and it was bigoted and narrow, it mistook circumspection for character, and I wanted to help him. "Come out of it," I said. "Come out of it, Tifty."

"Come out of what?"

"Come out of this gloominess. Come out of it. It's only a summer day. You're spoiling your own good time and you're spoiling everyone else's. We need a vacation, Tifty. I need one. I need to rest. We all do. And you've made everything tense and unpleasant. I only have two weeks in the year. Two weeks. I need to have a good time and so do all the others. We need to rest. You think that your pessimism is an advantage, but it's nothing but an unwillingness to grasp realities."

"What are the realities?" he said. "Diana is a foolish and a promiscuous woman. So is Odette. Mother is an alcoholic. If she doesn't discipline herself, she'll be in a hospital in a year or two. Chaddy is dishonest. He always has been. The house is going to fall into the sea." He looked at me and added, as an afterthought, "You're a fool."

"You're a gloomy son of a bitch," I said. "You're a gloomy son of a bitch."

"Get your fat face out of mine," he said. He walked along.

Then I picked up a root and, coming at his back—although I have never hit a man from the back before—I swung the root, heavy with sea water, behind me, and the momentum sped my arm and I gave him, my brother, a blow on the head that forced him to his knees on the sand, and I saw the blood come out and begin to darken his hair. Then I wished that he was dead, dead and about to be buried, not buried but about to be buried, because I did not want to be denied ceremony and decorum in putting him away, in putting him out of my consciousness, and I saw the rest of us—Chaddy and Mother and Diana and Helen—in mourning in the house on Belvedere Street that was torn down twenty years ago, greeting our guests and our relatives at the door and answering their mannerly condolences with mannerly grief. Nothing decorous was lacking so that even if he had been murdered on a beach, one would feel before the tiresome ceremony ended that he had come into the winter of his life and that it was a law of nature, and a beautiful one, that Tifty should be buried in the cold, cold ground.

He was still on his knees. I looked up and down. No one had seen us. The naked beach, like a piece of the moon, reached to invisibility. The spill of a wave, in a glancing run, shot up to where he knelt. I would still have liked to end him, but now I had begun to act like two men, the murderer and the Samaritan. With a swift roar, like hollowness made sound, a white wave reached him and encircled him, boiling over his shoulders, and I held him against the undertow. Then I led him to a higher place. The blood had spread all through his hair, so that it looked black. I took off my shirt and tore it to bind up his head. He was conscious, and I didn't think he was badly hurt. He didn't speak. Neither did I. Then I left him there.

I walked a little way down the beach and turned to watch him, and I was thinking of my own skin then. He had got to his feet and he seemed steady. The daylight was still clear, but on the sea wind fumes of brine were blowing in like a light fog, and when I had walked a little way from him, I could hardly see his dark figure in this obscurity. All down the beach I could see the heavy salt air blowing in. Then I turned my back on him, and as I got near to the house, I went swimming again, as I seem to have done after every encounter with Lawrence that summer.

When I got back to the house, I lay down on the terrace. The others came back. I could hear Mother defaming the flower arrangements that had won prizes. None of ours had won anything. Then the house quieted, as it always does at that hour. The children went into the kitchen to get supper and the others went upstairs to bathe. Then I heard Chaddy making cocktails, and the conversation about the flower-show judges was resumed. Then Mother cried, "Tifty! Tifty! Oh, Tifty!"

He stood in the door, looking half dead. He had taken off the bloody bandage and he held it in his hand. "My brother did this," he said. "My brother did it. He hit me with a stone—something—on the beach." His voice broke with self-pity. I thought he was going to cry. No one else spoke. "Where's Ruth?" he cried. "Where's Ruth? Where in hell is Ruth? I want her to start packing. I don't have any more time to waste here. I have important things to do. I have *important* things to do." And he went up the stairs.

They left for the mainland the next morning, taking the six-o'clock boat. Mother got up to say goodbye, but she was the only one, and it is a harsh and an easy scene to imagine—the matriarch and the changeling, looking at each other with a dismay that would seem like the powers of love reversed. I heard the children's voices and the car go down the drive, and I got up and went to the window, and what a morning that was! Jesus, what a morning! The wind was northerly. The air was clear. In the early heat, the roses in the garden smelled like strawberry jam. While I was dressing, I heard the boat whistle, first the warning signal and then the double blast, and I could see the good people on the top deck drinking coffee out of fragile paper cups, and Lawrence at the bow, saying to the sea, "*Thalassa, thalassa,*"[2] while his timid and unhappy children watched the creation from the encirclement of their mother's arms. The buoys would toll mournfully for Lawrence, and while the grace of the light would make it an exertion not to throw out your arms and swear exultantly, Lawrence's eyes would trace the black sea as it fell astern; he would think of the bottom, dark and strange, where full fathom five our father lies.

Oh, what can you do with a man like that? What can you do? How can you dissuade his eye in a crowd from seeking out the cheek with acne, the infirm hand; how can you teach him to respond to the inestimable greatness of the race, the harsh surface beauty of life; how can you put his finger for him on the obdurate truths before which fear and horror are powerless? The sea that morning was iridescent and dark. My wife and my sister were swimming— Diana and Helen—and I saw their uncovered heads, black and gold in the dark water. I saw them come out and I saw that they were naked, unshy, beautiful, and full of grace, and I watched the naked women walk out of the sea.

---

2. Sea (Greek).

John Updike

FRIENDS FROM PHILADELPHIA

This was the first story I ever sold, and I wrote it in Vermont, on my father-in-law's typewriter, in the June of my graduation from college. I had given myself five years to become a "writer," and my becoming one immediately has left me with an uneasy, apologetic sense of having blundered through the wrong door. Nevertheless, it is a story I am grateful to. . . . In it, Olinger, unnamed, is simply the world; its author was so young that everything outside Olinger—Harvard, marriage, Vermont—seemed relatively unreal. . . . I have been told that the story seems to have no point. The point, to me, is plain, and it is the point, more or less, of all these Olinger stories. *We are rewarded unexpectedly.*

JOHN UPDIKE,
preface to *Olinger Stories* (1964)

In the moment before the door was opened to him, he glimpsed her thigh below the half-drawn shade. Thelma was home, then. She was wearing the Camp Winniwoho T shirt and her quite short shorts.

"Why, my goodness: Janny!" she cried. She always pronounced his name, John, to rhyme with Ann. Earlier that vacation, she had visited in New York City, and tried to talk the way she thought they talked there. "What on earth ever brings you to me at this odd hour?"

"Hello, Thel," he said. "I hope—I guess this is a pretty bad time." She had been plucking her eyebrows again. He wished she wouldn't do that.

Thelma extended her arm and touched her fingers to the base of John's neck. It wasn't a fond gesture, just a hostesslike one. "Now, Janny. You know that I—my mother and I—are always happy to be seeing you. Mother, who do you ever guess is here at this odd hour?"

"Don't keep John Nordholm standing there," Mrs. Lutz said. Thelma's mother was settled in the deep red settee watching television and smoking.

140

A coffee cup being used as an ashtray lay in her lap, and her dress was hitched so her knees showed.

"Hello, Mrs. Lutz," John said, trying not to look at her broad, pale knees. "I really hate to bother you at this odd hour."

"I don't see anything odd about it." She took a deep-throated drag on her cigarette and exhaled through her nostrils, the way men do. "Some of the other kids were here earlier this afternoon."

"I would have come in if anybody had told me."

Thelma said, "Oh, Janny! Stop trying to make a martyr of yourself. Keep in touch, they say, if you want to keep up."

He felt his face grow hot and knew he was blushing, which made him blush all the more. Mrs. Lutz shook a wrinkled pack of Herbert Tareytons at him. "Smoke?" she said.

"I guess not, thanks a lot."

"You've stopped? It's a bad habit. I wish I had stopped at your age. I'm not sure I even *begun* at your age."

"No, it's just that I have to go home soon, and my mother would smell the smoke on my breath. She can smell it even through chewing gum."

"Why must you go home soon?" Thelma asked.

Mrs. Lutz sniffled. "I have sinus. I can't even smell the flowers in the garden or the food on the table any more. Let the kids smoke if they want, if it makes them feel better. I don't care. My Thelma, she can smoke right in her own home, her own living room, if she wants to. But she doesn't seem to have the taste for it. I'm just as glad, to tell the truth."

John hated interrupting, but it was close to five-thirty. "I have a problem," he said.

"A problem—how gruesome," Thelma said. "And here I thought, Mother, I was being favored with a social call."

"Don't talk like that," Mrs. Lutz said.

"It's sort of complex," John began.

"Talk like what, Mother? Talk like what?"

"Then let me turn this off," Mrs. Lutz said, snapping the right knob on the television set.

"Oh, Mother, and I was listening to it!" Thelma toppled into a chair, her legs flashing. John thought she was delicious when she pouted.

Mrs. Lutz had set herself to give sympathy. Her lap was broadened and her hands were laid palms upward in it.

"It's not much of a problem," John assured her. "But we're having some people up from Philadelphia." He turned to Thelma and added, "If anything is going on tonight, I can't get out."

"Life is just too, too full of disappointments," Thelma said.

"Look—is there?"

"Too, too full," Thelma said.

Mrs. Lutz made fluttery motions out of her lap. "These Philadelphia people."

John said, "Maybe I shouldn't bother you about this." He waited, but she just looked more and more patient, so he went on. "My mother wants to give them wine, and my father isn't home from teaching school yet. He might not get home before the liquor store closes. It's at six, isn't it? My mother's busy cleaning, so I walked in."

"She made you walk the whole mile? Poor thing, can't you drive?" Mrs. Lutz asked.

"*Sure* I can drive. But I'm not sixteen yet."

"You look a lot taller than sixteen."

John looked at Thelma to see how she took that one, but Thelma was pretending to read a rental library novel wrapped in cellophane.

"I walked all the way in to the liquor store," John told Mrs. Lutz, "but they wouldn't give me anything without written permission. It was a new man."

"Your sorrow has rent me in twain," Thelma said, as if she was reading it from the book.

"Pay no attention, Johnny," Mrs. Lutz said. "Now Frank will be home any time. Why not wait until he comes and let him run down with you for a bottle?"

"That sounds wonderful. Thanks an awful lot, really."

Mrs. Lutz's hand descended upon the television knob. Some smiling man was playing the piano. John didn't know who he was; there wasn't any television at his house. They watched in silence until Mr. Lutz thumped on the porch outside. The empty milk bottles tinkled. "Now don't be surprised if he has a bit of a load on," Mrs. Lutz said.

Actually, he didn't act at all drunk. He was like a happy husband in the movies. He called Thelma his little pookie-pie and kissed her on the forehead; then he called his wife his big pookie-pie and kissed her on the mouth. Then he solemnly shook John's hand and told him how very, very happy he was to see him here and asked after his parents. "Is that goon still on television?" he said finally.

"Daddy, please pay attention to somebody else," Thelma said, turning off the television set. "Janny wants to talk to you."

"And *I* want to talk to *Johnny*," Thelma's father said. He spread his arms suddenly, clenching and unclenching his fists. He was a big man, with shaved gray hair above his tiny ears. John couldn't think of the word to begin.

Mrs. Lutz explained the errand. When she was through, Mr. Lutz said, "People from Philadelphia. I bet their name isn't William L. Trexler, is it?"

"No. I forget their name, but it's not that. The man is an engineer. The woman went to college with my mother."

"Oh. College people. Then we must get them something very, very nice, I should say."

"Daddy," Thelma said. "*Please*. The store will close."

"Tessie, you hear John. People from college. People with diplomas. And it is very nearly closing time, and who isn't on their way?" He took John's shoulder in one hand and Thelma's arm in the other and hustled them through the door. "We'll be back in one minute, Mamma," he said.

"Drive carefully," Mrs. Lutz said from the shadowed porch, where her cigarette showed as an orange star.

Mr. Lutz's huge blue Buick was parked in front of the house. "I never went to college," he said, "yet I buy a new car whenever I want." His tone wasn't nasty, but soft and full of wonder.

"Oh, Daddy, not *this* again," Thelma said, shaking her head at John, so he could understand what all she had to go through. When she looks like that, John thought, I could bite her lip until it bleeds.

"Ever driven this kind of car, John?" Mr. Lutz asked.

"No. The only thing I can drive is my parents' Plymouth, and that not very well."

"What year car is it?"

"I don't know exactly." John knew perfectly well it was a 1940 model. "We got it after the war. It has a gear shift. This is automatic, isn't it?"

"Automatic shift, fluid transmission, directional lights, the works," Mr. Lutz said, "Now, isn't it funny, John? Here is your father, an educated man, with an old Plymouth, yet at the same time I, who never read more than twenty, thirty books in my life . . . it doesn't seem as if there's justice." He slapped the fender, bent over to get into the car, straightened up abruptly, and said, "Do you want to drive it?"

Thelma said, "Daddy's asking you something."

"I don't know how," John said.

"It's very easy to learn, very easy. You just slide in there—come on, it's getting late." John got in on the driver's side. He peered out of the windshield. It was a wider car than the Plymouth; the hood looked wide as a boat.

Mr. Lutz asked him to grip the little lever behind the steering wheel. "You pull it toward you like *that*, that's it, and fit it into one of these notches. 'P' stands for 'parking'—you start it in that one. 'N,' that's 'neutral,' like on the car you have, 'D' means 'drive'—just put it in there and the car does all the work for you. You are using that one ninety-nine per cent of the time. 'L' is 'low,' for very steep hills, going up or down. And 'R' stands for—what?"

"Reverse," John said.

"Very, very good. Tessie, he's a smart boy. He'll never own a new car. And when you put them all together, you can remember their order by the sentence, Paint No Dimes Light Red. I thought that up when I was teaching my oldest girl how to drive."

"Paint No Dimes Light Red," John said.

"Excellent. Now, let's go."

A bubble was developing in John's stomach. "What gear do you want it in to start?" he asked Mr. Lutz.

Mr. Lutz must not have heard him, because all he said was "Let's go" again, and he drummed on the dashboard with his fingertips. They were thick, square fingers, with fur between the knuckles.

Thelma leaned up from the back seat. Her cheek almost touched John's ear. She whispered, "Put it at 'P.'"

He did, then he looked for the starter. "How does he start it?" he asked Thelma.

"I never watch him," she said. "There was a button in the last car, but I don't see it in this one."

"Push on the pedal," Mr. Lutz sang, staring straight ahead and smiling, "and away we go. And ah, ah, waay we go."

"Just step on the gas," Thelma suggested. John pushed down firmly, to keep his leg from trembling. The motor roared. "Now 'D'," she said. The car bounded away from the curb. Within a block, though, he could manage the car pretty well.

"It rides like a boat on smooth water," he told his two passengers. The metaphor pleased him.

Mr. Lutz squinted ahead. "Like a what?"

"Like a boat."

"Don't go so fast," Thelma said.

"The motor's so quiet," John explained. "Like a sleeping cat."

Without warning, a truck pulled out of Pearl Street. Mr. Lutz, trying to brake, stamped his foot on the empty floor in front of him. John could hardly keep from laughing. "I see him," he said, easing his speed so that the truck had just enough room to make its turn. "Those trucks think they own the road," he said. He let one hand slide away from the steering wheel. One-handed, he whipped around a bus. "What'll she do on the open road?"

"That's a good question, John," Mr. Lutz said. "And I don't know the answer. Eighty, maybe."

"The speedometer goes up to a hundred and ten." Another pause—nobody seemed to be talking. John said, "Hell. A baby could drive one of these."

"For instance, you," Thelma said.

There were a lot of cars at the liquor store, so John had to double-park the big wide Buick. "That's close enough, close enough," Mr. Lutz said. "Don't get any closer, whoa!" He was out of the car before John could bring it to a complete stop. "You and Tessie wait here," he said. "I'll go in for the liquor."

"Mr. Lutz. Say, Mr. Lutz," John called.

"Daddy!" Thelma shouted.

Mr. Lutz returned. "What is it, boys and girls?" His tone, John noticed, was becoming reedy. He was probably getting hungry.

"Here's the money they gave me." John pulled two wadded dollars from the change pocket of his dungarees. "My mother said to get something inexpensive but nice."

"Inexpensive but nice?" Mr. Lutz repeated.

"She said something about California sherry."

"What did she say about it? To get it? Or not to?"

"I guess to get it."

"You guess." Mr. Lutz shoved himself away from the car and walked backward toward the store as he talked. "You and Tessie wait in the car. Don't go off somewhere. It's getting late. I'll be only one minute."

John leaned back in his seat and gracefully rested one hand at the top of the steering wheel. "I like your father."

"You don't know how he acts to Mother," Thelma said.

John studied the clean line under his wrist and thumb. He flexed his wrist and watched the neat little muscles move in his forearm. "You know what I need?" he said. "A wristwatch."

"Oh, Jan," Thelma said. "Stop admiring your own hand. It's really disgusting."

A ghost of a smile flickered over his lips, but he let his strong nervous fingers remain as they were. "I'd sell my soul for a drag right now."

"Daddy keeps a pack in the glove compartment," Thelma said. "I'd get them if my fingernails weren't so long."

"*I'll* get it open," John said, and he did. They fished one cigarette out of the tired pack of Old Golds they found and took alternate puffs. "Ah," John said, "that first drag of the day, clawing and scraping its way down your throat."

"Be on the lookout for Daddy. They hate my smoking."

"Thelma."

"Yes?" She stared deep into his eyes, her face half hidden in blue shadow.

"Don't pluck your eyebrows."

"I think it looks nice."

"It's like calling me 'Jan.' " There was a silence, not awkward, between them.

"Get rid of the rette, Jan. Daddy just passed the window."

Being in the liquor store had put Mr. Lutz into a soberer mood. "Here you be, John," he said, and in a businesslike way handed John a tall, velvet-red bottle with a neck wrapped in foil. "Better let me drive. You drive like a veteran, but I know the roads."

"I can walk from your house, Mr. Lutz," John said, knowing Mr. Lutz wouldn't make him walk. "Thanks an awful lot for all you've done."

"I'll drive you up. Philadelphians can't be kept waiting. We can't make this young man walk a mile, now can we, Tessie?" The sweeping way the man asked the question kept the young people quiet all the way out of town, although several things were bothering John.

When the car stopped in front of his house, he forced himself to ask, "Say, Mr. Lutz. I wonder if there was any change?"

"What? Oh. I nearly forgot. You'll have your daddy thinking I'm a crook." He reached into his pocket and without looking handed John a dollar, a quarter, and a penny.

"This seems like a lot," John said. The wine must be cheap. His stomach squirmed; maybe he had made a mistake. Maybe he should have let his mother phone his father, like she had wanted to, instead of begging her to let him walk in.

"It's your change," Mr. Lutz said.

"Well, thanks an awful lot."

"Goodbye now," Mr. Lutz said.

"So long." John slammed the door. "Goodbye, Thelma. Don't forget what I told you." He winked.

The car pulled out, and John walked up the path. "Don't forget what I told you," he repeated to himself, winking. The bottle was cool and heavy in his hand. He glanced at the label, which read *Château Mouton-Rothschild 1937*.

AMAHL AND THE NIGHT VISITORS: A GUIDE TO THE TENOR OF LOVE

11/30. Understand that your cat is a whore and can't help you. She takes on love with the whiskery adjustments of a gold-digger. She is a gorgeous nomad, an unfriend. Recall how just last month when you got her from Bob downstairs, after Bob had become suddenly allergic, she leaped into your lap and purred, guttural as a German chanteuse, familiar and furry as a mold. And Bob, visibly heartbroken, still in the room, sneezing and giving instructions, hoping for one last cat nuzzle, descended to his hands and knees and jiggled his fingers in the shag. The cat only blinked. For you, however, she smiled, gave a fish-breath peep, and settled.

"Oh, well," said Bob, getting up off the floor. "Now I'm just a thing of her kittenish past."

That's the way with Bob. He'll say to the cat, "You be a good girl now, honey," and then just shrug, go back downstairs to his apartment, play jagged, creepy jazz, drink wine, stare out at the wintry scalp of the mountain.

12/1. Moss Watson, the man you truly love like no other, is singing December 23 in the Owonta Opera production of *Amahl and the Night Visitors*. He's playing Kaspar, the partially deaf Wise Man. Wisdom, says Moss, arrives in all forms. And you think, Yes, sometimes as a king and sometimes as a hesitant phone call that says the king'll be late at rehearsal don't wait up, and then when you call back to tell him to be careful not to let the cat out when he comes home, you discover there's been no rehearsal there at all.

At three o'clock in the morning you hear his car in the driveway, the thud of the front door. When he comes into the bedroom, you see his huge height framed for a minute in the doorway, his hair lit bright as curry. When he stoops to take off his shoes, it is as if some small piece of his back has given way, allowing him this one slow bend. He is quiet. When he gets into bed he kisses one of your shoulders, then pulls the covers up to his chin. He knows you're awake. "I'm tired," he announces softly, to ward you off when you roll toward him. Say: "You didn't let the cat out, did you?"

He says no, but he probably should have. "You're turning into a cat mom. Cats, Trudy, are the worst sort of surrogates."

Tell him you've always wanted to run off and join the surrogates.

Tell him you love him.

Tell him you know he didn't have rehearsal tonight.

"We decided to hold rehearsal at the Montessori school, what are you now, *my* mother?"

In the dark, discern the fine hook of his nose. Smooth the hair off his forehead. Say: "I love you Moss are you having an affair with a sheep?" You saw a movie once where a man was having an affair with a sheep, and acted, with his girlfriend, the way Moss now acts with you: exhausted.

Moss's eyes close. "I'm a king, not a shepherd, remember? You're acting like my ex-wife."

His ex-wife is now an anchorwoman in Missouri.

"Are you having a regular affair? Like with a person?"

"Trudy," he sighs, turns away from you, taking more than his share of blanket. "You've got to stop this." Know you are being silly. Any second now he will turn and press against you, reassure you with kisses, tell you oh how much he loves you. "How on earth, Trudy," is what he finally says, "would I ever have the time for an affair?"

12/2. Your cat is growing, eats huge and sloppy as a racehorse. Bob named her Stardust Sweetheart, a bit much even for Bob, so you and Moss think up other names for her: Pudge, Pudge-muffin, Pooch, Poopster, Secretariat, Stephanie, Emily. Call her all of them. "She has to learn how to deal with confusion," says Moss. "And we've gotta start letting her outside."

Say: "No. She's still too little. Something could happen." Pick her up and away from Moss. Bring her into the bathroom with you. Hold her up to the mirror. Say: "Whossat? Whossat pretty kitty?" Wonder if you could turn into Bob.

12/3. Sometimes Moss has to rehearse in the living room. King Kaspar has a large black jewelry box about which he must sing to the young, enthralled Amahl. He must open drawers and haul out beads, licorice, magic stones. The drawers, however, keep jamming when they're not supposed to. Moss finally tears off his fake beard and screams, "I can't do this shit! I can't sing about money and gewgaws. I'm the tenor of love!" Last year they'd done *La Bohème* and Moss had been Rodolfo.

This is the sort of thing he needs you for: to help him with his box. Kneel down beside him. Show him how one of the drawers is off its runner. Show him how to pull it out just so far. He smiles and thanks you in his berserk King Kaspar voice: "Oh, thank you, thank you, thank you!" He begins his aria again: " 'This is my box. This is my box. I never travel without my box.' "

All singing is, says Moss, is sculpted howling.

Say, "Bye." Wheel the TV into the kitchen. Watch MacNeil-Lehrer. Worry about Congress.

Listen to the goose-call of trains, all night, trundling by your house.

12/4. Sometimes the phone rings, but then the caller hangs up.

12/5. Your cat now sticks her paws right in the water dish while she drinks, then steps out from her short wade and licks them, washes her face with them, repeatedly, over the ears and down, like an itch. Take to observing her. On her feet the gray and pink configurations of pads and fur look like tiny baboon faces. She sees you watching, freezes, blinks at you, then busies herself again, her face in her belly, one leg up at a time, an intent ballerina in a hairy body stocking. And yet she's growing so quickly, she's clumsy. She'll walk along and suddenly her hip will fly out of whack and she'll stop and look at it, not comprehending. Or her feet will stumble, or it's difficult for her to move her new bulk along the edges of furniture, her body pushing itself out into the world before she's really ready. It puts a dent in her confidence. She looks at you inquiringly: *What is happening to me?* She rubs against your ankles and bleats. You pick her up, tuck her under your chin, your teeth clenched in love, your voice cooey, gooey with maternity, you say things like, "How's my little dirt-nose, my little fuzz-face, my little honey-head?"

"Jesus, Trudy," Moss yells from the next room. "Listen to how you talk to that cat."

12/6. Though the Christmas shopping season is under way, the store you work at downtown, Owonta Flair, is not doing well. "The malls," groans Morgan, your boss. "Every Christmas the malls! We're doomed. These candy cane slippers. What am I gonna do with these?"

Tell her to put one slipper from each pair in the window along with a mammoth sign that says, MATES INSIDE. "People only see the sign. Thom McAn did it once. They got hordes."

"You're depressed," says Morgan.

12/7. You and Moss invite the principals, except Amahl, over to dinner one night before a rehearsal. You also invite Bob. Three kings, Amahl's unwed mother, you, and Bob: this way four people can tell cranky anecdotes about the production, and two people can listen.

"This really is a trashy opera," says Sonia, who plays Amahl's mother. "Sentimental as all get-out." Sonia is everything you've always wanted to be: smart, Jewish, friendly, full-haired as Easter basket grass. She speaks with a mouthful of your spinach pie. She says she likes it. When she has swallowed, a piece of spinach remains behind, wrapped like a gap around one of her front teeth. Other than that she is very beautiful. Nobody says anything about the spinach on her tooth.

Two rooms away the cat is playing with a marble in the empty bathtub. This is one of her favorite games. She bats the marble and it speeds around the porcelain like a stock car. The noise is rattley, continuous.

"What is that weird noise?" asks Sonia.

"It's the beast," says Moss. "We should put her outside, Trudy." He pours Sonia more wine, and she murmurs, "Thanks."

Jump up. Say: "I'll go take the marble away."

Behind you you can hear Bob: "She used to be mine. Her name is Stardust Sweetheart. I got allergic."

Melchior shouts after you: "Aw, leave the cat alone, Trudy. Let her have some fun." But you go into the bathroom and take the marble away anyhow. Your cat looks up at you from the tub, her head cocked to one side, sweet and puzzled as a child movie star. Then she turns and bats drips from the faucet. Scratch the scruff of her neck. Close the door when you leave. Put the marble in your pocket.

You can hear Balthazar making jokes about the opera. He calls it *Amyl and the Nitrates.*

"I've always found Menotti insipid," Melchior is saying when you return to the dining room.

"Written for NBC, what can you expect," Sonia says. Soon she is off raving about *La Bohème* and other operas. She uses words like *verismo, messa di voce*, Montserrat Caballe. She smiles. "An opera should be like contraception: about *sex*, not *children*."

Start clearing the plates. Tell people to keep their forks for dessert. Tell them that no matter what anyone says, you think *Amahl* is a beautiful opera and that the ending, when the mother sends her son off with the kings, always makes you cry. Moss gives you a wink. Get brave. Give your head a toss. Add: "Papageno, Papagena—to me, *La Bohème*'s just a lot of scarves."

There is some gulping of wine.

Only Bob looks at you and smiles. "Here. I'll help you with the plates," he says.

Moss stands and makes a diversionary announcement: "Sonia, you've got a piece of spinach on your tooth."

"Christ," she says, and her tongue tunnels beneath her lip like an elegant gopher.

12/8. Sometimes still Moss likes to take candlelight showers with you. You usually have ten minutes before the hot water runs out. Soap his back, the wide moguls of his shoulders registering in you like a hunger. Press yourself against him. Whisper: "I really do like *La Bohème,* you know."

"It's okay," Moss says, all forgiveness. He turns and grabs your buttocks.

"It's just that your friends make me nervous. Maybe it's work, Morgan that forty-watt hysteric making me crazy." Actually you like Morgan.

Begin to hum a Dionne Warwick song, then grow self-conscious and stop. Moss doesn't like to sing in the shower. He has his operas, his church jobs, his weddings and bar mitzvahs—in the shower he is strictly off-duty. Say: "I mean, it *could* be Morgan."

Moss raises his head up under the spray, beatific, absent. His hair slicks back, like a baby's or a gangster's, dark with water, shiny as a record album. "Does Bob make you nervous?" he asks.

"Bob? Bob suffers from terminal sweetness. I like Bob."

"So do I. He's a real gem."

Say: "Yeah, he's a real chum."

"I said *gem,*" says Moss. "Not *chum.*" Things fall quiet. Lately you've been mishearing each other. Last night in bed you said, "Moss, I usually don't like discussing sex, but—" And he said, "I don't like disgusting sex either." And then he fell asleep, his snores scratching in the dark like zombies.

Take turns rinsing. Don't tell him he's hogging the water. Ask finally, "Do you think Bob's gay?"

"Of course he's gay."

"How do you know?"

"Oh, I don't know. He hangs out at Sammy's in the mall."

"Is that a gay bar?"

"Bit of everything." Moss shrugs.

Think: Bit of everything. Just like a mall. "Have you ever been there?" Scrub vigorously between your breasts.

"A few times," says Moss, the water growing cooler.

Say: "Oh." Then turn off the faucet, step out onto the bath mat. Hand Moss a towel. "I guess because I work trying to revive our poor struggling downtown I don't get out to these places much."

"I guess not," says Moss, candle shadows wobbling on the shower curtain.

12/9. Two years ago when Moss first moved in, there was something exciting about getting up in the morning. You would rise, dress, and, knowing your lover was asleep in your bed, drive out into the early morning office and factory traffic, feeling that you possessed all things, Your Man, like a Patsy Cline song, at home beneath your covers, pumping blood through your day like a heart.

Now you have a morbid fascination with news shows. You get up, dress, flick on the TV, sit in front of it with a bowl of cereal in your lap, quietly curse all governments everywhere, get into your car, drive to work, wonder how the sun has the nerve to show its face, wonder why the world seems to be picking up speed, even old ladies pass you on the highway, why you don't have a single erotic fantasy that Moss isn't in, whether there really are such things as vitamins, and how would you rather die cancer or a car accident, the man you love, at home, asleep, like a heavy, heavy heart through your day.

"Goddamn slippers," says Morgan at work.

12/10. The cat now likes to climb into the bathtub and stand under the dripping faucet in order to clean herself. She lets the water bead up on her face, then wipes herself, neatly dislodging the gunk from her eyes.

"Isn't she wonderful?" you ask Moss.

"Yeah. Come here you little scumbucket," he says, slapping the cat on the haunches, as if she were a dog.

"She's not a dog, Moss. She's a cat."

"That's right. She's a cat. Remember that, Trudy."

12/11. The phone again. The ringing and hanging up.

12/12. Moss is still getting in very late. He goes about the business of fondling you, like someone very tired at night having to put out the trash and bolt-lock the door.

He sleeps with his arms folded behind his head, elbows protruding, treacherous as daggers, like the enemy chariot in *Ben-Hur.*

12/13. Buy a Christmas tree, decorations, a stand, and lug them home to assemble for Moss. Show him your surprise.

"Why are the lights all in a clump in the back?" he asks, closing the front door behind him.

Say: "I know. Aren't they great? Wait till you see me do the tinsel." Place handfuls of silver icicles, matted together like alfalfa sprouts, at the end of all the branches.

"Very cute," says Moss, kissing you, then letting go. Follow him into the bathroom. Ask how rehearsal went. He points to the kitty litter and sings: " 'This is my box. I never travel without my box.' "

Say: "You are not a well man, Moss." Play with his belt loops.

12/14. The white fur around the cat's neck is growing and looks like a stiff Jacobean collar. "A rabato," says Moss, who suddenly seems to know these things. "When are we going to let her go outside?"

"Someday when she's older." The cat has lately taken to the front window the way a hypochondriac takes to a bed. When she's there she's more interested in the cars, the burled fingers of the trees, the occasional squirrel, the train tracks like long fallen ladders, than she is in you. Call her: "Here pootchy-kootchy-honey." Ply her, bribe her with food.

12/15. There are movies in town: one about Brazil, and one about sexual abandonment in upstate New York. "What do you say, Moss. Wanna go to the movies this weekend?"

"I can't," says Moss. "You know how busy I am."

12/16. The evening news is full of death: young marines, young mothers, young children. By comparison you have already lived forever. In a kind of heaven.

12/17. Give your cat a potato and let her dribble it about soccer-style. She's getting more coordinated, conducts little dramas with the potato, pretends to have conquered it, strolls over it, then somersaults back after it again. She's not bombing around, crashing into the sideboards anymore. She's learning moves. She watches the potato by the dresser leg, stalks it, then pounces. When she gets bored she climbs up onto the sill and looks out, tail switching. Other cats have spotted her now, have started coming around at night. Though she will want to go, do not let her out the front door.

12/18. The phone rings. You say hello, and the caller hangs up. Two minutes later it rings again, only this time Moss answers it in the next room, speaks softly, cryptically, not the hearty phone voice of the Moss of yesteryear. When he hangs up, wander in and say, blasé as paste, "So, who was that?"

"Stop," says Moss. "Just stop."

Ask him what's the big deal, it was Sonia wasn't it.

"Stop," says Moss. "You're being my wife. Things are repeating themselves."

Say that nothing repeats itself. Nothing, nothing, nothing. "Sonia, right?"

"Trudy, you've got to stop this. You've been listening to too much *Tosca*. I'm going out to get a hamburger. Do you want anything?"

Say: "I'm the only person in the whole world who really knows you, Moss. And I don't know you at all anymore."

"That's a different opera," he says. "I'm going out to get a hamburger. Do you want anything?"

Do not cry. Stick to monosyllables. Say: "No. Fine. Go."

Say: "Please don't let the cat out."

Say: "You should wear a hat it's cold."

12/19. Actually what you've been listening to is Dionne Warwick's Golden Hits—musical open heart surgery enough for you. Sometimes you pick up the cat and waltz her around, her purr staticky and intermittent as a walkie-talkie.

On "Do You Know the Way to San Jose," you put her down, do an unfortunate Charleston, while she attacks your stockinged feet, thinking them large rodents.

Sometimes you knock into the Christmas tree.

Sometimes you collapse into a chair and convince yourself that things are still okay.

When Robert MacNeil talks about mounting inflation, you imagine him checking into a motel room with a life-size, blow-up doll. This is, once in a while, how you amuse yourself.

When Moss gets in at four in the morning, whisper: "There are lots of people in this world, Moss, but you can't be in love with them all."

"I'm not," he says, "in love with the mall."

12/20. The mall stores stay open late this last week before Christmas. Moss is supposed to be there, "in the gazebo next to the Santa gazebo," for an *Amahl and the Night Visitors* promotional. Decide to drive up there. Perhaps you can look around in the men's shops for a sweater for Moss, perhaps even one for Bob as well. Last year was a bad Christmas: you and Moss returned each other's gifts for cash. You want to do better this year. You want to buy: sweaters.

The mall parking lot, even at 7 p.m., is, as Moss would say, packed as a bag, though you do manage to find a space.

Inside the mall entranceway it smells of stale popcorn, dry heat, and three-day-old hobo urine. A drunk, slumped by the door, smiles and toasts you with nothing.

Say: "Cheers."

To make your journey down to the gazebos at the other end of the mall, first duck into all the single-item shops along the way. Compare prices with the prices at Owonta Flair: things are a little cheaper here. Buy stuff, mostly for Moss and the cat.

In the pet food store the cashier hands you your bagged purchase, smiles, and says, "Merry Christmas."

Say: "You, too."

In the men's sweater shop the cashier hands you your bagged purchase, smiles, and says, "Merry Christmas."

Say: "You, too."

In the belt shop the cashier hands you your bagged purchase, smiles, and says, "Come again."

Say: "You, too." Grow warm. Narrow your eyes to seeds.

In the gazebo next to the Santa gazebo there is only an older man in gray coveralls stacking some folding chairs.

Say: "Excuse me, wasn't *Amahl and the Night Visitors* supposed to be here?"

The man stops for a moment. "There's visitors," he says, pointing out and around, past the gazebo to all the shoppers. Shoppers in parkas. Shoppers moving slow as winter. Shoppers who haven't seen a crosswalk or a window in hours.

"I mean the opera promotional."

"The singers?" He looks at his watch. "They packed it in a while ago."

Say thank you, and wander over to Cinema 1-2-3 to read the movie posters. It's when you turn to go that you see Moss and Bob coming out together from the bar by the theater. They look tired.

Adjust your packages. Walk over. Say: "Hi. I guess I missed the promo, so I was thinking of going to a movie."

"We ended it early," says Moss. "Sonia wasn't feeling well. Bob and I just went into Sammy's for a drink."

Look and see the sign that, of course, reads SAMMY'S.

Bob smiles and says, "Hello, Trudy." Because Bob says *hello* and never *hi,* he always manages to sound a little like Mister Rogers.

You can see some of Moss's makeup and glue lines. His fake beard is sticking out from his coat pocket. Smile. Say: "Well, Moss. Here all along I thought it was Sonia, and it's really Bob." Chuck him under the chin. Keep your smile steady. You are the only one smiling. Not even Bob. You have clearly said the wrong thing.

"Fuck off, Trudy," Moss says finally, palming his hair back off his forehead.

Bob squirms in his coat. "I believe I forgot something," he says. "I'll see you both later." And he touches Moss's arm, turns, disappears back inside Sammy's.

"Jesus Christ, Trudy." Moss's voice suddenly booms through the mall. You can see a few stores closing up, men coming out to lower the metal night gates. Santa Claus has gotten down from the gazebo and is eating an egg roll.

Moss turns from you, charges toward the exit, an angry giant with a beard sticking out of his coat pocket. Run after him and grab his sleeve, make him stop. Say: "I'm sorry, Moss. What am I doing? Tell me. What am I doing wrong?" You look up at his face, with the orange and brown lines and the glue patches, and realize: He doesn't understand you've planned your lives together. That you have even planned your deaths together, not really deaths at all but more like a *pas de deux.* Like Gene Kelly and Leslie Caron in *An American in Paris,* only older.

"You just won't let people be," says Moss, each consonant spit like a fish bone.

Say: "People be? I don't understand. Moss, what is happening to us?" You want to help him, rescue him, build houses and magnificent lawns around him.

"To *us?*"

Moss's voice is loud. He puts on his gloves. He tells you you are a child. He needs to get away. For him you have managed to reduce love, like weather, to a map and a girl, and he needs to get away from you, live someplace else for a while, and think.

The bag with the cat food slips and falls. "The opera's in three days, Moss. Where are you going to go?"

"Right now," he says, "I'm going to get a hamburger." And he storms toward the mall doors, pushes against all of them until he finds the one that's open.

Stare and mumble at the theater candy concession. "Good and Plenty. There's no Good and Plenty." Your bangs droop into your vision. You keep hearing "Jingle Bells," over and over.

In the downtown theaters of your childhood, everything was made of carved wood, and in the ladies' rooms there were framed photographs of Elizabeth Taylor and Ava Gardner. The theaters had names: The Rialto, The Paramount. There were ushers and Good and Plenty. Ushers with flashlights and bow ties. That's the difference now. No ushers. Now you have to do everything by yourself.

"Trudy," says a voice behind you. "Would you like to be accompanied to the movies?" The passive voice. It's Bob's. Turn to look at him, but as with the Good and Plenty, you don't really see, everything around you vague and blurry as glop in your eye.

Say: "Sure. Why not."

In Cinema 3, sit in seats close to the aisle. Listen to the Muzak. The air smells like airplane air.

"It's a strange thing about Moss," Bob is saying, looking straight ahead. "He's so busy with the opera, it pushes him up against certain things. He ends up feeling restless and smothered. But, Trudy, Moss is a good man. He really is."

Don't say anything, and then say finally, "Moss who?"

Stare at the curtain with the rose-tinted lights on it. Try to concentrate on more important matters, things like acid rain.

Bob taps his fingers on the metal arm of the seat. Say: "Look, Bob. I'm no idiot. I was born in New York City. I lived there until I was four. Come on. Tell me: Who's Moss sleeping with?"

"As far as I know," says Bob, sure and serious as a tested hypothesis, "Moss isn't sleeping with anyone."

Continue staring at the rose lights. Then say in a loud contralto: "He's sleeping with *me,* Bob. That's who he's sleeping with."

When the lights dim and the curtains part, there arrive little cigarette lighters on the screen telling you not to smoke. Then there are coming attractions. Bob leans toward you, says, "These previews are horrible."

Say: "Yeah. Nothing Coming Soon."

There are so many previews you forget what movie you've come to see. When the feature presentation comes on, it takes you by surprise. The images melt together like a headache. The movie seems to be about a woman whose lover, losing interest in her, has begun to do inexplicable things like yell about the cat, and throw scenes in shopping malls.

"What is this movie about?"

"Brazil," whispers Bob.

The audience has begun to laugh at something someone is doing; you are tense with comic exile. Whisper: "Bob, I'm gonna go. Wanna go?"

"Yes, in fact, I do," says Bob.

It's ten-thirty and cold. The mall stores are finally closed. In the parking lot, cars are leaving. Say to Bob: "God, look how many people shop here." The whole world suddenly seems to you like a downtown dying slow.

Spot your car and begin to head toward it. Bob catches your sleeve. "My car's the other way. Listen. Trudy. About Moss: No matter what's going on with him, no matter what he decides he has to do, the man loves you. I know he does."

Gently pull your sleeve away. Take a step sideways toward your car. Headlights, everywhere headlights and tires crunching. Say: "Bob, you're a sweet person. But you're sentimental as all get-out." Turn on the nail of your boot and walk.

At home the cat refuses to dance to Dionne Warwick with you. She sits on the sill of the window, rumbling in her throat, her tail a pendulum of fluff. Outside, undoubtedly, there are suitors, begging her not to be so cold-hearted. "Ya got friends out there?" When you turn off the stereo, she jumps down from the sill and snakes lovingly about your ankles. Say something you never thought you'd say. Say: "Wanna go out?" She looks at you, all hope and supplication, and follows you to the door, carefully watching your hand as it moves for the knob: she wants you to let her go, to let her go and be. Begin slowly, turn, pull. The suction of door and frame gives way, and the cold night insinuates itself like a kind of future. She doesn't leave immediately. But her whole body is electrified, surveying the yard for eyes and rustles, and just to the left of the streetlight she suddenly spots them—four, five, phosphorescent glints—and, without a nudge, without ever looking back, she scurries out, off the porch, down after, into some sweet unknown, some somehow known unknown, some new yet very old religion.

12 / 21. Every adoration is seasonal as Christmas.

Moss stops by to get some things. He's staying with Balthazar for a few days, then after the opera and Christmas and all, he'll look for an efficiency somewhere.

Nod. "Efficiency. Great. That's what hell is: efficient." You want to ask him if this is all some silly opera where he's leaving in order to spare you his tragic, bluish death by consumption.

He says, "It's just something I've got to do." He opens cupboards in the kitchen, closets in the hallway, pulls down boxes, cups, boots. He is slow about it, doesn't do it in a mean way, you are grateful for that.

"What have you been doing tonight?" he asks, not looking, but his voice is urgent as a touch.

"I watched two hours of MacNeil-Lehrer. You can get it on channel seven and then later on channel four."

"Right," says Moss. "I know."

Pause. Then say: "Last night I let the cat out. Finally."

Moss looks at you and smiles.

Smile back and shrug, as if all the world were a comedy you were only just now appreciating. Moss begins to put a hand to your shoulder but then takes it back. "Congratulations, Trudy," he murmurs.

"But she hasn't come back yet. I haven't seen her since last night."

"She'll come back," says Moss. "It's only been a day."

"But it's been a whole day. Maybe I should put in ads."

"It's only been one day. She'll come back. You'll see."

Step away from him. Outside, in front of the streetlight, something like snow is falling. Think back again to MacNeil-Lehrer. Say in a level tone: "You know, there are people who know more about it than we do, who say that there is no circumnavigating a nuclear war, we will certainly have one, it's just a matter of time. And when it happens, it's going to dissolve all our communications systems, melt silicon chips—"

"Trudy, please." He wants you to stop. He knows this edge in your voice, this MacNeil-Lehrer edge. All of the world knotted and failing on your tongue.

"And then if you're off living someplace else, in some efficiency, how will I be able to get in touch with you? There I'll be, Moss, all alone in my pink pom-pom slippers, the entire planet exploding all around, and I won't be able to talk to you, to say—" In fifth grade you learned the first words ever spoken on the telephone: *Mr. Watson, come here, I want you.* And suddenly, as you look at him, at the potatoey fists of his cheeks, at his broom-blonde hair, it hits you as it would a child: Someday, like everybody, this man you truly love like no other is going to die. No matter how much you love him, you cannot save him. No matter how much you love: nothing, no one, lasts.

"Moss, we're not safe."

And though there's no flutter of walls, or heave of the floor, above the frayed-as-panic rug, shoes move, and Moss seems to come unstuck, to float toward you, his features beginning to slide in downward diagonals, some chip in his back dissolving, allowing him to bend. His arms reach out to bring you close to his chest. The buttons of his shirt poke against you, and his chin hooks, locks around your neck. When he is gone, the world will grow dull as Mars.

"It's okay," he whispers, his lips moving against your hair. Things grow fuzzy around the edge like a less than brilliant lie. "It's okay," says Moss.

THE NAKED LADY

FOR ALAN LEQUIRE

This is a thing that happened before Monroe started maken the heads, while he was still maken the naked ladies.

Monroe went to the college and it made him crazy for a while like it has done to many a one.

He about lost his mind on this college girl he had. She was just a little old bit of a thing and she talked like she had bugs in her mouth and she was just nothen but trouble. I never would of messed with her myself.

When she thown him over we had us a party to take his mind off it. Monroe had these rooms in a empty mill down by the railroad yard. He used to make his scultures there and we was both liven there too at the time.

We spent all the money on whiskey and beer and everybody we known come over. When it got late Monroe appeared to drop a stitch and went to thowin bottles at the walls. This caused some people to leave but some other ones stayed on to help him I think.

I had a bad case of drunk myself. A little before sunrise I crawled off and didn't wake up till up in the afternoon. I had a sweat from sleepin with clothes on. First thing I seen when I opened my eyes was this big old rat setten on the floor side the mattress. He had a look on his face like he was wonderen would it be safe if he come over and took a bite out of my leg.

It was the worst rats in that place you ever saw. I never saw nothin to match em for bold. If you chunked somethin at em they would just back off a ways and look at you mean. Monroe had him this tin sink which was full of plaster from the scultures and ever night these old rats would mess in it. In the mornin you could see they had left tracks goen places you wouldnt of believed somethin would go.

We had this twenty two pistol we used to shoot em up with but it wasnt a whole lot of good. You could hit one of these rats square with a twenty two and he would go off with it in him and just get meaner. About the only way to kill one was if you hit him spang in the head and that needs you to be a better shot than I am most of the time.

We did try a box of them exploden twenty twos like what that boy shot the president with. They would take a rat apart if you hit him but if you didnt they would bounce around the room and bust up the scultures and so on.

It happened I had put this pistol in my pocket before I went to bed so Monroe couldnt get up to nothin silly with it. I taken it out slow and thew down on this rat that was looken me over. Hit him in the hindquarter and he went off and clamb a pipe with one leg draggen.

I sat up and saw the fluorescents was on in the next room thew the door. When I went in there Monroe was messen around one of his sculture stands.

Did you get one, he said.

Winged him, I said.

That aint worth much, Monroe said. He off somewhere now plotten your doom.

I believe the noise hurt my head more'n the slug hurt that rat, I said. Is it any whiskey left that you know of.

Let me know if you find some, Monroe said. So I went to looken around. The place was nothin but trash and it was glass all over the floor.

I might of felt worse some time but I dont just remember when it was, I said.

They's coffee, Monroe said.

I went in the other room and found a half of a pint of Heaven Hill between the mattress and the wall where I must of hid it before I tapped out. Pretty slick for drunk as I was. I taken it in to the coffee pot and mixed half and half with some milk in it for the sake of my stomach.

Leave me some, Monroe said. I hadnt said a word, he must of smelt it. He tipped the bottle and took half what was left.

The hell, I said. What you maken anyway?

Naked lady, Monroe said.

I taken a look and it was this shape of a woman setten on a mess of clay. Monroe made a number of these things at the time. Some he kept and the rest he thown out. Never could tell the difference myself.

Thats all right, I said.

No it aint, Monroe said. Soon's I made her mouth she started in asken me for stuff. She wants new clothes and she wants a new car and she wants some jewry and a pair of Italian shoes.

And if I make her that stuff, Monroe said, I know she's just goen to take it out looken for some other fool. I'll set here all day maken stuff I dont care for and she'll be out just riden and riden.

Dont make her no clothes and she cant leave, I said.

She'll whine if I do that, Monroe said. The whole time you was asleep she been fussen about our relationship.

You know the worst thing, Monroe said. If I just even thought about maken another naked lady I know she would purely raise hell.

Why dont you just make her a naked man and forget it, I said.

Why dont I do this? Monroe said. He whopped the naked lady with his fist and she turned into a flat clay pancake, which Monroe put in a plastic bag to keep soft. He could hit a good lick when he wanted. I hear this is common among scultures.

Dont you feel like doen somethin, Monroe said.

I aint got the least dime, I said.

I got a couple dollars, he said. Lets go see if it might be any gas in the truck.

They was some. We had this old truck that wasnt too bad except it was slow to start. When we once got it goen we drove over to this pool hall in Antioch where nobody didnt know us. We stayed awhile and taught some fellers that was there how to play rotation and five in the side and some other games that Monroe was good at. When this was over with we had money and I thought we might go over to the Ringside and watch the fights. This was a bar with a ring in the middle so you could set there and drink and watch people get hurt.

We got in early enough to take seats right under the ropes. They was an exhibition but it wasnt much and Monroe started in on this little girl that was setten by herself at the next table.

Hey there Juicy Fruit, he said, come on over here and get somethin real good.

I wouldnt, I told him, haven just thought of what was obvious. Then this big old hairy thing came out from the back and sat down at her table. I known him from a poster out front. He was champion of some kind of karate and had come all the way up from Atlanta just to beat somebody to death and I didnt think he would care if it was Monroe. I got Monroe out of there. I was some annoyed with him because I would have admired to see them fights if I could do it without bein in one myself.

So Monroe said he wanted to hear music and we went some places where they had that. He kept after the girls but they wasnt any trouble beyond what we could handle. After while these places closed and we found us a little rail-road bar down on Lower Broad.

It wasnt nobody there but the pitifulest band you ever heard and six bikers, the big fat ugly kind. They wasnt the Hell's Angels but I believe they would have done until some come along. I would of left if it was just me.

Monroe played pool with one and lost. It wouldnt of happened if he hadnt been drunk. He did have a better eye than me which may be why he is a sculture and I am a second rate pool player.

How come all the fat boys in this joint got on black leather jackets? Monroe hollered out. Could that be a new way to lose weight?

The one he had played with come bellyen over. These boys like to look you up and down beforehand to see if you might faint. But Monroe hooked this one side of the head and he went down like a steer in the slaughterhouse. This didnt make me as happy as it might of because it was five of em left and the one that was down I thought apt to get up shortly.

I shoved Monroe out the door and told him to go start the truck. The band had done left already. I thown a chair and I thown some other stuff that was layen around and I ducked out myself.

The truck wasnt started yet and they was close behind. It was this old four ten I had under the seat that somebody had sawed a foot off the barrel. I taken it and shot the sidewalk in front of these boys. The pattern was wide on account of the barrel bein short like it was and I believe some of it must of hit all of em. It was a pump and took three shells and I kept two back in case I needed em for serious. But Monroe got the truck goen and we left out of there.

I was some mad at Monroe. Never said a word to him till he parked outside the mill. It was a nice moon up and thowin shadows in the cab when the headlights went out. I turned the shotgun across the seat and laid it into Monroe's ribs.

What you up to? he said.

You might want to die, I said, but I dont believe I want to go with you. I pumped the gun to where you could hear the shell fallen in the chamber.

If that's what you want just tell me now and I'll save us both some trouble.

It aint what I want, Monroe said.

I taken the gun off him.

I dont know what I do want, Monroe said.

Go up ther and make a naked lady and you feel better, I told him.

He was messen with clay when I went to sleep but that aint what he done. He set up a mirror and done a head of himself instead. I taken a look at the thing in the mornin and it was a fair likeness. It looked like it was thinkin about all the foolish things Monroe had got up to in his life so far.

That same day he done one of me that was so real it even looked like it had a hangover. Ugly too but that aint Monroe's fault.

He is makin money with it now.

How we finally fixed them rats was we brought on a snake. Monroe was the one to have the idea. It was a good-sized one and when it had just et a rat it was as big around as your arm. It didnt eat more than about one a week but it appeared to cause the rest of em to lay low.

You might say it was as bad to have snakes around as rats but at least it was only one of the snake.

The only thing was when it turned cold the old snake wanted to get in the bed with you. Snakes aint naturally warm like we are and this is how come people think they are slimy which is not the truth when you once get used to one.

This old snake just comes and goes when the spirit moves him. I aint seen him in a while but I expect he must be still around.

THE SUTTON PIE SAFE

A blacksnake lay stretched out on the cracked slab of concrete near the diesel tank. It kept still in a spot of sun. It had drawn clear membranes across its eyes, had puffed its glistening scales a little, soaking up the heat of the day. It must have been three feet long.

"There's one, dad," I said, pointing at it. My father was staring at the old pole barn, listening to the birds in the loft as they chattered and swooped from one sagging rafter to another. The pole barn was leaning hard to one side, the west wall buckling under. The next big summer storm would probably knock it down. The winter had been hard, the snows heavy, and the weight had snapped the ridgepole. I wondered where we would put that summer's hay.

"Where is he?" my dad asked. He held the cut-down .410 in one hand, the short barrel cradled in the crook of his elbow, stock tight against his bare ribs. We were looking for copperheads to kill, but I thought maybe I could coax my dad into shooting the sleeping blacksnake. I loved the crack of the gun, the smell of sulphur from the opened breech. Again I pointed to the snake.

"Whew," he said, "that's a big one there. What do you figure, two, two and a half feet?" "Three," I said. "Three at least." He grunted.

"You gonna kill it?" I asked.

"Boys want to kill everything, don't they?" he said to me, grinning. Then, more seriously, "Not too good an idea to kill a blacksnake. They keep the mice down, the rats. Better than a cat, really, a good-sized blacksnake."

He stood, considering the unmoving snake, his lips pursed. He tapped the stock of the gun against his forearm. Behind us, past the line of willow trees near the house, I heard the crunch of gravel in the driveway. Somebody was driving up. We both turned to watch as the car stopped next to the smokehouse. It was a big car, Buick Riviera, and I could see that the metallic flake finish had taken a beating on the way up our lane.

My father started forward, then stopped. A woman got out of the car, a tall woman in a blue sun dress. She looked over the car at us, half waved. She had honey-colored hair that hung to her shoulders, and beautiful, well-muscled arms. Her wave was uncertain. When I looked at my dad, he seemed embarrassed to have been caught without a shirt. He raised the gun in a salute, decided that wasn't right, lowered the gun and waved his other hand instead.

It was too far to talk without shouting, so we didn't say anything, and neither did the woman. We all stood there a minute longer. Then I started over toward her.

"Boy," my dad said. I stopped. "Don't you want to get that snake?" he said.

"Thought it wasn't good to kill blacksnakes," I said. I gestured toward the house. "Who is she?" I asked.

"Friend of your mother's," he said. His eyes were on her. She had turned from us, was at the screen porch. I could see her talking through the mesh to my mother, nodding her head. She had a purse in her hand, waved it to emphasize something she was saying. "Your mom'll take care of her," my dad said. The woman opened the porch door, entered. The blue sun dress was pretty much backless, and I watched her go. Once she was on the porch, she was no more than a silhouette.

"Sure is pretty," I said to my father. "Yeah," he said. He snapped the .410's safety off, stepped over to the diesel pump. The snake sensed his coming, turned hooded eyes on him. The sensitive tongue flicked from the curved mouth, testing the air, the warm concrete. For just a second, I saw the pink inner lining of the mouth, saw the rows of tiny, backward curving fangs. "When I was ten, just about your age," my dad said, levelling the gun at the snake, "my daddy killed a big old blacksnake out in our back yard."

The snake, with reluctance, started to crawl from the spot of sun. My dad steadied the gun on it with both hands. It was a short weapon, the barrel and stock both cut down. It couldn't have measured more than twenty inches overall. Easy to carry, quick to use: perfect for snake. "He killed that blacksnake, pegged the skin out, and give it to me for a belt," my dad said. He closed one eye, squeezed the trigger.

The shot tore the head off the snake. At the sound, a couple of barn swallows flew from the haymow, streaked around the barn, swept back into the dark loft. I watched the body of the snake vibrate and twitch, watched it crawl rapidly away from the place where it had died. It moved more quickly than I'd seen it move that afternoon. The blood was dark, darker than beets or raspberry juice. My dad snapped the bolt of the gun open, and the spent cartridge bounced on the concrete. When the snake's body twisted toward me, I stepped away from it.

My dad picked the snake up from the mess of its head. The dead snake, long and heavy, threw a couple of coils over his wrist. He shook them off, shook the body of the snake out straight, let it hang down from his hand. It was longer than one of his legs. "Wore that belt for a lot of years," he said, and I noticed that my ears were ringing. It took me a second to understand what he was talking about. "Wore it 'til it fell apart." He offered the snake to me, but I didn't want to touch it. He laughed.

"Let's go show your mother," he said, walking past me toward the house. I thought of the woman in the sun dress, wondered what she would think of the blacksnake. I followed my dad, watching the snake. Its movements were slowing now, lapsing into a rhythmic twitching along the whole length of its body.

As we passed the smokehouse and the parked Riviera, I asked him, "What's her name?" He looked at the car, back at me. I could hear my mother's voice, and the voice of the other woman, couldn't hear what they were saying.

"Hanson," he said. "Mrs. Hanson. Judge Hanson's wife." Judge Hanson was a circuit court judge in the county seat; he'd talked at my school once, a big man wearing a three-piece suit, even though the day had been hot. It seemed to me that his wife must be a good deal younger than he was.

The snake in my father's hand was motionless now, hung straight down toward the earth. His fingers were smeared with gore, and a line of blood streaked his chest.

"Why'd you kill the blacksnake?" I asked him. "After what you said, about rats and all?" I was still surprised he'd done it. He looked at me, and for a moment I didn't think he was going to answer me.

He reached for the doorknob with his free hand, twisted it. "Thought you'd know," he said. "My daddy made a belt for me. I'm gonna make one for you."

⸫ ⸫ ⸫

The woman in the sun dress, Mrs. Hanson, was talking to my mother when we entered the porch. "I was talking to Karen Spangler the other day," she said. My mother, sitting at the other end of the screen porch, nodded. Mrs. Spangler was one of our regular egg customers, came out about once every two weeks, just for a minute. Mrs. Hanson continued. "She says that you all have just the best eggs, and the Judge and I wondered if you might possibly . . ." She let the sentence trail off, turned to my father.

"Why, hello, Mr. Albright," she said. She saw the snake, but she had poise: she didn't react. My father nodded at her. "Mrs. Hanson," he said. He held the snake up for my mother to see. "Look here, Sara," he said. "Found this one sunning himself out near the diesel pump."

My mother stood. "You don't want to bring that thing on the porch, Jack," she said. She was a small woman, my mother, with quick movements, deft reactions. There was anger in her eyes.

"Thought I'd make a belt out of it for the boy," my dad said, ignoring her. He waved the snake, and a drop of blood fell from his hand to the floor. "You remember that old snakeskin belt I had?"

Mrs. Hanson came over to me, and I could smell her perfume. Her skin was tan, lightly freckled. "I don't think we've met," she said to me, like I was a man, and not just a boy. I tried to look her straight in the eye, found I couldn't. "No'm," I said. "Don't think we have."

"His name's Cates," my mother said. "He's ten." I didn't like it that she answered for me. Mrs. Hanson nodded, held out her hand. "Pleased to meet you, Cates," she said. I took her hand, shook it, realized I probably wasn't supposed to shake a lady's hand. I pulled back, noticed the grime under my fingernails, the dust on the backs of my hands. "Pleased," I said, and Mrs. Hanson gave out a laugh that was like nothing I'd ever heard from a woman before, loud and happy.

"You've a fine boy there," she said to my dad. I bent my head. To my father, my mother said, "Why don't you take that snake out of here, Jack. And get a shirt on. We've got company."

He darted a look at her. Then he waved the snake in the air, to point out to everybody what a fine, big blacksnake it was. He opened the screen door, leaned out, and dropped the snake in a coiled heap next to the steps. It looked almost alive lying there, the sheen of the sun still on the dark scales. "Mrs. Hanson," he said, and went on into the house. He let the door slam behind him, and I could hear him as he climbed the stairs inside.

Once he was gone, Mrs. Hanson seemed to settle back, to become more businesslike. "The Judge and I certainly would appreciate the opportunity to buy some of your eggs." She sat down in one of the cane bottom chairs we kept on the porch in summer, set her purse down beside her. "But Sara—may I call you Sara?" she asked, and my mother nodded. "Something else has brought me here as well." My mother sat forward in her chair, interested to hear. I leaned forward too, and Mrs. Hanson shot a glance my way. I could tell she wasn't sure she wanted me there.

"Sara," she said, "you have a Sutton pie safe." She pointed across the porch, and at first I thought she meant the upright freezer that stood there. Then I saw she was pointing at the old breadbox.

My mother looked at it. "Well, it's a pie safe," she said. "Sutton, I don't know—"

"Oh, yes, it's a Sutton," Mrs. Hanson said. "Mrs. Spangler told me so, and I can tell she was right." Mrs. Spangler, so far as I knew, had never said anything to us about a pie safe. Mrs. Hanson rose, knelt in front of the thing, touched first one part of it and then another.

"Here, you see," she said, pointing to the lower right corner of one of the pie safe's doors. We'd always called it a breadbox, kept all kinds of things in it: canned goods, my dad's ammunition and his reloading kit, things that needed to be kept cool in winter. The pie safe was made of cherry wood— you could tell even through the paint—with a pair of doors on the front. The doors had tin panels, and there were designs punched in the tin, swirls and circles and I don't know what all. I looked at the place where she was point- ing. "SS" I saw, stamped into the wood. The letters were mostly filled with paint; I'd never noticed them before.

Mrs. Hanson patted the thing, picked a chip of paint off it. My mother and I watched her. "Of course," Mrs. Hanson said, "this paint will have to come off. Oh, a complete refinishing job, I imagine. How lovely!" She sounded thrilled. She ran her hands down the tin, feeling the holes where the metal- punch had gone through.

"Damn," she said, and I was surprised to hear her curse. "What's the mat- ter?" my mother asked. Mrs. Hanson looked closely at the tin on the front of the pie safe. "It's been reversed," she said. "The tin panels on the front, you see how the holes were punched in? It wasn't put together that way, you know. When they punched this design in the tin, they poked it through from the back to the front, so the points were outside the pie safe."

"Oh," my mother said, sounding deflated. It sounded ridiculous to me. I couldn't figure why anyone would care which way the tin was put on the thing.

"Sometimes country people do that, reverse the tin panels," Mrs. Han- son said in a low voice, as if she weren't talking to country people. My mother didn't disagree. "Still, though," Mrs. Hanson said, "it is a Sutton, and I must have it. What will you take for it?"

I guess I should have known that she was angling to buy the thing all along, but still it surprised me. It surprised my mother too. "Take for it?" she said.

"Yes," Mrs. Hanson said, "it's our anniversary next week—mine and the Judge's—and I just know he would be thrilled with a Sutton piece. Especially one of the pie safes. Of course, I don't think it'll be possible to have it refin- ished by then, but he'll see the possibilities."

"I don't know," my mother said, and I couldn't believe she was consid- ering the idea. "Is it worth a lot?" It was an odd way to arrive at a price, and I laughed. Both women looked at me as if they had forgotten that I was on the porch with them. I wondered what my father would say when he came down from putting on a shirt.

Mrs. Hanson turned back to my mother. "Oh, yes," she said. "Samuel Sutton was quite a workman, very famous throughout the Valley. People are vying to buy his pieces. And here I've found one all for myself. And the Judge." Then, as if understanding that she wasn't being wise, she said, "Of course, the damage to it, the tin and all, that does lower the value a great deal. And the paint." My father had painted the breadbox, the pie safe, when it had been in the kitchen years ago, to match the walls. We'd since moved it out to the porch, when my mother picked up a free-standing cupboard she liked better.

"I don't know," my mother said. "After all, we don't use it much anymore, just let it sit out here. And if you really want it . . ." She sounded worried. She knew my father wasn't going to be pleased with the idea. "We should wait, ask my husband." Mrs. Hanson reached into her handbag, looking for her checkbook. I knew it wasn't going to be that easy.

"Didn't that belong to Granddad?" I asked my mother. She looked at me, didn't answer. "Dad's dad?" I said, pressing.

"It was in my husband's family," my mother said to Mrs. Hanson. "He might not like it."

"Could we say, then, three hundred dollars? Would that be possible?" Mrs. Hanson asked. She wasn't going to give up. Just then, my father opened the door and stepped out of the house onto the porch. He had washed his hands, put on a blue chambray shirt, one I'd given him for Christmas.

"Three hundred dollars?" my father said. "Three hundred dollars for what?" I saw my mother's face set into hard lines; she was determined to oppose him.

"She wants to buy the pie safe," my mother said. Her voice was soft, but not afraid.

My father walked over to the breadbox, struck the tin with two fingers. "This?" he said. "You're going to pay three hundred for this?" Both my mother and Mrs. Hanson nodded. "I think that's a fair enough price, Mr. Albright," Mrs. Hanson said. I noticed she didn't call him Jack.

"You could use it to get someone over to help you work on the barn," my mother said. My father didn't even look at her. I moved to his side.

"Didn't know the breadbox was for sale," he said. "Didn't know that it would be worth that much if it was for sale."

"My father owned that," he said. "Bought it for my mother, for this house, when they were first married." He turned to my mother. "You know that," he said.

"But what do we use it for, Jack?" she asked. "We use the barn. We need the barn. More than some pie safe."

My father put his hand on my shoulder. "You're not going to leave me anything, are you?" he said to my mother. She flushed, gestured at Mrs. Hanson. Mrs. Hanson managed to look unflustered.

My dad looked at Mrs. Hanson. Her calm seemed to infuriate him. "We aren't merchants," he said. "And this isn't a furniture shop." He turned to me. "Is it, boy?" I nodded, then shook my head no, not sure which was the correct response. "Mrs. Hanson," my mother began. You could tell she didn't like my father talking like that to Mrs. Hanson, who was a guest in her home.

"Don't apologize for me, Sara," my dad said. "Go ahead and sell the damn breadbox if you want, but just don't apologize for me." My mother opened her mouth, shut it again.

"Boy," he said to me, "you want a snakeskin belt like I was talking about? Like my daddy made?" He gestured out the porch door, to where the headless snake lay. A big fly, colored like blue glass, was crawling on the body.

"Yes, sir," I said, glad not to have to look at the high color rising in Mrs. Hanson's cheeks.

"You come out back with me, then, and I'll show you how to skin it, how to stretch the hide. How'd that be?" Neither my mother nor Mrs. Hanson said a word. My dad pushed me ahead of him, and I headed out the door.

As he came after me, he turned and spoke through the screen. "I'll tell you something, Mrs. Hanson," he said. "You ought not to try to buy what hasn't been put up for sale."

*　　*　　*

Outside, my father groped in his pocket for a second, came up with his old Barlow knife, flicked the blade out. "You hold the snake for me," he said. "We'll take that skin right off him." He held out the body to me. I hesitated, reached out and took it.

It was heavy and rope-like, cool and limp in my hands. The scales were dry as sand. "Set it down there," my dad said, "and hold it stretched out tight." I set the snake down.

"Belly up," my dad said. "We don't want to mess up the scales on his back. That's what makes a snakeskin belt so nice, so shiny, them back scales." I rolled the snake. The scales on the sausage-like belly were light-colored, looked soft, and I prodded them with a forefinger. The skin rasped against my fingernail.

"Here we go," my father said, and pressed the blade of the knife against the belly of the snake. He always kept the knife razor-sharp, had a whetstone at the house he kept specially for it. I looked away. The knife made a sound as it went in; I thought I could hear him slicing through muscle, thought I could hear the small, cartilaginous ribs giving way under the blade.

Mrs. Hanson left the porch, and I could tell from the way she was walking that she must have gotten what she wanted. She moved with a bounce in her step. She looked over at us where we were kneeling, shook her hair back out of her face, smiled. My father paused in his cutting for a second when he heard the car door open. Mrs. Hanson backed the Buick around, headed back down the lane, toward the highway. A couple of low-hanging branches lashed the windshield as she went.

My mother stood on the porch, an outline behind the mesh of the screen, watching her go. When the car was out of sight, she turned and went back into the house.

My father gave a low laugh. When I looked at him, he was holding something gray between two fingers, dangled it back and forth in front of my face. "I'll be damned," he said. I looked down at the snake, the open stomach cavity, realized that he was holding a dead mouse by its tail. "No wonder that snake was so sleepy," my dad said. "He just ate." I stood, turned away from him.

"What's the matter?" he asked. I didn't answer. "You aren't gonna let that bother you," he said, and there was disdain in his voice. I put my arms over the top rail of the board fence around our yard, leaned my weight on it. I closed my eyes, saying nothing.

My father lowered his voice. "Thought you wanted that belt," he said. I wanted to turn to him, tell him that I did want the belt, just to give me a minute. I wasn't sure I could trust my voice not to break. "Guess not," he said.

Once again, I heard the sound of the knife, two quick cuts. I turned to look, saw that he had deftly sliced the body of the snake, had carved it into three nearly equal sections. It looked like pieces of bicycle tire lying there, bloody bicycle tire. My father rose, wiped his hands on his jeans.

"You think about that, boy," he said. "You think about that, next time you decide you want something." He walked past me, not toward the house, but toward the ruined barn.

A PORTRAIT OF
A FATHER

My father gave me ten dollars when I went home and he said: "I wish I had somebody to give me ten dollars." He's still looking for somebody to take care of him, he did what he was told, but it didn't work out, so he's looking for a savior, and he wants me, his son, to be his father. And I love him, I look at him from far away sometimes like at temple when he's at the torah in front of the congregation and I'm sad suddenly to see how old he's become, I haven't really looked at him in so long. But then I'm proud to watch him make his faces and say his prayers, and I wonder if anyone in the congregation will remember Ira Vine as he stood there or do they not see him, as I haven't for so long. Who is that man up there that I want to say "I love you" to and how good that would make him feel, he's failed in everything else, but if he could be confident in his son's love . . . I know he tries to be strong for me, on the phone to New York he'll say, "Goodnight, son." And just from those two words I hear him trying, trying to be a father, saying son.

But then he comes back down from the torah and he's up close again, and the burden is too great for me to comfort him with my pride and love for him, and somehow it turns to the old repulsion. For years as a child I couldn't bear to watch him eat, I would move as far away into the corner of the table, it wasn't a big table, and I'd turn my head, I couldn't stand the sounds he made. And he would make me scratch his back, his hairy back, and somehow it was a test of my love if I didn't scratch hard enough, but I was horrified to get things under my fingernails and he didn't understand that. And he would take baths with my sister and myself, and he always wanted to cuddle, and I remember feeling his penis against the crack of my ass, and who knows what that has done to me.

And all I've heard for the last ten years is his crying and weeping, about how he would be better off dead, and his heart palpitations and anxiety attacks and a problem with his shoulder, hand, knee, wrist, eyes, What's bothering you today, Dad? He's a Depression-born child and all the values he had don't work, and he was a momma's boy because he had a hole in his ear, IRA DON'T GO SWIMMING, DON'T GET YOUR HEAD WET, IRA YOU HAVE TO GO TO THE DOCTOR. His mother, my grandmother, who babied him for a long time, died two years ago. (His father, long dead, never encouraged him, only told him, "Promise me you won't be a taxi driver," since he had been a taxi driver in Brooklyn during the Depression. So my father kept the promise and became a traveling salesman in the northeast corridor.) So now that his momma is dead, my father is more lost than ever—he has no one's expectation not to live up to anymore ("Why are you a salesman? Why couldn't you have been something?" she would say well into his fifties.) But he doesn't realize how freeing her death is, he still looks in the mirror and hears her saying "failure." So he takes naps all the time and doesn't feel well. Every time I've eaten at home the last ten years he starts the meal by saying, "I don't feel right," and one time I jumped up and screamed, "Dad, this is serious," so I dialed 911. My mother laughed with me. And even he smiled. He hasn't felt right for a decade.

I asked him once, "Dad, what were your dreams?" I was trying to figure out why he had been depressed for so long, and he said, "To marry your mother, have you kids, have a house, a car, and a dog." So I said, "What's the problem then? You've got everything." He just shook his head, somehow it isn't enough and he has no new dreams. He just keeps his job because he is afraid to quit, and afraid to lose his company car, he hasn't paid for his own gas in years. As a traveling salesman, he can tell you the year of a photograph if his car is in the background; he's had over twenty-five company cars since the fifties and he remembers each one. Sometimes I try to think of him as a brave knight of the roads traveling eight hundred miles a week to factories in East Stroudsburg and Gloversville to sell tool and die. And over the years he's learned all the roads without tolls and what number to order at Howard Johnson restaurants, and how to make his brakes last an extra ten thousand miles. He never stopped being a good father though, he'd bathe me and bring me juice at night and miss work to help my mother take care of me when I was sick. But he's defeated now, too many miles on roads through the Poconos dark and winding and his eyes burning from his own cigar smoke and fatigue, and one thing kept him from driving off the road, and that's his great love for my mother.

So now he is terrorized by his two young Jewish bosses, the Feldmans, who grow fantastically in size and evilness every year. I tell him, "Dad, stop worrying, they like you, it's all in your mind." And sure enough, they said, "Ira, we wouldn't hurt a Jewish boy." And he's fifteen years older than they are. And he fears they'll find the extra two hundred dollars a year worth of gas he puts in my mother's car. Now towards the end of his career they've struck him the greatest salesman's blow, after twelve years on salary they've put him on commission, to light a fire under his sixty-year-old ass.

And he's had one outlet over the years from his job as a salesman, and that outlet was guns. For a while he even rode in auxiliary police cars, he loved the uniform, but then the governor made it illegal for volunteers to carry guns (some volunteer shot somebody without warning). So now he just lies in front of the TV on a couch with a blanket wrapped around him, and our dog lying between his legs, and out of that blanket sticks his gun and he dry fires it at the TV, aiming between the eyes.

THE ART AND THE
CRAFT OF REVISION

THE ART AND THE
CRAFT OF REVISION

> **The last thing one settles in writing . . . is what one should put in first.**
>
> —*Blaise Pascal*

The advantage of writing over living is self-evident: writing can be revised, living cannot. For the serious writer, writing *is* revising. The writer who is impatient with revision, for all his or her natural gifts, will be disadvantaged; for, however good the work, it isn't so good as it might have been. Any artist who is impatient with revision is probably doomed to be forever an amateur: "promising" through a lifetime.

Writers are fascinated by early drafts and revisions of others' work. Unless one is Mozart or Shakespeare, gifted with a quicksilver ability to create art of surpassing genius without, evidently, toiling over it, one will have to revise, rework, reconsider—sometimes rewrite completely. And sometimes discard that which one has been working on with such hope and diligence.

We write in order to read what we've written in order to have the experience of reading: a mystery. Yet we're immersed in the mystery of why, out of the world's teeming billions, only each one of us, only the individual, could have created this singular work of art. We don't know what we've written until we read it through as a reader, expelled from the process of the work, and no longer as a writer enthralled by its creation. Sometimes it startles us— it reads so much more swiftly and smoothly than we'd dare to imagine. Sometimes it shocks us—it isn't what we'd meant to write at all but leaden, misconceived, *wrong*.

But only until we've read what we've been working to create do we understand, as Pascal says, what we should put in first. Sometimes we learn that the entire effort might be better discarded. This is a hurtful revelation, and some might wish valiantly to deny it; but like all genuine revelations, it is likely to be illuminating, and cleansing.

Students quickly learn, in workshops, that fiction writing is a process. The process may result in a product, or products; but it's the process in which one lives, and thinks, hour following hour, day following day. This process is not in any way alienated from or even detached from "life": it *is* life, as integral to life as eating, dreaming, breathing. Similarly, a work of art is not separate from or in opposition to or a mere "metaphor" for life: it *is* life, as rightfully in existence as any object, person, event.

Fiction and poetry workshops, like all courses in composition, music, art, dance, and theater, are for works-in-progress, works-in-process. The young (or not-young) writer who imagines that his work is already perfect has no need of a workshop, nor would anyone want this individual in one. In matters of art-in-process, in workshop situations in which criticism (of a constructive kind solely) is offered, it is wisest to leave one's ego at the door. The writer who imagines she hasn't any ego, or can easily control her ego, will soon discover otherwise. The more urgent the admonition, then: *leave one's ego at the door.*

Boxers sometimes say, with absolute seriousness, that in the ring, they're fighting for their lives. To be precise, they are fighting not to lose prematurely; they are fighting for a measure of "immortality." So too the ambitious artist is fighting not to fail, but to endure by way of his or her art. Ernest Hemingway, even as a young writer, rewrote and revised continually; it was his practice to write for hours, with a pencil, waiting patiently for his "one true sentence" to emerge. The most intuitive, inspired, and rapid of writers, D. H. Lawrence nonetheless assiduously rewrote: the massive *Women in Love,* for instance, required several complete drafts involving thousands of pages; *Lady Chatterly's Lover* exists in three quite distinctive manuscript versions of which the last was the one to be published, and became infamous.

James Joyce has the distinction of being perhaps the most meticulous of all writers, ceaselessly writing, rewriting, and revising the highly conceptualized prose works of his maturity, like a spider casting out an ever larger, ever more complex and labyrinthine web as if to capture the very universe. *Ulysses* required approximately seven years to write, *Finnegans Wake* approximately sixteen. When Joyce began working on the subtly modulated yet starkly realistic stories set in Dublin that would eventually make up his first book, *Dubliners,* he was twenty-two years old and immensely ambitious; he had been writing, and thinking about writing, for half his life. Early versions of "The Sisters," "Eveline," and "After the Race" appeared in the agricultural journal *The Irish Homestead* as one of its features, *Our Weekly Story,* in late 1904.

Though the completed manuscript of *Dubliners,* fourteen stories and the novella "The Dead," was accepted for publication as early as 1906, one publisher after another feared its "controversial" or "blasphemous" content (in Roman Catholic Ireland), and the book's publication was delayed until 1914. By that time, Joyce had not only completed his first, radically innovative novel, *A Portrait of the Artist as a Young Man,* which would be published in 1916, but had begun to draft *Ulysses.* The stories of *Dubliners* would have seemed to him the work of his vanished youth, created out of an aesthetic of simplicity and directness; in these stories, of which "The Sisters" is a prime example, the protagonist moves through space and time unimpeded by the net of impressions and thought that would characterize the later baroque Joycean style. It is fascinating to compare "The Sisters" of 1904 with "The Sisters" of 1914: the dramatically direct opening of the later version, the significant alterations in sentence structure and vocabulary, the deliberate excision of "God rest his soul!"—all are shrewdly chosen, the mark of an artist grown to maturity.

James Joyce

THE SISTERS

[*version of 1904*]

Three nights in succession I had found
myself in Great Britain Street at
that hour, as if by providence. Three
nights I had raised my eyes to that
lighted square of window and speculated.
I seemed to understand that it would
occur at night. But in spite of the
providence which had led my feet
and in spite of the reverent curiosity
of my eyes I had discovered nothing.
Each night the square was lighted
in the same way, faintly and evenly.
It was not the light of candles so
far as I could see. Therefore it had
not ~~yet~~ occurred yet.

On the fourth night at that
hour I was in another part of the
city. It may have been the same
providence that led me there—a
whimsical kind of providence—to
take me at a disadvantage. As I
went home I wondered was that
square of window lighted as before
or did it reveal the ceremonious
candles in the light of which the
Christian must take his last sleep.
I was not surprised, then, when at

supper I found myself a prophet.
Old Cotter and my uncle were talking
at the fire, smoking. Old Cotter was
a retired distiller who owned a batch
of prize setters. He used to be very
interesting when I knew him first,
talking about *faints* and *worms,* but[1]

afterwards he became tedious.
    While I was eating my stirabout
I heard him say to my uncle:
—Without a doubt. The upper storey
(he tapped an unnecessary hand
at his forehead) was gone—
—So they said. I never could see
much of it. I thought he was
sane enough—
—So he was, at times, said old
Cotter—
I sniffed the *was* apprehensively
and gulped down some stirabout.

Jack
—Is he any better, Uncle ~~John~~?—
—He's dead—
—O. . . . . —
—Died a few hours ago—
—Who told you?—
—Mr Cotter here brought us the
news. He was passing. . . .—
—Yes, I just happened to be passing
and I noticed the windows. . . . You
know. So I just knocked softly—
—Do you think they will bring him
to the chapel? asked my aunt—
—O, no, ma'am. I wouldn't say so—
—Very unlikely, my uncle agreed—
    So old Cotter had got the better
of me for all my vigilance of
three nights. It is often annoying
the way people will blunder on

1. Space breaks indicate where pages ended in the original manuscript.

what you have elaborately planned
for. I was sure he would die
at night.

The following morning after breakfast
I went down to look at the little
house in Great Britain Street.
It was an unassuming shop
registered under the vague name
of *Drapery.* The drapery consisted
chiefly of children's boots and
umbrellas and on ordinary days
there used to be a notice hanging
in the window which said *Umbrellas
Recovered.* There was no notice
visible now for the shop-blinds
were drawn down and a crape
bouquet was tied to the knocker
of the door with white ribbons.
Three women of the people and
a telegram boy were reading
the card pinned on the crape. I
also went over and read:
     July 2nd, 1890
    The Rev. James Flynn
    (formerly of S. Catherine's
    Church, Meath Street) aged
    Sixty-five Years.
       R.I.P.
    Only sixty-five! He looked
much older than that. I often saw
him sitting at the fire in the close
dark room behind the shop, nearly
smothered in his great coat. He
seemed to have almost stupefied
himself with heat and the gesture
of his large trembling hand to
his nostrils had grown automatic.
My aunt, who is what they call
good-hearted, never went into
the shop without bringing him

some High Toast; and he used to
take the packet of snuff from
her hands, gravely inclining his
head for sign of thanks. He used
to sit in that stuffy room for
the greater part of the day from
early morning while Nannie
(who was almost stone deaf)
read out the newspaper to him.
His other sister, Eliza, used to
mind the shop. These two old
women used to look after him,
feed him and clothe him. The
task of clothing him was not
difficult for his ancient priestly
clothes were quite green with
age and his dogskin slippers
were everlasting. When he was
tired of hearing the news he used
to rattle his snuff-box on the
arm of his chair to avoid
shouting at her and then he
used to make believe to read
his prayerbook. Make believe
because whenever Eliza brought
him a cup of soup from the
kitchen she had always to
waken him.

As I stood looking up at the
crape and the card which bore
his name I could not convince
myself that he was dead. He
seemed like one who could have
gone on living for ever if only
he had wanted to; his life was

so methodical and uneventful.
I think he said more to me than
to anyone else. He had an
egoistic contempt for all

women-folk and suffered all
their services to him in polite
silence. Of course neither of
his sisters was very intelligent.
Nannie, for instance, had been
reading out the newspaper
to him every day for years and
could read tolerably well and
yet she always spoke of it
as the *Freeman's General*.
Perhaps he found me more
intelligent and honoured me
with words for that reason.
Nothing, practically nothing,
ever happened to remind him
of his former life (I mean friends
or visitors) but still he could
remember every detail of it
in his own fashion. He had
studied at the college in Rome
pronounce and he taught me to ~~speak~~
Latin in the Italian way. He
often put me through the
responses of the Mass, smiling
often and pushing huge pinches
of snuff up each nostril
alternately. When he smiled
he used to uncover his big
discoloured teeth and let his
tongue lie on his lower lip.
At first this habit of his used

to make me feel uneasy. Then
I grew used to it.
  That evening my aunt
visited the house of mourning
and took me with her. It was
an oppressive summer evening
of faded gold. Nannie received
us in the hall and, as it was

no use saying anything to
her, my aunt shook hands
with her for all. We followed
the old woman upstairs and
into the dead-room. The room
through the lace end of the
blind was suffused with
dusky golden light amid
which the candles seemed
like pale thin flames. He
had been coffined. Nannie
gave the lead and we three
knelt down at the foot of
the bed. There was no sound
in the room for some minutes
except the sound of Nannie's
mutterings, for she prayed
noisily. The fancy came
to me that the old priest
was smiling as he lay there
in his coffin.

But no. When we rose
and went up to the head
of the bed I saw that he was
not smiling. There he lay

solemn and copious, vested
as for the altar, his large
hands loosely retaining a
cross. His face was very grey
and massive with distended
nostrils and circled with a
scanty white fur. There was
a heavy odour in the room, the
flowers.

We sat downstairs in the
little room behind the shop,
my aunt and I and the two
sisters. We, as visitors, were
given a glass of sherry each.

Nannie sat in a corner and
said nothing but her lips
moved from speaker to
speaker with a painfully
intelligent movement. I
said nothing either, being
too young, but my aunt said
a great deal for she was a
gossip, a harmless one.
—Ah, well, he's gone!—
—To enjoy his eternal reward,
Miss Flynn, I'm sure. He was
a good and holy man—
—He was a good man but. . . . .
you see. . . . he was a disappointed
man. You see. . . . his life was,
you might say, crossed—
—Ah, yes. I know what you mean—

—Not that he was anyway mad,
as you know yourself: but he
was always a little queer. Even
when we were all growing up
together he was queer. One
time he didn't speak hardly
for a month. You know, he
was that kind always—
—Perhaps he read too much,
Miss Flynn—
—O, he read a good deal but
not latterly. It was his
scrupulousness, you see, that
affected his mind. The duties
of the priesthood were too
much for him—
—Did he. . . . . . . peacefully?—
—O, quite peacefully, ma'am. You
couldn't tell when the breath
went out of him. He had a
beautiful death, God be

praised—
—And everything . . . . . . ?—
—Father O'Rourke was in with
him yesterday and gave him
the Last Sacrament—
—He knew then?—
—Yes. He was quite resigned—
Nannie gave a sleepy nod
and looked ashamed.
—Poor Nannie, said her sister,

she's worn out. All the work
we had getting in a woman
and laying him out! And
then the coffin and arranging
about the mass in the chapel.
God knows we did all we could,
as poor as we are. We wouldn't
see him want anything at
the last—
—Indeed you were both very
kind to him while he lived—
—Ah, poor James! He was no
great trouble to us. You wouldn't
hear him in the house any
more than now. Still I know
he's gone and all that I
won't be bringing him in
his soup any more nor Nannie
reading him out the paper
nor you, ma'am, bringing
him his snuff! Poor James!—
—O, yes, you'll miss him in a
day or two more than you
do now—
Silence invaded the room
until memory reawakened
it, Eliza speaking slowly:
—It was that chalice he broke.
Of course, it was all right.

I mean it contained nothing.
But still. . . . . They say it was
the boy's fault. But poor

James was so nervous. God be
merciful to him!—
—Yes, Miss Flynn, I heard that
about the chalice. He . . . . his
mind was a bit affected by
that—
—He began to mope by himself,
talking to no-one and wandering
about. Often he couldn't be
found. One night he was wanted
and they looked high up and
low down and couldn't find
him. Then the clerk suggested
the chapel. So they opened the
chapel (it was late at night)
and brought in a light to look
for him . . . . . And there, sure
enough, he was sitting in his
confession-box in the dark, wide
awake, and laughing like—
softly to himself. Then they knew
something was wrong—
—God rest his soul!—

THE SISTERS

[*version of 1914*]

There was no hope for him this time: it was the third stroke. Night after night I had passed the house (it was vacation time) and studied the lighted square of window: and night after night I had found it lighted in the same way, faintly and evenly. If he was dead, I thought, I would see the reflection of candles on the darkened blind for I knew that two candles must be set at the head of a corpse. He had often said to me: *I am not long for this world,* and I had thought his words idle. Now I knew they were true. Every night as I gazed up at the window I said softly to myself the word *paralysis.* It had always sounded strangely in my ears, like the word *gnomon* in the Euclid and the word *simony* in the Catechism. But now it sounded to me like the name of some maleficent and sinful being. It filled me with fear, and yet I longed to be nearer to it and to look upon its deadly work.

Old Cotter was sitting at the fire, smoking, when I came downstairs to supper. While my aunt was ladling out my stirabout he said, as if returning to some former remark of his:

—No, I wouldn't say he was exactly . . . but there was something queer . . . there was something uncanny about him. I'll tell you my opinion. . . .

He began to puff at his pipe, no doubt arranging his opinion in his mind. Tiresome old fool! When we knew him first he used to be rather interesting, talking of faints and worms; but I soon grew tired of him and his endless stories about the distillery.

—I have my own theory about it, he said. I think it was one of those . . . peculiar cases. . . . But it's hard to say. . . .

He began to puff again at his pipe without giving us his theory. My uncle saw me staring and said to me:

—Well, so your old friend is gone, you'll be sorry to hear.

—Who? said I.

——Father Flynn.

——Is he dead?

——Mr Cotter here has just told us. He was passing by the house.

I knew that I was under observation so I continued eating as if the news had not interested me. My uncle explained to old Cotter.

——The youngster and he were great friends. The old chap taught him a great deal, mind you; and they say he had a great wish for him.

——God have mercy on his soul, said my aunt piously.

Old Cotter looked at me for a while. I felt that his little beady black eyes were examining me but I would not satisfy him by looking up from my plate. He returned to his pipe and finally spat rudely into the grate.

——I wouldn't like children of mine, he said, to have too much to say to a man like that.

——How do you mean, Mr Cotter? asked my aunt.

——What I mean is, said old Cotter, it's bad for children. My idea is: let a young lad run about and play with young lads of his own age and not be . . . Am I right, Jack?

——That's my principle, too, said my uncle. Let him learn to box his corner. That's what I'm always saying to that Rosicrucian there: take exercise. Why, when I was a nipper every morning of my life I had a cold bath, winter and summer. And that's what stands to me now. Education is all very fine and large. . . . Mr Cotter might take a pick of that leg of mutton, he added to my aunt.

——No, no, not for me, said old Cotter.

My aunt brought the dish from the safe and laid it on the table.

——But why do you think it's not good for children, Mr Cotter? she asked.

——It's bad for children, said old Cotter, because their minds are so impressionable. When children see things like that, you know, it has an effect. . . .

I crammed my mouth with stirabout for fear I might give utterance to my anger. Tiresome old red-nosed imbecile!

It was late when I fell asleep. Though I was angry with old Cotter for alluding to me as a child I puzzled my head to extract meaning from his unfinished sentences. In the dark of my room I imagined that I saw again the heavy grey face of the paralytic. I drew the blankets over my head and tried to think of Christmas. But the grey face still followed me. It murmured; and I understood that it desired to confess something. I felt my soul receding into some pleasant and vicious region; and there again I found it waiting for me. It began to confess to me in a murmuring voice and I wondered why it smiled continually and why the lips were so moist with spittle. But then I remembered that it had died of paralysis and I felt that I too was smiling feebly as if to absolve the simoniac of his sin.

The next morning after breakfast I went down to look at the little house in Great Britain Street. It was an unassuming shop, registered under the vague name of *Drapery*. The drapery consisted mainly of children's bootees and umbrellas; and on ordinary days a notice used to hang in the window, saying: *Umbrellas Re-covered*. No notice was visible now for the shutters were up. A crape bouquet was tied to the door-knocker with ribbon. Two poor women and a telegram boy were reading the card pinned on the crape. I also approached and read:

July 1st, 1895

The Rev. James Flynn (formerly of S. Catherine's Church,
Meath Street), aged sixty-five years.

R.I.P.

The reading of the card persuaded me that he was dead and I was disturbed to find myself at check. Had he not been dead I would have gone into the little dark room behind the shop to find him sitting in his arm-chair by the fire, nearly smothered in his great-coat. Perhaps my aunt would have given me a packet of High Toast for him and this present would have roused him from his stupefied doze. It was always I who emptied the packet into his black snuff-box for his hands trembled too much to allow him to do this without spilling half the snuff about the floor. Even as he raised his large trembling hand to his nose little clouds of smoke dribbled through his fingers over the front of his coat. It may have been these constant showers of snuff which gave his ancient priestly garments their green faded look for the red handkerchief, blackened, as it always was, with the snuff-stains of a week, with which he tried to brush away the fallen grains, was quite inefficacious.

I wished to go in and look at him but I had not the courage to knock. I walked away slowly along the sunny side of the street, reading all the theatrical advertisements in the shop-windows as I went. I found it strange that neither I nor the day seemed in a mourning mood and I felt even annoyed at discovering in myself a sensation of freedom as if I had been freed from something by his death. I wondered at this for, as my uncle had said the night before, he had taught me a great deal. He had studied in the Irish college in Rome and he had taught me to pronounce Latin properly. He had told me stories about the catacombs and about Napoleon Bonaparte, and he had explained to me the meaning of the different ceremonies of the Mass and of the different vestments worn by the priest. Sometimes he had amused himself by putting difficult questions to me, asking me what one should do in certain circumstances or whether such and such sins were mortal or venial or only imperfections. His questions showed me how complex and mysterious were certain institutions of the Church which I had always regarded as the simplest acts. The duties of the priest towards the Eucharist and towards the secrecy of the confessional seemed so grave to me that I wondered how anybody had ever found in himself the courage to undertake them; and I was not surprised when he told me that the fathers of the Church had written books as thick as the *Post Office Directory* and as closely printed as the law notices in the newspaper, elucidating all these intricate questions. Often when I thought of this I could make no answer or only a very foolish and halting one upon which he used to smile and nod his head twice or thrice. Sometimes he used to put me through the responses of the Mass which he had made me learn by heart; and, as I pattered, he used to smile pensively and nod his head, now and then pushing huge pinches of snuff up each nostril alternately. When he smiled he used to uncover his big discoloured teeth and let his tongue lie upon his lower lip— a habit which had made me feel uneasy in the beginning of our acquaintance before I knew him well.

As I walked along in the sun I remembered old Cotter's words and tried to remember what had happened afterwards in the dream. I remembered that I had noticed long velvet curtains and a swinging lamp of antique fashion. I felt that I had been very far away, in some land where the customs were strange—in Persia, I thought. . . . But I could not remember the end of the dream.

In the evening my aunt took me with her to visit the house of mourning. It was after sunset; but the window-panes of the houses that looked to the west reflected the tawny gold of a great bank of clouds. Nannie received us in the hall; and, as it would have been unseemly to have shouted at her, my aunt shook hands with her for all. The old woman pointed upwards interrogatively and, on my aunt's nodding, proceeded to toil up the narrow staircase before us, her bowed head being scarcely above the level of the banister-rail. At the first landing she stopped and beckoned us forward encouragingly towards the open door of the dead-room. My aunt went in and the old woman, seeing that I hesitated to enter, began to beckon to me again repeatedly with her hand.

I went in on tiptoe. The room through the lace end of the blind was suffused with dusky golden light amid which the candles looked like pale thin flames. He had been coffined. Nannie gave the lead and we three knelt down at the foot of the bed. I pretended to pray but I could not gather my thoughts because the old woman's mutterings distracted me. I noticed how clumsily her skirt was hooked at the back and how the heels of her cloth boots were trodden down all to one side. The fancy came to me that the old priest was smiling as he lay there in his coffin.

But no. When we rose and went up to the head of the bed I saw that he was not smiling. There he lay, solemn and copious, vested as for the altar, his large hands loosely retaining a chalice. His face was very truculent, grey and massive, with black cavernous nostrils and circled by a scanty white fur. There was a heavy odour in the room—the flowers.

We blessed ourselves and came away. In the little room downstairs we found Eliza seated in his arm-chair in state. I groped my way towards my usual chair in the corner while Nannie went to the sideboard and brought out a decanter of sherry and some wine-glasses. She set these on the table and invited us to take a little glass of wine. Then, at her sister's bidding, she poured out the sherry into the glasses and passed them to us. She pressed me to take some cream crackers also but I declined because I thought I would make too much noise eating them. She seemed to be somewhat disappointed at my refusal and went over quietly to the sofa where she sat down behind her sister. No one spoke: we all gazed at the empty fireplace.

My aunt waited until Eliza sighed and then said:

—Ah, well, he's gone to a better world.

Eliza sighed again and bowed her head in assent. My aunt fingered the stem of her wine-glass before sipping a little.

—Did he . . . peacefully? she asked.

—O, quite peacefully, ma'am, said Eliza. You couldn't tell when the breath went out of him. He had a beautiful death, God be praised.

—And everything . . . ?

—Father O'Rourke was in with him a Tuesday and anointed him and prepared him and all.

—He knew then?

—He was quite resigned.

—He looks quite resigned, said my aunt.

—That's what the woman we had in to wash him said. She said he just looked as if he was asleep, he looked that peaceful and resigned. No one would think he'd make such a beautiful corpse.

—Yes, indeed, said my aunt.

She sipped a little more from her glass and said:

—Well, Miss Flynn, at any rate it must be a great comfort for you to know that you did all you could for him. You were both very kind to him, I must say.

Eliza smoothed her dress over her knees.

—Ah, poor James! she said. God knows we done all we could, as poor as we are—we wouldn't see him want anything while he was in it.

Nannie had leaned her head against the sofa-pillow and seemed about to fall asleep.

—There's poor Nannie, said Eliza, looking at her, she's wore out. All the work we had, she and me, getting in the woman to wash him and then laying him out and then the coffin and then arranging about the Mass in the chapel. Only for Father O'Rourke I don't know what we'd have done at all. It was him brought us all them flowers and them two candlesticks out of the chapel and wrote out the notice for the *Freeman's General* and took charge of all the papers for the cemetery and poor James's insurance.

—Wasn't that good of him? said my aunt.

Eliza closed her eyes and shook her head slowly.

—Ah, there's no friends like the old friends, she said, when all is said and done, no friends that a body can trust.

—Indeed, that's true, said my aunt. And I'm sure now that he's gone to his eternal reward he won't forget you and all your kindness to him.

—Ah, poor James! said Eliza. He was no great trouble to us. You wouldn't hear him in the house any more than now. Still, I know he's gone and all to that. . . .

—It's when it's all over that you'll miss him, said my aunt.

—I know that, said Eliza. I won't be bringing him in his cup of beef-tea any more, nor you, ma'am, sending him his snuff. Ah, poor James!

She stopped, as if she were communing with the past and then said shrewdly:

—Mind you, I noticed there was something queer coming over him latterly. Whenever I'd bring in his soup to him I'd find him with his breviary fallen to the floor, lying back in the chair and his mouth open.

She laid a finger against her nose and frowned: then she continued:

—But still and all he kept on saying that before the summer was over he'd go out for a drive one fine day just to see the old house again where we were all born down in Irishtown and take me and Nannie with him. If we could only get one of them new-fangled carriages that makes no noise that Father O'Rourke told him about—them with the rheumatic wheels—for the day cheap, he said, at Johnny Rush's over the way there and drive out the three of us together of a Sunday evening. He had his mind set on that. . . . Poor James!

—The Lord have mercy on his soul! said my aunt.

Eliza took out her handkerchief and wiped her eyes with it. Then she put it back again in her pocket and gazed into the empty grate for some time without speaking.

—He was too scrupulous always, she said. The duties of the priesthood was too much for him. And then his life was, you might say, crossed.

—Yes, said my aunt. He was a disappointed man. You could see that.

A silence took possession of the little room and, under cover of it, I approached the table and tasted my sherry and then returned quietly to my chair in the corner. Eliza seemed to have fallen into a deep revery. We waited respectfully for her to break the silence: and after a long pause she said slowly:

—It was that chalice he broke. . . . That was the beginning of it. Of course, they say it was all right, that it contained nothing, I mean. But still. . . . They say it was the boy's fault. But poor James was so nervous, God be merciful to him!

—And was that it? said my aunt. I heard something. . . .

Eliza nodded.

—That affected his mind, she said. After that he began to mope by himself, talking to no one and wandering about by himself. So one night he was wanted for to go on a call and they couldn't find him anywhere. They looked high up and low down; and still they couldn't see a sight of him anywhere. So then the clerk suggested to try the chapel. So then they got the keys and opened the chapel and the clerk and Father O'Rourke and another priest that was there brought in a light for to look for him. . . . And what do you think but there he was, sitting up by himself in the dark in his confession-box, wide-awake and laughing-like softly to himself?

She stopped suddenly as if to listen. I too listened; but there was no sound in the house: and I knew that the old priest was lying still in his coffin as we had seen him, solemn and truculent in death, an idle chalice on his breast.

Eliza resumed:

—Wide-awake and laughing-like to himself. . . . So then, of course, when they saw that, that made them think that there was something gone wrong with him. . . .

RE-VISIONS:
REAPPROPRIATIONS

RE-VISIONS:
REAPPROPRIATIONS

At the heart of ancient myths, legends, tales are archetypes that are both time-less and susceptible to ever-new interpretations. This is the secret of their en-durance through the centuries.

Sometimes, we "create" fictions that adumbrate preexisting, timeless fic-tions without knowing what we do. Often in our dreams the impersonal shape of an archetype pushes through the personal, intimate material of the dream. There is an "I" that is an adventurer bold as Odysseus, night following night.

The very choice of an ancient myth to "re-vision" will tell us something revealing about ourselves. Which, among so many, is *your* myth?

Contemporary "re-visionings" of older texts are likely, for obvious rea-sons, to be feminist. Women writers have long known that myths, fairy tales, legends—indeed, history itself—have been the province of men; in contem-porary times, classic texts have been deconstructed, or dissected, and reimag-ined from radically different perspectives. Alicia Ostriker's playfully serious, or seriously playful, prose poem "The Cave" is part of her reinterpretation of the Hebrew Bible from the perspective of a late-twentieth-century Jewish woman (daughter, wife, mother), *The Nakedness of the Fathers: Biblical Visions and Revisions.* (See also Ostriker's significantly titled *Stealing the Language: The Emergence of Women's Poetry in America.*) In another era, in another culture, such writing would be considered blasphemous. Angela Carter's re-visioning of the traditional tale "Little Red-Cap" is shocking, almost obscene in its depiction of female violation and betrayal by females. Anne Sexton's re-visioning of "Lit-tle Snow-White" from her collection *Transformations* is disturbingly ironic, rich with metaphorical language and, in its denouement, jarring in a way that the original fairy tale—with its childlike simplicity and primitive sense of jus-tice—is not. "Beauty is a simple passion," Sexton warns, "but, oh my friends, in the end / you will dance the fire dance in iron shoes."

C. K. Williams's characteristically brooding poem on "Hercules, Deianira, Nessus" is as much about the problematic act of comprehending "in our age of scrutiny and dissection" as it is about the bizarre violence of Hercules' fate in that long-ago ancient world of "metamorphoses" described by Ovid. Harlan Ellison's poetic fantasy upon the survival of Icarus dares to refute its Ovidian source, locating "Icarus" as a yearning impulse in us all. (See also Robert Taylor, Jr.'s "Mourning" in part VIII of this anthology, a balladlike story based on the life of the American desperado of the 1880s, Jesse James.)

Biblical texts, sacred myths, fairy tales, legends, ballads, folktales: these constitute a rich legacy for imaginative re-visioning in our time. By appropriating an archetype of the past, the contemporary writer "makes it new" in his or her unique terms.

GENESIS 19

And there came two angels to Sodom at even; and Lot sat in the gate of Sodom: and Lot seeing them rose up to meet them; and he bowed himself with his face toward the ground;

2 And he said, Behold now, my lords, turn in, I pray you, into your servant's house, and tarry all night, and wash your feet, and ye shall rise up early, and go on your ways. And they said, Nay; but we will abide in the street all night.

3 And he pressed upon them greatly; and they turned in unto him, and entered into his house; and he made them a feast, and did bake unleavened bread, and they did eat.

4 But before they lay down, the men of the city, even the men of Sodom, compassed the house round, both old and young, all the people from every quarter:

5 And they called unto Lot, and said unto him, Where are the men which came in to thee this night? bring them out unto us, that we may know them.

6 And Lot went out at the door unto them, and shut the door after him,

7 And said, I pray you, brethren, do not so wickedly.

8 Behold now, I have two daughters which have not known man; let me, I pray you, bring them out unto you, and do ye to them as is good in your eyes: only unto these men do nothing; for therefore came they under the shadow of my roof.

9 And they said, Stand back. And they said again, This one fellow came in to sojourn, and he will needs be a judge: now will we deal worse with thee, than with them. And they pressed sore upon the man, even Lot, and came near to break the door.

10 But the men put forth their hand, and pulled Lot into the house to them, and shut to the door.

11 And they smote the men that were at the door of the house with blindness, both small and great: so that they wearied themselves to find the door.

12 And the men said unto Lot, Hast thou here any besides? son in law, and thy sons, and thy daughters, and whatsoever thou hast in the city, bring them out of this place:

13 For we will destroy this place, because the cry of them is waxen great before the face of the LORD; and the LORD hath sent us to destroy it.

14 And Lot went out, and spake unto his sons in law, which married his daughters, and said, Up, get you out of this place; for the LORD will destroy this city. But he seemed as one that mocked unto his sons in law.

15 And when the morning arose, then the angels hastened Lot, saying, Arise, take thy wife, and thy two daughters, which are here; lest thou be consumed in the iniquity of the city.

16 And while he lingered, the men laid hold upon his hand, and upon the hand of his wife, and upon the hand of his two daughters; the LORD being merciful unto him; and they brought him forth, and set him without the city.

17 And it came to pass, when they had brought them forth abroad, that he said, Escape for thy life; look not behind thee, neither stay thou in all the plain; escape to the mountain, lest thou be consumed.

18 And Lot said unto them, Oh, not so, my Lord:

19 Behold now, thy servant hath found grace in thy sight, and thou hast magnified thy mercy, which thou hast shewed unto me in saving my life; and I cannot escape to the mountain, lest some evil take me, and I die:

20 Behold now, this city is near to flee unto, and it is a little one: Oh, let me escape thither, (is it not a little one?) and my soul shall live.

21 And he said unto him, See, I have accepted thee concerning this thing also, that I will not overthrow this city, for the which thou hast spoken.

22 Haste thee, escape thither; for I cannot do any thing till thou be come thither. Therefore the name of the city was called Zō-̈är.

23 The sun was risen upon the earth when Lot entered into Zō-̈är.

24 Then the LORD rained upon Sodom and upon Gō-mŏr′-răh brimstone and fire from the LORD out of heaven;

25 And he overthrew those cities, and all the plain, and all the inhabitants of the cities, and that which grew upon the ground.

26 But his wife looked back from behind him, and she became a pillar of salt.

27 And Abraham gat up early in the morning to the place where he stood before the LORD:

28 And he looked toward Sodom and Gō-mŏr′-răh, and toward all the land of the plain, and beheld, and, lo, the smoke of the country went up as the smoke of a furnace.

29 And it came to pass, when God destroyed the cities of the plain, that God remembered Abraham, and sent Lot out of the midst of the overthrow, when he overthrew the cities in the which Lot dwelt.

30 And Lot went up out of Zŏ-är, and dwelt in the mountain, and his two daughters with him; for he feared to dwell in Zŏ-är: and he dwelt in a cave, he and his two daughters.

31 And the firstborn said unto the younger, Our father is old, and there is not a man in the earth to come in unto us after the manner of all the earth:

32 Come, let us make our father drink wine, and we will lie with him, that we may preserve seed of our father.

33 And they made their father drink wine that night: and the firstborn went in, and lay with her father; and he perceived not when she lay down, nor when she arose.

34 And it came to pass on the morrow, that the firstborn said unto the younger, Behold, I lay yesternight with my father: let us make him drink wine this night also; and go thou in, and lie with him, that we may preserve seed of our father.

35 And they made their father drink wine that night also: and the younger arose, and lay with him; and he perceived not when she lay down, nor when she arose.

36 Thus were both the daughters of Lot with child by their father.

37 And the firstborn bare a son, and called his name Moab: the same is the father of the Moabites unto this day.

38 And the younger, she also bare a son, and called his name Bĕn-ăm-mī: the same is the father of the children of Ammon unto this day.

King James translation

THE CAVE

> *Come, let us make our father drink wine,*
> *and we will lie with him, that we may*
> *preserve the seed of the father.*
> GENESIS 19:32

> *Cave girl mama*
> *Don't you go down on me.*
> *Oh cave girl mama*
> *Don't you go down on me.*
> *Take your pretty legs and your tangled hair*
> *Away and just leave me be.*

What is a cave, and how deep must it go, they must have wondered. The girls, they were really women, the daughters, the daughters of their father. They had never known a man. You remember the daughters. The first important ones. Daughters of Lot, nieces of Abraham, temporary inhabitants of Sodom, a city of the plain which is no longer in existence. They themselves had not looked back, unlike their mother. Unlike, unlike. Unlike who? Long afterward they might have hung on a ledge, peering, back there, at the widths of the flat landscape, so difficult really to discern anything, a mineral formation, back there, a mineral formation in the middle of what was flat and burnt-out, really, standing up it could have been white and salty, it could have been shaped like a pillar, only it was difficult, really, to see anything.

The hawks, they spiral. I wish I could be like them. Blindingly cruel, the floating, on the airdrafts, far below one's feet, gradually ascending until you can distinguish the feathers at the wing-ends dipping, lightly, to steer them. Now time goes by, I'm hypnotized by the breeze. And then when they drop, it is just like a thunderbolt, the talons come out, the beak widens, it is over in a minute. The killing is over in a minute, a swift crunch, a swallow, and the gliding begins again, the volumes of space, the shadowy cliffs, the hypnosis.

A holocaust is unlike this. Unlike, unlike. For example, it takes much longer. It is much louder. It stinks worse. It is much more redness. Far, far more redness. (How do the girls know, if they don't see it? If they obey and don't look back? They still know. How could they fail to know. Perhaps they know by the heat, perhaps by the roar. For everyone has heard a fire roaring, and felt the terrifying heat when you come too close, that whips at your back even when you are running away, until you are finally to freshness). While you are running away it is going on, on, on.

Afterward the smoke of the country goes up like smoke from a furnace.

A cave mouth. You go inside the mouth, it becomes cool, it can be comfortable, it can be home. Deep in, here you are, fix it up, girls. You have to be hiding. You have to keep on hiding here. But why?

They were wicked people. But is it true that the girls can never go back, can never in fact leave these cliffs where they are hiding out, and this cave here? The cities were all full of wicked people, so the girls must not (they do not) remember the girls who used to be their friends, or the mothers of those girls. They must not (do not) think about their clothing, their jewelry, or their makeup. Bad girls. Bad mothers. Now they are cinders.

Innocence means: we have never known a man. Father says: we are good girls. He tries to pet our heads but his hand slides over the fronts of our faces. It is like having a blind person touch you. He cries all of the time. It is disgusting.

Innocence means: we do not remember the night the two men were staying at our house, the night the drunken crowd was roaring outside our door (we used to see them in daytime, our girlfriends' fathers, brothers, and uncles) banging at the windows (wanting to fuck our visitors), the night our father took us by the elbows and tried to push us outside the door instead. He thought we might be a substitute, and yelled through the door that they should do whatever they wanted with us. He was pulling one way, we were pulling the other, screaming our heads off. Our mother was screaming, hitting him, trying to get his face with her nails. Innocence means we do not remember our mother.

Here we are in the cave. Cool and nice, cool and safe. Some of the rocks look like dragons and some like camels, we eat over here and we sleep over here, using skins. But he cries all of the time and it is disgusting. Tears and snot and dribble mingling on his face. We ask him about husbands. Where is he going to find us husbands, because we have to have children. But he dribbles and bawls, and it is really disgusting. Also he gets drunk every night.

It is easy to get him drunk.

Now it is easy, when he is drunk and asleep. We are giggling for days beforehand. You go first. No, you.

Oily, I've used the fat of a wildcat I skinned. Candle steady, shadows on his nipples he's sound asleep, I can look him over head to knees. Unlike, unlike. Unlike ourselves, less soft but more meaty. I circle the dove brown aureoles with my index finger, skim lightly by the hairs until the nipples harden like snaps. I use my tongue tip and, very carefully, my teeth. I crouch until my breasts flap against his face like hot towels. The air grows denser and the room heats from the single candle's brilliant orange cone, edged gold, diffused to smoke lifted like a string. His red body resembles clay which invites the fingers to burrow in. I pursue the rivulets of his fur down the center, downstream, I make it wet and greasy, I make it shine. Now here is his baby thing, a sleepy puppy. Now here we go, a dog sitting up begging. Oh my mama I'm happy filling up my mouth with figs, another breast, the blissful childhood I can't remember. And slip now and slide. Mama, no giggling. A gush of blood, but it feels good. God, it feels finally good.

First me then her. Tomorrow her then me.

Do you guess he was only pretending to be asleep, on the ledge, the skins, the leaves, in the warm room in the cave.

▪ ▪ ▪

> Cave Girl Mama
> Go put your red dress on
> Yeah Cave Girl Mama
> Go put your red dress on
> Put some lipstick on your mouth and we'll
> Cakewalk into town.

Ovid

THE STORY OF HERCULES, NESSUS, AND DEIANIRA

from *Metamorphoses*, Book 9

But the Centaur Nessus burned for Deianira
As if an arrow had pierced him. Hercules
Was coming home with his bride, and reached the river,
Evenus, swollen to flood with the rains of winter,
Too dangerous to cross, with its whirling eddies.
It was not for himself that Hercules was worried,
But what of Deianira? At this point Nessus
Came stalking up; he knew the fords, he told them:
"You swim it, Hercules; I'll carry her over!"
So Hercules entrusted her to Nessus,
And she was pale and trembling, afraid of the river,
Afraid of Nessus, but Hercules, undaunted,
Threw club and bow across the stream, but wearing
The lion-skin and quiver, faced the river
Knowing that he must finish what he started,
And had no hesitation, did not even
Look for the smoothest current, scorning favors
From any river. So he reached the bank,
Was picking up his bow, and heard his bride
Calling for help: Nessus was full of evil.
"So," Hercules cried, "this double-bodied monster
Has so much pride of strength and swiftness in him
He turns to violence. Now hear me, Nessus!
Let things of mine alone! The wheel your father
Rides in eternal Hell should be warning
Against forbidden loves. You will not escape me,
No matter how much you trust your vaunted horse-power!"

I will catch up with you, if not by running,
By deeds, by wounds." And as he spoke, he proved it:
The arrow pierced the back, came out at the shoulder,
So two wounds bled, and the blood had poison in it
For the barb was dipped in the venom of the serpent,
And Nessus wrenched it loose. "I shall not die,"
He thought, "Without revenge," and gave his robe,
Dyed in warm crimson, as a gift to her,
The girl he would have ravished, as a token,
To help to make her love him.

                       Time went by
And Hercules' great deeds, and Juno's hatred
Spread over all the world. He was returning
Victorious from Oechalia, making ready
To pay his vows to Jove, when Rumor, lover
Of truth and falsehood both, the tattletale
Who makes big things of little ones, comes rushing
To Deianira, and her story has it
That Hercules burns with passion for Iole.
She loves him, she believes it, she is frightened,
Gives way, at first, to tears, pities herself,
Makes her grief grow by weeping, and recovers
A little, thinking: "What's the good of weeping?
Tears would delight my rival, and she is coming,
Is on her way: what I had better do
Is hurry, figure out something, while I can,
Before she is in my bed. Shall I complain,
Shall I keep silent? Shall I go again
To Calydon, or linger here? Shall I
Forsake this house, or keep her out? I might
Remember Meleager was my brother,
Might plan some desperate deed, murder my rival
To show her what a woman in grief and outrage
Can do by way of vengeance." So her mind
Wavers in all directions, but at last
She thinks it best to send the robe of Nessus,
Dyed with his blood, *to help to make her love him,*
To send this on to Hercules. Not knowing
What she is giving, the cause of her own sorrow,
She hands it over to Lichas, unsuspecting,
And with most gentle words bids him deliver

The robe to Hercules, and the hero takes it
Throwing it over his shoulder, Lerna's poison.
He was offering incense on the rising flames,
Praying and pouring wine on the marble altar,
And the warmth brought out the virulence of the garment,
Whose molten deadliness spread over his limbs,
And, while he could, his usual fortitude
Kept back his groans, but even his endurance
Could not hold out forever, and in his madness
He knocked the altars down, filled woody Oeta
With horrible cries, tried to tear off the robe,
And where he tore it, there it tore the skin,
Or, where it could not be torn, clung to the limbs,
Or burned to the naked muscles and great bones.
And the blood hissed, as white-hot metal does
Dipped in cold water, and the mixture boiled,
Poison and blood together, the hungry fever
Eating his very marrow, and the tendons,
Half-burnt, made cracking sounds, and livid sweat
Poured from all over his body. He raised his hands:
"Gloat on my suffering, gloat, O cruel Juno,
Sate that relentless heart, watching me burn!
Or if an enemy—and I am yours,
That much is certain—could find some reason
For pity, take away this life of mine,
Sick from its torture, hateful, born for anguish.
Stepmother, I ask a favor: give me death!
Was it for this that I subdued Busiris
Who fouled the temples of the gods with blood
Of strangers slain? Was it for this I lifted
Antaeus from supporting earth, for this
Slew Geryon, dragged off Cerberus? My hands
Seized the bull's horns, and Elis was the gainer
With the Parthenian groves, Stymphalian waters.
My hands brought back the golden belt, my hands
The golden apples from the sleepless dragon.
Centaurs could not resist me, nor the boar
That ravaged Arcady. I slew the Hydra
That gained by its own loss, and little good
That did the monster! And the Thracian horses,
Fed fat on human blood, the mangers filled

With human bodies, I found, and when I found them
Tore them to pieces. These were the hands that choked
The lion of Nemea, these the shoulders
That held the weight of the world, one time, for Atlas.
Juno grew tired of giving orders; I
Was never tired obeying them. But now
A new doom comes upon me, one I cannot
Fight off by arms or courage, and the fire
Devours my lungs, and feeds on all my members.
But still Eurystheus keeps his health: who is there
To think that gods exist?" So, racked with pain,
He wandered over Oeta, as a tiger
Drags off the spears that wounded him, when the hunter
Has fled in fear. There you could see him groaning,
Gnashing his teeth, still tearing at the garment,
Leveling trees, raging against the mountains,
Or holding out his hands to his father's Heaven.
Then he saw Lichas, trembling, lying hidden
Under the hollow of a rock, and pain
Roused all his fury: "You were the one who did it,
You, Lichas, brought me death!" And Lichas shuddered,
Turned pale, tried to say something, came to his knees
In supplication, and found himself raised high,
Whirled through the air, three times, four times, flung far
Toward the Euboean waters, as a stone
Flies from a catapult, and high in the air,
In the cold wind, he felt his body stiffen
As showers in cold wind are turned to snow
And snow to sleet and sleet to hail, so Lichas
Hurled through the air by Hercules, grew colder,
The blood, by fear, made rigid, and the body
All stone and hardness. To this very day
Euboean sailors show the traveler
A low rock rising, as if with human features,
Out of the water, and they call it Lichas,
And will not step there; they are never sure
It would not feel their tread, and be offended.

And Hercules cut down trees from lofty Oeta
To make himself a funeral pyre, and called
On Poeas' son to take the bow, the quiver,

The arrows that would visit Troy again,
And Philoctetes had the fire made ready
Under the barrow, and as the flames went roaring
Above, around, Hercules spread as quilt
The lion's skin, and used his club as pillow,
And lay there, no more troubled than a feaster
At a great banquet, garland-crowned, among
The brimming cups of wine. And the flame grew stronger,
Spread, sought the care-free limbs of its despiser,
And the gods were troubled for earth's champion
As Jove, with joyful voice addressed them: "Gods,
This fear of yours is my delight; my heart
Rejoices that the people I rule and father
Is grateful, that your favor guards my son.
He has earned that favor by his deeds, but I
Am under obligation for that favor.
Let not your hearts be troubled; Oeta's flames
Are nothing, and the conqueror will conquer
These also. Only his mother's heritage,
His mortal part, will feel the fire; that part
Which comes from me, no flames will ever master,
It will live always, safe from death and burning,
And I shall take it to the shores of Heaven
When it is done with earth, and you, I trust,
Will, all of you, approve. If anyone
Should grieve that Hercules becomes a god,
Should be unwilling that he have this honor,
Well, let him grieve, and let him grant, and let him,
Even against his will, own it was proper."
The gods agreed, and even royal Juno
Looked willing enough, only a little sullen
At Jove's last words, aimed, as she knew, at her,
And meanwhile anything that fire could conquer
Was conquered: there was nothing left, a form,
A shape, not to be recognized, of Hercules,
With nothing human about it, only spirit,
The proof of Jove, shining, the way a serpent
Shines with the old skin cast, when the new life glistens.
So Hercules put off the mortal body,
Thriving, and in his better part becoming greater,
More worthy of veneration, and Jove raised him

Through hollow clouds to the bright stars, a rider
In the chariot drawn by the four heavenly horses.
And Atlas, who bears Heaven on his shoulders,
Felt the new weight, and Sthenelus' son, Eurystheus,
Held to his ancient grudge at Hercules,
And, troubled with long suffering for her son,
Alcmena had one comforter, Iole,
To whom to tell her sorrows, an old woman
Proud of the world-wide glory of her son,
Unhappy in her misfortunes.

Translated by Rolfe Humphries

C. K. Williams

HERCULES, DEIANIRA, NESSUS

There was absolutely no reason after the centaur had pawed her and tried to
    mount her,
after Hercules waiting across the raging river for the creature to carry her to
    him
heard her cry out and launched an arrow soaked in the Hydra's incurable
    venom into the monster,
that Deianira should have believed him, Nessus, horrible thing, as he died,
    but she did.

We see the end of the story: Deianira anguished, aghast, suicide-sword in her
    hand;
Hercules's blood hissing and seething like water into which molten rods are
    plunged to anneal,
but how could a just-married girl hardly out of her father's house have envi-
    sioned all that,
and even conjecturing that Nessus was lying, plotting revenge, how could she
    have been sure?

We see the centaur as cunning, malignant, a hybrid from the savage time be-
    fore ours
when emotion always was passion and passion was always unchecked by com-
    mandment or conscience;
she sees only a man-horse, mortally hurt, suddenly harmless, eyes suddenly
    soft as a foal's,
telling her, "Don't be afraid, come closer, listen": offering homage, friendship,
    a favor.

In our age of scrutiny and dissection we know Deianira's mind better than
she does herself:
we know the fortune of women as chattel and quarry, objects to be won then
shunted aside;
we understand the cost of repression, the repercussions of unsatisfied rage
and resentment,
but consciousness then was still new, Deianira inhabited hers like the light from
a fire.

Or might she have glimpsed with that mantic prescience the gods hadn't
taken away yet
her hero a lifetime later on the way home with another king's daughter, callow, but lovely,
lovely enough to erase from Hercules's scruples not only his vows but the simple convention
that tells you you don't bring a rival into your aging wife's weary, sorrowful
bed?

. . . No, more likely the centaur's promise intrigued in itself: an infallible po-
tion of love.
"Just gather the clots of blood from my wound: here, use my shirt, then hide
it away.
Though so exalted, so regal a woman as you never would need it, it might
still be of use:
whoever's shoulders it touches, no matter when, will helplessly, hopelessly
love you forever."

See Hercules now, in the shirt Deianira has sent him, approaching the fire of
an altar,
the garment suddenly clinging, the Hydra, his long-vanquished foe, alive in
its threads,
each thread a tentacle clutching at him, each chemical tentacle acid, adher-
ing, consuming,
charring before his horrified eyes skin from muscle, muscle from tendon, tendon from bone.

Now Deianira, back then, the viscous gouts of Nessus's blood dyeing her dif-
fident hands:
if she could imagine us watching her there in her myth, how would she want
us to see her?

Surely as symbol, a petal of sympathy caught in the perilous rift between culture and chaos,
not as the nightmare she is, a corpse with a slash of tardy self-knowledge deep
  in its side.

What Hercules sees as he pounds up the bank isn't himself cremated alive on
  his pyre,
shrieking as Jove his Olympian father extracts his immortal essence from its
  agonized sheath:
he sees what's before him: the woman, his bride, kneeling to the dark, rushing river,
obsessively scrubbing away, he must think, the nocuous, mingled reek of
  horse, Hydra, human.

THE STORY OF
DAEDALUS AND ICARUS

from *Metamorphoses*, Book 8

Homesick for homeland, Daedalus hated Crete
And his long exile there, but the sea held him.
"Though Minos blocks escape by land or water,"
Daedalus said, "surely the sky is open,
And that's the way we'll go. Minos' dominion
Does not include the air." He turned his thinking
Toward unknown arts, changing the laws of nature.
He laid out feathers in order, first the smallest,
A little larger next it, and so continued,
The way that pan-pipes rise in gradual sequence.
He fastened them with twine and wax, at middle,
At bottom, so, and bent them, gently curving,
So that they looked like wings of birds, most surely.
And Icarus, his son, stood by and watched him,
Not knowing he was dealing with his downfall,
Stood by and watched, and raised his shiny face
To let a feather, light as down, fall on it,
Or stuck his thumb into the yellow wax,
Fooling around, the way a boy will, always,
Whenever a father tries to get some work done.
Still, it was done at last, and the father hovered,
Poised, in the moving air, and taught his son:
"I warn you, Icarus, fly a middle course:
Don't go too low, or water will weigh the wings down;
Don't go too high, or the sun's fire will burn them.
Keep to the middle way. And one more thing,
No fancy steering by star or constellation,

Follow my lead!" That was the flying lesson,
And now to fit the wings to the boy's shoulders.
Between the work and warning the father found
His cheeks were wet with tears, and his hands trembled.
He kissed his son (*Good-bye,* if he had known it),
Rose on his wings, flew on ahead, as fearful
As any bird launching the little nestlings
Out of high nest into thin air. *Keep on,*
Keep on, he signals, *follow me!* He guides him
In flight—O fatal art!—and the wings move
And the father looks back to see the son's wings moving.
Far off, far down, some fisherman is watching
As the rod dips and trembles over the water,
Some shepherd rests his weight upon his crook,
Some ploughman on the handles of the ploughshare,
And all look up, in absolute amazement,
At those air-borne above. They must be gods!
They were over Samos, Juno's sacred island,
Delos and Paros toward the left, Lebinthus
Visible to the right, and another island,
Calymne, rich in honey. And the boy
Thought *This is wonderful!* and left his father,
Soared higher, higher, drawn to the vast heaven,
Nearer the sun, and the wax that held the wings
Melted in that fierce heat, and the bare arms
Beat up and down in air, and lacking oarage
Took hold of nothing. *Father!* he cried, and *Father!*
Until the blue sea hushed him, the dark water
Men call the Icarian now. And Daedalus,
Father no more, called "Icarus, where are you!
Where are you, Icarus? Tell me where to find you!"
And saw the wings on the waves, and cursed his talents,
Buried the body in a tomb, and the land
Was named for Icarus.
                    During the burial
A noisy partridge, from a muddy ditch,
Looked out, drummed with her wings in loud approval.
No other bird, those days, was like the partridge,
Newcomer to the ranks of birds; the story
Reflects no credit on Daedalus. His sister,
Ignorant of the fates, had sent her son

To Daedalus as apprentice, only a youngster,
Hardly much more than twelve years old, but clever,
With an inventive turn of mind. For instance,
Studying a fish's backbone for a model,
He had notched a row of teeth in a strip of iron,
Thus making the first saw, and he had bound
Two arms of iron together with a joint
To keep them both together and apart,
One standing still, the other traversing
In a circle, so men came to have the compass.
And Daedalus, in envy, hurled the boy
Headlong from the high temple of Minerva,
And lied about it, saying he had fallen
Through accident, but Minerva, kind protectress
Of all inventive wits, stayed him in air,
Clothed him with plumage; he still retained his aptness
In feet and wings, and kept his old name, Perdix,
But in the new bird-form, Perdix, the partridge,
Never flies high, nor nests in trees, but flutters
Close to the ground, and the eggs are laid in hedgerows.
The bird, it seems, remembers, and is fearful
Of all high places.

Translated by Rolfe Humphries

FEVER

Icarus did not die in the fall.

What his father, Daedalus, never saw was this:

Icarus fell toward the Aegean Sea; fell through clouds; through billows and canopies and flotillas of clouds; and was lost to the sight of his father. The wings melted and fell away. They were carried on the stratospheric currents, miles away from the drop point at which Icarus had vanished through the cloud foam. When Daedalus banked and swooped and did his air-search, he found the pinions floating in the Sea. But he did not find his son, because Icarus had come down miles away.

In a wagon filled with sheep's wool.

But even from that height, even falling that distance, even though he had blacked out with fear and the air wrenched from his throat . . . the impact was enormous. And Icarus broke both legs. And Icarus slipped an intervertebral disk. And Icarus went into total systemic shock. And Icarus had his memory smashed out of him.

When he awoke in the hospital, he could not tell his name, could not relate the facts of his accident, could not offer a clue as to where he had come from, who he was, what he did for a living. He was *tabula rasa*.

He was taken in by a kindly family; and they raised him as their own son. The family was poor, but honest. Traditionally, they were vineyard hands and Certified Public Accountants during the months of October through April.

After many years, Icarus left home and immigrated to Switzerland, where the need for vintners and notaries and young men who never seemed to age was limitless.

He settled in Berne. Where he works to this day. Frugal, fair-haired, unmarried, and neat, he shares his two-room flat with a small gray dog, and gets nine hours sleep every night. And dreams of the sky.

Every morning he washes the fever sweat from his body.

And sees unfamiliar faces in the clouds.

LITTLE RED-CAP

Once upon a time there was a dear little girl who was loved by every one who looked at her, but most of all by her grandmother, and there was nothing that she would not have given to the child. Once she gave her a little cap of red velvet, which suited her so well that she would never wear anything else; so she was always called 'Little Red-Cap.'

One day her mother said to her: "Come, Little Red-Cap, here is a piece of cake and a bottle of wine; take them to your grandmother, she is ill and weak, and they will do her good. Set out before it gets hot, and when you are going, walk nicely and quietly and do not run off the path, or you may fall and break the bottle, and then your grandmother will get nothing; and when you go into her room, don't forget to say, 'Good-morning,' and don't peep into every corner before you do it."

"I will take great care," said Little Red-Cap to her mother, and gave her hand on it.

The grandmother lived out in the wood, half a league from the village, and just as Little Red-Cap entered the wood, a wolf met her. Red-Cap did not know what a wicked creature he was, and was not at all afraid of him.

"Good-day, Little Red-Cap," said he.

"Thank you kindly, wolf."

"Whither away so early, Little Red-Cap?"

"To my grandmother's."

"What have you got in your apron?"

"Cake and wine; yesterday was baking-day, so poor sick grandmother is to have something good, to make her stronger."

"Where does your grandmother live, Little Red-Cap?"

"A good quarter of a league farther on in the wood; her house stands under the three large oak-trees, the nut-trees are just below; you surely must know it," replied Little Red-Cap.

The wolf thought to himself: "What a tender young creature! what a nice plump mouthful—she will be better to eat than the old woman. I must act craftily, so as to catch both." So he walked for a short time by the side of Little Red-Cap, and then he said: "See, Little Red-Cap, how pretty the flowers are about here—why do you not look round? I believe, too, that you do not hear how sweetly the little birds are singing; you walk gravely along as if you were going to school, while everything else out here in the wood is merry."

Little Red-Cap raised her eyes, and when she saw the sunbeams dancing here and there through the trees, and pretty flowers growing everywhere, she thought: "Suppose I take grandmother a fresh nosegay; that would please her too. It is so early in the day that I shall still get there in good time"; and so she ran from the path into the wood to look for flowers. And whenever she had picked one, she fancied that she saw a still prettier one farther on, and ran after it, and so got deeper and deeper into the wood.

Meanwhile the wolf ran straight to the grandmother's house and knocked at the door.

"Who is there?"

"Little Red-Cap," replied the wolf. "She is bringing cake and wine; open the door."

"Lift the latch," called out the grandmother, "I am too weak, and cannot get up."

The wolf lifted the latch, the door sprang open, and without saying a word he went straight to the grandmother's bed, and devoured her. Then he put on her clothes, dressed himself in her cap, laid himself in bed and drew the curtains.

Little Red-Cap, however, had been running about picking flowers, and when she had gathered so many that she could carry no more, she remembered her grandmother, and set out on the way to her.

She was surprised to find the cottage-door standing open, and when she went into the room, she had such a strange feeling that she said to herself: "Oh dear! how uneasy I feel to-day, and at other times I like being with grandmother so much." She called out: "Good morning," but received no answer; so she went to the bed and drew back the curtains. There lay her grandmother with her cap pulled far over her face, and looking very strange.

"Oh! grandmother," she said, "what big ears you have!"

"The better to hear you with, my child," was the reply.

"But, grandmother, what big eyes you have!" she said.

"The better to see you with, my dear."

"But, grandmother, what large hands you have!"

"The better to hug you with."

"Oh! but, grandmother, what a terrible big mouth you have!"

"The better to eat you with!"

And scarcely had the wolf said this, than with one bound he was out of bed and swallowed up Red-Cap.

When the wolf had appeased his appetite, he lay down again in the bed, fell asleep and began to snore very loud. The huntsman was just passing the house, and thought to himself: "How the old woman is snoring! I must just see if she wants anything." So he went into the room, and when he came to the bed, he saw that the wolf was lying in it. "Do I find you here, you old sinner!" said he. "I have long sought you!" Then just as he was going to fire at him, it occurred to him that the wolf might have devoured the grandmother, and that she might still be saved, so he did not fire, but took a pair of scissors, and began to cut open the stomach of the sleeping wolf. When he had made two snips, he saw the little Red-Cap shining, and then he made two snips more, and the little girl sprang out, crying: "Ah, how frightened I have been! How dark it was inside the wolf"; and after that the aged grandmother came out alive also, but scarcely able to breathe. Red-Cap, however, quickly fetched great stones with which they filled the wolf's belly, and when he awoke, he wanted to run away, but the stones were so heavy that he collapsed at once, and fell dead.

Then all three were delighted. The huntsman drew off the wolf's skin and went home with it; the grandmother ate the cake and drank the wine which Red-Cap had brought, and revived, but Red-Cap thought to herself: "As long as I live, I will never by myself leave the path, to run into the wood, when my mother has forbidden me to do so."

Translated by Margaret Hunt, revised and completed by James Stern

THE WEREWOLF

It is a northern country; they have cold weather, they have cold hearts.

Cold; tempest; wild beasts in the forest. It is a hard life. Their houses are built of logs, dark and smoky within. There will be a crude icon of the virgin behind a guttering candle, the leg of a pig hung up to cure, a string of drying mushrooms. A bed, a stool, a table. Harsh, brief, poor lives.

To these upland woodsmen, the Devil is as real as you or I. More so; they have not seen us nor even know that we exist, but the Devil they glimpse often in the graveyards, those bleak and touching townships of the dead where the graves are marked with portraits of the deceased in the naïf style and there are no flowers to put in front of them, no flowers grow there, so they put out small, votive offerings, little loaves, sometimes a cake that the bears come lumbering from the margins of the forest to snatch away. At midnight especially on Walpurgisnacht, the Devil holds picnics in the graveyards and invites the witches; then they dig up fresh corpses, and eat them. Anyone will tell you that.

Wreaths of garlic on the doors keep out the vampires. A blue-eyed child born feet first on the night of St John's Eve will have second sight. When they discover a witch—some old woman whose cheeses ripen when her neighbour's do not, another old woman whose black cat, oh, sinister! *follows her about all the time,* they strip the crone, search her for marks, for the supernumary nipple her familiar sucks. They soon find it. Then they stone her to death.

Winter and cold weather.

Go and visit grandmother, who has been sick. Take her the oatcakes I've baked for her on the hearthstone and a little pot of butter.

The good child does as her mother bids—five miles' trudge through the forest; do not leave the path because of the bears, the wild boar, the starving wolves. Here, take your father's hunting knife; you know how to use it.

The child had a scabby coat of sheepskin to keep out the cold, she knew the forest too well to fear it but she must always be on her guard. When she heard that freezing howl of a wolf, she dropped her gifts, seized her knife and turned on the beast.

It was a huge one, with red eyes and running, grizzled chops; any but a mountaineer's child would have died of fright at the sight of it. It went for her throat, as wolves do, but she made a great swipe at it with her father's knife and slashed off its right forepaw.

The wolf let out a gulp, almost a sob, when she saw what had happened to it; wolves are less brave than they seem. It went lolloping off disconsolately between the trees as well as it could on three legs, leaving a trail of blood behind it. The child wiped the blade of her knife clean on her apron, wrapped up the wolf's paw in the cloth in which her mother had packed the oatcakes and went on towards her grandmother's house. Soon it came on to snow so thickly that the path and any footsteps, track or spoor that might have been upon it were obscured.

She found her grandmother was so sick she had taken to her bed and fallen into a fretful sleep, moaning and shaking so that the child guessed she had a fever. She felt the forehead, it burned. She shook out the cloth from her basket, to use it to make the old woman a cold compress, and the wolf's paw fell to the floor.

But it was no longer a wolf's paw. It was a hand, chopped off at the wrist, a hand toughened with work and freckled with age. There was a wedding ring on the third finger and a wart on the index finger. By the wart, she knew it for her grandmother's hand.

She pulled back the sheet but the old woman woke up, at that, and began to struggle, squawking, and shrieking like a thing possessed. But the child was strong, and armed with her father's hunting knife; she managed to hold her grandmother down long enough to see the cause of her fever. There was a bloody stump where her right hand should have been, festering already.

The child crossed herself and cried out so loud the neighbours heard her and came rushing in. They knew the wart on the hand at once for a witch's nipple; they drove the old woman, in her shift as she was, out into the snow with sticks, beating her old carcass as far as the edge of the forest, and pelted her with stones until she fell down dead.

Now the child lived in her grandmother's house; she prospered.

LITTLE SNOW-WHITE

Once upon a time in the middle of winter, when the flakes of snow were falling like feathers from the sky, a Queen sat at a window sewing, and the frame of the window was made of black ebony. And whilst she was sewing and looking out of the window at the snow, she pricked her finger with the needle, and three drops of blood fell upon the snow. And the red looked pretty upon the white snow, and she thought to herself: "Would that I had a child as white as snow, as red as blood, and as black as the wood of the window-frame."

Soon after that she had a little daughter, who was as white as snow, and as red as blood, and her hair was as black as ebony; and she was therefore called Little Snow-white. And when the child was born, the Queen died.

After a year had passed the King took to himself another wife. She was a beautiful woman, but proud and haughty, and she could not bear that any-one else should surpass her in beauty. She had a wonderful looking-glass, and when she stood in front of it and looked at herself in it, and said:

> "Looking-glass, Looking-glass, on the wall,
> Who in this land is the fairest of all?"

the looking-glass answered:

> "Thou, O Queen, art the fairest of all!"

Then she was satisfied, for she knew that the looking-glass spoke the truth.

But Snow-white was growing up, and grew more and more beautiful; and when she was seven years old she was as beautiful as the day, and more

beautiful than the Queen herself. And once when the Queen asked her
looking-glass:

> "Looking-glass, Looking-glass, on the wall,
> Who in this land is the fairest of all?"

It answered:

> "Thou art fairer than all who are here, Lady Queen.
> But more beautiful still is Snow-white, as I ween."

Then the Queen was shocked, and turned yellow and green with envy. From
that hour, whenever she looked at Snow-white, her heart heaved in her breast,
she hated the girl so much.

And envy and pride grew higher and higher in her heart like a weed, so
that she had no peace day or night. She called a huntsman, and said: "Take the
child away into the forest; I will no longer have her in my sight. Kill her, and
bring me back her lung and liver as a token." The huntsman obeyed, and took
her away; but when he had drawn his knife, and was about to pierce Snow-
white's innocent heart, she began to weep, and said: "Ah, dear huntsman, leave
me my life! I will run away into the wild forest, and never come home again."

And as she was so beautiful the huntsman had pity on her and said: "Run
away, then, you poor child." "The wild beasts will soon have devoured you,"
thought he, and yet it seemed as if a stone had been rolled from his heart since
it was no longer needful for him to kill her. And as a young boar just then
came running by he stabbed it, and cut out its lung and liver and took them
to the Queen as proof that the child was dead. The cook had to salt them, and
the wicked Queen ate them, and thought she had eaten the lung and liver of
Snow-white.

But now the poor child was all alone in the great forest, and so terrified that she looked at all the leaves on the trees, and did not know what to
do. Then she began to run, and ran over sharp stones and through thorns, and
the wild beasts ran past her, but did her no harm.

She ran as long as her feet would go until it was almost evening; then
she saw a little cottage and went into it to rest herself. Everything in the cottage was small, but neater and cleaner than can be told. There was a table on
which was a white cover, and seven little plates, and on each plate a little
spoon; moreover, there were seven little knives and forks, and seven little
mugs. Against the wall stood seven little beds side by side, and covered with
snow-white counterpanes.

Little Snow-white was so hungry and thirsty that she ate some vegetables and bread from each plate and drank a drop of wine out of each mug, for she did not wish to take all from one only. Then, as she was so tired, she laid herself down on one of the little beds, but none of them suited her; one was too long, another too short, but at last she found that the seventh one was right, and so she remained in it, said a prayer and went to sleep.

When it was quite dark the owners of the cottage came back; they were seven dwarfs who dug and delved in the mountains for ore. They lit their seven candles, and as it was now light within the cottage they saw that someone had been there, for everything was not in the same order in which they had left it.

The first said: "Who has been sitting on my chair?"

The second: "Who has been eating off my plate?"

The third: "Who has been taking some of my bread?"

The fourth: "Who has been eating my vegetables?"

The fifth: "Who has been using my fork?"

The sixth: "Who has been cutting with my knife?"

The seventh: "Who has been drinking out of my mug?"

Then the first looked round and saw that there was a little hollow on his bed, and he said: "Who has been getting into my bed?" The others came up and each called out: "Somebody has been lying in my bed too." But the seventh when he looked at his bed saw little Snow-white, who was lying asleep therein. And he called the others, who came running up, and they cried out with astonishment, and brought their seven little candles and let the light fall on little Snow-white. "Oh, heavens! oh, heavens!" cried they, "what a lovely child!" and they were so glad that they did not wake her up, but let her sleep on in the bed. And the seventh dwarf slept with his companions, one hour with each, and so passed the night.

When it was morning little Snow-white awoke, and was frightened when she saw the seven dwarfs. But they were friendly and asked her what her name was. "My name is Snow-white," she answered. "How have you come to our house?" said the dwarfs. Then she told them that her step-mother had wished to have her killed, but that the huntsman had spared her life, and that she had run for the whole day, until at last she had found their dwelling. The dwarfs said: "If you will take care of our house, cook, make the beds, wash, sew, and knit, and if you will keep everything neat and clean, you can stay with us and you shall want for nothing." "Yes," said Snow-white, "with all my heart," and she stayed with them. She kept the house in order for them; in the mornings they went to the mountains and looked for copper and gold, in the evenings they came back, and then their supper had to be ready. The girl was alone the whole day, so the good dwarfs warned her and said: "Beware of your step-mother, she will soon know that you are here; be sure to let no one come in."

But the Queen, believing that she had eaten Snow-white's lung and liver, could not but think that she was again the first and most beautiful of all; and she went to her looking-glass and said:

> "Looking-glass, Looking-glass, on the wall,
> Who in this land is the fairest of all?"

And the glass answered:

> "Oh, Queen, thou art fairest of all I see,
> But over the hills, where the seven dwarfs dwell,
> Snow-white is still alive and well,
> And none is so fair as she."

Then she was astounded, for she knew that the looking-glass never spoke falsely, and she knew that the huntsman had betrayed her, and that lit-tle Snow-white was still alive.

And so she thought and thought again how she might kill her, for so long as she was not the fairest in the whole land, envy let her have no rest. And when she had at last thought of something to do, she painted her face, and dressed herself like an old pedlar-woman, and no one could have known her. In this disguise she went over the seven mountains to the seven dwarfs, and knocked at the door and cried: "Pretty things to sell, very cheap, very cheap." Little Snow-white looked out of the window and called out: "Good-day, my good woman, what have you to sell?" "Good things, pretty things," she an-swered; "stay-laces of all colors," and she pulled out one which was woven of bright-colored silk. "I may let the worthy old woman in," thought Snow-white, and she unbolted the door and bought the pretty laces. "Child," said the old woman, "what a fright you look; come, I will lace you properly for once." Snow-white had no suspicion, but stood before her, and let herself be laced with the new laces. But the old woman laced so quickly and laced so tightly that Snow-white lost her breath and fell down as if dead. "Now I am the most beautiful," said the Queen to herself, and ran away.

Not long afterwards, in the evening, the seven dwarfs came home, but how shocked they were when they saw their dear little Snow-white lying on the ground, and that she neither stirred nor moved, and seemed to be dead. They lifted her up, and, as they saw that she was laced too tightly, they cut the laces; then she began to breathe a little, and after a while came to life again. When the dwarfs heard what had happened they said: "The old pedlar-woman was no one else than the wicked Queen; take care and let no one come in when we are not with you."

But the wicked woman when she had reached home went in front of the glass and asked:

> "Looking-glass, Looking-glass, on the wall,
> Who in this land is the fairest of all?"

And it answered as before:

> "Oh, Queen, thou art fairest of all I see,
> But over the hills, where the seven dwarfs dwell,
> Snow-white is still alive and well,
> And none is so fair as she."

When she heard that, all her blood rushed to her heart with fear, for she saw plainly that little Snow-white was again alive. "But now," she said, "I will think of something that shall really put an end to you," and by the help of witchcraft, which she understood, she made a poisonous comb. Then she disguised herself and took the shape of another old woman. So she went over the seven mountains to the seven dwarfs, knocked at the door, and cried: "Good things to sell, cheap, cheap!" Little Snow-white looked out and said: "Go away; I cannot let anyone come in." "I suppose you can look," said the old woman, and pulled the poisonous comb out and held it up. It pleased the girl so well that she let herself be beguiled, and opened the door. When they had made a bargain the old woman said: "Now I will comb you properly for once." Poor little Snow-white had no suspicion, and let the old woman do as she pleased, but hardly had she put the comb in her hair than the poison in it took effect, and the girl fell down senseless. "You paragon of beauty," said the wicked woman, "you are done for now," and she went away.

But fortunately it was almost evening, when the seven dwarfs came home. When they saw Snow-white lying as if dead upon the ground they at once suspected the step-mother, and they looked and found the poisoned comb. Scarcely had they taken it out when Snow-white came to herself, and told them what had happened. Then they warned her once more to be upon her guard and to open the door to no one.

The Queen, at home, went in front of the glass and said:

> "Looking-glass, Looking-glass, on the wall,
> Who in this land is the fairest of all?"

then it answered as before:

> "Oh, Queen, thou art fairest of all I see,
> But over the hills, where the seven dwarfs dwell,
> Snow-white is still alive and well,
> And none is so fair as she."

When she heard the glass speak thus she trembled and shook with rage. "Snow-white shall die," she cried, "even if it costs me my life!"

Thereupon she went into a quite secret, lonely room, where no one ever came, and there she made a very poisonous apple. Outside it looked pretty, white with a red cheek, so that everyone who saw it longed for it; but whoever ate a piece of it must surely die.

When the apple was ready she painted her face, and dressed herself up as a farmer's wife, and so she went over the seven mountains to the seven dwarfs. She knocked at the door. Snow-white put her head out of the window and said: "I cannot let anyone in; the seven dwarfs have forbidden me." "It is all the same to me," answered the woman, "I shall soon get rid of my apples. There, I will give you one."

"No," said Snow-white, "I dare not take anything." "Are you afraid of poison?" said the old woman; "look, I will cut the apple in two pieces; you eat the red cheek, and I will eat the white." The apple was so cunningly made that only the red cheek was poisoned. Snow-white longed for the fine apple, and when she saw that the woman ate part of it she could resist no longer, and stretched out her hand and took the poisonous half. But hardly had she a bit of it in her mouth than she fell down dead. Then the Queen looked at her with a dreadful look, and laughed aloud and said: "White as snow, red as blood, black as ebony-wood! this time the dwarfs cannot wake you up again."

And when she asked of the looking-glass at home:

> "Looking-glass, Looking-glass, on the wall,
> Who in this land is the fairest of all?"

it answered at last:

> "Oh, Queen, in this land thou art fairest of all."

Then her envious heart had rest, so far as an envious heart can have rest.

The dwarfs, when they came home in the evening, found Snow-white lying upon the ground; she breathed no longer and was dead. They lifted

her up, looked to see whether they could find anything poisonous, unlaced
her, combed her hair, washed her with water and wine, but it was all of no
use; the poor child was dead, and remained dead. They laid her upon a bier,
and all seven of them sat round it and wept for her, and wept three days
long.

Then they were going to bury her, but she still looked as if she were living, and still had her pretty red cheeks. They said: "We could not bury her in
the dark ground," and they had a transparent coffin of glass made, so that she
could be seen from all sides, and they laid her in it, and wrote her name upon
it in golden letters, and that she was a king's daughter. Then they put the coffin out upon the mountain, and one of them always stayed by it and watched
it. And birds came too, and wept for Snow-white; first an owl, then a raven,
and last a dove.

And now Snow-white lay a long, long time in the coffin, and she did not
change, but looked as if she were asleep; for she was as white as snow, as red
as blood, and her hair was as black as ebony.

It happened, however, that a king's son came into the forest, and went
to the dwarfs' house to spend the night. He saw the coffin on the mountain,
and the beautiful Snow-white within it, and read what was written upon it in
golden letters. Then he said to the dwarfs: "Let me have the coffin, I will give
you whatever you want for it." But the dwarfs answered: "We will not part
with it for all the gold in the world." Then he said: "Let me have it as a gift,
for I cannot live without seeing Snow-white. I will honor and prize her as my
dearest possession." As he spoke in this way the good dwarfs took pity upon
him, and gave him the coffin.

And now the King's son had it carried away by his servants on their shoulders. And it happened that they stumbled over a tree-stump, and with the
shock the poisonous piece of apple which Snow-white had bitten off came out
of her throat. And before long she opened her eyes, lifted up the lid of the
coffin, sat up, and was once more alive. "Oh, heavens, where am I?" she cried.
The King's son, full of joy, said: "You are with me," and told her what had happened, and said: "I love you more than everything in the world; come with
me to my father's palace, you shall be my wife."

And Snow-white was willing, and went with him, and their wedding was
held with great show and splendor. But Snow-white's wicked step-mother was
also bidden to the feast. When she had arrayed herself in beautiful clothes she
went before the Looking-glass, and said:

> "Looking-glass, Looking-glass, on the wall,
> Who in this land is the fairest of all?"

the glass answered:

> "Oh, Queen, of all here the fairest art thou,
> But the young Queen is fairer by far as I trow."

Then the wicked woman uttered a curse, and was so wretched, so utterly wretched, that she knew not what to do. At first she would not go to the wedding at all, but she had no peace, and had to go to see the young Queen. And when she went in she recognized Snow-white; and she stood still with rage and fear, and could not stir. But iron slippers had already been put upon the fire, and they were brought in with tongs, and set before her. Then she was forced to put on the red-hot shoes, and dance until she dropped down dead.

Translated by Margaret Hunt, revised and completed by James Stern

Anne Sexton

SNOW WHITE AND
THE SEVEN DWARFS

No matter what life you lead
the virgin is a lovely number:
cheeks as fragile as cigarette paper,
arms and legs made of Limoges,
lips like Vin du Rhône,
rolling her china-blue doll eyes
open and shut.
Open to say,
Good Day Mama,
and shut for the thrust
of the unicorn.
She is unsoiled.
She is as white as a bonefish.
Once there was a lovely virgin
called Snow White.
Say she was thirteen.
Her stepmother,
a beauty in her own right,
though eaten, of course, by age,
would hear of no beauty surpassing her own.
Beauty is a simple passion,
but, oh my friends, in the end
you will dance the fire dance in iron shoes.
The stepmother had a mirror to which she referred—
something like the weather forecast—
a mirror that proclaimed
the one beauty of the land.

She would ask,
Looking glass upon the wall,
who is fairest of us all?
And the mirror would reply,
You are fairest of us all.
Pride pumped in her like poison.

Suddenly one day the mirror replied,
Queen, you are full fair, 'tis true,
but Snow White is fairer than you.
Until that moment Snow White
had been no more important
than a dust mouse under the bed.
But now the queen saw brown spots on her hand
and four whiskers over her lip
so she condemned Snow White
to be hacked to death.
Bring me her heart, she said to the hunter,
and I will salt it and eat it.
The hunter, however, let his prisoner go
and brought a boar's heart back to the castle.
The queen chewed it up like a cube steak.
Now I am fairest, she said,
lapping her slim white fingers.

Snow White walked in the wildwood
for weeks and weeks.
At each turn there were twenty doorways
and at each stood a hungry wolf,
his tongue lolling out like a worm.
The birds called out lewdly,
talking like pink parrots,
and the snakes hung down in loops,
each a noose for her sweet white neck.
On the seventh week
she came to the seventh mountain
and there she found the dwarf house.
It was as droll as a honeymoon cottage
and completely equipped with
seven beds, seven chairs, seven forks

and seven chamber pots.
Snow White ate seven chicken livers
and lay down, at last, to sleep.

The dwarfs, those little hot dogs,
walked three times around Snow White,
the sleeping virgin. They were wise
and wattled like small czars.
Yes. It's a good omen,
they said, and will bring us luck.
They stood on tiptoes to watch
Snow White wake up. She told them
about the mirror and the killer-queen
and they asked her to stay and keep house.
Beware of your stepmother,
they said.
Soon she will know you are here.
While we are away in the mines
during the day, you must not
open the door.

Looking glass upon the wall . . .
The mirror told
and so the queen dressed herself in rags
and went out like a peddler to trap Snow White.
She went across seven mountains.
She came to the dwarf house
and Snow White opened the door
and bought a bit of lacing.
The queen fastened it tightly
around her bodice,
as tight as an Ace bandage,
so tight that Snow White swooned.
She lay on the floor, a plucked daisy.
When the dwarfs came home they undid the lace
and she revived miraculously.
She was as full of life as soda pop.
Beware of your stepmother,
they said.
She will try once more.

Looking glass upon the wall . . .
Once more the mirror told
and once more the queen dressed in rags
and once more Snow White opened the door.
This time she bought a poison comb,
a curved eight-inch scorpion,
and put it in her hair and swooned again.
The dwarfs returned and took out the comb
and she revived miraculously.
She opened her eyes as wide as Orphan Annie.
Beware, beware, they said,
but the mirror told,
the queen came,
Snow White, the dumb bunny,
opened the door
and she bit into a poison apple
and fell down for the final time.
When the dwarfs returned
they undid her bodice,
they looked for a comb,
but it did no good.
Though they washed her with wine
and rubbed her with butter
it was to no avail.
She lay as still as a gold piece.

The seven dwarfs could not bring themselves
to bury her in the black ground
so they made a glass coffin
and set it upon the seventh mountain
so that all who passed by
could peek in upon her beauty.
A prince came one June day
and would not budge.
He stayed so long his hair turned green
and still he would not leave.
The dwarfs took pity upon him
and gave him the glass Snow White—
its doll's eyes shut forever—
to keep in his far-off castle.

As the prince's men carried the coffin
they stumbled and dropped it
and the chunk of apple flew out
of her throat and she woke up miraculously.

And thus Snow White became the prince's bride.
The wicked queen was invited to the wedding feast
and when she arrived there were
red-hot iron shoes,
in the manner of red-hot roller skates,
clamped upon her feet.
First your toes will smoke
and then your heels will turn black
and you will fry upward like a frog,
she was told.
And so she danced until she was dead,
a subterranean figure,
her tongue flicking in and out
like a gas jet.
Meanwhile Snow White held court,
rolling her china-blue doll eyes open and shut
and sometimes referring to her mirror
as women do.

NARRATIVE IN OTHER MODES

NARRATIVE
IN OTHER MODES

Perhaps there are as many ways of storytelling, story invention, as there are individuals. The creation of "formal" stories is, contrary to general assumption, but one way. That it is the traditional way does not mean that it is superior to all others; nor does it mean that, for certain individuals, another mode of expression may not be far more liberating, and far more interesting.

The first-person account nearly always possesses an air of immediacy and authenticity lacking in third-person "fictitious" prose. Compare the elaborately allegorical, highly stylized prose parables of Nathaniel Hawthorne with the vivid directness of his superb *Notebook;* compare Virginia Woolf's impressionistic, oddly impersonal (and bodiless) novels with the zest, vigor, color, motion, and idiosyncratic wit of her famous diary. Zora Neale Hurston's "How It Feels to Be Colored Me" is about just that: the peculiar puzzle of the very designation "color"—"colored"—in America. Richard Wright's seminal memoir *Black Boy* ("American Hunger") frequently reads like a work of prose fiction; Jack Kerouac's alleged work of fiction, *Desolation Angels,* always reads like a memoir. "Borges and I" and "Updike and I"— the latter wittily inspired by the former, a contemporary classic—are of particular interest to aspiring writers, as well as to anyone intrigued by the riddle of personality.

Maxine Hong Kingston's "No Name Woman," from the influential *The Woman Warrior: Memoirs of a Childhood among Ghosts,* is a painfully candid autobiographical work that manages to be, at the same time, about an entire culture and an inheritance specific to a young Chinese American woman of our time. M. F. K. Fisher's "Those Who Must Leap" is a poetic meditation on a "confessional" subject; Mikal Gilmore's memoir of his brother Gary Gilmore, *Shot in the Heart,* is a confession of another sort, elegiac and fiercely loving. It has been remarked that ours is an age of memoir (see such outstanding examples as Tobias Wolff's *This Boy's Life,* John Edgar Wideman's *Brothers and Keepers,* Brent Staples's *Parallel Time: Growing Up in Black and White,* Henry Louis Gates, Jr.'s *Colored People,* Veronica Chambers's *Mama's Girl,* Mary Gordon's *The Shadow Man,* and Mary Karr's *The Liar's Club,* among others); to read such powerful yet intimate prose is to feel the urge to speak of one's own life, to "memorialize" a family, a place, a way of life uniquely experienced.

(Memoirist writing, like monologues, is also an excellent means to stimulate inspiration. The emotions released by "remembering in prose" can be astonishing; such writing need not be graphically confessional, still less shocking, to strike resonant chords in others.)

It is likely that poetry predates prose as a vehicle for the telling of tales of symbolic social or religious significance. From Homer's *Iliad* and *Odyssey* through the Old English *Beowulf,* Chaucer's *Canterbury Tales,* Dante's *Comedy,* Milton's *Paradise Lost,* and ambitious narrative poems by Blake, Wordsworth, Byron, Shelley, Tennyson, and the Brownings—poetry has been a natural means of such expression. In recent times the long narrative poem has become something of a rarity, its function taken over by prose fiction and films; but the narrative impulse is still potent in short, colloquial, often highly dramatic poems and monologues of the kind included here. Note the recurring use of the first-person voice.

Memoir, Diary, Personal Document

Nathaniel Hawthorne

from *The American Notebooks*

1845

On the night of July 9th, a search for the dead body of a drowned girl. She was a Miss Hunt, about nineteen years old; a girl of education and refinement, but depressed and miserable for want of sympathy—her family being an affectionate one, but uncultivated, and incapable of responding to her demands. She was of a melancholic temperament, accustomed to solitary walks in the woods. At this time, she had the superintendence of one of the district-schools, comprising sixty scholars, particularly difficult of management. Well; Ellery Channing[1] knocked at the door, between 9 and 10 in the evening, in order to get my boat, to go in search of this girl's drowned body. He took the oars, and I the paddle, and we went rapidly down the river, until, a good distance below the bridge, we saw lights on the bank, and the dim figures of a number of people waiting for us. Her bonnet and shoes had already been found on this spot, and her handkerchief, I believe, on the edge of the water; so that the body was probably at no great distance, unless the current (which is gentle, and almost imperceptible) had swept her down.

We took in General Buttrick, and a young man in a blue frock, and commenced the search; the general and the other man having long poles, with hooks at the end, and Ellery a hay-rake, while I steered the boat. It was a very eligible place to drown one's self. On the verge of the river, there were water-weeds; but after a few steps, the bank goes off very abruptly, and the water speedily becomes fifteen or twenty feet deep. It must be one of the deepest spots in the whole river; and, holding a lantern over it, it was black as mid-night, smooth, impenetrable, and keeping its secrets from the eye as perfectly as mid-ocean could. We caused the boat to float once or twice past the spot

---

1. Ellery Channing (1818–1901), a Concord writer and friend of Hawthorne and Henry David Thoreau, was Thoreau's first biographer (*Thoreau, the Poet-Naturalist*, 1873).

where the bonnet &c had been found; carefully searching the bottom at different distances from the shore—but, for a considerable time without success. Once or twice the poles or the rake caught in bunches of water-weed, which, in the star-light, looked like garments; and once Ellery and the General struck some substance at the bottom, which they at first mistook for the body; but it was probably a sod that had rolled in from the bank. All this time, the persons on the bank were anxiously waiting, and sometimes giving us their advice to search higher or lower, or at such and such a point. I now paddled the boat again past the point where she was supposed to have entered the river, and then turned it, so as to let it float broadside downwards, about midway from bank to bank. The young fellow in the blue frock sat on the next seat to me, plying his long pole.

We had drifted a little distance below the group of men on the bank, when this fellow gave a sudden start—"What's this?" cried he. I felt in a moment what it was; and I suppose the same electric shock went through everybody in the boat. "Yes; I've got her!" said he; and heaving up his pole with difficulty, there was an appearance of light garments on the surface of the water; he made a strong effort, and brought so much of the body above the surface, that there could be no doubt about it. He drew her towards the boat, grasped her arm or hand; and I steered the boat to the bank, all the while looking at this dead girl, whose limbs were swaying in the water, close at the boat's side. The fellow evidently had the same sort of feeling in his success as if he had caught a particularly fine fish; though mingled, no doubt, with horror. For my own part, I felt my voice tremble a little, when I spoke, at the first shock of the discovery; and at seeing the body come to the surface, dimly in the starlight. When close to the bank, some of the men stepped into the water and drew out the body; and then, by their lanterns, I could see how rigid it was. There was nothing flexible about it; she did not droop over the arms of those who supported her, with her hair hanging down, as a painter would have represented her; but was all as stiff as marble. And it was evident that her wet garments covered limbs perfectly inflexible. They took her out of the water, and deposited her under an oak-tree; and by the time we had got ashore, they were examining her by the light of two or three lanterns.

I never saw nor imagined a spectacle of such perfect horror. The rigidity, above spoken of, was dreadful to behold. Her arms had stiffened in the act of struggling; and were bent before her, with the hands clenched. She was the very image of a death-agony; and when the men tried to compose her figure, her arms would still return to that same position; indeed it was almost impossible to force them out of it for an instant. One of the men put his foot upon her arm, for the purpose of reducing it by her side; but, in a moment, it rose again. The lower part of the body had stiffened into a more quiet attitude; the legs were slightly bent, and the feet close together. But that rigidity!—it is impossible to express the effect of it; it seemed as if she would keep the same posture in the grave, and that her skeleton would keep it too, and that when she rose at the day of Judgment, it would be in the same attitude.

As soon as she was taken out of the water, the blood began to stream from her nose. Something seemed to have injured her eye, too; perhaps it was the pole, when it first struck the body. The complexion was a dark red, almost purple; the hands were white, with the same rigidity in their clench as in all the rest of the body. Two of the men got water, and began to wash away the blood from her face; but it flowed and flowed, and continued to flow; and an old carpenter, who seemed to be skilful in such matters, said that this was always the case, and that she would continue to "purge," as he called it, in this manner, until her burial, I believe. He said, too, that the body would swell, by morning, so that nobody would know her. Let it take what change it might, it could scarcely look more horrible than it did now, in its rigidity; certainly, she did not look as if she had gotten grace in the world whither she had precipitated herself; but rather, her stiffened death-agony was an emblem of inflexible judgment pronounced upon her. If she could have foreseen, while she stood, at 5 o'clock that morning, on the bank of the river, how her maiden corpse would have looked, eighteen hours afterwards, and how coarse men would strive with hand and foot to reduce it to a decent aspect, and all in vain—it would surely have saved her from this deed. So horribly did she look, that a middle-aged man, David Buttrick, absolutely fainted away, and was found lying on the grass, at a little distance, perfectly insensible. It required much rubbing of hands and limbs to restore him.

Meantime, General Buttrick had gone to give notice to the family that the body was found; and others had gone in search of rails, to make a bier. Another boat now arrived, and added two or three more horror-struck spectators. There was a dog with them, who looked at the body, as it seemed to me, with pretty much the same feelings as the rest of us—horror and curiosity. A young brother of the deceased, apparently about twelve or fourteen years old, had been on the spot from the beginning. He seemed not much moved, externally, but answered questions about his sister, and the number of the brothers and sisters, (ten in all,) with composure. No doubt, however, he was stunned and bewildered with the scene—to see his sister lying there, in such terrific guise, at midnight, under an oak, on the verge of the black river, with strangers clustering about her, holding their lanterns over her face; and that old carpenter washing the blood away, which still flowed forth, though from a frozen fountain. Never was there a wilder scene. All the while, we were talking about the circumstances, and about an inquest, and whether or no it was necessary, and of how many it should consist; and the old carpenter was talking of dead people, and how he would as lief handle them as living ones.

By this time, two rails had been procured, across which were laid some boards or broken oars from the bottom of a boat; and the body, being wrapt in an old quilt, was laid upon this rude bier. All of us took part in bearing the corpse, or in steadying it. From the bank of the river to her father's house, there was nearly half a mile of pasture-ground, on the ascent of the hill; and our burthen grew very heavy, before we reached the door. What a midnight procession it was! How strange and fearful it would have seemed, if it could have been foretold, a day beforehand, that I should help carry a dead body along that track! At last, we reached the door, where appeared an old gray-haired man, holding a light; he said nothing, seemed calm, and after the body was laid upon a large table, in what seemed to be the kitchen, the old man disappeared. This was the grandfather. Good Mrs. Pratt was in the room, having been sent for to assist in laying out the body; but she seemed wholly at a loss how to proceed; and no wonder—for it was an absurd idea to think of composing that rigidly distorted figure into the decent quiet of the coffin. A Mrs. Lee had likewise been summoned, and shortly appeared, a withered, skin-and-bone looking woman; but she, too, though a woman of skill, was in despair at the job, and confessed her ignorance how to set about it. Whether the poor girl did finally get laid out, I know not, but can scarcely think it possible. I have since been told that, on stripping the body, they found a strong cord wound round the waist, and drawn tight—for what purpose is impossible to guess.

"Ah, poor child!"—that was the exclamation of an elderly man, as he helped draw her out of the water. I suppose one friend would have saved her; but she died for want of sympathy—a severe penalty for having cultivated and refined herself out of the sphere of her natural connections.

She is said to have gone down to the river at 5 in the morning, and to have been seen walking to and fro on the bank, so late as 7—there being all that space of final struggle with her misery. She left a diary, which is said to exhibit (as her whole life did) many high and remarkable traits. The idea of suicide was not a new one with her; she had before attempted, walking up to her chin into the water, but coming out again, in compassion to the agony of a sister, who stood on the bank. She appears to have been religious, and of a high morality.

The reason, probably, that the body remained so near the spot where she drowned herself, was, that it had sunk to the bottom of perhaps the deepest spot in the river, and so was out of the action of the current.

Henry David Thoreau

from *The Journal*

May 22, 1853

When yesterday Sophia[1] and I were rowing past Mr. Prichard's land, where the river is bordered by a row of elms and low willows, at 6 P.M., we heard a singular note of distress as it were from a catbird—a loud, vibrating, catbird sort of note, as if the catbird's mew were imitated by a smart vibrating spring. Blackbirds and others were flitting about, apparently attracted by it. At first, thinking it was merely some peevish catbird or red-wing, I was disregarding it, but on second thought turned the bows to the shore, looking into the trees as well as over the shore, thinking some bird might be in distress, caught by a snake or in a forked twig. The hovering birds dispersed at my approach; the note of distress sounded louder and nearer as I approached the shore covered with low osiers. The sound came from the ground, not from the trees. I saw a little black animal making haste to meet the boat under the osiers. A young muskrat? a mink? No, it was a little dot of a kitten. It was scarcely six inches long from the face to the base—or I might as well say the tip—of the tail, for the latter was a short, sharp pyramid, perfectly perpendicular but not swelled in the least. It was a very handsome and very precocious kitten, in perfectly good condition, its breadth being considerably more than one third of its length. Leaving its mewing, it came scrambling over the stones as fast as its weak legs would permit, straight to me. I took it up and dropped it into the boat, but while I was pushing off it ran the length of the boat to Sophia, who held it while we rowed homeward. Evidently it had not been weaned—was smaller than we remembered that kittens ever were—almost infinitely small; yet it had hailed a boat, its life being in danger, and saved itself. Its performance, considering its age and amount of experience, was more wonderful than that of any young mathematician or musician that I have read of. Various were the conjectures as to how the kitten came there, a

---

1. Thoreau's younger sister.

quarter of a mile from a house. The possible solutions were finally reduced to three: first, it must either have been born there, or, secondly, carried there by its mother, or, thirdly, by human hands. In the first case, it had possibly brothers and sisters, one or both, and its mother had left them to go a-hunting on her own account and might be expected back. In the second, she might equally be expected to return. At any rate, not having thought of all this till we got home, we found that we had got ourselves into a scrape; for this kitten, though exceedingly interesting, required one nurse to attend it constantly for the present, and, of course, another to spell the first; and, beside, we had already a cat well-nigh grown, who manifested such a disposition toward the young stranger that we had no doubt it would have torn it in pieces in a moment if left alone with it. As nobody made up his or her mind to have it drowned, and still less to drown it,—having once looked into its innocent extremely pale blue eyes (as of milk thrice skimmed) and had his finger or his chin sucked by it, while, its eyes being shut, its little paws played a soothing tune,—it was resolved to keep it till it could be suitably disposed of. It rested nowhere, in no lap, under no covert, but still faintly cried for its mother and its accustomed supper. It ran toward every sound or movement of a human being, and whoever crossed the room it was sure to follow at a rapid pace. It had all the ways of a cat of the maturest years; could purr divinely and raised its back to rub all boots and shoes. When it raised its foot to scratch its ear, which by the way it never hit, it was sure to fall over and roll on the floor. It climbed straight up the sitter, faintly mewing all the way, and sucked his chin. In vain, at first, its head was bent down into saucers of milk which its eyes did not see, and its chin was wetted. But soon it learned to suck a finger that had been dipped in it, and better still a rag; and then at last it slept and rested. The street was explored in vain to find its owner, and at length an Irish family took it into their cradle. Soon after we learned that a neighbor who had heard the mewing of kittens in the partition had sent for a carpenter, taken off a board, and found two the very day at noon that we sailed. That same hour it was first brought to the light a coarse Irish cook had volunteered to drown it, had carried it to the river, and without bag or sinker had cast it in! It saved itself and hailed a boat! What an eventful life! What a precocious kitten! We feared it owed its first plump condition to the water. How strong and effective the instinct of self-preservation!

January 5, 1856

The thin snow now driving from the north and lodging on my coat consists of those beautiful star crystals, not cottony and chubby spokes, as on the 13th December, but thin and partly transparent crystals. They are about a tenth of an inch in diameter, perfect little wheels with six spokes without a tire, or rather with six perfect little leafets, fernlike, with a distinct straight and slender midrib, raying from the centre. On each side of each midrib there is a transparent thin blade with a crenate edge, thus: How full of the creative genius is the air in which these are gener-   ated! I should hardly admire more if real stars fell and lodged on my coat. Nature is full of genius, full of the divinity; so that not a snowflake escapes its fashioning hand. Nothing is cheap and coarse, neither dewdrops nor snowflakes. Soon the storm increases,——it was already very severe to face,——and the snow comes finer, more white and powdery. Who knows but this is the original form of all snowflakes, but that when I observe these crystal stars falling around me they are but just generated in the low mist next the earth? I am nearer to the source of the snow, its primal, auroral, and golden hour [of] infancy, but commonly the flakes reach us travel-worn and agglomerated, comparatively without order or beauty, far down in their fall, like men in their advanced age.

As for the circumstances under which this phenomenon occurs, it is quite cold, and the driving storm is bitter to face,[2] though very little snow is falling. It comes almost horizontally from the north. Methinks this kind of snow never falls in any quantity.[3]

October 8, 1857

Walking through the Lee farm swamp, a dozen or more rods from the river, I found a large box trap closed. I opened it and found in it the remains of a gray rabbit,——skin, bones, and mould,——closely fitting the right-angled corner of one side. It was wholly inoffensive, as so much vegetable mould, and must have been dead some years. None of the furniture of the trap remained, but the box itself, with a lid which just moved on two rusty nails; the stick which held the bait, the string, etc., etc., were all gone. The box had the appearance of having been floated off in an upright position by a freshet. It had been a rabbit's living tomb. He had gradually starved to death in it. What a tragedy to have occurred within a box in one of our quiet swamps! The trapper lost his box, the rabbit its life. The box had not been gnawed. After days and nights of moaning and struggle, heard for a few rods through the swamp, increasing weakness and emaciation and delirium, the rabbit breathes its last. They tell you of opening the tomb and finding by the contortions of the body that it was buried alive. This was such a case. Let the trapping boy dream of the dead rabbit in its ark, as it sailed, like a small meeting-house with its rude spire, slowly, with a grand and solemn motion, far amid the alders.

2. *Vide* Mar. 19th [Thoreau's note].
3. Yes, it does [Thoreau's note].

Virginia Woolf

from *The Diary*

Monday 17 February 1930

And this temperature is up;
but it has now gone down; & now

[Thursday 20 February]

Feb. 20th, I must canter my wits if I can. Perhaps some character sketches.

Snow:[1]
She came in wrapped in a dark fur coat; which being taken off, she appeared in nondescript grey stockinette & jay blue stripes. Her eyes too are jay blue, but have an anguished starved look, as of a cat that has climbed on to a chimney piece & looks down at a dog. Her face is pale, & very small; indeed, has a curious preserved innocency which makes it hard to think that she is 50. However, her neck is very loose skinned; & there are the dewlaps of middle age. The preserved look seems to indicate lack of experience; as if life had put her in a refrigerator. And we talked—She brought me a parcel, & this was a book from Ethel Smyth,[2] with a letter, which to veil the embarrassment which I supposed her to feel, I read aloud. Her comment was "What miles away all this is from Cheltenham!" Then we talked—but it was her starved & anguished look that remains & the attitude of mind. She seemed to be saying inwardly "I have missed everything. There are Vanessa[3] & Virginia,

---

1. Margaret (Margery) Kemplay Snowden (1878–1966?), daughter of a Yorkshire vicar, had been a fellow student of Vanessa's at the Royal Academy Schools at the beginning of the century and remained her faithful friend and correspondent.
2. Dame Ethel Smyth (1858–1944), composer, author, and feminist.
3. Vanessa Stephen Bell (1879–1961), Virginia's elder sister; a painter.

They have lives full of novels & husbands & exhibitions. I am fifty & it has all slipped by." I gathered this from the jocose pertinacity with which she kept referring to herself. She said the climate of Cheltenham is so sleepy that she often cant paint; & after lunch they put on the gramophone; & then she goes most days to her mother at Bockhampton, where she likes meeting the village people. Farmers wives shake hands. After her mothers death—but she is only 80 & as firm as a rock—she & Lily who is political, but of course that doesn't take up all her time exactly, are going to live at Harrogate, where the climate is not so sleepy, & they know more people. Nothing long distracted her from her central concern—I have had no life & life is over. Even clothes suggested the same old theme. A dressmaker had told her that one enjoyed life more if one was well dressed. So she was trying this specific, to the tune of £8.8 at Pomeroy's in Old Burlington Street. But this worried & fretted her too. In fact I have seldom got a more dismal impression of suffering—too ignoble & petty to be called suffering: call it rather frustration, non-entity; being lifted on a shelf, & seeing things pass; "but then I am very lazy—thats what it is—I lapse into comfort." I should call it lapsing into despair. "What can three women do alone in the country?" Lord, how I praise God that I had a bent strong enough to coerce every minute of my life since I was born! This fiddling & drifting & not impressing oneself upon anything—this always refraining & fingering & cutting things up into little jokes & facetiousness—thats whats so annihilating. Yet given little money, little looks, no special gift, but only enough to make her devastatingly aware that other people have more gift, so that she sees her still lives against the superior still lives of Margaret Gere & the Cotswold school,—what can one do?[4] How could one battle? How could one leap on the back of life & wring its scruff? One would joke, bitterly; & become egotistical & anxious to explain & excuse; & plaintive. What I thought most pathetic was the fact that about 5.30 she began to fidget (she never does anything boldly & directly) with her gloves, & say she must be going. But where? I asked. To the Polytechnic to hear a lecture upon French literature. But why? "Oh one never hears French talked in Cheltenham." Dear dear, but I could tell you all about French literature, I said. However, she shillied shallied; & whether she wanted to go or to stay, I don't know. And when I asked her what she was going to do that night, Well that depends how long the lecture lasts, she said, feebly laughing. Wont you go to a play? No I think I shall have what is called a snack at the Temperance hotel;—Lord Lord, I repeat again. And it isn't as if she were unconscious & oblivious: no,

---

4. Margaret Gere (1878–1965) studied painting at Birmingham and at the Slade. She lived at Painswick in Gloucestershire and was, like Margery Snowden, a member of the Cheltenham Group of Artists. She was primarily a figure painter.

she knows that the dog is there, & arches her back & puts out her paw, but ever so feebly & fussily.

Friday 21 February 1930

No two women could be more extravagantly contraposed than Marjorie Snowden & Ethel Smyth. I was lying here at four yesterday when I heard the bell ring then a brisk tramp up the stairs; & then behold a bluff, military old woman (older than I expected), bounced into the room, a little glazed fly-away & abrupt; in a three cornered hat & tailor made suit.

"Let me look at you".

That over, Now I have brought a book & pencil. I want to ask.

Here there was a ring at the bell. I went to look over. Then we went to tea.

First I want to make out the genealogy of your mothers family. Old Pattle—have you a picture? No. Well now—the names of his daughters.

This lasted out tea. Afterwards, on the sofa, with Ethel stretching her legs out on Pinker's basket, we talked ceaselessly till 7—when L.⁵ came in. We talked—she talked considerably more than I. (On the stairs going up to tea I had asked to be Virginia; about ten minutes after tea she asked to be Ethel: all was settled; the basis of an undying friendship made in 15 minutes:—how sensible; how rapid;) & she got off; oh about music—"I am said to be an egoist. I am a fighter. I feel for the underdog. I rang up Hugh Allen & suggested lunch.⁶ My dear Sir Hugh—my dear Ethel—there are facts you dont know about your sex. Believe me I have to go on coming to London, bullying, badgering—at last, they promise me 14 women in the orchestra. I go & find 2. So I begin ringing up." She has a vein, like a large worm, in her temple which swells. Her cheeks redden. Her faded eyes flash. She has a broad rounded forehead. She recurred to dress. I have to go to Bath to hear dear Maurice Baring's little plays; & then we go to (here Elly interrupted) Rottingdean.⁷ And I must take an evening suit. Thats what worries me. I'm only happy in this— I have one gown I wear for conducting. And then I have to pack (here is a pineapple from Leonard's mother who waits outside). "My maid? But she's only a general—an Irish woman. "Dr (she calls me Dr) Mrs Woolf doesn't mean to see you. Heres another letter from her—to put you off." But I've come. And dont it show that my appetite for life is still great? I've thought of

---

5. Leonard Woolf (1880–1969), Virginia's husband, a writer and, with her, publisher of Hogarth Press.

6. Sir Hugh Percy Allen (1869–1946), professor of music at Oxford from 1918 until his death and director of the Royal College of Music, 1918–37.

7. Maurice Baring, since 1893 one of Ethel Smyth's closest friends, had a house at Rottingdean, near Brighton.

nothing but seeing you for 10 days. And this friendship has come to me now."
So sincere & abrupt is she, & discriminating withal—judging Vita[8] & her secondrate women friends shrewdly—that perhaps something gritty & not the
usual expansive fluff, may come of it. I like to hear her talk of music. She has
written a piece—on Brewster's Prisoner; & will have the gorgeous fun of or-
chestrating it this summer.[9] She says writing music is like writing novels. One
thinks of the sea—naturally one gets a phrase for it. Orchestration is colour-
ing. And one has to be very careful with one's 'technique'. Rhapsodies about
A Room; about Miss Williamson;[1] about the end of some book of Maurice
Baring's. "I'm in the street. I belong to the crowd. I say the crowd is right."
Perhaps she is right to belong to the crowd. There is something fine & tried
& experienced about her besides the rant & the riot & the egotism—& I'm
not sure that she is the egotist that people make out. She said she never had
anybody to admire her, & therefore might write good music to the end. Has
to live in the country because of her passion for games. Plays golf, rides a bicycle; was thrown hunting two years ago. Then fell on her arm & was in despair, because life wd. be over if she could not play games. 'I am very strong'
which she proved by talking till 7.30; then eating a biscuit & drinking a glass
of vermouth & going off to eat a supper of maccaroni when she got to Wok-
ing at 9.

"I'll tell you all about it" she grinned at her maid, who asked if I was a
nice woman. A fine old creature, certainly, Ethel. She talks French 'méringues'
with a highly French accent.

Saturday 22 February 1930

I had meant to write a sketch of George—Sir George Duck-worth[2]—
as he announced himself to Nelly—& of Lytton;[3] both unexpected visitors
yesterday—for I'm not to go down to the studio till Monday; & so must canter my pen amateurishly here; but ten minutes ago the idea came to me of a
possible broadsheet; which I wd. like to adumbrate, before discussing with
L. My notion is a single sheet, containing say 2,000 or if printed back & front
4,000 words. Art, politics, Lit., music: an essay by a single writer to be
printed at irregular intervals; sent to subscribers; costing 6d. Sometimes only

8. Vita Sackville-West (1892–1962), novelist and poet, and a close friend of Virginia's.
9. Henry Bennet Brewster (1859–1908), a cosmopolitan Anglo-American philosopher and writer; Smyth's
last large-scale work, the oratorio *The Prison*, took its inspiration from his metaphysical work *The Prison: A
Dialogue* (1891).
1. Elizabeth Williamson (b. 1903), a great-niece of Ethel Smyth, was an astronomer and a mathematician
who taught at University College, London.
2. George Herbert Duckworth (1868–1934), the elder of Virginia's half-brothers, knighted in 1927.
3. Lytton Strachey (1880–1932), critic and biographer, close friend of Virginia's.

a reproduction. It should be a statement about life: something somebody wants to say; not a regular comment. Very little expense wd. be involved. It would have a spring & an urgency about it wh. the regular sheets lack. Sometimes only a picture. To be closely under L. & my thumbs, so as to give character & uniformity. To lapse for a month if necessary. No incubus of regular appearance. A circular signed by L. & me to be sent round. Young writers enlisted. Signed articles. Everything of the humblest, least ostentatious. The Hogarth News. The Broadsheet.——name to be decided. You see I wd. like to write on Scott this week, & cant, because Richmond has sent the book already. L. wd. do politics. Roger art. The young would have their fling. Possibly, if expenses were kept down, they could get £5 or so, & have their names. But they must not be essays——always——must be topical to some extent.

And in June, I was offered the Editorship of a 4ly; by <the Graphic> Mr Bott & Mr Turner of the Book Club: L. is refusing it at this moment (30th June)

That being enough to go upon in talk after lunch——& it is a fine still day & perhaps we may drive to Richmond & try my legs walking——I will obediently, like a student in the art school——sketch Sir George. First his jowl: it is of the finest semi-transparent flesh; so that one longs to slice it, as it rests, infinitely tender, upon his collar. Otherwise he is as tight as a drum. One expects his trousers to split as he sits down. This he does slowly & rises with difficulty. Still some sentiment begins to form misty between us. He speaks of 'Mother'. I daresay finds in me some shadowy likeness——well——& then he is not now in a position to do me harm. His conventions amuse me. I suppose these family affections are somehow self-protection. He preserves a grain or two of what is me——my unknown past; myself; so that if George died, I should feel something of myself buried. He is endlessly self-complacent. His stories, once started, roll comfortably——he is immensely comfortable——into the pocket of his solid self esteem. I ask, What about the hogs (the Chesterfield hogs) & he replies that the cowman's wife has had a very long labour. Margaret has been very worried. Dalingridge was lit up all night. They had to use the telephone——to send for the dr. The womans mother slept in the house——& so it goes on, singing cosily & contentedly the praises of the good master & mistress——which I have no doubt they are. And he trots out his little compliments——asked to be Sheriff. And he wishes to know if I am making fabulous sums——& he chuckles & dimples & respects me for being asked to a party by the Lord Mayor. And he twits Eddy Marsh for being fond of the society of the great. And he deplores the nudity of Nessa's pictures——& so prattles & chortles & gives me

See Sir George Duckworth on 'Pigs' in todays Times. "Pigs are the most intelligent of animals. I own a small herd of white pedigree hogs."

turtle soup & advises about the preparation & so takes himself off, to meet Henry & return to Dalingridge & the cowman & the hogs—a very incestuous race—& his cook Janet & his Bronnie, home on leave from the Navy— well, it does appear as if human life were perfectly tolerable; his voltage is absolutely normal. The world has been made for him.

Lytton came in after dinner. Very twinkly, lustrous, easy & even warm. Leonard made cigarettes. I lay on the sofa in the twilight of cushions. Lytton had been sent a book about Columbus & told us the story making it into a fantastic amusing Lytton book—Columbus a mad religious fanatic who sailed west & west because he had read in Isaiah a prophesy; his crew being convicts let out from prison; & they came to Cuba & he made them sign a statement that this was India, because it was too large to be an island; & they picked up gold & gems & went back to Spain & the King & Queen rose as he came in. Here are all the elements of a Lytton concoction, told with great gusto; irony; a sense of the incongruous & dramatic. Then we warbled melodiously about Dadie, & Cambridge; & Charlie; & so on. He has a new gramophone. He is editing Greville. He is very content too—not for George's reasons; & very well equipped, & buys books; & likes us; & is going to Cambridge this week end. Its odd how little one remembers what is actually said. I am thinking of the new paper.

Saturday 1 March 1930

And then I went for a walk & brought on a headache, & so lay down again till today, Saturday—a fine day—when we propose to drive off—oh Thank God a thousand times—to Rod- mell & there be at rest. This little affair has taken 3 weeks, & will land me in 4, of non-writing inexpressiveness. Yet I'm not sure that this is not the very thing for The Waves. It was dragging too much out of my head— If ever a book drained me, this one does. If I had wisdom, no doubt I should potter at Rodmell for a fortnight, not writing. I shall take a look at it one of these mornings in my sunny room.

To Hampstead Garden suburb [*on 22 February*]

One evening here I had the odd experience of perfect rest & satisfaction. All the bayonets that prod me sank. There I lay (I daresay for an hour) happy. And the quality was odd. Not an anxiety, not a stir, anywhere. No one coming. Nothing to do. All strain ceased. A supreme sailing with . . . through the dominion (I am quoting—I think Shelley—& it makes nonsense.) This is the rarest of all my moods. I cant recall another. Perhaps at Rodmell sometimes. Everything is shut off. It depends upon having been in the stir of London for some time. Not to have to get up & see Sibyl or Ethel or anybody—what a supreme relief! And now I have a chance to brew a little quiet thought. Yesterday I was offered £2,000 to write

[*word illegible*]

a life of Boswell by Doran Heinemann. L. is writing my polite refusal this moment. I have bought my freedom. A queer thought that I have actually paid for the power to go to Rodmell & only think of The Waves by refusing this offer. If I accepted I would buy houses, tables & go to Italy; not worth it. Yesterday we went over 57 Russell Sqre wh. we may take. But I rather dread the noise & the size—I dont know. A lovely view.

Monday 3 March 1930

Rodmell again. My new bedroom again. Children playing in the school. A thick pearl grey blue day; water drops on the window. Suppose health were shown on a thermometer I have gone up 10 degrees since yesterday, when I lay, mumbling the bones of Dodo: if it had bones;[4] now I sit up, but cannot face going down & bringing an MS to read. Curiosity begins to stir all the same. Such is the effect of 24 hours here, & one ramble for 30 minutes on the flats. The sunwells up, like a pulse, behind the clouds. Tremendous shoals of birds are flying,—& the flop eared trains meeting as usual under Caburn.[5]

Molly Hamilton writes a d—d bad novel.[6] She has the wits to construct a method of telling a story; & then heaps it with the dreariest, most confused litter of old clothes. When I stop to read a page attentively I am shocked by the dishabille of her English. It is like hearing cooks & scullions chattering; she scarcely articulates, dashes it off, I imagine, on blocks of paper, on her knee, at the House of Commons perhaps; or in the Tube. And the quality of the emotion is so thick & squab, the emotions of secondrate women painters, of spotted & pimpled young men: I dont know how she conveys such a sense of the secondrate without gift: the soft pedal too, & the highminded pedal; & no wit; & not precision; & no word standing alone, but each flopping on to the shoulder of another—Lord what a style! What a mind. It has energy & some ability—chiefly shown in the method; but that breaks down; & that too is laboriously lifted. Now being still flabby in the march of the mind, I must read Sea Air—a good manuscript.

Tuesday 11 March 1930

all because I have to buy myself a dress this afternoon, & cant think what I want, I cannot read. I have written, fairly well—but it is a difficult book—at Waves; but cant keep on after 12; & now shall write here, for 20 minutes.

---

4. *Dodo* (1893) was a once celebrated novel by E. F. Benson, with characters based on Margot Tennant and Ethel Smyth.

5. This train image occurs in *II VW Diary*, 7 January 1920, and in *The Waves*; but the word used is *lop* not *flop*.

6. Mary Agnes (Molly) Hamilton (1882–1966), a writer and journalist whom Virginia knew; she had been elected Labour MP for Blackburn in 1929. Her latest novel was *Special Providence* (1930).

My impressions of Margaret [Llewelyn Davies] & Lilian [Harris] at Monks House were of great lumps of grey coat; straggling wisps of hair; hats floppy & home made; thick woollen stockings; black shoes, many wraps, shabby handbags, & shapelessness, & shabbiness & dreariness & drabness unspeakable. A tragedy in its way. Margaret at any rate deserved better of life than this dishevelled & undistinguished end. They are in lodgings—as usual. Have, as usual, a wonderful Xtian Scientist landlady; are somehow rejected by active life; sit knitting perhaps & smoking cigarettes in the parlour where they have their meals, where there is always left a dish of oranges & bananas. I doubt if they have enough to eat. They seemed to me flabby & bloodless, spread into rather toneless chunks of flesh; having lost any commerce with looking glasses. So we showed them the garden, gave them tea (& I dont think an iced cake had come Lilian's way this 6 weeks) & then—oh the dismal sense of people stranded, wanting to be energised; drifting—all woollen & hairy. (It is odd how the visual impression dominates.) There is a jay blue spark in Margaret's eye, now & then, But she had not been out of the lodging for 5 weeks because of the East wind. Her mind has softened & wrinkled, sitting indoors with the oranges & cigarettes. Lilian is almost stone deaf, & mumbles & crumbles, emerging clearly only once, to discuss politics. Something has blunted Margaret's edge, rusted it, worn it, long before its time. Must old age be so shapeless? The only escape is to work the mind. I shall write a history of English literature, I think, in those days. And I shall walk. And I shall buy clothes, & keep my hair tidy, & make myself dine out. But perhaps life becomes repetitious, & one takes no trouble; is glad to be shovelled about in motor cars. M. has her tragic past. She is pathetic to me now—conciliatory & nervous where she used to be trenchant & severe. Janet she says writes endless notes; has sisters for ever staying with her to convalesce; & Emphie caught up their little white dog the other day from a wild herd of racing greyhounds, & had it bitten to death in her arms.[7] This is the sort of adventure that only befalls elderly unmarried women, on whom it makes a tremendous & very painful impression—so defenceless are they, so unable to throw off the damp blanket that surrounds them. What I miss is colour, energy, any clear reflection of the moment. I see those thick stockings & grey hairy wraps everywhere.

---

7. Janet Case lived with her sister Emphie at Minstead in the New Forest; she was the youngest of six sisters.

MOMENTS OF BEING

from "A Sketch of the Past"

Often when I have been writing one of my so-called novels I have been baffled by this same problem: that is, how to describe what I call in my private shorthand—"non-being." Every day includes much more non-being than being. Yesterday for example, Tuesday the 18th of April, was [as] it happened a good day; above the average in "being." It was fine; I enjoyed writing these first pages; my head was relieved of the pressure of writing about Roger; I walked over Mount Misery and along the river; and save that the tide was out, the country, which I notice very closely always, was coloured and shaded as I like—there were the willows, I remember, all plumy and soft green and purple against the blue. I also read Chaucer with pleasure; and began a book— the memoirs of Madame de la Fayette—which interested me. These separate moments of being were however embedded in many more moments of nonbeing. I have already forgotten what Leonard and I talked about at lunch; and at tea; although it was a good day the goodness was embedded in a kind of nondescript cotton wool. This is always so. A great part of every day is not lived consciously. One walks, eats, sees things, deals with what has to be done; the broken vacuum cleaner; ordering dinner; writing orders to Mabel; washing; cooking dinner; bookbinding. When it is a bad day the proportion of nonbeing is much larger. I had a slight temperature last week; almost the whole day was non-being. The real novelist can somehow convey both sorts of being. I think Jane Austen can; and Trollope; perhaps Thackeray and Dickens and Tolstoy. I have never been able to do both. I tried—in "Nights and Days"; and in "The Years." But I will leave the literary side alone for the moment.

As a child ~~then,~~ my days, ~~just as they do now,~~ contained a large proportion of ~~this cotton wool, this~~ non-being. Week after week passed at St. Ives and nothing made any dint upon me. Then, for no reason that I know about, there was a sudden violent shock; something happened so violently that I have remembered it all my life. I will give a few instances. The first: I was fighting with Thoby on the lawn. We were pommelling each other with our fists. Just as I raised my fist to hit him, I felt: why hurt another person? I dropped my hand instantly, and stood there, and let him beat me. I remember the feeling. It was a feeling of hopeless sadness. It was as if I became aware of something terrible; and of my own powerlessness. I slunk off alone, feeling horribly depressed. The second instance was also in the garden at St. Ives. I was looking at the flower bed by the front door; "That is the whole," I said. I was looking at a plant with a spread of leaves; and it seemed suddenly plain that the flower itself was a part of the earth; that a ring enclosed what was the flower; and that was the real flower; part earth; part flower. It was a thought I put away as being likely to be very useful to me later. The third case was also at St. Ives. Some people called Valpy had been staying at St. Ives, and had left. We were waiting at dinner one night, when somehow I overheard my father or my mother say that Mr. Valpy had killed himself. The next thing I remember is being in the garden at night and walking on the path by the apple tree. It seemed to me that the apple tree was connected with the horror of Mr. Valpy's suicide. I could not pass it. I stood there looking at the grey-green creases of the bark—it was a moonlit night—in a trance of horror. I seemed to be dragged down, hopelessly, into some pit of absolute despair from which I could not escape. My body seemed paralysed.

These are three instances of exceptional moments. I often tell them over, or rather they come to the surface unexpectedly. But now that for the first time I have written them down, I realise something that I have never realised before. Two of these moments ended in a state of despair. The other ended, on the contrary, in a state of satisfaction. When I said about the flower "That is the whole," I felt that I had made a discovery. I felt that I had put away in my mind something that I should go back to turn over and explore. It strikes me now that this was a profound difference. It was the difference in the first place between despair and satisfaction. This difference I think arose from the fact that I was quite unable to deal with the pain of discovering that people hurt each other; that a man I had seen had killed himself. The sense of horror held me powerless. But in the case of the flower I found a reason; and was thus able to deal with the sensation. I was not powerless, I was conscious— if only at a distance—that I should in time explain it. I do not know if I was older when I saw the flower than I was when I had the other two experiences. I only know that many of these exceptional moments brought with them a peculiar horror and a physical collapse; they seemed dominant; myself passive. This suggests that as one gets older one has a greater power through reason to provide an explanation; and that this explanation blunts the sledge-hammer force of the blow. I think this is true, because though I still have the peculiarity that I receive these sudden shocks, they are now always welcome; after the first surprise, I always feel instantly that they are particularly valuable. And so I go on to suppose that the shock-receiving capacity is what makes me a writer. I hazard the explanation that a shock is at once in my case followed by the desire to explain it. I feel that I have had a blow; but it is not, as I thought as a child, simply a blow from an enemy hidden behind the cotton wool of daily life; it is or will become a revelation of some order; it is a token of some real thing behind appearances; and I make it real by putting it into words. It is only by putting it into words that I make it whole; this wholeness means that it has lost its power to hurt me; it gives me, perhaps because by doing so I take away the pain, a great delight to put the severed parts together. Perhaps this is the strongest pleasure known to me. It is the rapture I get when in writing I seem to be discovering what belongs to what; making a scene come right; making a character come together. From this I reach what I might call a philosophy; at any rate it is a constant idea of mine; that behind the cotton wool is hidden a pattern; that we—I mean all human beings—are connected with this; that the whole world is a work of art; that we are parts of the work of art. "Hamlet" or a Beethoven quartet is the truth about this vast mass that we call the world. But there is no Shakespeare, there is no Beethoven; certainly and emphatically there is no God; we are the words; we are the music; we are the thing itself. And I see this when I have a shock.

Richard Wright

AMERICAN HUNGER

from *Black Boy*

One summer morning I stood at a sink in the rear of the factory washing a pair of eyeglasses that had just come from the polishing machines whose throbbing shook the floor upon which I stood. At each machine, a white man was bent forward, working intently. To my left sunshine poured through a window, lighting up the rouge smears and making the factory look garish, violent, dangerous. It was nearing noon and my mind was drifting toward my daily lunch of a hamburger and a bag of peanuts. It had been a routine day, a day more or less like the other days I had spent on the job as errand boy and washer of eyeglasses. I was at peace with the world, that is, at peace in the only way in which a black boy in the South can be at peace with a world of white men.

Perhaps it was the mere sameness of the day that soon made it different from the other days; maybe the white men who operated the machines felt bored with their dull, automatic tasks and hankered for some kind of excitement. Anyway, I presently heard footsteps behind me and turned my head. At my elbow stood a young white man, Mr. Olin, the immediate foreman under whom I worked. He was smiling and observing me as I cleaned emery dust from the eyeglasses.

"Boy, how's it going?" he asked.

"Oh, fine, sir!" I answered with false heartiness, falling quickly into that nigger-being-a-good-natured-boy-in-the-presence-of-a-white-man pattern, a pattern into which I could now slide easily; although I was wondering if he had any criticism to make of my work.

He continued to hover wordlessly at my side. What did he want? It was unusual for him to stand there and watch me; I wanted to look at him, but was afraid to.

"Say, Richard, do you believe that I'm your friend?" he asked me.

The question was so loaded with danger that I could not reply at once. I scarcely knew Mr. Olin. My relationship to him had been the typical relationship of Negroes to southern whites. He gave me orders and I said, "Yes, sir," and obeyed them. Now, without warning, he was asking me if I thought that he was my friend; and I knew that all southern white men fancied themselves as friends of niggers. While fishing for an answer that would say nothing, I smiled.

"I mean," he persisted, "do you think I'm your friend?"

"Well," I answered, skirting the vast racial chasm between us, "I hope you are."

"I am," he said emphatically.

I continued to work, wondering what motives were prompting him. Already apprehension was rising in me.

"I want to tell you something," he said.

"Yes, sir," I said.

"We don't want you to get hurt," he explained. "We like you round here. You act like a good boy."

"Yes, sir," I said. "What's wrong?"

"You don't deserve to get into trouble," he went on.

"Have I done something that somebody doesn't like?" I asked, my mind frantically sweeping over all my past actions, weighing them in the light of the way southern white men thought Negroes should act.

"Well, I don't know," he said and paused, letting his words sink meaningfully into my mind. He lit a cigarette. "Do you know Harrison?"

He was referring to a Negro boy of about my own age who worked across the street for a rival optical house. Harrison and I knew each other casually, but there had never been the slightest trouble between us.

"Yes, sir," I said. "I know him."

"Well, be careful," Mr. Olin said. "He's after you."

"After me? For what?"

"He's got a terrific grudge against you," the white man explained. "What have you done to him?"

The eyeglasses I was washing were forgotten. My eyes were upon Mr. Olin's face, trying to make out what he meant. Was this something serious? I did not trust the white man, and neither did I trust Harrison. Negroes who worked on jobs in the South were usually loyal to their white bosses; they felt that that was the best way to ensure their jobs. Had Harrison felt that I had in some way jeopardized his job? Who was my friend: the white man or the black boy?

"I haven't done anything to Harrison," I said.

"Well, you better watch that nigger Harrison," Mr. Olin said in a low, confidential tone. "A little while ago I went down to get a Coca-Cola and Harrison was waiting for you at the door of the building with a knife. He asked me when you were coming down. Said he was going to get you. Said you called him a dirty name. Now, we don't want any fighting or bloodshed on the job."

I still doubted the white man, yet thought that perhaps Harrison had really interpreted something I had said as an insult.

"I've got to see that boy and talk to him," I said, thinking out loud.

"No, you'd better not," Mr. Olin said. "You'd better let some of us white boys talk to him."

"But how did this start?" I asked, still doubting but half believing.

"He just told me that he was going to get even with you, going to cut you and teach you a lesson," he said. "But don't you worry. Let me handle this."

He patted my shoulder and went back to his machine. He was an important man in the factory and I had always respected his word. He had the authority to order me to do this or that. Now, why would he joke with me? White men did not often joke with Negroes, therefore what he had said was serious. I was upset. We black boys worked long hard hours for what few pennies we earned and we were edgy and tense. Perhaps that crazy Harrison was really after me. My appetite was gone. I had to settle this thing. A white man had walked into my delicately balanced world and had tipped it and I had to right it before I could feel safe. Yes, I would go directly to Harrison and ask what was the matter, what I had said that he resented. Harrison was black and so was I; I would ignore the warning of the white man and talk face to face with a boy of my own color.

At noon I went across the street and found Harrison sitting on a box in the basement. He was eating lunch and reading a pulp magazine. As I approached him, he ran his hand into his pocket and looked at me with cold, watchful eyes.

"Say, Harrison, what's this all about?" I asked, standing cautiously four feet from him.

He looked at me a long time and did not answer.

"I haven't done anything to you," I said.

"And I ain't got nothing against you," he mumbled, still watchful. "I don't bother nobody."

"But Mr. Olin said that you came over to the factory this morning, looking for me with a knife."

"Aw, naw," he said, more at ease now. "I ain't been in your factory all day." He had not looked at me as he spoke.

"Then what did Mr. Olin mean?" I asked. "I'm not angry with you."

"Shucks, I thought *you* was looking for me to cut me," Harrison explained. "Mr. Olin, he came over here this morning and said you was going to kill me with a knife the moment you saw me. He said you was mad at me because I had insulted you. But I ain't said nothing about you." He still had not looked at me. He rose.

"And I haven't said anything about you," I said.

Finally he looked at me and I felt better. We two black boys, each working for ten dollars a week, stood staring at each other, thinking, comparing the motives of the absent white man, each asking himself if he could believe the other.

"But why would Mr. Olin tell me things like that?" I asked.

Harrison dropped his head; he laid his sandwich aside.

"I . . . I . . ." he stammered and pulled from his pocket a long, gleaming knife; it was already open. "I was just waiting to see what you was gonna do to me . . ."

I leaned weakly against a wall, feeling sick, my eyes upon the sharp steel blade of the knife.

"You were going to cut me?" I asked.

"If you had cut me, I was gonna cut you first," he said. "I ain't taking no chances."

"Are you angry with me about something?" I asked.

"Man, I ain't mad at nobody," Harrison said uneasily.

I felt how close I had come to being slashed. Had I come suddenly upon Harrison, he would have thought I was trying to kill him and he would have stabbed me, perhaps killed me. And what did it matter if one nigger killed another?

"Look here," I said. "Don't believe what Mr. Olin says."

"I see now," Harrison said. "He's playing a dirty trick on us."

"He's trying to make us kill each other for nothing."

"How come he wanna do that?" Harrison asked.

I shook my head. Harrison sat, but still played with the open knife. I began to doubt. Was he really angry with me? Was he waiting until I turned my back to stab me? I was in torture.

"I suppose it's fun for white men to see niggers fight," I said, forcing a laugh.

"But you might've killed me," Harrison said.

"To white men we're like dogs or cocks," I said.

"I don't want to cut you," Harrison said.

"And I don't want to cut you," I said.

Standing well out of each other's reach, we discussed the problem and decided that we would keep silent about our conference. We would not let Mr. Olin know that we knew that he was egging us to fight. We agreed to ignore any further provocations. At one o'clock I went back to the factory. Mr. Olin was waiting for me, his manner grave, his face serious.

"Did you see that Harrison nigger?" he asked.

"No, sir," I lied.

"Well, he still has that knife for you," he said.

Hate tightened in me. But I kept a dead face.

"Did you buy a knife yet?" he asked me.

"No, sir," I answered.

"Do you want to use mine?" he asked. "You've got to protect yourself, you know."

"No, sir. I'm not afraid," I said.

"Nigger, you're a fool," he spluttered. "I thought you had some sense! Are you going to just let that nigger cut your heart out? His boss gave *him* a knife to use against *you!* Take this knife, nigger, and stop acting crazy!"

I was afraid to look at him; if I had looked at him I would have had to tell him to leave me alone, that I knew he was lying, that I knew he was no friend of mine, that I knew if anyone had thrust a knife through my heart he would simply have laughed. But I said nothing. He was the boss and he could fire me if he did not like me. He laid an open knife on the edge of his work-bench, about a foot from my hand. I had a fleeting urge to pick it up and give it to him, point first into his chest. But I did nothing of the kind. I picked up the knife and put it into my pocket.

"Now, you're acting like a nigger with some sense," he said.

As I worked Mr. Olin watched me from his machine. Later when I passed him he called me.

"Now, look here, boy," he began. "We told that Harrison nigger to stay out of this building, and leave you alone, see? But I can't protect you when you go home. If that nigger starts at you when you are on your way home, you stab him before he gets a chance to stab you, see?"

I avoided looking at him and remained silent.

"Suit yourself, nigger," Mr. Olin said. "But don't say I didn't warn you."

I had to make my round of errands to deliver eyeglasses and I stole a few minutes to run across the street to talk to Harrison. Harrison was sullen and bashful, wanting to trust me, but afraid. He told me that Mr. Olin had telephoned his boss and had told him to tell Harrison that I had planned to wait for him at the back entrance of the building at six o'clock and stab him. Harrison and I found it difficult to look at each other; we were upset and distrustful. We were not really angry at each other; we knew that the idea of murder had been planted in each of us by the white men who employed us. We told ourselves again and again that we did not agree with the white men;

we urged ourselves to keep faith in each other. Yet there lingered deep down in each of us a suspicion that maybe one of us was trying to kill the other.

"I'm not angry with you, Harrison," I said.

"I don't wanna fight nobody," Harrison said bashfully, but he kept his hand in his pocket on his knife.

Each of us felt the same shame, felt how foolish and weak we were in the face of the domination of the whites.

"I wish they'd leave us alone," I said.

"Me too," Harrison said.

"There are a million black boys like us to run errands," I said. "They wouldn't care if we killed each other."

"I know it," Harrison said.

Was he acting? I could not believe in him. We were toying with the idea of death for no reason that stemmed from our own lives, but because the men who ruled us had thrust the idea into our minds. Each of us depended upon the whites for the bread we ate, and we actually trusted the whites more than we did each other. Yet there existed in us a longing to trust men of our own color. Again Harrison and I parted, vowing not to be influenced by what our white boss men said to us.

The game of egging Harrison and me to fight, to cut each other, kept up for a week. We were afraid to tell the white men that we did not believe them, for that would have been tantamount to calling them liars or risking an argument that might have ended in violence being directed against us.

One morning a few days later Mr. Olin and a group of white men came to me and asked me if I was willing to settle my grudge with Harrison with gloves, according to boxing rules. I told them that, though I was not afraid of Harrison, I did not want to fight him and that I did not know how to box. I could feel now that they knew I no longer believed them.

When I left the factory that evening, Harrison yelled at me from down the block. I waited and he ran toward me. Did he want to cut me? I backed away as he approached. We smiled uneasily and sheepishly at each other. We spoke haltingly, weighing our words.

"Did they ask you to fight me with gloves?" Harrison asked.

"Yes," I told him. "But I didn't agree."

Harrison's face became eager.

"They want us to fight four rounds for five dollars apiece," he said. "Man, if I had five dollars, I could pay down on a suit. Five dollars is almost half a week's wages for me."

"I don't want to," I said.

"We won't hurt each other," he said.

"But why do a thing like that for white men?"

"To get that five dollars."

"I don't need five dollars that much."

"Aw, you're a fool," he said. Then he smiled quickly.

"Now, look here," I said. "Maybe you *are* angry with me . . ."

"Naw, I'm not." He shook his head vigorously.

"I don't want to fight for white men. I'm no dog or rooster."

I was watching Harrison closely and he was watching me closely. Did he really want to fight me for some reason of his own? Or was it the money? Harrison stared at me with puzzled eyes. He stepped toward me and I stepped away. He smiled nervously.

"I need that money," he said.

"Nothing doing," I said.

He walked off wordlessly, with an air of anger. Maybe he will stab me now, I thought. I got to watch that fool . . .

For another week the white men of both factories begged us to fight. They made up stories about what Harrison had said about me; and when they saw Harrison they lied to him in the same way. Harrison and I were wary of each other whenever we met. We smiled and kept out of arm's reach, ashamed of ourselves and of each other.

Again Harrison called to me one evening as I was on my way home.

"Come on and fight," he begged.

"I don't want to and quit asking me," I said in a voice louder and harder than I had intended.

Harrison looked at me and I watched him. Both of us still carried the knives that the white men had given us.

"I wanna make a payment on a suit of clothes with that five dollars," Harrison said.

"But those white men will be looking at us, laughing at us," I said.

"What the hell," Harrison said. "They look at you and laugh at you every day, nigger."

It was true. But I hated him for saying it. I ached to hit him in his mouth, to hurt him.

"What have we got to lose?" Harrison asked.

"I don't suppose we have anything to lose," I said.

"Sure," he said. "Let's get the money. We don't care."

"And now they know that we know what they tried to do to us," I said, hating myself for saying it. "And they hate us for it."

"Sure," Harrison said. "So let's get the money. You can use five dollars, can't you?"

"Yes."

"Then let's fight for 'em."

"I'd feel like a dog."

"To them, both of us are dogs," he said.

"Yes," I admitted. But again I wanted to hit him.

"Look, let's fool them white men," Harrison said. "We won't hurt each other. We'll just pretend, see? We'll show 'em we ain't dumb as they think, see?"

"I don't know."

"It's just exercise. Four rounds for five dollars. You scared?"

"No."

"Then come on and fight."

"All right," I said. "It's just exercise. I'll fight."

Harrison was happy. I felt that it was all very foolish. But what the hell. I would go through with it and that would be the end of it. But I still felt a vague anger that would not leave.

When the white men in the factory heard that we had agreed to fight, their excitement knew no bounds. They offered to teach me new punches. Each morning they would tell me in whispers that Harrison was eating raw onions for strength. And—from Harrison—I heard that they told him I was eating raw meat for strength. They offered to buy me my meals each day, but I refused. I grew ashamed of what I had agreed to do and wanted to back out of the fight, but I was afraid that they would be angry if I tried to. I felt that if white men tried to persuade two black boys to stab each other for no reason save their own pleasure, then it would not be difficult for them to aim a wanton blow at a black boy in a fit of anger, in a passing mood of frustration.

The fight took place one Saturday afternoon in the basement of a Main Street building. Each white man who attended the fight dropped his share of the pot into a hat that sat on the concrete floor. Only white men were allowed in the basement; no women or Negroes were admitted. Harrison and I were stripped to the waist. A bright electric bulb glowed above our heads. As the gloves were tied on my hands, I looked at Harrison and saw his eyes watching me. Would he keep his promise? Doubt made me nervous.

We squared off and at once I knew that I had not thought sufficiently about what I had bargained for. I could not pretend to fight. Neither Harrison nor I knew enough about boxing to deceive even a child for a moment. Now shame filled me. The white men were smoking and yelling obscenities at us.

"Crush that nigger's nuts, nigger!"

"Hit that nigger!"

"Aw, fight, you goddamn niggers!"

"Sock 'im in his f——k——g piece!"

"Make 'im bleed!"

I lashed out with a timid left. Harrison landed high on my head and, before I knew it, I had landed a hard right on Harrison's mouth and blood came. Harrison shot a blow to my nose. The fight was on, was on against our will. I felt trapped and ashamed. I lashed out even harder, and the harder I fought the harder Harrison fought. Our plans and promises now meant nothing. We fought four hard rounds, stabbing, slugging, grunting, spitting, cursing, crying, bleeding. The shame and anger we felt for having allowed ourselves to be duped crept into our blows and blood ran into our eyes, half blinding us. The hate we felt for the men whom we had tried to cheat went into the blows we threw at each other. The white men made the rounds last as long as five minutes and each of us was afraid to stop and ask for time for fear of receiving a blow that would knock us out. When we were on the point of collapsing from exhaustion, they pulled us apart.

I could not look at Harrison. I hated him and I hated myself. I clutched my five dollars in my fist and walked home. Harrison and I avoided each other after that and we rarely spoke. The white men attempted to arrange other fights for us, but we had sense enough to refuse. I heard of other fights being staged between other black boys, and each time I heard those plans falling from the lips of the white men in the factory I eased out of earshot. I felt that I had done something unclean, something for which I could never properly atone.

Zora Neale Hurston

HOW IT FEELS
TO BE COLORED ME

I am colored but I offer nothing in the way of extenuating circumstances except the fact that I am the only Negro in the United States whose grandfather on the mother's side was *not* an Indian chief.

I remember the very day that I became colored. Up to my thirteenth year I lived in the little Negro town of Eatonville, Florida. It is exclusively a colored town. The only white people I knew passed through the town going to or coming from Orlando. The native whites rode dusty horses, the Northern tourists chugged down the sandy village road in automobiles. The town knew the Southerners and never stopped cane chewing when they passed. But the Northerners were something else again. They were peered at cautiously from behind the curtains by the timid. The more venturesome would come out on the porch to watch them go past and got just as much pleasure out of the tourists as the tourists got out of the village.

The front porch might seem a daring place for the rest of the town, but it was a gallery seat for me. My favorite place was atop the gate-post. Proscenium box for a born first-nighter. Not only did I enjoy the show, but I didn't mind the actors knowing that I liked it. I usually spoke to them in passing. I'd wave at them and when they returned my salute, I would say something like this: "Howdy-do-well-I-thank-you-where-you-goin'?" Usually automobile or the horse paused at this, and after a queer exchange of compliments, I would probably "go a piece of the way" with them, as we say in farthest Florida. If one of my family happened to come to the front in time to see me, of course negotiations would be rudely broken off. But even so, it is clear that I was the first "welcome-to-our-state" Floridian, and I hope the Miami Chamber of Commerce will please take notice.

During this period, white people differed from colored to me only in that they rode through town and never lived there. They liked to hear me "speak pieces" and sing and wanted to see me dance the parse-me-la, and gave me generously of their small silver for doing these things, which seemed strange to me for I wanted to do them so much that I needed bribing to stop. Only they didn't know it. The colored people gave no dimes. They deplored any joyful tendencies in me, but I was their Zora nevertheless. I belonged to them, to the nearby hotels, to the county—everybody's Zora.

But changes came in the family when I was thirteen, and I was sent to school in Jacksonville. I left Eatonville, the town of the oleanders, as Zora. When I disembarked from the river-boat at Jacksonville, she was no more. It seemed that I had suffered a sea change. I was not Zora of Orange County any more, I was now a little colored girl. I found it out in certain ways. In my heart as well as in the mirror, I became a fast brown—warranted not to rub nor run.

But I am not tragically colored. There is no great sorrow dammed up in my soul, nor lurking behind my eyes. I do not mind at all. I do not belong to the sobbing school of Negrohood who hold that nature somehow has given them a lowdown dirty deal and whose feelings are all hurt about it. Even in the helter-skelter skirmish that is my life, I have seen that the world is to the strong regardless of a little pigmentation more or less. No, I do not weep at the world—I am too busy sharpening my oyster knife.

Someone is always at my elbow reminding me that I am the grand-daughter of slaves. It fails to register depression with me. Slavery is sixty years in the past. The operation was successful and the patient is doing well, thank you. The terrible struggle that made me an American out of a potential slave said "On the line!" The Reconstruction said "Get set!"; and the generation be-fore said "Go!" I am off to a flying start and I must not halt in the stretch to look behind and weep. Slavery is the price I paid for civilization, and the choice was not with me. It is a bully adventure and worth all that I have paid through my ancestors for it. No one on earth ever had a greater chance for glory. The world to be won and nothing to be lost. It is thrilling to think—to know that for any act of mine, I shall get twice as much praise or twice as much blame. It is quite exciting to hold the center of the national stage, with the specta-tors not knowing whether to laugh or to weep.

The position of my white neighbor is much more difficult. No brown specter pulls up a chair beside me when I sit down to eat. No dark ghost thrusts its leg against mine in bed. The game of keeping what one has is never so ex-citing as the game of getting.

I do not always feel colored. Even now I often achieve the unconscious Zora of Eatonville before the Hegira. I feel most colored when I am thrown against a sharp white background.

For instance at Barnard. "Besides the waters of the Hudson" I feel my race. Among the thousand white persons, I am a dark rock surged upon, and overswept, but through it all, I remain myself. When covered by the waters, I am: and the ebb but reveals me again.

Sometimes it is the other way around. A white person is set down in our midst, but the contrast is just as sharp for me. For instance, when I sit in the drafty basement that is The New World Cabaret with a white person, my color comes. We enter chatting about any little nothing that we have in common and are seated by the jazz waiters. In the abrupt way that jazz orchestras have, this one plunges into a number. It loses no time in circumlocutions, but gets right down to business. It constricts the thorax and splits the heart with its tempo and narcotic harmonies. This orchestra grows rambunctious, rears on its hind legs and attacks the tonal veil with primitive fury, rending it, clawing it until it breaks through to the jungle beyond. I follow those heathen— follow them exultingly. I dance wildly inside myself; I yell within, I whoop; I shake my assegai above my head, I hurl it true to the mark *yeeeeooww!* I am in the jungle and living in the jungle way. My face is painted red and yellow and my body is painted blue. My pulse is throbbing like a war drum. I want to slaughter something—give pain, give death to what, I do not know. But the piece ends. The men of the orchestra wipe their lips and rest their fingers. I creep back slowly to the veneer we call civilization with the last tone and find the white friend sitting motionless in his seat smoking calmly.

"Good music they have here," he remarks, drumming the table with his fingertips.

Music. The great blobs of purple and red emotion have not touched him. He has only heard what I felt. He is far away and I see him but dimly across the ocean and the continent that have fallen between us. He is so pale with his whiteness then and I am *so* colored.

At certain times I have no race, I am *me*. When I set my hat at a certain angle and saunter down Seventh Avenue, Harlem City, feeling as snooty as the lions in front of the Forty-Second Street Library, for instance. So far as my feelings are concerned, Peggy Hopkins Joyce on the Boule Mich with her gorgeous raiment, stately carriage, knees knocking together in a most aristocratic manner, has nothing on me. The cosmic Zora emerges. I belong to no race nor time. I am the eternal feminine with its string of beads.

I have no separate feeling about being an American citizen and colored. I am merely a fragment of the Great Soul that surges within the boundaries. My country, right or wrong.

Sometimes, I feel discriminated against, but it does not make me angry. It merely astonishes me. How *can* any deny themselves the pleasure of my company? It's beyond me.

But in the main, I feel like a brown bag of miscellany propped against a wall. Against a wall in company with other bags, white, red and yellow. Pour out the contents, and there is discovered a jumble of small things priceless and worthless. A first-water diamond, an empty spool, bits of broken glass, lengths of string, a key to a door long since crumbled away, a rusty knife-blade, old shoes saved for a road that never was and never will be, a nail bent under the weight of things too heavy for any nail, a dried flower or two still a little fragrant. In your hand is the brown bag. On the ground before you is the jumble it held—so much like the jumble in the bags, could they be emptied, that all might be dumped in a single heap and the bags refilled without altering the content of any greatly. A bit of colored glass more or less would not matter. Perhaps that is how the Great Stuffer of Bags filled them in the first place—who knows?

Jorge Luis Borges

BORGES AND I

It is to my other self, to Borges, that things happen. I walk about Buenos Aires and I pause, almost mechanically, to contemplate the arch of an entry or the portal of a church: news of Borges comes to me in the mail, and I see his name on a short list of professors or in a biographical dictionary. I am fond of hour-glasses, maps, eighteenth-century typography, the etymology of words, the tang of coffee, and the prose of Stevenson: the other one shares these enthu-siasms, but in a rather vain, theatrical way. It would be an exaggeration to call our relationship hostile. I live, I agree to go on living, so that Borges may fash-ion his literature; that literature justifies me. I do not mind admitting that he has managed to write a few worthwhile pages, but these pages cannot save me, perhaps because good writing belongs to nobody, not even to my other, but rather to language itself, to the tradition. Beyond that, I am doomed to oblivion, utterly doomed, and no more than certain flashes of my existence can survive in the work of my other. Little by little I am surrendering every-thing to him, although I am well aware of his perverse habit of falsifying and exaggerating. Spinoza understood that everything wishes to continue in its own being: a stone wishes to be a stone, eternally, a tiger a tiger. I must go on in Borges, not in myself (if I am anyone at all). But I recognize myself much less in the books he writes than in many others or in the clumsy plucking of a gui-tar. Years ago I tried to cut free from him and I went from myths of suburban life to games with time and infinity; but those games belong to Borges now and I will have to come up with something else. And so my life leaks away and I lose everything, and everything passes into oblivion, or to my other.

    I cannot tell which one of us is writing this page.

Translated by Alastair Reid

THOSE WHO
MUST JUMP

Now I am thinking about jumping from the Golden Gate Bridge, and about
other places where people have jumped to their deaths for many years. I think
I should find out more about this, for I have an idea that there is some sort of
collection of spirit strength or power or love in those places that says, *no,* or
yes, or *now.*

I feel very strongly that this is true of the Golden Gate Bridge. Today I
heard that people are trying once more to build a kind of suicide-prevention
railing along its side, which would keep us from seeing the bay and the beautiful view of the city. I haven't read much about suicide lately, but I believe
that 98 percent of such deaths leave more evil than good after them. Even my
husband Dillwyn's death, which I still feel was justified, left many of us with
some bad things. And when my brother David died, about a year after my
brother Timmy did, my mother asked me very seriously if I felt that Timmy's
death had influenced David to commit his own suicide, which to me remains
a selfish one, compared with the first. I said, "Of course, yes! I do think so,
Mother." And I *did* think then that Timmy's doing away with himself helped
David to kill himself. But there was *really* no connection; we don't know what
the limit of tolerance is in any human being.

I do think, though, that there *has* to be a place where one can jump to
one's death. There have always been such places. There is one in Japan that is
quite famous. I believe it has something to do with Mount Fuji, which I saw
in a strange breathtaking view from far away one day when Norah and I were
in Japan in 1978. We had gone out with our chauffeur to meet some people
for lunch, and suddenly the driver stopped the car abruptly. He said in an odd
voice, "Look! Look!" And there, rising above a most dramatic Japanese-carved
bank of mist and dark and light and lavender and white, was Fujiyama.

Even from a distance I could feel some of its enormous magic, and my hair prickled on my head. It was exactly like all the bad pictures I had seen on calendars and cans of beer. But it was there, and it was beautiful beyond the face of any god. It was all-powerful, and I felt like dying.

I have always known that there are some people who must jump, but I never really knew about it myself until I was almost overcome once by a need to go off the Golden Gate Bridge. I feel quite impersonal about it now, just as I did the day Arnold Gingrich came out to California and dedicated one whole day to me.

He said, "Please, let's make a list of everything you like to plan but never really do." It was all very touristy: we went to the Cliff House first, and then we drove to the San Francisco end of the Golden Gate Bridge, where I thought we would walk halfway across and then walk back. I never did tell Arnold about what happened, but about a quarter of a mile onto the bridge I realized that the whizzing cars on one side and the peaceful bay on the other were splitting me in two. The stronger half looked toward the city, the tranquil city, and I was almost overcome with the terrible need to jump off and be more peaceful.

I know it wasn't the sound of the traffic. It was a kind of force that was almost as strong as I, and I felt sick at the effort to resist it. I remember I took Arnold's arm and said, very coolly, "Let's go back now. Let's not go any further." And without question we turned around, and I stayed on the inside track, near the bridge rail, and as long as I kept my hand firmly on Arnold's arm I knew I would not do anything foolish. But I know that I have never had such a strong feeling of forces outside myself, except once at Stonehenge—

No, now that is not exactly true; there *were* two or three other times. One time, I remember, when Al and I were living in a room in Dijon above a pastry shop on the rue Monge, I felt a wave of horror. I didn't know it then, but the little square where I went to get water in big pitchers for our cooking and washing and so on had been an execution spot during the French Revolution. The guillotine was set up in that little *place,* and many fine Burgundians had their heads roll there.

I remember our apartment was charming—one large room with three windows looking down onto the old *place.* There was an alcove with a bed in it, and Al slept on the outside of the bed and I was on the inside, and one night I jumped right over him and stood in the middle of the room, overcome by a sense of horror and fear. I felt filthy. Al woke up and asked what was wrong. I said, "Nothing! Nothing!" But I felt absolutely clammy and horror-stricken by something I did not understand.

Such times have made me believe that there are congregations of evil and that they are stronger than any of us. This is why people who are perhaps weak to begin with jump to their death at times. Perhaps many of them, like me, do not want to jump off into the deep water far, far below, but something says: Jump!

This is why I have often said, in a rather casual way, that I don't think there should be a fence on the Golden Gate Bridge. Some people are going to jump. And if they can't join the waters deep below and be swept out to sea, I think there should be someplace else for them. But that place and others like it have always been chosen not by the citizens of San Francisco or elsewhere and not by the people who built the bridge but by something much stronger than we know.

Perhaps there is something about water, or anything bridging a body of water, that seems to attract people to jump off out down into it. Very few people jump down into a pit of manure, except by accident, but there is something about a bridge over clear water, no matter how far down (perhaps the farther the better), that does pull people down into it, toward it. I know this pull well, and I have no feeling of impatience or anything but tolerance for the people who jump. There *must* be those places. There are those places.

I have not said that the Golden Gate itself had a feeling of evil when I almost jumped off it. Rather, I felt an urging toward oblivion, I suppose, toward peace. I do not believe it was bad. I do feel the Golden Gate Bridge is a place of great beauty, where many people merge with that beauty into a kind of serenity, a compulsion to get out of this world and into a better one. And that is not evil at all. But I do know that there are many evil things that lurk in the minds of all people who are left after the suicide of somebody they love.

Jack Kerouac

PASSING THROUGH
TANGIERS

from *Desolation Angels*

50

What a crazy picture, maybe the picture of the typical American, sitting on a boat mulling over fingernails wondering where to really go, what to do next—I suddenly realized I had nowhere to turn at all.

But it was on this trip that the great change took place in my life which I called a "complete turningabout" on that earlier page, turning from a youthful brave sense of adventure to a complete nausea concerning experience in the world at large, a *revulsion* in all the six senses. And as I say the first sign of that revulsion had appeared during the dreamy solitary comfort of the two months on Desolation mountain, before Mexico, since which time I'd been melanged again with all my friends and old adventures, as you saw, and not so 'sweetly,' but now I was alone again. And the same feeling came to me: Avoid the World, it's just a lot of dust and drag and means nothing in the end. But what to do instead? And here I was relentlessly being carried to further "adventures" across the sea. But it was really in Tangiers after an overdose of opium the turningabout really clicked down and locked. In a minute—but meanwhile another experience, at sea, put the fear of the world in me, like an omen warning. This was a huge tempest that whacked at our C-4 from the North, from the Januaries and Pleniaries of Iceland and Baffin Bay. During wartime I'd actually sailed in those Northern seas of the Arctic but it was only in summertime: now, a thousand miles south of these in the void of January Seas, gloom, the cappers came glurring in gray spray as high as a house and plowed rivers all over our bow and down the washes. Furyiating howling Blakean glooms, thunders of thumping, washing waving sick manship diddling like a long cork for nothing in the mad waste. Some old Breton knowledge of the sea still in my blood now shuddered. When I saw those walls of water advancing one by one for miles in gray carnage I cried in my soul WHY DIDNT I STAY HOME!? But it was too late. When the third night came the ship was heaving from side to side so badly even the Yugoslavs went to bed and jammed themselves down between pillows and blankets. The kitchen was insane all night with crashing and toppling pots even tho they'd been secured. It scares a seaman to hear the Kitchen scream in fear. For eating at first the steward had placed dishes on a wet table-cloth, and of course no soup in soupbowls but in deep cups, but now it was too late for even that. The men chewed at biscuits as they staggered to their knees in their wet sou'westers. Out on deck where I went a minute the heel of the ship was enough to kick you over the gunwale straight *at* walls of water, sperash. Deck lashed trucks groaned and broke their cables and smashed around. It was a Biblical Tempest like an old dream. In the night I prayed with fear to God Who was now taking all of us, the souls on board, at this dread particular time, for reasons of His own, at last. In my semi delirium I thought I saw a snow white ladder being held down to us from the sky. I saw Stella Maris over the Sea like a statue of Liberty in all shining white. I thought of all the sailors that ever drowned and O the choking thought of it, from Phoenicians of 3000 years ago to poor little teenage sailors of America only last war (some of whom I'd sailed in safety with)— The carpets of sinking water all deep blue *green* in the middle of the ocean, with their damnable patterns of foam, the sickening choking *too-much* of it even tho you're only looking at the surface—beneath all that the upwell of cold miles of fathoms—swaying, rolling, smashing, the tonnages of Peligroso Roar beating, heaving, swirling—not a face in sight! Here comes more! Duck! The whole ship (only as long as a Village) ducks into it shuddering, the crazy screws furiously turn in nothingness, shaking the ship, slap, the bow's now up, thrown up, the screws are dreaming deep below, the ship hasnt gained ten feet—it's like that— It's like frost in your face, like the cold mouths of ancient fathers, like wood cracking in the sea. Not even a fish in sight. It's the thunderous jubilation of Neptune and his bloody wind god canceling men. "All I had to do was stay home, give it all up, get a little home for me and Ma, meditate, live quiet, read in the sun, drink wine in the moon in old clothes, pet my kitties, sleep good dreams—now look at this *petrain* I got me in, Oh dammit!" ("Petrain" is a 16th Century French word meaning "mess.") But God chose to let us live as at dawn the captain turned the ship the other way and gradually left the storm behind, then headed back east towards Africa and the stars.

51

I feel I didnt explain that right, but it's too late, the moving finger crossed the storm and that's the storm.

I thereafter spent ten quiet days as that old freighter chugged and chugged across the calmest seas without seeming to get anywhere and I read a book on world history, wrote notes, and paced the deck at night. (How insouciantly they write about the sinking of the Spanish fleet in the storm off Ireland, ugh!) (Or even one little Galilean fisherman, drowned forever.) But even in so peaceful and simple an act as reading world history in a comfortable cabin on comfortable seas I felt that awful revulsion for everything—the insane things done in human history even before us, enough to make Apollo cry or Atlas drop his load, my God the massacres, purges, tithes stolen, thieves hanged, crooks imperatored, dubs praetorian'd, benches busted on people's heads, wolves attacked nomad campfires, Genghiz Khans ruining—testes smashed in battle, women raped in smoke, children belted, animals slaughtered, knives raised, bones thrown— Clacking big slurry meatjuiced lips the dub Kings crapping on everybody thru silk— The beggars crapping thru burlap— The mistakes everywhere the mistakes! The smell of old settlements and their cookpots and dungheaps—The Cardinals like "Silk stockings full of mud," the American congressmen who "shine and stink like rotten mackerel in the moonlight"— The scalpings from Dakota to Tamurlane— And the human eyes at Guillotine and burning stake at dawn, the glooms, bridges, mists, nets, raw hands and old dead vests of poor mankind in all these thousands of years of "history" (they call it) and all of it an awful mistake. Why did God do it? or is there really a Devil who led the Fall? Souls in Heaven said "We want to try mortal existence, O God, Lucifer said it's great!"—Bang, down we fall, to this, to concentration camps, gas ovens, barbed wire, atom bombs, television murders, Bolivian starvation, thieves in silk, thieves in neckties, thieves in office, paper shufflers, bureaucrats, insult, rage, dismay, horror, terrified nightmares, secret death of hangovers, cancer, ulcers, strangulation, pus, old age, old age homes, canes, puffed flesh, dropped teeth, stink, tears, and goodbye. Somebody else write it, I dont know how.

How to live with glee and peace therefore? By roaming around with your baggage from state to state each one worse deeper into the darkness of the fearful heart? And the heart only a thumping tube all delicately murderable with snips of artery and vein, with chambers that shut, finally someone eats it with the knife and fork of malice, laughing. (Laughing for awhile anyway.)

Ah but as Julien would say "There's nothing you can do about it, revel in it boy— Bottoms up in every way, Fernando." I think of Fernando his puffed alcoholic eyes like mine looking out on bleak palmettos at dawn, shivering in his scarf: beyond the last Frisian Hill a big scythe is cutting down the daisies of his hope tho he's urged to celebrate this each New Years Eve in Rio or in

Bombay. In Hollywood they swiftly slide the old director in his crypt. Aldous Huxley half blind watches his house burn down, seventy years old and far from the happy walnut chair of Oxford. Nothing, nothing, nothing O but *nothing* could interest me any more for one god damned minute in anything in the *world*. But where else to go?

On the overdose of opium this was intensified to the point where I actually got up and packed to go back to America and find a *home*.

Maxine Hong Kingston

NO NAME WOMAN

from *The Woman Warrior*

"You must not tell anyone," my mother said, "what I am about to tell you. In China your father had a sister who killed herself. She jumped into the family well. We say that your father has all brothers because it is as if she had never been born.

"In 1924 just a few days after our village celebrated seventeen hurry-up weddings—to make sure that every young man who went 'out on the road' would responsibly come home—your father and his brothers and your grandfather and his brothers and your aunt's new husband sailed for America, the Gold Mountain. It was your grandfather's last trip. Those lucky enough to get contracts waved goodbye from the decks. They fed and guarded the stowaways and helped them off in Cuba, New York, Bali, Hawaii. 'We'll meet in California next year,' they said. All of them sent money home.

"I remember looking at your aunt one day when she and I were dressing; I had not noticed before that she had such a protruding melon of a stomach. But I did not think, 'She's pregnant,' until she began to look like other pregnant women, her shirt pulling and the white tops of her black pants showing. She could not have been pregnant, you see, because her husband had been gone for years. No one said anything. We did not discuss it. In early summer she was ready to have the child, long after the time when it could have been possible.

"The village had also been counting. On the night the baby was to be born the villagers raided our house. Some were crying. Like a great saw, teeth strung with lights, files of people walked zigzag across our land, tearing the rice. Their lanterns doubled in the disturbed black water, which drained away through the broken bunds. As the villagers closed in, we could see that some of them, probably men and women we knew well, wore white masks. The people with long hair hung it over their faces. Women with short hair made it stand up on end. Some had tied white bands around their foreheads, arms, and legs.

"At first they threw mud and rocks at the house. Then they threw eggs and began slaughtering our stock. We could hear the animals scream their deaths—the roosters, the pigs, a last great roar from the ox. Familiar wild heads flared in our night windows; the villagers encircled us. Some of the faces stopped to peer at us, their eyes rushing like searchlights. The hands flattened against the panes, framed heads, and left red prints.

"The villagers broke in the front and the back doors at the same time, even though we had not locked the doors against them. Their knives dripped with the blood of our animals. They smeared blood on the doors and walls. One woman swung a chicken, whose throat she had slit, splattering blood in red arcs about her. We stood together in the middle of our house, in the family hall with the pictures and tables of the ancestors around us, and looked straight ahead.

"At that time the house had only two wings. When the men came back, we would build two more to enclose our courtyard and a third one to begin a second courtyard. The villagers pushed through both wings, even your grandparents' rooms, to find your aunt's, which was also mine until the men returned. From this room a new wing for one of the younger families would grow. They ripped up her clothes and shoes and broke her combs, grinding them underfoot. They tore her work from the loom. They scattered the cooking fire and rolled the new weaving in it. We could hear them in the kitchen breaking our bowls and banging the pots. They overturned the great waist-high earthenware jugs; duck eggs, pickled fruits, vegetables burst out and mixed in acrid torrents. The old woman from the next field swept a broom through the air and loosed the spirits-of-the-broom over our heads. 'Pig.' 'Ghost.' 'Pig,' they sobbed and scolded while they ruined our house.

"When they left, they took sugar and oranges to bless themselves. They cut pieces from the dead animals. Some of them took bowls that were not broken and clothes that were not torn. Afterward we swept up the rice and sewed it back up into sacks. But the smells from the spilled preserves lasted. Your aunt gave birth in the pigsty that night. The next morning when I went for the water, I found her and the baby plugging up the family well.

"Don't let your father know that I told you. He denies her. Now that you have started to menstruate, what happened to her could happen to you. Don't humiliate us. You wouldn't like to be forgotten as if you had never been born. The villagers are watchful."

Whenever she had to warn us about life, my mother told stories that ran like this one, a story to grow up on. She tested our strength to establish realities. Those in the emigrant generations who could not reassert brute survival died young and far from home. Those of us in the first American generations have had to figure out how the invisible world the emigrants built around our childhoods fits in solid America.

The emigrants confused the gods by diverting their curses, misleading them with crooked streets and false names. They must try to confuse their offspring as well, who, I suppose, threaten them in similar ways—always trying to get things straight, always trying to name the unspeakable. The Chinese I know hide their names; sojourners take new names when their lives change and guard their real names with silence.

Chinese-Americans, when you try to understand what things in you are Chinese, how do you separate what is peculiar to childhood, to poverty, insanities, one family, your mother who marked your growing with stories, from what is Chinese? What is Chinese tradition and what is the movies?

If I want to learn what clothes my aunt wore, whether flashy or ordinary, I would have to begin, "Remember Father's drowned-in-the-well sister?" I cannot ask that. My mother has told me once and for all the useful parts. She will add nothing unless powered by Necessity, a riverbank that guides her life. She plants vegetable gardens rather than lawns; she carries the odd-shaped tomatoes home from the fields and eats food left for the gods.

Whenever we did frivolous things, we used up energy; we flew high kites. We children came up off the ground over the melting cones our parents brought home from work and the American movie on New Year's Day—*Oh, You Beautiful Doll* with Betty Grable one year, and *She Wore a Yellow Ribbon* with John Wayne another year. After the one carnival ride each, we paid in guilt; our tired father counted his change on the dark walk home.

Adultery is extravagance. Could people who hatch their own chicks and eat the embryos and the heads for delicacies and boil the feet in vinegar for party food, leaving only the gravel, eating even the gizzard lining—could such people engender a prodigal aunt? To be a woman, to have a daughter in starvation time was a waste enough. My aunt could not have been the lone romantic who gave up everything for sex. Women in the old China did not choose. Some man had commanded her to lie with him and be his secret evil. I wonder whether he masked himself when he joined the raid on her family.

Perhaps she had encountered him in the fields or on the mountain where the daughters-in-law collected fuel. Or perhaps he first noticed her in the marketplace. He was not a stranger because the village housed no strangers. She had to have dealings with him other than sex. Perhaps he worked an adjoining field, or he sold her the cloth for the dress she sewed and wore. His demand must have surprised, then terrified her. She obeyed him; she always did as she was told.

When the family found a young man in the next village to be her husband, she had stood tractably beside the best rooster, his proxy, and promised before they met that she would be his forever. She was lucky that he was her age and she would be the first wife, an advantage secure now. The night she first saw him, he had sex with her. Then he left for America. She had almost forgotten what he looked like. When she tried to envision him, she only saw the black and white face in the group photograph the men had had taken before leaving.

The other man was not, after all, much different from her husband. They both gave orders: she followed. "If you tell your family, I'll beat you. I'll kill you. Be here again next week." No one talked sex, ever. And she might have separated the rapes from the rest of living if only she did not have to buy her oil from him or gather wood in the same forest. I want her fear to have lasted just as long as rape lasted so that the fear could have been contained. No drawn-out fear. But women at sex hazarded birth and hence lifetimes. The fear did not stop but permeated everywhere. She told the man, "I think I'm pregnant." He organized the raid against her.

On nights when my mother and father talked about their life back home, sometimes they mentioned an "outcast table" whose business they still seemed to be settling, their voices tight. In a commensal tradition, where food is precious, the powerful older people made wrongdoers eat alone. Instead of letting them start separate new lives like the Japanese, who could become samurais and geishas, the Chinese family, faces averted but eyes glowering sideways, hung on to the offenders and fed them leftovers. My aunt must have lived in the same house as my parents and eaten at an outcast table. My mother spoke about the raid as if she had seen it, when she and my aunt, a daughter-in-law to a different household, should not have been living together at all. Daughters-in-law lived with their husbands' parents, not their own; a synonym for marriage in Chinese is "taking a daughter-in-law." Her husband's parents could have sold her, mortgaged her, stoned her. But they had sent her back to her own mother and father, a mysterious act hinting at disgraces not told me. Perhaps they had thrown her out to deflect the avengers.

She was the only daughter; her four brothers went with her father, husband, and uncles "out on the road" and for some years became western men. When the goods were divided among the family, three of the brothers took land, and the youngest, my father, chose an education. After my grandparents gave their daughter away to her husband's family, they had dispensed all the adventure and all the property. They expected her alone to keep the traditional ways, which her brothers, now among the barbarians, could fumble without detection. The heavy, deep-rooted women were to maintain the past against the flood, safe for returning. But the rare urge west had fixed upon our family, and so my aunt crossed boundaries not delineated in space.

The work of preservation demands that the feelings playing about in one's guts not be turned into action. Just watch their passing like cherry blossoms. But perhaps my aunt, my forerunner, caught in a slow life, let dreams grow and fade and after some months or years went toward what persisted. Fear at the enormities of the forbidden kept her desires delicate, wire and bone. She looked at a man because she liked the way the hair was tucked behind his ears, or she liked the question-mark line of a long torso curving at the shoulder and straight at the hip. For warm eyes or a soft voice or a slow walk—that's all—a few hairs, a line, a brightness, a sound, a pace, she gave up family. She offered us up for a charm that vanished with tiredness, a pigtail that didn't toss when the wind died. Why, the wrong lighting could erase the dearest thing about him.

It could very well have been, however, that my aunt did not take subtle enjoyment of her friend, but, a wild woman, kept rollicking company. Imagining her free with sex doesn't fit, though. I don't know any women like that, or men either. Unless I see her life branching into mine, she gives me no ancestral help.

To sustain her being in love, she often worked at herself in the mirror, guessing at the colors and shapes that would interest him, changing them frequently in order to hit on the right combination. She wanted him to look back.

On a farm near the sea, a woman who tended her appearance reaped a reputation for eccentricity. All the married women blunt-cut their hair in flaps about their ears or pulled it back in tight buns. No nonsense. Neither style blew easily into heart-catching tangles. And at their weddings they displayed themselves in their long hair for the last time. "It brushed the backs of my knees," my mother tells me. "It was braided, and even so, it brushed the backs of my knees."

At the mirror my aunt combed individuality into her bob. A bun could have been contrived to escape into black streamers blowing in the wind or in quiet wisps about her face, but only the older women in our picture album wear buns. She brushed her hair back from her forehead, tucking the flaps behind her ears. She looped a piece of thread, knotted into a circle between her index fingers and thumbs, and ran the double strand across her forehead. When she closed her fingers as if she were making a pair of shadow geese bite, the string twisted together catching the little hairs. Then she pulled the thread away from her skin, ripping the hairs out neatly, her eyes watering from the needles of pain. Opening her fingers, she cleaned the thread, then rolled it along her hairline and the tops of her eyebrows. My mother did the same to me and my sisters and herself. I used to believe that the expression "caught by the short hairs" meant a captive held with a depilatory string. It especially hurt at the temples, but my mother said we were lucky we didn't have to have our feet bound when we were seven. Sisters used to sit on their beds and cry together, she said, as their mothers or their slaves removed the bandages for a few minutes each night and let the blood gush back into their veins. I hope that the man my aunt loved appreciated a smooth brow, that he wasn't just a tits-and-ass man.

Once my aunt found a freckle on her chin, at a spot that the almanac said predestined her for unhappiness. She dug it out with a hot needle and washed the wound with peroxide.

More attention to her looks than these pullings of hairs and pickings at spots would have caused gossip among the villagers. They owned work clothes and good clothes, and they wore good clothes for feasting the new seasons. But since a woman combing her hair hexes beginnings, my aunt rarely found an occasion to look her best. Women looked like great sea snails—the corded wood, babies, and laundry they carried were the whorls on their backs. The Chinese did not admire a bent back; goddesses and warriors stood straight. Still there must have been a marvelous freeing of beauty when a worker laid down her burden and stretched and arched.

Such commonplace loveliness, however, was not enough for my aunt. She dreamed of a lover for the fifteen days of New Year's, the time for families to exchange visits, money, and food. She plied her secret comb. And sure enough she cursed the year, the family, the village, and herself.

Even as her hair lured her imminent lover, many other men looked at her. Uncles, cousins, nephews, brothers would have looked, too, had they been home between journeys. Perhaps they had already been restraining their curiosity, and they left, fearful that their glances, like a field of nesting birds, might be startled and caught. Poverty hurt, and that was their first reason for leaving. But another, final reason for leaving the crowded house was the never-said.

She may have been unusually beloved, the precious only daughter, spoiled and mirror gazing because of the affection the family lavished on her. When her husband left, they welcomed the chance to take her back from the in-laws; she could live like the little daughter for just a while longer. There are stories that my grandfather was different from other people, "crazy ever since the little Jap bayoneted him in the head." He used to put his naked penis on the dinner table, laughing. And one day he brought home a baby girl, wrapped up inside his brown western-style greatcoat. He had traded one of his sons, probably my father, the youngest, for her. My grandmother made him trade back. When he finally got a daughter of his own, he doted on her. They must have all loved her, except perhaps my father, the only brother who never went back to China, having once been traded for a girl.

Brothers and sisters, newly men and women, had to efface their sexual color and present plain miens. Disturbing hair and eyes, a smile like no other, threatened the ideal of five generations living under one roof. To focus blurs, people shouted face to face and yelled from room to room. The immigrants I know have loud voices, unmodulated to American tones even after years away from the village where they called their friendships out across the fields. I have not been able to stop my mother's screams in public libraries or over telephones. Walking erect (knees straight, toes pointed forward, not pigeon-toed, which is Chinese-feminine) and speaking in an inaudible voice, I have tried to turn myself American-feminine. Chinese communication was loud, public. Only sick people had to whisper. But at the dinner table, where the family members came nearest one another, no one could talk, not the outcasts nor any eaters. Every word that falls from the mouth is a coin lost. Silently they gave and accepted food with both hands. A preoccupied child who took his bowl with one hand got a sideways glare. A complete moment of total attention is due everyone alike. Children and lovers have no singularity here, but my aunt used a secret voice, a separate attentiveness.

She kept the man's name to herself throughout her labor and dying; she did not accuse him that he be punished with her. To save her inseminator's name she gave silent birth.

He may have been somebody in her own household, but intercourse with a man outside the family would have been no less abhorrent. All the village were kinsmen, and the titles shouted in loud country voices never let kinship be forgotten. Any man within visiting distance would have been neutralized as a lover—"brother," "younger brother," "older brother"—one hundred and fifteen relationship titles. Parents researched birth charts probably not so much to assure good fortune as to circumvent incest in a population that has but one hundred surnames. Everybody has eight million relatives. How useless then sexual mannerisms, how dangerous.

As if it came from an atavism deeper than fear, I used to add "brother" silently to boys' names. It hexed the boys, who would or would not ask me to dance, and made them less scary and as familiar and deserving of benevolence as girls.

But, of course, I hexed myself also—no dates. I should have stood up, both arms waving, and shouted out across libraries, "Hey, you! Love me back." I had no idea, though, how to make attraction selective, how to control its direction and magnitude. If I made myself American-pretty so that the five or six Chinese boys in the class fell in love with me, everyone else—the Caucasian, Negro, and Japanese boys—would too. Sisterliness, dignified and honorable, made much more sense.

Attraction eludes control so stubbornly that whole societies designed to organize relationships among people cannot keep order, not even when they bind people to one another from childhood and raise them together. Among the very poor and the wealthy, brothers married their adopted sisters, like doves. Our family allowed some romance, paying adult brides' prices and providing dowries so that their sons and daughters could marry strangers. Marriage promises to turn strangers into friendly relatives—a nation of siblings.

In the village structure, spirits shimmered among the live creatures, balanced and held in equilibrium by time and land. But one human being flaring up into violence could open up a black hole, a maelstrom that pulled in the sky. The frightened villagers, who depended on one another to maintain the real, went to my aunt to show her a personal, physical representation of the break she had made in the "roundness." Misallying couples snapped off the future, which was to be embodied in true offspring. The villagers punished her for acting as if she could have a private life, secret and apart from them.

If my aunt had betrayed the family at a time of large grain yields and peace, when many boys were born, and wings were being built on many houses, perhaps she might have escaped such severe punishment. But the men—hungry, greedy, tired of planting in dry soil—had been forced to leave the village in order to send food-money home. There were ghost plagues, bandit plagues, wars with the Japanese, floods. My Chinese brother and sister had died of an unknown sickness. Adultery, perhaps only a mistake during good times, became a crime when the village needed food.

The round moon cakes and round doorways, the round tables of graduated sizes that fit one roundness inside another, round windows and rice bowls—these talismans had lost their power to warn this family of the law: a family must be whole, faithfully keeping the descent line by having sons to feed the old and the dead, who in turn look after the family. The villagers came to show my aunt and her lover-in-hiding a broken house. The villagers were speeding up the circling of events because she was too shortsighted to see that her infidelity had already harmed the village, that waves of consequences would return unpredictably, sometimes in disguise, as now, to hurt her. This roundness had to be made coin-sized so that she would see its circumference: punish her at the birth of her baby. Awaken her to the inexorable. People who refused fatalism because they could invent small resources insisted on culpability. Deny accidents and wrest fault from the stars.

After the villagers left, their lanterns now scattering in various directions toward home, the family broke their silence and cursed her. "Aiaa, we're going to die. Death is coming. Death is coming. Look what you've done. You've killed us. Ghost! Dead ghost! Ghost! You've never been born." She ran out into the fields, far enough from the house so that she could no longer hear their voices, and pressed herself against the earth, her own land no more. When she felt the birth coming, she thought that she had been hurt. Her body seized together. "They've hurt me too much," she thought. "This is gall, and it will kill me." With forehead and knees against the earth, her body convulsed and then relaxed. She turned on her back, lay on the ground. The black well of sky and stars went out and out and out forever; her body and her complexity seemed to disappear. She was one of the stars, a bright dot in blackness, without home, without a companion, in eternal cold and silence. An agoraphobia rose in her, speeding higher and higher, bigger and bigger; she would not be able to contain it; there would no end to fear.

Flayed, unprotected against space, she felt pain return, focusing her body. This pain chilled her—a cold, steady kind of surface pain. Inside, spasmodically, the other pain, the pain of the child, heated her. For hours she lay on the ground, alternately body and space. Sometimes a vision of normal comfort obliterated reality: she saw the family in the evening gambling at the dinner table, the young people massaging their elders' backs. She saw them congratulating one another, high joy on the mornings the rice shoots came up. When these pictures burst, the stars drew yet further apart. Black space opened.

She got to her feet to fight better and remembered that old-fashioned women gave birth in their pigsties to fool the jealous, pain-dealing gods, who do not snatch piglets. Before the next spasms could stop her, she ran to the pigsty, each step a rushing out into emptiness. She climbed over the fence and knelt in the dirt. It was good to have a fence enclosing her, a tribal person alone.

Laboring, this woman who had carried her child as a foreign growth that sickened her every day, expelled it at last. She reached down to touch the hot, wet, moving mass, surely smaller than anything human, and could feel that it was human after all—fingers, toes, nails, nose. She pulled it up on to her belly, and it lay curled there, butt in the air, feet precisely tucked one under the other. She opened her loose shirt and buttoned the child inside. After resting, it squirmed and thrashed and she pushed it up to her breast. It turned its head this way and that until it found her nipple. There, it made little snuffling noises. She clenched her teeth at its preciousness, lovely as a young calf, a piglet, a little dog.

She may have gone to the pigsty as a last act of responsibility: she would protect this child as she had protected its father. It would look after her soul, leaving supplies on her grave. But how would this tiny child without family find her grave when there would be no marker for her anywhere, neither in the earth nor the family hall? No one would give her a family hall name. She had taken the child with her into the wastes. At its birth the two of them had felt the same raw pain of separation, a wound that only the family pressing tight could close. A child with no descent line would not soften her life but only trail after her, ghostlike, begging her to give it purpose. At dawn the villagers on their way to the fields would stand around the fence and look.

Full of milk, the little ghost slept. When it awoke, she hardened her breasts against the milk that crying loosens. Toward morning she picked up the baby and walked to the well.

Carrying the baby to the well shows loving. Otherwise abandon it. Turn its face into the mud. Mothers who love their children take them along. It was probably a girl; there is some hope of forgiveness for boys.

"Don't tell anyone you had an aunt. Your father does not want to hear her name. She has never been born." I have believed that sex was unspeakable and words so strong and fathers so frail that "aunt" would do my father mysterious harm. I have thought that my family, having settled among immigrants who had also been their neighbors in the ancestral land, needed to clean their name, and a wrong word would incite the kinspeople even here. But there is more to this silence: they want me to participate in her punishment. And I have.

In the twenty years since I heard this story I have not asked for details nor said my aunt's name; I do not know it. People who can comfort the dead can also chase after them to hurt them further—a reverse ancestor worship. The real punishment was not the raid swiftly inflicted by the villagers, but the family's deliberately forgetting her. Her betrayal so maddened them, they saw to it that she would suffer forever, even after death. Always hungry, always needing, she would have to beg food from other ghosts, snatch and steal it from those whose living descendants give them gifts. She would have to fight the ghosts massed at crossroads for the buns a few thoughtful citizens leave to decoy her away from village and home so that the ancestral spirits could feast unharassed. At peace, they could act like gods, not ghosts, their descent lines providing them with paper suits and dresses, spirit money, paper houses, paper automobiles, chicken, meat, and rice into eternity—essences delivered up in smoke and flames, steam and incense rising from each rice bowl. In an attempt to make the Chinese care for people outside the family, Chairman Mao encourages us now to give our paper replicas to the spirits of outstanding soldiers and workers, no matter whose ancestors they may be. My aunt remains forever hungry. Goods are not distributed evenly among the dead.

My aunt haunts me—her ghost drawn to me because now, after fifty years of neglect, I alone devote pages of paper to her, though not origamied into houses and clothes. I do not think she always means me well. I am telling on her, and she was a spite suicide, drowning herself in the drinking water. The Chinese are always very frightened of the drowned one, whose weeping ghost, wet hair hanging and skin bloated, waits silently by the water to pull down a substitute.

John Updike

UPDIKE AND I

I created Updike out of the sticks and mud of my Pennsylvania boyhood, so I can scarcely resent it when people, mistaking me for him, stop me on the street and ask me for his autograph. I am always surprised that I resemble him so closely that we can be confused. Meeting strangers, I must cope with an extra brightness in their faces, an expectancy that I will say something worthy of him; they do not realize that he works only in the medium of the written word, where other principles apply, and hours of time can be devoted to a moment's effect. Thrust into "real" time, he can scarcely function, and his awkward pleasantries and anxious stutter emerge through my lips. Myself, I am rather suave. I think fast, on my feet, and have no use for the qualificatory complexities and lame *double entendres* and pained exactations of language in which he is customarily mired. I move swiftly and rather blindly through life, spending the money he earns.

I early committed him to a search for significance, to philosophical issues that give direction and point to his verbal inventions, but am not myself aware of much point or meaning to things. Things *are,* rather unsayably, and when I force myself to peruse his elaborate scrims of words I wonder where he gets it all—not from *me,* I am sure. The distance between us is so great that the bad reviews he receives do not touch me, though I treasure his few prizes and mount them on the walls and shelves of my house, where they instantly yellow and tarnish. That he takes up so much of my time, answering his cloying mail and reading his incessant proofs, I resent. I feel that the fractional time of day he spends away from being Updike is what feeds and inspires him, and yet, perversely, he spends more and more time being Updike, that monster of whom my boyhood dreamed.

Each morning I awake from my dreams, which as I age leave an ever more sour taste. Men once thought dreams to be messages from the gods, and then from something called the subconscious, as it sought a salubrious rearrangement of the contents of the day past; but now it becomes hard to believe that they partake of any economy. Instead, a basic chaos seems expressed: a random play of electricity generates images of inexplicable specificity.

I brush my teeth, I dress and descend to the kitchen, where I eat and read the newspaper, which has been dreaming its own dreams in the night. Postponing the moment, savoring every small news item and vitamin pill and sip of unconcentrated orange juice, I at last return to the upstairs and face the rooms that Updike has filled with his books, his papers, his trophies, his projects. The abundant clutter stifles me, yet I am helpless to clear away much of it. It would be a blasphemy. He has become a sacred reality to me. I gaze at his worn wooden desk, his boxes of dull pencils, his blank-faced word processor, with a religious fear.

Suppose, some day, he fails to show up? I would attempt to do his work, but no one would be fooled.

Mikal Gilmore

THE DREAM

from *Shot in the Heart*

I have dreamed a terrible dream.

In this dream, it is always night. We are in my father's house—an old charred-brown, 1950s-era home. Shingled, two-story, and weather-worn, it is located on the far outskirts of a dead-end American town, pinioned between the night-lights and smoking chimneys of towering industrial factories. In front of the house, forming the border to a forest I am forbidden to trespass, lies a moonlit stretch of railroad track. Throughout the night of the dreams, you can hear a train whistle howling in the distance, heralding the approach of a passenger car from the outside world. For some reason, no train ever follows this signal. There is only the howl.

In the house, people come and go, moving between the darkness outside and the darkness inside. These people are my family, and in the dream, they are all back from the dead. There is my mother, Bessie Gilmore, who lived a life of bitter losses, who died spitting blood, calling the names of her father and her husband—men who had long before brutalized her hopes and her love—crying to them for mercy, for a passage into the darkness that she had so long feared. There is my brother Gaylen, who died young of old wounds, as his new bride sat at his side, holding his hand, watching the life pass from his sunken face. There is my brother Gary, who murdered innocent men in rage against the way life had robbed him of too much time and too much love, and who died when a volley of bullets tore his violent, tortured heart from his chest. There is my brother Frank, who turned increasingly quiet and distant with each new death, who was last seen walking down a road nearby the night-house of this dream, his hands rammed deep into his pockets, a look of uncomprehending pain seizing his face. And there is my father, Frank Sr., who died from the ravages and insults of cancer. Of all the family members, he is in these dreams the least, and when he is there, I end

297

up feeling guilt over his presence: I am always hapy to see him, it turns out, but nobody else is. That's because, in the dreams, as in life, there is the fear that my father will spread anger and ruin too far for his family to survive, that he will somehow find a way to kill those who have already been killed, who have already paid dearly for his legacy. When he appears, sometimes the point of the dream is to convince him that the only cure for all the bitterness, for all the bad blood, is for him to return to death. Lie down, Father, we say. Let us bury you again.

Finally, there is me. I watch my family in these dreams and seem always to feel apart from the fraternity—as if there is a struggle here for love and participation that, somehow, I always fail. And so I watch as my brothers come and go. I look out the windows and see them move in the darkness outside, through the bushes, across the yard, toward the driveway. I watch cars cross the railway tracks. I watch them come and take my brothers and deliver them back, and I know they are moving to and from underworlds that I cannot take part in, because for some reason I cannot leave this house.

Then, one night, years into these dreams, Gary tells me why I can never join my family in its comings and goings, why I am left alone sitting in the living room as they leave: It is because I have not yet entered death. I cannot follow them across the tracks, into the forest where their real lives take place, he says, until I die. He pulls a gun from his coat pocket. He lays it on my lap. There is a door across the room, and he moves toward it. Through the door, there is the night. I see the glimmer of the train tracks. Beyond them, my family. "See you in the darkness beyond," he says.

I do not hesitate. I pick the pistol up. I put its barrel in my mouth. I pull the trigger. I feel the back of my head erupt. It is a softer feeling than I expect. I feel my teeth fracture and disintegrate and pass in a gush of blood out of my mouth. I also feel my life pass out of my mouth, and in that instant I feel a collapse into nothingness. There is darkness, but there is no beyond. There is never any beyond, only the sudden, certain rush of extinction. I know that it is death I am feeling—that is, I know this is how death must truly feel—and I know that this is where beyond ceases to be a possibility.

I have had this dream more than once, in various forms. I always wake at this point, my heart hammering hard, hurting for being torn back from the void that I know is the gateway to the refuge of my ruined family. Or is it the gateway to hell? Either way, I want back into the dream, but in those haunted hours of the night, there is no way back.

Poems That
Tell Stories

Homer

ODYSSEUS BLINDS THE CYCLOPS

from *The Odyssey*, Book 9

In this famous adventure, Odysseus and his men reach the land of "high and mighty Cyclops, / lawless brutes" who live in caverns on mountain peaks, "each a law to himself." They enter the cave of the one-eyed giant Polyphemus in his absence and await his return hoping to be welcomed as guests—"suppliants at [the Cyclops's] mercy."

> There we built a fire, set our hands on the cheeses,
> offered some to the gods and ate the bulk ourselves
> and settled down inside, awaiting his return . . .
> And back he came from pasture, late in the day,
> herding his flocks, lugging a huge load
> of good dry logs to fuel his fire at supper.
> He flung them down in the cave—a jolting crash—
> we scuttled in panic into the deepest dark recess.
> And next he drove his sleek flocks into the open vault,
> all he'd milk at least, but he left the males outside,
> rams and billy goats out in the high-walled yard.
> Then to close his door he hoisted overhead
> a tremendous, massive slab—
> no twenty-two wagons, rugged and four-wheeled,
> could budge that boulder off the ground, I tell you,
> such an immense stone the monster wedged to block his cave!
> Then down he squatted to milk his sheep and bleating goats,
> each in order, and put a suckling underneath each dam.
> And half of the fresh white milk he curdled quickly,
> set it aside in wicker racks to press for cheese,

the other half let stand in pails and buckets,
ready at hand to wash his supper down.
As soon as he'd briskly finished all his chores
he lit his fire and spied us in the blaze and
"*Strangers!*" he thundered out, "now who are you?
Where did you sail from, over the running sea-lanes?
Out on a trading spree or roving the waves like pirates,
sea-wolves raiding at will, who risk their lives
to plunder other men?"
                              The hearts inside us shook,
terrified by his rumbling voice and monstrous hulk.
Nevertheless I found the nerve to answer, firmly,
"Men of Achaea we are and bound now from Troy!
Driven far off course by the warring winds,
over the vast gulf of the sea—battling home
on a strange tack, a route that's off the map,
and so we've come to you . . .
so it must please King Zeus's plotting heart.

We're glad to say we're men of Atrides Agamemnon,
whose fame is the proudest thing on earth these days,
so great a city he sacked, such multitudes he killed!
But since we've chanced on you, we're at your knees
in hopes of a warm welcome, even a guest-gift,
the sort that hosts give strangers. That's the custom.
Respect the gods, my friend. We're suppliants—at your mercy!
Zeus of the Strangers guards all guests and suppliants:
strangers are sacred—Zeus will avenge their rights!"

     "Stranger," he grumbled back from his brutal heart,
"you must be a fool, stranger, or come from nowhere,
telling *me* to fear the gods or avoid their wrath!
We Cyclops never blink at Zeus and Zeus's shield
of storm and thunder, or any other blessed god—
we've got more force by far.
I'd never spare you in fear of Zeus's hatred,
you or your comrades here, unless I had the urge.
But tell me, where did you moor your sturdy ship
when you arrived? Up the coast or close in?
I'd just like to know."

So he laid his trap
but he never caught me, no, wise to the world
I shot back in my crafty way, "My ship?
Poseidon god of the earthquake smashed my ship,
he drove it against the rocks at your island's far cape,
dashed it against a cliff as the winds rode us in.
I and the men you see escaped a sudden death."

Not a word in reply to that, the ruthless brute.
Lurching up, he lunged out with his hands toward my men
and snatching two at once, rapping them on the ground
he knocked them dead like pups—
their brains gushed out all over, soaked the floor—
and ripping them limb from limb to fix his meal
he bolted them down like a mountain-lion, left no scrap,
devoured entrails, flesh and bones, marrow and all!
We flung our arms to Zeus, we wept and cried aloud,
looking on at his grisly work—paralyzed, appalled.
But once the Cyclops had stuffed his enormous gut
with human flesh, washing it down with raw milk,
he slept in his cave, stretched out along his flocks.
And I with my fighting heart, I thought at first
to steal up to him, draw the sharp sword at my hip
and stab his chest where the midriff packs the liver—
I groped for the fatal spot but a fresh thought held me back.
There at a stroke we'd finish off ourselves as well—
how could *we* with our bare hands heave back
that slab he set to block his cavern's gaping maw?
So we lay there groaning, waiting Dawn's first light.

When young Dawn with her rose-red fingers shone once more
the monster relit his fire and milked his handsome ewes,
each in order, putting a suckling underneath each dam,
and as soon as he'd briskly finished all his chores
he snatched up two more men and fixed his meal.
Well-fed, he drove his fat sheep from the cave,
lightly lifting the huge doorslab up and away,
then slipped it back in place
as a hunter flips the lid of his quiver shut.
Piercing whistles—turning his flocks to the hills

he left me there, the heart inside me brooding on revenge:
how could I pay him back? would Athena give me glory?
Here was the plan that struck my mind as best . . .
the Cyclops' great club: there it lay by the pens,
olivewood, full of sap. He'd lopped it off to brandish
once it dried. Looking it over, we judged it big enough
to be the mast of a pitch-black ship with her twenty oars,
a freighter broad in the beam that plows through miles of sea—
so long, so thick it bulked before our eyes. Well,
flanking it now, I chopped off a fathom's length,
pushed it to comrades, told them to plane it down,
and they made the club smooth as I bent and shaved
the tip to a stabbing point. I turned it over
the blazing fire to char it good and hard,
then hid it well, buried deep under the dung
that littered the cavern's floor in thick wet clumps.
And now I ordered my shipmates all to cast lots—
who'd brave it out with me
to hoist our stake and grind it into his eye
when sleep had overcome him? Luck of the draw:
I got the very ones I would have picked myself,
four good men, and I in the lead made five . . .

    Nightfall brought him back, herding his woolly sheep,
and he quickly drove the sleek flock into the vaulted cavern,
rams and all—none left outside in the walled yard—
his own idea, perhaps, or a god led him on.
Then he hoisted the huge slab to block the door
and squatted to milk his sheep and bleating goats,
each in order, putting a suckling underneath each dam,
and as soon as he'd briskly finished all his chores
he snatched up two more men and fixed his meal.
But this time I lifted a carved wooden bowl,
brimful of my ruddy wine,
and went right up to the Cyclops, enticing,
"Here, Cyclops, try this wine—to top off
the banquet of human flesh you've bolted down!
Judge for yourself what stock our ship had stored.
I brought it here to make you a fine libation,
hoping you would pity me, Cyclops, send me home,
but your rages are insufferable. You barbarian—

how can any man on earth come visit you after *this?*
What you've done outrages all that's right!"

At that he seized the bowl and tossed it off
and the heady wine pleased him immensely. "More"—
he demanded a second bowl—"a hearty helping!
And tell me your name now, quickly,
so I can hand my guest a gift to warm *his* heart.
Our soil yields the Cyclops powerful, full-bodied wine
and the rains from Zeus build its strength. But this,
this is nectar, ambrosia—this flows from heaven!"

So he declared. I poured him another fiery bowl—
three bowls I brimmed and three he drank to the last drop,
the fool, and then, when the wine was swirling round his brain,
I approached my host with a cordial, winning word:
"So, you ask me the name I'm known by, Cyclops?
I will tell you. But you must give me a guest-gift
as you've promised. Nobody—that's my name. Nobody—
so my mother and father call me, all my friends."

But he boomed back at me from his ruthless heart,
"Nobody? I'll eat Nobody last of all his friends—
I'll eat the others first! That's my gift to *you!"*
                                             With that
he toppled over, sprawled full-length, flat on his back
and lay there, his massive neck slumping to one side,
and sleep that conquers all overwhelmed him now
as wine came spurting, flooding up from his gullet
with chunks of human flesh—he vomited, blind drunk.
Now, at last, I thrust our stake in a bed of embers
to get it glowing hot and rallied all my comrades:
"Courage—no panic now, don't hang back!"
And green as it was, just as the olive stake
was about to catch fire—the glow terrific, yes—
I dragged it from the flames, my men clustering round
as some god breathed enormous courage through us all.
Hoisting high that olive stake with its stabbing point,
straight into the monster's eye they rammed it hard—
I drove my weight on it from above and bored it home
as a shipwright bores his beam with a shipwright's drill

that men below, whipping the strap back and forth, whirl
and the drill keeps twisting faster, never stopping—
So we seized our stake with its fiery tip
and bored it round and round in the giant's eye
till blood came boiling up around that smoking shaft
and the hot blast singed his brow and eyelids round the core
and the broiling eyeball burst—
                                        its crackling roots blazed
and hissed—
                    as a blacksmith plunges a heavy ax or adze
in an ice-cold bath and the metal screeches steam
and its temper hardens—that's the iron's strength—
so the eye of the Cyclops sizzled round that stake!
He loosed a hideous roar, the rock walls echoed round
and we scuttled back in terror. The monster wrenched the spike
from his eye and out it came with a red geyser of blood—
he flung it aside with frantic hands, and mad with pain
he bellowed out for help from his neighbor Cyclops
living round about in caves on windswept crags.
Hearing his cries, they lumbered up from every side
and hulking around his cavern, asked what ailed him:
"What, Polyphemus, what in the world's the trouble?
Roaring out in the godsent night to rob us of our sleep.
Surely no one's rustling your flocks against your will—
surely no one's trying to kill you now by fraud or force!"

         "Nobody, friends"—Polyphemus bellowed back from his cave—
"Nobody's killing me now by fraud and not by force!"

         "If you're alone," his friends boomed back at once,
"and nobody's trying to overpower you now—look,
it must be a plague sent here by mighty Zeus
and there's no escape from that.
You'd better pray to your father, Lord Poseidon."

         They lumbered off, but laughter filled my heart
to think how nobody's name—my great cunning stroke—
had duped them one and all. But the Cyclops there,
still groaning, racked with agony, groped around
for the huge slab, and heaving it from the doorway,
down he sat in the cave's mouth, his arms spread wide,

hoping to catch a comrade stealing out with sheep—
such a blithering fool he took me for!
But I was already plotting . . .
what was the best way out? how could I find
escape from death for my crew, myself as well?
My wits kept weaving, weaving cunning schemes—
life at stake, monstrous death staring us in the face—
till this plan struck my mind as best. That flock,
those well-fed rams with their splendid thick fleece,
sturdy, handsome beasts with their dark weight of wool:
I lashed them abreast, quietly, twisting the willow-twigs
the Cyclops slept on—giant, lawless brute—I took them
three by three; each ram in the middle bore a man
while the two rams either side would shield him well.
So three beasts to bear each man, but as for myself?
There was one bellwether ram, the prize of all the flock,
and clutching him by his back, tucked up under
his shaggy belly, there I hung, face upward,
both hands locked in his marvelous deep fleece,
clinging for dear life, my spirit steeled, enduring . . .
So we held on, desperate, waiting Dawn's first light.

As soon

as young Dawn with her rose-red fingers shone once more
the rams went rumbling out of the cave toward pasture,
the ewes kept bleating round the pens, unmilked,
their udders about to burst. Their master now,
heaving in torment, felt the back of each animal
halting before him here, but the idiot never sensed
my men were trussed up under their thick fleecy ribs.
And last of them all came my great ram now, striding out,
weighed down with his dense wool and my deep plots.
Stroking him gently, powerful Polyphemus murmured,
"Dear old ram, why last of theflock to quit the cave?
In the good old days you'd never lag behind the rest—
you with your long marching strides, first by far
of the flock to graze the fresh young grasses,
first by far to reach the rippling streams,
first to turn back home, keen for your fold
when night comes on—but now you're last of all.
And why? Sick at heart for your master's eye
that coward gouged out with his wicked crew?—

only after he'd stunned my wits with wine—
that, that Nobody . . .
who's not escaped his death, I swear, not yet.
Oh if only you thought like *me,* had words like *me*
to tell me where that scoundrel is cringing from my rage!
I'd smash him against the ground, I'd spill his brains—
flooding across my cave—and that would ease my heart
of the pains that good-for-nothing Nobody made me suffer!"

And with that threat he let my ram go free outside.
But soon as we'd got one foot past cave and courtyard,
first I loosed myself from the ram, then loosed my men,
then quickly, glancing back again and again we drove
our flock, good plump beasts with their long shanks,
straight to the ship, and a welcome sight we were
to loyal comrades—we who'd escaped our deaths—
but for all the rest they broke down and wailed.
I cut it short, I stopped each shipmate's cries,
my head tossing, brows frowning, silent signals
to hurry, tumble our fleecy herd on board,
launch out on the open sea!
They swung aboard, they sat to the oars in ranks
and in rhythm churned the water white with stroke on stroke.
But once offshore as far as a man's shout can carry,
I called back to the Cyclops, stinging taunts:
"So, Cyclops, no weak coward it was whose crew
you bent to devour there in your vaulted cave—
you with your brute force! Your filthy crimes
came down on your own head, you shameless cannibal,
daring to eat your guests in your own house—
so Zeus and the other gods have paid you back!"

That made the rage of the monster boil over.
Ripping off the peak of a towering crag, he heaved it
so hard the boulder landed just in front of our dark prow
and a huge swell reared up as the rock went plunging under—
a tidal wave from the open sea. The sudden backwash
drove us landward again, forcing us close inshore
but grabbing a long pole, I thrust us off and away,
tossing my head for dear life, signaling crews
to put their backs in the oars, escape grim death.

They threw themselves at the labor, rowed on fast
but once we'd plowed the breakers twice as far,
again I began to taunt the Cyclops—men around me
trying to check me, calm me, left and right,
"So headstrong—why? Why rile the beast again?"

    "That rock he flung in the sea just now, hurling our ship
to shore once more—we thought we'd die on the spot!"

    "If he'd caught a sound from *one* of us, just a whisper,
he would have crushed our heads and ship timbers
with one heave of another flashing, jagged rock!"

    "Good god, the brute can throw!"
                            So they begged
but they could not bring my fighting spirit round.
I called back with another burst of anger, "Cyclops—
if any man on the face of the earth should ask you
who blinded you, shamed you so—say Odysseus,
raider of cities, *he* gouged out your eye,
Laertes' son who makes his home in Ithaca!"

    So I vaunted and he groaned back in answer,
"Oh no, no—that prophecy years ago . . .
it all comes home to me with a vengeance now!
We once had a prophet here, a great tall man,
Telemus, Eurymus' son, a master at reading signs,
who grew old in his trade among his fellow-Cyclops.
All this, he warned me, would come to pass someday—
that I'd be blinded here at the hands of one Odysseus.
But I always looked for a handsome giant man to cross my path,
some fighter clad in power like armor-plate, but now,
look what a dwarf, a spineless good-for-nothing,
stuns me with wine, then gouges out my eye!
Come here, Odysseus, let me give you a guest-gift
and urge Poseidon the earthquake god to speed you home.
I am his son and he claims to be my father, true,
and he himself will heal me if he pleases—
no other blessed god, no man can do the work!"

"Heal you!"—
here was my parting shot—"Would to god I could strip you
of life and breath and ship you down to the House of Death
as surely as no one will ever heal your eye,
not even your earthquake god himself!"

But at that he bellowed out to lord Poseidon,
thrusting his arms to the starry skies, and prayed, "Hear me—
Poseidon, god of the sea-blue mane who rocks the earth!
If I really *am* your son and you claim to be my father—
come, grant that Odysseus, raider of cities,
Laertes' son who makes his home in Ithaca,
never reaches home. Or if he's fated to see
his people once again and reach his well-built house
and his own native country, let him come home late
and come a broken man—all shipmates lost,
alone in a stranger's ship—
and let him find a world of pain at home!"

                                        So he prayed
and the god of the sea-blue mane Poseidon heard his prayer.
The monster suddenly hoisted a boulder—far larger—
wheeled and heaved it, putting his weight behind it,
massive strength, and the boulder crashed close,
landing just in the wake of our dark stern,
just failing to graze the rudder's bladed edge.
A huge swell reared up as the rock went plunging under,
yes, and the tidal breaker drove us out to our island's
far shore where all my well-decked ships lay moored,
clustered, waiting, and huddled round them, crewmen
sat in anguish, waiting, chafing for our return.
We beached our vessel hard ashore on the sand,
we swung out in the frothing surf ourselves
and herding Cyclops' sheep from our deep holds
we shared them round so no one, not on my account,
would go deprived of his fair share of spoils.
But the splendid ram—as we meted out the flocks
my friends-in-arms made *him* my prize of honor,
mine alone, and I slaughtered him on the beach
and burnt his thighs to Cronus' mighty son,

Zeus of the thundercloud who rules the world.
But my sacrifices failed to move the god:
Zeus was still obsessed with plans to destroy
my entire oarswept fleet and loyal crew of comrades.
Now all day long till the sun went down we sat
and feasted on sides of meat and heady wine.
Then when the sun had set and night came on
we lay down and slept at the water's shelving edge.
When young Dawn with her rose-red fingers shone once more
I roused the men straight off, ordering all crews
to man the ships and cast off cables quickly.
They swung aboard at once, they sat to the oars in ranks
and in rhythm churned the water white with stroke on stroke.
And from there we sailed on, glad to escape our death
yet sick at heart for the comrades we had lost.

Translated by Robert Fagles

Ovid

THE STORY OF ACTAEON

from *Metamorphoses*, Book 3

One of these grandsons was the lad Actaeon,
First cause of Cadmus' sorrow. On his forehead
Horns sprouted, and his hound-dogs came to drink
The blood of their young master. In the story
You will find Actaeon guiltless; put the blame
On luck, not crime: what crime is there in error?

There was a mountain, on whose slopes had fallen
The blood of many kinds of game: high noon,
Short shadows, and Actaeon, at ease, and friendly
Telling his company: "Our nets and spears
Drip with the blood of our successful hunting.
To-day has brought us luck enough; to-morrow
We try again. The Sun-god, hot and burning,
Is halfway up his course. Give up the labor,
Bring home the nets." And they obeyed his orders.

There was a valley there, all dark and shaded
With pine and cypress, sacred to Diana,
Gargaphie, its name was, and it held
Deep in its inner shade a secret grotto
Made by no art, unless you think of Nature
As being an artist. Out of rock and tufa
She had formed an archway, where the shining water
Made slender watery sound, and soon subsided
Into a pool, and grassy banks around it.
The goddess of the woods, when tired from hunting,

Came here to bathe her limbs in the cool crystal.
She gave her armor-bearer spear and quiver
And loosened bow; another's arm received
The robe, laid off; two nymphs unbound her sandals,
And one, Crocale, defter than the others,
Knotted the flowing hair; others brought water,
Psecas, Phyale, Nephele, and Rhanis,
Pouring it out from good-sized urns, as always.
But look! While she was bathing there, all naked,
Actaeon came, with no more thought of hunting
Till the next day, wandering, far from certain,
Through unfamiliar woodland till he entered
Diana's grove, as fate seemed bound to have it.
And when he entered the cool dripping grotto,
The nymphs, all naked, saw him, saw a man,
And beat their breasts and screamed, and all together
Gathered around their goddess, tried to hide her
With their own bodies, but she stood above them,
Taller by head and shoulders. As the clouds
Grow red at sunset, as the daybreak reddens,
Diana blushed at being seen, and turned
Aside a little from her close companions,
Looked quickly for her arrows, found no weapon
Except the water, but scooped up a handful
And flung it in the young man's face, and over
The young man's hair. Those drops had vengeance in them.
She told him so: "Tell people you have seen me,
Diana, naked! Tell them if you can!"
She said no more, but on the sprinkled forehead
Horns of the long-lived stag began to sprout,
The neck stretched out, the ears were long and pointed,
The arms were legs, the hands were feet, the skin
A dappled hide, and the hunter's heart was fearful.
Away in flight he goes, and, going, marvels
At his own speed, and finally sees, reflected,
His features in a quiet pool. "Alas!"
He tries to say, but has no words. He groans,
The only speech he has, and the tears run down
Cheeks that are not his own. There is one thing only
Left him, his former mind. What should he do?
Where should he go—back to the royal palace

Or find some place of refuge in the forest?
Fear argues against one, and shame the other.
And while he hesitates, he sees his hounds,
Blackfoot, Trailchaser, Hungry, Hurricane,
Gazelle and Mountain-Ranger, Spot and Sylvan,
Swift Wingfoot, Glen, wolf-sired, and the bitch Harpy
With her two pups, half-grown, ranging beside her,
Tigress, another bitch, Hunter, and Lanky,
Chop-jaws, and Soot, and Wolf, with the white marking
On his black muzzle, Mountaineer, and Power,
The Killer, Whirlwind, Whitey, Blackskin, Grabber,
And others it would take too long to mention,
Arcadian hounds, and Cretan-bred, and Spartan.
The whole pack, with the lust of blood upon them,
Come baying over cliffs and crags and ledges
Where no trail runs: Actaeon, once pursuer
Over this very ground, is now pursued,
Fleeing his old companions. He would cry
"I am Actaeon: recognize your master!"
But the words fail, and nobody could hear him
So full the air of baying. First of all
The Killer fastens on him, then the Grabber,
Then Mountaineer gets hold of him by a shoulder.
These three had started last, but beat the others
By a short-cut through the mountains. So they run him
To stand at bay until the whole pack gathers
And all together nip and slash and fasten
Till there is no more room for wounds. He groans,
Making a sound not human, but a sound
No stag could utter either, and the ridges
Are filled with that heart-breaking kind of moaning.
Actaeon goes to his knees, like a man praying,
Faces them all in silence, with his eyes
In mute appeal, having no arms to plead with,
To stretch to them for mercy. His companions,
The other hunting lads, urge on the pack
With shouts as they did always, and not knowing
What has become of him, they call *Actaeon!*
Actaeon! each one louder than the others,
As if they thought him miles away. He answers,
Hearing his name, by turning his head toward them,

And hears them growl and grumble at his absence,
Calling him lazy, missing the good show
Of quarry brought to bay. Absence, for certain,
He would prefer, but he is there; and surely
He would rather see and hear the dogs than feel them.
They circle him, dash in, and nip, and mangle
And lacerate and tear their prey, not master,
No master whom they know, only a deer.
And so he died, and so Diana's anger
Was satisfied at last.

Translated by Rolf Humphries

Robert Frost

HOME BURIAL

He saw her from the bottom of the stairs
Before she saw him. She was starting down,
Looking back over her shoulder at some fear.
She took a doubtful step and then undid it
To raise herself and look again. He spoke
Advancing toward her: "What is it you see
From up there always—for I want to know."
She turned and sank upon her skirts at that,
And her face changed from terrified to dull.
He said to gain time: "What is it you see,"
Mounting until she cowered under him.
"I will find out now—you must tell me, dear."
She, in her place, refused him any help
With the least stiffening of her neck and silence
She let him look, sure that he wouldn't see,
Blind creature; and a while he didn't see.
But at last he murmured, "Oh," and again, "Oh."

"What is it—what?" she said.

                              "Just that I see."

"You don't," she challenged. "Tell me what it is."

"The wonder is I didn't see at once.
I never noticed it from here before.
I must be wonted to it—that's the reason.

The little graveyard where my people are!
So small the window frames the whole of it.
So as to please you. But I might be taught
I should suppose. I can't say I see how.
A man must partly give up being a man
With women-folk. We could have some arrangement
By which I'd bind myself to keep hands off
Anything special you're a-mind to name.
Though I don't like such things 'twixt those that love.
Two that don't love can't live together without them.
But two that do can't live together with them."
She moved the latch a little. "Don't—don't go.
Don't carry it to someone else this time.
Tell me about it if it's something human.
Let me into your grief. I'm not so much
Unlike other folks as your standing there
Apart would make me out. Give me my chance.
I do think, though, you overdo it a little.
What was it brought you up to think it the thing
To take your mother-loss of a first child
So inconsolably—in the face of love.
You'd think his memory might be satisfied—"

"There you go sneering now!"

                             "I'm not, I'm not!
You make me angry. I'll come down to you.
God, what a woman! And it's come to this,
A man can't speak of his own child that's dead."

"You can't because you don't know how to speak.
If you had any feelings, you that dug
With your own hand—how could you?—his little grave;
I saw you from that very window there,
Making the gravel leap and leap in air,
Leap up, like that, like that, and land so lightly
And roll back down the mound beside the hole.
I thought, Who is that man? I didn't know you.
And I crept down the stairs and up the stairs
To look again, and still your spade kept lifting.
Then you came in. I heard your rumbling voice

Out in the kitchen, and I don't know why,
But I went near to see with my own eyes.
You could sit there with the stains on your shoes
Of the fresh earth from your own baby's grave
And talk about your everyday concerns.
You had stood the spade up against the wall
Outside there in the entry, for I saw it."

"I shall laugh the worst laugh I ever laughed.
I'm cursed. God, if I don't believe I'm cursed."

"I can repeat the very words you were saying.
'Three foggy mornings and one rainy day
Will rot the best birch fence a man can build.'
Think of it, talk like that at such a time!
What had how long it takes a birch to rot
To do with what was in the darkened parlour.
You *couldn't* care! The nearest friends can go
With anyone to death, comes so far short
They might as well not try to go at all.
No, from the time when one is sick to death,
One is alone, and he dies more alone.
Friends make pretence of following to the grave,
But before one is in it, their minds are turned
And making the best of their way back to life
And living people, and things they understand.
But the world's evil. I won't have grief so
If I can change it. Oh, I won't, I won't!"

"There, you have said it all and you feel better.
You won't go now. You're crying. Close the door.
The heart's gone out of it: why keep it up.
Amy! There's someone coming down the road!"

"*You*—oh, you think the talk is all. I must go—
Somewhere out of this house. How can I make you—"

"If—you—do!" She was opening the door wider.
"Where do you mean to go? First tell me that.
I'll follow and bring you back by force. I *will!*—"

James Dickey

CHERRYLOG ROAD

Off Highway 106
At Cherrylog Road I entered
The '34 Ford without wheels,
Smothered in kudzu,
With a seat pulled out to run
Corn whiskey down from the hills,

And then from the other side
Crept into an Essex
With a rumble seat of red leather
And then out again, aboard
A blue Chevrolet, releasing
The rust from its other color,

Reared up on three building blocks.
None had the same body heat;
I changed with them inward, toward
The weedy heart of the junkyard,
For I knew that Doris Holbrook
Would escape from her father at noon

And would come from the farm
To seek parts owned by the sun
Among the abandoned chassis,
Sitting in each in turn
As I did, leaning forward
As in a wild stock-car race

•

In the parking lot of the dead.
Time after time, I climbed in
And out the other side, like
An envoy or movie star
Met at the station by crickets.
A radiator cap raised its head,

Become a real toad or a kingsnake
As I neared the hub of the yard,
Passing through many states,
Many lives, to reach
Some grandmother's long Pierce-Arrow
Sending platters of blindness forth

From its nickel hubcaps
And spilling its tender upholstery
On sleepy roaches,
The glass panel in between
Lady and colored driver
Not all the way broken out,

The back-seat phone
Still on its hook.
I got in as though to exclaim,
"Let us go to the orphan asylum,
John; I have some old toys
For children who say their prayers."

I popped with sweat as I thought
I heard Doris Holbrook scrape
Like a mouse in the southern-state sun
That was eating the paint in blisters
From a hundred car tops and hoods.
She was tapping like code,

Loosening the screws,
Carrying off headlights,
Sparkplugs, bumpers,
Cracked mirrors and gear-knobs,

Getting ready, already,
To go back with something to show

Other than her lips' new trembling
I would hold to me soon, soon,
Where I sat in the ripped back seat
Talking over the interphone,
Praying for Doris Holbrook
To come from her father's farm

And to get back there
With no trace of me on her face
To be seen by her red-haired father
Who would change, in the squalling barn,
Her back's pale skin with a strop,
Then lay for me

In a bootlegger's roasting car
With a string-triggered 12-gauge shotgun
To blast the breath from the air.
Not cut by the jagged windshields,
Through the acres of wrecks she came
With a wrench in her hand,

Through dust where the blacksnake dies
Of boredom, and the beetle knows
The compost has no more life.
Someone outside would have seen
The oldest car's door inexplicably
Close from within:

I held her and held her and held her,
Convoyed at terrific speed
By the stalled, dreaming traffic around us,
So the blacksnake, stiff
With inaction, curved back
Into life, and hunted the mouse

With deadly overexcitement,
The beetles reclaimed their field
As we clung, glued together,

With the hooks of the seat springs
Working through to catch us red-handed
Amidst the gray breathless batting

That burst from the seat at our backs.
We left by separate doors
Into the changed, other bodies
Of cars, she down Cherrylog Road
And I to my motorcycle
Parked like the soul of the junkyard

Restored, a bicycle fleshed
With power, and tore off
Up Highway 106, continually
Drunk on the wind in my mouth,
Wringing the handlebar for speed,
Wild to be wreckage forever.

THE CAR

The car with a cracked windshield.
The car that threw a rod.
The car without brakes.
The car with a faulty U-joint.
The car with a hole in its radiator.
The car I picked peaches for.
The car with a cracked block.
The car with no reverse gear.
The car I traded for a bicycle.
The car with steering problems.
The car with generator trouble.
The car with no back seat.
The car with the torn front seat.
The car that burned oil.
The car with rotten hoses.
The car that left the restaurant without paying.
The car with bald tires.
The car with no heater or defroster.
The car with its front end out of alignment.
The car the child threw up in.
The car *I* threw up in.
The car with the broken water pump.
The car whose timing gear was shot.
The car with a blown head-gasket.
The car I left on the side of the road.
The car that leaked carbon monoxide.
The car with a sticky carburetor.

The car that hit the dog and kept going.
The car with a hole in its muffler.
The car with no muffler.
The car my daughter wrecked.
The car with the twice-rebuilt engine.
The car with corroded battery cables.
The car bought with a bad check.
Car of my sleepless nights.
The car with a stuck thermostat.
The car whose engine caught fire.
The car with no headlights.
The car with a broken fan belt.
The car with wipers that wouldn't work.
The car I gave away.
The car with transmission trouble.
The car I washed my hands of.
The car I struck with a hammer.
The car with payments that couldn't be met.
The repossessed car.
The car whose clutch-pin broke.
The car waiting on the back lot.
Car of my dreams.
My car.

Maxine Kumin

400-METER FREESTYLE

The gun full swing the swimmer catapults and cracks

$\qquad$ s

$\qquad$ i

$\qquad$ x

feet away onto that perfect glass he catches at

a

n

d

throws behind him scoop after scoop cunningly moving

$\qquad$ t

$\qquad$ h

$\qquad$ e

water back to move him forward. Thrift is his wonderful

s

e

c

ret; he has schooled out all extravagance. No muscle

$\qquad$ r

$\qquad$ i

$\qquad$ p

ples without compensation wrist cock to heel snap to

h

i

s

mobile mouth that siphons in the air that nurtures

$\qquad$ h

$\qquad$ i

$\qquad$ m

at half an inch above sea level so to speak.
T
h
e
astonishing whites of the soles of his feet rise
                     a
                        n
                        d
salute us on the turns. He flips, converts, and is gone
a
l
l
in one. We watch him for signs. His arms are steady at
                           t
                            h
           .   e
catch, his cadent feet tick in the stretch, they know
t
h
e
lesson well. Lungs know, too; he does not list for
                      a
                        i
                     r
he drives along on little sips carefully expended
b
u
t
that plum red heart pumps hard cries hurt how soon
                         i
                         t
                       s
near one more and makes its final surge   TIME: 4:25:9

Annie Dillard

EMERGENCIES

—Brent Q. Hafen, Ph.D., and Keith J. Karren, Ph.D.,

Prehospital Emergency Care and Crisis

Intervention, 1989

(Few people are initially prepared for the sights, smells, and sounds of intense human suffering.)

FIRST THINGS FIRST

Introduce yourself to the patient.
If you have time and are in doubt,
Simply ask, "What
Would you like me to call you?"

Cut clothing away quickly
To see a bleeding site clearly.
Put on a pair of latex
Or surgical gloves to protect yourself . . .

Many religious people
Attach great significance
To religious symbols.
Unless it is necessary for treatment,
Do not remove crosses or amulets.

Observe circumstances, collect
Suicide notes, and compile

The relevant materials. Is the patient
Restless, irritable, or combative?
It is best to wait rather
Than try to remove weapons
Or potential weapons from unstable
Victims, relatives, bystanders.

Ask someone, "Will you please
Turn off the TV?" Or do it yourself.

Say, "Please sit
On the ground on her left side,
Ma'am, and hold her hand.
Talk to her. Don't move
Her arm, and don't let her move
Her head. I'm going
To be checking her hips and legs."

Comment positively on the aid
Already given (for example,
"You've done a good job
Of immobilizing the head").

TOUCH

Take a hand, pat
A shoulder. Remember that
You have to be comfortable doing it,
And not just trying it as a gimmick.

Squeezing a foot or patting
An ankle, if you are working
Near the foot is not
Usually considered intimate.
Patting above the knee is.
Sometimes a man receiving
Help from a woman EMT
Or a woman patient being treated
By a male EMT will automatically
Respond to comforting physical

Gestures with flirtatious behavior.
Do not respond by flirting back.

ASK

Ask questions about an area
Or organ *before* you examine it.

Ask: What's your name?
        What's happening to you?
        Where were you going, or where
        Are you? Can you tell me the date
        (Day of the week, year)?
Document the patient's condition
Precisely—"disoriented to time."

Depending on the urgency of the situation,
Either ask yes-or-no questions
        ("Have you eaten today?" "Does it hurt
        When you move your arm?")
Or open-ended questions
        ("When does the pain come on?"
        "Tell me about your last meal").

How intense is the pain?
        Dull? Throbbing? Sharp?
        Crushing? Stabbing? Does
        The pain change in intensity
        Or remain constant? What
        Started it? How long ago?

RESPONSIVENESS

What can the patient feel?
Can he identify the stimulus?
How does he respond to pain?
With unconscious or sleeping patients,
Determine how easily
They can be aroused.

If they cannot be aroused
By verbal stimuli, can
They be aroused by a pain
Stimulus like a pinch?

If the patient does not respond
To voice, try pain.

Your patient is RESPONSIVE
If he seems to be unconscious but will:
  • Open his eyes if you speak to him.
  • Respond to a light touch on the hand.
  • Try to avoid pain.

The answer you receive from the patient
When you ask, "Can you tell me where
You are hurt?" is the CHIEF COMPLAINT.
In many instances, this
Will be obvious, such as the patient
Who lies bleeding in the street
After being struck by an automobile.

Even in this circumstance, however,
It is useful to determine
What is bothering the patient most.
Check the Facial Features.
Feel the Head and Neck.
Check the Clavicles and Arms.
Check the Chest. In injury
        Patients, feel for air
        Crackling beneath the skin.
Check the Abdominal Region.
        Sudden pokes will make
        The muscles tense.
Check the Pelvic Region
        For Tenderness. Damage here
        Can cause great pain,
        So be gentle.
Check the Back.
Check the Feet, Ankles, and Legs.

•

Describe pulse amplitude by using the following scale:
    4+ Bounding
    3+ Normal
    2+ Difficult to palpate
    1+ Weak and rapid, thready
    0 Absent

HELPFUL TIPS

Avoid traffic accidents
While going to the scene of an accident
Or to the hospital. Use a seat belt . . .
Park safely and carefully.

Check all equipment.
Keep the interior clean.
Are all your bandage wraps cleaned up?
About the patient's condition, assume
The worst and work from there.

If a patient requests
That you pray with him, do so.

LEGAL SITUATIONS

What Happens if a Patient
Files Suit? [How to document:]
    Draw a thin line
    Through an error.
    Never erase an error.

Another legal situation
Is death. If a person is obviously
Dead (crushed, decapitated,
Rigor mortis setting in),
You may be required
To leave the body at the site.

ANSWER

If death is imminent either
On the scene or in the ambulance,
Be supportive and reassuring
To the patient, but do not lie.

If a patient asks, "I'm dying,
Aren't I?" respond
With something like, "You
Have some very serious injuries,
But I'm not giving up on you."

AND BEAR IN MIND

The heart is a hollow, muscular
Organ the size of the fist.

Once the patient remains
In clinical death for a certain time
(Typically four to six minutes),
Brain cells begin to die.

Along the edges of the eyelids
Are openings of many small oil glands
Which help prevent the tears
From evaporating too rapidly.

CATTLE-KILLING WINTER,
1 8 8 9 – 9 0

We walked, of course.
Omaha to Walla Walla: 5 months, 3 days.
My husband, Nathan Sloan (known as Kentucky),
a fireman on the Missouri-Louisville line,
worked years tallowing valves
before the railroads fell on slack times.
He lost his job and the farm.

In Walla Walla, rested our oxen before
the baby—christened Caleb—was born,
walked another week north to where
Loop Loop Creek crosses the Okanogan.

Long days, high clouds, temperatures in the 90's.

Made a land claim, went to Buzzard Lake
to wash and water our stock,
met a miner, Dutch Jake, and his dog,
who infected my husband with gold fever.
Came back, found our claim jumped,
went up creek, made another. The only law
against selling black powder to an Indian.

Milled lumber too costly—not even a board
for a coffin. So cut and hewed logs for a cabin,
our lead ox hauling through mire.

Local talk had it winters too mild
to necessitate a barn.

Humidity high. Nighttime temperatures falling.

Mosquitoes so thick, Nathan had to stand
above me as I cooked, battling them off
with a towel. Morning coffee required
constant skimming, while bugs
in our mash appeared as caraway.
Deer were so plentiful they staggered
for lack of forage and could be had by clubbing.
November 1, ten venison hams hung from our eaves.

Nights getting longer, though unseasonably warm.

Just before New Year's, I awoke to ice
in the washbasin. Snowed nineteen inches.
Temperatures dropped. Snow crusted hard enough
to cut the lead ox's tendon.
John Other Day, Cut Nose, and their squaws
came daily to our door demanding flour.
Oats: six cents a pound; potatoes, five;
hay, a hundred a ton if you could find it.

Forty below by mid-month. The sun never shone.

Our oxen froze in the fields,
the twin calves dead at the milch cow's side,
the last of our hay in front of her.
Five feet of snow and blizzarding winds
for thirteen consecutive days.

The only drinking water, melted snow;
the only wood, our furniture.
Nathan sawed frozen meat from the dead,
feeding it to what stock remained.
I soaked rags in the blood of offal, giving
the baby suck. God Be Praised, he thrived.

•

Up on Buzzard Mountain, prospectors
were trapped in their mines—the artillery
of avalanche thundered through our valley.
When he tried to leave, Dutch, his mule and hound,
were buried—the dog dug its way out.
Ours was the first cabin he came to.

Brought the two living cows and one horse
into our lean-to kitchen, supped with us
on flour mash and seed potato.
If we went anywhere, it was hand-over-hand
over ice. No mail for weeks,
river frozen, the railroad snowbound.
A stranger who went through on snowshoes,
said a neighbor's wife died of laudanum
taken with suicidal intent.
Flour and sugar gone, rumor our daily bread.

When the ice melted, the creeks swelled
bringing typhoid which weakened my husband.
After pneumonia, he looked worse
than any at Andersonville and was unable
to help with chores.

First day of March. Days longer. Heavy fog.

The stock were enfeebled by hunger.
Balding from rain scald, hair fell in sheets
from their hides. When the spring grass
came on, they were too weak to graze,
collapsing like long-legged insects.
Ill myself, I crawled out to help, Caleb on my back:
right hoof forward, left knee bent, sometimes
it took a rail under the rump to raise them.

Most ranchers went under.
Some took twenty years to repay loans
on herds that perished, and then
only when they sold off their farms.
But the two cows left to us begat others

who begat the thousand head
Caleb and his sons graze in this valley.

I was born Effie Rebecca, named for my mother,
but forever after that cattle-killing winter,
my husband called me by another.
Years ago he went to the stone orchard,
my place beside him ready: "SLOAN, Nathan
known as Kentucky, and Wife, Born Again '89
as God's handmaiden, Faith."

Long Days. High clouds. Temperatures in the 90's.

Jana Harris

AVALANCHE

**MARY BRISKY,
RATTLESNAKE CANYON,
FEBRUARY 1888**

i.
I remember it this way:
That morning we sat down to breakfast,
me, mama, and the traveling Reverend.
My baby sister was on the floor
next to the sewing machine.
On the table, three blue bowls
filled with oatmeal.
It had a smoky taste that I'll never forget.
Sepin was outside shoveling snow
off the roof. My father was up on the bluff
cutting trees, snaking them down the mountain.
When a tree fell, there was the noise
of lightning lash and as it hit the ground,
thunder shook our cabin—those trees
were twenty feet around, some of them.
When baby crawled under the table,
I was afraid she'd burn herself
on the hot stones mama had
put there to warm our feet,
so I stooped to pick her up.

ii.
"What is your only comfort in life and death?"
Reverend Beggs's voice was far away.

I was lying on top of baby
who was screaming. I didn't

realize what was smothering me,
until her breath melted the snow.
Mama was nearby. I could hear,
but couldn't see or touch her.
She spoke calmly to us:
"Lie quietly and breathe as lightly as possible."
The baby kept screaming 'til I thought
my head would split.
"Are you hurt?" mama asked,
"Can you wiggle your arms and legs?"
I could. The baby was thrashing beneath me,
beating with her fists.

The Reverend's voice was shallow.
"From whence do you know your sin and misery?"
No one answered. Mama said to me:
"Mary, the first thing to know about a baby
is to keep her warm and dry."
The baby howled louder. Everything around us
was wet and cold.
"Don't let her little butt get red," mama said.
"For croup, rub her chest
in rendered mutton and turpentine."

The Reverend asked, "How are you delivered?"
Mama said, "Mary, you can get sixty loaves
of bread from a sack of flour,
if you're frugal. I always could."
I said, yes, and then she said, "Remember
to seal your crock of sourdough
with a layer of water, seal your buttermilk
the same way." I reminded her
it was my job to milk the cow and hers to churn.
She said now I would have to both milk
and churn. "Roasted barley is the best
substitute for coffee," she said.
"Use the juice of boiled corn cobs
for sweetener, and don't drink it up
faster than you make it."

"Jesus did not die for everyone
as some believe," Reverend Beggs droned.

"If God chooses to elect you,
you cannot fight it."
"I want father," I said. Mama said I'd see him,
but she wasn't sure when.
"And your brother, too," she added.

Though I shivered, I felt sleepy.
The baby screamed herself out.
She was soaking, my body kept her warm.
"Mary," mother said, startling me awake.
"If Pokamiakin comes to the door with a knife,
hide the baby in the bread box." By now
Reverend's voice was barely a whisper.
This time when he asked, What is your only
comfort in life and death? Mama answered,
"That I am not my own.
That I belong to Jesus Christ."

"And from whence do you know your sin
and misery?" "From the word of God,"
mother and I said, our voices one.

"And how are you delivered?"
I waited for mama to answer, but she did not.

iii.
We sat down to oatmeal at 8:30 that morning.
At 5:00, they pulled us out.
The wall of falling snow knocked
my brother out of the way.
It was the baby's screaming that told father
and Sepin where to dig.
The Reverend Beggs was dead.
Mama was dead.
The cow could not be saved.
High up on the opposite canyon wall
were splintered logs, bits of furniture,
the wheel of the sewing machine, and one
blue bowl amid shards of all the others.

The smoky taste of oatmeal
was still inside my mouth.

Tom Wayman

VIOLENCE

The cars leap out of the plant parking lot
lay rubber, fishtail, and disappear.

Bill says: "The scar? When I was up in Ashcroft
I was coming out of the pub one day and a guy I'd never seen
smacked me in the face with a piece of wood.
Broke these teeth and split me open along here: nose, lips, chin.
I got stitched up, and the next day
had a buddy drive me around town looking for the guy.
I saw him, told my buddy to stop
and leaped out holding a tire iron behind my back.

"The guy recognized me. He comes up and says:
'I'm sure sorry about yesterday. I thought you were somebody else.'
I said to him: 'You have three seconds to start running.'
He turned to get away, and I let him have it across the back of the head.
Cold-cocked him right there in the street.
Then I kicked the shit out of him, broke a couple of his ribs
and me and my buddy got out of there fast."

And Magnowski, the giant partsman, on his wedding night:
"They put shaving cream, lather, all over my car.
I stopped in at a garage to wash it off
and as I was using the hose the attendant comes out
and just stands there, making all these dumb comments
like: 'I guess you're really gonna screw her tonight, boy.'
I couldn't believe it. He was big, but

I'm a head taller than him. I was going to deck him
but it was our wedding night. Debbie was right there in the car
and I'm wearing a tuxedo and everything.
So I just said: 'Do you have a hose with some *pressure*
in it, asshole?' He got kind of choked up at that.
He could see I was really mad, just holding myself in.

"But I didn't want to ruin it for Debbie on our wedding.
I think I'm going back this Saturday and see if the guy is still on."

And Don Grayson, another partsman, limping around
with a broken foot he got kicking someone
in a fight in the Duff beer parlor.
He and his friends took exception to some remarks
that were made about the woman who brings the food.
And me always careful not to get in a fight.
Chris and Ernie, Bucket and Phil at lunch one day
talking about a brawl, and me saying:
"It takes two to fight. If you don't want to
you can always walk away." And Ernie really horrified
at this: "Oh no, Tom, no, no.
There are times when you have to fight, you just have to."
And me maintaining that you don't
and everybody looking disgusted at my idea.

How is it I have clung all my life to my life
as though to the one thing I never wanted to lose?

Bob changes the subject. We begin to talk about car accidents.

SURE SHOT

The only way to tell this life
is to squint away the details.
America is huge and all-consuming:
I've got little girls dressed up like me
in fringed skirts and holsters;
I've got kinetographs and headlines,
a name in history—Annie Oakley,
Maid of the Western Plains.

Everything on the periphery is waiting
hungry and cruel—call it wilderness,
call it fancy, call it signs of the times.
The West was dying and we brought it back.
We were legends almost before we began—
Buffalo Bill Cody, Pony Express rider,
and Chief Sitting Bull, who had defeated Custer
after receiving a vision of soldiers
falling upside down from the clouds.

In your own life, you're either a native
or a paying guest. Either way, restlessness
is the only sure way around memory.
Call it attention, call it avoidance,
after dark call it no sleep allowed.

Night after night I tossed new dimes
into the sky to make the sky disappear.

I'd watch the coin grow huge as a dinner plate
before I fired my hole through its center.
People were pleased I got what I aimed for.
They never reckoned I'd crawled inside
the ragged circumference,
splayed my Winchester across the hot ceiling
to guarantee the shot-up silver
came home to the dust.

At the age of eight, capable and healthy,
I was delivered by my mother
to the County Infirmary,
asylum of the bent and the broken,
the abandoned at birth.

I leave nothing out here.
We rode there together on a wagon, mute as eggs.
She did not say a widowed nurse
could not afford to keep her daughter;
she did not say my younger sisters suffered;
she did not say how far she planned to stretch
the weekly quarter she would be sent
in exchange for my hours
stitching pinafores and drawers.
She said only, "It won't be long,
Phoebe Anne Moses,"
and she would not kiss my lips.

I must have suspected. Why else
would I have packed in my new cloth bag
the single ruby button, the tawny stone
like a half-sad moon,
my sister Mary Jane's dented thimble,
and the hammer I'd stolen from the rifle?
My dead father's muzzle loader:
no one would fire it while I was gone.

While Mama had been traveling the district
nursing fevers, Mary Jane had taught me

to fire the garden clear of birds.
I was six and in it for the ritual and the noise.
I measured each load more carefully than flour,
welcomed the ache of learning in my shoulder.

Until you're strong, you're stuck
with ground creatures—
dumb squirrel or, if you're quiet, rabbit.
By the time I was seven I was hunting
in the waist-high grass.

You never saw such grass as licked me then,
kept me upright as I tried for quail,
letting my mind go plump and finicky
so I'd know ahead of time whether fear
would pull the birds up east or west.

What you learn from a moving target
is to stay ahead of it, to meet your bird
while it's still rising, just before
it finds the height of its climb.
Soon I was shooting dinner every night.
A year later I was lying in a row of cots
with nothing in my hands but the stolen hammer.
This is how I passed the night:
slowly, carefully, I took the rifle from the shelf
and cleaned the movable parts with oil
that brought my father back into the room.
I measured the load, showing him
the care the task deserved, and then I took him
outside into the grass that hid us
from every future except success.

We stood inside the audience of grass,
never speaking until my quail lit up,
and when I dropped it my father would say, "Fine,"
and I would load the gun again.

       ▩   ▩   ▩

I've seen other children lose and find
themselves in the folds of their mother's skirt,

in the creases of a father's infrequent speech.
In the Darke County Infirmary
I had to ask myself: Against whose living form
will I take shape?

In my rifle I found the great all-returning pleasure
others find in place or family.
Wide-eyed is not for me.
I squint even in my dreams.
No, a made thing is what I chose to love:
butt, comb, trigger, guard, barrel.

▪ ▪ ▪

Who came for me, a year later,
was not my mother but a new master,
the County Commissioner, a bank trustee.
He got me for fifty cents a week,
this man obese with socially progressive theories.
I would sleep upstairs beside the family;
I would learn to recite poetry and the presidents.

At nine I was impressed with the flowered wallpaper,
the damask roses indoors and out.
In my room there was the pier-glass mirror
where I first saw my whole body:
compact, quick, eyes as silver
as the air between the leaves of aspen.

Always the rifle of my dreams
stood by me in the mirror,
the well-worn grain easy against my palm,
the polished hammer my only heirloom.
During my hours off, I posed
and shot into the mirror's endless presence.

▪ ▪ ▪

The first time I faltered on a sonnet
my master struck me on the mouth.
The second time he threw me off a wagon.
"You asked for that," he screamed
as my knees scraped the ground.
When the words to "She Walks in Beauty"

went muddy in my mouth,
he pressed my hand against a flame.
His son was watching. The next day
I was surrounded by boys
who forced me toward the open pants
of one whose meanness stiffened
like a turkey's neck. The son screamed,
"Lick it or we'll kill you."

My master moved me to the room behind the kitchen.
I found a grayness in the grease-stained walls
that preserved me for another year.
Then one night—I was going on eleven—
the dreamgun in my arms spoke up:
"Run home. It's now or never."

If I tell you I returned to the asylum,
I hope you can forgive me.
Looking forward, the mind
may see only the distant past.
So what if we ate boiled cabbage twice a day?
So what if the children moaned all night?
My treadle made a noise like wind in grass,
the white spools roosted at my side.
The infirmary was where my mother had left me,
where she would come looking when she could.

                    ▩   ▩   ▩

For my homecoming my mother chose
my sister Lydia's wedding day.
All I remember is the fit of the hammer
as I pressed it back into the muzzle loader
after all those years.
This is the real beginning, I told myself,
the part where fact meets fancy,
where every question I toss up
will have an angle of flight
I comprehend in plenty of time.

My body had a message of its own.
I was that age where surreptitious contours
make their way upward for all to see,

but I stayed far inside, a miner
obedient to the mineral glow
of priceless discovery.

⬛   ⬛   ⬛

On the day my husband and I met
I beat him at a shooting match.
Everyone in Cincinnati except Butler
knew I was a better shot.
For years I'd been sending quail
down to the finest restaurants.
Drawn and gutted, wrapped in swamp grass,
I sold the birds for twenty-five cents a brace.

Do you know how good it feels to win
when you're fifteen and already you've paid off
your mother's mortgage?
I remember my load—three drams powder,
one ounce number eight shot.
I was fifteen when Frank and I were married.
First thing he did was teach me how to read.
That's Butler—I've got nothing bad to say
about the man: way he holds my aces up,
lets me trim the edges without flinching,
way he rubs my shoulders with witch hazel.
No matter where we are, the guns are clean and oiled,
a pot of tea is warming on the spirit lamp.
When the show is over it's always Butler
lets me fold up like a spyglass in his arms.

⬛   ⬛   ⬛

The spring of 1885 we started to play with Cody.
He called his Wild West Show "genuine living history"
to irritate the circus men.
Genuine Sioux and Wichita,
genuine buffalo and cowboys.

Already the West was so far gone
Cody felt free to turn it into theater—
the Deadwood Stage, the Oregon Trail,

cattle drives and Indian massacres
staged in front of canvas buttes.

The thing is, people needed the Wild West.
In the big cities and in the skinniest backwaters,
people put their money down
and got what they came for.
They walked out of the show feeling lean and rugged.
They loped home singing a song.
No matter where they lay their heads that night,
they believed they were sleeping under stars.
Maybe a whiff of gunsmoke crossed their pillows.
Maybe they heard ponies nickering in the dark.

⬚　⬚　⬚

I could play to that audience.
We were telling a story that was already over.
Men who'd been scouts and squatters
in the territories were wearing
made-to-order fringe, arguing
over the trimwork on their saddles.

I whipped up my own disguises in the evening—
roses on my skirt, or buckskin knickers—
and Butler ironed them in the morning.
I ran through my routines 'til they were flawless,
imported smokeless powder from London,
and bought a gun chest big enough to carry
the Damascus and the Stevens,
a gold-plated Winchester,
the pearl-handled Smith and Wesson
I'd used to shoot the cigarette
from the mouth of the Crown Prince of Germany.

What else did I shoot? Flame from a candle,
apple from the head of a miniature poodle,
.22 through a spread of aces.
Why did I do it? I tell you,
to narrow my gaze over the plain open sight,
to spot what I was looking for

where I knew I would find it,
to bring it down like I do so well.

                    ▩   ▩   ▩

Sitting Bull came to the Wild West
straight out of prison,
villain of Little Big Horn.
First night he opened with us in Buffalo,
the crowd booed him and called him a bastard.
What they'd come for was make-believe,
not the medicine man of the Hunkpapa Sioux,
genuine braids, genuine pockmarks.

The Chief and I went riding every morning.
Just watching him taught me
how the parts of the horse come together
in a good rider's hands.
I learned to wear cream-colored doeskin,
to make a bonnet of white eagle plumes.
He adopted me and gave me the name
Little Sure Shot.
Listening to him inside his smoky tepee,
I believed in the country of our kinship.

By the winter of 1890,
the Chief had returned to his restless people
and the Wild West Show was quartered in Alsace.
All through Europe we'd been hearing about the Ghost Dances
stirring up hope among the Sioux and Paiute.
Maybe the dances would bring back the buffalo.
Maybe the plains would be given back
to the original hunters.
Maybe the fighting wasn't over.
This was the old-style talk that fired up Sitting Bull.
Of course the government grew nervous.
Their soldiers surrounded Pine Ridge and Rosebud,
ordered the arrest of Sitting Bull.
I learned all this in a letter from Cody—
a huckster, you might say, but he spoke the Chief's language;
he'd left us in Europe and wangled himself orders
to visit Sitting Bull's reservation.

He was there when the Chief walked out of his cabin
to saddle up the sure-footed gray
I'd seen him on every morning.
He was watching when the two Indian police,
Shave Head and Red Tomahawk,
shot the Chief before he'd fastened his bridle.

The minute Sitting Bull fell down, Cody wrote,
the horse kneeled like his master had taught him.
Kneeled and bowed and pawed the hard ground,
cued by the sound of the rifles.
You can fire at a thousand glass balls
and hit every one and still there will be a pain
that flies straight for the opening in your heart.

                  ■   ■   ■

I began to ask myself,
What if there'd been no Wild West?
Where would I have gone with my shooting?
My whole act consisted of picking things out
of the sky. You don't so much sight them
as swing with them;
when it feels right
you pull and go on to the next.
Things I knew nothing about
were flowers coming up in the same bed
year after year, washing hung fresh on the line,
the comfort of a butcher who knows you by name.

Butler found us a house on a river,
but the whole thing was cursed from the start.
When the chimney wouldn't draw,
we took turns firing up the flue.
When the corn seed was planted,
the crows dropped in by the dozen.
We had a few good afternoons owning a house,
Butler and I, when we filled all the cornfields
with fresh-shot crow, but in the meantime
we'd let the watering go
and we lost the whole crop anyhow.

◼ ◼ ◼

I'd rather do anything than live in a house.
When night came to me in a house of my own,
the shaky window I looked out of
showed me nothing but the night's heavy back
backing into me. No thanks.
In boarding houses, people are proud
of staying up all night,
proud to be peeling an orange
when you knock on their door close to dawn.

◼ ◼ ◼

Hard as you look, you can't tell
where the new light will come from.
It's out there somewhere in the audience
like a pair of bright eyes among leaves.
I was thirty-six before my mother saw me perform.
In Picqua, Ohio, not far from my birthplace.
For nearly twenty years I'd been telling myself
she'd missed the show because she was Quaker
and the Wild West was show business.
No mention of her coming,
not so much as a wave when I spotted her
during the opening parade.

She sat through the whole performance
in that black Sunday dress,
lips dry as chalk, never a hint
of excitement or regret.
Afterward she came to my tent,
called me the name I had run from, Phoebe Anne,
saying it crisp enough to leave wrinkles.

"What do you think?" I asked,
knowing from the start it was wrong.
I can still see her spindly fingers
cautious on the flap of the tent
as if it were satin from Paris.

●

I look at her wondering who I am.
She looks at me wondering where I came from.
Why is there never someone who enters
at these moments to answer our questions?
I am sorry the West needed a child.
I am sorry the child needed a West.
She stood there forever without speaking.
A different daughter would have offered
camomile tea. In my own heart,
there was nothing but prairie and sagebrush
and a silhouette of myself poised to fire,
taller than anything in sight.

When at last she spoke,
she said, "Mighty fine tent." That was it.
I knew what she meant, what she saw
in the canvas opaque as fine paper.
I knew how hard she was working
to narrow her glance.

※　※　※

Where are we tonight? The Imperial,
or the Royal, or the velvet-fringed stateroom
of the train racing from Charlotte to Danbury.
We have entered a new century:
a Rough Rider is president,
Cody has added Prussians to the show.
Cowboys and Indians don't sell
like they used to.

One stunt I'll never give up
is shooting behind my back with a mirror.
I can't tell you the pleasure it brings.
I use a hand mirror no larger
than the eye of a bull.
Trimmed in silver, it narrows down the choices
without preaching or applause.
With one hand I rest my rifle on my shoulder;
with the other I hold up the mirror

until it brings me the candles
set out on an old wagon wheel.

In my life—call it skill,
call it necessity—I have tried
to be as certain as that mirror.
One by one, the flames enter the glass
and I stop them.
I know where the next one will come from.
I have never missed yet.

Jon Davis

TESTIMONY

"I want to take this time so 'generously' given
by the court to tell you of my genius for
destruction, the drugs that slide like honey
through my veins, the nights I've spent with
women you can't even dream of—the model who
crashed our Labor Day picnic with her hand-
shaking boyfriend, who left and came back
alone at two a.m. to take her dress off and
lie down in Tony's van . . . That was my life
until some idiot baby-faced hero jumped from
behind a wall and I pulled my piece. And
blew him backwards to nowhere, and past that
to where the devil picked his heart up like
a magazine, flipped the pages of his life, hissed
like a blown piston, and tossed it on the fire
if you believe the crap they hand you . . ."

That's not what he said, the man who killed Larry Johnson (who bowled
on my uncle's Thursday night bowling team), the man who lived with a friend
of mine named Jack until Jack decided to move out because "You hang around
with guys like that too long and pretty soon you're in trouble, too." So now
Jack paints houses and tries not to drink too much and every once in a while
he remembers his life with Lisa, how he chose the only direction he could,
and chose wrong. He feels sorry for the guy on my uncle's bowling team who
lived down the street from my wife's father's house and never did anything
wrong, but had a half-sister who stole a bag of cocaine from a man with a .38
and a quick finger because "If you led the life I lead you'd understand I had to

kill any man who turned a corner or came down the stairs like that." So now he's in prison while the guy on my uncle's bowling team is dead, and my friend who lived with a murderer paints houses, and my uncle continues to bowl, holding a 200 average in several leagues. I can't say I feel anything for the dead man. And I can't stop thinking about the man who pulled the trigger. But what I wrote is not what he said, the man who killed a man on my uncle's bowling team. The reporters asked him what he thought of the life sentence, and he said, "I thought it was a good sentence. A damn good sentence. I'm getting a warm place to sleep and a good hot meal. Larry Johnson's dead in his grave and I'm getting free room and board. What do I think of the sentence? I think it sucks, you stupid assholes." Then he pushed the microphones away and sang "The worms crawl in, the worms crawl out." Then they took him away.

Robert Phillips

AFTER THE FACT:
TO TED BUNDY

1.

The thing of it was,
you looked so handsome
and trustworthy—
such a nice smile.

The thing of it was,
you showed me
a laminated ID card,
said you were police.

The thing was, you see,
I was seventeen,
didn't know people
could buy fake IDs.

Thing of it was,
you told me someone
had been arrested
breaking into my car,

Did I want to go
down to the station
and press charges?
You'd drive me.

●

355

You had a hot car,
smooth, brand-new,
smelled like leather.
A turn-on. Like you.

2.

Not far down the road
you pulled over,
quickly handcuffed me,
unzipped yourself,

started waving a pistol.
You said you'd blow
my brains all over
the highway if I didn't

do what I was told.
Whatever reason, I didn't
think you would.
(Your cock was tiny,

soft as a slug.) Somehow
I got the door open,
ran. You didn't fire,
but came after me

waving a tire jack.
I wore high heels,
couldn't run fast.
Thought I was a goner.

Then a VW came along.
I lifted my handcuffed
hands and hollered.
It stopped for me.

3.

I'm one of the lucky few.
I've seen your picture
in all the newspapers.
No question, it was you.

I've seen your face
most nights in dreams,
big as the harvest moon,
grinning like a goon.

It's the good-looking
ones I distrust most—
the way they try to
sweet-talk their way.

Last week in a bar
a guy reached over,
touched my shoulder.
In the ladies' room

I puked my guts out.
I'll find one so homely,
so uncomplicated, I'll
simply go along. Okay?

Fifteen years after,
you finally got fried.
Clean-shaven bastard!
Inside me, you're still alive.

Gary Soto

TARGET PRACTICE

When we fired our rifles
We spooked sparrows from the tree.
Bottles burst when we aimed,
Tin cans did more than *ping*
And throw themselves in dry grass.
The dog pulled in tail and ears,
Saddened his eyes and crawled under the car.
We smiled at this, Leonard and I,
And went to look at the tin cans
And push our fingers into the holes—
Pink worms wagging at our happiness.
We set them up again, blew jagged zeros
On all sides, and then sat down
To eat sandwiches, talk about girls,
School, and how to get by on five-dollar dates.
Finished eating, we called the dog
With finger snaps and tongue clicks,
But he crawled deeper into shadow.
We searched the car trunk for Coke cans,
Found three, and set them farther away.
We raised the rifles, winced an eye,
And fired, Leonard hitting
On the third try, me on the fifth.
We jumped up and down, laughed, and waved
A hand through the drifts of gun smoke,
Then the two of us returned to the car
Where we dragged the dog into the back seat.

We started the engine, let it idle in smoke,
And raised our rifles one last time,
The grass and dirt leaping into air.
We laughed and took a step back,
Packed the rifles in oily blankets,
And revved the engine. We turned onto the road
Without a good thought in our heads,
Ready for life.

THE LEVEE

At seventeen, I liked driving around,
Breaking the backs of leaves and casting long shadows
Where the lawns were burned. I didn't like home,
Especially in summer. But eventually I returned to watch
My stepfather eat fried chicken on a TV tray.
He ate for bulk, not taste,
And every night he drank to flood the hole inside him.
I couldn't believe my life. I was a Mexican
Among relatives with loud furniture. I knew most
Of us wouldn't get good jobs, some
Would die, others pull over
On the sides of roads to fix their Nova Super Sports
For a hundred years. I wanted out
Because the TV wouldn't stop until eleven.
The summer heat billowed near the ceiling.
Flies mingled among the smells
Of pried-apart chicken wings. I sweated
When I drank water from a dirty glass. I thought of
Putting my fingers in the box fan, of standing up
Nails under the tires of our neighbor's car.
That's why at night I drove to the levee
And played the radio. The water
Was constant, and the blown tires that bumped along
On a filthy current no longer surprised me.
The bushes breathed dust and hamburger wrappers,
The faint stink of dead birds. After a while
I talked to myself because the songs on the radio

Didn't seem honest. I was tired of home,
Of our TV wreathed in doilies
And the glow-in-the-night Christ on the windowsill.
I was sickened by the sound of toads flopping
In the dark, of a dying fish gasping among reeds.
I began to realize that we deserved each other,
Son to his stepfather, daughter to her real mother.
That it would take more than a car to make us happy.
We deserved this life, where a canal rushed
Black water, and the stars held for a while,
Then washed away as tires floated by in twos.

THE TREES THAT
CHANGE OUR LIVES

When I was twenty I walked past
The lady I would marry
Cross-legged on the porch.
She was cracking walnuts
With a hammer, a jar
At her side. I had come
From the store, swinging
A carton of cold beers,
And when I looked she smiled.
And that was all, until
I came back, flushed,
Glowing like a lantern
Against a backdrop
Of silly one-liners—
Cute-face, peaches, baby-lips.

We talked rain, cats,
About rain on cats,
And later went inside
For a sandwich, a glass
Of milk, sweets.
Still later, a month later,
We were going at one
Another on the couch, bed,
In the bathtub
And its backwash of bubbles,
Snapping. So it went,

And how strangely: the walnut
Tree had dropped its hard
Fruit, and they, in turn,
Were dropped into a paper
Bag, a jar, then into
The dough that was twisted
Into bread for the love
Of my mouth, so
It might keep talking.

Gary Soto

THE WRESTLER'S HEART

I had no choice but to shave my hair
And wrestle—thirty guys humping one another
On a mat. I didn't like high school.
There were no classes in archeology,
And the girls were too much like flowers
To bother with them. My brother, I think,
Was a hippie, and my sister, I know,
Was the runner-up queen of the Latin American Club.
When I saw her in the cafeteria, waved
And said things like, Debbie, is it your turn
To do the dishes tonight? she would smile and
Make real scary eyes. When I saw my brother
In his long hair and sissy bell-bottom pants,
He would look through me at a little snotty
Piece of gum on the ground. Neither of them
Liked me. So I sided with the wrestling coach,
The same person who taught you how to drive.
But first there was wrestling, young dudes
In a steamy room, and coach with his silver whistle,
His clipboard, his pencil behind his clubbed ear.
I was no good. Everyone was better
Than me. Everyone was larger
In the showers, their cocks like heavy wrenches,
Their hair like the scribbling of a mad child.
I would lather as best I could to hide
What I didn't have, then walk home
In the dark. When we wrestled

Madera High, I was pinned in twelve seconds.
My Mom threw me a half stick of gum
From the bleachers. She shouted, It's Juicy Fruit!
And I just looked at her. I looked at
The three spectators, all crunching corn nuts,
Their faces like punched-in paper bags.
We lost that night. The next day in Biology
I chewed my half stick of Juicy Fruit
And thought about what can go wrong
In twelve seconds. The guy who pinned
Me was named Bloodworth, a meaningful name.
That night I asked Mom what our name meant in Spanish.
She stirred crackling *papas* and said it meant Mexican.
I asked her what was the worst thing that happened
To her in the shortest period
Of time. She looked at my stepfather's chair
And told me to take out the garbage.
That year I gained weight, lost weight,
And lost more matches, nearly all by pins.
I wore my arm in a sling when
I got blood poisoning from a dirty fingernail.
I liked that. I liked being hurt. I even went so far
As limping, which I thought would attract girls.

One day at lunch the counselor called me to his office.
I killed my sandwich in three bites. In his
Office of unwashed coffee mugs,
He asked what I wanted from life.
I told him I wanted to be an archeologist,
And if not that, then an oceanographer.
I told him that I had these feelings
I was Chinese, that I had lived before
And was going to live again. He told me
To get a drink of water and that by fifth period
I should reconsider what I was saying.
I studied some, dated once, ate the same sandwich
Until it was spring in most of the trees
That circled the campus, and wrestling was over.
Then school was over. That summer I mowed lawns,
Picked grapes, and rode my bike
Up and down my block because it was good

For heart and legs. The next year I took Driver's Ed.
Coach was the teacher. He said, Don't be scared
But you're going to see some punks
Getting killed. If you're going to cry,
Do it later. He turned on the projector,
A funnel of silver light that showed motes of dust,
Then six seconds of car wreck from different angles.
The narrator with a wrestler's haircut came on.
His face was thick like a canned ham
Sliding onto a platter. He held up a black tennis shoe.
He said, The boy who wore this sneaker is dead.
Two girls cried. Three boys laughed.
Coach smiled and slapped the clipboard
Against his leg, kind of hard.
With one year of wrestling behind me,
I barely peeked but thought,
Six seconds for the kid with the sneakers,
Twelve seconds for Bloodworth to throw me on my back.
Tough luck in half the time.

Carlos Cumpián

WHEN JESUS WALKED

"You don't wanna die like Crow McDonald, do ya?"
My cousin just shook his dark bushy hair,
took another beer and tossed his jean jacket on a chair.

I was talking 'bout Crow, a tall hook-nose peddler
in a black leather cabretta and jeans, who flew face first
into a soda delivery truck outside of Ragos food shop,
the truck's red and white logo branding his
beer-soaked brain.

Crow's casket was draped with biker colors while
ganja laughter closed the lid on that cold day,
six-feet under, after a Chicago Outlaw's funeral.

Weeks later on a sleepy Sunday afternoon
I struggled to stay awake, and asked in a daze,
"Cuz, you used ta be an altar boy.
Think there's something in the incense that makes
people slower before dinner and Disney?"
"I wouldn't know, I haven't been to church in years,"
he replied. Then I drifted off and dreamt of Crow's
bony arms all folded up like wings as he said,
"Caw caw, I'm doing fine," and disappeared into the egg of darkness.

Waking up I sing, "We got to get up off this couch
        and find someone with a car.
See ya later Mom, I'll be back around eight."

Then who pulls up in his daddy's white Cadillac—Italian Tony,
with music pulsating the plush-padded interior,
we hop in and take a quick spin,
seven guys filling front and back seats,
it's so crowded we had no need for restraints, with our bony
shoulders pinned against each other, we bobbed ridiculously
to each tune, until fuzzy-haired Charlie Olsen squeaked,
"Let me out at 111th and the Ave,
I want to get somethin' to eat . . ."
Bye to the guy whose cremated parents
were kept at home in two rice-colored jars.

We drove on to find something
to smoke at Finchum's West Pullman pad,
after ten minutes of knocking, we agreed,
nothing could rouse Finchum from his lair,
if he was inside, he must've been out cold.
"Nah, I called him yesterday," Larry claimed,
"Said he's been wide awake for days on speed
reading books, *The Idiot* and *The Stranger*.
Weird, I can hear some mumbling, but there's no answer."

Under late September's autumnal rays
car windows rolled up, I clapped to full-throated
rock gospel on the car's radio,
"O happy days, when Jesus walked, O, when He walked."
In contrast my companions sat, stoned grass-eyed mystics.

Pausing at a four corner stop in a residential block,
normally as uneventful as changing a channel,
we philosophers at leisure missed
the pale blue transparent flashes
that grew bigger as it bounced
off a parked car's window,
too late,
we rolled out
to be struck broadside
by speeding Chicago cops,
Tony's daddy's caddy wavered,
then flipped onto its side,
as the song echoed the chorus.

●

Each shaggy head emerged from that tycoon's chariot
with the grave spoor of fear
mixed with the hashish breath
that greeted the huckleberries
as they peered in and asked,
"You ladies alright?" Hell, they changed their tunes
as soon as they saw Blackie's and Tom's mustaches,
while the rest of us held the unblinking golden
stare of the zig-zag rolling papers man,
before we heard,
"You're all under arrest, climb out
and assume the position,"
mixed with the radio's blissful,
"O, when Jesus walked, He took my pains away."

AISLE OF DOGS

In the first cage
a hunk of raw flesh.
No, it was alive, but skinned.

Or its back was skinned.
The knobs of the spine

poked through the bluish meat.

It was a pit bull, held by the shelter
for evidence until the case
could come to trial,

then they'd put him down. The dog,
not the human whose cruelty

lived on in the brindled body,
unmoving except for the enemy eyes.

Not for adoption, said the sign.

All the other cages held adoptable pets,
the manic yappers, sad matted mongrels,
the dumb slobbering abandoned ones,

the sick, the shaved, the scratching,
the wounded and terrified, the lost,

one to a cage, their water dishes
overturned, their shit tracked around,
on both sides of a long echoey
concrete aisle—clank of chain mesh gates,
the attendant hosing down the gutters

with his headphones on, half-dancing
to the song in his head.

I'd come for kittens. There were none.
So I stood in front of the pit bull's
quivering carcass, its longdrawn death,

its untouched food, its incurable hatred
of my species, until the man with the hose
touched my arm and steered me away,

shaking his head in a way that said
Don't look. Leave him alone.
I don't know why, either.

THE CLEAVING

He gossips like my grandmother, this man
with my face, and I could stand
amused all afternoon
in the Hon Kee Grocery,
amid hanging meats he
chops: roast pork cut
from a hog hung
by nose and shoulders,
his entire skin burnt
crisp, his
flesh I know
to be sweet,
his shining
face grinning
up at ducks
dangling single file,
each pierced by black
hooks through breast, bill,
and steaming from a hole
stitched shut at the ass.
I step to the counter, recite,
and he, without even slightly
varying the rhythm of his current confession or harangue,
scribbles my order on a greasy receipt,
and chops it up quick.
Such a sorrowful Chinese face,
nomad, Gobi, Northern

in its boniness
clear from the high
warlike forehead
to the sheer edge of the jaw.
He could be my brother, but slighter,
and except for his left forearm—engorged,
sinewy from his daily grip and
wield of a two-pound tool—
he's delicate, narrow-
waisted, his frame
so slight a lover, some
rough other,
might break it down
its smooth, oily length.
In his light-handed calligraphy
on receipts, and in his
moodiness, he is
a Southerner from a river province;
suited for scholarship, his face poised
above an open book, he'd mumble
his favorite passages.
He could be my grandfather;
come to America to get a Western education
in 1917, but too homesick to study,
he sits in the park all day, reading poems
and writing letters to his mother.

He lops the head off, chops
the neck of the duck
into six, slits
the body
open, groin
to breast, and drains
the scalding juices,
then quarters the carcass
with two fast hacks of the cleaver,
which blade has worn
into the surface of the round
foot-thick clop-block
a scoop that cradles precisely the curved steel.

●

The head, flung from the body, opens
down the middle where the butcher
cleanly halved it between
the eyes, and I
see, foetal-crouched
inside the skull, the homunculus,
gray brain grainy
to eat.
Did this animal, after all, at the moment
its neck broke,
image the way his executioner
shrinks from his own death?
Is this how
I, too, recoil from my day?
See how this shape
hordes itself, see how
little it is.
See its grease on the blade.
Is this how I'll be found
when judgment is passed, when names
are called, when crimes are tallied?
This is also how I looked before I tore my mother open.
Is this how I presided over my century, is this how
I regarded the murders?
This is also how I prayed.
Was it me in the Other
I prayed to when I prayed?
This too was how I slept, clutching my wife.
Was it me in the other I loved
when I loved another?
The butcher sees me eye this delicacy.
With a finger, he picks it
out of the skull-cradle
and offers it to me.
I take it gingerly between my fingers
and suck it down.
I eat my man.
The noise the body makes
when the body meets
the soul over the soul's ocean and penumbra
is the old sound of up-and-down, in-and-out,

a lump of muscle chug-chugging blood
into the ear; a lover's
heart-shaped tongue;
flesh rocking flesh until flesh comes;
the butcher working
at his block and blade to marry their shapes
by violence and time;
an engine crossing,
recrossing salt water, hauling

immigrants and the junk
of the poor. These
are the faces I love, the bodies
and scents of bodies
for which I long
in various ways, at various times,
thirteen gathered around the redwood,
happy, talkative, voracious
at day's end,
eager to eat
four kinds of meat
prepared four different ways,
numerous plates and bowls of rice and vegetables,
each made by distinct affections
and brought to table by many hands.
Brothers and sisters by blood and design,
who sit in separate bodies of varied shapes,
we constitute a many-membered
body of love.
In a world of shapes
of my desires, each one here
is a shape of one of my desires, and each
is known to me and dear by virtue
of each one's
unique corruption
of those texts, face, body:
that jut jaw
to gnash tendon;
that wide nose to meet the blows
a face like that invites;
those long eyes closing on the seen;

those thick lips
to suck the meat of animals
or recite 300 poems of the T'ang;
these teeth to bite my monosyllables;
these cheekbones to make
those syllables sing the soul.
Puffed or sunken
according to the life,
dark or light according
to the birth, straight
or humped, whole, manque, quasi, each pleases, verging
to utter grotesquery.
All are beautiful by variety.
The soul too
is a debasement
of a text, but, thus, it
acquires salience, although a
human salience, but
inimitable, and, hence, memorable.
God is the text.
The soul is a corruption
and a mnemonic.

A bright moment
I hold up an old head
from the sea, and admire the haughty
down-curved mouth
that seems to disdain
all the eyes are blind to,
including me, the eater.
Whole unto itself, complete
without me, yet its
shape complements the shape of my mind.
I take it as text and evidence
of the world's love for me,
and I feel urged to utterance,
urged to read the body of the world,
urged to say it
in human terms,
any reading a kind of eating, my eating
a kind of reading,

my saying a diminishment, my noise
a love-in-answer.

What is it in me would
devour the world to utter it?
What is it in me will not let
the world be, would eat
not just this fish
but the one who killed it,
that butcher who cleaned it.
I would eat the way he
squats, the way he
reaches into the plastic tubs
and pulls out a fish, clubs it, takes it
to the sink, guts it, drops it on the weighing pan.
I would eat that thrash
and plunge of the watery body
in the water, that liquid violence
between the man's hands,
I would eat
the gutless twitching on the scales,
three pounds of dumb
nerve and pulse, I would eat it all
to utter it.
The deaths at the sinks, those bodies prepared
for eating, I would eat,
and the standing deaths
at the counters, in the aisles,
the walking deaths in the streets,
the death-far-from-home, the death-
in-a-strange-land, these Chinatown
deaths, these American deaths.
I would devour this race to sing it,
this race that according to Emerson
managed to preserve to a hair
for three or four thousand years
the ugliest features in the world.
I would eat these features, eat
the last three or four thousand years, every hair.
And I would eat Emerson, his transparent soul, his
boring transcendence.

I would eat this head,
glazed in pepper-speckled sauce,
the cooked eyes opaque in their sockets.
I bring it to my mouth and—
the way I was taught, the way I've watched
others before me do—
with a stiff tongue lick out
the cheek-meat and the meat
over the armored jaw, my eating—
its sensual, salient nowness—
punctuating the void
from which such hunger springs and to which it proceeds.

And what
is this
I excavate
with my mouth?
What is this
plated, ribbed, hinged
architecture, this *carp head,*
but one more
articulation of a single nothing
severally manifested?
What is my eating,
rapt as it is,
but another
shape of going,
my immaculate expiration?
O, nothing is so
steadfast it won't go
the way the body goes.
The body goes.
The body's grave,
so serious
in its dying,
arduous as martyrs
in that task and as
glorious. It goes
empty always
and announces its going
by spasms and groans, farts and sweats.

•

What I thought were the arms
aching *cleave,* were the knees trembling *leave.*
What I thought were the muscles
insisting *resist, persist, exist,*
were the pores
hissing *mist* and *waste.*
What I thought was the body humming *reside, reside,*
was the body sighing *revise, revise.*
O, the murderous deletions,
the keening down
to nothing, the cleaving.
All of the body's revisions end
in death.
All of the body's revisions end.

Bodies eating bodies, heads eating heads,
we are nothing eating nothing,
and though we feast,
are filled, overfilled,
we go famished.
We gang the doors of death.
That is, our deaths are fed
that we may continue our daily dying,
our bodies going
down, while the plates-soon-empty
are passed around, that true
direction of our true prayers,
while the butcher spells
his message, manifold,
in the mortal air.
He coaxes, cleaves, brings change
before our very eyes, and at every
moment of our being.
As we eat we're eaten.
Else what is this
violence, this salt, this
passion, this heaven?

I thought the soul an airy thing.
I did not know the soul

is cleaved so that the soul might be restored.
Live wood hewn,
its sap springs from a sticky wound.
No seed, no egg has he
whose business calls for an axe.
In the trade of my soul's shaping,
he traffics in hews and hacks.

No easy thing, violence.
One of its names? Change. Change
resides in the embrace
of the effaced and the effacer,
in the covenant of the opened and the opener;
the axe accomplishes it on the soul's axis.
What then may I do
but cleave to what cleaves me.
I kiss the blade and eat my meat,
I thank the wielder and receive,

while terror spirits
my change, sorrow also.
The terror the butcher
scripts in the unhealed
air, the sorrow of his Shang
dynasty face,
African face with slit eyes. He is
my sister, this
beautiful Bedouin, this Shulamite,
keeper of sabbaths, diviner
of holy texts, this dark
dancer, this Jew, this Asian, this one
with the Cambodian face, Vietnamese face, this Chinese
I daily face,
this immigrant,
this man with my own face.

Joy Harjo

THE FLOOD

It had been years since I'd seen the watermonster, the snake who lived at the bottom of the lake. He had disappeared in the age of reason, as a mystery that never happened.

For in the muggy lake was the girl I could have been at sixteen, wrested from the torment of exaggerated fools, one version anyway, though the story at the surface would say car accident, or drowning while drinking, all of it eventually accidental.

This story is not an accident, nor is the existence of the watersnake in the memory of the people as they carried the burden of the myth from Alabama to Oklahoma. Each reluctant step pounded memory into the broken heart and no one will ever forget it.

When I walk the stairway of water into the abyss, I return as the wife of the watermonster, in a blanket of time decorated with swatches of cloth and feathers from our favorite clothes.

The stories of the battles of the watersnake are forever ongoing, and those stories soaked into my blood since infancy like deer gravy, so how could I resist the watersnake, who appeared as the most handsome man in the tribe, or any band whose visits I'd been witness to since childhood?

This had been going on for centuries: the first time he appeared I carried my baby sister on my back as I went to get water. She laughed at a woodpecker flitting like a small sun above us and before I could deter the symbol we were in it.

My body was already on fire with the explosion of womanhood as if I were flint, hot stone, and when he stepped out of the water he was the first myth I had ever seen uncovered. I had surprised him in a human moment. I looked aside but I could not discount what I had seen.

My baby sister's cry pinched reality, the woodpecker a warning of a disjuncture in the brimming sky, and then a man who was not a man but a myth.

What I had seen there were no words for except in the sacred language of the most holy recounting, so when I ran back to the village, drenched in salt, how could I explain the water jar left empty by the river to my mother who deciphered my burning lips as shame?

My imagination swallowed me like a mica sky, but I had seen the watermonster in the fight of lightning storms, breaking trees, stirring up killing winds, and had lost my favorite brother to a spear of the sacred flame, so certainly I would know my beloved if he were hidden in the blushing skin of the suddenly vulnerable.

I was taken with a fever and nothing cured it until I dreamed my fiery body dipped in the river where it fed into the lake. My father carried me as if I were newborn, as if he were presenting me once more to the world, and when he dipped me I was quenched, pronounced healed.

My parents immediately made plans to marry me to an important man who was years older but would provide me with everything I needed to survive in this world, a world I could no longer perceive, as I had been blinded with a ring of water when I was most in need of a drink by a snake who was not a snake, and how did he know my absolute secrets, those created at the brink of acquired language?

When I disappeared it was in a storm that destroyed the houses of my relatives; my baby sister was found sucking on her hand in the crook of an oak.

And though it may have appeared otherwise, I did not go willingly. That night I had seen my face strung on the shell belt of my ancestors, and I was standing next to a man who could not look me in the eye.

The oldest woman in the tribe wanted to remember me as a symbol in the story of a girl who disobeyed, who gave in to her desires before marriage and was destroyed by the monster disguised as the seductive warrior.

Others saw the car I was driving as it drove into the lake early one morning, the time the carriers of tradition wake up, before the sun or the approach of woodpeckers, and found the emptied six-pack on the sandy shores of the lake.

The power of the victim is a power that will always be reckoned with, one way or the other. When the proverbial sixteen-year-old woman walked down to the lake within her were all sixteen-year-old women who had questioned their power from time immemorial.

Her imagination was larger than the small frame house at the north edge of town, with the broken cars surrounding it like a necklace of futility, larger than the town itself leaning into the lake. Nothing could stop it, just as no one could stop the bearing-down thunderheads as they gathered overhead in the war of opposites.

Years later when she walked out of the lake and headed for town, no one recognized her, or themselves, in the drench of fire and rain. The watersnake was a story no one told anymore. They'd entered a drought that no one recognized as drought, the convenience store a signal of temporary amnesia.

I had gone out to get bread, eggs and the newspaper before breakfast and hurried the cashier for my change as the crazy woman walked in, for I could not see myself as I had abandoned her some twenty years ago in a blue windbreaker at the edge of the man-made lake as everyone dove naked and drunk off the sheer cliff, as if we had nothing to live for, not then or ever.

It was beginning to rain in Oklahoma, the rain that would flood the world.

※　※　※

Embedded in Muscogee tribal memory is the creature the tie snake, a huge snake of a monster who lives in waterways and will do what he can to take us with him. He represents the power of the underworld.

He is still present today in the lakes and rivers of Oklahoma and Alabama, a force we reckon with despite the proliferation of inventions that keep us from ourselves.

V I I

GENRE:
HORROR

GENRE:
HORROR

The oldest and strongest emotion of mankind is fear,
and the oldest and strongest kind of fear is fear of the
unknown.

—H. P. Lovecraft

Here are two exemplary works of horror (sometimes called "dark fantasy"):
one classic, published in 1923; the other by America's most popular contemporary horror writer, and one of the most popular writers in American
history, published in 1995. The pairing is doubly instructive: Stephen King,
like numerous other practitioners of the genre, has been richly influenced by
H. P. Lovecraft; and, though arriving at antithetical conclusions about evil and
our power to escape it, "The Rats in the Walls" and "The Man in the Black
Suit" are thematically related.

    "Genre" means "category, type, kind": the deliberate shaping of imagi-
native work in terms of *mystery-suspense, mystery-detective, romance, science fiction, fantasy,* and *dark fantasy,* among other conventions. Genre is usually popular, mass-market writing, though it can be "literary" as well. (Henry James's
great novella "The Turn of the Screw" is an ingenious ghost story; Angela
Carter's *The Bloody Chamber,* from which "Werewolf" is taken, is a contemporary example of reimaginings of traditional fairy tales that is both literary
and very popular.) Implicit in genre is the promise of a strong, clearly defined,
and cinematically vivid story; probability is subordinated to plot, and while
there is often a specificity of setting (as in the Lovecraft and King stories),
there is rarely development of character in the introspective, psychological
sense.

Horror fiction, like most genre writing, often begins with a concept. (Virtually all blockbuster Hollywood films of our era are "high-concept" genre films, systematically produced by filmmakers and consumed by uncritical fans.) In the Lovecraft story, the concept has to do with an ordinary, well-intentioned, and seemingly decent man succumbing to the curse of his ancestors: a reversion through human evolution back to cannibalism; in the King story, the concept has to do with a young boy, protected by parental love, resisting the Devil. Notoriously, horror fiction risks stereotypes and banalities precisely because it is so popular and because its emphasis is usually upon visual, simplistically plotted elements. Yet a more original and meaningful form of gothic horror may be generated by an individual's private experience transposed into "images," as well as by dreams or nightmares with which the writer can consciously experiment. (Lovecraft was haunted since childhood, for instance, by terrifying dreams to which he gave the name "night-haunts.")

H. P. Lovecraft (1890–1937) is generally considered the most significant writer of horror since Edgar Allan Poe, whose work influenced him greatly. His tales are unremittingly dark, savage, pessimistic about mankind, yet highly compelling, even addictive, as narratives; evil pervades his work, as it pervades his vision of the universe. By contrast, Stephen King's vision, while equally dark and macabre, allows frequently for human redemption and the repudiation of evil (as in "The Man in the Black Suit"). Lovecraft died in obscurity and has received only posthumous celebrity; King is enormously popular because, apart from the invention and narrative energy of his prose, he reaffirms traditional American values of free will, familial bonds, and common human decency.

THE RATS
IN THE WALLS

On July 16, 1923, I moved into Exham Priory after the last workman had finished his labors. The restoration had been a stupendous task, for little had remained of the deserted pile but a shell-like ruin; yet because it had been the seat of my ancestors, I let no expense deter me. The place had not been inhabited since the reign of James the First, when a tragedy of intensely hideous, though largely unexplained, nature had struck down the master, five of his children, and several servants; and driven forth under a cloud of suspicion and terror the third son, my lineal progenitor and the only survivor of the abhorred line.

With this sole heir denounced as a murderer, the estate had reverted to the crown, nor had the accused man made any attempt to exculpate himself or regain his property. Shaken by some horror greater than that of conscience or the law, and expressing only a frantic wish to exclude the ancient edifice from his sight and memory, Walter de la Poer, eleventh Baron Exham, fled to Virginia and there founded the family which by the next century had become known as Delapore.

Exham Priory had remained untenanted, though later allotted to the estates of the Norrys family and much studied because of its peculiarly composite architecture; an architecture involving Gothic towers resting on a Saxon or Romanesque substructure, whose foundation in turn was of a still earlier order or blend of orders—Roman, and even Druidic or native Cymric, if legends speak truly. This foundation was a very singular thing, being merged on one side with the solid limestone of the precipice from whose brink the priory overlooked a desolate valley three miles west of the village of Anchester.

Architects and antiquarians loved to examine this strange relic of forgotten centuries, but the country folk hated it. They had hated it hundreds of years before, when my ancestors lived there, and they hated it now, with the moss and mould of abandonment on it. I had not been a day in Anchester before I knew I came of an accursed house. And this week workmen have blown up Exham Priory, and are busy obliterating the traces of its foundations. The bare statistics of my ancestry I had always known, together with the fact that my first American forbear had come to the colonies under a strange cloud. Of details, however, I had been kept wholly ignorant through the policy of reticence always maintained by the Delapores. Unlike our planter neighbors, we seldom boasted of crusading ancestors or other mediaeval and Renaissance heroes; nor was any kind of tradition handed down except what may have been recorded in the sealed envelope left before the Civil War by every squire to his eldest son for posthumous opening. The glories we cherished were those achieved since the migration; the glories of a proud and honorable, if somewhat reserved and unsocial Virginia line.

During the war our fortunes were extinguished and our whole existence changed by the burning of Carfax, our home on the banks of the James. My grandfather, advanced in years, had perished in that incendiary outrage, and with him the envelope that had bound us all to the past. I can recall that fire today as I saw it then at the age of seven, with the Federal soldiers shouting, the women screaming, and the negroes howling and praying. My father was in the army, defending Richmond, and after many formalities my mother and I were passed through the lines to join him.

When the war ended we all moved north, whence my mother had come; and I grew to manhood, middle age, and ultimate wealth as a stolid Yankee. Neither my father nor I ever knew what our hereditary envelope had contained, and as I merged into the greyness of Massachusetts business life I lost all interest in the mysteries which evidently lurked far back in my family tree. Had I suspected their nature, how gladly I would have left Exham Priory to its moss, bats, and cobwebs!

My father died in 1904, but without any message to leave to me, or to my only child, Alfred, a motherless boy of ten. It was this boy who reversed the order of family information, for although I could give him only jesting conjectures about the past, he wrote me of some very interesting ancestral legends when the late war took him to England in 1917 as an aviation officer. Apparently the Delapores had a colorful and perhaps sinister history, for a friend of my son's, Capt. Edward Norrys of the Royal Flying Corps, dwelt near the family seat at Anchester and related some peasant superstitions which few novelists could equal for wildness and incredibility. Norrys himself, of course, did not take them so seriously; but they amused my son and made good material for his letters to me. It was this legendry which definitely turned my attention to my transatlantic heritage, and made me resolve to purchase and restore the family seat which Norrys showed to Alfred in its picturesque desertion, and offered to get for him at a surprisingly reasonable figure, since his own uncle was the present owner.

I bought Exham Priory in 1 9 1 8, but was almost immediately distracted from my plans of restoration by the return of my son as a maimed invalid. During the two years that he lived I thought of nothing but his care, having even placed my business under the direction of partners.

In 1 9 2 1, as I found myself bereaved and aimless, a retired manufacturer no longer young, I resolved to divert my remaining years with my new possession. Visiting Anchester in December, I was entertained by Capt. Norrys, a plump, amiable young man who had thought much of my son, and secured his assistance in gathering plans and anecdotes to guide in the coming restoration. Exham Priory itself I saw without emotion, a jumble of tottering mediaeval ruins covered with lichens and honeycombed with rooks' nests, perched perilously upon a precipice, and denuded of floors or other interior features save the stone walls of the separate towers.

As I gradually recovered the image of the edifice as it had been when my ancestors left it over three centuries before, I began to hire workmen for the reconstruction. In every case I was forced to go outside the immediate locality, for the Anchester villagers had an almost unbelievable fear and hatred of the place. This sentiment was so great that it was sometimes communicated to the outside laborers, causing numerous desertions; whilst its scope appeared to include both the priory and its ancient family.

My son had told me that he was somewhat avoided during his visits because he was a de la Poer, and I now found myself subtly ostracised for a like reason until I convinced the peasants how little I knew of my heritage. Even then they sullenly disliked me, so that I had to collect most of the village traditions through the mediation of Norrys. What the people could not forgive, perhaps, was that I had come to restore a symbol so abhorrent to them; for, rationally or not, they viewed Exham Priory as nothing less than a haunt of fiends and werewolves.

Piecing together the tales which Norrys collected for me, and supplementing them with the accounts of several savants who had studied the ruins, I deduced that Exham Priory stood on the site of a prehistoric temple; a Druidical or ante-Druidical thing which must have been contemporary with Stonehenge. That indescribable rites had been celebrated there, few doubted, and there were unpleasant tales of the transference of these rites into the Cybele-worship which the Romans had introduced.

Inscriptions still visible in the subcellar bore such unmistakable letters as "DIV . . . OPS . . . MAGNA.MAT . . ." sign of the Magna Mater whose dark worship was once vainly forbidden to Roman citizens. Anchester had been the camp of the third Augustan legion, as many remains attest, and it was said that the temple of Cybele was splendid and thronged with worshippers who performed nameless ceremonies at the bidding of a Phrygian priest. Tales added that the fall of the old religion did not end the orgies at the temple, but that the priests lived on in the new faith without real change. Likewise was it said that the rites did not vanish with the Roman power, and that certain among the Saxons added to what remained of the temple, and gave it the essential outline it subsequently preserved, making it the center of a cult feared through half the heptarchy. About 1000 A.D. the place is mentioned in a chronicle as being a substantial stone priory housing a strange and powerful monastic order and surrounded by extensive gardens which needed no walls to exclude a frightened populace. It was never destroyed by the Danes, though after the Norman Conquest it must have declined tremendously; since there was no impediment when Henry the Third granted the site to my ancestor, Gilbert de la Poer, First Baron Exham, in 1261.

Of my family before this date there is no evil report, but something strange must have happened then. In one chronicle there is a reference to a de la Poer as "cursed of God" in 1307, whilst village legendry had nothing but evil and frantic fear to tell of the castle that went up on the foundations of the old temple and priory. The fireside tales were of the most grisly description, all the ghastlier because of their frightened reticence and cloudy evasiveness. They represented my ancestors as a race of hereditary daemons beside whom Gilles de Retz and the Marquis de Sade would seem the veriest tyros, and hinted whisperingly at their responsibility for the occasional disappearances of villagers through several generations.

The worst characters, apparently, were the barons and their direct heirs; at least, most was whispered about these. If of healthier inclinations, it was said, an heir would early and mysteriously die to make way for another more typical scion. There seemed to be an inner cult in the family, presided over by the head of the house, and sometimes closed except to a few members. Temperament rather than ancestry was evidently the basis of this cult, for it was entered by several who married into the family. Lady Margaret Trevor from Cornwall, wife of Godfrey, the second son of the fifth baron, became a favorite bane of children all over the countryside, and the daemon heroine of a particularly horrible old ballad not yet extinct near the Welsh border. Preserved in balladry, too, though not illustrating the same point, is the hideous tale of Lady Mary de la Poer, who shortly after her marriage to the Earl of Shrewsfield was killed by him and his mother, both of the slayers being absolved and blessed by the priest to whom they confessed what they dared not repeat to the world.

These myths and ballads, typical as they were of crude superstition, repelled me greatly. Their persistence, and their application to so long a line of my ancestors, were especially annoying; whilst the imputations of monstrous habits proved unpleasantly reminiscent of the one known scandal of my immediate forbears—the case of my cousin, young Randolph Delapore of Carfax, who went among the negroes and became a voodoo priest after he returned from the Mexican War.

I was much less disturbed by the vaguer tales of wails and howlings in the barren, windswept valley beneath the limestone cliff; of the graveyard stenches after the spring rains; of the floundering, squealing white thing on which Sir John Clave's horse had trod one night in a lonely field; and of the servant who had gone mad at what he saw in the priory in the full light of day. These things were hackneyed spectral lore, and I was at that time a pronounced skeptic. The accounts of vanished peasants were less to be dismissed, though not especially significant in view of mediaeval custom. Prying curiosity meant death, and more than one severed head had been publicly shown on the bastions—now effaced—around Exham Priory.

A few of the tales were exceedingly picturesque, and made me wish I had learnt more of the comparative mythology in my youth. There was, for instance, the belief that a legion of batwinged devils kept witches' sabbath each night at the priory—a legion whose sustenance might explain the disproportionate abundance of coarse vegetables harvested in the vast gardens. And, most vivid of all, there was the dramatic epic of the rats—the scampering army of obscene vermin which had burst forth from the castle three months after the tragedy that doomed it to desertion—the lean, filthy, ravenous army which had swept all before it and devoured fowl, cats, dogs, hogs, sheep, and even two hapless human beings before its fury was spent. Around that unforgettable rodent army a whole separate cycle of myths revolves, for it scattered among the village homes and brought curses and horrors in its train.

Such was the lore that assailed me as I pushed to completion, with an elderly obstinacy, the work of restoring my ancestral home. It must not be imagined for a moment that these tales formed my principal psychological environment. On the other hand, I was constantly praised and encouraged by Capt. Norrys and the antiquarians who surrounded and aided me. When the task was done, over two years after its commencement, I viewed the great rooms, wainscotted walls, vaulted ceilings, mullioned windows, and broad staircases with a pride which fully compensated for the prodigious expense of the restoration.

Every attribute of the Middle Ages was cunningly reproduced, and the new parts blended perfectly with the original walls and foundations. The seat of my fathers was complete, and I looked forward to redeeming at last the local fame of the line which ended in me. I would reside here permanently, and prove that a de la Poer (for I had adopted again the original spelling of the name) need not be a fiend. My comfort was perhaps augmented by the fact that, although Exham Priory was mediaevally fitted, its interior was in truth wholly new and free from old vermin and old ghosts alike.

As I have said, I moved in on July 16, 1923. My household consisted of seven servants and nine cats, of which latter species I am particularly fond. My eldest cat, "Nigger-Man," was seven years old and had come with me from my home in Bolton, Massachusetts; the others I had accumulated whilst living with Capt. Norrys' family during the restoration of the priory.

For five days our routine proceeded with the utmost placidity, my time being spent mostly in the codification of old family data. I had now obtained some very circumstantial accounts of the final tragedy and flight of Walter de la Poer, which I conceived to be the probable contents of the hereditary paper lost in the fire at Carfax. It appeared that my ancestor was accused with much reason of having killed all the other members of his household, except four servant confederates, in their sleep, about two weeks after a shocking discovery which changed his whole demeanor, but which, except by implication, he disclosed to no one save perhaps the servants who assisted him and afterward fled beyond reach.

This deliberate slaughter, which included a father, three brothers, and two sisters, was largely condoned by the villagers, and so slackly treated by the law that its perpetrator escaped honored, unharmed, and undisguised to Virginia; the general whispered sentiment being that he had purged the land of immemorial curse. What discovery had prompted an act so terrible, I could scarcely even conjecture. Walter de la Poer must have known for years the sinister tales about his family, so that this material could have given him no fresh impulse. Had he, then, witnessed some appalling ancient rite, or stumbled upon some frightful and revealing symbol in the priory or its vicinity? He was reputed to have been a shy, gentle youth in England. In Virginia he seemed not so much hard or bitter as harassed and apprehensive. He was spoken of in the diary of another gentleman adventurer, Francis Harley of Bellview, as a man of unexampled justice, honor, and delicacy.

On July 22 occurred the first incident which, though lightly dismissed at the time, takes on a preternatural significance in relation to later events. It was so simple as to be almost negligible, and could not possibly have been noticed under the circumstances; for it must be recalled that since I was in a building practically fresh and new except for the walls, and surrounded by a well-balanced staff of servitors, apprehension would have been absurd despite the locality.

What I afterward remembered is merely this—that my old black cat, whose moods I know so well, was undoubtedly alert and anxious to an extent wholly out of keeping with his natural character. He roved from room to room, restless and disturbed, and sniffed constantly about the walls which formed part of the Gothic structure. I realize how trite this sounds—like the inevitable dog in the ghost story, which always growls before his master sees the sheeted figure—yet I cannot consistently suppress it.

The following day a servant complained of restlessness among all the cats in the house. He came to me in my study, a lofty west room on the second story, with groined arches, black oak panelling, and a triple Gothic window overlooking the limestone cliff and desolate valley; and even as he spoke I saw the jetty form of Nigger-Man creeping along the west wall and scratching at the new panels which overlaid the ancient stone.

I told the man that there must be some singular odor or emanation from the old stonework, imperceptible to human senses, but affecting the delicate organs of cats even through the new woodwork. This I truly believed, and when the fellow suggested the presence of mice or rats, I mentioned that there had been no rats there for three hundred years, and that even the field mice of the surrounding country could hardly be found in these high walls, where they had never been known to stray. That afternoon I called on Capt. Norrys, and he assured me that it would be quite incredible for field mice to infest the priory in such a sudden and unprecedented fashion.

That night, dispensing as usual with a valet, I retired in the west tower chamber which I had chosen as my own, reached from the study by a stone staircase and short gallery—the former partly ancient, the latter entirely restored. This room was circular, very high, and without wainscotting, being hung with arras which I had myself chosen in London.

Seeing that Nigger-Man was with me, I shut the heavy Gothic door and retired by the light of the electric bulbs which so cleverly counterfeited candles, finally switching off the light and sinking on the carved and canopied four-poster, with the venerable cat in his accustomed place across my feet. I did not draw the curtains, but gazed out at the narrow north window which I faced. There was a suspicion of aurora in the sky, and the delicate traceries of the window were pleasantly silhouetted.

At some time I must have fallen quietly asleep, for I recall a distinct sense of leaving strange dreams, when the cat started violently from his placid position. I saw him in the faint auroral glow, head strained forward, forefeet on my ankles, and hind feet stretched behind. He was looking intensely at a point on the wall somewhat west of the window, a point which to my eye had nothing to mark it, but toward which all my attention was now directed.

And as I watched, I knew that Nigger-Man was not vainly excited. Whether the arras actually moved I cannot say. I think it did, very slightly. But what I can swear to is that behind it I heard a low, distinct scurrying as of rats or mice. In a moment the cat had jumped bodily on the screening tapestry, bringing the affected section to the floor with his weight, and exposing a damp, ancient wall of stone; patched here and there by the restorers, and devoid of any trace of rodent prowlers.

Nigger-Man raced up and down the floor by this part of the wall, clawing the fallen arras and seemingly trying at times to insert a paw between the wall and the oaken floor. He found nothing, and after a time returned wearily to his place across my feet. I had not moved, but I did not sleep again that night.

In the morning I questioned all the servants, and found that none of them had noticed anything unusual, save that the cook remembered the actions of a cat which had rested on her windowsill. This cat had howled at some unknown hour of the night, awaking the cook in time for her to see him dart purposefully out of the open door down the stairs. I drowsed away the noontime, and in the afternoon called again on Capt. Norrys, who became exceedingly interested in what I told him. The odd incidents—so slight yet so curious—appealed to his sense of the picturesque, and elicited from him a number of reminiscences of local ghostly lore. We were genuinely perplexed at the presence of rats, and Norrys lent me some traps and Paris green, which I had the servants place in strategic localities when I returned.

I retired early, being very sleepy, but was harassed by dreams of the most horrible sort. I seemed to be looking down from an immense height upon a twilit grotto, knee-deep with filth, where a white-bearded daemon swineherd drove about with his staff a flock of fungous, flabby beasts whose appearance filled me with unutterable loathing. Then, as the swineherd paused and nodded over his task, a mighty swarm of rats rained down on the stinking abyss and fell to devouring beasts and man alike.

From this terrific vision I was abruptly awaked by the motions of Nigger-Man, who had been sleeping as usual across my feet. This time I did not have to question the source of his snarls and hisses, and of the fear which made him sink his claws into my ankle, unconscious of their effect; for on every side of the chamber the walls were alive with nauseous sound—the verminous slithering of ravenous, gigantic rats. There was now no aurora to show the state of the arras—the fallen section of which had been replaced—but I was not too frightened to switch on the light.

As the bulbs leapt into radiance I saw a hideous shaking all over the tapestry, causing the somewhat peculiar designs to execute a singular dance of death. This motion disappeared almost at once, and the sound with it. Springing out of bed, I poked at the arras with the long handle of a warming-pan that rested near, and lifted one section to see what lay beneath. There was nothing but the patched stone wall, and even the cat had lost his tense realization of abnormal presences. When I examined the circular trap that had been placed in the room, I found all of the openings sprung, though no trace remained of what had been caught and had escaped.

Further sleep was out of the question, so, lighting a candle, I opened the door and went out in the gallery toward the stairs to my study, Nigger-Man following at my heels. Before we had reached the stone steps, however, the cat darted ahead of me and vanished down the ancient flight. As I descended the stairs myself, I became suddenly aware of sounds in the great room below; sounds of a nature which could not be mistaken.

The oak-panelled walls were alive with rats, scrampering and milling, whilst Nigger-Man was racing about with the fury of a baffled hunter. Reaching the bottom, I switched on the light, which did not this time cause the noise to subside. The rats continued their riot, stampeding with such force and distinctness that I could finally assign to their motions a definite direction. These creatures, in numbers apparently inexhaustible, were engaged in one stupendous migration from inconceivable heights to some depth conceivably or inconceivably below.

I now heard steps in the corridor, and in another moment two servants pushed open the massive door. They were searching the house for some unknown source of disturbance which had thrown all the cats into a snarling panic and caused them to plunge precipitately down several flights of stairs and squat, yowling, before the closed door to the sub-cellar. I asked them if they had heard the rats, but they replied in the negative. And when I turned to call their attention to the sounds in the panels, I realized that the noise had ceased.

With the two men, I went down to the door of the sub-cellar, but found the cats already dispersed. Later I resolved to explore the crypt below, but for the present I merely made a round of the traps. All were sprung, yet all were tenantless. Satisfying myself that no one had heard the rats save the felines and me, I sat in my study till morning, thinking profoundly and recalling every scrap of legend I had unearthed concerning the building I inhabited.

I slept some in the forenoon, leaning back in the one comfortable library chair which my mediaeval plan of furnishing could not banish. Later I telephoned to Capt. Norrys, who came over and helped me explore the sub-cellar. Absolutely nothing untoward was found, although we could not repress a thrill at the knowledge that this vault was built by Roman hands. Every low arch and massive pillar was Roman—not the debased Romanesque of the bungling Saxons, but the severe and harmonious classicism of the age of the Caesars; indeed, the walls abounded with inscriptions familiar to the antiquarians who had repeatedly explored the place—things like "P. GETAE. PROP ...TEMP ... DONA ..." and "L. PRAEC ... VS ... PONTIFI ... ATYS ...."

The reference to Atys made me shiver, for I had read Catullus and knew something of the hideous rites of the Eastern god, whose worship was so mixed with that of Cybele. Norrys and I, by the light of lanterns, tried to interpret the odd and nearly effaced designs on certain irregularly rectangular blocks of stone generally held to be altars, but could make nothing of them. We remembered that one pattern, a sort of rayed sun, was held by students to imply a non-Roman origin, suggesting that these altars had merely been adopted by the Roman priests from some older and perhaps aboriginal temple on the same site. On one of these blocks were some brown stains which made me wonder. The largest, in the center of the room, had certain features on the upper surface which indicated its connection with fire—probably burnt offerings.

Such were the sights in that crypt before whose door the cats howled, and where Norrys and I now determined to pass the night. Couches were brought down by the servants, who were told not to mind any nocturnal actions of the cats, and Nigger-Man was admitted as much for help as for companionship. We decided to keep the great oak door—a modern replica with slits for ventilation—tightly closed; and, with this attended to, we retired with lanterns still burning to await whatever might occur.

The vault was very deep in the foundations of the priory, and undoubtedly far down on the face of the beetling limestone cliff overlooking the waste valley. That it had been the goal of the scuffling and unexplainable rats I could not doubt, though why, I could not tell. As we lay there expectantly, I found my vigil occasionally mixed with half-formed dreams from which the uneasy motions of the cat across my feet would rouse me.

These dreams were not wholesome, but horribly like the one I had had the night before. I saw again the twilit grotto, and the swineherd with his unmentionable fungous beasts wallowing in filth, and as I looked at these things they seemed nearer and more distinct—so distinct that I could almost observe their features. Then I did observe the flabby features of one of them—and awaked with such a scream that Nigger-Man started up, whilst Capt. Norrys, who had not slept, laughed considerably. Norrys might have laughed more—or perhaps less—had he known what it was that made me scream. But I did not remember myself till later. Ultimate horror often paralyses memory in a merciful way.

Norrys waked me when the phenomena began. Out of the same frightful dream I was called by his gentle shaking and his urging to listen to the cats. Indeed, there was much to listen to, for beyond the closed door at the head of the stone steps was a veritable nightmare of feline yelling and clawing, whilst Nigger-Man, unmindful of his kindred outside, was running excitedly around the bare stone walls, in which I heard the same babel of scurrying rats that had troubled me the night before.

An acute terror now rose within me, for here were anomalies which nothing normal could well explain. These rats, if not the creatures of a madness which I shared with the cats alone, must be burrowing and sliding in Roman walls I had thought to be of solid limestone blocks . . . unless perhaps the action of water through more than seventeen centuries had eaten winding tunnels which rodent bodies had worn clear and ample. . . . But even so, the spectral horror was no less; for if these were living vermin why did not Norrys hear their disgusting commotion? Why did he urge me to watch Nigger-Man and listen to the cats outside, and why did he guess wildly and vaguely at what could have aroused them?

By the time I had managed to tell him, as rationally as I could, what I thought I was hearing, my ears gave me the last fading impression of the scurrying; which had retreated *still downward,* far underneath this deepest of sub-cellars till it seemed as if the whole cliff below were riddled with questing rats. Norrys was not as skeptical as I had anticipated, but instead seemed profoundly moved. He motioned to me to notice that the cats at the door had ceased their clamor, as if giving up the rats for lost; whilst Nigger-Man had a burst of renewed restlessness, and was clawing frantically around the bottom of the large stone altar in the center of the room, which was nearer Norrys' couch than mine.

My fear of the unknown was at this point very great. Something astounding had occurred, and I saw that Capt. Norrys, a younger, stouter, and presumably more naturally materialistic man, was affected fully as much as myself—perhaps because of his lifelong and intimate familiarity with local legend. We could for the moment do nothing but watch the old black cat as he pawed with decreasing fervor at the base of the altar, occasionally looking up and mewing to me in that persuasive manner which he used when he wished me to perform some favor for him.

Norrys now took a lantern close to the altar and examined the place where Nigger-Man was pawing; silently kneeling and scraping away the lichens of the centuries which joined the massive pre-Roman block to the tesselated floor. He did not find anything, and was about to abandon his efforts when I noticed a trivial circumstance which made me shudder, even though it implied nothing more than I had already imagined.

I told him of it, and we both looked at its almost imperceptible manifestation with the fixedness of fascinated discovery and acknowledgment. It was only this—that the flame of the lantern set down near the altar was slightly but certainly flickering from a draught of air which it had not before received, and which came indubitably from the crevice between floor and altar where Norrys was scraping away the lichens.

We spent the rest of the night in the brilliantly-lighted study, nervously discussing what we should do next. The discovery that some vault deeper than the deepest known masonry of the Romans underlay this accursed pile; some vault unsuspected by the curious antiquarians of three centuries; would have been sufficient to excite us without any background of the sinister. As it was, the fascination became two-fold; and we paused in doubt whether to abandon our search and quit the priory forever in superstitious caution, or to gratify our sense of adventure and brave whatever horrors might await us in the unknown depths.

By morning we had compromised, and decided to go to London to gather a group of archaeologists and scientific men fit to cope with the mystery. It should be mentioned that before leaving the sub-cellar we had vainly tried to move the central altar which we now recognized as the gate to a new pit of nameless fear. What secret would open the gate, wiser men than we would have to find.

During many days in London Capt. Norrys and I presented our facts, conjectures, and legendary anecdotes to five eminent authorities, all men who could be trusted to respect any family disclosures which future explorations might develop. We found most of them little disposed to scoff, but, instead, intensely interested and sincerely sympathetic. It is hardly necessary to name them all, but I may say that they included Sir William Brinton, whose excavations in the Troad excited most of the world in their day. As we all took the train for Anchester I felt myself poised on the brink of frightful revelations, a sensation symbolized by the air of mourning among the many Americans at the unexpected death of the President on the other side of the world.

On the evening of August 7 we reached Exham Priory, where the servants assured me that nothing unusual had occurred. The cats, even old Nigger-Man, had been perfectly placid; and not a trap in the house had been sprung. We were to begin exploring on the following day, awaiting which I assigned well-appointed rooms to all my guests.

I myself retired in my own tower chamber, with Nigger-Man across my feet. Sleep came quickly, but hideous dreams assailed me. There was a vision of a Roman feast like that of Trimalchio, with a horror in a covered platter. Then came that damnable, recurrent thing about the swineherd and his filthy drove in the twilit grotto. Yet when I awoke it was full daylight, with normal sounds in the house below. The rats, living or spectral, had not troubled me; and Nigger-Man was still quietly asleep. On going down, I found that the same tranquillity had prevailed elsewhere; a condition which one of the assembled savants—a fellow named Thornton, devoted to the psychic—rather absurdly laid to the fact that I had now been shown the thing which certain forces had wished to show me.

All was now ready, and at 11 A.M. our entire group of seven men, bearing

powerful electric searchlights and implements of excavation, went down to
the sub-cellar and bolted the door behind us. Nigger-Man was with us, for
the investigators found no occasion to despise his excitability, and were indeed anxious that he be present in case of obscure rodent manifestations. We
noted the Roman inscriptions and unknown altar designs only briefly, for three
of the savants had already seen them, and all knew their characteristics. Prime
attention was paid to the momentous central altar, and within an hour Sir
William Brinton had caused it to tilt backward, balanced by some unknown
species of counterweight.

There now lay revealed such a horror as would have overwhelmed us
had we not been prepared. Through a nearly square opening in the tiled floor,
sprawling on a flight of stone steps so prodigiously worn that it was little more
than an inclined plane at the center, was a ghastly array of human or semi-
human bones. Those which retained their collocation as skeletons showed attitudes of panic fear, and over all were the marks of rodent gnawing. The skulls
denoted nothing short of utter idiocy, cretinism, or primitive semi-apedom.

Above the hellishly littered steps arched a descending passage seemingly
chiseled from the solid rock, and conducting a current of air. This current was
not a sudden and noxious rush as from a closed vault, but a cool breeze with
something of freshness in it. We did not pause long, but shiveringly began to
clear a passage down the steps. It was then that Sir William, examining the
hewn walls, made the odd observation that the passage, according to the direction of the strokes, must have been chiseled *from beneath.*

I must be very deliberate now, and choose my words.

After ploughing down a few steps amidst the gnawed bones we saw that
there was light ahead; not any mystic phosphorescence, but a filtered daylight
which could not come except from unknown fissures in the cliff that overlooked the waste valley. That such fissures had escaped notice from outside
was hardly remarkable, for not only is the valley wholly uninhabited, but the
cliff is so high and beetling that only an aeronaut could study its face in detail. A few steps more, and our breaths were literally snatched from us by what
we saw; so literally that Thornton, the psychic investigator, actually fainted
in the arms of the dazed man who stood behind him. Norrys, his plump face
utterly white and flabby, simply cried out inarticulately; whilst I think that
what I did was to gasp or hiss, and cover my eyes.

The man behind me—the only one of the party older than I—croaked
the hackneyed "My God!" in the most cracked voice I ever heard. Of seven
cultivated men, only Sir William Brinton retained his composure, a thing the
more to his credit because he led the party and must have seen the sight first.

It was a twilit grotto of enormous height, stretching away farther than
any eye could see; a subterranean world of limitless mystery and horrible

suggestion. There were buildings and other architectural remains—in one ter-rified glance I saw a weird pattern of tumuli, a savage circle of monoliths, a low-domed Roman ruin, a sprawling Saxon pile, and an early English edifice of wood—but all these were dwarfed by the ghoulish spectacle presented by the general surface of the ground. For yards about the steps extended an in-sane tangle of human bones, or bones at least as human as those on the steps. Like a foamy sea they stretched, some fallen apart, but others wholly or partly articulated as skeletons; these latter invariably in postures of daemo-niac frenzy, either fighting off some menace or clutching other forms with cannibal intent.

When Dr. Trask, the anthropologist, stopped to classify the skulls, he found a degraded mixture which utterly baffled him. They were mostly lower than the Piltdown man in the scale of evolution, but in every case definitely human. Many were of higher grade, and a very few were the skulls of supremely and sensitively developed types. All the bones were gnawed, mostly by rats, but somewhat by others of the half-human drove. Mixed with them were many tiny bones of rats—fallen members of the lethal army which closed the ancient epic.

I wonder that any man among us lived and kept his sanity through that hideous day of discovery. Not Hoffman or Huysmans could conceive a scene more wildly incredible, more frenetically repellent, or more Gothically grotesque than the twilit grotto through which we seven staggered; each stumbling on revelation after revelation, and trying to keep for the nonce from thinking of the events which must have taken place there three hundred, or a thousand, or two thousand, or ten thousand years ago. It was the an-techamber of hell, and poor Thornton fainted again when Trask told him that some of the skeleton things must have descended as quadrupeds through the last twenty or more generations.

Horror piled on horror as we began to interpret the architectural re-mains. The quadruped things—with their occasional recruits from the biped class—had been kept in stone pens, out of which they must have broken in their last delirium of hunger or rat-fear. There had been great herds of them, evidently fattened on the coarse vegetables whose remains could be found as a sort of poisonous ensilage at the bottom of huge stone bins older than Rome. I knew now why my ancestors had had such excessive gardens—would to heaven I could forget! The purpose of the herds I did not have to ask.

Sir William, standing with his searchlight in the Roman ruin, translated aloud the most shocking ritual I have ever known; and told of the diet of the antediluvian cult which the priests of Cybele found and mingled with their own. Norrys, used as he was to the trenches, could not walk straight when he came out of the English building. It was a butcher shop and kitchen—he had expected that—but it was too much to see familiar English implements in such a place, and to read familiar English *graffiti* there, some as recent as 1610. I could not go in that building—that building whose daemon activities were stopped only by the dagger of my ancestor Walter de la Poer.

What I did venture to enter was the low Saxon building whose oaken door had fallen, and there I found a terrible row of ten stone cells with rusty bars. Three had tenants, all skeletons of high grade, and on the bony forefinger of one I found a seal ring with my own coat-of-arms. Sir William found a vault with far older cells below the Roman chapel, but these cells were empty. Below them was a low crypt with cases of formally arranged bones, some of them bearing terrible parallel inscriptions carved in Latin, Greek, and the tongue of Phrygia.

Meanwhile, Dr. Trask had opened one of the prehistoric tumuli, and brought to light skulls which were slightly more human than a gorilla's, and which bore indescribably ideographic carvings. Through all this horror my cat stalked unperturbed. Once I saw him monstrously perched atop a mountain of bones, and wondered at the secrets that might lie behind his yellow eyes.

Having grasped to some slight degree the frightful revelations of this twilit area—an area so hideously foreshadowed by my recurrent dream—we turned to that apparently boundless depth of midnight cavern where no ray of light from the cliff could penetrate. We shall never know what sightless Stygian worlds yawn beyond the little distance we went, for it was decided that such secrets are not good for mankind. But there was plenty to engross us close at hand, for we had not gone far before the searchlights showed that accursed infinity of pits in which the rats had feasted, and whose sudden lack of replenishment had driven the ravenous rodent army first to turn on the living herds of starving things, and then to burst forth from the priory in that historic orgy of devastation which the peasants will never forget.

God! those carrion black pits of sawed, picked bones and opened skulls! Those nightmare chasms choked with the pithecanthropoid, Celtic, Roman, and English bones of countless unhallowed centuries! Some of them were full, and none can say how deep they had once been. Others were still bottomless to our searchlights, and peopled by unnamable fancies. What, I thought, of the hapless rats that stumbled into such traps amidst the blackness of their quests in this grisly Tartarus?

Once my foot slipped near a horribly yawning brink, and I had a moment of ecstatic fear. I must have been musing a long time, for I could not see any of the party but the plump Capt. Norrys. Then there came a sound from that inky, boundless, farther distance that I thought I knew; and I saw my old black cat dart past me like a winged Egyptian god, straight into the illimitable gulf of the unknown. But I was not far behind, for there was no doubt after another second. It was the eldritch scurrying of those fiend-born rats, always questing for new horrors, and determined to lead me on even unto those grinning caverns of earth's center where Nyarlathotep, the mad faceless god, howls blindly in the darkness to the piping of two amorphous idiot flute-players.

My searchlight expired, but still I ran. I heard voices, and yowls, and echoes, but above all there gently rose that impious, insidious scurrying; gently rising, rising, as a stiff bloated corpse gently rises above an oily river that flows under endless onyx bridges to a black, putrid sea.

Something bumped into me—something soft and plump. It must have been the rats; the viscous, gelatinous, ravenous army that feast on the dead and the living. . . . Why shouldn't rats eat a de la Poer as a de la Poer eats forbidden things? . . . The war ate my boy, damn them all . . . and the Yanks ate Carfax with flames and burnt Grandsire Delapore and the secret . . . No, no, I tell you, I am *not* that daemon swineherd in the twilit grotto! It was *not* Edward Norrys' fat face on that flabby fungous thing! Who says I am a de la Poer? He lived, but my boy died! . . . Shall a Norrys hold the lands of a de la Poer? . . . It's voodoo, I tell you . . . that spotted snake . . . Curse you, Thornton, I'll teach you to faint at what my family do! . . . 'Sblood, thou stinkard, I'll learn ye how to gust . . . wolde ye swynke me thilke wys? . . . *Magna Mater! Magna Mater! . . . Atys . . . Dia ad aghaidh 's ad aodaun . . . agus bas dunach ort! Dhonas 's dholas ort, agus leat-sa! . . . Ungl . . . ungl . . . rrlh . . . chchch . . .*

That is what they say I said when they found me in the blackness after three hours; found me crouching in the blackness over the plump, half-eaten body of Capt. Norrys, with my own cat leaping and tearing at my throat. Now they have blown up Exham Priory, taken my Nigger-Man away from me, and shut me into this barred room at Hanwell with fearful whispers about my heredity and experience. Thornton is in the next room, but they prevent me from talking to him. They are trying, too, to suppress most of the facts concerning the priory. When I speak of poor Norrys they accuse me of a hideous thing, but they must know that I did not do it. They must know it was the rats; the slithering scurrying rats whose scampering will never let me sleep; the daemon rats that race behind the padding in this room and beckon me down to greater horrors than I have ever known; the rats they can never hear; the rats, the rats in the walls.

Stephen King

THE MAN
IN THE BLACK SUIT

I am now a very old man and this is something that happened to me when I was very young—only nine years old. It was 1914, the summer after my brother, Dan, died in the west field and not long before America got into the First World War. I've never told anyone about what happened at the fork in the stream that day, and I never will. I've decided to write it down, though, in this book, which I will leave on the table beside my bed. I can't write long, because my hands shake so these days and I have next to no strength, but I don't think it will take long.

Later, someone may find what I have written. That seems likely to me, as it is pretty much human nature to look in a book marked "Diary" after its owner has passed along. So, yes—my words will probably be read. A better question is whether anyone will believe them. Almost certainly not, but that doesn't matter. It's not belief I'm interested in but freedom. Writing can give that, I've found. For twenty years I wrote a column called "Long Ago and Far Away" for the Castle Rock *Call,* and I know that sometimes it works that way—what you write down sometimes leaves you forever, like old photographs left in the bright sun, fading to nothing but white.

I pray for that sort of release.

A man in his eighties should be well past the terrors of childhood, but as my infirmities slowly creep up on me, like waves licking closer and closer to some indifferently built castle of sand, that terrible face grows clearer and clearer in my mind's eye. It glows like a dark star in the constellations of my childhood. What I might have done yesterday, who I might have seen here in my room at the nursing home, what I might have said to them or they to me— those things are gone, but the face of the man in the black suit grows ever clearer, ever closer, and I remember every word he said. I don't want to think of him but I can't help it, and sometimes at night my old heart beats so hard and so fast I think it will tear itself right clear of my chest. So I uncap my fountain pen and force my trembling old hand to write this pointless anecdote in the diary one of my great-grandchildren—I can't remember her name for sure, at least not right now, but I know it starts with an "S"—gave to me last Christmas, and which I have never written in until now. Now I will write in it. I will write the story of how I met the man in the black suit on the bank of Castle Stream one afternoon in the summer of 1914.

The town of Motton was a different world in those days—more different than I could ever tell you. That was a world without airplanes droning overhead, a world almost without cars and trucks, a world where the skies were not cut into lanes and slices by overhead power lines. There was not a single paved road in the whole town, and the business district consisted of nothing but Corson's General Store, Thut's Livery & Hardware, the Methodist church at Christ's Corner, the school, the town hall, and half a mile down from there, Harry's Restaurant, which my mother called, with unfailing disdain, "the liquor house."

Mostly, though, the difference was in how people lived—how *apart* they were. I'm not sure people born after the middle of the century could quite credit that, although they might say they could, to be polite to old folks like me. There were no phones in western Maine back then, for one thing. The first one wouldn't be installed for another five years, and by the time there was a phone in our house, I was nineteen and going to college at the University of Maine in Orono.

But that is only the roof of the thing. There was no doctor closer than Casco, and there were no more than a dozen houses in what you would call town. There were no neighborhoods (I'm not even sure we knew the word, although we had a verb—"neighboring"—that described church functions and barn dances), and open fields were the exception rather than the rule. Out of town the houses were farms that stood far apart from each other, and from December until the middle of March we mostly hunkered down in the little pockets of stove warmth we called families. We hunkered and listened to the wind in the chimney and hoped no one would get sick or break a leg or get a headful of bad ideas, like the farmer over in Castle Rock who had chopped up his wife and kids three winters before and then said in court that the ghosts made him do it. In those days before the Great War, most of Motton was woods and bog—dark long places full of moose and mosquitoes, snakes and secrets. In those days there were ghosts everywhere.

This thing I'm telling about happened on a Saturday. My father gave me a whole list of chores to do, including some that would have been Dan's, if he'd still been alive. He was my only brother, and he'd died of a bee sting. A

year had gone by, and still my mother wouldn't hear that. She said it was something else, *had* to have been, that no one ever died of being stung by a bee.
When Mama Sweet, the oldest lady in the Methodist Ladies' Aid, tried to tell
her—at the church supper the previous winter, this was—that the same thing
had happened to her favorite uncle back in '73, my mother clapped her hands
over her ears, got up, and walked out of the church basement. She'd never
been back since, and nothing my father could say to her would change her
mind. She claimed she was done with church, and that if she ever had to see
Helen Robichaud again (that was Mama Sweet's real name) she would slap
her eyes out. She wouldn't be able to help herself, she said.

That day Dad wanted me to lug wood for the cookstove, weed the beans
and the cukes, pitch hay out of the loft, get two jugs of water to put in the
cold pantry, and scrape as much old paint off the cellar bulkhead as I could.
Then, he said, I could go fishing, if I didn't mind going by myself—he had to
go over and see Bill Eversham about some cows. I said I sure didn't mind going
by myself, and my dad smiled as if that didn't surprise him so very much. He'd
given me a bamboo pole the week before—not because it was my birthday
or anything but just because he liked to give me things sometimes—and I was
wild to try it in Castle Stream, which was by far the troutiest brook I'd ever
fished.

"But don't you go too far in the woods," he told me. "Not beyond where
the water splits."

"No, sir."

"Promise me."

"Yessir, I promise."

"Now promise your mother."

We were standing on the back stoop; I had been bound for the spring-
house with the water jugs when my dad stopped me. Now he turned me
around to face my mother, who was standing at the marble counter in a flood
of strong morning sunshine falling through the double windows over the
sink. There was a curl of hair lying across the side of her forehead and touching her eyebrow—you see how well I remember it all? The bright light turned
that little curl to filaments of gold and made me want to run to her and put
my arms around her. In that instant I saw her as a woman, saw her as my father must have seen her. She was wearing a housedress with little red roses
all over it, I remember, and she was kneading bread. Candy Bill, our little black
Scottie dog, was standing alertly beside her feet, looking up, waiting for anything that might drop. My mother was looking at me.

"I promise," I said.

She smiled, but it was the worried kind of smile she always seemed to
make since my father brought Dan back from the west field in his arms. My

father had come sobbing and bare-chested. He had taken off his shirt and draped it over Dan's face, which had swelled and turned color. *My boy!* he had been crying. *Oh, look at my boy! Jesus, look at my boy!* I remember that as if it were yesterday. It was the only time I ever heard my dad take the Saviour's name in vain.

"What do you promise, Gary?" she asked.

"Promise not to go no further than where the stream forks, Ma'am."

"Any further."

"Any."

She gave me a patient look, saying nothing as her hands went on working in the dough, which now had a smooth, silky look.

"I promise not to go any further than where the stream forks, Ma'am."

"Thank you, Gary," she said. "And try to remember that grammar is for the world as well as for school."

"Yes, Ma'am."

Candy Bill followed me as I did my chores, and sat between my feet as I bolted my lunch, looking up at me with the same attentiveness he had shown my mother while she was kneading her bread, but when I got my new bamboo pole and my old, splintery creel and started out of the dooryard, he stopped and only stood in the dust by an old roll of snow fence, watching. I called him but he wouldn't come. He yapped a time or two, as if telling me to come back, but that was all.

"Stay, then," I said, trying to sound as if I didn't care. I did, though, at least a little. Candy Bill *always* went fishing with me.

My mother came to the door and looked out at me with her left hand held up to shade her eyes. I can see her that way still, and it's like looking at a photograph of someone who later became unhappy, or died suddenly. "You mind your dad now, Gary!"

"Yes, Ma'am, I will."

She waved. I waved, too. Then I turned my back on her and walked away.

The sun beat down on my neck, hard and hot, for the first quartermile or so, but then I entered the woods, where double shadow fell over the road and it was cool and fir-smelling and you could hear the wind hissing through the deep, needled groves. I walked with my pole on my shoulder the way boys did back then, holding my creel in my other hand like a valise or a salesman's sample case. About two miles into the woods along a road that was really nothing but a double rut with a grassy strip growing up the center hump, I began to hear the hurried, eager gossip of Castle Stream. I thought of trout with bright speckled backs and pure-white bellies, and my heart went up in my chest.

The stream flowed under a little wooden bridge, and the banks leading down to the water were steep and brushy. I worked my way down carefully, holding on where I could and digging my heels in. I went down out of summer and back into mid-spring, or so it felt. The cool rose gently off the water, and there was a green smell like moss. When I got to the edge of the water I only stood there for a little while, breathing deep of that mossy smell and watching the dragonflies circle and the skitterbugs skate. Then, further down, I saw a trout leap at a butterfly—a good big brookie, maybe fourteen inches long—and remembered I hadn't come here just to sightsee.

I walked along the bank, following the current, and wet my line for the first time, with the bridge still in sight upstream. Something jerked the tip of my pole down once or twice and ate half my worm, but whatever it was was too sly for my nine-year-old hands—or maybe just not hungry enough to be careless—so I quit that place.

I stopped at two or three other places before I got to the place where Castle Stream forks, going southwest into Castle Rock and southeast into Kashwakamak Township, and at one of them I caught the biggest trout I have ever caught in my life, a beauty that measured nineteen inches from tip to tail on the little ruler I kept in my creel. That was a monster of a brook trout, even for those days.

If I had accepted this as gift enough for one day and gone back, I would not be writing now (and this is going to turn out longer than I thought it would, I see that already), but I didn't. Instead I saw to my catch right then and there as my father had shown me—cleaning it, placing it on dry grass at the bottom of the creel, then laying damp grass on top of it—and went on. I did not, at age nine, think that catching a nineteen-inch brook trout was particularly remarkable, although I do remember being amazed that my line had not broken when I, netless as well as artless, had hauled it out and swung it toward me in a clumsy tail-flapping arc.

Ten minutes later, I came to the place where the stream split in those days (it is long gone now; there is a settlement of duplex homes where Castle Stream once went its course, and a district grammar school as well, and if there is a stream it goes in darkness), dividing around a huge gray rock nearly the size of our outhouse. There was a pleasant flat space here, grassy and soft, overlooking what my dad and I called South Branch. I squatted on my heels, dropped my line into the water, and almost immediately snagged a fine rainbow trout. He wasn't the size of my brookie—only a foot or so—but a good fish, just the same. I had it cleaned out before the gills had stopped flexing, stored it in my creel, and dropped my line back into the water.

This time there was no immediate bite, so I leaned back, looking up at the blue stripe of sky I could see along the stream's course. Clouds floated by, west to east, and I tried to think what they looked like. I saw a unicorn, then a rooster, then a dog that looked like Candy Bill. I was looking for the next one when I drowsed off.

Or maybe slept. I don't know for sure. All I know is that a tug on my line so strong it almost pulled the bamboo pole out of my hand was what brought me back into the afternoon. I sat up, clutched the pole, and suddenly became aware that something was sitting on the tip of my nose. I crossed my eyes and saw a bee. My heart seemed to fall dead in my chest, and for a horrible second I was sure I was going to wet my pants.

The tug on my line came again, stronger this time, but although I maintained my grip on the end of the pole so it wouldn't be pulled into the stream and perhaps carried away (I think I even had the presence of mind to snub the line with my forefinger), I made no effort to pull in my catch. All my horrified attention was fixed on the fat black-and-yellow thing that was using my nose as a rest stop.

I slowly poked out my lower lip and blew upward. The bee ruffled a little but kept its place. I blew again and it ruffled again—but this time it also seemed to shift impatiently, and I didn't dare blow anymore, for fear it would lose its temper completely and give me a shot. It was too close for me to focus on what it was doing, but it was easy to imagine it ramming its stinger into one of my nostrils and shooting its poison up toward my eyes. And my brain.

A terrible idea came to me: that this was the very bee that had killed my brother. I knew it wasn't true, and not only because honeybees probably didn't live longer than a single year (except maybe for the queens; about them I was not so sure). It couldn't be true, because honeybees died when they stung, and even at nine I knew it. Their stingers were barbed, and when they tried to fly away after doing the deed, they tore themselves apart. Still, the idea stayed. This was a special bee, a devil-bee, and it had come back to finish the other of Albion and Loretta's two boys.

And here is something else: I had been stung by bees before, and although the stings had swelled more than is perhaps usual (I can't really say for sure), I had never died of them. That was only for my brother, a terrible trap that had been laid for him in his very making—a trap that I had somehow escaped. But as I crossed my eyes until they hurt, in an effort to focus on the bee, logic did not exist. It was the *bee* that existed, only that—the bee that had killed my brother, killed him so cruelly that my father had slipped down the straps of his overalls so he could take off his shirt and cover Dan's swollen, engorged face. Even in the depths of his grief he had done that, because he didn't want his wife to see what had become of her firstborn. Now the bee had returned, and now it would kill me. I would die in convulsions on the bank, flopping just as a brookie flops after you take the hook out of its mouth. As I sat there trembling on the edge of panic—ready to bolt to my feet and then bolt anywhere—there came a report from behind me. It was as sharp and peremptory as a pistol shot, but I knew it wasn't a pistol shot; it was someone clapping his hands. One single clap. At that moment, the bee tumbled off my nose and fell into my lap. It lay there on my pants with its legs sticking up and its stinger a threatless black thread against the old scuffed brown of the corduroy. It was dead as a doornail, I saw that at once. At the same moment, the pole gave another tug—the hardest yet—and I almost lost it again.

I grabbed it with both hands and gave it a big stupid yank that would have made my father clutch his head with both hands, if he had been there to see. A rainbow trout, a good bit larger than either of the ones I had already caught, rose out of the water in a wet flash, spraying fine drops of water from its tail—it looked like one of those fishing pictures they used to put on the covers of men's magazines like *True* and *Man's Adventure* back in the forties and fifties. At that moment hauling in a big one was about the last thing on my mind, however, and when the line snapped and the fish fell back into the stream, I barely noticed. I looked over my shoulder to see who had clapped. A man was standing above me, at the edge of the trees. His face was very long and pale. His black hair was combed tight against his skull and parted with rigorous care on the left side of his narrow head. He was very tall. He was wearing a black three-piece suit, and I knew right away that he was not a human being, because his eyes were the orangey red of flames in a woodstove. I don't mean just the irises, because he *had* no irises, and no pupils, and certainly no whites. His eyes were completely orange—an orange that shifted and flickered. And it's really too late not to say exactly what I mean, isn't it? He was on fire inside, and his eyes were like the little isinglass portholes you sometimes see in stove doors.

My bladder let go, and the scuffed brown the dead bee was lying on went a darker brown. I was hardly aware of what had happened, and I couldn't take my eyes off the man standing on top of the bank and looking down at me— the man who had apparently walked out of thirty miles of trackless western Maine woods in a fine black suit and narrow shoes of gleaming leather. I could see the watch chain looped across his vest glittering in the summer sunshine. There was not so much as a single pine needle on him. And he was smiling at me.

"Why, it's a fisherboy!" he cried in a mellow, pleasing voice. "Imagine that! Are we well met, fisherboy?"

"Hello, sir," I said. The voice that came out of me did not tremble, but it didn't sound like my voice, either. It sounded older. Like Dan's voice, maybe. Or my father's, even. And all I could think was that maybe he would let me go if I pretended not to see what he was. If I pretended I didn't see there were flames glowing and dancing where his eyes should have been.

"I've saved you a nasty sting, perhaps," he said, and then, to my horror, he came down the bank to where I sat with a dead bee in my wet lap and a bamboo fishing pole in my nerveless hands. His slicksoled city shoes should have slipped on the low, grassy weeds dressing the steep bank, but they didn't; nor did they leave tracks, I saw. Where his feet had touched—or seemed to touch—there was not a single broken twig, crushed leaf, or trampled shoe-shape.

Even before he reached me, I recognized the aroma baking up from the skin under the suit—the smell of burned matches. The smell of sulfur. The man in the black suit was the Devil. He had walked out of the deep woods between Motton and Kashwakamak, and now he was standing here beside me. From the corner of one eye I could see a hand as pale as the hand of a storewindow dummy. The fingers were hideously long.

He hunkered beside me on his hams, his knees popping just as the knees of any normal man might, but when he moved his hands so they dangled between his knees, I saw that each of those long fingers ended in not a fingernail but a long yellow claw.

"You didn't answer my question, fisherboy," he said in his mellow voice. It was, now that I think of it, like the voice of one of those radio announcers on the big-band shows years later, the ones that would sell Geritol and Serutan and Ovaltine and Dr. Grabow pipes. "Are we well met?"

"Please don't hurt me," I whispered, in a voice so low I could barely hear it. I was more afraid than I could ever write down, more afraid than I want to remember. But I do. I do. It never crossed my mind to hope I was having a dream, although it might have, I suppose, if I had been older. But I was nine, and I knew the truth when it squatted down beside me. I knew a hawk from a handsaw, as my father would have said. The man who had come out of the woods on that Saturday afternoon in midsummer was the Devil, and inside the empty holes of his eyes his brains were burning.

"Oh, do I smell something?" he asked, as if he hadn't heard me, although I knew he had. "Do I smell something . . . wet?"

He leaned toward me with his nose stuck out, like someone who means to smell a flower. And I noticed an awful thing; as the shadow of his head traveled over the bank, the grass beneath it turned yellow and died. He lowered his head toward my pants and sniffed. His glaring eyes half closed, as if he had inhaled some sublime aroma and wanted to concentrate on nothing but that.

"Oh, bad!" he cried. "Lovely-bad!" And then he chanted: "Opal! Diamond! Sapphire! Jade! I smell Gary's lemonade!" He threw himself on his back in the little flat place and laughed.

I thought about running, but my legs seemed two counties away from my brain. I wasn't crying, though; I had wet my pants, but I wasn't crying. I was too scared to cry. I suddenly knew that I was going to die, and probably painfully, but the worst of it was that that might not be the worst of it. The worst might come later. *After* I was dead.

He sat up suddenly, the smell of burnt matches fluffing out from his suit and making me feel gaggy in my throat. He looked at me solemnly from his narrow white face and burning eyes, but there was a sense of laughter about him, too. There was always that sense of laughter about him.

"Sad news, fisherboy," he said. "I've come with sad news."

I could only look at him—the black suit, the fine black shoes, the long white fingers that ended not in nails but in talons.

"Your mother is dead."

"No!" I cried. I thought of her making bread, of the curl lying across her forehead and just touching her eyebrow, of her standing there in the strong morning sunlight, and the terror swept over me again, but not for myself this time. Then I thought of how she'd looked when I set off with my fishing pole, standing in the kitchen doorway with her hand shading her eyes, and how she had looked to me in that moment like a photograph of someone you expected to see again but never did. "No, you lie!" I screamed.

He smiled—the sadly patient smile of a man who has often been accused falsely. "I'm afraid not," he said. "It was the same thing that happened to your brother, Gary. It was a bee."

"No, that's not true," I said, and now I *did* begin to cry. "She's old, she's thirty-five—if a bee sting could kill her the way it did Danny she would have died a long time ago, and you're a lying bastard!"

I had called the Devil a lying bastard. I was aware of this, but the entire front of my mind was taken up by the enormity of what he'd said. My mother dead? He might as well have told me that the moon had fallen on Vermont. But I believed him. On some level I believed him completely, as we always believe, on some level, the worst thing our hearts can imagine.

"I understand your grief, little fisherboy, but that particular argument just doesn't hold water, I'm afraid." He spoke in a tone of bogus comfort that was horrible, maddening, without remorse or pity. "A man can go his whole life without seeing a mockingbird, you know, but does that mean mocking-birds don't exist? Your mother—"

A fish jumped below us. The man in the black suit frowned, then pointed a finger at it. The trout convulsed in the air, its body bending so strenuously that for a split second it appeared to be snapping at its own tail, and when it fell back into Castle Stream it was floating lifelessly. It struck the big gray rock where the waters divided, spun around twice in the whirlpool eddy that formed there, and then floated away in the direction of Castle Rock. Mean-while, the terrible stranger turned his burning eyes on me again, his thin lips pulled back from tiny rows of sharp teeth in a cannibal smile.

"Your mother simply went through her entire life without being stung by a bee," he said. "But then—less than an hour ago, actually—one flew in through the kitchen window while she was taking the bread out of the oven and putting it on the counter to cool."

I raised my hands and clapped them over my ears. He pursed his lips as if to whistle and blew at me gently. It was only a little breath, but the stench was foul beyond belief—clogged sewers, outhouses that have never known a single sprinkle of lime, dead chickens after a flood.

My hands fell away from the sides of my face.

"Good," he said. "You need to hear this, Gary; you need to hear this, my little fisherboy. It was your mother who passed that fatal weakness on to your brother. You got some of it, but you also got a protection from your father that poor Dan somehow missed." He pursed his lips again, only this time he made a cruelly comic little *tsk-tsk* sound instead of blowing his nasty breath at me. "So although I don't like to speak ill of the dead, it's almost a case of poetic justice, isn't it? After all, she killed your brother Dan as surely as if she had put a gun to his head and pulled the trigger."

"No," I whispered. "No, it isn't true."

"I assure you it is," he said. "The bee flew in the window and lit on her neck. She slapped at it before she even knew what she was doing—*you* were wiser than that, weren't you, Gary?—and the bee stung her. She felt her throat start to close up at once. That's what happens, you know, to people who can't tolerate bee venom. Their throats close and they drown in the open air. That's why Dan's face was so swollen and purple. That's why your father covered it with his shirt."

I stared at him, now incapable of speech. Tears streamed down my cheeks. I didn't want to believe him, and knew from my church schooling that the Devil is the father of lies, but I *did* believe him just the same.

"She made the most wonderfully awful noises," the man in the black suit said reflectively, "and she scratched her face quite badly, I'm afraid. Her eyes bulged out like a frog's eyes. She wept." He paused, then added: "She wept as she died, isn't that sweet? And here's the most beautiful thing of all. After she was dead, after she had been lying on the floor for fifteen minutes or so with no sound but the stove ticking and with that little thread of a bee stinger still poking out of the side of her neck—so small, so small—do you know what Candy Bill did? That little rascal licked away her tears. First on one side, and then on the other."

He looked out at the stream for a moment, his face sad and thoughtful. Then he turned back to me and his expression of bereavement disappeared like a dream. His face was as slack and as avid as the face of a corpse that has died hungry. His eyes blazed. I could see his sharp little teeth between his pale lips.

"I'm starving," he said abruptly. "I'm going to kill you and eat your guts, little fisherboy. What do you think about that?"

No, I tried to say, *please no,* but no sound came out. He meant to do it, I saw. He really meant to do it.

"I'm just so *hungry,*" he said, both petulant and teasing. "And you won't want to live without your precious mommy, anyhow, take my word for it. Because your father's the sort of man who'll have to have some warm hole to stick it in, believe me, and if you're the only one available, you're the one who'll have to serve. I'll save you all that discomfort and unpleasantness. Also, you'll go to Heaven, think of that. Murdered souls *always* go to Heaven. So we'll both be serving God this afternoon, Gary. Isn't that nice?"

He reached for me again with his long, pale hands, and without thinking what I was doing, I flipped open the top of my creel, pawed all the way down to the bottom, and brought out the monster brookie I'd caught earlier—the one I should have been satisfied with. I held it out to him blindly, my fingers in the red slit of its belly, from which I had removed its insides as the man in the black suit had threatened to remove mine. The fish's glazed eye stared dreamily at me, the gold ring around the black center reminding me of my mother's wedding ring. And in that moment I saw her lying in her coffin with the sun shining off the wedding band and knew it was true—she had been stung by a bee, she had drowned in the warm, bread-smelling kitchen air, and Candy Bill had licked her dying tears from her swollen cheeks.

"Big fish!" the man in the black suit cried in a guttural, greedy voice. "Oh, *biiig fiiish!*"

He snatched it away from me and crammed it into a mouth that opened wider than any human mouth ever could. Many years later, when I was sixty-five (I know it was sixty-five, because that was the summer I retired from teaching), I went to the aquarium in Boston and finally saw a shark. The mouth of the man in the black suit was like that shark's mouth when it opened, only his gullet was blazing orange, the same color as his eyes, and I felt heat bake out of it and into my face, the way you feel a sudden wave of heat come pushing out of a fireplace when a dry piece of wood catches alight. And I didn't imagine that heat, either—I know I didn't—because just before he slid the head of my nineteen-inch brook trout between his gaping jaws, I saw the scales along the sides of the fish rise up and begin to curl like bits of paper floating over an open incinerator.

He slid the fish in like a man in a traveling show swallowing a sword. He didn't chew, and his blazing eyes bulged out, as if in effort. The fish went in and went in, his throat bulged as it slid down his gullet, and now he began to cry tears of his own—except his tears were blood, scarlet and thick.

I think it was the sight of those bloody tears that gave me my body back.

I don't know why that should have been, but I think it was. I bolted to my feet like a Jack released from its box, turned with my bamboo pole still in one hand, and fled up the bank, bending over and tearing tough bunches of weeds out with my free hand in an effort to get up the slope more quickly.

He made a strangled, furious noise—the sound of any man with his mouth too full—and I looked back just as I got to the top. He was coming after me, the back of his suit coat flapping and his thin gold watch chain flashing and winking in the sun. The tail of the fish was still protruding from his mouth and I could smell the rest of it, roasting in the oven of his throat.

He reached for me, groping with his talons, and I fled along the top of the bank. After a hundred yards or so I found my voice and went to screaming—screaming in fear, of course, but also screaming in grief for my beautiful dead mother.

He was coming after me. I could hear snapping branches and whipping bushes, but I didn't look back again. I lowered my head, slitted my eyes against the bushes and low-hanging branches along the stream's bank, and ran as fast as I could. And at every step I expected to feel his hands descending on my shoulders, pulling me back into a final burning hug.

That didn't happen. Some unknown length of time later—it couldn't have been longer than five or ten minutes, I suppose, but it seemed like forever—I saw the bridge through layerings of leaves and firs. Still screaming, but breathlessly now, sounding like a teakettle that has almost boiled dry, I reached this second, steeper bank and charged up.

Halfway to the top, I slipped to my knees, looked over my shoulder, and saw the man in the black suit almost at my heels, his white face pulled into a convulsion of fury and greed. His cheeks were splattered with his bloody tears and his shark's mouth hung open like a hinge.

"Fisherboy!" he snarled, and started up the bank after me, grasping at my foot with one long hand. I tore free, turned, and threw my fishing pole at him. He batted it down easily, but it tangled his feet up somehow and he went to his knees. I didn't wait to see any more; I turned and bolted to the top of the slope. I almost slipped at the very top, but managed to grab one of the support struts running beneath the bridge and save myself.

"You can't get away, fisherboy!" he cried from behind me. He sounded furious, but he also sounded as if he were laughing. "It takes more than a mouthful of trout to fill *me* up!"

"Leave me alone!" I screamed back at him. I grabbed the bridge's railing and threw myself over it in a clumsy somersault, filling my hands with splinters and bumping my head so hard on the boards when I came down that I saw stars. I rolled over on my belly and began crawling. I lurched to my feet just before I got to the end of the bridge, stumbled once, found my rhythm, and then began to run. I ran as only nine-year-old boys can run, which is like the wind. It felt as if my feet only touched the ground with every third or fourth stride, and, for all I know, that may be true. I ran straight up the right-hand wheel rut in the road, ran until my temples pounded and my eyes pulsed in their sockets, ran until I had a hot stitch in my left side from the bottom of my ribs to my armpit, ran until I could taste blood and something like metal shavings in the back of my throat. When I couldn't run anymore I stumbled to a stop and looked back over my shoulder, puffing and blowing like a wind-broken horse. I was convinced I would see him standing right there behind me in his natty black suit, the watch chain a glittering loop across his vest and not a hair out of place.

But he was gone. The road stretching back toward Castle Stream between the darkly massed pines and spruces was empty. And yet I sensed him somewhere near in those woods, watching me with his grassfire eyes, smelling of burned matches and roasted fish.

I turned and began walking as fast as I could, limping a little—I'd pulled muscles in both legs, and when I got out of bed the next morning I was so sore I could barely walk. I kept looking over my shoulder, needing again and again to verify that the road behind me was still empty. It was each time I looked, but those backward glances seemed to increase my fear rather than lessen it. The firs looked darker, massier, and I kept imagining what lay behind the trees that marched beside the road—long, tangled corridors of forest, leg-breaking deadfalls, ravines where anything might live. Until that Saturday in 1914, I had thought that bears were the worst thing the forest could hold.

A mile or so farther up the road, just beyond the place where it came out of the woods and joined the Geegan Flat Road, I saw my father walking toward me and whistling "The Old Oaken Bucket." He was carrying his own rod, the one with the fancy spinning reel from Monkey Ward. In his other hand he had his creel, the one with the ribbon my mother had woven through the handle back when Dan was still alive. "Dedicated to Jesus" that ribbon said. I had been walking, but when I saw him I started to run again, screaming *Dad! Dad! Dad!* at the top of my lungs and staggering from side to side on my tired, sprung legs like a drunken sailor. The expression of surprise on his face when he recognized me might have been comical under other circumstances. He dropped his rod and creel into the road without so much as a downward glance at them and ran to me. It was the fastest I ever saw my dad run in his life; when we came together it was a wonder the impact didn't knock us both senseless, and I struck my face on his belt buckle hard enough to start a little nosebleed. I didn't notice that until later, though. Right then I only reached out my arms and clutched him as hard as I could. I held on and rubbed my hot face back and forth against his belly, covering his old blue workshirt with blood and tears and snot.

"Gary, what is it? What happened? Are you all right?"

"Ma's dead!" I sobbed. "I met a man in the woods and he told me! Ma's dead! She got stung by a bee and it swelled her all up just like what happened to Dan, and she's dead! She's on the kitchen floor and Candy Bill . . . licked the t-t-tears . . . off her . . . off her . . ."

Face was the last word I had to say, but by then my chest was hitching so bad I couldn't get it out. My own tears were flowing again, and my dad's startled, frightened face had blurred into three overlapping images. I began to howl—not like a little kid who's skinned his knee but like a dog that's seen something bad by moonlight—and my father pressed my head against his hard flat stomach again. I slipped out from under his hand, though, and looked back over my shoulder. I wanted to make sure the man in the black suit wasn't coming. There was no sign of him; the road winding back into the woods was completely empty. I promised myself I would never go back down that road again, not ever, no matter what, and I suppose now that God's greatest blessing to His creatures below is that they can't see the future. It might have broken my mind if I had known I *would* be going back down that road, and not two hours later. For that moment, though, I was only relieved to see we were still alone. Then I thought of my mother—my beautiful dead mother—and laid my face back against my father's stomach and bawled some more.

"Gary, listen to me," he said a moment or two later. I went on bawling. He gave me a little longer to do that, then reached down and lifted my chin so he could look down into my face and I could look up into his. "Your mom's fine," he said.

I could only look at him with tears streaming down my cheeks. I didn't believe him.

"I don't know who told you different, or what kind of dirty dog would want to put a scare like that into a little boy, but I swear to God your mother's fine."

"But . . . but he said . . ."

"I don't care *what* he said. I got back from Eversham's earlier than I expected—he doesn't want to sell any cows, it's all just talk—and decided I had time to catch up with you. I got my pole and my creel and your mother made us a couple of jelly fold-overs. Her new bread. Still warm. So she was fine half an hour ago, Gary, and there's nobody knows any different that's come from this direction, I guarantee you. Not in just half an hour's time." He looked over my shoulder. "Who was this man? And where was he? I'm going to find him and thrash him within an inch of his life."

I thought a thousand things in just two seconds—that's what it seemed like, anyway—but the last thing I thought was the most powerful: if my Dad met up with the man in the black suit, I didn't think my Dad would be the one to do the thrashing. Or the walking away.

I kept remembering those long white fingers, and the talons at the ends of them.

"Gary?"

"I don't know that I remember," I said.

"Were you where the stream splits? The big rock?"

I could never lie to my father when he asked a direct question—not to save his life or mine. "Yes, but don't go down there." I seized his arm with both hands and tugged it hard. "Please don't. He was a scary man." Inspiration struck like an illuminating lightning bolt. "I think he had a gun."

He looked at me thoughtfully. "Maybe there wasn't a man," he said, lifting his voice a little on the last word and turning it into something that was almost but not quite a question. "Maybe you fell asleep while you were fishing, son, and had a bad dream. Like the ones you had about Danny last winter."

I *had* had a lot of bad dreams about Dan last winter, dreams where I would open the door to our closet or to the dark, fruity interior of the cider shed and see him standing there and looking at me out of his purple strangulated face; from many of these dreams I had awakened screaming, and awakened my parents as well. I had fallen asleep on the bank of the stream for a little while, too—dozed off, anyway—but I hadn't dreamed, and I was sure I had awakened just before the man in the black suit clapped the bee dead, sending it tumbling off my nose and into my lap. I hadn't dreamed him the way I had dreamed Dan, I was quite sure of that, although my meeting with him had already attained a dreamlike quality in my mind, as I suppose supernatural occurrences always must. But if my Dad thought that the man had only existed in my own head, that might be better. Better for him.

"It might have been, I guess," I said.

"Well, we ought to go back and find your rod and your creel."

He actually started in that direction, and I had to tug frantically at his arm to stop him again and turn him back toward me.

"Later," I said. "Please, Dad? I want to see Mother. I've got to see her with my own eyes."

He thought that over, then nodded. "Yes, I suppose you do. We'll go home first, and get your rod and creel later."

So we walked back to the farm together, my father with his fish pole propped on his shoulder just like one of my friends, me carrying his creel, both of us eating folded-over slices of my mother's bread smeared with black-currant jam.

"Did you catch anything?" he asked as we came in sight of the barn.

"Yes, sir," I said. "A rainbow. Pretty good-sized." *And a brookie that was a lot bigger,* I thought but didn't say.

"That's all? Nothing else?"

"After I caught it I fell asleep." This was not really an answer but not really a lie, either.

"Lucky you didn't lose your pole. You didn't, did you, Gary?"

"No, sir," I said, very reluctantly. Lying about that would do no good even if I'd been able to think up a whopper—not if he was set on going back to get my creel anyway, and I could see by his face that he was.

Up ahead, Candy Bill came racing out of the back door, barking his shrill bark and wagging his whole rear end back and forth the way Scotties do when they're excited. I couldn't wait any longer. I broke away from my father and ran to the house, still lugging his creel and still convinced, in my heart of hearts, that I was going to find my mother dead on the kitchen floor with her face swollen and purple, as Dan's had been when my father carried him in from the west field, crying and calling the name of Jesus.

But she was standing at the counter, just as well and fine as when I had left her, humming a song as she shelled peas into a bowl. She looked around at me, first in surprise and then in fright as she took in my wide eyes and pale cheeks.

"Gary, what is it? What's the matter?"

I didn't answer, only ran to her and covered her with kisses. At some point my father came in and said, "Don't worry, Lo—he's all right. He just had one of his bad dreams, down there by the brook."

"Pray God it's the last of them," she said, and hugged me tighter while Candy Bill danced around our feet, barking his shrill bark.

"You don't have to come with me if you don't want to, Gary," my father said, although he had already made it clear that he thought I should—that I should go back, that I should face my fear, as I suppose folks would say nowadays. That's very well for fearful things that are make-believe, but two hours hadn't done much to change my conviction that the man in the black suit had been real. I wouldn't be able to convince my father of that, though. I don't think there was a nine-year-old who ever lived who would have been able to convince his father he'd seen the Devil walking out of the woods in a black suit.

"I'll come," I said. I had come out of the house to join him before he left, mustering all my courage to get my feet moving, and now we were standing by the chopping block in the side yard, not far from the woodpile.

"What you got behind your back?" he asked.

I brought it out slowly. I would go with him, and I would hope the man in the black suit with the arrow-straight part down the left side of his head was gone. But if he wasn't, I wanted to be prepared. As prepared as I could be, anyway. I had the family Bible in the hand I had brought out from behind my back. I'd set out just to bring my New Testament, which I had won for memorizing the most psalms in the Thursday-night Youth Fellowship competition (I managed eight, although most of them except the Twenty-third had floated out of my mind in a week's time), but the little red Testament didn't seem like enough when you were maybe going to face the Devil himself, not even when the words of Jesus were marked out in red ink.

My father looked at the old Bible, swollen with family documents and pictures, and I thought he'd tell me to put it back, but he didn't. A look of mixed grief and sympathy crossed his face, and he nodded. "All right," he said. "Does your mother know you took that?"

"No, sir."

He nodded again. "Then we'll hope she doesn't spot it gone before we get back. Come on. And don't drop it."

Half an hour or so later, the two of us stood on the bank at the place where Castle Stream forked, and at the flat place where I'd had my encounter with the man with the red-orange eyes. I had my bamboo rod in my hand—I'd picked it up below the bridge—and my creel lay down below, on the flat place. Its wicker top was flipped back. We stood looking down, my father and I, for a long time, and neither of us said anything.

Opal! Diamond! Sapphire! Jade! I smell Gary's lemonade! That had been his unpleasant little poem, and once he had recited it, he had thrown himself on his back, laughing like a child who has just discovered he has enough courage to say bathroom words like shit or piss. The flat place down there was as green and lush as any place in Maine that the sun can get to in early July. Except where the stranger had lain. There the grass was dead and yellow in the shape of a man.

I was holding our lumpy old family Bible straight out in front of me with both thumbs pressing so hard on the cover that they were white. It was the way Mama Sweet's husband, Norville, held a willow fork when he was trying to dowse somebody a well.

"Stay here," my father said at last, and skidded sideways down the bank, digging his shoes into the rich soft soil and holding his arms out for balance. I stood where I was, holding the Bible stiffly out at the ends of my arms, my heart thumping. I don't know if I had a sense of being watched that time or not; I was too scared to have a sense of anything, except for a sense of wanting to be far away from that place and those woods.

My dad bent down, sniffed at where the grass was dead, and grimaced.

I knew what he was smelling: something like burnt matches. Then he grabbed my creel and came on back up the bank, hurrying. He snagged one fast look over his shoulder to make sure nothing was coming along behind. Nothing was. When he handed me the creel, the lid was still hanging back on its cunning little leather hinges. I looked inside and saw nothing but two handfuls of grass.

"Thought you said you caught a rainbow," my father said, "but maybe you dreamed that, too."

Something in his voice stung me. "No, sir," I said. "I caught one."

"Well, it sure as hell didn't flop out, not if it was gutted and cleaned. And you wouldn't put a catch into your fisherbox without doing that, would you, Gary? I taught you better than that."

"Yes, sir, you did, but—"

"So if you didn't dream catching it and if it was dead in the box, something must have come along and eaten it," my father said, and then he grabbed another quick glance over his shoulder, eyes wide, as if he had heard something move in the woods. I wasn't exactly surprised to see drops of sweat standing out on his forehead like big clear jewels. "Come on," he said. "Let's get the hell out of here."

I was for that, and we went back along the bank to the bridge, walking quick without speaking. When we got there, my dad dropped to one knee and examined the place where we'd found my rod. There was another patch of dead grass there, and the lady's slipper was all brown and curled in on itself, as if a blast of heat had charred it. I looked in my empty creel again. "He must have gone back and eaten my other fish, too," I said.

My father looked up at me. "*Other* fish!"

"Yes, sir. I didn't tell you, but I caught a brookie, too. A big one. He was awful hungry, that fella." I wanted to say more, and the words trembled just behind my lips, but in the end I didn't.

We climbed up to the bridge and helped each other over the railing. My father took my creel, looked into it, then went to the railing and threw it over. I came up beside him in time to see it splash down and float away like a boat, riding lower and lower in the stream as the water poured in between the wicker weavings.

"It smelled bad," my father said, but he didn't look at me when he said it, and his voice sounded oddly defensive. It was the only time I ever heard him speak just that way.

"Yes, sir."

"We'll tell your mother we couldn't find it. If she asks. If she doesn't ask, we won't tell her anything."

"No, sir, we won't."

And she didn't and we didn't, and that's the way it was.

That day in the woods is eighty years gone, and for many of the years in between I have never even thought of it—not awake, at least. Like any other man or woman who ever lived, I can't say about my dreams, not for sure. But now I'm old, and I dream awake, it seems. My infirmities have crept up like waves that will soon take a child's abandoned sand castle, and my memories have also crept up, making me think of some old rhyme that went, in part, "Just leave them alone / And they'll come home / Wagging their tails behind them." I remember meals I ate, games I played, girls I kissed in the school cloakroom when we played post office, boys I chummed with, the first drink I ever took, the first cigarette I ever smoked (cornshuck behind Dicky Hamner's pig shed, and I threw up). Yet of all the memories the one of the man in the black suit is the strongest, and glows with its own spectral, haunted light. He was real, he was the Devil, and that day I was either his errand or his luck. I feel more and more strongly that escaping him was my luck—*just* luck, and not the intercession of the God I have worshiped and sung hymns to all my life.

As I lie here in my nursing-home room, and in the ruined sand castle that is my body, I tell myself that I need not fear the Devil—that I have lived a good, kindly life, and I need not fear the Devil. Sometimes I remind myself that it was I, not my father, who finally coaxed my mother back to church later on that summer. In the dark, however, these thoughts have no power to ease or comfort. In the dark comes a voice that whispers that the nine-year-old fisherboy I was had done nothing for which he might legitimately fear the Devil, either, and yet the Devil came—to him. And in the dark I sometimes hear that voice drop even lower, into ranges that are inhuman. *Big fish!* it whispers in tones of hushed greed, and all the truths of the moral world fall to ruin before its hunger.

VIII

CLASSICS AND CONTEMPORARIES

CLASSICS AND
CONTEMPORARIES

To write, one must read.

To write well, one must read well.

Which means: to read widely, to read with enthusiasm, to read for pleasure, to read with an eye for another's craft. To read both "classics" and "contemporaries": works that are immediately engaging, and works that demand effort.

A writer must read not only for stimulation and inspiration but in order to know what has been written, and written well, by others preceding him or her. There are certain inevitable styles in prose fiction that evolve through the decades; what is new, exciting, and controversial in one era, like Hemingway's minimalist language or Faulkner's labyrinthine, lushly constructed sentences, will be familiar and dated in another.

These stories have been selected to give the young writer a sense of the variegated nature of "the short story" as a form, with an emphasis upon contemporary work. There are traditionally structured stories here, among them D. H. Lawrence's "Tickets, Please," Flannery O'Connor's "A Temple of the Holy Ghost," and E. L. Doctorow's "The Writer in the Family"; there are very short, compact stories, virtually miniature narratives, like Grace Paley's "Anxiety"; there are playful, fantastical fictions, like Donald Barthelme's "The Balloon," T. Coraghessan Boyle's "I Dated Jane Austen," and Ian Frazier's "Dating Your Mom." There are stories comprised almost entirely of dialogue, like William Faulkner's "That Evening Sun" and Richard Bausch's "Aren't You Happy For Me?" There are stories that are virtuoso feats of "voice"—Toni Cade Bambara's "My Man Bovanne," Jamaica Kincaid's "My Mother," Jewel Mogan's "X and O," Russell Banks's "Just Don't Touch Anything," Thom Jones's "The Pugilist at Rest." There are frankly intimate, personal stories like David Leavitt's "Gravity" and Abby Frucht's "Fruit of the Month"; there is John Edgar Wideman's "Damballah," the opening story of his novel of interlocked stories, *Damballah,* a boldly mythic, visionary work. There are stories that begin as mysteries, like C. E. Poverman's "Cutter." A number of stories are impossible to define except as expressions of their authors' singular use of language: Katherine Mansfield's dream-generated "Sun and Moon" (see note), William Heyen's "Any Sport," Robert Taylor, Jr.'s "Mourning," Gish Jen's "In the American Society."

D. H. Lawrence

TICKETS, PLEASE

There is in the Midlands a single-line tramway system which boldly leaves the county town and plunges off into the black, industrial country-side, up hill and down dale, through the long ugly villages of workmen's houses, over canals and railways, past churches perched high and nobly over the smoke and shadows, through stark, grimy cold little market-places, tilting away in a rush past cinemas and shops down to the hollow where the collieries are, then up again, past a little rural church, under the ash trees, on in a rush to the terminus, the last little ugly place of industry, the cold little town that shivers on the edge of the wild, gloomy country beyond. There the green and creamy coloured tram-cars seem to pause and purr with curious satisfaction. But in a few minutes—the clock on the turret of the Co-operative Wholesale Society's shops gives the time—away it starts once more on the adventure. Again there are the reckless swoops downhill, bouncing the loops: again the chilly wait in the hill-top market-place: again the breathless slithering round the precipitous drop under the church: again the patient halts at the loops, waiting for the outcoming car: so on and on, for two long hours, till at last the city looms beyond the fat gas-works, the narrow factories draw near, we are in the sordid streets of the great town, once more we sidle to a standstill at our terminus, abashed by the great crimson and cream-coloured city cars, but still perky, jaunty, somewhat dare-devil, green as a jaunty sprig of parsley out of a black colliery garden.

To ride on these cars is always an adventure. Since we are in war-time, the drivers are men unfit for active service: cripples and hunchbacks. So they have the spirit of the devil in them. The ride becomes a steeplechase. Hurray! we have leapt in a clear jump over the canal bridge—now for the four-lane corner. With a shriek and a trail of sparks we are clear again. To be sure, a tram often leaps the rails—but what matter! It sits in a ditch till other trams come to haul it out. It is quite common for a car, packed with one solid mass of living people, to come to a dead halt in the midst of unbroken blackness, the heart of nowhere on a dark night, and for the driver and the girl conductor to call: "All get off—car's on fire!" Instead, however, of rushing out in a panic, the passengers stolidly reply: "Get on—get on! We're not coming out. We're stopping where we are. Push on, George." So till flames actually appear.

The reason for this reluctance to dismount is that the nights are howlingly cold, black, and windswept, and a car is a haven of refuge. From village to village the miners travel, for a change of cinema, of girl, of pub. The trams are desperately packed. Who is going to risk himself in the black gulf outside, to wait perhaps an hour for another tram, then to see the forlorn notice 'Depot Only', because there is something wrong! Or to greet a unit of three bright cars all so tight with people that they sail past with a howl of derision. Trams that pass in the night.

This, the most dangerous tram-service in England, as the authorities themselves declare, with pride, is entirely conducted by girls, and driven by rash young men, a little crippled, or by delicate young men, who creep forward in terror. The girls are fearless young hussies. In their ugly blue uniform, skirts up to their knees, shapeless old peaked caps on their heads, they have all the *sang-froid* of an old non-commissioned officer. With a tram packed with howling colliers, roaring hymns downstairs and a sort of antiphony of obscenities upstairs, the lasses are perfectly at their ease. They pounce on the youths who try to evade their ticket-machine. They push off the men at the end of their distance. They are not going to be done in the eye—not they. They fear nobody—and everybody fears them.

"Hello, Annie!"

"Hello, Ted!"

"Oh, mind my corn, Miss Stone. It's my belief you've got a heart of stone, for you've trod on it again."

"You should keep it in your pocket," replies Miss Stone, and she goes sturdily upstairs in her high boots.

"Tickets, please."

She is peremptory, suspicious, and ready to hit first. She can hold her own against ten thousand. The step of that tram-car is her Thermopylæ.

Therefore, there is a certain wild romance aboard these cars—and in the sturdy bosom of Annie herself. The time for soft romance is in the morning, between ten o'clock and one, when things are rather slack: that is, except market-day and Saturday. Thus Annie has time to look about her. Then she often hops off her car and into a shop where she has spied something, while the driver chats in the main road. There is very good feeling between the girls and the drivers. Are they not companions in peril, shipments aboard this careering vessel of a tram-car, for ever rocking on the waves of a stormy land.

Then, also, during the easy hours, the inspectors are most in evidence. For some reason, everybody employed in this tram-service is young: there are no grey heads. It would not do. Therefore the inspectors are of the right age, and one, the chief, is also good-looking. See him stand on a wet, gloomy morning, in his long oilskin, his peaked cap well down over his eyes, waiting to board a car. His face ruddy, his small brown moustache is weathered, he has a faint impudent smile. Fairly tall and agile, even in his waterproof, he springs aboard a car and greets Annie.

"Hello, Annie! Keeping the wet out?"

"Trying to."

There are only two people in the car. Inspecting is soon over. Then for a long and impudent chat on the foot-board, a good, easy, twelve-mile chat.

The inspector's name is John Thomas Raynor—always called John Thomas, except sometimes, in malice, Coddy. His face sets in fury when he is addressed, from a distance, with this abbreviation. There is considerable scandal about John Thomas in half a dozen villages. He flirts with the girl conductors in the morning, and walks out with them in the dark night, when they leave their tram-car at the depôt. Of course, the girls quit the service frequently. Then he flirts and walks out with the newcomer: always providing she is sufficiently attractive, and that she will consent to walk. It is remarkable, however, that most of the girls are quite comely, they are all young, and this roving life aboard the car gives them a sailor's dash and recklessness. What matter how they behave when the ship is in port? To-morrow they will be aboard again.

Annie, however, was something of a Tartar, and her sharp tongue had kept John Thomas at arm's length for many months. Perhaps, therefore, she liked him all the more: for he always came up smiling, with impudence. She watched him vanquish one girl, then another. She could tell by the movement of his mouth and eyes, when he flirted with her in the morning, that he had been walking out with this lass, or the other, the night before. A fine cock-of-the-walk he was. She could sum him up pretty well.

In this subtle antagonism they knew each other like old friends, they were as shrewd with one another almost as man and wife. But Annie had always kept him sufficiently at arm's length. Besides, she had a boy of her own.

The Statutes fair, however, came in November, at Bestwood. It happened that Annie had the Monday night off. It was a drizzling ugly night, yet she dressed herself up and went to the fair-ground. She was alone, but she expected soon to find a pal of some sort.

The roundabouts were veering round and grinding out their music, the side-shows were making as much commotion as possible. In the coconut shies there were no coconuts, but artificial war-time substitutes, which the lads declared were fastened into the irons. There was a sad decline in brilliance and luxury. None the less, the ground was muddy as ever, there was the same crush, the press of faces lighted up by the flares and the electric lights, the same smell of naphtha and a few potatoes, and of electricity.

Who should be the first to greet Miss Annie on the showground but John Thomas. He had a black overcoat buttoned up to his chin, and a tweed cap pulled down over his brows, his face between was ruddy and smiling and handy as ever. She knew so well the way his mouth moved.

She was very glad to have a 'boy'. To be at the Statutes without a fellow was no fun. Instantly, like the gallant he was, he took her on the Dragons, grim-toothed, roundabout switchbacks. It was not nearly so exciting as a tram-car actually. But, then, to be seated in a shaking, green dragon, uplifted above the sea of bubble faces, careering in a rickety fashion in the lower heavens, whilst John Thomas leaned over her, his cigarette in his mouth, was after all the right style. She was a plump, quick, alive little creature. So she was quite excited and happy.

John Thomas made her stay on for the next round. And therefore she could hardly for shame repulse him when he put his arm round her and drew her a little nearer to him, in a very warm and cuddly manner. Besides, he was fairly discreet, he kept his movement as hidden as possible. She looked down, and saw that his red, clean hand was out of sight of the crowd. And they knew each other so well. So they warmed up to the fair.

After the dragons they went on the horses. John Thomas paid each time, so she could but be complaisant. He, of course, sat astride on the outer horse—named 'Black Bess'—and she sat sideways, towards him, on the inner horse—named 'Wildfire'. But of course John Thomas was not going to sit discreetly on 'Black Bess', holding the brass bar. Round they spun and heaved, in the light. And round he swung on his wooden steed, flinging one leg across her mount, and perilously tipping up and down, across the space, half lying back, laughing at her. He was perfectly happy; she was afraid her hat was on one side, but she was excited.

He threw quoits on a table, and won for her two large, pale blue hat-pins. And then, hearing the noise of the cinemas, announcing another performance, they climbed the boards and went in.

Of course, during these performances pitch darkness falls from time to time, when the machine goes wrong. Then there is a wild whooping, and a loud smacking of simulated kisses. In these moments John Thomas drew Anne towards him. After all, he had a wonderfully warm, cosy way of holding a girl with his arm, he seemed to make such a nice fit. And, after all, it was pleasant to be so held: so very comforting and cosy and nice. He leaned over her and she felt his breath on her hair; she knew he wanted to kiss her on the lips. And, after all, he was so warm and she fitted in to him so softly. After all, she wanted him to touch her lips.

But the light sprang up; she also started electrically, and put her hat straight. He left his arm lying nonchalantly behind her. Well, it was fun, it was exciting to be at the Statutes with John Thomas.

When the cinema was over they went for a walk across the dark, damp fields. He had all the arts of love-making. He was especially good at holding a girl, when he sat with her on a stile in the black, drizzling darkness. He seemed to be holding her in space, against his own warmth and gratification. And his kisses were soft and slow and searching.

So Annie walked out with John Thomas, though she kept her own boy dangling in the distance. Some of the tram-girls chose to be huffy. But there, you must take things as you find them, in this life.

There was no mistake about it, Annie liked John Thomas a good deal. She felt so rich and warm in herself whenever he was near. And John Thomas really liked Annie, more than usual. The soft, melting way in which she could flow into a fellow, as if she melted into his very bones, was something rare and good. He fully appreciated this.

But with a developing acquaintance there began a developing intimacy. Annie wanted to consider him a person, a man: she wanted to take an intelligent interest in him, and to have an intelligent response. She did not want a mere nocturnal presence, which was what he was so far. And she prided herself that he could not leave her.

Here she made a mistake. John Thomas intended to remain a nocturnal presence; he had no idea of becoming an all-round individual to her. When she started to take an intelligent interest in him and his life and his character, he sheered off. He hated intelligent interest. And he knew that the only way to stop it was to avoid it. The possessive female was aroused in Annie. So he left her.

It is no use saying she was not surprised. She was at first startled, thrown out of her count. For she had been so *very* sure of holding him. For a while she was staggered, and everything became uncertain to her. Then she wept with fury, indignation, desolation, and misery. Then she had a spasm of despair. And then, when he came, still impudently, on to her car, still familiar, but letting her see by the movement of his head that he had gone away to somebody else for the time being, and was enjoying pastures new, then she determined to have her own back.

She had a very shrewd idea what girls John Thomas had taken out. She went to Nora Purdy. Nora was a tall, rather pale, but well-built girl, with beautiful yellow hair. She was rather secretive.

"Hey!" said Annie, accosting her; then softly: "Who's John Thomas on with now?"

"I don't know," said Nora.

"Why, tha does," said Annie, ironically lapsing into dialect. "Tha knows as well as I do."

"Well, I do, then," said Nora. "It isn't me, so don't bother."

"It's Cissy Meakin, isn't it?"

"It is, for all I know."

"Hasn't he got a face on him!" said Annie. "I don't half like his cheek. I could knock him off the foot-board when he comes round at me."

"He'll get dropped on one of these days," said Nora.

"Ay, he will, when somebody makes up their mind to drop it on him. I should like to see him taken down a peg or two, shouldn't you?"

"I shouldn't mind," said Nora.

"You've got quite as much cause to as I have," said Annie. "But we'll drop on him one of these days, my girl. What? Don't you want to?"

"I don't mind," said Nora.

But as a matter of fact, Nora was much more vindictive than Annie.

One by one Annie went the round of the old flames. It so happened that Cissy Meakin left the tramway service in quite a short time. Her mother made her leave. Then John Thomas was on the *qui vive*. He cast his eyes over his old flock. And his eyes lighted on Annie. He thought she would be safe now. Besides, he liked her.

She arranged to walk home with him on Sunday night. It so happened that her car would be in the depôt at half-past nine: the last car would come in at 10.15. So John Thomas was to wait for her there.

At the depôt the girls had a little waiting-room of their own. It was quite rough, but cosy, with a fire and an oven and a mirror, and table and wooden chairs. The half-dozen girls who knew John Thomas only too well had arranged to take service this Sunday afternoon. So, as the cars began to come in, early, the girls dropped into the waiting-room. And instead of hurrying off home, they sat around the fire and had a cup of tea. Outside was the darkness and lawlessness of war-time.

John Thomas came on the car after Annie, at about a quarter to ten. He poked his head easily into the girls' waiting-room.

"Prayer-meeting?" he asked.

"Ay," said Laura Sharp. "Ladies only."

"That's me!" said John Thomas. It was one of his favourite exclamations.

"Shut the door, boy," said Muriel Baggaley.

"Oh, which side of me?" said John Thomas.

"Which tha likes," said Polly Birkin.

He had come in and closed the door behind him. The girls moved in their circle, to make a place for him near the fire. He took off his great-coat and pushed back his hat.

"Who handles the teapot?" he said.

Nora Purdy silently poured him out a cup of tea.

"Want a bit o' my bread and drippin'?" said Muriel Baggaley to him.

"Ay, give us a bit."

And he began to eat his piece of bread.

"There's no place like home, girls," he said.

They all looked at him as he uttered this piece of impudence. He seemed to be sunning himself in the presence of so many damsels.

"Especially if you're not afraid to go home in the dark," said Laura Sharp.

"Me! By myself I am."

They sat till they heard the last tram come in. In a few minutes Emma Houselay entered.

"Come on, my old duck!" cried Polly Birkin.

"It *is* perishing," said Emma, holding her fingers to the fire.

"But—I'm afraid to, go home in, the dark," sang Laura Sharp, the tune having got into her mind.

"Who're you going with to-night, John Thomas?" asked Muriel Baggaley coolly.

"To-night?" said John Thomas. "Oh, I'm going home by myself to-night—all on my lonely-o."

"That's me!" said Nora Purdy, using his own ejaculation.

The girls laughed shrilly.

"Me as well, Nora," said John Thomas.

"Don't know what you mean," said Laura.

"Yes, I'm toddling," said he, rising and reaching for his overcoat.

"Nay," said Polly. "We're all here waiting for you."

"We've got to be up in good time in the morning," he said, in the benevolent official manner.

They all laughed.

"Nay," said Muriel. "Don't leave us all lonely, John Thomas. Take one!"

"I'll take the lot, if you like," he responded gallantly.

"That you won't, either," said Muriel. "Two's company; seven's too much of a good thing."

"Nay—take one," said Laura. "Fair and square, all above board and say which."

"Ay," cried Annie, speaking for the first time. "Pick, John Thomas; let's hear thee."

"Nay," he said. "I'm going home quiet to-night. Feeling good, for once."

"Whereabouts?" said Annie. "Take a good 'un, then. But tha's got to take one of us!"

"Nay, how can I take one," he said, laughing uneasily. "I don't want to make enemies."

"You'd only make *one,*" said Annie.

"The chosen *one,*" added Laura.

"Oh, my! Who said girls!" exclaimed John Thomas, again turning, as if to escape. "Well—good-night."

"Nay, you've got to make your pick," said Muriel. "Turn your face to the wall, and say which one touches you. Go on—we shall only just touch your back—one of us. Go on—turn your face to the wall, and don't look, and say which one touches you."

He was uneasy, mistrusting them. Yet he had not the courage to break away. They pushed him to a wall and stood him there with his face to it. Behind his back they all grimaced, tittering. He looked so comical. He looked around uneasily.

"Go on!" he cried.

"You're looking—you're looking!" they shouted.

He turned his head away. And suddenly, with a movement like a swift cat, Annie went forward and fetched him a box on the side of the head that sent his cap flying and himself staggering. He started round.

But at Annie's signal they all flew at him, slapping him, pinching him, pulling his hair, though more in fun than in spite or anger. He, however, saw red. His blue eyes flamed with strange fear as well as fury, and he butted through the girls to the door. It was locked. He wrenched at it. Roused, alert, the girls stood round and looked at him. He faced them, at bay. At that moment they were rather horrifying to him, as they stood in their short uniforms. He was distinctly afraid.

"Come on, John Thomas! Come on! Choose!" said Annie.

"What are you after? Open the door," he said.

"We shan't—not till you've chosen!" said Muriel.

"Chosen what?" he said.

"Chosen the one you're going to marry," she replied.

He hesitated a moment.

"Open the blasted door," he said, "and get back to your senses." He spoke with official authority.

"You've got to choose!" cried the girls.

"Come on!" cried Annie, looking him in the eye. "Come on! Come on!"

He went forward, rather vaguely. She had taken off her belt, and swinging it, she fetched him a sharp blow over the head with the buckle end. He sprang and seized her. But immediately the other girls rushed upon him, pulling and tearing and beating him. Their blood was now thoroughly up. He was their sport now. They were going to have their own back, out of him. Strange, wild creatures, they hung on him and rushed at him to bear him down. His tunic was torn right up the back, Nora had hold at the back of his collar, and was actually strangling him. Luckily the button burst. He struggled in a wild frenzy of fury and terror, almost mad terror. His tunic was simply torn off his back, his shirt-sleeves were torn away, his arms were naked. The girls rushed at him, clenched their hands on him and pulled at him: or they rushed at him and pushed him, butted him with all their might: or they struck him wild blows. He ducked and cringed and struck sideways. They became more intense.

At last he was down. They rushed on him, kneeling on him. He had neither breath nor strength to move. His face was bleeding with a long scratch, his brow was bruised.

Annie knelt on him, the other girls knelt and hung on to him. Their faces were flushed, their hair wild, their eyes were all glittering strangely. He lay at last quite still, with face averted, as an animal lies when it is defeated and at the mercy of the captor. Sometimes his eye glanced back at the wild faces of the girls. His breast rose heavily, his wrists were torn.

"Now, then, my fellow!" gasped Annie at length. "Now then—now——"

At the sound of her terrifying, cold triumph, he suddenly started to struggle as an animal might, but the girls threw themselves upon him with unnatural strength and power, forcing him down.

"Yes—now, then!" gasped Annie at length.

And there was a dead silence, in which the thud of heartbeating was to be heard. It was a suspense of pure silence in every soul.

"Now you know where you are," said Annie.

The sight of his white, bare arm maddened the girls. He lay in a kind of trance of fear and antagonism. They felt themselves filled with supernatural strength.

Suddenly Polly started to laugh—to giggle wildly—helplessly—and Emma and Muriel joined in. But Annie and Nora and Laura remained the same, tense, watchful, with gleaming eyes. He winced away from these eyes.

"Yes," said Annie, in a curious low tone, secret and deadly. "Yes! You've got it now. You know what you've done, don't you? You know what you've done."

He made no sound nor sign, but lay with bright, averted eyes, and averted, bleeding face.

"You ought to be *killed,* that's what you ought," said Annie, tensely. "You ought to be *killed.*" And there was a terrifying lust in her voice.

Polly was ceasing to laugh, and giving long-drawn Oh-h-hs and sighs as she came to herself.

"He's got to choose," she said vaguely.

"Oh, yes, he has," said Laura, with vindictive decision.

"Do you hear—do you hear?" said Annie. And with a sharp movement, that made him wince, she turned his face to her.

"Do you hear?" she repeated, shaking him.

But he was quite dumb. She fetched him a sharp slap on the face. He started, and his eyes widened. Then his face darkened with defiance, after all.

"Do you hear?" she repeated.

He only looked at her with hostile eyes.

"Speak!" she said, putting her face devilishly near his.

"What?" he said, almost overcome.

"You've got to *choose!*" she cried, as if it were some terrible menace, and as if it hurt her that she could not exact more.

"What?" he said, in fear.

"Choose your girl, Coddy. You've got to choose her now. And you'll get your neck broken if you play any more of your tricks, my boy. You're settled now."

There was a pause. Again he averted his face. He was cunning in his overthrow. He did not give in to them really—no, not if they tore him to bits.

"All right, then," he said, "I choose Annie." His voice was strange and full of malice. Annie let go of him as if he had been a hot coal.

"He's chosen Annie!" said the girls in chorus.

"Me!" cried Annie. She was still kneeling, but away from him. He was still lying prostrate, with averted face. The girls grouped uneasily around.

"Me!" repeated Annie, with a terrible bitter accent.

Then she got up, drawing away from him with strange disgust and bitterness.

"I wouldn't touch him," she said.

But her face quivered with a kind of agony, she seemed as if she would fall. The other girls turned aside. He remained lying on the floor, with his torn clothes and bleeding, averted face.

"Oh, if he's chosen——" said Polly.

"I don't want him—he can choose again," said Annie, with the same rather bitter hopelessness.

"Get up," said Polly, lifting his shoulder. "Get up."

He rose slowly, a strange, ragged, dazed creature. The girls eyed him from a distance, curiously, furtively, dangerously.

"Who wants him?" cried Laura, roughly.

"Nobody," they answered, with contempt. Yet each one of them waited for him to look at her, hoped he would look at her. All except Annie, and something was broken in her.

He, however, kept his face closed and averted from them all. There was a silence of the end. He picked up the torn pieces of his tunic, without knowing what to do with them. The girls stood about uneasily, flushed, panting, tidying their hair and their dress unconsciously, and watching him. He looked at none of them. He espied his cap in a corner, and went and picked it up. He put it on his head, and one of the girls burst into a shrill, hysteric laugh at the sight he presented. He, however, took no heed, but went straight to where his overcoat hung on a peg. The girls moved away from contact with him as if he had been an electric wire. He put on his coat and buttoned it down. Then he rolled his tunic-rags into a bundle, and stood before the locked door, dumbly.

"Open the door, somebody," said Laura.

"Annie's got the key," said one.

Annie silently offered the key to the girls. Nora unlocked the door.

"Tit for tat, old man," she said. "Show yourself a man, and don't bear a grudge."

But without a word or sign he had opened the door and gone, his face closed, his head dropped.

"That'll learn him," said Laura.

"Coddy!" said Nora.

"Shut up, for God's sake!" cried Annie fiercely, as if in torture.

"Well, I'm about ready to go, Polly. Look sharp!" said Muriel.

The girls were all anxious to be off. They were tidying themselves hurriedly, with mute, stupefied faces.

SUN AND MOON

This extraordinary story, seemingly so fluid, effortless, and "real," is one of those rare instances when a dream has directly inspired a work of art. As anyone knows who has been inspired by a dream, the experience is nearly always confused and frustrating; we labor to express, in language, that which we experienced so naturally while asleep.

Katherine Mansfield was thirty years old when she wrote "Sun and Moon," noting in her journal:

I *dreamed* a short story last night, even down to its name, which was "Sun and Moon." It was very light. I dreamed it all—about children. I got up at 6:30 and wrote a note or two because I knew it would fade. . . . I didn't dream that I read it. No, I was in it, part of it, and it played round invisible me. But the hero is not more than 5. In my dream I saw a supper table with the eyes of 5. It was awfully queer—especially a plate of half-melted ice-cream.

(Katherine Mansfield,
Letters and Journals, 10 February 1918)

In the afternoon the chairs came, a whole big cart full of little gold ones with their legs in the air. And then the flowers came. When you stared down from the balcony at the people carrying them the flower pots looked like funny awfully nice hats nodding up the path.

Moon thought they were hats. She said: "Look. There's a man wearing a palm on his head." But she never knew the difference between real things and not real ones.

There was nobody to look after Sun and Moon. Nurse was helping Annie alter Mother's dress which was much-too-long-and-tight-under-the-arms and Mother was running all over the house and telephoning Father to be sure not to forget things. She only had time to say: "Out of my way, children!"

They kept out of her way—at any rate Sun did. He did so hate being sent stumping back to the nursery. It didn't matter about Moon. If she got tangled in people's legs they only threw her up and shook her till she squeaked. But Sun was too heavy for that. He was so heavy that the fat man who came to dinner on Sundays used to say: "Now, young man, let's try to lift you." And then he'd put his thumbs under Sun's arms and groan and try and give it up at last saying: "He's a perfect little ton of bricks!"

Nearly all the furniture was taken out of the dining-room. The big piano was put in a corner and then there came a row of flower pots and then there came the goldy chairs. That was for the concert. When Sun looked in a white faced man sat at the piano—not playing, but banging at it and then looking inside. He had a bag of tools on the piano and he had stuck his hat on a statue against the wall. Sometimes he just started to play and then he jumped up again and looked inside. Sun hoped he wasn't the concert.

But of course the place to be in was the kitchen. There was a man helping in a cap like a blancmange, and their real cook, Minnie, was all red in the face and laughing. Not cross at all. She gave them each an almond finger and lifted them up on to the flour bin so that they could watch the wonderful things she and the man were making for supper. Cook brought in the things and he put them on dishes and trimmed them. Whole fishes, with their heads and eyes and tails still on, he sprinkled with red and green and yellow bits; he made squiggles all over the jellies, he stuck a collar on a ham and put a very thin sort of a fork in it; he dotted almonds and tiny round biscuits on the creams. And more and more things kept coming.

"Ah, but you haven't seen the ice pudding," said Cook. "Come along." Why was she being so nice, thought Sun as she gave them each a hand. And they looked into the refrigerator.

Oh! Oh! Oh! It was a little house. It was a little pink house with white snow on the roof and green windows and a brown door and stuck in the door there was a nut for a handle.

When Sun saw the nut he felt quite tired and had to lean against Cook.

"Let me touch it. Just let me put my finger on the roof," said Moon, dancing. She always wanted to touch all the food. Sun didn't.

"Now, my girl, look sharp with the table," said Cook as the housemaid came in.

"It's a picture, Min," said Nellie. "Come along and have a look." So they all went into the dining-room. Sun and Moon were almost frightened. They wouldn't go up to the table at first; they just stood at the door and made eyes at it.

It wasn't real night yet but the blinds were down in the dining-room and the lights turned on—and all the lights were red roses. Red ribbons and bunches of roses tied up the table at the corners. In the middle was a lake with rose petals floating on it.

"That's where the ice pudding is to be," said Cook.

Two silver lions with wings had fruit on their backs, and the salt cellars were tiny birds drinking out of basins.

And all the winking glasses and shining plates and sparkling knives and forks—and all the food. And the little red table napkins made into roses. . . .

"Are people going to eat the food?" asked Sun.

"I should just think they were," laughed Cook, laughing with Nellie. Moon laughed, too; she always did the same as other people. But Sun didn't want to laugh. Round and round he walked with his hands behind his back. Perhaps he never would have stopped if Nurse hadn't called suddenly: "Now then, children. It's high time you were washed and dressed." And they were marched off to the nursery.

While they were being unbuttoned Mother looked in with a white thing over her shoulders; she was rubbing stuff on her face.

"I'll ring for them when I want them, Nurse, and then they can just come down and be seen and go back again," said she.

Sun was undressed, first nearly to his skin, and dressed again in a white shirt with red and white daisies speckled on it, breeches with strings at the sides and braces that came over, white socks and red shoes.

"Now you're in your Russian costume," said Nurse, flattening down his fringe.

"Am I?" said Sun.

"Yes. Sit quiet in that chair and watch your little sister."

Moon took ages. When she had her socks put on she pretended to fall back on the bed and waved her legs at Nurse as she always did, and every time Nurse tried to make her curls with a finger and a wet brush she turned round and asked Nurse to show her the photo of her brooch or something like that. But at last she was finished too. Her dress stuck out, with fur on it, all white; there was even fluffy stuff on the legs of her drawers. Her shoes were white with big blobs on them.

"There you are, my lamb," said Nurse. "And you look like a sweet little cherub of a picture of a powder-puff?" Nurse rushed to the door. "Ma'am, one moment."

Mother came in again with half her hair down.

"Oh," she cried. "What a picture!"

"Isn't she," said Nurse.

And Moon held out her skirts by the tips and dragged one of her feet. Sun didn't mind people not noticing him—much. . . .

After that they played clean tidy games up at the table while Nurse stood at the door, and when the carriages began to come and the sound of laughter and voices and soft rustlings came from down below she whispered: "Now then, children, stay where you are." Moon kept jerking the table cloth so that it all hung down her side and Sun hadn't any—and then she pretended she didn't do it on purpose.

At last the bell rang. Nurse pounced at them with the hair brush, flattened his fringe, made her bow stand on end and joined their hands together.

"Down you go!" she whispered.

And down they went. Sun did feel silly holding Moon's hand like that but Moon seemed to like it. She swung her arm and the bell on her coral bracelet jingled.

At the drawing-room door stood Mother fanning herself with a black fan. The drawing-room was full of sweet smelling, silky, rustling ladies and men in black with funny tails on their coats—like beetles. Father was among them, talking very loud, and rattling something in his pocket.

"What a picture!" cried the ladies. "Oh, the ducks! Oh, the lambs! Oh, the sweets! Oh, the pets!"

All the people who couldn't get at Moon kissed Sun, and a skinny old lady with teeth that clicked said: "Such a serious little poppet," and rapped him on the head with something hard.

Sun looked to see if the same concert was there, but he was gone. Instead, a fat man with a pink head leaned over the piano talking to a girl who held a violin at her ear.

There was only one man that Sun really liked. He was a little grey man, with long grey whiskers, who walked about by himself. He came up to Sun and rolled his eyes in a very nice way and said: "Hullo, my lad." Then he went away. But soon he came back again and said: "Fond of dogs?" Sun said: "Yes." But then he went away again, and though Sun looked for him everywhere he couldn't find him. He thought perhaps he'd gone outside to fetch in a puppy.

"Good night, my precious babies," said Mother, folding them up in her bare arms. "Fly up to your little nest."

Then Moon went and made a silly of herself again. She put up her arms in front of everybody and said: "My Daddy must carry me."

But they seemed to like it, and Daddy swooped down and picked her up as he always did.

Nurse was in such a hurry to get them to bed that she even interrupted Sun over his prayers and said: "Get on with them, child, *do.*" And the moment after they were in bed and in the dark except for the nightlight in its little saucer.

"Are you asleep?" asked Moon.

"No," said Sun. "Are you?"

"No," said Moon.

A long while after Sun woke up again. There was a loud, loud noise of clapping from downstairs, like when it rains. He heard Moon turn over.

"Moon, are you awake?"

"Yes, are you?"

"Yes. Well, let's go and look over the stairs."

They had just got settled on the top step when the drawing-room door opened and they heard the party cross over the hall into the dining-room. Then that door was shut; there was a noise of "pops" and laughing. Then that stopped and Sun saw them all walking round and round the lovely table with their hands behind their backs like he had done. . . . Round and round they walked, looking and staring. The man with the grey whiskers liked the little house best. When he saw the nut for a handle he rolled his eyes like he did before and said to Sun: "Seen the nut?"

"Don't nod your head like that, Moon."

"I'm not nodding. It's you."

"It is not. I never nod my head."

"O-oh, you do. You're nodding it now."

"I'm not. I'm only showing you how not to do it."

When they woke up again they could only hear Father's voice very loud, and Mother, laughing away. Father came out of the dining-room, bounded up the stairs, and nearly fell over them.

"Hullo!" he said. "By Jove, Kitty, come and look at this."

Mother came out. "Oh, you naughty children," said she from the hall.

"Let's have 'em down and give 'em a bone," said Father. Sun had never seen him so jolly.

"No, certainly not," said Mother.

"Oh, my Daddy, do! Do have us down," said Moon.

"I'm hanged if I won't," cried Father. "I won't be bullied. Kitty—way there." And he caught them up, one under each arm.

Sun thought Mother would have been dreadfully cross. But she wasn't. She kept on laughing at Father.

"Oh, you dreadful boy!" said she. But she didn't mean Sun.

"Come on, kiddies. Come and have some pickings," said this jolly Father. But Moon stopped a minute.

"Mother—your dress is right off one side."

"Is it?" said Mother. And Father said "Yes" and pretended to bite her white shoulder, but she pushed him away.

And so they went back to the beautiful dining-room.

But—oh! oh! what had happened? The ribbons and the roses were all pulled untied. The little red table napkins lay on the floor, all the shining plates were dirty and all the winking glasses. The lovely food that the man had trimmed was all thrown about, and there were bones and bits and fruit peels and shells everywhere. There was even a bottle lying down with stuff coming out of it on to the cloth and nobody stood it up again.

And the little pink house with the snow roof and the green windows was broken—broken—half melted away in the centre of the table.

"Come on, Sun," said Father, pretending not to notice.

Moon lifted up her pyjama legs and shuffled up to the table and stood on a chair, squeaking away.

"Have a bit of this ice," said Father, smashing in some more of the roof.

Mother took a little plate and held it for him; she put her other arm round his neck.

"Daddy. Daddy," shrieked Moon. "The little handle's left. The little nut. Kin I eat it?" And she reached across and picked it out of the door and scrunched it up, biting hard and blinking.

"Here, my lad," said Father.

But Sun did not move from the door. Suddenly he put up his head and gave a loud wail.

"I think it's horrid—horrid—horrid!" he sobbed.

"There, you see!" said Mother. "You see!"

"Off with you," said Father, no longer jolly. "This moment. Off you go!"

And wailing loudly, Sun stumped off to the nursery.

William Faulkner

THAT EVENING SUN

Monday is no different from any other weekday in Jefferson now. The streets are paved now, and the telephone and electric companies are cutting down more and more of the shade trees—the water oaks, the maples and locusts and elms—to make room for iron poles bearing clusters of bloated and ghostly and bloodless grapes, and we have a city laundry which makes the rounds on Monday morning, gathering the bundles of clothes into bright-colored, specially made motorcars: the soiled wearing of a whole week now flees apparitionlike behind alert and irritable electric horns, with a long diminishing noise of rubber and asphalt like tearing silk, and even the Negro women who still take in white people's washing after the old custom, fetch and deliver it in automobiles.

But fifteen years ago, on Monday morning the quiet, dusty, shady streets would be full of Negro women with, balanced on their steady, turbaned heads, bundles of clothes tied up in sheets, almost as large as cotton bales, carried so without touch of hand between the kitchen door of the white house and the blackened washpot beside a cabin door in Negro Hollow.

Nancy would set her bundle on top of her head, then upon the bundle in turn she would set the black straw sailor hat which she wore winter and summer. She was tall, with a high, sad face sunken a little where her teeth were missing. Sometimes we would go a part of the way down the lane and across the pasture with her, to watch the balanced bundle and the hat that never bobbed or wavered, even when she walked down into the ditch and up the other side and stooped through the fence. She would go down on her hands and knees and crawl through the gap, her head rigid, uptilted, the bundle steady as a rock or a balloon, and rise to her feet again and go on.

Sometimes the husbands of the washing women would fetch and deliver the clothes, but Jesus never did that for Nancy, even before Father told him to stay away from our house, even when Dilsey was sick and Nancy would come to cook for us.

And then about half the time we'd have to go down the lane to Nancy's cabin and tell her to come on and cook breakfast. We would stop at the ditch, because Father told us to not have anything to do with Jesus—he was a short black man, with a razor scar down his face—and we would throw rocks at Nancy's house until she came to the door, leaning her head around it without any clothes on.

"What yawl mean, chunking my house?" Nancy said. "What you little devils mean?"

"Father says for you to come on and get breakfast," Caddy said. "Father says it's over a half an hour now, and you've got to come this minute."

"I ain't studying no breakfast," Nancy said. "I going to get my sleep out."

"I bet you're drunk," Jason said. "Father says you're drunk. Are you drunk, Nancy?"

"Who says I is?" Nancy said. "I got to get my sleep out. I ain't studying no breakfast."

So after a while we quit chunking the cabin and went back home. When she finally came, it was too late for me to go to school. So we thought it was whiskey until that day they arrested her again and they were taking her to jail and they passed Mr. Stovall. He was the cashier in the bank and a deacon in the Baptist church, and Nancy began to say:

"When you going to pay me, white man? When you going to pay me, white man? It's been three times now since you paid me a cent—" Mr. Stovall knocked her down, but she kept on saying, "When you going to pay me, white man? It's been three times now since—" until Mr. Stovall kicked her in the mouth with his heel and the marshal caught Mr. Stovall back, and Nancy lying in the street, laughing. She turned her head and spat out some blood and teeth and said, "It's been three times now since he paid me a cent."

That was how she lost her teeth, and all that day they told about Nancy and Mr. Stovall, and all that night the ones that passed the jail could hear Nancy singing and yelling. They could see her hands holding to the window bars, and a lot of them stopped along the fence, listening to her and the jailer trying to make her stop. She didn't shut up until almost daylight, when the jailer began to hear a bumping and scraping upstairs and he went up there and found Nancy hanging from the window bar. He said that it was cocaine and not whiskey, because no nigger would try to commit suicide unless he was full of cocaine, because a nigger full of cocaine wasn't a nigger any longer.

The jailer cut her down and revived her; then he beat her, whipped her. She had hung herself with her dress. She had fixed it all right, but when they arrested her she didn't have on anything except a dress and so she didn't have anything to tie her hands with and she couldn't make her hands let go of the window ledge. So the jailer heard the noise and ran up there and found Nancy hanging from the window, stark naked, her belly already swelling out a little, like a little balloon.

When Dilsey was sick in her cabin and Nancy was cooking for us, we could see her apron swelling out; that was before Father told Jesus to stay away from the house. Jesus was in the kitchen, sitting behind the stove, with his razor scar on his black face like a piece of dirty string. He said it was a watermelon that Nancy had under her dress.

"It never come off of your vine, though," Nancy said.

"Off of what vine?" Caddy said.

"I can cut down the vine it did come off of," Jesus said.

"What makes you want to talk like that before these chillen?" Nancy said. "Whyn't you go on to work? You done et. You want Mr. Jason to catch you hanging around his kitchen, talking that way before these chillen?"

"Talking what way?" Caddy said. "What vine?"

"I can't hang around white man's kitchen," Jesus said. "But white man can hang around mine. White man can come in my house, but I can't stop him. When white man want to come in my house, I ain't got no house. I can't stop him, but he can't kick me outen it. He can't do that."

Dilsey was still sick in her cabin. Father told Jesus to stay off our place. Dilsey was still sick. It was a long time. We were in the library after supper.

"Isn't Nancy through in the kitchen yet?" Mother said. "It seems to me that she has had plenty of time to have finished the dishes."

"Let Quentin go and see," Father said. "Go and see if Nancy is through, Quentin. Tell her she can go on home."

I went to the kitchen. Nancy was through. The dishes were put away and the fire was out. Nancy was sitting in a chair, close to the cold stove. She looked at me.

"Mother wants to know if you are through," I said.

"Yes," Nancy said. She looked at me. "I done finished." She looked at me.

"What is it?" I said. "What is it?"

"I ain't nothing but a nigger," Nancy said. "It ain't none of it my fault."

She looked at me, sitting in the chair before the cold stove, the sailor hat on her head. I went back to the library. It was the cold stove and all, when you think of a kitchen being warm and busy and cheerful. And with a cold stove and the dishes all put away, and nobody wanting to eat at that hour.

"Is she through?" Mother said.

"Yessum," I said.

"What is she doing?" Mother said.

"She's not doing anything. She's through."

"I'll go and see," Father said.

"Maybe she's waiting for Jesus to come and take her home," Caddy said.

"Jesus is gone," I said. Nancy told us how one morning she woke up and Jesus was gone.

"He quit me," Nancy said. "Done gone to Memphis, I reckon. Dodging them city *po*-lice for a while, I reckon."

"And a good riddance," Father said. "I hope he stays there."

"Nancy's scaired of the dark," Jason said.

"So are you," Caddy said.

"I'm not," Jason said.

"Scairy cat," Caddy said.

"I'm not," Jason said.

"You, Candace!" Mother said. Father came back.

"I am going to walk down the lane with Nancy," he said. "She says that Jesus is back."

"Has she seen him?" Mother said.

"No. Some Negro sent her word that he was back in town. I won't be long."

"You'll leave me alone, to take Nancy home?" Mother said. "Is her safety more precious to you than mine?"

"I won't be long," Father said.

"You'll leave these children unprotected, with that Negro about?"

"I'm going, too," Caddy said. "Let me go, Father."

"What would he do with them, if he were unfortunate enough to have them?" Father said.

"I want to go, too," Jason said.

"Jason!" Mother said. She was speaking to Father. You could tell that by the way she said the name. Like she believed that all day Father had been trying to think of doing the thing she wouldn't like the most, and that she knew all the time that after a while he would think of it. I stayed quiet, because Father and I both knew that Mother would want him to make me stay with her if she just thought of it in time. So Father didn't look at me. I was the oldest. I was nine and Caddy was seven and Jason was five.

"Nonsense," Father said. "We won't be long."

Nancy had her hat on. We came to the lane. "Jesus always been good to me," Nancy said. "Whenever he had two dollars, one of them was mine." We walked in the lane. "If I can just get through the lane," Nancy said, "I be all right then."

The lane was always dark. "This is where Jason got scaired on Halloween," Caddy said.

"I didn't," Jason said.

"Can't Aunt Rachel do anything with him?" Father said. Aunt Rachel was old. She lived in a cabin beyond Nancy's by herself. She had white hair and she smoked a pipe in the door, all day long; she didn't work any more. They said she was Jesus' mother. Sometimes she said she was and sometimes she said she wasn't any kin to Jesus.

"Yes you did," Caddy said. "You were scairder than Frony. You were scairder than T. P. even. Scairder than niggers."

"Can't nobody do nothing with him," Nancy said. "He say I done woke up the devil in him and ain't but one thing going to lay it down again."

"Well, he's gone now," Father said. "There's nothing for you to be afraid of now. And if you'd just let white men alone."

"Let what white men alone?" Caddy said. "How let them alone?"

"He ain't gone nowhere," Nancy said. "I can feel him. I can feel him now, in this lane. He hearing us talk, every word, hid somewhere, waiting. I ain't seen him, and I ain't going to see him again but once more, with that razor in his mouth. That razor on that string down his back, inside his shirt. And then I ain't going to be even surprised."

"I wasn't scaired," Jason said.

"If you'd behave yourself, you'd have kept out of this," Father said. "But it's all right now. He's probably in Saint Louis now. Probably got another wife by now and forgot all about you."

"If he has, I better not find out about it," Nancy said. "I'd stand there right over them, and every time he wropped her, I'd cut that arm off. I'd cut his head off and I'd slit her belly and I'd shove—"

"Hush," Father said.

"Slit whose belly, Nancy?" Caddy said.

I wasn't scaired, Jason said. "I'd walk right down this lane by myself."

"Yah," Caddy said. "You wouldn't dare to put your foot down in it if we were not here too."

2

Dilsey was still sick, so we took Nancy home every night until Mother said, "How much longer is this going on? I to be left alone in this big house while you take home a frightened Negro?"

We fixed a pallet in the kitchen for Nancy. One night we waked up, hearing the sound. It was not singing and it was not crying, coming up the dark stairs. There was a light in Mother's room and we heard Father going down the hall, down the back stairs, and Caddy and I went into the hall. The floor was cold. Our toes curled away from it while we listened to the sound. It was like singing and it wasn't like singing, like the sound that Negroes make.

Then it stopped and we heard Father going down the back stairs, and we went to the head of the stairs. Then the sound began again, in the stairway, not loud, and we could see Nancy's eyes halfway up the stairs, against the wall. They looked like cat's eyes do, like a big cat against the wall, watching us. When we came down the steps to where she was, she quit making the sound again, and we stood there until Father came back up from the kitchen, with his pistol in his hand. He went back down with Nancy and they came back with Nancy's pallet.

We spread the pallet in our room. After the light in Mother's room went off, we could see Nancy's eyes again. "Nancy," Caddy whispered, "are you asleep, Nancy?"

Nancy whispered something. It was oh or no. I don't know which. Like nobody had made it, like it came from nowhere and went nowhere, until it was like Nancy was not there at all; that I had looked so hard at her eyes on the stairs that they had got printed on my eyeballs, like the sun does when you have closed your eyes and there is no sun. "Jesus," Nancy whispered. "Jesus."

"Was it Jesus?" Caddy said. "Did he try to come into the kitchen?"

"Jesus," Nancy said. Like this: Jeeeeeeeeeeeeesus, until the sound went out, like a match or a candle does.

"It's the other Jesus she means," I said.

"Can you see us, Nancy?" Caddy whispered. "Can you see our eyes too?"

"I ain't nothing but a nigger," Nancy said. "God knows. God knows."

"What did you see down there in the kitchen?" Caddy whispered. "What tried to get in?"

"God knows," Nancy said. We could see her eyes. "God knows."

Dilsey got well. She cooked dinner. "You'd better stay in bed a day or two longer," Father said.

"What for?" Dilsey said. "If I had been a day later, this place would be to rack and ruin. Get on out of here now, and let me get my kitchen straight again."

Dilsey cooked supper too. And that night, just before dark, Nancy came into the kitchen.

"How do you know he's back?" Dilsey said. "You ain't seen him."

"Jesus is a nigger," Jason said.

"I can feel him," Nancy said. "I can feel him laying yonder in the ditch."

"Tonight?" Dilsey said. "Is he there tonight?"

"Dilsey's a nigger too," Jason said.

"You try to eat something," Dilsey said.

"I don't want nothing," Nancy said.

"I ain't a nigger," Jason said.

"Drink some coffee," Dilsey said. She poured a cup of coffee for Nancy. "Do you know he's out there tonight? How come you know it's tonight?"

"I know," Nancy said. "He's there, waiting. I know. I done lived with him too long. I know what he is fixing to do fore he know it himself."

"Drink some coffee," Dilsey said. Nancy held the cup to her mouth and blew into the cup. Her mouth pursed out like a spreading adder's, like a rubber mouth, like she had blown all the color out of her lips with blowing the coffee.

"I ain't a nigger," Jason said. "Are you a nigger, Nancy?"

"I hellborn, child," Nancy said. "I won't be nothing soon. I going back where I come from soon."

3

She began to drink the coffee. While she was drinking, holding the cup in both hands, she began to make the sound again. She made the sound into the cup and the coffee sploshed out onto her hands and her dress. Her eyes looked at us and she sat there, her elbows on her knees, holding the cup in both hands, looking at us across the wet cup, making the sound.

"Look at Nancy," Jason said. "Nancy can't cook for us now. Dilsey's got well now."

"You hush up," Dilsey said. Nancy held the cup in both hands, looking at us, making the sound, like there were two of them: one looking at us and the other making the sound. "Whyn't you let Mr. Jason telefoam the marshal?" Dilsey said. Nancy stopped then, holding the cup in her long brown hands. She tried to drink some coffee again, but it sploshed out of the cup, onto her hands and her dress, and she put the cup down. Jason watched her.

"I can't swallow it," Nancy said. "I swallows but it won't go down me."

"You go down to the cabin," Dilsey said. "Frony will fix you a pallet and I'll be there soon."

"Won't no nigger stop him," Nancy said.

"I ain't a nigger," Jason said. "Am I, Dilsey?"

"I reckon not," Dilsey said. She looked at Nancy. "I don't reckon so. What you going to do, then?"

Nancy looked at us. Her eyes went fast, like she was afraid there wasn't time to look, without hardly moving at all. She looked at us, at all three of us at one time. "You remember that night I stayed in yawls' room?" she said. She told about how we waked up early the next morning, and played. We had to play quiet, on her pallet, until Father woke up and it was time to get breakfast. "Go and ask your maw to let me stay here tonight," Nancy said. "I won't need no pallet. We can play some more."

Caddy asked Mother. Jason went too. "I can't have Negroes sleeping in the bedrooms," Mother said. Jason cried. He cried until Mother said he couldn't have any dessert for three days if he didn't stop. Then Jason said he would stop if Dilsey would make a chocolate cake. Father was there.

"Why don't you do something about it?" Mother said. "What do we have officers for?"

"Why is Nancy afraid of Jesus?" Caddy said. "Are you afraid of Father, Mother?"

"What could the officer do?" Father said. "If Nancy hasn't seen him, how could the officers find him?"

"Then why is she afraid?" Mother said.

"She says he is there. She says she knows he is there tonight."

"Yet we pay taxes," Mother said. "I must wait here alone in this big house while you take a Negro woman home."

"You know that I am not lying outside with a razor," Father said.

"I'll stop if Dilsey will make a chocolate cake," Jason said. Mother told us to go out and Father said he didn't know if Jason would get a chocolate cake or not, but he knew what Jason was going to get in about a minute. We went back to the kitchen and told Nancy.

"Father said for you to go home and lock the door, and you'll be all right," Caddy said. "All right from what, Nancy? Is Jesus mad at you?" Nancy was holding the coffee cup in her hands again, her elbows on her knees and her hands holding the cup between her knees. She was looking into the cup. "What have you done that made Jesus mad?" Caddy said. Nancy let the cup go. It didn't break on the floor, but the coffee spilled out, and Nancy sat there with her hands still making the shape of the cup. She began to make the sound again, not loud. Not singing and not unsinging. We watched her.

"Here," Dilsey said. "You quit that, now. You get aholt of yourself. You wait here. I going to get Versh to walk home with you." Dilsey went out.

We looked at Nancy. Her shoulders kept shaking, but she quit making the sound. We stood and watched her.

"What's Jesus going to do to you?" Caddy said. "He went away."

Nancy looked at us. "We had fun that night I stayed in yawls' room, didn't we?"

"I didn't," Jason said. "I didn't have any fun."

"You were asleep in Mother's room," Caddy said. "You were not there."

"Let's go down to my house and have some more fun," Nancy said.

"Mother won't let us," I said. "It's too late now."

"Don't bother her," Nancy said. "We can tell her in the morning. She won't mind."

"She wouldn't let us," I said.

"Don't ask her now," Nancy said. "Don't bother her now."

"She didn't say we couldn't go," Caddy said.

"We didn't ask," I said.

"If you go, I'll tell," Jason said.

"We'll have fun," Nancy said. "They won't mind, just to my house. I been working for yawl a long time. They won't mind."

"I'm not afraid to go," Caddy said. "Jason is the one that's afraid. He'll tell."

"I'm not," Jason said.

"Yes, you are," Caddy said. "You'll tell."

"I won't tell," Jason said. "I'm not afraid."

"Jason ain't afraid to go with me," Nancy said. "Is you, Jason?"

"Jason is going to tell," Caddy said. The lane was dark. We passed the pasture gate. "I bet if something was to jump out from behind that gate, Jason would holler."

"I wouldn't," Jason said. We walked down the lane. Nancy was talking loud.

"What are you talking so loud for, Nancy?" Caddy said.

"Who, me?" Nancy said. "Listen at Quentin and Caddy and Jason saying I'm talking loud."

"You talk like there was five of us here," Caddy said. "You talk like Father was here too."

"Who; me talking loud, Mr. Jason?" Nancy said.

"Nancy called Jason 'Mister,' " Caddy said.

"Listen how Caddy and Quentin and Jason talk," Nancy said.

"We're not talking loud," Caddy said. "You're the one that's talking like Father—"

"Hush," Nancy said; "hush, Mr. Jason."

"Nancy called Jason 'Mister' aguh—"

"Hush," Nancy said. She was talking loud when we crossed the ditch and stooped through the fence where she used to stoop through with the clothes on her head. Then we came to her house. We were going fast then. She opened the door. The smell of the house was like the lamp and the smell of Nancy was like the wick, like they were waiting for one another to begin to smell. She lit the lamp and closed the door and put the bar up. Then she quit talking loud, looking at us.

"What're we going to do?" Caddy said.

"What do yawl want to do?" Nancy said.

"You said we would have some fun," Caddy said.

There was something about Nancy's house; something you could smell besides Nancy and the house. Jason smelled it, even. "I don't want to stay here," he said. "I want to go home."

"Go home, then," Caddy said.

"I don't want to go by myself," Jason said.

"We're going to have some fun," Nancy said.

"How?" Caddy said.

Nancy stood by the door. She was looking at us, only it was like she had emptied her eyes, like she had quit using them. "What do you want to do?" she said.

"Tell us a story," Caddy said. "Can you tell a story?"

"Yes," Nancy said.

"Tell it," Caddy said. We looked at Nancy. "You don't know any stories."

"Yes," Nancy said. "Yes I do."

She came and sat in a chair before the hearth. There was a little fire there. Nancy built it up, when it was already hot inside. She built a good blaze. She told a story. She talked like her eyes looked, like her eyes watching us and her voice talking to us did not belong to her. Like she was living somewhere else, waiting somewhere else. She was outside the cabin. Her voice was inside and the shape of her, that Nancy that could stoop under a barbed wire fence with a bundle of clothes balanced on her head as though without weight, like a balloon, was there. But that was all. "And so this here queen come walking up to the ditch, where that bad man was hiding. She was walking up to the ditch, and she say, 'If I can just get past this here ditch,' was what she say . . ."

"What ditch?" Caddy said. "A ditch like that one out there? Why did a queen want to go into a ditch?"

"To get to her house," Nancy said. She looked at us. "She had to cross the ditch to get into her house quick and bar the door."

"Why did she want to go home and bar the door?" Caddy said.

4

Nancy looked at us. She quit talking. She looked at us. Jason's legs stuck straight out of his pants where he sat on Nancy's lap. "I don't think that's a good story," he said. "I want to go home."

"Maybe we had better," Caddy said. She got up from the floor. "I bet they are looking for us right now." She went toward the door.

"No," Nancy said. "Don't open it." She got up quick and passed Caddy. She didn't touch the door, the wooden bar.

"Why not?" Caddy said.

"Come back to the lamp," Nancy said. "We'll have fun. You don't have to go."

"We ought to go," Caddy said. "Unless we have a lot of fun." She and Nancy came back to the fire, the lamp.

"I want to go home," Jason said. "I'm going to tell."

"I know another story," Nancy said. She stood close to the lamp. She looked at Caddy, like when your eyes look up at a stick balanced on your nose. She had to look down to see Caddy, but her eyes looked like that, like when you are balancing a stick.

"I won't listen to it," Jason said. "I'll bang on the door."

"It's a good one," Nancy said. "It's better than the other one."

"What's it about?" Caddy said. Nancy was standing by the lamp. Her hand was on the lamp, against the light, long and brown.

"Your hand is on that hot globe," Caddy said. "Don't it feel hot to your hand?"

Nancy looked at her hand on the lamp chimney. She took her hand away, slow. She stood there, looking at Caddy, wringing her long hand as though it were tied to her wrist with a string.

"Let's do something else," Caddy said.

"I want to go home," Jason said.

"I got some popcorn," Nancy said. She looked at Caddy and then at Jason and then at me and then at Caddy again. "I got some popcorn."

"I don't like popcorn," Jason said. "I'd rather have candy."

Nancy looked at Jason. "You can hold the popper." She was still wringing her hand; it was long and limp and brown.

"All right," Jason said. "I'll stay a while if I can do that. Caddy can't hold it. I'll want to go home again if Caddy holds the popper."

Nancy built up the fire. "Look at Nancy putting her hands in the fire," Caddy said. "What's the matter with you, Nancy?"

"I got popcorn," Nancy said. "I got some." She took the popper from under the bed. It was broken. Jason began to cry.

"Now we can't have any popcorn," he said.

"We ought to go home anyway," Caddy said. "Come on, Quentin."

"Wait," Nancy said; "wait. I can fix it. Don't you want to help me fix it?"

"I don't think I want any," Caddy said. "It's too late now."

"You help me, Jason," Nancy said. "Don't you want to help me?"

"No," Jason said. "I want to go home."

"Hush," Nancy said; "hush. Watch. Watch me. I can fix it so Jason can hold it and pop the corn." She got a piece of wire and fixed the popper.

"It won't hold good," Caddy said.

"Yes it will," Nancy said. "Yawl watch. Yawl help me shell some corn."

The popcorn was under the bed too. We shelled it into the popper and Nancy helped Jason hold the popper over the fire.

"It's not popping," Jason said. "I want to go home."

"You wait," Nancy said. "It'll begin to pop. We'll have fun then."

She was sitting close to the fire. The lamp was turned up so high it was beginning to smoke. "Why don't you turn it down some?" I said.

"It's all right," Nancy said. "I'll clean it. Yawl wait. The popcorn will start in a minute."

"I don't believe it's going to start," Caddy said. "We ought to start home, anyway. They'll be worried."

"No," Nancy said. "It's going to pop. Dilsey will tell um yawl with me. I been working for yawl long time. They won't mind if yawl at my house. You wait, now. It'll start popping any minute now."

Then Jason got some smoke in his eyes and he began to cry. He dropped the popper into the fire. Nancy got a wet rag and wiped Jason's face, but he didn't stop crying.

"Hush," she said. "Hush." He didn't hush. Caddy took the popper out of the fire.

"It's burned up," she said. "You'll have to get some more popcorn, Nancy."

"Did you put all of it in?" Nancy said.

"Yes," Caddy said. Nancy looked at Caddy. Then she took the popper and opened it and poured the cinders into her apron and began to sort the grains, her hands long and brown, and we watched her.

"Haven't you got any more?" Caddy said.

"Yes," Nancy said; "yes. Look. This here ain't burnt. All we need to do is—"

"I want to go home," Jason said. "I'm going to tell."

"Hush," Caddy said. We all listened. Nancy's head was already turned toward the door, her eyes filled with red lamplight. "Somebody is coming," Caddy said.

Then Nancy began to make that sound again, not loud, sitting there above the fire, her long hands dangling between her knees; all of a sudden water began to come out on her face in big drops, running down her face, carrying in each one a little turning ball of firelight like a spark until it dropped off her chin. "She's not crying," I said.

"I ain't crying," Nancy said. Her eyes were closed. "I ain't crying. Who is it?"

"I don't know," Caddy said. She went to the door and looked out. "We've got to go now," she said. "Here comes Father."

"I'm going to tell," Jason said. "Yawl made me come."

The water still ran down Nancy's face. She turned in her chair. "Listen. Tell him. Tell him we going to have fun. Tell him I take good care of yawl until in the morning. Tell him to let me come home with yawl and sleep on the floor. Tell him I won't need no pallet. We'll have fun. You member last time how we had so much fun?"

"I didn't have fun," Jason said. "You hurt me. You put smoke in my eyes. I'm going to tell."

5

Father came in. He looked at us. Nancy did not get up.

"Tell him," she said.

"Caddy made us come down here," Jason said. "I didn't want to."

Father came to the fire. Nancy looked up at him. "Can't you go to Aunt Rachel's and stay?" he said. Nancy looked up at Father, her hands between her knees. "He's not here," Father said. "I would have seen him. There's not a soul in sight."

"He in the ditch," Nancy said. "He waiting in the ditch yonder."

"Nonsense," Father said. He looked at Nancy. "Do you know he's there?"

"I got the sign," Nancy said.

"What sign?"

"I got it. It was on the table when I came in. It was a hog-bone, with blood meat still on it, laying by the lamp. He's out there. When yawl walk out that door, I gone."

"Gone where, Nancy?" Caddy said.

"I'm not a tattletale," Jason said.

"Nonsense," Father said.

"He out there," Nancy said. "He looking through that window this minute, waiting for yawl to go. Then I gone."

"Nonsense," Father said. "Lock up your house and we'll take you on to Aunt Rachel's."

" 'Twon't do no good," Nancy said. She didn't look at Father now, but he looked down at her, at her long limp, moving hands. "Putting it off won't do no good."

"Then what do you want to do?" Father said.

"I don't know," Nancy said. "I can't do nothing. Just put it off. And that don't do no good. I reckon it belong to me. I reckon what I going to get ain't no more than mine."

"Get what?" Caddy said. "What's yours?"

"Nothing," Father said. "You all must get to bed."

"Caddy made me come," Jason said.

"Go on to Aunt Rachel's," Father said.

"It won't do no good," Nancy said. She sat down before the fire, her elbows on her knees, her long hands between her knees. "When even your own kitchen wouldn't do no good. When even if I was sleeping on the floor in the room with your chillen, and the next morning there I am, and blood—"

"Hush," Father said. "Lock your door and put out the lamp and go to bed."

"I scaired of the dark," Nancy said. "I scaired for it to happen in the dark."

"You mean you're going to sit right here with the lamp lighted?" Father said. Then Nancy began to make the sound again, sitting before the fire, her long hands between her knees. "Ah, damnation," Father said. "Come along, chillen. It's past bedtime."

"When yawl go home, I gone," Nancy said. She talked quieter now, and her face looked quiet, like her hands. "Anyway, I got my coffin money saved up with Mr. Lovelady." Mr. Lovelady was a short, dirty man who collected the Negro insurance, coming around to the cabins or the kitchens every Saturday morning, to collect fifteen cents. He and his wife lived at the hotel. One morning his wife committed suicide. They had a child, a little girl. He and the child went away. After a week or two he came back alone. We would see him going along the lanes and the back streets on Saturday mornings.

"Nonsense," Father said. "You'll be the first thing I'll see in the kitchen tomorrow morning."

"You'll see what you'll see, I reckon," Nancy said. "But it will take the Lord to say what that will be."

6

We left her sitting before the fire.

"Come and put the bar up," Father said. But she didn't move. She didn't look at us again, sitting quietly there between the lamp and the fire. From some distance down the lane we could look back and see her through the open door.

"What, Father?" Caddy said. "What's going to happen?"

"Nothing," Father said. Jason was on Father's back, so Jason was the tallest of all of us. We went down into the ditch. I looked at it, quiet. I couldn't see much where the moonlight and the shadows tangled.

"If Jesus *is* hid here, he can see us, can't he?" Caddy said.

"He's not there," Father said. "He went away a long time ago."

"You made me come," Jason said, high; against the sky it looked like Father had two heads, a little one and a big one. "I didn't want to."

We went up out of the ditch. We could still see Nancy's house and the open door, but we couldn't see Nancy now, sitting before the fire with the door open, because she was tired. "I just done got tired," she said. "I just a nigger. It ain't no fault of mine."

But we could hear her, because she began just after we came up out of the ditch, the sound that was not singing and not unsinging. "Who will do our washing now, Father?" I said.

"I'm not a nigger," Jason said, high and close above Father's head.

"You're worse," Caddy said, "you are a tattletale. If something was to jump out, you'd be scairder than a nigger."

"I wouldn't," Jason said.

"You'd cry," Caddy said.

"Caddy," Father said.

"I wouldn't!" Jason said.

"Scairy cat," Caddy said.

"Candace!" Father said.

Flannery O'Connor

A TEMPLE OF
THE HOLY GHOST

All week end the two girls were calling each other Temple One and Temple Two, shaking with laughter and getting so red and hot that they were positively ugly, particularly Joanne who had spots on her face anyway. They came in the brown convent uniforms they had to wear at Mount St. Scholastica but as soon as they opened their suitcases, they took off the uniforms and put on red skirts and loud blouses. They put on lipstick and their Sunday shoes and walked around in the high heels all over the house, always passing the long mirror in the hall slowly to get a look at their legs. None of their ways were lost on the child. If only one of them had come, that one would have played with her, but since there were two of them, she was out of it and watched them suspiciously from a distance.

They were fourteen—two years older than she was—but neither of them was bright, which was why they had been sent to the convent. If they had gone to a regular school, they wouldn't have done anything but think about boys; at the convent the sisters, her mother said, would keep a grip on their necks. The child decided, after observing them for a few hours, that they were practically morons and she was glad to think that they were only second cousins and she couldn't have inherited any of their stupidity. Susan called herself Su-zan. She was very skinny but she had a pretty pointed face and red hair. Joanne had yellow hair that was naturally curly but she talked through her nose and when she laughed, she turned purple in patches. Neither one of them could say an intelligent thing and all their sentences began, "You know this boy I know well one time he . . ."

They were to stay all week end and her mother said she didn't see how she would entertain them since she didn't know any boys their age. At this, the child, struck suddenly with genius, shouted, "There's Cheat! Get Cheat to come! Ask Miss Kirby to get Cheat to come show them around!" and she nearly choked on the food she had in her mouth. She doubled over laughing and hit the table with her fist and looked at the two bewildered girls while water started in her eyes and rolled down her fat cheeks and the braces she had in her mouth glared like tin. She had never thought of anything so funny before.

Her mother laughed in a guarded way and Miss Kirby blushed and carried her fork delicately to her mouth with one pea on it. She was a long-faced blonde schoolteacher who boarded with them and Mr. Cheatam was her admirer, a rich old farmer who arrived every Saturday afternoon in a fifteen-year-old baby-blue Pontiac powdered with red clay dust and black inside with Negroes that he charged ten cents apiece to bring into town on Saturday afternoons. After he dumped them he came to see Miss Kirby, always bringing a little gift—a bag of boiled peanuts or a watermelon or a stalk of sugar cane and once a wholesale box of Baby Ruth candy bars. He was bald-headed except for a little fringe of rust-colored hair and his face was nearly the same color as the unpaved roads and washed like them with ruts and gulleys. He wore a pale green shirt with a thin black stripe in it and blue galluses and his trousers cut across a protruding stomach that he pressed tenderly from time to time with his big flat thumb. All his teeth were backed with gold and he would roll his eyes at Miss Kirby in an impish way and say, "Haw haw," sitting in their porch swing with his legs spread apart and his hightopped shoes pointing in opposite directions on the floor.

"I don't think Cheat is going to be in town this week end," Miss Kirby said, not in the least understanding that this was a joke, and the child was convulsed afresh, threw herself backward in her chair, fell out of it, rolled on the floor and lay there heaving. Her mother told her if she didn't stop this foolishness she would have to leave the table.

Yesterday her mother had arranged with Alonzo Myers to drive them the forty-five miles to Mayville, where the convent was, to get the girls for the week end and Sunday afternoon he was hired to drive them back again. He was an eighteen-year-old boy who weighed two hundred and fifty pounds and worked for the taxi company and he was all you could get to drive you anywhere. He smoked or rather chewed a short black cigar and he had a round sweaty chest that showed through the yellow nylon shirt he wore. When he drove all the windows of the car had to be open.

"Well there's Alonzo!" the child roared from the floor. "Get Alonzo to show em around! Get Alonzo!"

The two girls, who had seen Alonzo, began to scream their indignation.

Her mother thought this was funny too but she said, "That'll be about enough out of you," and changed the subject. She asked them why they called each other Temple One and Temple Two and this sent them off into gales of giggles. Finally they managed to explain. Sister Perpetua, the oldest nun at the Sisters of Mercy in Mayville, had given them a lecture on what to do if a young man should—here they laughed so hard they were not able to go on without going back to the beginning—on what to do if a young man should— they put their heads in their laps—on what to do if—they finally managed to shout it out—if he should "behave in an ungentlemanly manner with them in the back of an automobile." Sister Perpetua said they were to say, "Stop sir! I am a Temple of the Holy Ghost!" and that would put an end to it. The child sat up off the floor with a blank face. She didn't see anything so funny in this. What was really funny was the idea of Mr. Cheatam or Alonzo Myers beau- ing them around. That killed her.

Her mother didn't laugh at what they had said. "I think you girls are pretty silly," she said. "After all, that's what you are—Temples of the Holy Ghost."

The two of them looked up at her, politely concealing their giggles, but with astonished faces as if they were beginning to realize that she was made of the same stuff as Sister Perpetua.

Miss Kirby preserved her set expression and the child thought, it's all over her head anyhow. I am a Temple of the Holy Ghost, she said to herself, and was pleased with the phrase. It made her feel as if somebody had given her a present.

After dinner, her mother collapsed on the bed and said, "Those girls are going to drive me crazy if I don't get some entertainment for them. They're awful."

"I bet I know who you could get," the child started.

"Now listen. I don't want to hear any more about Mr. Cheatam," her mother said. "You embarrass Miss Kirby. He's her only friend. Oh my Lord," and she sat up and looked mournfully out the window, "that poor soul is so lonesome she'll even ride in that car that smells like the last cir- cle in hell."

And she's a Temple of the Holy Ghost too, the child reflected. "I wasn't thinking of him," she said. "I was thinking of those two Wilkinses, Wendell and Cory, that visit old lady Buchell out on her farm. They're her grandsons. They work for her."

"Now that's an idea," her mother murmured and gave her an apprecia- tive look. But then she slumped again. "They're only farm boys. These girls would turn up their noses at them."

"Huh," the child said. "They wear pants. They're sixteen and they got a car. Somebody said they were both going to be Church of God preachers because you don't have to know nothing to be one."

"They would be perfectly safe with those boys all right," her mother said and in a minute she got up and called their grandmother on the telephone and after she had talked to the old woman a half an hour, it was arranged that Wendell and Cory would come to supper and afterwards take the girls to the fair.

Susan and Joanne were so pleased that they washed their hair and rolled it up on aluminum curlers. Hah, thought the child, sitting cross-legged on the bed to watch them undo the curlers, wait'll you get a load of Wendell and Cory! "You'll like these boys," she said. "Wendell is six feet tall ands got red hair. Cory is six feet six inches talls got black hair and wears a sport jacket and they gottem this car with a squirrel tail on the front."

"How does a child like you know so much about these men?" Susan asked and pushed her face up close to the mirror to watch the pupils in her eyes dilate.

The child lay back on the bed and began to count the narrow boards in the ceiling until she lost her place. I know them all right, she said to someone. We fought in the world war together. They were under me and I saved them five times from Japanese suicide divers and Wendell said I am going to marry that kid and the other said oh no you ain't I am and I said neither one of you is because I will court marshall you all before you can bat an eye. "I've seen them around is all," she said.

When they came the girls stared at them a second and then began to giggle and talk to each other about the convent. They sat in the swing together and Wendell and Cory sat on the banisters together. They sat like monkeys, their knees on a level with their shoulders and their arms hanging down between. They were short thin boys with red faces and high cheekbones and pale seed-like eyes. They had brought a harmonica and a guitar. One of them began to blow softly on the mouth organ, watching the girls over it, and the other started strumming the guitar and then began to sing, not watching them but keeping his head tilted upward as if he were only interested in hearing himself. He was singing a hillbilly song that sounded half like a love song and half like a hymm.

The child was standing on a barrel pushed into some bushes at the side of the house, her face on a level with the porch floor. The sun was going down and the sky was turning a bruised violet color that seemed to be connected with the sweet mournful sound of the music. Wendell began to smile as he sang and to look at the girls. He looked at Susan with a dog-like loving look and sang,

> "I've found a friend in Jesus,
> He's everything to me,
> He's the lily of the valley,
> He's the One who's set me free!"

Then he turned the same look on Joanne and sang,

> "A wall of fire about me,
> I've nothing now to fear,
> He's the lily of the valley,
> And I'll always have Him near!"

The girls looked at each other and held their lips stiff so as not to giggle but Susan let out one anyway and clapped her hand on her mouth. The singer frowned and for a few seconds only strummed the guitar. Then he began "The Old Rugged Cross" and they listened politely but when he had finished they said, "Let us sing one!" and before he could start another, they began to sing with their convent-trained voices,

> *"Tantum ergo Sacramentum*
> *Veneremur Cernui:*
> *Et antiquum documentum*
> *Novo cedat ritui:"*

The child watched the boys' solemn faces turn with perplexed frowning stares at each other as if they were uncertain whether they were being made fun of.

> *"Praestet fides supplementum*
> *Sensuum defectui.*
> *Genitori, Genitoque*
> *Laus et jubilatio*
>
> *Salus, honor, virtus quoque . . ."*

The boys' faces were dark red in the gray-purple light. They looked fierce and startled.

> *"Sit et benedictio;*
> *Procedenti ab utroque*

> *Compar sit laudatio.*
> *Amen.*"[1]

The girls dragged out the Amen and then there was a silence.

"That must be Jew singing," Wendell said and began to tune the guitar.

The girls giggled idiotically but the child stamped her foot on the barrel. "You big dumb ox!" she shouted. "You big dumb Church of God ox!" she roared and fell off the barrel and scrambled up and shot around the corner of the house as they jumped from the banister to see who was shouting.

Her mother had arranged for them to have supper in the back yard and she had a table laid out there under some Japanese lanterns that she pulled out for garden parties. "I ain't eating with them," the child said and snatched her plate off the table and carried it to the kitchen and sat down with the thin blue-gummed cook and ate her supper.

"Howcome you be so ugly sometime?" the cook asked.

"Those stupid idiots," the child said.

The lanterns gilded the leaves of the trees orange on the level where they hung and above them was black-green and below them were different dim muted colors that made the girls sitting at the table look prettier than they were. From time to time, the child turned her head and glared out the kitchen window at the scene below.

"God could strike you deaf dumb and blind," the cook said, "and then you wouldn't be as smart as you is."

"I would still be smarter than some," the child said.

After supper they left for the fair. She wanted to go to the fair but not with them so even if they had asked her she wouldn't have gone. She went upstairs and paced the long bedroom with her hands locked together behind her back and her head thrust forward and an expression, fierce and dreamy both, on her face. She didn't turn on the electric light but let the darkness collect and make the room smaller and more private. At regular intervals a

---

1. The Latin excerpt here is from *Pange lingua*, a hymn written by St. Thomas Aquinas. Roughly translated, it reads:

> Let us worship this great sacrament,
> and let the ancient ceremonies
> yield to new rites.
>
> Faith supplements what the senses lack.
>
> To the Father and the Son
> be praise, rejoicing, salvation, honor, and might;
> And to the One who proceeds from them both
> let there be equal praise.
>
> Amen.

light crossed the open window and threw shadows on the wall. She stopped and stood looking out over the dark slopes, past where the pond glinted silver, past the wall of woods to the speckled sky where a long finger of light was revolving up and around and away, searching the air as if it were hunting for the lost sun. It was the beacon light from the fair.

She could hear the distant sound of the calliope and she saw in her head all the tents raised up in a kind of gold sawdust light and the diamond ring of the ferris wheel going around and around up in the air and down again and the screeking merry-go-round going around and around on the ground. A fair lasted five or six days and there was a special afternoon for school children and a special night for niggers. She had gone last year on the afternoon for school children and had seen the monkeys and the fat man and had ridden on the ferris wheel. Certain tents were closed then because they contained things that would be known only to grown people but she had looked with interest at the advertising on the closed tents, at the faded-looking pictures on the canvas of people in tights, with stiff stretched composed faces like the faces of the martyrs waiting to have their tongues cut out by the Roman soldier. She had imagined that what was inside these tents concerned medicine and she had made up her mind to be a doctor when she grew up.

She had since changed and decided to be an engineer but as she looked out the window and followed the revolving searchlight as it widened and shortened and wheeled in its arc, she felt that she would have to be much more than just a doctor or an engineer. She would have to be a saint because that was the occupation that included everything you could know; and yet she knew she would never be a saint. She did not steal or murder but she was a born liar and slothful and she sassed her mother and was deliberately ugly to almost everybody. She was eaten up also with the sin of Pride, the worst one. She made fun of the Baptist preacher who came to the school at commencement to give the devotional. She would pull down her mouth and hold her forehead as if she were in agony and groan, "Fawther, we thank Thee," exactly the way he did and she had been told many times not to do it. She could never be a saint, but she thought she could be a martyr if they killed her quick.

She could stand to be shot but not to be burned in oil. She didn't know if she could stand to be torn to pieces by lions or not. She began to prepare her martyrdom, seeing herself in a pair of tights in a great arena, lit by the early Christians hanging in cages of fire, making a gold dusty light that fell on her and the lions. The first lion charged forward and fell at her feet, converted. A whole series of lions did the same. The lions liked her so much she even slept with them and finally the Romans were obliged to burn her but to their astonishment she would not burn down and finding she was so hard to kill, they finally cut off her head very quickly with a sword and she went immediately to heaven. She rehearsed this several times, returning each time at the entrance of Paradise to the lions.

Finally she got up from the window and got ready for bed and got in without saying her prayers. There were two heavy double beds in the room. The girls were occupying the other one and she tried to think of something cold and clammy that she could hide in their bed but her thought was fruitless. She didn't have anything she could think of, like a chicken carcass or a piece of beef liver. The sound of the calliope coming through the window kept her awake and she remembered that she hadn't said her prayers and got up and knelt down and began them. She took a running start and went through to the other side of the Apostle's Creed and then hung by her chin on the side of the bed, empty-minded. Her prayers, when she remembered to say them, were usually perfunctory but sometimes when she had done something wrong or heard music or lost something, or sometimes for no reason at all, she would be moved to fervor and would think of Christ on the long journey to Calvary, crushed three times under the rough cross. Her mind would stay on this a while and then get empty and when something roused her, she would find that she was thinking of a different thing entirely, of some dog or some girl or something she was going to do some day. Tonight, remembering Wendell and Cory, she was filled with thanksgiving and almost weeping with delight, she said, "Lord, Lord, thank You that I'm not in the Church of God, thank You Lord, thank You!" and got back in bed and kept repeating it until she went to sleep.

The girls came in at a quarter to twelve and waked her up with their giggling. They turned on the small blue-shaded lamp to see to get undressed by and their skinny shadows climbed up the wall and broke and continued moving about softly on the ceiling. The child sat up to hear what all they had seen at the fair. Susan had a plastic pistol full of cheap candy and Joanne a pasteboard cat with red polka dots in it. "Did you see the monkeys dance?" the child asked. "Did you see that fat man and those midgets?"

"All kinds of freaks," Joanne said. And then she said to Susan, "I enjoyed it all but the you-know-what," and her face assumed a peculiar expression as if she had bit into something that she didn't know if she liked or not.

The other stood still and shook her head once and nodded slightly at the child. "Little pitchers," she said in a low voice but the child heard it and her heart began to beat very fast.

She got out of her bed and climbed onto the footboard of theirs. They turned off the light and got in but she didn't move. She sat there, looking hard at them until their faces were well defined in the dark. "I'm not as old as you all," she said, "but I'm about a million times smarter."

"There are some things," Susan said, "that a child of your age doesn't know," and they both began to giggle.

"Go back to your own bed," Joanne said.

The child didn't move. "One time," she said, her voice hollow-sounding in the dark, "I saw this rabbit have rabbits."

There was a silence. Then Susan said, "How?" in an indifferent tone and she knew that she had them. She said she wouldn't tell until they told about the you-know-what. Actually she had never seen a rabbit have rabbits but she forgot this as they began to tell what they had seen in the tent.

It had been a freak with a particular name but they couldn't remember the name. The tent where it was had been divided into two parts by a black curtain, one side for men and one for women. The freak went from one side to the other, talking first to the men and then to the women, but everyone could hear. The stage ran all the way across the front. The girls heard the freak say to the men, "I'm going to show you this and if you laugh, God may strike you the same way." The freak had a country voice, slow and nasal and neither high nor low, just flat. "God made me thisaway and if you laugh He may strike you the same way. This is the way He wanted me to be and I ain't disputing His way. I'm showing you because I got to make the best of it. I expect you to act like ladies and gentlemen. I never done it to myself nor had a thing to do with it but I'm making the best of it. I don't dispute hit." Then there was a long silence on the other side of the tent and finally the freak left the men and came over onto the women's side and said the same thing.

The child felt every muscle strained as if she were hearing the answer to a riddle that was more puzzling than the riddle itself. "You mean it had two heads?" she said.

"No," Susan said, "it was a man and woman both. It pulled up its dress and showed us. It had on a blue dress."

The child wanted to ask how it could be a man and woman both without two heads but she did not. She wanted to get back into her own bed and think it out and she began to climb down off the footboard.

"What about the rabbit?" Joanne asked.

The child stopped and only her face appeared over the footboard, abstracted, absent. "It spit them out of its mouth," she said, "six of them."

She lay in bed trying to picture the tent with the freak walking from side to side but she was too sleepy to figure it out. She was better able to see the faces of the country people watching, the men more solemn than they were in church, and the women stern and polite, with painted-looking eyes, standing as if they were waiting for the first note of the piano to begin the hymn. She could hear the freak saying, "God made me thisaway and I don't dispute hit," and the people saying, "Amen. Amen."

"God done this to me and I praise Him."

"Amen. Amen."

"He could strike you thisaway."

"Amen. Amen."

"But he has not."

"Amen."

"Raise yourself up. A temple of the Holy Ghost. You! You are God's temple, don't you know? Don't you know? God's Spirit has a dwelling in you, don't you know?"

"Amen. Amen."

"If anybody desecrates the temple of God, God will bring him to ruin and if you laugh, He may strike you thisaway. A temple of God is a holy thing. Amen. Amen."

"I am a temple of the Holy Ghost."

"Amen."

The people began to slap their hands without making a loud noise and with a regular beat between the Amens, more and more softly, as if they knew there was a child near, half asleep.

The next afternoon the girls put on their brown convent uniforms again and the child and her mother took them back to Mount St. Scholastica. "Oh glory, oh Pete!" they said. "Back to the salt mines." Alonzo Myers drove them and the child sat in front with him and her mother sat in back between the two girls, telling them such things as how pleased she was to have had them and how they must come back again and then about the good times she and their mothers had had when they were girls at the convent. The child didn't listen to any of this twaddle but kept as close to the locked door as she could get and held her head out the window. They had thought Alonzo would smell better on Sunday but he did not. With her hair blowing over her face she could look directly into the ivory sun which was framed in the middle of the blue afternoon but when she pulled it away from her eyes she had to squint.

Mount St. Scholastica was a red brick house set back in a garden in the center of town. There was a filling station on one side of it and a firehouse on the other. It had a high black grillework fence around it and narrow bricked walks between old trees and japonica bushes that were heavy with blooms. A big moon-faced nun came bustling to the door to let them in and embraced her mother and would have done the same to her but that she stuck out her hand and preserved a frigid frown, looking just past the sister's shoes at the wainscoting. They had a tendency to kiss even homely children, but the nun shook her hand vigorously and even cracked her knuckles a little and said they must come to the chapel, that benediction was just beginning. You put your foot in their door and they got you praying, the child thought as they hurried down the polished corridor.

You'd think she had to catch a train, she continued in the same ugly vein as they entered the chapel where the sisters were kneeling on one side and the girls, all in brown uniforms, on the other. The chapel smelled of incense. It was light green and gold, a series of springing arches that ended with the one over the altar where the priest was kneeling in front of the monstrance, bowed low. A small boy in a surplice was standing behind him, swinging the censer. The child knelt down between her mother and the nun and they were well into the *"Tantum Ergo"* before her ugly thoughts stopped and she began to realize that she was in the presence of God. Hep me not to be so mean, she began mechanically. Hep me not to give her so much sass. Hep me not to talk like I do. Her mind began to get quiet and then empty but when the priest raised the monstrance with the Host shining ivory-colored in the center of it, she was thinking of the tent at the fair that had the freak in it. The freak was saying, "I don't dispute hit. This is the way He wanted me to be."

As they were leaving the convent door, the big nun swooped down on her mischievously and nearly smothered her in the black habit, mashing the side of her face into the crucifix hitched onto her belt and then holding her off and looking at her with little periwinkle eyes.

On the way home she and her mother sat in the back and Alonzo drove by himself in the front. The child observed three folds of fat in the back of his neck and noted that his ears were pointed almost like a pig's. Her mother, making conversation, asked him if he had gone to the fair.

"Gone," he said, "and never missed a thing and it was good I gone when I did because they ain't going to have it next week like they said they was."

"Why?" asked her mother.

"They shut it on down," he said. "Some of the preachers from town gone out and inspected it and got the police to shut it on down."

Her mother let the conversation drop and the child's round face was lost in thought. She turned it toward the window and looked out over a stretch of pasture land that rose and fell with a gathering greenness until it touched the dark woods. The sun was a huge red ball like an elevated Host drenched in blood and when it sank out of sight, it left a line in the sky like a red clay road hanging over the trees.

Grace Paley

ANXIETY

The young fathers are waiting outside the school. What curly heads! Such graceful brown mustaches. They're sitting on their haunches eating pizza and exchanging information. They're waiting for the 3 P.M. bell. It's springtime, the season of first looking out the window. I have a window box of greenhouse marigolds. The young fathers can be seen through the ferny leaves.

The bell rings. The children fall out of school, tumbling through the open door. One of the fathers sees his child. A small girl. Is she Chinese? A little. Up u-u-p, he says, and hoists her to his shoulders. U-u-p, says the second father, and hoists his little boy. The little boy sits on top of his father's head for a couple of seconds before sliding to his shoulders. Very funny, says the father.

They start off down the street, right under and past my window. The two children are still laughing. They try to whisper a secret. The fathers haven't finished their conversation. The frailer father is uncomfortable; his little girl wiggles too much.

Stop it this minute, he says.

Oink oink, says the little girl.

What'd you say?

Oink oink, she says.

The young father says What! three times. Then he seizes the child, raises her high above his head, and sets her hard on her feet.

What'd I do so bad, she says, rubbing her ankle.

Just hold my hand, screams the frail and angry father.

I lean far out the window. Stop! Stop! I cry.

The young father turns, shading his eyes, but sees. What? he says. His friend says, Hey? Who's that? He probably thinks I'm a family friend, a teacher maybe.

Who're you? he says.

I move the pots of marigold aside. Then I'm able to lean on my elbow way out into unshadowed visibility. Once, not too long ago, the tenements were speckled with women like me in every third window up to the fifth story, calling the children from play to receive orders and instruction. This memory enables me to say strictly, Young man, I am an older person who feels free because of that to ask questions and give advice.

Oh? he says, laughs with a little embarrassment, says to his friend, Shoot if you will that old gray head. But he's joking, I know, because he has established himself, legs apart, hands behind his back, his neck arched to see and hear me out.

How old are you? I call. About thirty or so?

Thirty-three.

First I want to say you're about a generation ahead of your father in your attitude and behavior toward your child.

Really? Well? Anything else, ma'am.

Son, I said, leaning another two, three dangerous inches toward him. Son, I must tell you that madmen intend to destroy this beautifully made planet. That the murder of our children by these men has got to become a terror and a sorrow to you, and starting now, it had better interfere with any daily pleasure.

Speech speech, he called.

I waited a minute, but he continued to look up. So, I said, I can tell by your general appearance and loping walk that you agree with me.

I do, he said, winking at his friend; but turning a serious face to mine, he said again, Yes, yes, I do.

Well then, why did you become so angry at that little girl whose future is like a film which suddenly cuts to white. Why did you nearly slam this little doomed person to the ground in your uncontrollable anger.

Let's not go too far, said the young father. She *was* jumping around on my poor back and hollering oink oink.

When were you angriest—when she wiggled and jumped or when she said oink?

He scratched his wonderful head of dark well-cut hair. I guess when she said oink.

Have you ever said oink oink? Think carefully. Years ago, perhaps?

No. Well maybe. Maybe.

Whom did you refer to in this way?

He laughed. He called to his friend, Hey Ken, this old person's got something. The cops. In a demonstration. Oink oink, he said, remembering, laughing.

The little girl smiled and said, Oink oink.

Shut up, he said.

What do you deduce from this?

That I was angry at Rosie because she was dealing with me as though I was a figure of authority, and it's not my thing, never has been, never will be.

I could see his happiness, his nice grin, as he remembered this.

So, I continued, since those children are such lovely examples of what may well be the last generation of humankind, why don't you start all over again, right from the school door, as though none of this had ever happened.

Thank you, said the young father. Thank you. It would be nice to be a horse, he said, grabbing little Rosie's hand. Come on Rosie, let's go. I don't have all day.

U-up, says the first father. U-up, says the second.

Giddap, shout the children, and the fathers yell neigh neigh, as horses do. The children kick their fathers' horsechests, screaming giddap giddap, and they gallop wildly westward.

I lean way out to cry once more, Be careful! Stop! But they've gone too far. Oh, anyone would love to be a fierce fast horse carrying a beloved beautiful rider, but they are galloping toward one of the most dangerous street corners in the world. And they may live beyond that trisection across other dangerous avenues.

So I must shut the window after patting the April-cooled marigolds with their rusty smell of summer. Then I sit in the nice light and wonder how to make sure that they gallop safely home through the airy scary dreams of scientists and the bulky dreams of automakers. I wish I could see just how they sit down at their kitchen tables for a healthy snack (orange juice or milk and cookies) before going out into the new spring afternoon to play.

Donald Barthelme

THE BALLOON

The balloon, beginning at a point on Fourteenth Street, the exact location of which I cannot reveal, expanded northward all one night, while people were sleeping, until it reached the Park. There, I stopped it, at dawn the northernmost edges lay over the Plaza, the free-hanging motion was frivolous and gentle. But experiencing a faint irritation at stopping, even to protect the trees, and seeing no reason the balloon should not be allowed to expand upward, over the parts of the city it was already covering, into the "air space" to be found there, I asked the engineers to see to it. This expansion took place throughout the morning, soft imperceptible sighing of gas through the valves. The balloon then covered forty-five blocks north-south and an irregular area east-west, as many as six crosstown blocks on either side of the Avenue in some places. That was the situation, then.

But it is wrong to speak of "situations," implying sets of circumstances leading to some resolution, some escape of tension, there were no situations, simply the balloon hanging there—muted heavy grays and browns for the most part, contrasting with walnut and soft yellows. A deliberate lack of finish, enhanced by skillful installation, gave the surface a rough, forgotten quality, sliding weights on the inside, carefully adjusted, anchored the great, varishaped mass at a number of points. Now we have had a flood of original ideas in all media, works of singular beauty as well as significant milestones in the history of inflation, but at that moment there was only *this balloon,* concrete particular, hanging there.

There were reactions. Some people found the balloon "interesting." As a response this seemed inadequate to the immensity of the balloon, the suddenness of its appearance over the city, on the other hand, in the absence of hysteria or other societally induced anxiety, it must be judged a calm, "mature" one. There was a certain amount of initial argumentation about the "meaning" of the balloon, this subsided, because we have learned not to insist on meanings, and they are rarely even looked for now, except in cases involving the simplest, safest phenomena. It was agreed that since the meaning of the balloon could never be known absolutely, extended discussion was pointless, or at least less purposeful than the activities of those who, for example, hung green and blue paper lanterns from the warm gray underside, in certain streets, or seized the occasion to write messages on the surface, announcing their availability for the performance of unnatural acts, or the availability of acquaintances.

Daring children jumped, especially at those points where the balloon hovered close to a building, so that the gap between balloon and building was a matter of a few inches, or points where the balloon actually made contact, exerting an ever-so-slight pressure against the side of a building, so that balloon and building seemed a unity. The upper surface was so structured that a "landscape" was presented, small valleys as well as slight knolls, or mounds, once atop the balloon, a stroll was possible, or even a trip, from one place to another. There was pleasure in being able to run down an incline, then up the opposing slope, both gently graded, or in making a leap from one side to the other. Bouncing was possible, because of the pneumaticity of the surface, and even falling, if that was your wish. That all these varied motions, as well as others, were within one's possibilities, in experiencing the "up" side of the balloon, was extremely exciting for children, accustomed to the city's flat, hard skin. But the purpose of the balloon was not to amuse children.

Too, the number of people, children and adults, who took advantage of the opportunities described was not so large as it might have been: a certain timidity, lack of trust in the balloon, was seen. There was, furthermore, some hostility. Because we had hidden the pumps, which fed helium to the interior, and because the surface was so vast that the authorities could not determine the point of entry—that is, the point at which the gas was injected—a degree of frustration was evidenced by those city officers into whose province such manifestations normally fell. The apparent purposelessness of the balloon was vexing (as was the fact that it was "there" at all). Had we painted, in great letters, LABORATORY TESTS PROVE or 18 PERCENT MORE EFFECTIVE on the sides of the balloon, this difficulty would have been circumvented. But I could not bear to do so. On the whole, these officers were remarkably tolerant, considering the dimensions of the anomaly, this tolerance being the result of, first, secret tests conducted by night that convinced them that little or nothing could be done in the way of removing or destroying the balloon, and, secondly, a public warmth that arose (not uncolored by touches of the aforementioned hostility) toward the balloon, from ordinary citizens.

As a single balloon must stand for a lifetime of thinking about balloons, so each citizen expressed, in the attitude he chose, a complex of attitudes. One man might consider that the balloon had to do with the notion *sullied,* as in the sentence *The big balloon sullied the otherwise clear and radiant Manhattan sky.* That is, the balloon was, in this man's view, an imposture, something inferior to the sky that had formerly been there, something interposed between the people and their "sky." But in fact it was January, the sky was dark and ugly, it was not a sky you could look up into, lying on your back in the street, with pleasure, unless pleasure, for you, proceeded from having been threatened, from having been misused. And the underside of the balloon was a pleasure to look up into, we had seen to that, muted grays and browns for the most part, contrasted with walnut and soft, forgotten yellows. And so, while this man was thinking *sullied,* still there was an admixture of pleasurable cognition in his thinking, struggling with the original perception.

Another man, on the other hand, might view the balloon as if it were part of a system of unanticipated rewards, as when one's employer walks in and says, "Here, Henry, take this package of money I have wrapped for you, because we have been doing so well in the business here, and I admire the way you bruise the tulips, without which bruising your department would not be a success, or at least not the success that it is." For this man the balloon might be a brilliantly heroic "muscle and pluck" experience, even if an experience poorly understood.

Another man might say, "Without the example of ———? it is doubtful that ——— would exist today in its present form," and find many to agree with him, or to argue with him. Ideas of "bloat" and "float" were introduced, as well as concepts of dream and responsibility. Others engaged in remarkably detailed fantasies having to do with a wish either to lose themselves in the balloon, or to engorge it. The private character of these wishes, of their origins, deeply buried and unknown, was such that they were not much spoken of, yet there is evidence that they were widespread. It was also argued that what was important was what you felt when you stood under the balloon, some people claimed that they felt sheltered, warmed, as never before, while enemies of the balloon felt, or reported feeling, constrained, a "heavy" feeling.

Critical opinion was divided:

"monstrous pourings"

"harp"

XXXXXXX "certain contrasts with darker portions"

"inner joy"

"large, square corners"

"conservative eclecticism that has so far governed
   modern balloon design"

::::::: "abnormal vigor"

   "warm, soft lazy passages"

"Has unity been sacrificed for a sprawling quality?"

   "Quelle catastrophe!"

   "munching"

   People began, in a curious way, to locate themselves in relation to aspects of the balloon: "I'll be at that place where it dips down into Forty-seventh Street almost to the sidewalk, near the Alamo Chili House," or, "Why don't we go stand on top, and take the air, and maybe walk about a bit, where it forms a tight, curving line with the façade of the Gallery of Modern Art——" Marginal intersections offered entrances within a given time duration, as well as "warm, soft, lazy passages" in which . . . But it is wrong to speak of "marginal intersections," each intersection was crucial, none could be ignored (as if, walking there, you might not find someone capable of turning your attention, in a flash, from old exercises to new exercises, risks and escalations). Each intersection was crucial, meeting of balloon and building, meeting of balloon and man, meeting of balloon and balloon.
   It was suggested that what was admired about the balloon was finally this: that it was not limited, or defined. Sometimes a bulge, blister, or subsection would carry all the way east to the river on its own initiative, in the manner of an army's movements on a map, as seen in a headquarters remote from the fighting. Then that part would be, as it were, thrown back again, or would withdraw into new dispositions; the next morning, that part would have made another sortie, or disappeared altogether. This ability of the balloon to shift its shape, to change, was very pleasing, especially to people whose lives were rather rigidly patterned, persons to whom change, although desired, was not available. The balloon, for the twenty-two days of its existence, offered the possibility, in its randomness, of mislocation of the self, in contradistinction to the grid of precise, rectangular pathways under our feet. The amount of specialized training currently needed, and the consequent desirability of long-term commitments, has been occasioned by the steadily growing importance of complex machinery, in virtually all kinds of operations; as this tendency increases, more and more people will turn, in

bewildered inadequacy, to solutions for which the balloon may stand as a prototype, or "rough draft."

I met you under the balloon, on the occasion of your return from Norway, you asked if it was mine, I said it was. The balloon, I said, is a spontaneous autobiographical disclosure, having to do with the unease I felt at your absence, and with sexual deprivation, but now that your visit to Bergen has been terminated, it is no longer necessary or appropriate. Removal of the balloon was easy; trailer trucks carried away the depleted fabric, which is now stored in West Virginia, awaiting some other time of unhappiness, some time, perhaps, when we are angry with one another.

E. L. Doctorow

THE WRITER
IN THE FAMILY

In 1955 my father died with his ancient mother still alive in a nursing home. The old lady was ninety and hadn't even known he was ill. Thinking the shock might kill her, my aunts told her that he had moved to Arizona for his bronchitis. To the immigrant generation of my grandmother, Arizona was the American equivalent of the Alps, it was where you went for your health. More accurately, it was where you went if you had the money. Since my father had failed in all the business enterprises of his life, this was the aspect of the news my grandmother dwelled on, that he had finally had some success. And so it came about that as we mourned him at home in our stocking feet, my grandmother was bragging to her cronies about her son's new life in the dry air of the desert.

My aunts had decided on their course of action without consulting us. It meant neither my mother nor my brother nor I could visit Grandma because we were supposed to have moved west too, a family, after all. My brother Harold and I didn't mind—it was always a nightmare at the old people's home, where they all sat around staring at us while we tried to make conversation with Grandma. She looked terrible, had numbers of ailments, and her mind wandered. Not seeing her was no disappointment either for my mother, who had never gotten along with the old woman and did not visit when she could have. But what was disturbing was that my aunts had acted in the manner of that side of the family of making government on everyone's behalf, the true citizens by blood and the lesser citizens by marriage. It was exactly this attitude that had tormented my mother all her married life. She claimed Jack's family had never accepted her. She had battled them for twenty-five years as an outsider.

A few weeks after the end of our ritual mourning my Aunt Frances phoned us from her home in Larchmont. Aunt Frances was the wealthier of my father's sisters. Her husband was a lawyer, and both her sons were at Amherst. She had called to say that Grandma was asking why she didn't hear from Jack. I had answered the phone. "You're the writer in the family," my aunt said. "Your father had so much faith in you. Would you mind making up something? Send it to me and I'll read it to her. She won't know the difference."

That evening, at the kitchen table, I pushed my homework aside and composed a letter. I tried to imagine my father's response to his new life. He had never been west. He had never traveled anywhere. In his generation the great journey was from the working class to the professional class. He hadn't managed that either. But he loved New York, where he had been born and lived his life, and he was always discovering new things about it. He especially loved the old parts of the city below Canal Street, where he would find ships' chandlers or firms that wholesaled in spices and teas. He was a salesman for an appliance jobber with accounts all over the city. He liked to bring home rare cheeses or exotic foreign vegetables that were sold only in certain neighborhoods. Once he brought home a barometer, another time an antique ship's telescope in a wooden case with a brass snap.

"Dear Mama," I wrote. "Arizona is beautiful. The sun shines all day and the air is warm and I feel better than I have in years. The desert is not as barren as you would expect, but filled with wildflowers and cactus plants and peculiar crooked trees that look like men holding their arms out. You can see great distances in whatever direction you turn and to the west is a range of mountains maybe fifty miles from here, but in the morning with the sun on them you can see the snow on their crests."

My aunt called some days later and told me it was when she read this letter aloud to the old lady that the full effect of Jack's death came over her. She had to excuse herself and went out in the parking lot to cry. "I wept so," she said. "I felt such terrible longing for him. You're so right, he loved to go places, he loved life, he loved everything."

We began trying to organize our lives. My father had borrowed money against his insurance and there was very little left. Some commissions were still due but it didn't look as if his firm would honor them. There was a couple of thousand dollars in a savings bank that had to be maintained there until the estate was settled. The lawyer involved was Aunt Frances' husband and he was very proper. "The estate!" my mother muttered, gesturing as if to pull out her hair. "The estate!" She applied for a job part-time in the admissions office of the hospital where my father's terminal illness had been diagnosed, and where he had spent some months until they had sent him home to die. She knew a lot of the doctors and staff and she had learned "from bitter experience," as she told them, about the hospital routine. She was hired.

I hated that hospital, it was dark and grim and full of tortured people. I thought it was masochistic of my mother to seek out a job there, but did not tell her so.

We lived in an apartment on the corner of 175th Street and the Grand Concourse, one flight up. Three rooms. I shared the bedroom with my brother. It was jammed with furniture because when my father had required a hospital bed in the last weeks of his illness we had moved some of the living-room pieces into the bedroom and made over the living room for him. We had to navigate bookcases, beds, a gateleg table, bureaus, a record player and radio console, stacks of 78 albums, my brother's trombone and music stand, and so on. My mother continued to sleep on the convertible sofa in the living room that had been their bed before his illness. The two rooms were connected by a narrow hall made even narrower by bookcases along the wall. Off the hall were a small kitchen and dinette and a bathroom. There were lots of appliances in the kitchen—broiler, toaster, pressure cooker, counter-top dishwasher, blender—that my father had gotten through his job, at cost. A treasured phrase in our house: *at cost*. But most of these fixtures went unused because my mother did not care for them. Chromium devices with timers or gauges that required the reading of elaborate instructions were not for her. They were in part responsible for the awful clutter of our lives and now she wanted to get rid of them. "We're being buried," she said. "Who needs them!"

So we agreed to throw out or sell anything inessential. While I found boxes for the appliances and my brother tied the boxes with twine, my mother opened my father's closet and took out his clothes. He had several suits because as a salesman he needed to look his best. My mother wanted us to try on his suits to see which of them could be altered and used. My brother refused to try them on. I tried on one jacket which was too large for me. The lining inside the sleeves chilled my arms and the vaguest scent of my father's being came to me.

"This is way too big," I said.

"Don't worry," my mother said. "I had it cleaned. Would I let you wear it if I hadn't?"

It was the evening, the end of winter, and snow was coming down on the windowsill and melting as it settled. The ceiling bulb glared on a pile of my father's suits and trousers on hangers flung across the bed in the shape of a dead man. We refused to try on anything more, and my mother began to cry.

"What are you crying for?" my brother shouted. "You wanted to get rid of things, didn't you?"

●

A few weeks later my aunt phoned again and said she thought it would be necessary to have another letter from Jack. Grandma had fallen out of her chair and bruised herself and was very depressed.

"How long does this go on?" my mother said.

"It's not so terrible," my aunt said, "for the little time left to make things easier for her."

My mother slammed down the phone. "He can't even die when he wants to!" she cried. "Even death comes second to Mama! What are they afraid of, the shock will kill her? Nothing can kill her. She's indestructible! A stake through the heart couldn't kill her!"

When I sat down in the kitchen to write the letter I found it more difficult than the first one. "Don't watch me," I said to my brother. "It's hard enough."

"You don't have to do something just because someone wants you to," Harold said. He was two years older than me and had started at City College; but when my father became ill he had switched to night school and gotten a job in a record store.

"Dear Mama," I wrote. "I hope you're feeling well. We're all fit as a fiddle. The life here is good and the people are very friendly and informal. Nobody wears suits and ties here. Just a pair of slacks and a short-sleeved shirt. Perhaps a sweater in the evening. I have bought into a very successful radio and record business and I'm doing very well. You remember Jack's Electric, my old place on Forty-third Street? Well, now it's Jack's Arizona Electric and we have a line of television sets as well."

I sent that letter off to my Aunt Frances, and as we all knew she would, she phoned soon after. My brother held his hand over the mouthpiece. "It's Frances with her latest review," he said.

"Jonathan? You're a very talented young man. I just wanted to tell you what a blessing your letter was. Her whole face lit up when I read the part about Jack's store. That would be an excellent way to continue."

"Well, I hope I don't have to do this anymore, Aunt Frances. It's not very honest."

Her tone changed. "Is your mother there? Let me talk to her."

"She's not here," I said.

"Tell her not to worry," my aunt said. "A poor old lady who has never wished anything but the best for her will soon die."

I did not repeat this to my mother, for whom it would have been one more in the family anthology of unforgivable remarks. But then I had to suffer it myself for the possible truth it might embody. Each side defended its position with rhetoric, but I, who wanted peace, rationalized the snubs and rebuffs each inflicted on the other, taking no stands, like my father himself.

Years ago his life had fallen into a pattern of business failures and missed opportunities. The great debate between his family on the one side, and my mother Ruth on the other, was this: who was responsible for the fact that he had not lived up to anyone's expectations?

As to the prophecies, when spring came my mother's prevailed. Grandma was still alive.

One balmy Sunday my mother and brother and I took the bus to the Beth El cemetery in New Jersey to visit my father's grave. It was situated on a slight rise. We stood looking over rolling fields embedded with monuments. Here and there processions of black cars wound their way through the lanes, or clusters of people stood at open graves. My father's grave was planted with tiny shoots of evergreen but it lacked a headstone. We had chosen one and paid for it and then the stonecutters had gone on strike. Without a headstone my father did not seem to be honorably dead. He didn't seem to me properly buried.

My mother gazed at the plot beside his, reserved for her coffin. "They were always too fine for other people," she said. "Even in the old days on Stanton Street. They put on airs. Nobody was ever good enough for them. Finally Jack himself was not good enough for them. Except to get them things wholesale. Then he was good enough for them."

"Mom, please," my brother said.

"If I had known. Before I ever met him he was tied to his mama's apron strings. And Essie's apron strings were like chains, let me tell you. We had to live where we could be near them for the Sunday visits. Every Sunday, that was my life, a visit to mamaleh. Whatever she knew I wanted, a better apartment, a stick of furniture, a summer camp for the boys, she spoke against it. You know your father, every decision had to be considered and reconsidered. And nothing changed. Nothing ever changed."

She began to cry. We sat her down on a nearby bench. My brother walked off and read the names on stones. I looked at my mother, who was crying, and I went off after my brother.

"Mom's still crying," I said. "Shouldn't we do something?"

"It's all right," he said. "It's what she came here for."

"Yes," I said, and then a sob escaped from my throat. "But I feel like crying too."

My brother Harold put his arm around me. "Look at this old black stone here," he said. "The way it's carved. You can see the changing fashion in monuments—just like everything else."

Somewhere in this time I began dreaming of my father. Not the robust father of my childhood, the handsome man with healthy pink skin and brown eyes and a mustache and the thinning hair parted in the middle. My dead father. We were taking him home from the hospital. It was understood that he had come back from death. This was amazing and joyous. On the other hand, he was terribly mysteriously damaged, or, more accurately, spoiled and unclean. He was very yellowed and debilitated by his death, and there were no guarantees that he wouldn't soon die again. He seemed aware of this and his entire personality was changed. He was angry and impatient with all of us. We were trying to help him in some way, struggling to get him home, but something prevented us, something we had to fix, a tattered suitcase that had sprung open, some mechanical thing: he had a car but it wouldn't start; or the car was made of wood; or his clothes, which had become too large for him, had caught in the door. In one version he was all bandaged and as we tried to lift him from his wheelchair into a taxi the bandage began to unroll and catch in the spokes of the wheelchair. This seemed to be some unreasonableness on his part. My mother looked on sadly and tried to get him to cooperate.

That was the dream. I shared it with no one. Once when I woke, crying out, my brother turned on the light. He wanted to know what I'd been dreaming but I pretended I didn't remember. The dream made me feel guilty. I felt guilty *in* the dream too because my enraged father knew we didn't want to live with him. The dream represented us taking him home, or trying to, but it was nevertheless understood by all of us that he was to live alone. He was this derelict back from death, but what we were doing was taking him to some place where he would live by himself without help from anyone until he died again.

At one point I became so fearful of this dream that I tried not to go to sleep. I tried to think of good things about my father and to remember him before his illness. He used to call me "matey." "Hello, matey," he would say when he came home from work. He always wanted us to go someplace—to the store, to the park, to a ball game. He loved to walk. When I went walking with him he would say: "Hold your shoulders back, don't slump. Hold your head up and look at the world. Walk as if you meant it!" As he strode down the street his shoulders moved from side to side, as if he was hearing some kind of cakewalk. He moved with a bounce. He was always eager to see what was around the corner.

The next request for a letter coincided with a special occasion in the house: My brother Harold had met a girl he liked and had gone out with her several times. Now she was coming to our house for dinner.

We had prepared for this for days, cleaning everything in sight, giving the house a going-over, washing the dust of disuse from the glasses and good dishes. My mother came home early from work to get the dinner going. We opened the gateleg table in the living room and brought in the kitchen chairs. My mother spread the table with a laundered white cloth and put out her silver. It was the first family occasion since my father's illness.

I liked my brother's girlfriend a lot. She was a thin girl with very straight hair and she had a terrific smile. Her presence seemed to excite the air. It was amazing to have a living breathing girl in our house. She looked around and what she said was: "Oh, I've never seen so many books!" While she and my brother sat at the table my mother was in the kitchen putting the food into serving bowls and I was going from the kitchen to the living room, kidding around like a waiter, with a white cloth over my arm and a high style of service, placing the serving dish of green beans on the table with a flourish. In the kitchen my mother's eyes were sparkling. She looked at me and nodded and mimed the words: "She's adorable!"

My brother suffered himself to be waited on. He was wary of what we might say. He kept glancing at the girl—her name was Susan—to see if we met with her approval. She worked in an insurance office and was taking courses in accounting at City College. Harold was under a terrible strain but he was excited and happy too. He had bought a bottle of Concord-grape wine to go with the roast chicken. He held up his glass and proposed a toast. My mother said: "To good health and happiness," and we all drank, even I. At that moment the phone rang and I went into the bedroom to get it.

"Jonathan? This is your Aunt Frances. How is everyone?"

"Fine, thank you."

"I want to ask one last favor of you. I need a letter from Jack. Your grandma's very ill. Do you think you can?"

"Who is it?" my mother called from the living room.

"OK, Aunt Frances," I said quickly. "I have to go now, we're eating dinner." And I hung up the phone.

"It was my friend Louie," I said, sitting back down. "He didn't know the math pages to review."

The dinner was very fine. Harold and Susan washed the dishes and by the time they were done my mother and I had folded up the gateleg table and put it back against the wall and I had swept the crumbs up with the carpet sweeper. We all sat and talked and listened to records for a while and then my brother took Susan home. The evening had gone very well.

Once when my mother wasn't home my brother had pointed out something: the letters from Jack weren't really necessary. "What is this ritual?" he said, holding his palms up. "Grandma is almost totally blind, she's half deaf and crippled. Does the situation really call for a literary composition? Does it need verisimilitude? Would the old lady know the difference if she was read the phone book?"

"Then why did Aunt Frances ask me?"

"That is the question, Jonathan. Why did she? After all, she could write the letter herself—what difference would it make? And if not Frances, why not Frances' sons, the Amherst students? They should have learned by now to write."

"But they're not Jack's sons," I said.

"That's exactly the point," my brother said. "The idea is *service*. Dad used to bust his balls getting them things wholesale, getting them deals on things. Frances of Westchester really needed things at cost. And Aunt Molly. And Aunt Molly's husband, and Aunt Molly's ex-husband. Grandma, if she needed an errand done. He was always on the hook for something. They never thought his time was important. They never thought every favor he got was one he had to pay back. Appliances, records, watches, china, opera tickets, any goddamn thing. Call Jack."

"It was a matter of pride to him to be able to do things for them," I said. "To have connections."

"Yeah, I wonder why," my brother said. He looked out the window.

Then suddenly it dawned on me that I was being implicated.

"You should use your head more," my brother said.

Yet I had agreed once again to write a letter from the desert and so I did. I mailed it off to Aunt Frances. A few days later, when I came home from school, I thought I saw her sitting in her car in front of our house. She drove a black Buick Roadmaster, a very large clean car with whitewall tires. It was Aunt Frances all right. She blew the horn when she saw me. I went over and leaned in at the window.

"Hello, Jonathan," she said. "I haven't long. Can you get in the car?"

"Mom's not home," I said. "She's working."

"I know that. I came to talk to you."

"Would you like to come upstairs?"

"I can't, I have to get back to Larchmont. Can you get in for a moment, please?"

I got in the car. My Aunt Frances was a very pretty white-haired woman, very elegant, and she wore tasteful clothes. I had always liked her and from the time I was a child she had enjoyed pointing out to everyone that I looked more like her son than Jack's. She wore white gloves and held the steering wheel and looked straight ahead as she talked, as if the car was in traffic and not sitting at the curb.

"Jonathan," she said, "there is your letter on the seat. Needless to say I didn't read it to Grandma. I'm giving it back to you and I won't ever say a word to anyone. This is just between us. I never expected cruelty from you. I never thought you were capable of doing something so deliberately cruel and perverse."

I said nothing.

"Your mother has very bitter feelings and now I see she has poisoned you with them. She has always resented the family. She is a very strong-willed, selfish person."

"No she isn't," I said.

"I wouldn't expect you to agree. She drove poor Jack crazy with her demands. She always had the highest aspirations and he could never fulfill them to her satisfaction. When he still had his store he kept your mother's brother, who drank, on salary. After the war when he began to make a little money he had to buy Ruth a mink jacket because she was so desperate to have one. He had debts to pay but she wanted a mink. He was a very special person, my brother, he should have accomplished something special, but he loved your mother and devoted his life to her. And all she ever thought about was keeping up with the Joneses."

I watched the traffic going up the Grand Concourse. A bunch of kids were waiting at the bus stop at the corner. They had put their books on the ground and were horsing around.

"I'm sorry I have to descend to this," Aunt Frances said. "I don't like talking about people this way. If I have nothing good to say about someone, I'd rather not say anything. How is Harold?"

"Fine."

"Did he help you write this marvelous letter?"

"No."

After a moment she said more softly: "How are you all getting along?"

"Fine."

"I would invite you up for Passover if I thought your mother would accept."

I didn't answer.

She turned on the engine. "I'll say good-bye now, Jonathan. Take your letter. I hope you give some time to thinking about what you've done."

That evening when my mother came home from work I saw that she wasn't as pretty as my Aunt Frances. I usually thought my mother was a good-looking woman, but I saw now that she was too heavy and that her hair was undistinguished.

"Why are you looking at me?" she said.

"I'm not."

"I learned something interesting today," my mother said. "We may be eligible for a V.A. pension because of the time your father spent in the Navy."

That took me by surprise. Nobody had ever told me my father was in the Navy.

"In World War I," she said, "he went to Webb's Naval Academy on the Harlem River. He was training to be an ensign. But the war ended and he never got his commission."

After dinner the three of us went through the closets looking for my father's papers, hoping to find some proof that could be filed with the Veterans Administration. We came up with two things, a Victory medal, which my brother said everyone got for being in the service during the Great War, and an astounding sepia photograph of my father and his shipmates on the deck of a ship. They were dressed in bell-bottoms and T-shirts and armed with mops and pails, brooms and brushes.

"I never knew this," I found myself saying. "I never knew this."

"You just don't remember," my brother said.

I was able to pick out my father. He stood at the end of the row, a thin, handsome boy with a full head of hair, a mustache, and an intelligent smiling countenance.

"He had a joke," my mother said. "They called their training ship the S.S. *Constipation* because it never moved."

Neither the picture nor the medal was proof of anything, but my brother thought a duplicate of my father's service record had to be in Washington somewhere and that it was just a matter of learning how to go about finding it.

"The pension wouldn't amount to much," my mother said. "Twenty or thirty dollars. But it would certainly help."

I took the picture of my father and his shipmates and propped it against the lamp at my bedside. I looked into his youthful face and tried to relate it to the Father I knew. I looked at the picture a long time. Only gradually did my eye connect it to the set of Great Sea Novels in the bottom shelf of the bookcase a few feet away. My father had given that set to me: it was uniformly bound in green with gilt lettering and it included works by Melville, Conrad, Victor Hugo and Captain Marryat. And lying across the top of the books, jammed in under the sagging shelf above, was his old ship's telescope in its wooden case with the brass snap.

I thought how stupid, and imperceptive, and self-centered I had been never to have understood while he was alive what my father's dream for his life had been.

On the other hand, I had written in my last letter from Arizona—the one that had so angered Aunt Frances—something that might allow me, the writer in the family, to soften my judgment of myself. I will conclude by giving the letter here in its entirety.

Dear Mama,

This will be my final letter to you since I have been told by the doctors that I am dying.

I have sold my store at a very fine profit and am sending Frances a check for five thousand dollars to be deposited in your account. My present to you, Mamaleh. Let Frances show you the passbook.

As for the nature of my ailment, the doctors haven't told me what it is, but I know that I am simply dying of the wrong life. I should never have come to the desert. It wasn't the place for me.

I have asked Ruth and the boys to have my body cremated and the ashes scattered in the ocean.

Your loving son,
Jack

Raymond Carver

WHY DON'T YOU DANCE?

In the kitchen, he poured another drink and looked at the bedroom suite in his front yard. The mattress was stripped and the candy-striped sheets lay beside two pillows on the chiffonier. Except for that, things looked much the way they had in the bedroom—nightstand and reading lamp on his side of the bed, nightstand and reading lamp on her side.

His side, her side.

He considered this as he sipped the whiskey.

The chiffonier stood a few feet from the foot of the bed. He had emptied the drawers into cartons that morning, and the cartons were in the living room. A portable heater was next to the chiffonier. A rattan chair with a decorator pillow stood at the foot of the bed. The buffed aluminum kitchen set took up a part of the driveway. A yellow muslin cloth, much too large, a gift, covered the table and hung down over the sides. A potted fern was on the table, along with a box of silverware and a record player, also gifts. A big console-model television set rested on a coffee table, and a few feet away from this stood a sofa and chair and a floor lamp. The desk was pushed against the garage door. A few utensils were on the desk, along with a wall clock and two framed prints. There was also in the driveway a carton with cups, glasses, and plates, each object wrapped in newspaper. That morning he had cleared out the closets, and except for the three cartons in the living room, all the stuff was out of the house. He had run an extension cord on out there and everything was connected. Things worked, no different from how it was when they were inside.

Now and then a car slowed and people stared. But no one stopped.

It occurred to him that he wouldn't, either.

•

"It must be a yard sale," the girl said to the boy.

This girl and this boy were furnishing a little apartment.

"Let's see what they want for the bed," the girl said.

"And for the TV," the boy said.

The boy pulled into the driveway and stopped in front of the kitchen table.

They got out of the car and began to examine things, the girl touching the muslin cloth, the boy plugging in the blender and turning the dial to MINCE, the girl picking up a chafing dish, the boy turning on the television set and making little adjustments.

He sat down on the sofa to watch. He lit a cigarette, looked around, flipped the match into the grass.

The girl sat on the bed. She pushed off her shoes and lay back. She thought she could see a star.

"Come here, Jack. Try this bed. Bring one of those pillows," she said.

"How is it?" he said.

"Try it," she said.

He looked around. The house was dark.

"I feel funny," he said. "Better see if anybody's home."

She bounced on the bed.

"Try it first," she said.

He lay down on the bed and put the pillow under his head.

"How does it feel?" she said.

"It feels firm," he said.

She turned on her side and put her hand to his face.

"Kiss me," she said.

"Let's get up," he said.

"Kiss me," she said.

She closed her eyes. She held him.

He said, "I'll see if anybody's home."

But he just sat up and stayed where he was, making believe he was watching the television.

Lights came on in houses up and down the street.

"Wouldn't it be funny if," the girl said and grinned and didn't finish.

The boy laughed, but for no good reason. For no good reason, he switched the reading lamp on.

The girl brushed away a mosquito, whereupon the boy stood up and tucked in his shirt.

"I'll see if anybody's home," he said. "I don't think anybody's home. But if anybody is, I'll see what things are going for."

"Whatever they ask, offer ten dollars less. It's always a good idea," she said. "And, besides, they must be desperate or something."

"It's a pretty good TV," the boy said.

"Ask them how much," the girl said.

The man came down the sidewalk with a sack from the market. He had sandwiches, beer, whiskey. He saw the car in the driveway and the girl on the bed. He saw the television set going and the boy on the porch.

"Hello," the man said to the girl. "You found the bed. That's good."

"Hello," the girl said, and got up. "I was just trying it out." She patted the bed. "It's a pretty good bed."

"It's a good bed," the man said, and put down the sack and took out the beer and the whiskey.

"We thought nobody was here," the boy said. "We're interested in the bed and maybe in the TV. Also maybe the desk. How much do you want for the bed?"

"I was thinking fifty dollars for the bed," the man said.

"Would you take forty?" the girl asked.

"I'll take forty," the man said.

He took a glass out of the carton. He took the newspaper off the glass. He broke the seal on the whiskey.

"How about the TV?" the boy said.

"Twenty-five."

"Would you take fifteen?" the girl said.

"Fifteen's okay. I could take fifteen," the man said.

The girl looked at the boy.

"You kids, you'll want a drink," the man said. "Glasses in that box. I'm going to sit down. I'm going to sit down on the sofa."

The man sat on the sofa, leaned back, and stared at the boy and the girl.

The boy found two glasses and poured whiskey.

"That's enough," the girl said. "I think I want water in mine."

She pulled out a chair and sat at the kitchen table.

"There's water in that spigot over there," the man said. "Turn on that spigot."

The boy came back with the watered whiskey. He cleared his throat and sat down at the kitchen table. He grinned. But he didn't drink anything from his glass.

The man gazed at the television. He finished his drink and started another. He reached to turn on the floor lamp. It was then that his cigarette dropped from his fingers and fell between the cushions.

The girl got up to help him find it.

"So what do you want?" the boy said to the girl.

The boy took out the checkbook and held it to his lips as if thinking.

"I want the desk," the girl said. "How much money is the desk?"

The man waved his hand at this preposterous question.

"Name a figure," he said.

He looked at them as they sat at the table. In the lamplight, there was something about their faces. It was nice or it was nasty. There was no telling.

"I'm going to turn off this TV and put on a record," the man said. "This record-player is going, too. Cheap. Make me an offer."

He poured more whiskey and opened a beer.

"Everything goes," said the man.

The girl held out her glass and the man poured.

"Thank you," she said. "You're very nice," she said.

"It goes to your head," the boy said. "I'm getting it in the head." He held up his glass and jiggled it.

The man finished his drink and poured another, and then he found the box with the records.

"Pick something," the man said to the girl, and he held the records out to her.

The boy was writing the check.

"Here," the girl said, picking something, picking anything, for she did not know the names on these labels. She got up from the table and sat down again. She did not want to sit still.

"I'm making it out to cash," the boy said.

"Sure," the man said.

They drank. They listened to the record. And then the man put on another.

Why don't you kids dance? he decided to say, and then he said it. "Why don't you dance?"

"I don't think so," the boy said.

"Go ahead," the man said. "It's my yard. You can dance if you want to."

Arms about each other, their bodies pressed together, the boy and the girl moved up and down the driveway. They were dancing. And when the record was over, they did it again, and when that one ended, the boy said, "I'm drunk."

The girl said, "You're not drunk."

"Well, I'm drunk," the boy said.

The man turned the record over and the boy said, "I am."

"Dance with me," the girl said to the boy and then to the man, and when the man stood up, she came to him with her arms wide open.

"Those people over there, they're watching," she said.

"It's okay," the man said. "It's my place," he said.

"Let them watch," the girl said.

"That's right," the man said. "They thought they'd seen everything over here. But they haven't seen this, have they?" he said.

He felt her breath on his neck.

"I hope you like your bed," he said.

The girl closed and then opened her eyes. She pushed her face into the man's shoulder. She pulled the man closer.

"You must be desperate or something," she said.

Weeks later, she said: "The guy was about middle-aged. All his things right there in his yard. No lie. We got real pissed and danced. In the driveway. Oh, my God. Don't laugh. He played us these records. Look at this record-player. The old guy gave it to us. And all these crappy records. Will you look at this shit?"

She kept talking. She told everyone. There was more to it, and she was trying to get it talked out. After a time, she quit trying.

THE MAN FROM MARS

A long time ago Christine was walking through the park. She was still wearing her tennis dress; she hadn't had time to shower and change, and her hair was held back with an elastic band. Her chunky reddish face, exposed with no softening fringe, looked like a Russian peasant's, but without the elastic band the hair got in her eyes. The afternoon was too hot for April; the indoor courts had been steaming, her skin felt poached.

The sun had brought the old men out from wherever they spent the winter: she had read a story recently about one who lived for three years in a manhole. They sat weedishly on the benches or lay on the grass with their heads on squares of used newspaper. As she passed, their wrinkled toadstool faces drifted towards her, drawn by the movement of her body, then floated away again, uninterested.

The squirrels were out too, foraging; two or three of them moved towards her in darts and pauses, eyes fixed on her expectantly, mouths with the rat-like receding chins open to show the yellowed front teeth. Christine walked faster, she had nothing to give them. People shouldn't feed them, she thought, it makes them anxious and they get mangy.

Halfway across the park she stopped to take off her cardigan. As she bent over to pick up her tennis racquet again someone touched her on her freshly bared arm. Christine seldom screamed; she straightened up suddenly, gripping the handle of her racquet. It was not one of the old men, however: it was a dark-haired boy of twelve or so.

"Excuse me," he said, "I search for Economics Building. It is there?" He motioned towards the west.

Christine looked at him more closely. She had been mistaken: he was not young, just short. He came a little above her shoulder, but then, she was above the average height; "statuesque," her mother called it when she was straining. He was also what was referred to in their family as "a person from another culture": oriental without a doubt, though perhaps not Chinese. Christine judged he must be a foreign student and gave him her official welcoming smile. In high school she had been President of the United Nations Club; that year her school had been picked to represent the Egyptian delegation at the Mock Assembly. It had been an unpopular assignment—nobody wanted to be the Arabs—but she had seen it through. She had made rather a good speech about the Palestinian refugees.

"Yes," she said, "that's it over there. The one with the flat roof. See it?"

The man had been smiling nervously at her the whole time. He was wearing glasses with transparent plastic rims, through which his eyes bulged up at her as though through a goldfish bowl. He had not followed where she was pointing. Instead he thrust towards her a small pad of green paper and a ballpoint pen.

"You make map," he said.

Christine set down her tennis racquet and drew a careful map. "We are here," she said, pronouncing distinctly. "You go this way. The building is here." She indicated the route with a dotted line and an X. The man leaned close to her, watching the progress of the map attentively; he smelled of cooked cauliflower and an unfamiliar brand of hair grease. When she had finished Christine handed the paper and pen back to him with a terminal smile.

"Wait," the man said. He tore the piece of paper with the map off the pad, folded it carefully and put it in his jacket pocket; the jacket sleeves came down over his wrists and had threads at the edges. He began to write something; she noticed with a slight feeling of revulsion that his nails and the ends of his fingertips were so badly bitten they seemed almost deformed. Several of his fingers were blue from the leaky ballpoint.

"Here is my name," he said, holding the pad out to her.

Christine read an odd assemblage of G's, Y's and N's, neatly printed in block letters. "Thank you," she said.

"You now write *your* name," he said, extending the pen.

Christine hesitated. If this had been a person from her own culture she would have thought he was trying to pick her up. But then, people from her own culture never tried to pick her up: she was too big. The only one who had made the attempt was the Moroccan waiter at the beer parlour where they sometimes went after meetings, and he had been direct. He had just intercepted her on the way to the Ladies' Room and asked and she said no; that had been that. This man was not a waiter though but a student; she didn't want to offend him. In his culture, whatever it was, this exchange of names on pieces of paper was probably a formal politeness, like saying Thank You. She took the pen from him.

"That is a very pleasant name," he said. He folded the paper and placed it in his jacket pocket with the map.

Christine felt she had done her duty. "Well, goodbye," she said. "It was nice to have met you." She bent for her tennis racquet but he had already stooped and retrieved it and was holding it with both hands in front of him, like a captured banner.

"I carry this for you."

"Oh no, please. Don't bother, I am in a hurry," she said, articulating clearly. Deprived of her tennis racquet she felt weaponless. He started to saunter along the path; he was not nervous at all now, he seemed completely at ease.

"Vous parlez français?" he asked conversationally.

"Oui, un petit peu," she said. "Not very well." How am I going to get my racquet away from him without being rude? she was wondering.

"Mais vous avez un bel accent."[1] His eyes goggled at her through the glasses: was he being flirtatious? She was well aware that her accent was wretched.

"Look," she said, for the first time letting her impatience show, "I really have to go. Give me my racquet, please."

He quickened his pace but gave no sign of returning the racquet. "Where you are going?"

"Home," she said. "My house."

"I go with you now," he said hopefully.

"*No,*" she said: she would have to be firm with him. She made a lunge and got a grip on her racquet; after a brief tug of war it came free.

"Goodbye," she said, turning away from his puzzled face and setting off at what she hoped was a discouraging jog-trot. It was like walking away from a growling dog, you shouldn't let on you were frightened. Why should she be frightened anyway? He was only half her size and she had the tennis racquet, there was nothing he could do to her.

Although she did not look back she could tell he was still following. Let there be a streetcar, she thought, and there was one, but it was far down the line, stuck behind a red light. He appeared at her side, breathing audibly, a moment after she reached the stop. She gazed ahead, rigid.

"You are my friend," he said tentatively.

Christine relented: he hadn't been trying to pick her up after all, he was a stranger, he just wanted to meet some of the local people; in his place she would have wanted the same thing.

"Yes," she said, doling him out a smile.

---

1. Their exchange in French: "Do you speak French?" "Yes, a little bit." "But you have a good accent."

"That is good," he said. "My country is very far."

Christine couldn't think of an apt reply. "That's interesting," she said. "Très interessant."[2] The streetcar was coming at last; she opened her purse and got out a ticket.

"I go with you now," he said. His hand clamped on her arm above the elbow.

"You . . . stay . . . *here,*" Christine said, resisting the impulse to shout but pausing between each word as though for a deaf person. She detached his hand—his hold was quite feeble and could not compete with her tennis biceps—and leapt off the curb and up the streetcar steps, hearing with relief the doors grind shut behind her. Inside the car and a block away she permitted herself a glance out a side window. He was standing where she had left him; he seemed to be writing something on his little pad of paper.

When she reached home she had only time for a snack, and even then she was almost late for the Debating Society. The topic was, "Resolved: That War Is Obsolete." Her team took the affirmative, and won.

Christine came out of her last examination feeling depressed. It was not the exam that depressed her but the fact it was the last one: it meant the end of the school year. She dropped into the coffee shop as usual, then went home early because there didn't seem to be anything else to do.

"Is that you, dear?" her mother called from the living room. She must have heard the front door close. Christine went in and flopped on the sofa, disturbing the neat pattern of the cushions.

"How was your exam, dear?" her mother asked.

"Fine," said Christine flatly. It had been fine, she had passed. She was not a brilliant student, she knew that, but she was conscientious. Her professors always wrote things like "A serious attempt" and "Well thought out but perhaps lacking in *élan*" on her term papers; they gave her B's, the occasional B+. She was taking Political Science and Economics, and hoped for a job with the Government after she graduated; with her father's connections she had a good chance.

"That's nice."

Christine felt, resentfully, that her mother had only a hazy idea of what an exam was. She was arranging gladioli in a vase; she had rubber gloves on to protect her hands as she always did when engaged in what she called "housework." As far as Christine could tell her housework consisted of arranging flowers in vases: daffodils and tulips and hyacinths through gladioli, iris and roses, all the way to asters and mums. Sometimes she cooked, elegantly and with chafing

2. Very interesting.

dishes, but she thought of it as a hobby. The girl did everything else. Christine thought it faintly sinful to have a girl. The only ones available now were either foreign or pregnant; their expressions usually suggested they were being taken advantage of somehow. But her mother asked what they would do otherwise, they'd either have to go into a Home or stay in their own countries, and Christine had to agree this was probably true. It was hard anyway to argue with her mother, she was so delicate, so preserved-looking, a harsh breath would scratch the finish.

"An interesting young man phoned today," her mother said. She had finished the gladioli and was taking off her rubber gloves. "He asked to speak with you and when I said you weren't in we had quite a little chat. You didn't tell me about him, dear." She put on the glasses which she wore on a decorative chain around her neck, a signal that she was in her modern, intelligent mood rather than her old-fashioned whimsical one.

"Did he leave his name?" Christine asked. She knew a lot of young men but they didn't often call her, they conducted their business with her in the coffee shop or after meetings.

"He's a person from another culture. He said he would call back later."

Christine had to think a moment. She was vaguely acquainted with several people from other cultures, Britain mostly; they belonged to the Debating Society.

"He's studying Philosophy in Montreal," her mother prompted. "He sounded French."

Christine began to remember the man in the park. "I don't think he's French, exactly," she said.

Her mother had taken off her glasses again and was poking absent-mindedly at a bent gladiolus. "Well, he sounded French." She meditated, flowery sceptre in hand. "I think it would be nice if you had him to tea."

Christine's mother did her best. She had two other daughters, both of whom took after her. They were beautiful, one was well married already and the other would clearly have no trouble. Her friends consoled her about Christine by saying, "She's not fat, she's just big-boned, it's the father's side," and "Christine is so healthy." Her other daughters had never gotten involved in activities when they were at school, but since Christine could not possibly ever be beautiful even if she took off weight, it was just as well she was so athletic and political, it was a good thing she had interests. Christine's mother tried to encourage her interests whenever possible. Christine could tell when she was making an extra effort, there was a reproachful edge to her voice.

She knew her mother expected enthusiasm but she could not supply it. "I don't know, I'll have to see," she said dubiously.

"You look tired, darling," said her mother. "Perhaps you'd like a glass of milk."

Christine was in the bathtub when the phone rang. She was not prone to fantasy but when she was in the bathtub she often pretended she was a dolphin, a game left over from one of the girls who used to bathe her when she was small. Her mother was being bell-voiced and gracious in the hall; then there was a tap at the door.

"It's that nice young French student, Christine," her mother said.

"Tell him I'm in the bathtub," Christine said, louder than necessary. "He isn't French."

She could hear her mother frowning. "That wouldn't be very polite, Christine. I don't think he'd understand."

"Oh all right," Christine said. She heaved herself out of the bathtub, swathed her pink bulk in a towel and splattered to the phone.

"Hello," she said gruffly. At a distance he was not pathetic, he was a nuisance. She could not imagine how he had tracked her down: most likely he went through the phone book, calling all the numbers with her last name until he hit on the right one.

"It is your friend."

"I know," she said. "How are you?"

"I am very fine." There was a long pause, during which Christine had a vicious urge to say, "Well, goodbye then," and hang up; but she was aware of her mother poised figurine-like in her bedroom doorway. Then he said, "I hope you also are very fine."

"Yes," said Christine. She wasn't going to participate.

"I come to tea," he said.

This took Christine by surprise. "You do?"

"Your pleasant mother ask me. I come Thursday, four o'clock."

"Oh," Christine said, ungraciously.

"See you then," he said, with the conscious pride of one who has mastered a difficult idiom.

Christine set down the phone and went along the hall. Her mother was in her study, sitting innocently at her writing desk.

"Did you ask him to tea on Thursday?"

"Not exactly, dear," her mother said. "I did mention he might come round to tea *some*time, though."

"Well, he's coming Thursday. Four o'clock."

"What's wrong with that?" her mother said serenely. "I think it's a very nice gesture for us to make. I do think you might try to be a little more co-operative." She was pleased with herself.

"Since you invited him," said Christine, "you can bloody well stick around and help me entertain him. I don't want to be left making nice gestures all by myself."

"Christine *dear,*" her mother said, above being shocked. "You ought to put on your dressing gown, you'll catch a chill."

After sulking for an hour Christine tried to think of the tea as a cross between an examination and an executive meeting: not enjoyable, certainly, but to be got through as tactfully as possible. And it *was* a nice gesture. When the cakes her mother had ordered arrived from *The Patisserie* on Thursday morning she began to feel slightly festive; she even resolved to put on a dress, a good one, instead of a skirt and blouse. After all, she had nothing against him, except the memory of the way he had grabbed her tennis racquet and then her arm. She suppressed a quick impossible vision of herself pursued around the living room, fending him off with thrown sofa cushions and vases of gladioli; nevertheless she told the girl they would have tea in the garden. It would be a treat for him, and there was more space outdoors.

She had suspected her mother would dodge the tea, would contrive to be going out just as he was arriving: that way she could size him up and then leave them alone together. She had done things like that to Christine before; the excuse this time was the Symphony Committee. Sure enough, her mother carefully mislaid her gloves and located them with a faked murmur of joy when the doorbell rang. Christine relished for weeks afterwards the image of her mother's dropped jaw and flawless recovery when he was introduced: he wasn't quite the foreign potentate her optimistic, veil-fragile mind had concocted.

He was prepared for celebration. He had slicked on so much hair cream that his head seemed to be covered with a tight black patent-leather cap, and he had cut the threads off his jacket sleeves. His orange tie was overpoweringly splendid. Christine noticed however as he shook her mother's suddenly braced white glove that the ballpoint ink on his fingers was indelible. His face had broken out, possibly in anticipation of the delights in store for him; he had a tiny camera slung over his shoulder and was smoking an exotic-smelling cigarette.

Christine led him through the cool flowery softly padded living room and out by the French doors into the garden. "You sit here," she said. "I will have the girl bring tea."

This girl was from the West Indies: Christine's parents had been enraptured with her when they were down at Christmas and had brought her back with them. Since that time she had become pregnant, but Christine's mother had not dismissed her. She said she was slightly disappointed but what could you expect, and she didn't see any real difference between a girl who was pregnant before you hired her and one who got that way afterwards. She prided herself on her tolerance; also there was a scarcity of girls. Strangely enough, the girl became progressively less easy to get along with. Either she did not share Christine's mother's view of her own generosity, or she felt she had gotten away with something and was therefore free to indulge in contempt. At first Christine had tried to treat her as an equal. "Don't call me 'Miss Christine,' " she had said with an imitation of light, comradely laughter. "What you want me to call you then?" the girl had said, scowling. They had begun to have brief, surly arguments in the kitchen, which Christine decided were like the arguments between one servant and another: her mother's attitude towards each of them was similar, they were not altogether satisfactory but they would have to do.

The cakes, glossy with icing, were set out on a plate and the teapot was standing ready; on the counter the electric kettle boiled. Christine headed for it, but the girl, till then sitting with her elbows on the kitchen table and watching her expressionlessly, made a dash and intercepted her. Christine waited until she had poured the water into the pot. Then, "I'll carry it out, Elvira," she said. She had just decided she didn't want the girl to see her visitor's orange tie; already, she knew, her position in the girl's eyes had suffered because no one had yet attempted to get *her* pregnant.

"What you think they pay me for, Miss Christine?" the girl said insolently. She swung towards the garden with the tray; Christine trailed her, feeling lumpish and awkward. The girl was at least as big as she was but she was big in a different way.

"Thank you, Elvira," Christine said when the tray was in place. The girl departed without a word, casting a disdainful backward glance at the frayed jacket sleeves, the stained fingers. Christine was now determined to be especially kind to him.

"You are very rich," he said.

"No," Christine protested, shaking her head; "we're not." She had never thought of her family as rich, it was one of her father's sayings that nobody made any money with the Government.

"Yes," he repeated, "you are very rich." He sat back in his lawn chair, gazing about him as though dazed.

Christine set his cup of tea in front of him. She wasn't in the habit of paying much attention to the house or the garden; they were nothing special, far from being the largest on the street; other people took care of them. But now she looked where he was looking, seeing it all as though from a different height: the long expanses, the border flowers blazing in the early-summer sunlight, the flagged patio and walks, the high walls and the silence.

He came back to her face, sighing a little. "My English is not good," he said, "but I improve."

"You do," Christine said, nodding encouragement.

He took sips of his tea, quickly and tenderly as though afraid of injuring the cup. "I like to stay here."

Christine passed him the cakes. He took only one, making a slight face as he ate it; but he had several more cups of tea while she finished the cakes. She managed to find out from him that he had come over on a Church fellowship—she could not decode the denomination—and was studying Philosophy or Theology, or possibly both. She was feeling well-disposed towards him: he had behaved himself, he had caused her no inconvenience.

The teapot was at last empty. He sat up straight in his chair, as though alerted by a soundless gong. "You look this way, please," he said. Christine saw that he had placed his miniature camera on the stone sundial her mother had shipped back from England two years before: he wanted to take her picture. She was flattered, and settled herself to pose, smiling evenly.

He took off his glasses and laid them beside his plate. For a moment she saw his myopic, unprotected eyes turned towards her, with something tremulous and confiding in them she wanted to close herself off from knowing about. Then he went over and did something to the camera, his back to her. The next instant he was crouched beside her, his arm around her waist as far as it could reach, his other hand covering her own hands which she had folded in her lap, his cheek jammed up against hers. She was too startled to move. The camera clicked.

He stood up at once and replaced his glasses, which glittered now with a sad triumph. "Thank you, Miss," he said to her. "I go now." He slung the camera back over his shoulder, keeping his hand on it as though to hold the lid on and prevent escape. "I send to my family; they will like."

He was out the gate and gone before Christine had recovered; then she laughed. She had been afraid he would attack her, she could admit it now, and he had; but not in the usual way. He had raped, *rapeo, rapere, rapui, to seize and carry off,* not herself but her celluloid image, and incidently that of the silver tea service, which glinted mockingly at her as the girl bore it away, carrying it regally, the insignia, the official jewels.

Christine spent the summer as she had for the past three years: she was the sailing instructress at an expensive all-girls camp near Algonquin Park. She had been a camper there, everything was familiar to her; she sailed almost better than she played tennis.

The second week she got a letter from him, postmarked Montreal and forwarded from her home address. It was printed in block letters on a piece of green paper, two or three sentences. It began, "I hope you are well," then described the weather in monosyllables and ended, "I am fine." It was signed "Your friend." Each week she got another of these letters, more or less identical. In one of them a colour print was enclosed: himself, slightly cross-eyed and grinning hilariously, even more spindly than she remembered him against her billowing draperies, flowers exploding around them like firecrackers, one of his hands an equivocal blur in her lap, the other out of sight; on her own face, astonishment and outrage, as though he was sticking her in the behind with his hidden thumb.

She answered the first letter, but after that the seniors were in training for the races. At the end of the summer, packing to go home, she threw all the letters away.

When she had been back for several weeks she received another of the green letters. This time there was a return address printed at the top which Christine noted with foreboding was in her own city. Every day she waited for the phone to ring; she was so certain his first attempt at contact would be a disembodied voice that when he came upon her abruptly in mid-campus she was unprepared.

"How are you?"

His smile was the same, but everything else about him had deteriorated. He was, if possible, thinner; his jacket sleeves had sprouted a lush new crop of threads, as though to conceal hands now so badly bitten they appeared to have been gnawed by rodents. His hair fell over his eyes, uncut, ungreased; his eyes in the hollowed face, a delicate triangle of skin stretched on bone, jumped behind his glasses like hooked fish. He had the end of a cigarette in the corner of his mouth and as they walked he lit a new one from it.

"I'm fine," Christine said. She was thinking, I'm not going to get involved again, enough is enough, I've done my bit for internationalism. "How are you?"

"I live here now," he said. "Maybe I study Economics."

"That's nice." He didn't sound as though he was enrolled anywhere.

"I come to see you."

Christine didn't know whether he meant he had left Montreal in order to be near her or just wanted to visit her at her house as he had done in the spring; either way she refused to be implicated. They were outside the Political Science building. "I have a class here," she said. "Goodbye." She was being callous, she realized that, but a quick chop was more merciful in the long run, that was what her beautiful sisters used to say.

Afterwards she decided it had been stupid of her to let him find out where her class was. Though a timetable was posted in each of the colleges: all he had to do was look her up and record her every probable movement in block letters on his green notepad. After that day he never left her alone.

Initially he waited outside the lecture rooms for her to come out. She said Hello to him curtly at first and kept on going, but this didn't work; he followed her at a distance, smiling his changeless smile. Then she stopped speaking altogether and pretended to ignore him, but it made no difference, he followed her anyway. The fact that she was in some way afraid of him— or was it just embarrassment?—seemed only to encourage him. Her friends started to notice, asking her who he was and why he was tagging along behind her; she could hardly answer because she hardly knew.

As the weekdays passed and he showed no signs of letting up, she began to jog-trot between classes, finally to run. He was tireless, and had an amazing wind for one who smoked so heavily: he would speed along behind her, keeping the distance between them the same, as though he was a pull-toy attached to her by a string. She was aware of the ridiculous spectacle they must make, galloping across campus, something out of a cartoon short, a lumbering elephant stampeded by a smiling, emaciated mouse, both of them locked in the classic pattern of comic pursuit and flight; but she found that to race made her less nervous than to walk sedately, the skin on the back of her neck crawling with the feel of his eyes on it. At least she could use her muscles. She worked out routines, escapes: she would dash in the front door of the Ladies' Room in the coffee shop and out the back door, and he would lose the trail, until he discovered the other entrance. She would try to shake him by detours through baffling archways and corridors, but he seemed as familiar with the architectural mazes as she was herself. As a last refuge she could head for the women's dormitory and watch from safety as he was skidded to a halt by the receptionist's austere voice: men were not allowed past the entrance.

Lunch became difficult. She would be sitting, usually with other members of the Debating Society, just digging nicely into a sandwich, when he would appear suddenly as though he'd come up through an unseen manhole. She then had the choice of barging out through the crowded cafeteria, sandwich half-eaten, or finishing her lunch with him standing behind her chair, everyone at the table acutely aware of him, the conversation stilting and dwindling. Her friends learned to spot him from a distance; they posted lookouts. "Here he comes," they would whisper, helping her collect her belongings for the sprint they knew would follow.

Several times she got tired of running and turned to confront him. "What do you want?" she would ask, glowering belligerently down at him, almost clenching her fists; she felt like shaking him, hitting him.

"I wish to talk with you."

"Well, here I am," she would say. "What do you want to talk about?"

But he would say nothing; he would stand in front of her, shifting his feet, smiling perhaps apologetically (though she could never pinpoint the exact tone of that smile, chewed lips stretched apart over the nicotine-yellowed teeth, rising at the corners, flesh held stiffly in place for an invisible photographer), his eyes jerking from one part of her face to another as though he saw her in fragments.

Annoying and tedious though it was, his pursuit of her had an odd result: mysterious in itself, it rendered her equally mysterious. No-one had ever found Christine mysterious before. To her parents she was a beefy heavyweight, a plodder, lacking in flair, ordinary as bread. To her sisters she was the plain one, treated with an indulgence they did not give to each other: they did not fear her as a rival. To her male friends she was the one who could be relied on. She was helpful and a hard worker, always good for a game of tennis with the athletes among them. They invited her along to drink beer with them so they could get into the cleaner, more desirable Ladies and Escorts side of the beer parlour, taking it for granted she would buy her share of the rounds. In moments of stress they confided to her their problems with women. There was nothing devious about her and nothing interesting.

Christine had always agreed with these estimates of herself. In childhood she had identified with the False Bride or the ugly sister; whenever a story had begun, "Once there was a maiden as beautiful as she was good," she had known it wasn't her. That was just how it was, but it wasn't so bad. Her parents never expected her to be a brilliant social success and weren't overly disappointed when she wasn't. She was spared the maneuvering and anxiety she witnessed among others her age, and she even had a kind of special position among men: she was an exception, she fitted none of the categories they commonly used when talking about girls, she wasn't a cockteaser, a cold fish, an easy lay or a snarky bitch; she was an honorary person. She had grown to share their contempt for most women.

Now however there was something about her that could not be explained. A man was chasing her, a peculiar sort of man, granted, but still a man, and he was without doubt attracted to her, he couldn't leave her alone. Other men examined her more closely than they ever had, appraising her, trying to find out what it was those twitching bespectacled eyes saw in her. They started to ask her out, though they returned from these excursions with their curiosity unsatisfied, the secret of her charm still intact. Her opaque dumpling face, her solid bear-shaped body became for them parts of a riddle no-one could solve. Christine knew this and began to use it. In the bathtub she no longer imagined she was a dolphin; instead she imagined she was an elusive water-nixie, or sometimes, in moments of audacity, Marilyn Monroe. The daily chase was becoming a habit; she even looked forward to it. In addition to its other benefits she was losing weight.

All those weeks he had never phoned her or turned up at the house. He must have decided however that his tactics were not having the desired result, or perhaps he sensed she was becoming bored. The phone began to ring in the early morning or late at night when he could be sure she would be there. Sometimes he would simply breathe (she could recognize, or thought she could, the quality of his breathing), in which case she would hang up. Occasionally he would say again that he wanted to talk to her, but even when she gave him lots of time nothing else would follow. Then he extended his range: she would see him on her streetcar, smiling at her silently from a seat never closer than three away; she could feel him tracking her down her own street, though when she would break her resolve to pay no attention and would glance back he would be invisible or in the act of hiding behind a tree or hedge.

Among crowds of people and in daylight she had not really been afraid of him; she was stronger than he was and he had made no recent attempt to touch her. But the days were growing shorter and colder, it was almost November, often she was arriving home in twilight or a darkness broken only by the feeble orange streetlamps. She brooded over the possibility of razors, knives, guns; by acquiring a weapon he could quickly turn the odds against her. She avoided wearing scarves, remembering the newspaper stories about girls who had been strangled by them. Putting on her nylons in the morning gave her a funny feeling. Her body seemed to have diminished, to have become smaller than his.

Was he deranged, was he a sex maniac? He seemed so harmless, yet it was that kind who often went berserk in the end. She pictured those ragged fingers at her throat, tearing at her clothes, though she could not think of herself as screaming. Parked cars, the shrubberies near her house, the driveways on either side of it, changed as she passed them from unnoticed background to sinisterly shadowed foreground, every detail distinct and harsh: they were places a man might crouch, leap out from. Yet every time she saw him in the clear light of morning or afternoon (for he still continued his old methods of pursuit), his aging jacket and jittery eyes convinced her that it was she herself who was the tormentor, the persecutor. She was in some sense responsible; from the folds and crevices of the body she had treated for so long as a reliable machine was emanating, against her will, some potent invisible odour, like a dog's in heat or a female moth's, that made him unable to stop following her.

Her mother, who had been too preoccupied with the unavoidable fall entertaining to pay much attention to the number of phone calls Christine was getting or to the hired girl's complaints of a man who hung up without speaking, announced that she was flying down to New York for the weekend; her father decided to go too. Christine panicked: she saw herself in the bathtub with her throat slit, the blood drooling out of her neck and running in a little spiral down the drain (for by this time she believed he could walk through walls, could be everywhere at once). The girl would do nothing to help; she might even stand in the bathroom door with her arms folded, watching. Christine arranged to spend the weekend at her married sister's.

When she arrived back Sunday evening she found the girl close to hysterics. She said that on Saturday she had gone to pull the curtains across the French doors at dusk and had found a strangely contorted face, a man's face, pressed against the glass, staring in at her from the garden. She claimed she had fainted and had almost had her baby a month too early right there on the living-room carpet. Then she had called the police. He was gone by the time they got there but she had recognized him from the afternoon of the tea; she had informed them he was a friend of Christine's.

They called Monday evening to investigate, two of them; they were very polite, they knew who Christine's father was. Her father greeted them heartily; her mother hovered in the background, fidgeting with her porcelain hands, letting them see how frail and worried she was. She didn't like having them in the living room but they were necessary.

Christine had to admit he'd been following her around. She was relieved he'd been discovered, relieved also that she hadn't been the one to tell, though if he'd been a citizen of the country she would have called the police a long time ago. She insisted he was not dangerous, he had never hurt her.

"That kind don't hurt you," one of the policemen said. "They just kill you. You're lucky you aren't dead."

"Nut cases," the other one said.

Her mother volunteered that the thing about people from another culture was that you could never tell whether they were insane or not because their ways were so different. The policeman agreed with her, deferential but also condescending, as though she was a royal halfwit who had to be humoured.

"You know where he lives?" the first policeman asked. Christine had long ago torn up the letter with his address on it; she shook her head.

"We'll have to pick him up tomorrow then," he said. "Think you can keep him talking outside your class if he's waiting for you?"

After questioning her they held a murmured conversation with her father in the front hall. The girl, clearing away the coffee cups, said if they didn't lock him up she was leaving, she wasn't going to be scared half out of her skin like that again.

Next day when Christine came out of her Modern History lecture he was there, right on schedule. He seemed puzzled when she did not begin to run. She approached him, her heart thumping with treachery and the prospect of freedom. Her body was back to its usual size; she felt herself a giantess, self-controlled, invulnerable.

"How are you?" she asked, smiling brightly.

He looked at her with distrust.

"How have you been?" she ventured again. His own perennial smile faded; he took a step back from her.

"This the one?" said the policeman, popping out from behind a notice board like a Keystone Cop and laying a competent hand on the worn jacket shoulder. The other policeman lounged in the background; force would not be required.

"Don't *do* anything to him," she pleaded as they took him away. They nodded and grinned, respectful, scornful. He seemed to know perfectly well who they were and what they wanted.

The first policeman phoned that evening to make his report. Her father talked with him, jovial and managing. She herself was now out of the picture; she had been protected, her function was over.

"What did they *do* to him?" she asked anxiously as he came back into the living room. She was not sure what went on in police stations.

"They didn't do anything to him," he said, amused by her concern. "They could have booked him for Watching and Besetting, they wanted to know if I'd like to press charges. But it's not worth a court case: he's got a visa that says he's only allowed in the country as long as he studies in Montreal, so I told them to just ship him up there. If he turns up here again they'll deport him. They went around to his rooming house, his rent's two weeks overdue; the landlady said she was on the point of kicking him out. He seems happy enough to be getting his back rent paid and a free train ticket to Montreal." He paused. "They couldn't get anything out of him though."

"*Out* of him?" Christine asked.

"They tried to find out why he was doing it; following you, I mean." Her father's eyes swept her as though it was a riddle to him also. "They said when they asked him about that he just clammed up. Pretended he didn't understand English. He understood well enough, but he wasn't answering."

Christine thought it was the end, but somehow between his arrest and the departure of the train he managed to elude his escort long enough for one more phone call.

"I see you again," he said. He didn't wait for her to hang up.

Now that he was no longer an embarrassing present reality he could be talked about, he could become an amusing story. In fact he was the only amusing story Christine had to tell, and telling it preserved both for herself and for others the aura of her strange allure. Her friends and the men who continued to ask her out speculated about his motives. One suggested he had wanted to marry her so he could remain in the country; another said that oriental men were fond of well-built women: "It's your Rubens quality."

Christine thought about him a lot. She had not been attracted to him, rather the reverse, but as an idea only he was a romantic figure, the one man who had found her irresistible; though she often wondered, inspecting her unchanged pink face and hefty body in her full-length mirror, just what it was about her that had done it. She avoided whenever it was proposed the theory of his insanity: it was only that there was more than one way of being sane.

But a new acquaintance, hearing the story for the first time, had a different explanation. "So he got you too," he said, laughing. "That has to be the same guy who was hanging around our day camp a year ago this summer. He followed all the girls like that. A short guy, Japanese or something, glasses, smiling all the time."

"Maybe it was another one," Christine said.

"There couldn't be two of them, everything fits. This was a pretty weird guy."

"What . . . kind of girls did he follow?" Christine asked.

"Oh, just anyone who happed to be around. But if they paid any attention to him at first, if they were nice to him or anything, he was unshakeable. He was a bit of a pest, but harmless."

Christine ceased to tell her amusing story. She had been one among many, then. She went back to playing tennis, she had been neglecting her game.

A few months later the policeman who had been in charge of the case telephoned her again.

"Like you to know, Miss, that fellow you were having the trouble with was sent back to his own country. Deported."

"What for?" Christine asked. "Did he try to come back here?" Maybe she had been special after all, maybe he had dared everything for her.

"Nothing like it," the policeman said. "He was up to the same tricks in Montreal but he really picked the wrong woman this time—a Mother Superior of a convent. They don't stand for things like that in Quebec—had him out of here before he knew what happened. I guess he'll be better off in his own place."

"How old was she?" Christine asked, after a silence.

"Oh, around sixty, I guess."

"Thank you very much for letting me know," Christine said in her best official manner. "It's such a relief." She wondered if the policeman had called to make fun of her.

She was almost crying when she put down the phone. What had he wanted from her then? A Mother Superior. Did she really look sixty, did she look like a mother? What did convents mean? Comfort, charity? Refuge? Was it that something had happened to him, some intolerable strain just from being in this country; her tennis dress and exposed legs too much for him, flesh and money seemingly available everywhere but withheld from him wherever he turned, the nun the symbol of some final distortion, the robe and the veil reminiscent to his nearsighted eyes of the women of his homeland, the ones he was able to understand? But he was back in his own country, remote from her as another planet; she would never know.

He hadn't forgotten her though. In the spring she got a postcard with a foreign stamp and the familiar block-letter writing. On the front was a picture of a temple. He was fine, he hoped she was fine also, he was her friend. A month later another print of the picture he had taken in the garden arrived, in a sealed manila envelope otherwise empty.

Christine's aura of mystery soon faded away; anyway, she herself no longer believed in it. Life became again what she had always expected. She graduated with mediocre grades and went into the Department of Health and Welfare; she did a good job, and was seldom discriminated against for being a woman because nobody thought of her as one. She could afford a pleasant-sized apartment, though she did not put much energy into decorating it. She played less and less tennis; what had been muscle with a light coating of fat turned gradually to fat with a thin substratum of muscle. She began to get headaches.

As the years were used up and the war began to fill the newspapers and magazines, she realized which eastern country he had actually been from. She had known the name but it hadn't registered at the time, it was such a minor place; she could never keep them separate in her mind.

But though she tried, she couldn't remember the name of the city, and the postcard was long gone—had he been from the North or the South, was he near the battle zone or safely from it? Obsessively she bought the magazines and poured over the available photographs, dead villagers, soldiers on the march, colour blow-ups of frightened or angry faces, spies being executed; she studied maps, she watched the late-night newscasts, the distant country and terrain becoming almost more familiar to her than her own. Once or twice she thought she could recognize him but it was no use, they all looked like him.

Finally she had to stop looking at the pictures. It bothered her too much, it was bad for her; she was beginning to have nightmares in which he was coming through the French doors of her mother's house in his shabby jacket, carrying a packsack and a rifle and a huge bouquet of richly-coloured flowers. He was smiling in the same way but with blood streaked over his face, partly blotting out the features. She gave her television set away and took to reading nineteenth century novels instead; Trollope and Galsworthy were her favourites. When, despite herself, she would think about him, she would tell herself that he had been crafty and agile-minded enough to survive, more or less, in her country, so surely he would be able to do it in his own, where he knew the language. She could not see him in the army, on either side; he wasn't the type, and to her knowledge he had not believed in any particular ideology. He would be something nondescript, something in the background, like herself; perhaps he had become an interpreter.

JASMINE

Jasmine came to Detroit from Port-of-Spain, Trinidad, by way of Canada. She crossed the border at Windsor in the back of a gray van loaded with mattresses and box springs. The plan was for her to hide in an empty mattress box if she heard the driver say, "All bad weather seems to come down from Canada, doesn't it?" to the customs man. But she didn't have to crawl into a box and hold her breath. The customs man didn't ask to look in.

The driver let her off at a scary intersection on Woodward Avenue and gave her instructions on how to get to the Plantations Motel in Southfield. The trick was to keep changing vehicles, he said. That threw off the immigration guys real quick.

Jasmine took money for cab fare out of the pocket of the great big raincoat that the van driver had given her. The raincoat looked like something that nuns in Port-of-Spain sold in church bazaars. Jasmine was glad to have a coat with wool lining, though; and anyway, who would know in Detroit that she was Dr. Vassanji's daughter?

All the bills in her hand looked the same. She would have to be careful when she paid the cabdriver. Money in Detroit wasn't pretty the way it was back home, or even in Canada, but she liked this money better. Why should money be pretty, like a picture? Pretty money is only good for putting on your walls maybe. The dollar bills felt businesslike, serious. Back home at work, she used to count out thousands of Trinidad dollars every day and not even think of them as real. Real money was worn and green, American dollars. Holding the bills in her fist on a street corner meant she had made it in okay. She'd outsmarted the guys at the border. Now it was up to her to use her wits to do something with her life. As her Daddy kept saying, "Girl, is opportunity come only once." The girls she'd worked with at the bank in Port-of-Spain had gone green as bananas when she'd walked in with her ticket on Air

Canada. Trinidad was too tiny. That was the trouble. Trinidad was an island stuck in the middle of nowhere. What kind of place was that for a girl with ambition?

The Plantations Motel was run by a family of Trinidad Indians who had come from the tuppennyha'penny country town, Chaguanas. The Daboos were nobodies back home. They were lucky, that's all. They'd gotten here before the rush and bought up a motel and an ice cream parlor. Jasmine felt very superior when she saw Mr. Daboo in the motel's reception area. He was a pumpkin-shaped man with very black skin and Elvis Presley sideburns turning white. They looked like earmuffs. Mrs. Daboo was a bumpkin, too; short, fat, flapping around in house slippers. The Daboo daughters seemed very American, though. They didn't seem to know that they were nobodies, and kept looking at her and giggling.

She knew she would be short of cash for a great long while. Besides, she wasn't sure she wanted to wear bright leather boots and leotards like Viola and Loretta. The smartest move she could make would be to put a down payment on a husband. Her Daddy had told her to talk to the Daboos first chance. The Daboos ran a service fixing up illegals with islanders who had made it in legally. Daddy had paid three thousand back in Trinidad, with the Daboos and the mattress man getting part of it. They should throw in a good-earning husband for that kind of money.

The Daboos asked her to keep books for them and to clean the rooms in the new wing, and she could stay in 16B as long as she liked. They showed her 16B. They said she could cook her own roti; Mr. Daboo would bring in a stove, two gas rings that you could fold up in a metal box. The room was quite grand, Jasmine thought. It had a double bed, a TV, a pink sink and matching bathtub. Mrs. Daboo said Jasmine wasn't the big-city Port-of-Spain type she'd expected. Mr. Daboo said that he wanted her to stay because it was nice to have a neat, cheerful person around. It wasn't a bad deal, better than stories she'd heard about Trinidad girls in the States.

All day every day except Sundays Jasmine worked. There wasn't just the bookkeeping and the cleaning up. Mr. Daboo had her working on the match-up marriage service. Jasmine's job was to check up on social security cards, call clients' bosses for references, and make sure credit information wasn't false. Dermatologists and engineers living in Bloomfield Hills, store owners on Canfield and Woodward: she treated them all as potential liars. One of the first things she learned was that Ann Arbor was a magic word. A boy goes to Ann Arbor and gets an education, and all the barriers come crashing down. So Ann Arbor was the place to be.

She didn't mind the work. She was learning about Detroit, every side of it. Sunday mornings she helped unload packing crates of Caribbean spices in a shop on the next block. For the first time in her life, she was working for a black man, an African. So what if the boss was black? This was a new life, and she wanted to learn everything. Her Sunday boss, Mr. Anthony, was a courtly, Christian, church-going man, and paid her the only wages she had in her pocket. Viola and Loretta, for all their fancy American ways, wouldn't go out with blacks.

One Friday afternoon she was writing up the credit info on a Guyanese Muslim who worked in an assembly plant when Loretta said that enough was enough and that there was no need for Jasmine to be her father's drudge.

"Is time to have fun," Viola said. "We're going to Ann Arbor."

Jasmine filed the sheet on the Guyanese man who probably now would never get a wife and got her raincoat. Loretta's boyfriend had a Cadillac parked out front. It was the longest car Jasmine had ever been in and louder than a country bus. Viola's boyfriend got out of the front seat. "Oh, oh, sweet things," he said to Jasmine. "Get in front." He was a talker. She'd learned that much from working on the matrimonial match-ups. She didn't believe him for a second when he said that there were dudes out there dying to ask her out.

Loretta's boyfriend said, "You have eyes I could leap into, girl."

Jasmine knew he was just talking. They sounded like Port-of-Spain boys of three years ago. It didn't surprise her that these Trinidad country boys in Detroit were still behind the times, even of Port-of-Spain. She sat very stiff between the two men, hands on her purse. The Daboo girls laughed in the back seat.

On the highway the girls told her about the reggae night in Ann Arbor. Kevin and the Krazee Islanders. Malcolm's Lovers. All the big reggae groups in the Midwest were converging for the West Indian Students Association fall bash. The ticket didn't come cheap but Jasmine wouldn't let the fellows pay. She wasn't that kind of girl.

The reggae and steel drums brought out the old Jasmine. The rum punch, the dancing, the dreadlocks, the whole combination. She hadn't heard real music since she got to Detroit, where music was supposed to be so famous. The Daboos girls kept turning on rock stuff in the motel lobby whenever their father left the area. She hadn't danced, really *danced,* since she'd left home. It felt so good to dance. She felt hot and sweaty and sexy. The boys at the dance were more than sweet talkers; they moved with assurance and spoke of their futures in America. The bartender gave her two free drinks and said, "Is ready when you are, girl." She ignored him but she felt all hot and good deep inside. She knew Ann Arbor was a special place.

When it was time to pile back into Loretta's boyfriend's Cadillac, she just couldn't face going back to the Plantations Motel and to the Daboos with their accounting books and messy files.

"I don't know what happen, girl," she said to Loretta. "I feel all crazy inside. Maybe is time for me to pursue higher studies in this town."

"This Ann Arbor, girl, they don't just take you off the street. It *cost* like hell."

She spent the night on a bashed-up sofa in the Student Union. She was a well-dressed, respectable girl, and she didn't expect anyone to question her right to sleep on the furniture. Many others were doing the same thing. In the morning, a boy in an army parka showed her the way to the Placement Office. He was a big, blond, clumsy boy, not bad-looking except for the blond eyelashes. He didn't scare her, as did most Americans. She let him buy her a Coke and a hotdog. That evening she had a job with the Moffitts.

Bill Moffitt taught molecular biology and Lara Hatch-Moffitt, his wife, was a performance artist. A performance artist, said Lara, was very different from being an actress, though Jasmine still didn't understand what the difference might be. The Moffitts had a little girl, Muffin, whom Jasmine was to look after, though for the first few months she might have to help out with the housework and the cooking because Lara said she was deep into performance rehearsals. That was all right with her, Jasmine said, maybe a little too quickly. She explained she came from a big family and was used to heavy-duty cooking and cleaning. This wasn't the time to say anything about Ram, the family servant. Americans like the Moffitts wouldn't understand about keeping servants. Ram and she weren't in similar situations. Here mother's helpers, which is what Lara had called her—Americans were good with words to cover their shame—seemed to be as good as anyone.

Lara showed her the room she would have all to herself in the finished basement. There was a big, old TV, not in color like the motel's and a portable typewriter on a desk which Lara said she would find handy when it came time to turn in her term papers. Jasmine didn't say anything about not being a student. She was a student of life, wasn't she? There was a scary moment after they'd discussed what she could expect as salary, which was three times more than anything Mr. Daboo was supposed to pay her but hadn't. She thought Bill Moffitt was going to ask her about her visa or her green card number and social security. But all Bill did was smile and smile at her—he had a wide, pink, baby face—and play with a button on his corduroy jacket. The button would need sewing back on, firmly.

Lara said, "I think I'm going to like you, Jasmine. You have a something about you. A something real special. I'll just bet you've acted, haven't you?" The idea amused her, but she merely smiled and accepted Lara's hug. The interview was over.

Then Bill opened a bottle of Soave and told stories about camping in northern Michigan. He'd been raised there. Jasmine didn't see the point in sleeping in tents; the woods sounded cold and wild and creepy. But she said, "Is exactly what I want to try out come summer, man. Campin and huntin."

Lara asked about Port-of-Spain. There was nothing to tell about her hometown that wouldn't shame her in front of nice white American folk like the Moffitts. The place was shabby, the people were grasping and cheating and lying and life was full of despair and drink and wanting. But by the time she finished, the island sounded romantic. Lara said, "It wouldn't surprise me one bit if you were a writer, Jasmine."

Ann Arbor was a huge small town. She couldn't imagine any kind of school the size of the University of Michigan. She meant to sign up for courses in the spring. Bill brought home a catalogue bigger than the phonebook for all of Trinidad. The university had courses in everything. It would be hard to choose; she'd have to get help from Bill. He wasn't like a professor, not the ones back home where even high school teachers called themselves professors and acted like little potentates. He wore blue jeans and thick sweaters with holes in the elbows and used phrases like "in vitro" as he watched her curry up fish. Dr. Parveen back home—he called himself "doctor" when everybody knew he didn't have even a Master's degree—was never seen without his cotton jacket which had gotten really ratty at the cuffs and lapel edges. She hadn't learned anything in the two years she'd put into college. She'd learned more from working in the bank for two months than she had at college. It was the assistant manager, Personal Loans Department, Mr. Singh, who had turned her on to the Daboos and to smooth, bargain-priced emigration.

Jasmine liked Lara. Lara was easygoing. She didn't spend the time she had between rehearsals telling Jasmine how to cook and clean American-style. Mrs. Daboo did that in 16B. Mrs. Daboo would barge in with a plate of stale samosas and snoop around giving free advice on how mainstream Americans did things. As if she were dumb or something! As if she couldn't keep her own eyes open and make her mind up for herself. Sunday mornings she had to share the butcher-block workspace in the kitchen with Bill. He made the Sunday brunch from new recipes in *Gourmet* and *Cuisine*. Jasmine hadn't seen a man cook who didn't have to or wasn't getting paid to do it. Things were topsy-turvy in the Moffitt house. Lara went on two- and three-day road trips and Bill stayed home. But even her Daddy, who'd never poured himself a cup of tea, wouldn't put Bill down as a woman. The mornings Bill tried out something complicated, a Cajun shrimp, sausage, and beans dish, for instance, Jasmine skipped church services. The Moffitts didn't go to church, though they seemed to be good Christians. They just didn't talk church talk, which suited her fine.

Two months passed. Jasmine knew she was lucky to have found a small, clean, friendly family like the Moffitts to build her new life around. "Man!" she'd exclaim as she vacuumed the wide-plank wood floors or ironed (Lara wore pure silk or pure cotton). "In this country Jesus givin out good luck only!" By this time they knew she wasn't a student, but they didn't care and said they wouldn't report her. They never asked if she was illegal on top of it.

To savor her new sense of being a happy, lucky person, she would put herself through a series of "what ifs": what if Mr. Singh in Port-of-Spain hadn't turned her on to the Daboos and loaned her two thousand! What if she'd been ugly like the Mintoo girl and the manager hadn't even offered! What if the customs man had unlocked the door of the van! Her Daddy liked to say, "You is a helluva girl, Jasmine."

"Thank you, Jesus," Jasmine said, as she carried on.

Christmas Day the Moffitts treated her just like family. They gave her a red cashmere sweater with a V neck so deep it made her blush. If Lara had worn it, her bosom wouldn't hang out like melons. For the holiday weekend Bill drove her to the Daboos in Detroit. "You work too hard," Bill said to her. "Learn to be more selfish. Come on, throw your weight around." She'd rather not have spent time with the Daboos, but that first afternoon of the interview she'd told Bill and Lara that Mr. Daboo was her mother's first cousin. She had thought it shameful in those days to have no papers, no family, no roots. Now Loretta and Viola in tight, bright pants seemed trashy like girls at Two-Johnny Bissoondath's Bar back home. She was stuck with the story of the Daboos being family. Village bumpkins, ha! She would break out. Soon.

Jasmine had Bill drop her off at the RenCen. The Plantations Motel, in fact, the whole Riverfront area, was too seamy. She'd managed to cut herself off mentally from anything too islandy. She loved her Daddy and Mummy, but she didn't think of them that often anymore. Mummy had expected her to be homesick and come flying right back home. "Is blowin sweat-of-brow money is what you doin, Pa," Mummy had scolded. She loved them, but she'd become her own person. That was something that Lara said: "I am my own person."

The Daboos acted thrilled to see her back. "What you drinkin, Jasmine girl?" Mr. Daboo kept asking. "You drinkin sherry or what?" Pouring her little glasses of sherry instead of rum was a sure sign he thought she had become whitefolk-fancy. The Daboo sisters were very friendly, but Jasmine considered them too wild. Both Loretta and Viola had changed boyfriends. Both were seeing black men they'd danced with in Ann Arbor. Each night at bedtime, Mr. Daboo cried. "In Trinidad we stayin we side, they stayin they side. Here, everything mixed up. Is helluva confusion, no?"

On New Year's Eve the Daboo girls and their black friends went to a dance. Mr. and Mrs. Daboo and Jasmine watched TV for a while. Then Mr.

Daboo got out a brooch from his pocket and pinned it on Jasmine's red sweater. It was a Christmasy brooch, a miniature sleigh loaded down with snowed-on mistletoe. Before she could pull away, he kissed her on the lips. "Good luck for the New Year!" he said. She lifted her head and saw tears. "Is year for dreams comin true."

Jasmine started to cry, too. There was nothing wrong, but Mr. Daboo, Mrs. Daboo, she, everybody was crying.

What for? This is where she wanted to be. She'd spent some damned uncomfortable times with the assistant manager to get approval for her loan. She thought of Daddy. He would be playing poker and fanning himself with a magazine. Her married sisters would be rolling out the dough for stacks and stacks of roti, and Mummy would be steamed purple from stirring the big pot of goat curry on the stove. She missed them. But. It felt strange to think of anyone celebrating New Year's Eve in summery clothes.

In March Lara and her performing group went on the road. Jasmine knew that the group didn't work from scripts. The group didn't use a stage, either; instead, it took over supermarkets, senior citizens' centers, and school halls, without notice. Jasmine didn't understand the performance world. But she was glad that Lara said, "I'm not going to lay a guilt trip on myself. Muffie's in super hands," before she left.

Muffie didn't need much looking after. She played Trivial Pursuit all day, usually pretending to be two persons, sometimes Jasmine, whose accent she could imitate. Since Jasmine didn't know any of the answers, she couldn't help. Muffie was a quiet, precocious child with see-through blue eyes like her dad's, and red braids. In the early evenings Jasmine cooked supper, something special she hadn't forgotten from her island days. After supper she and Muffie watched some TV, and Bill read. When Muffie went to bed, Bill and she sat together for a bit with their glasses of Soave. Bill, Muffie, and she were a family, almost.

Down in her basement room that late, dark winter, she had trouble sleeping. She wanted to stay awake and think of Bill. Even when she fell asleep it didn't feel like sleep because Bill came barging into her dreams in his funny, loose-jointed, clumsy way. It was mad to think of him all the time, and stupid and sinful; but she couldn't help it. Whenever she put back a book he'd taken off the shelf to read or whenever she put his clothes through the washer and dryer, she felt sick in a giddy, wonderful way. When Lara came back things would get back to normal. Meantime she wanted the performance group miles away.

Lara called in at least twice a week. She said things like, "We've finally obliterated the margin between realspace and performancespace." Jasmine filled her in on Muffie's doings and the mail. Bill always closed with, "I love you. We miss you, hon."

One night after Lara had called—she was in Lincoln, Nebraska—Bill said to Jasmine, "Let's dance."

She hadn't danced since the reggae night she'd had too many rum punches. Her toes began to throb and clench. She untied her apron and the fraying, knotted-up laces of her running shoes.

Bill went around the downstairs rooms turning down lights. "We need atmosphere," he said. He got a small, tidy fire going in the living room grate and pulled the Turkish scatter rug closer to it. Lara didn't like anybody walking on the Turkish rug, but Bill meant to have his way. The hissing logs, the plants in the dimmed light, the thick patterned rug: everything was changed. This wasn't the room she cleaned every day.

He stood close to her. She smoothed her skirt down with both hands.

"I want you to choose the record," he said.

"I don't know your music."

She brought her hand high to his face. His skin was baby smooth.

"I want *you* to pick," he said. "You are your own person now."

"You got island music?"

He laughed, "What do you think?" The stereo was in a cabinet with albums packed tight alphabetically into the bottom three shelves. "Calypso has not been a force in my life."

She couldn't help laughing. "Calypso? Oh, man." She pulled dust jackets out at random. Lara's records. The Flying Lizards. The Violent Fems. There was so much still to pick up on!

"This one," she said, finally.

He took the record out of her hand. "God!" he laughed. "Lara must have found this in a garage sale!" He laid the old record on the turntable. It was "Music for Lovers," something the nuns had taught her to fox-trot to way back in Port-of-Spain.

They danced so close that she could feel his heart heaving and crashing against her head. She liked it, she liked it very much. She didn't care what happened.

"Come on," Bill whispered. "If it feels right, do it." He began to take her clothes off.

"Don't, Bill," she pleaded.

"Come on, baby," he whispered again. "You're a blossom, a flower."

He took off his fisherman's knit pullover, the corduroy pants, the blue shorts. She kept pace. She'd never had such an effect on a man. He nearly flung his socks and Adidas into the fire. "You feel so good," he said. "You smell so good. You're really something, flower of Trinidad."

"Flower of Ann Arbor," she said, "not Trinidad."

She felt so good she was dizzy. She'd never felt this good on the island where men did this all the time, and girls went along with it always for favors. You couldn't feel really good in a nothing place. She was thinking this as they made love on the Turkish carpet in front of the fire: she was a bright, pretty girl with no visa, no papers, and no birth certificate. No nothing other than what she wanted to invent and tell. She was a girl rushing wildly into the future.

His hand moved up her throat and forced her lips apart and it felt so good, so right, that she forgot all the dreariness of her new life and gave herself up to it.

Tobias Wolff

SISTER

There was a park at the bottom of the hill. Now that the leaves were down Marty could see the exercise stations and part of a tennis court from her kitchen window, through a web of black branches. She took another doughnut from the box on the table and ate it slowly, watching the people at the exercise stations: two men and a woman. The woman was doing leg-raises. The men were just standing there. Though the day was cold one of the men had taken his shirt off, and even from this distance Marty was struck by the deep brown color of his skin. You hardly ever saw great tans like that on people around here, not even in summer. He had come from somewhere else.

She went into the bedroom and put on a running suit and an old pair of Adidas. The seams were giving out but her other pair was new and their whiteness made her feet look big. She took off her glasses and put her contacts in. Tears welled up under the lenses. For a few moments she lost her image in the mirror; then it returned and she saw the excitement in her face, the eagerness. *Whoa,* she thought. She sat there for a while, feeling the steady thump of the stereo in the apartment overhead. Then she rolled a joint and stuck it in the pocket of her sweatshirt.

A dog barked at Marty as she walked down the hallway. It barked at her every time she passed its door and it always took her by surprise, leaving her fluttery and breathless. The dog was a big shepherd whose owners were gone all the time. She could hear its feet scrabbling and see its nose pushed under the door. "Easy," she said, "easy there," but it kept trying to get at her, and Marty heard it barking all the way down the corridor until she reached the door and stepped outside.

It was late afternoon and cold, so cold she could see her breath. As always on Sunday the street was dead quiet, except for the skittering of leaves on the sidewalk as the breeze swept through them and ruffled the cold-looking pools of water from last night's rain. With the trees bare, the sky seemed vast. Two dark clouds drifted overhead, and in the far distance an angle of geese flew across the sky. Honkers, her brother called them. Right now he and his buddies would be banging away at them from one of the marshes outside town. By nightfall they'd all be drunk. She smiled, thinking of that.

Marty did a couple of knee-bends and headed toward the park, forcing herself to walk against the urge she felt to run. She considered taking a couple of hits off the joint in her pocket but decided against it. She didn't want to lose her edge.

The woman she'd seen at the exercise station was gone, but the two men were still there. Marty held back for a while, did a few more knee-bends and watched some boys playing football on the field behind the tennis courts. They couldn't have been more than ten or eleven but they moved like men, hunching up their shoulders and shaking their wrists as they jogged back to the huddle, grunting when they came off the line as if their bodies were big and weighty. You could tell that in their heads they had a whole stadium of people watching them. It tickled her. Marty watched them run several plays, then she walked over to the exercise stations.

When she got there she had a shock. Marty recognized one of the men, and she was so afraid he would recognize her that she almost turned around and went home. He was a regular at the Kon-Tiki. A few weeks earlier he had taken notice of Marty and they'd matched daiquiris for a couple of hours and things looked pretty good. Then she went out to the car to get this book she'd been describing to him, a book about Edgar Cayce and reincarnation, and when she got back he was sitting on the other side of the room with someone else. He hadn't left anything for the drinks, so she got stuck with the bar bill. And her lighter was missing. The man's name was Jack. When she saw him leaning against the chin-up station she didn't know what to do. She wanted to vanish right into the ground.

But he seemed not to remember her. In fact, he was the one who said hello. "Hey there," he said.

She smiled at him. Then she looked at the tan one and said, "Hi."

He didn't answer. His eyes moved over her for a moment, and he looked away. He'd put on a warm-up jacket with a hood but left the zipper open nearly to his waist. His chest was covered with little curls of glistening golden hair. The other one, Jack, had on faded army fatigues with dark patches where the insignia had been removed. He needed a shave. He was holding a quart bottle of beer.

The two men had been talking when she walked up but now they were silent. Marty felt them watching her as she did her stretches. They had been talking about sex, she was sure of that. What they'd been saying was still in the air somehow, with the ripe smell of wet leaves and the rain-soaked earth. She took a deep breath.

Then she said, "You didn't get that tan around here." She kept rocking back and forth on her knuckles but looked up at him.

"You bet your buns I didn't," he said. "The only thing you get around here is arthritis." He pulled the zipper of his jacket up and down. "Hawaii. Waikiki Beach."

"Waikiki," Jack said. "Bikini-watching capital of the world."

"Brother, you speak true," the tan one said. "They've got this special breed over there that they raise just to walk back and forth in front of you. They ought to parachute about fifty of them into Russia. Those old farts in the Kremlin would go out of their skulls. We could just walk in and take the place over."

"They could drop a couple on this place while they're at it," Jack said.

"Amen." The tan one nodded. "Make it four—two apiece."

"Aloha," Marty said. She rolled over on her back and raised her feet a few inches off the ground. She held them there for a moment, then lowered them. "That's all the Hawaiian I know," she said. "Aloha and Maui Zowie. They grow some killer weed over there."

"For sure," the tan one said. "It's God's country, sister, and that's a fact."

Jack walked up closer. "I know you from somewhere," he said.

Oh no, Marty thought. She smiled at him. "Maybe," she said. "What's your name?"

"Bill," he said.

Right, Marty wanted to say. *You bet, Jack.*

Jack looked down at her. "What's yours?"

She raised her feet again. "Elizabeth."

"Elizabeth," he repeated, slowly, so that it struck Marty how beautiful the name was. Fairfield, she almost added, but she hesitated, and the moment passed.

"I guess not," he said.

She lowered her feet and sat up. "A lot of people look like me."

He nodded.

Just then something flew past Marty's head. She jerked to one side and threw her hands up in front of her face. She gave a shudder and looked around. "Jesus," she said.

"Sorry!" someone shouted.

"Goddam Frisbees," Jack said.

"It's all right," Marty told him, and waved at the man who'd thrown it. She turned and waved again at another man some distance behind her, who was wiping the Frisbee on his shirt. He waved back.

"Frisbee freaks," Jack said. "I'm sick of them." He lifted the bottle and drank from it, then held it out to Marty. "Go on," he told her.

She took a swig. "There's more than beer in here," she said.

Jack shrugged.

"What's in here?" she asked.

"Secret formula," he answered. "Go for two. You're behind."

Marty looked at the bottle, then drank again and passed it to the other man. Even his fingers were brown. He wore a thick wedding band and a gold chain-link bracelet. She held on to the bottle for an extra moment, long enough for him to notice and give her a look; then she let go. The hood of his jacket fell back as he tilted his head to drink. Marty saw that he was nearly bald. He had parted his hair just above one ear and swept it sideways to cover the skin on top, which was even darker than the rest of him.

"What's your name?" she asked.

Jack answered for him. "His name is Jack," he said.

The tan one laughed. "Brother," he said, "you are too much."

"You aren't from around here," she said. "I would have seen you."

He shook his head. "I was running and I ended up here."

Jack said, "Don't hog the fuel, Jack," and made a drinking motion with his hand.

The tan one nodded. He took a long pull and wiped his mouth and passed the bottle to Jack.

Marty stood and brushed off her warm-ups. "Hawaii," she said. "I've always wanted to go to Hawaii. Just kick back for about three weeks. Check out the volcanoes. Do some mai tais."

"Get leis," Jack said.

All three of them laughed.

"Well," she said. She touched her toes a couple of times.

Jack kept laughing.

"Hawaii's amazing," said the other man. "Anything goes."

"Stop talking about Hawaii," Jack told him. "It makes me cold."

"Me too," Marty said. She rubbed her hands together. "I'm always cold. When I come back, I just hope I come back as a native of some place warm. California, maybe."

"Right," Jack said. "Bitchin' Cal," but there was something in his voice that made her look over at him. He was studying her. She could tell that he was trying to place her again, trying to recall where he'd met her. She wished she hadn't made that remark about coming back. That was what had set him off. She wasn't even sure she actually believed in it—believed that she was going to return as a different entity later on, someone new and different. She had serious doubts, sometimes. But at other times she thought it had to be true; this couldn't be everything.

"So," she said, "do you guys know each other?"

Jack stared at her a moment longer, then nodded. "All our lives," he said.

The tan one shook his head and laughed. "Too much," he said.

"We're inseparable," Jack said. "Aren't we, Jack?"

The tan one laughed again.

"Is that right?" Marty asked him. "Are you inseparable?"

He pulled the zipper of his jacket up and down, hiding and then revealing the golden hairs on his chest, though not in a conscious way. His cheeks puffed out and his brow thickened just above his eyes, so that his face seemed heavier. Marty could see that he was thinking. He looked at her and said, "I guess we are. For the time being."

"That's fine," she said. "That's all right." That was all right, she thought. She could call Jill, Jill was always up for a party, and if Jill was out or had company then she'd think of something else. It would work out.

"Okay," she said, but before she could say anything else someone yelled "Heads up!" and they all looked around. The Frisbee was coming straight at them. Marty felt her body tighten. "Got it," she said, and balanced herself for the catch. Suddenly the breeze gusted and the Frisbee seemed to stop cold, a quivering red line, and then it jerked upwards and flew over their heads and past them. She ran after it, one arm raised, gathering herself to jump, but it stayed just out of reach and finally she gave up.

The Frisbee flew a short distance farther, then fell to the sidewalk and skidded halfway across the street. Marty scooped it up and flipped it back into the park. She stood there, wanting to laugh but completely out of breath. Too much weed, she thought. She put her hands on her knees and rocked back and forth. It was quiet. Then, from up the hill, she heard a low rumble that grew steadily louder, and a few seconds later a big white car came around the corner. Its tires squealed and then went silent as the car slid through a long sheet of water lying in the road. It was moving sideways in her direction. She watched it come. The car cleared the water and the tires began to squeal again but it kept sliding, and Marty saw the faces inside getting bigger and bigger. There was a girl staring at her from the front window. The girl's mouth was open, her arms braced against the dashboard. Then the tires caught and the car shot forward, so close that Marty could have reached out and touched the girl's cheek as they went past.

The car fish-tailed down the street. It ran a stop sign at the corner and turned left back up the hill, coughing out bursts of black exhaust.

Marty turned toward the park and saw the two men looking at her. They were looking at her as if they had seen her naked, and that was how she felt—naked. She had nearly been killed and now she was an embarrassment, like someone in need. She wasn't welcome in the park.

Marty crossed the street and started up the hill toward her apartment building. She felt as if she were floating, as if there were nothing to her. She passed a grey cat curled up on the hood of a car. There was smoke on the breeze and the smell of decay. It seemed to Marty that she drifted with the smoke through the yellow light, over the dull grass and the brown clumps of leaves. In the park behind her a boy called football signals, his voice perfectly distinct in the thin cold air.

She climbed the steps to the building but did not go inside. She knew that the dog would bark at her, and she didn't think she could handle that right now.

She sat on the steps. From somewhere nearby a bird cried out in a hoarse, ratcheting voice like chain being jerked through a pulley. Marty did some breathing exercises to get steady, to quiet the fluttering sensation in her shoulders and knees, but she could not calm herself. A few minutes ago she had nearly been killed and now there was nobody to talk to about it, to see how afraid she was and tell her not to worry, that it was over now. That she was still alive. That everything was going to be all right.

At this moment, sitting here, Marty understood that there was never going to be anyone to tell her these things. She had no idea why this should be so; it was just something she knew. There was no need for her to make a fool of herself again.

The sun was going down. Marty couldn't see it from where she sat, but the windows of the house across the street had turned crimson, and the breeze was colder. A broken kite flapped in a tree. Marty fingered the joint in her pocket but left it there; she felt empty and clean, and did not want to lose the feeling.

She watched the sky darken. Her brother and his friends would be coming off the marsh about now, flushed with cold and drink, their dogs running ahead through the reeds and the tall grass. When they reach the car they'll compare birds and pass a bottle around, and after the bottle is empty they will head for the nearest bar. Do boilermakers. Stuff themselves with pickled eggs and jerky. Throw dice from a leather cup. And outside in the car the dogs will be waiting, ears pricked for the least sound, sometimes whimpering to themselves but mostly silent, tense, and still, watching the bright door the men have closed behind them.

Richard Ford

COMMUNIST

My mother once had a boyfriend named Glen Baxter. This was in 1961. We—my mother and I—were living in the little house my father had left her up the Sun River, near Victory, Montana, west of Great Falls. My mother was thirty-one at the time. I was sixteen. Glen Baxter was somewhere in the middle, between us, though I cannot be exact about it.

We were living then off the proceeds of my father's life insurance policies, with my mother doing some part-time waitressing work up in Great Falls and going to the bars in the evenings, which I know is where she met Glen Baxter. Sometimes he would come back with her and stay in her room at night, or she would call up from town and explain that she was staying with him in his little place on Lewis Street by the GN yards. She gave me his number every time, but I never called it. I think she probably thought that what she was doing was terrible, but simply couldn't help herself. I thought it was all right, though. Regular life it seemed and still does. She was young, and I knew that even then.

Glen Baxter was a Communist and liked hunting, which he talked about a lot. Pheasants. Ducks. Deer. He killed all of them, he said. He had been to Vietnam as far back as then, and when he was in our house he often talked about shooting the animals over there—monkeys and beautiful parrots—using military guns just for sport. We did not know what Vietnam was then, and Glen, when he talked about that, referred to it only as "the far east." I think now he must've been in the CIA and been disillusioned by something he saw or found out about and had been thrown out, but that kind of thing did not matter to us. He was a tall, dark-eyed man with thick black hair, and was usually in a good humor. He had gone halfway through college in Peoria, Illinois, he said, where he grew up. But when he was around our life he worked wheat farms as a ditcher, and stayed out of work winters and in the bars drinking with women like my mother, who had work and some money. It is not an uncommon life to lead in Montana.

What I want to explain happened in November. We had not been seeing Glen Baxter for some time. Two months had gone by. My mother knew other men, but she came home most days from work and stayed inside watching television in her bedroom and drinking beers. I asked about Glen once, and she said only that she didn't know where he was, and I assumed they had had a fight and that he was gone off on a flyer back to Illinois or Massachusetts, where he said he had relatives. I'll admit that I liked him. He had something on his mind always. He was a labor man as well as a Communist, and liked to say that the country was poisoned by the rich, and strong men would need to bring it to life again, and I liked that because my father had been a labor man, which was why we had a house to live in and money coming through. It was also true that I'd had a few boxing bouts by then—just with town boys and one with an Indian from Choteau—and there were some girlfriends I knew from that. I did not like my mother being around the house so much at night, and I wished Glen Baxter would come back, or that another man would come along and entertain her somewhere else.

At two o'clock on a Saturday, Glen drove up into our yard in a car. He had had a big brown Harley-Davidson that he rode most of the year, in his black-and-red irrigators and a baseball cap turned backwards. But this time he had a car, a blue Nash Ambassador. My mother and I went out on the porch when he stopped inside the olive trees my father had planted as a shelter belt, and my mother had a look on her face of not much pleasure. It was starting to be cold in earnest by then. Snow was down already onto the Fairfield Bench, though on this day a chinook was blowing, and it could as easily have been spring, though the sky above the Divide was turning over in silver and blue clouds of winter.

"We haven't seen you in a long time, I guess," my mother said coldly.

"My little retarded sister died," Glen said, standing at the door of his old car. He was wearing his orange VFW jacket and canvas shoes we called wino shoes, something I had never seen him wear before. He seemed to be in a good humor. "We buried her in Florida near the home."

"That's a good place," my mother said in a voice that meant she was a wronged party in something.

"I want to take this boy hunting today, Aileen," Glen said. "There're snow geese down now. But we have to go right away or they'll be gone to Idaho by tomorrow."

"He doesn't care to go," my mother said.

"Yes I do," I said and looked at her.

My mother frowned at me. "Why do you?"

"Why does he need a reason?" Glen Baxter said and grinned.

"I want him to have one, that's why." She looked at me oddly. "I think Glen's drunk, Les."

"No, I'm not drinking," Glen said, which was hardly ever true. He looked at both of us, and my mother bit down on the side of her lower lip and stared at me in a way to make you think she thought something was being put over on her and she didn't like you for it. She was very pretty, though when she was mad her features were sharpened and less pretty by a long way. "All right then, I don't care," she said to no one in particular. "Hunt, kill, maim. Your father did that too." She turned to go back inside.

"Why don't you come with us, Aileen?" Glen was smiling still, pleased.

"To do what?" my mother said. She stopped and pulled a package of cigarettes out of her dress pocket and put one in her mouth.

"It's worth seeing."

"See dead animals?" my mother said.

"These geese are from Siberia, Aileen," Glen said. "They're not like a lot of geese. Maybe I'll buy us dinner later. What do you say?"

"Buy what with?" my mother said. To tell the truth, I didn't know why she was so mad at him. I would've thought she'd be glad to see him. But she just suddenly seemed to hate everything about him.

"I've got some money," Glen said. "Let me spend it on a pretty girl tonight."

"Find one of those and you're lucky," my mother said, turning away toward the front door.

"I already found one," Glen Baxter said. But the door slammed behind her, and he looked at me then with a look I think now was helplessness, though I could not see a way to change anything.

My mother sat in the back seat of Glen's Nash and looked out the window while we drove. My double gun was in the seat between us beside Glen's Belgian pump, which he kept loaded with five shells in case, he said, he saw something beside the road he wanted to shoot. I had hunted rabbits before, and had ground-sluiced pheasants and other birds, but I had never been on an actual hunt before, one where you drove out to some special place and did it formally. And I was excited. I had a feeling that something important was about to happen to me and that this would be a day I would always remember.

My mother did not say anything for a long time, and neither did I. We drove up through Great Falls and out the other side toward Fort Benton, which was on the benchland where wheat was grown.

"Geese mate for life," my mother said, just out of the blue, as we were driving. "I hope you know that. They're special birds."

"I know that," Glen said in the front seat. "I have every respect for them."

"So where were you for three months?" she said. "I'm only curious."

"I was in the Big Hole for a while," Glen said, "and after that I went over to Douglas, Wyoming."

"What were you planning to do there?" my mother asked.

"I wanted to find a job, but it didn't work out."

"I'm going to college," she said suddenly, and this was something I had never heard about before. I turned to look at her, but she was staring out her window and wouldn't see me.

"I knew French once," Glen said. "Rose's pink. Rouge's red." He glanced at me and smiled. "I think that's a wise idea, Aileen. When are you going to start?"

"I don't want Les to think he was raised by crazy people all his life," my mother said.

"Les ought to go himself," Glen said.

"After I go, he will."

"What do you say about that, Les?" Glen said, grinning.

"He says it's just fine," my mother said.

"It's just fine," I said.

Where Glen Baxter took us was out onto the high flat prairie that was disked for wheat and had high, high mountains out to the east, with lower heartbreak hills in between. It was, I remember, a day for blues in the sky, and down in the distance we could see the small town of Floweree and the state highway running past it toward Fort Benton and the high line. We drove out on top of the prairie on a muddy dirt road fenced on both sides, until we had gone about three miles, which is where Glen stopped.

"All right," he said, looking up in the rearview mirror at my mother. "You wouldn't think there was anything here, would you?"

"*We're* here," my mother said. "You brought us here."

"You'll be glad though," Glen said, and seemed confident to me. I had looked around myself but could not see anything. No water or trees, nothing that seemed like a good place to hunt anything. Just wasted land. "There's a big lake out there, Les," Glen said. "You can't see it now from here because it's low. But the geese are there. You'll see."

"It's like the moon out here, I recognize that," my mother said, "only it's worse." She was staring out at the flat, disked wheatland as if she could actually see something in particular and wanted to know more about it. "How'd you find this place?"

"I came once on the wheat push," Glen said.

"And I'm sure the owner told you just to come back and hunt any time you like and bring anybody you wanted. Come one, come all. Is that it?"

"People shouldn't own land anyway," Glen said. "Anybody should be able to use it."

"Les, Glen's going to poach here," my mother said. "I just want you to know that, because that's a crime and the law will get you for it. If you're a man now, you're going to have to face the consequences."

"That's not true," Glen Baxter said, and looked gloomily out over the steering wheel down the muddy road toward the mountains. Though for myself I believed it was true, and didn't care. I didn't care about anything at that moment except seeing geese fly over me and shooting them down.

"Well, I'm certainly not going out there," my mother said. "I like towns better, and I already have enough trouble."

"That's okay," Glen said. "When the geese lift up you'll get to see them. That's all I wanted. Les and me'll go shoot them, won't we, Les?"

"Yes," I said, and I put my hand on my shotgun, which had been my father's and was heavy as rocks.

"Then we should go on," Glen said, "or we'll waste our light."

We got out of the car with our guns. Glen took off his canvas shoes and put on his pair of black irrigators out of the trunk. Then we crossed the barbed-wire fence and walked out into the high, tilled field toward nothing. I looked back at my mother when we were still not so far away, but I could only see the small, dark top of her head, low in the back seat of the Nash, staring out and thinking what I could not then begin to say.

On the walk toward the lake, Glen began talking to me. I had never been alone with him and knew little about him except what my mother said—that he drank too much, or other times that he was the nicest man she had ever known in the world and that some day a woman would marry him, though she didn't think it would be her. Glen told me as we walked that he wished he had finished college, but that it was too late now, that his mind was too old. He said he had liked "the far east" very much, and that people there knew how to treat each other, and that he would go back some day but couldn't go now. He said also that he would like to live in Russia for a while and mentioned the names of people who had gone there, names I didn't know. He said it would be hard at first, because it was so different, but that pretty soon anyone would learn to like it and wouldn't want to live anywhere else, and that Russians treated Americans who came to live there like kings. There were Communists everywhere now, he said. You didn't know them, but they were there. Montana had a large number, and he was in touch with all of them. He said that Communists were always in danger and that he had to protect himself all the time. And when he said that he pulled back his VFW jacket and showed me the butt of a pistol he had stuck under his shirt against his bare skin. "There are people who want to kill me right now," he said, "and I would kill a man myself if I thought I had to." And we kept walking. Though in a while he said, "I don't think I know much about you, Les. But I'd like to. What do you like to do?"

"I like to box," I said. "My father did it. It's a good thing to know."

"I suppose you have to protect yourself too," Glen said.

"I know how to," I said.

"Do you like to watch TV?" Glen said, and smiled.

"Not much."

"I love to," Glen said. "I could watch it instead of eating if I had one."

I looked out straight ahead over the green tops of sage that grew at the edge of the disked field, hoping to see the lake Glen said was there. There was an airishness and a sweet smell that I thought might be the place we were going, but I couldn't see it. "How will we hunt these geese?" I said.

"It won't be hard," Glen said. "Most hunting isn't even hunting. It's only shooting. And that's what this will be. In Illinois you would dig holes in the ground to hide in and set out your decoys. Then the geese come to you, over and over again. But we don't have time for that here." He glanced at me. "You have to be sure the first time here."

"How do you know they're here now?" I asked. And I looked toward the Highwood Mountains twenty miles away, half in snow and half dark blue at the bottom. I could see the little town of Floweree then, looking shabby and dimly lighted in the distance. A red bar sign shone. A car moved slowly away from the scattered buildings.

"They always come November first," Glen said.

"Are we going to poach them?"

"Does it make any difference to you?" Glen asked.

"No, it doesn't."

"Well then we aren't," he said.

We walked then for a while without talking. I looked back once to see the Nash far and small in the flat distance. I couldn't see my mother, and I thought that she must've turned on the radio and gone to sleep, which she always did, letting it play all night in her bedroom. Behind the car the sun was nearing the rounded mountains southwest of us, and I knew that when the sun was gone it would be cold. I wished my mother had decided to come along with us, and I thought for a moment of how little I really knew her at all.

Glen walked with me another quarter mile, crossed another barbed-wire fence where sage was growing, then went a hundred yards through wheatgrass and spurge until the ground went up and formed a kind of long hillock bunker built by a farmer against the wind. And I realized the lake was just beyond us. I could hear the sound of a car horn blowing and a dog barking all the way down in the town, then the wind seemed to move and all I could hear then and after then were geese. So many geese, from the sound of them, though I still could not see even one. I stood and listened to the high-pitched shouting sound, a sound I had never heard so close, a sound with size to it— though it was not loud. A sound that meant great numbers and that made your chest rise and your shoulders tighten with expectancy. It was a sound to make you feel separate from it and everything else, as if you were of no importance in the grand scheme of things.

"Do you hear them singing?" Glen asked. He held his hand up to make me stand still. And we both listened. "How many do you think, Les, just hearing?"

"A hundred," I said. "More than a hundred."

"Five thousand," Glen said. "More than you can believe when you see them. Go see."

I put down my gun and on my hands and knees crawled up the earth-work through the wheatgrass and thistle until I could see down to the lake and see the geese. And they were there, like a white bandage laid on the water, wide and long and continuous, a white expanse of snow geese, seventy yards from me, on the bank, but stretching onto the lake, which was large itself— a half mile across, with thick tules on the far side and wild plums farther and the blue mountain behind them.

"Do you see the big raft?" Glen said from below me, in a whisper.

"I see it," I said, still looking. It was such a thing to see, a view I had never seen and have not since.

"Are any on the land?" he said.

"Some are in the wheatgrass," I said, "but most are swimming."

"Good," Glen said. "They'll have to fly. But we can't wait for that now."

And I crawled backwards down the heel of land to where Glen was, and my gun. We were losing our light, and the air was purplish and cooling. I looked toward the car but couldn't see it, and I was no longer sure where it was below the lighted sky.

"Where do they fly to?" I said in a whisper, since I did not want anything to be ruined because of what I did or said. It was important to Glen to shoot the geese, and it was important to me.

"To the wheat," he said. "Or else they leave for good. I wish your mother had come, Les. Now she'll be sorry."

I could hear the geese quarreling and shouting on the lake surface. And I wondered if they knew we were here now. "She might be," I said with my heart pounding, but I didn't think she would be much.

It was a simple plan he had. I would stay behind the bunker, and he would crawl on his belly with his gun through the wheatgrass as near to the geese as he could. Then he would simply stand up and shoot all the ones he could close up, both in the air and on the ground. And when all the others flew up, with luck some would turn toward me as they came into the wind, and then I could shoot them and turn them back to him, and he would shoot them again. He could kill ten, he said, if he was lucky, and I might kill four. It didn't seem hard.

"Don't show them your face," Glen said. "Wait till you think you can touch them, then stand up and shoot. To hesitate is lost in this."

"All right," I said. "I'll try it."

"Shoot one in the head, and then shoot another one," Glen said. "It won't be hard." He patted me on the arm and smiled. Then he took off his VFW jacket and put it on the ground, climbed up the side of the bunker, cradling his shotgun in his arms, and slid on his belly into the dry stalks of yellow grass out of my sight.

Then for the first time in that entire day I was alone. And I didn't mind it. I sat squat down in the grass, loaded my double gun, and took my other two shells out of my pocket to hold. I pushed the safety off and on to see that it was right. The wind rose a little then, scuffed the grass and made me shiver. It was not the warm chinook now, but a wind out of the north, the one geese flew away from if they could.

Then I thought about my mother in the car alone, and how much longer I would stay with her, and what it might mean to her for me to leave. And I wondered when Glen Baxter would die and if someone would kill him, or whether my mother would marry him and how I would feel about it. And though I didn't know why, it occurred to me then that Glen Baxter and I would not be friends when all was said and done, since I didn't care if he ever married my mother or didn't.

Then I thought about boxing and what my father had taught me about it. To tighten your fists hard. To strike out straight from the shoulder and never punch backing up. How to cut a punch by snapping your fist inwards, how to carry your chin low, and to step toward a man when he is falling so you can hit him again. And most important, to keep your eyes open when you are hitting in the face and causing damage, because you need to see what you're doing to encourage yourself, and because it is when you close your eyes that you stop hitting and get hurt badly. "Fly all over your man, Les," my father said. "When you see your chance, fly on him and hit him till he falls." That, I thought, would always be my attitude in things.

And then I heard the geese again, their voices in unison, louder and shouting, as if the wind had changed and put all new sounds in the cold air. And then a *boom*. And I knew Glen was in among them and had stood up to shoot. The noise of geese rose and grew worse, and my fingers burned where

I held my gun too tight to the metal, and I put it down and opened my fist to make the burning stop so I could feel the trigger when the moment came. *Boom,* Glen shot again, and I heard him shuck a shell, and all the sounds out beyond the bunker seemed to be rising—the geese, the shots, the air itself going up. *Boom,* Glen shot another time, and I knew he was taking his careful time to make his shots good. And I held my gun and started to crawl up the bunker so as not to be surprised when the geese came over me and I could shoot.

From the top I saw Glen Baxter alone in the wheatgrass field, shooting at a white goose with black tips of wings that was on the ground not far from him, but trying to run and pull into the air. He shot it once more, and it fell over dead with its wings flapping.

Glen looked back at me and his face was distorted and strange. The air around him was full of white rising geese and he seemed to want them all. "Behind you, Les," he yelled at me and pointed. "They're all behind you now." I looked behind me, and there were geese in the air as far as I could see, more than I knew how many, moving so slowly, their wings wide out and working calmly and filling the air with noise, though their voices were not as loud or as shrill as I had thought they would be. And they were so close! Forty feet, some of them. The air around me vibrated and I could feel the wind from their wings and it seemed to me I could kill as many as the times I could shoot—a hundred or a thousand—and I raised my gun, put the muzzle on the head of a white goose and fired. It shuddered in the air, its wide feet sank below its belly, its wings cradled out to hold back air, and it fell straight down and landed with an awful sound, a noise a human would make, a thick, soft, *hump* noise. I looked up again and shot another goose, could hear the pellets hit its chest, but it didn't fall or even break its pattern for flying. *Boom,* Glen shot again. And then again. "Hey," I heard him shout. "Hey, hey." And there were geese flying over me, flying in line after line. I broke my gun and reloaded, and thought to myself as I did: I need confidence here, I need to be sure with this. I pointed at another goose and shot it in the head, and it fell the way the first one had, wings out, its belly down, and with the same thick noise of hitting. Then I sat down in the grass on the bunker and let geese fly over me.

By now the whole raft was in the air, all of it moving in a slow swirl above me and the lake and everywhere, finding the wind and heading out south in long wavering lines that caught the last sun and turned to silver as they gained a distance. It was a thing to see, I will tell you now. Five thousand white geese all in the air around you, making a noise like you have never heard before. And I thought to myself then: This is something I will never see again. I will never forget this. And I was right.

Glen Baxter shot twice more. One shot missed, but with the other he hit a goose flying away from him and knocked it half-falling and flying into the empty lake not far from shore, where it began to swim as though it was fine and make its noise.

Glen stood in the stubbly grass, looking out at the goose, his gun lowered. "I didn't need to shoot that, did I, Les?"

"I don't know," I said, sitting on the little knoll of land, looking at the goose swimming in the water.

"I don't know why I shoot 'em. They're so beautiful." He looked at me.

"I don't know either," I said.

"Maybe there's nothing else to do with them." Glen stared at the goose again and shook his head. "Maybe this is exactly what they're put on earth for."

I did not know what to say because I did not know what he could mean by that, though what I felt was embarrassment at the great number of geese there were, and a dulled feeling like a hunger because the shooting had stopped and it was over for me now.

Glen began to pick up his geese, and I walked down to my two that had fallen close together and were dead. One had hit with such an impact that its stomach had split and some of its inward parts were knocked out. Though the other looked unhurt, its soft white belly turned up like a pillow, its head and jagged bill-teeth and its tiny black eyes looking as if it were alive.

"What's happened to the hunters out here?" I heard a voice speak. It was my mother, standing in her pink dress on the knoll above us, hugging her arms. She was smiling though she was cold. And I realized that I had lost all thought of her in the shooting. "Who did all this shooting? Is this your work, Les?"

"No," I said.

"Les is a hunter, though, Aileen," Glen said. "He takes his time." He was holding two white geese by their necks, one in each hand, and he was smiling. He and my mother seemed pleased.

"I see you didn't miss too many," my mother said and smiled. I could tell she admired Glen for his geese, and that she had done some thinking in the car alone. "It *was* wonderful, Glen," she said. "I've never seen anything like that. They were like snow."

"It's worth seeing once, isn't it?" Glen said. "I should've killed more, but I got excited."

My mother looked at me then. "Where's yours, Les?"

"Here," I said and pointed to my two geese on the ground beside me.

My mother nodded in a nice way, and I think she liked everything then and wanted the day to turn out right and for all of us to be happy. "Six, then. You've got six in all."

"One's still out there," I said and motioned where the one goose was swimming in circles on the water.

"Okay," my mother said and put her hand over her eyes to look. "Where is it?"

Glen Baxter looked at me then with a strange smile, a smile that said he wished I had never mentioned anything about the other goose. And I wished I hadn't either. I looked up in the sky and could see the lines of geese by the thousands shining silver in the light, and I wished we could just leave and go home.

"That one's my mistake there," Glen Baxter said and grinned. "I shouldn't have shot that one, Aileen. I got too excited."

My mother looked out on the lake for a minute, then looked at Glen and back again. "Poor goose." She shook her head. "How will you get it, Glen?"

"I can't get that one now," Glen said.

My mother looked at him. "What do you mean?" she said.

"I'm going to leave that one," Glen said.

"Well, no. You can't leave one," my mother said. "You shot it. You have to get it. Isn't that a rule?"

"No," Glen said.

And my mother looked from Glen to me. "Wade out and get it, Glen," she said, in a sweet way, and my mother looked young then for some reason, like a young girl, in her flimsy short-sleeved waitress dress, and her skinny, bare legs in the wheatgrass.

"No." Glen Baxter looked down at his gun and shook his head. And I didn't know why he wouldn't go, because it would've been easy. The lake was shallow. And you could tell that anyone could've walked out a long way before it got deep, and Glen had on his boots.

My mother looked at the white goose, which was not more than thirty yards from the shore, its head up, moving in slow circles, its wings settled and relaxed so you could see the black tips. "Wade out and get it, Glenny, won't you please?" she said. "They're special things."

"You don't understand the world, Aileen," Glen said. "This can happen. It doesn't matter."

"But that's so cruel, Glen," she said, and a sweet smile came on her lips.

"Raise up your own arms, Leeny," Glen said. "I can't see any angel's wings, can you Les?" He looked at me, but I looked away.

"Then you go on and get it, Les," my mother said. "You weren't raised by crazy people." I started to go, but Glen Baxter suddenly grabbed me by my shoulder and pulled me back hard, so hard his fingers made bruises in my skin that I saw later.

"Nobody's going," he said. "This is over with now."

And my mother gave Glen a cold look then. "You don't have a heart, Glen," she said. "There's nothing to love in you. You're just a son of a bitch, that's all."

And Glen Baxter nodded at my mother as if he understood something that he had not understood before, but something that he was willing to know. "Fine," he said, "that's fine." And he took his big pistol out from against his belly, the big blue revolver I had only seen part of before and that he said protected him, and he pointed it out at the goose on the water, his arm straight away from him, and shot and missed. And then he shot and missed again. The goose made its noise once. And then he hit it dead, because there was no splash. And then he shot it three times more until the gun was empty and the goose's head was down and it was floating toward the middle of the lake where it was empty and dark blue. "Now who has a heart?" Glen said. But my mother was not there when he turned around. She had already started back to the car and was almost lost from sight in the darkness. And Glen smiled at me then and his face had a wild look on it. "Okay, Les?" he said.

"Okay," I said.

"There're limits to everything, right?"

"I guess so," I said.

"Your mother's a beautiful woman, but she's not the only beautiful woman in Montana." I did not say anything. And Glen Baxter suddenly said, "Here," and he held the pistol out at me. "Don't you want this? Don't you want to shoot me? Nobody thinks they'll die. But I'm ready for it right now." And I did not know what to do then. Though it is true that what I wanted to do was to hit him, hit him as hard in the face as I could, and see him on the ground bleeding and crying and pleading for me to stop. Only at that moment he looked scared to me, and I had never seen a grown man scared before—though I have seen one since—and I felt sorry for him, as though he was already a dead man. And I did not end up hitting him at all.

A light can go out in the heart. All of this went on years ago, but I still can feel now how sad and remote the world was to me. Glen Baxter, I think now, was not a bad man, only a man scared of something he'd never seen before—something soft in himself—his life going a way he didn't like. A woman with a son. Who could blame him there? I don't know what makes people do what they do or call themselves what they call themselves, only that you have to live someone's life to be the expert.

My mother had tried to see the good side of things, tried to be hopeful in the situation she was handed, tried to look out for us both, and it hadn't worked. It was a strange time in her life then and after that, a time when she had to adjust to being an adult just when she was on the thin edge of things. Too much awareness too early in life was her problem, I think.

And what I felt was only that I had somehow been pushed out into the world, into the real life then, the one I hadn't lived yet. In a year I was gone to hardrock mining and no-paycheck jobs and not to college. And I have thought more than once about my mother saying that I had not been raised by crazy people, and I don't know what that could mean or what difference it could make, unless it means that love is a reliable commodity, and even that is not always true, as I have found out.

Late on the night that all this took place I was in bed when I heard my mother say, "Come outside, Les. Come and hear this." And I went out onto the front porch barefoot and in my underwear, where it was warm like spring, and there was a spring mist in the air. I could see the lights of the Fairfield Coach in the distance on its way up to Great Falls.

And I could hear geese, white birds in the sky, flying. They made their high-pitched sound like angry yells, and though I couldn't see them high up, it seemed to me they were everywhere. And my mother looked up and said, "Hear them?" I could smell her hair wet from the shower. "They leave with the moon," she said. "It's still half wild out here."

And I said, "I hear them," and I felt a chill come over my bare chest, and the hair stood up on my arms the way it does before a storm. And for a while we listened.

"When I first married your father, you know, we lived on a street called Bluebird Canyon, in California. And I thought that was the prettiest street and the prettiest name. I suppose no one brings you up like your first love. You don't mind if I say that, do you?" She looked at me hopefully.

"No," I said.

"We have to keep civilization alive somehow." And she pulled her little housecoat together because there was a cold vein in the air, a part of the cold that would be on us the next day. "I don't feel part of things tonight, I guess."

"It's all right," I said.

"Do you know where I'd like to go?" she said.

"No," I said. And I suppose I knew she was angry then, angry with life but did not want to show me that.

"To the Straits of Juan de Fuca. Wouldn't that be something? Would you like that?"

"I'd like it," I said. And my mother looked off for a minute, as if she could see the Straits of Juan de Fuca out against the line of mountains, see the lights of things alive and a whole new world.

"I know you liked him," she said after a moment. "You and I both suffer fools too well."

"I didn't like him too much," I said. "I didn't really care."

"He'll fall on his face. I'm sure of that," she said. And I didn't say anything because I didn't care about Glen Baxter anymore, and was happy not to talk about him. "Would you tell me something if I asked you? Would you tell me the truth?"

"Yes," I said.

And my mother did not look at me. "Just tell the truth," she said.

"All right," I said.

"Do you think I'm still very feminine? I'm thirty-two years old now. You don't know what that means. But do you think I am?"

And I stood at the edge of the porch, with the olive trees before me, looking straight up into the mist where I could not see geese but could still hear them flying, could almost feel the air move below their white wings. And I felt the way you feel when you are on a trestle all alone and the train is coming, and you know you have to decide. And I said, "Yes, I do." Because that was the truth. And I tried to think of something else then and did not hear what my mother said after that.

And how old was I then? Sixteen. Sixteen is young, but it can also be a grown man. I am forty-one years old now, and I think about that time without regret, though my mother and I never talked in that way again, and I have not heard her voice now in a long, long time.

William Heyen

ANY SPORT

I

Four men in a new Buick LeSabre are driving west on the New York State Thruway from Rochester to Buffalo's Rich Stadium where the Bills are to play the Cleveland Browns in a late-season game. After meeting at a bar in Rochester, they piled into Burke's big car, believing it to be the safest in case of an accident. It was snowing as they left, big flakes down from Lake Ontario in the north, beginning to stick, and now they are doing 25 mph in driving sleet getting icier by the minute, the weather coming at them now from Lake Erie in the west.

"Relax, they'll play," says Burke, checking to make sure he has his lights on. "Rich drains good, the tarp's on. This'll let up. Maybe they'll start late, but they'll get it in. They got to, they can't postpone it, they got to get it in."

From the back seat behind Burke, Squeak hits them with a question. "Who were the starting guards in 1960 for the College All Stars against the Knicks at the Garden?"

"1960, 1960," Jerry says. He's looking out his front-seat window to his right at the sleet slanting into a turf farm near Batavia. A few days before, he saw that same angle of lines on the screen of his new IBM PC as he went through an introductory program. He made the lines move. His wife had just told him she was sick of him. That's what she said, "sick." Now, seeing the broken lines of sleet angle down to the flat land, he is depressed. "1960—West and the 'O'."

"Right," says Squeak.

Jerry feels a little better, an obscure veil dissolving from around his heart.

"Jerry," Russ says from behind, "which Knick did they call 'The Horse'?"

"Shit, I don't know," Jerry says. "He must have picked up splinters. I don't

543

fuck around with bench-warmers." The veil forms again. "Sick" was the word she used.

"Harry Gallatin," Burke says. "I saw that big mother once. He spoke at our senior sports dinner. He was a . . ." Burke's voice trails off as he peers low to see through the splash of sleet thrown up on his windshield by a passing truck.

"If this shit freezes," Russ says, "they'll never get it in."

"If this shit freezes," Jerry says, "they can look for us out here in the morning."

"Who invented the doughnut that replaced lead bats in the on-deck circle?" Russ asks.

The other three are silent, thinking hard. The LeSabre swerves right with other cars into the lane for the Rich Stadium exit. As they leave the Thruway behind them and slow for the toll booth, Russ answers his own question.

"Elston Howard. You guys never give the niggers credit for anything."

"I love the niggers," Burke says. "I just hate the fucking Yankees."

"You and your fucking underdogs," Russ says. "All your life you're betting losers. You'd think you'd get tired of putting my kids through college."

They all laugh. Burke has lost $100 to Russ on last season's NBA playoffs, and the C-note is a delicious bone that Russ keeps chewing.

"What was the name of the Russian who made that basket to beat us in the '76 Olympics?" Squeak asks.

"They never beat us," Russ says. Now he is angry. "You call that game legal? Three plays for the fucking Russians in the last six seconds? Shit, we didn't even bother to pick up the silver at the awards ceremonies. That was bullshit. It was fixed. They'll never beat us. Stop asking asshole questions, Squeak."

Squeak wants to say the name, but knows Russ well enough by now not to. They went to high school together in Rochester. Squeak managed the basketball team for four years while Russ started on the varsity his junior and senior years. Squeak got by, he himself knew, by being quick with his mouth. He was a wise-ass who had hustled water and basketballs and uniforms and orange slices for the section-champion varsity for two years before Russ made it up from jay vees. Russ had always been a hothead. Squeak had seen him kick a cheerleader when untangling himself from the crowd after not quite being able to save a bad pass. Squeak had read a book on Elvis Presley, and Russ reminded him of Red West, one of Elvis's friends, a quick-tempered bodyguard. Russ had red hair, too. So Squeak does not mention the name of the Russian who beat America with that basket, though the diminutive Squeak, out of work from his job in a print shop, somehow cherishes that name as though it were a little prayer, or spell.

Burke presses the lever to roll down his window. At first, ice clutches the window, but the glass breaks free and rolls down. The toll is $2.60. He hands three singles to the woman in the booth and tells her to keep the change.

"Burke," says Jerry, "I never saw anyone tip a fucking toll booth collector before."

"Jerry," Burke says, "if you'd had a good look at her, as I did, you'd have seen that they were worth twenty cents each."

Jerry is thinking of his wife, thinking of the first time they were in bed together. It was their wedding night. He knelt between her legs and was kissing her belly, his hands on her breasts. She was writhing under him. It was as though, holding her breasts in his palms and fingers . . .

"I knew it," Russ says. The LeSabre is being waved past the Rich Stadium parking lot entrance by red-tipped flashlights held by men in yellow slickers. The sleet is not letting up. It's noon, but visibility is only about a first down in front of them. The LeSabre is sliding in ruts of slush and ice.

"What true-blue All American college did Bevo Francis play for?" Squeak asks.

II

A waitress has just brought a third round of drinks to their booth. "This time I'd bid fifty cents each," Burke says, straight-faced, as he flips a folded buck onto her tray.

"If her husband's as big as her diamond, you'd better watch your ass," Squeak says.

"She's got that available look," Burke says.

Driving away from the stadium, they'd found this place by luck, its blue neon rooftop sign flashing CHEKKO'S—TRUCKERS WELCOME at them just as Burke was wondering where the hell to go, what to do. He pushed the LeSabre as far as he could into a slushbank beside the place, trying to get her ass end out of the way. They've got a corner booth. Waylon Jennings is on the juke, singing about how he loves America.

Shit, Burke was thinking, he'd really wanted to see that football game. He'd *needed* to see it. He'd wanted to sit in their end-zone seats with Jerry and Russ and Squeak and get sloshed, yelling like hell for Cribbs to bust one or for Butler to make assholes out of the Cleveland defense. He wanted to yell all afternoon, watch the scoreboard post other NFL scores, and cheer or moan with the crowd. He wanted to drink stadium beer and his flask of Jack Daniels and sleep in the back seat while one of the others drove back to Rochester. Now he was sitting in a booth at a fucking truck stop. At least he was with his three friends. At least there was that. In about eighteen fucking hours (weather allowing, and it was just his luck it would) he'd be at work at Kodak, busting his ass in the gloom and stink of the silver recovery building. He couldn't wait to retire.

Burke had played some high school football. Chugging half his beer, he imagined the Bills down in their locker room under Rich, some still in pads, some in civvies already and heading home, one or two in whirlpools and glad to rest their injuries, some maybe playing poker. Maybe he and Jerry and Russ and Squeak ought to try to make it back to Rochester and get up a poker game. They could play all night and call in sick in the morning. But the fucking Thruway was probably closed by now. He'd never seen the weather this bad.

Squeak was thinking what Burke was thinking. "Good thing this shithole is open 24 hours," he said.

"Fucking A, Squeak," Russ said, lifting his mug of Bud to Squeak, making amends for his outburst in the car.

"Fucking A," said Jerry, lifting his shot of Seagrams to his friends and then downing it. Who was the bitch to say *he* made *her* sick? She'd gained thirty pounds. Fuck her. Let her go. There were plenty of women around, like this waitress whose buns he'd like to palm. He'd been voted "best looking" in high school, and hadn't lost it. He'd proved that enough times. Fuck her. She made *him* sick.

They took turns walking past the pool table over to the picture window. The stop's parking lot was criss-crossed with vehicles stuck in foot-deep slush, and the weather wasn't letting up—freezing rain, hail.

The place was crowded with truckers and with disappointed football fans like themselves. Every few minutes, the power winked off, but came back on right away.

"Squeak, let's you and me show these assholes how to shoot some pool," Russ said. He got up to put a quarter on the rail of the pool table behind several other quarters. They wouldn't have the table for about a half hour.

"How can a pitcher be both the winning pitcher and the losing pitcher in the same ball game?" Jerry asked. He'd heard this one at the salesroom from old man Wiczorek, who would call tomorrow, Jerry predicted, to buy that clean pickup Jerry had offered him. Jerry could pick up a fast four hundred on that one.

"He can't," Russ said. "Impossible . . . No, wait a fucking minute. What if it was only four innings, and he was winning or losing, and the game was rained out, and he was traded to the other team, and . . ." Russ sold insurance. He unravelled the complicated process by which a pitcher could appear in just one game and end up 1-1.

"Close enough," Jerry said. "You get the idea."

"Jerry, that was a shit question," Russ said, but this time he wasn't angry. It felt good answering one of those shit questions. Jerry was okay. Old Squeak was okay, too. They were all okay. Squeak couldn't help it if all he could do was carry water.

Jerry said "Fucking A," smiled at Russ, got up to find the john. He passed the register and asked the waitress. She lifted her hand to point. Her bosom rose, swelling her pink satiny blouse toward him. Jerry asked her to do him a favor and serve up another round for his friends back there, and he told her he wished she'd have a drink herself. Jerry noticed that she had some hard miles on her, this woman, and serving this whole truckstop today made her appear as old as she was, about forty, but she had what seemed to be natural honey-blond hair, and good teeth—he wanted to tongue those teeth—and a body that wouldn't quit.

She said she would. She said she'd heard them talking sports back there. She said her favorite baseball player was her namesake, and could Jerry guess? She turned and went to the bar, two or three men calling to her. That's what you call a body, Jerry said to himself.

Standing at the urinal, holding his pecker in his fingertips, Jerry realized he was glad he was here. Even before he was done pissing, thinking of the waitress, he began to get an erection. This was more like it, he said to himself.

The four men drank and smoked. They shot pool. They ate burgers and eggs. They began drinking again. Chekko, jolly at the killing he was making, a Ukie with a thick accent, ordered up a round on the house. "Ve vill trink no more," he shouted, pounding the bar, then waited a second. "But ve vill trink no less," he thundered. Burke kept supplementing bar drinks with jolts from his flask of Lynchburg. Strangers bought one another drinks, swapped life stories.

It was dark out now. A trooper stopped in to tell everybody to stay put. Burke was playing "goalposts" with Squeak and Russ, one holding up fingers while the other tried to flick a pack of matches through. They played "edges," sliding quarters across the table. Waylon and Willy and Dolly and Johnny kept singing to these western New Yorkers, telling them that country is in the heart and you shouldn't raise your sons to be cowboys and you were always on my mind, honey, even when I was drinking in town because we're broke and I can't take it no more and the crops have burned out and the cows need milking. Jerry, car salesman at Rochester Motors, was helping his Rose behind the bar now, touching her when he had a chance, following her into the kitchen and holding her from behind when she went to the bread drawer.

She turned around and faced him squarely. She licked her lips with her tongue and said, "You look like you could swing a mean bat, honey, but we better not, maybe I'll see you later." She turned him around and put her hands on his buttocks and said "Now march." Jerry left the kitchen, following his erection back out to his friends.

Jerry was going to go to bed with this woman even if he had to hitch home a week later. Let his wife think he was lost in Buffalo ice, let his three friends say they got separated in a blizzard and he was probably dead, but he was going to sink into Rose. He went back to the booth to check on his friends.

"Burke," Jerry said, "I don't know if you can take this, but if you're so goddamned smart, what's the record for World Series homers, and who hit them? . . . The *Mick,*" Jerry shouted, answering his own question. "Who the fuck else? Your fucking Pirates ain't even been *up* eighteen times. They can't even get it *up,*" he shouted. "God made a mistake, and you know it. Clemente should have been a Yankee!"

III

At 4:30 in the morning, sleet has lightened to snow, but the snow is heavy and drifting in this squall area near the lake. No traffic, nothing moving. Russ, Squeak, and Burke are shooting pool. Half the men are still awake, drinking and talking quietly, others are sleeping or trying to sleep, leaning back in corners of the booths or stretched out, chairs extending their beds. The only other woman in the place besides Rose is sleeping in her husband's arms along a wall where he has spread blankets for them. A trucker gets up every five or ten minutes to try to call Detroit, Chicago, New York, but the phone is out. The stop smells of stale beer and cigar smoke.

Squeak banks in the 8-ball. He says he's had enough fucking pool. Russ and Burke throw bills on the table. Squeak, master in the use of the bridge, has won a total of about $200 in about ten games. Burke looks around for the broad or for Chekko, but Chekko is asleep in his trailer out behind the stop, and who knows where the broad is? He wants a poker deck. He's got one out in the LeSabre. "I'll go with you," Russ says, "I need some fucking air." Stuffing the bills into his pocket, Squeak goes back to their booth.

Jerry is with Rose. She is sitting up on a table in the kitchen. The only light is coming in over the half-door from beer signs in the windows out past the bar. Jerry is standing between her legs, feeling a nyloned thigh with each hand, working his thumbs close to her sweet vee. Rose has her arms around his neck, alternately, teasingly, pushing him away and drawing him forward. "Now honey," she is saying, "I like pinch hitters, but not here, we just can't do it here."

"They're all asleep," Jerry is saying, feeling Rose's legs, pressing his erection up against the metal table. He feels like he could split the table.

Burke and Russ are watching their breath steam against the gray morning light. The snow has let up, but they know it's going to be a long time before this parking lot unclogs. They'd pushed their way to the LeSabre through chest-high drifts. Burke liked the way his car waited in the dark for him. It would get him to the next game no matter what. He fishes a deck of cards from his glove compartment.

"Russ," Burke says, "I wanted to see that fucking game. The Bills would've whipped Cleveland's ass, I just knew it."

"So what," Russ says.

"What do you mean so what?"

"Who gives a fuck?" Russ is angry, glaring at Burke. He'd like to hit Burke.

"Russ, it's for the fucking *playoffs,*" Burke says carefully. He knows that Russ hated losing that money to Squeak. Insurance isn't as steady as Kodak checks, and there's all that tuition Russ is paying.

"Fuck the playoffs. Man, Burke, grow up, will you? We're standing in the dark here outside a truck stop and we don't know our asses from a hole in the ground and you're talking about the playoffs. Where's the dough in *your* pocket if they win the fucking Super Bowl? Fuck the Bills. I'm never going to another fucking game."

"I know what you mean," Burke says, though he knows he simply doesn't know what Russ is talking about. The game was for the *playoffs!* The two stand there another ten seconds, scanning the blank gray heavens for a sign of who knows what, then push their way back through their paths through the drifts.

"You know, Russ," Burke says, "we recover twenty-six million ounces of silver a year from old film and shit. That stuff is awfully pretty when you burn it out." Walking behind Burke, Russ thinks of snapping Burke's neck in two and burying Burke in a drift. "Burke, go fuck yourself with your silver," Russ says.

In the kitchen, Jerry has his hands inside Rose's pants. He has buried his nose between those basketballs he's wanted to palm all his life. Then she says it.

"Jerry, honey, maybe we could for a little money." But she's not much of a businesswoman. She has her hands half over Jerry's ears, and he can't quite hear her. Jerry is pulling her panty hose down. Maybe he heard "we could." Whatever. He has pulled her off the table onto him. She didn't want to do this, not without three or five of his twenties to take back to her husband in the trailer—when she does that he does things to her that sometimes make this life worth it—but she's doing it, and it's too late now, too late, and Chekko's a pig next to this Jerry, and this is wonderful, and any sport in a storm, she says to herself, this is wonderful, but in five or ten thrusts Jerry has fucked her, but, damn it, she hasn't come.

Jerry hoists her back up onto the table. "At last," he thinks, "at last, God," he thinks, "Jesus," he thinks, "that was something." Rose sits up, begins putting herself together. She's thinking of her sister, living on a farm out in Kendall with her husband and kids. They plant a whole acre of sunflowers out there every spring. You can stand among them in the summer and almost listen to them. And they bend down those beautiful heads to listen to you, those gold-rimmed heads. You could just stand there for a long time inside those sunflowers, watching the bumblebees in their faces, and the butterflies flutter around them and land on them and open and close their wings. You could just stand there for a long time, "a rose in the sunflowers," her sister said.

Jerry joins his three friends at their booth. He's sitting next to Burke, and sees Burke fold three aces to Russ's two-pair in a game of draw for a good-sized pot. What the fuck is Burke doing, Jerry wonders. Jerry wonders if he should call Wiczorek about that pickup today. He doesn't want to seem to be too anxious, but sometimes you can play too nonchalant.

Morning light begins to fill the stop, washing out the neon beer signs. A plow rumbles along the highway. Jerry sees Chekko in the parking lot with his snowblower, arcing the whitestuff high over the roofs of cars. Jerry thinks his new PC is going to change his life. Maybe his wife had the rag on. She's probably sorry about that word. She's probably worried about him right now.

Squeak is thinking about Gayle Sayers, how a linebacker said that when you tried to tackle him straight on he seemed to divide in half, go around you, and reassemble. You just couldn't lay a hand on him, you were left there with air in your arms. Another defensive back swore that one time he looked behind him after Sayers flew over him and saw wings sprouting between Sayers' shoulders.

Burke hits a flush, and knows he has a winner.

"Who scored six touchdowns against . . ."

"Gayle Sayers, old #38," says Russ, as he rakes in another big pot.

MOURNING

Jesse James had a wife
Who mourned for his life. . . .

I

1876–1881

He's a blue-eyed handsome man but he makes you worry. She watches him ride away, his linen duster flying and the dust swirling up behind him, and she thinks: this is to be my portion. A skillet. Little Jesse crying. Mary moaning. This plank floor and these thick windows, the bright fire, the distant trees. Zee, he says, I'm going. She knows, has known long ago. He comes in and paces. He wrings his hands. He stares, his blue eyes glazing over, then commencing to blink.

Stay here with me, she says.

Zee, I have got to go.

She knows, but regrets. Zerelda, his mother and her aunt and namesake, also regrets.

I see he's gone again, she says.

Yes, he's gone again.

Say where?

He never says.

No. He wouldn't.

She walks her mother-in-law to the door. The trees sway and clouds move across the sky as though in a great rush to get someplace else. The clouds look like great dark hands, big fists. She closes the door, fixes the latch, turns to her children, who are hungry, one crying, one tugging at her hand.

In Saratoga they ride out the long boulevard in a grand phaeton, past the mansions with the wonderful turrets and spacious porches, the driver sitting tall and rigid in front of them in a narrow-brimmed, flat-topped gray hat that she is certain will blow away in one of the warm gusts of wind but that remains firmly in place while she almost loses the scarf she's tied so carefully in a broad bow around her neck. Jesse wears the dark suit he's purchased in New York City. Quiet, he sits as rigid as the driver, his hands folded in his lap. You would think he sat in church, listened to a sermon. Wouldn't it be wonderful, she wants to say, to live in a home such as one of these. She sees herself moving from room to room, her silk gown rustling, Jesse in the parlor with his newspaper, his cigar, the children in the playroom two floors above, watched by a selfless nursemaid. She loves little Jesse, sweet Mary, but can she help it if she sometimes desires her husband, wants him all alone to herself, the way it used to be?

But of course it has never been as it should be. Not even now, in this fine carriage, is it as it should be. Look at him. What is he thinking, what is he feeling. Shouldn't she know, have some inkling. Why does he so seldom speak, take her into his confidence. There has been a time—but no, there hasn't been a time. Nothing has been provided. She must grasp, she must always be pulling at him, at life itself. He has no self. Don't his actions say as much? She believes everything she has ever heard about him. He is an outlaw, a thief. He has nothing of his own, not even a name.

At the baths the woman helps her down into the warm water. She thinks of Jesse, wonders what he thinks as he feels the water's warmth. No doubt nothing. Probably he thinks nothing at all, a secret even to himself. Is the water warm enough, the woman asks. It is very warm. Warm and calming. She lowers herself into it. I might drown, she thinks. I might let my head come with my body down into the water. Then I would be the mystery.

Aunt Zeralda waves the stump of her right arm as though it were a stick. Zee, she says, men are all the same. Even my dear Dr. Samuel, why, he's no more with me sometimes than my dead father, just a memory of himself in the flesh. There's much we must resign ourselves to.

Little Jesse jumps at his grandmother when she comes, and Zee thinks he will knock her over surely, for he's a growing boy, heavy as sin, but Ma Zeralda clasps her good arm around him and lets him hang onto the other and together they stagger towards the high-back rocker. Tell me about the Pinkertons, he says. Tell me how they blew off your arm, Nanna. He has his father's tact, as well as his blue eyes and the same shuffling gait. Mary looks like her grandmother in the eyes, their sockets set back as if for better safety, and like her father in the mouth, the lips small in proportion to the chin and nose and customarily drawn tight. When I grow up, she says frequently, I'm going to marry a rich, rich man and live in a big house with tall trees all around it so that nobody can ever find us.

I won't think about him, she tells herself. He is dead to me and I will go on with my life. And she rides into town, the children left with their grandmother. She rides in the little cabriolet Jesse has brought her from St. Louis, rides with her head high, her hands tight around the thick reins. I'm permitting myself to be seen, she thinks. I want the gentlemen on Messanie Street to turn their heads when I pass. There goes a fine-looking woman, I want them to say, tipping their high-crowned hats.

He says it was the war that changed everything. That is what he used to say, his voice lowering so that it doesn't sound like a voice, the vowels firm as fruit fresh-picked. Before the war, he says, a man had a chance. There was rich farms, prosperous towns, and for them of a mind to seek fortune in other climes there was California and the promise of gold.

California. Hasn't his father gone to California. Left his mother behind with three young children. Gone and found nothing, sent nothing back. In fact never heard from again. And all this *before the war.*

Oh, he could be tiresome sometimes. Lord, yes. Before the war! Before the war indeed. Before the war as well as during it he was a boy, no man at all, hardly out of knee britches when the redlegs start their raiding and the Federals their burning, scarce eighteen when Lee surrenders. But with two years of fighting with Quantrill's raiders, he points out, his blue eyes fierce and rapidly blinking, as if he suddenly sees the whole war again, everything all at once, the fire and the bloodshed, himself in the midst of it, pistols brandished and smoking. *I'm with child,* she tells him, and off he goes, not saying where, climbing onto the big horse, and she lies there alone in the bed and thinks maybe he is only a dream, everything that has happened to her since she has left the home of her parents in Kansas City a dream, this house on the hill, these children who survive and those poor dead twins, this child in her womb tinier surely than a finger, all a dream. She will wake up and there he will be, a man with Jesse's eyes—only thy will not blink like his do. Unflinching, this man looks deep into her eyes and says, You are my life. Let me be yours. A lover to love, this one. An outlaw, perhaps, but alive, hidden in her heart.

Hotter, she tells the attendant. I want the water hotter. I want it steaming hot. And then he says, It's time, Zee. It's time we moved on. The baths make her feel as though she might live a life, after all, of perfect loveliness, in warmth, submerged but breathing fine. It's time, he says, and they are on the train again, headed south, the land through the windows passing as if it were in fact another kind of river, swift and dangerous to cross, whose dirt you might drown in.

She is with child, the fourth time in their marriage. When Jesse and Mary learn to walk, they move so like their father that she expects them to come to her any minute, say, Now it's time. We have got to move on. We don't know when we'll be back. They will not, she is certain, ever be able to stay put, doomed with a double dose of the blood that dooms their father, their uncle. Getting even takes a long time, at least a life. Young, lying wounded in her father's house, he tells her what has happened. They found me in the cornfield, he says. They was Jim Lane's men, come looking for Quantrill. Frank'd been riding with Quantrill, and I guess they found that out and so naturally came to us. But we wasn't saying a word. I lit out for the fields, nary a thought in my head about what fate I was leaving behind for my dear mother. I tore through them fields, run through the corn rows, and all the time I hear the horses tromping over the stalks and know it ain't no escaping. They get me down there all right, but I swear they'll pay. I'll be harder to find next time.

He could've been a preacher like his runaway daddy, yes, he could if he could only preach on the wrongs done to him and to his brother and to his beloved maimed mother. On that subject he might speak for hours and keep your attention.

She has heard him sing hymns, a pure and lovely tenor, when he comes to visit her, his cousin Zerelda Mims of Kansas City, and takes her to the Baptist Church, later to ride with her to the river, the Missouri, wider and bluer in those sweet summers before the war, with tufts of columbine and chicory spread across its banks like decoration put there for their pleasure alone. I am a family man, he tells her later, courting her while she nurses his war wound. I want to be a husband to a good woman, a loving father. Do you think that is possible, Zee. Can you see your way to helping me. Lord, how could any woman resist, him there in her bed, lying so peaceful between her sheets, the blue comforter tucked beneath his chin, his blue eyes always filling with tears, and not a single complaint, not once a word about the pain she knows he's feeling, his lung, the doctor says, punctured clean through by a Federal's bullet, a fingertip shot away.

Mama, she says, I think I love him.

Lord help us, her mama says.

II

1882

She doesn't look forward to the visits from Frank and Annie. In his tight suit with the black bow tie, the pin-striped trousers, the shiny boots, Frank talks like a schoolteacher, puffing his big cigar and looking at her as if amused with something, as if he finds her stupid, comical. And how, he asks, is the little mama. Annie glides through the doorway as if pretending to be a swan. She is a plump woman with large hands and feet, given to the wearing of pearly brooches above her commodious breast and many thick rattling crinolines beneath her bell-shaped skirts. Hello, Zerelda-dear, she says. It's *so* good to see you again. Frank sits in the rocker, creaking and puffing, in his schoolteacher's tight collar.

We been through hell and high water, Jesse says. Frank's the only man in the world I trust. He'll never betray me, Zee, not Frank, not for any sum of money. I don't know why you don't like him better.

She tries to. She tries to make conversation with him. And what, she asks him, pouring hot coffee into the delicate cup, do you think will ever become of the Indians? The subject interests her. It is a topic of interest in the East, she has noted, as well as in the West. The Easterner's point of view, she has observed, differs sharply from that of the Westerner. Is there room for all the tribes in the Indian Territory? Is it right that they should all be moved there—and can they really be guaranteed permanent asylum anywhere. Grant's policy was perhaps radical, though idealistic to be sure, but what will a man like Arthur do with the mess Hayes left. Frank has no opinions. He quotes her Shakespeare—he *says* it's Shakespeare. He reckons things will work out. He puffs his cigar, sips his coffee. Maybe, he says to Jesse, you and me'd best step into the other room. Ladies, will you excuse us for a moment.

Have you heard, Annie says, leaning forward in her chair, what the Indians do with the white women they capture.

She has read accounts, has Annie, true-life accounts, and the things they say will make your blood boil. Savages. Why, it's ridiculous to even think that a wild Cheyenne such as them that raid in Kansas will ever turn Christian. They are savage through and through, and the only solution to the problem is to show them we won't stand for any more of their outrages.

At least she has an opinion. As for herself, why, listen, what if you *were* captured by a savage Cheyenne, Annie. What would you do. Be honest now.

What would I do! Fight tooth and nail for my freedom, of course. I'd not give in. I'd run. I'd escape.

Would you. Well. I think I might not. Not if my brave had enough passion in him. Not if he wanted me so badly that he couldn't bear the thought of life without me and would hold onto me whether I loved him in return or not.

Oh, certainly, Zee, but I don't think that's the way it is, at least not in the accounts I've read.

Accounts! Why you don't think a woman is going to speak of such pleasure when she's recaptured by her family, do you. Would you? No. You'd have to protect *their* honor, save their pride. Or else be treated as the lowest of the low. No, I don't place much faith in the accounts.

Really, Zee? Don't you.

She shakes her head. Little Jesse pulls at her skirt. Mayn't he please go in the room where his daddy and Uncle Frank are? Mary sits in the middle of the room, legs crossed in front of her, her rag doll, a present from Ma Zerelda, flat on its face being whipped vigorously. Indian children would be quiet, well-behaved, trained from an early age to do their share. The air in the dark tipi would be sweet and leathery, her brave's eyes dark brown and unflinching, his touch, as he draws her to him, gentle.

She hasn't wanted this return. Missouri, he tells her, is our home, but she's been happy in Tennessee, as happy, at any rate, as she has ever been since their marriage. The death of the twins brings him closer to her for a time, and he begins to take an interest in farming. Then it's: We must return to Missouri. It is time. I feel it in my bones. There's no use arguing. When he brings up his bones, she knows it's no use quarreling, he's made up his mind, he's got to go.

What surprises her is the feeling of warmth she has. The Mississippi seems to move with the same pace and thickness as her blood. She feels steady, calm. Perhaps, she thinks, it *is* right, this return of the family to Missouri. How white the rocks that rim the hills, how thick and swirling the snow-washed grass in the valleys, how stately the rows of willow and cottonwood along the creekbanks, bark shining in the late winter sunlight like fine silk stretched tight and brushed perfectly clean. Then, at last in St. Joseph, bold in the spring sun, she walks past the storefronts along Messanie Street. *Mrs. Howard. I am Mrs. Howard of Lafayette Street.*

The house on the hill commands a view of St. Joseph, the Missouri River, and all of Kansas beyond. Home, she thinks, yes, he's right this time. This is our home. A child will be born here. It is 1882. The world is not the same as when Jesse lies wounded in my father's house and talks so foolish of families. Because it wasn't possible then—even I must have known that it wasn't possible to live in peace, not for him nor for me, not then, not in those times.

Merchants smile pleasantly, offer assistance. They are not suspicious. Why should they be. We are at last living the life we have planned for ourselves. She tells him she is with child and he kisses her hand, clasps it almost with tenderness. Mr. and Mrs. Thomas Howard, of Lafayette Street, St. Joseph, Missouri.

But then he goes. He rides off alone, leaving before daybreak, returns in a week, two weeks, a month, she doesn't know. His mother sits in the rocker by the fire, the chair not moving, and talks to her of burdens and injustices while the children loll about on the floor, calm as dolls for a change, drawing stick figures on their slates.

Things get worse, the old woman says, waving her stump, before they get better. I raised them up to be good boys, my Frank and my Jesse. They never gave me heartache such as my Susan did. They are gentlemen. I raised them up to be gentlemen. But they have no peace, while Susan, who has shamed her mother and her brothers more than once, prospers in Texas with that scoundrel Parmer. Lord a-mercy.

In the middle of March the chill winds give way to warm breezes from the south and the rain falls like mist. When the gray has gone, she takes the children to the river. We'll have a picnic, she tells them, with Aunt Annie and your cousin Bob. But the river's high and muddy, the banks thick with briars and silt. Annie sees a snake. And so they have their picnic lunch in the yard of the house on the hill. We can see the river anyway, says Annie. Who needs to be close to it.

When Jesse comes back it is the eve of April and the Ford boys come with him. Well, he says, you're swelling up just fine, but she's in no mood for sweet talk. She needs love and knows there's no getting it from him, not any-more, not ever, though it breaks her heart to think it. Where is she to get it, if not from her husband. She looks at her children and they seem not hers, some other woman's, and the child within her might be rock. She remem-bers, she tries to imagine the moments when his touch thrilled, his glance warmed. There was a gentleness, a tenderness. It was trust, she remembers, trust that we had. When, now, might that have been.

What do you think, Annie asks, of that Charley Ford.

Not at all, she says. I don't think of him at all.

Have you noticed the way he looks at me? Zee, he gives me the shivers.

Stop ogling him. Stop flirting with him, Annie.

Zee! You're one to talk.

They sit in the straight chairs by the south window, the dark curtains drawn back, the morning sun streaming through the panes. It is a warmth, she thinks, but not the warmth I need. She has lost that warmth, just when she believed she had it back, lost it as sure as she has lost her youth. When she hears the gun, she thinks it is the sound of her soul breaking loose from its skin. She closes her eyes, a girl again in Old Missouri, Missouri before the war, waking to the sound of the mourning dove, the footsteps of her father, birds, so many of them, singing in the trees, beautiful, something fine and beautiful, her mother calling, Zee! Zee! and now the sun lighting up every-thing, Jesse her cousin, her lover, on his way to pay her a secret visit, him just a boy trying to look like a man by strapping that big pistol around his waist and letting the fuzz above his sweet boy's lips stay, blonding in the sunshine, curling ever so slightly at the corners of his mouth, where the cheeks soften and the chin drops like it wants speech, a tongue and mouth of its own. What has happened. What in God's name has happened. Zerelda, they're calling her name, but isn't it his mother they want and not his wife. It's always somebody, Shepherds or Hiteses or Cumminses or Liddils or Ryans, who could keep track of them, these mean-eyed men with their guns and their grins, their matted hair, their small teeth. Pleased to meet you, Ma'am. She is sure. How does he know, her blue-eyed Jesse, who he can trust. This one, no. This one, yes. And Frank, Frank forever.

What has happened. A gunshot or a slamming door. Jesse doesn't slam a door, leaves a room quietly, enters in silence. He is there or he is not and in either case you think that is the way it will always be, his presence all one with his absence, eternal his comings and goings. And so it is not like him, she thinks, rising from her chair, to go so noisily. Perhaps it is thunder. Perhaps nothing at all, her soul, her bursting heart, her wild imagination, her unsettled mind.

Charley Ford, what have you done.

No. It's Bob that's done it. Bob, my brother Bob Ford. Yonder he goes. Zerelda, you mustn't look.

He seems to embrace the wall, her Jesse, the red coming on the back of his head like another set of lips that she might more conveniently kiss while the other pair, those pale thin ones she remembers always drawn tight like stays, squeeze against the skin of the room. Oh, she'll look, all right. She sees him lying there, for sure not wanting her, wanting no one to hold him back, a secret and safe, you bet, her Mr. Howard, gone for good.

MY MAN BOVANNE

Blind people got a hummin jones if you notice. Which is understandable completely once you been around one and notice what no eyes will force you into to see people, and you get past the first time, which seems to come out of nowhere, and it's like you in church again with fat-chest ladies and old gents gruntin a hum low in the throat to whatever the preacher be saying. Shakey Bee bottom lip all swole up with Sweet Peach and me explainin how come the sweet-potato bread was a dollar-quarter this time stead of dollar regular and he say uh huh he understand, then he break into this *thizzin* kind of hum which is quiet, but fiercesome just the same, if you ain't ready for it. Which I wasn't. But I got used to it and the onliest time I had to say somethin bout it was when he was playin checkers on the stoop one time and he commenst to hummin quite churchy seem to me. So I says, "Look here Shakey Bee, I can't beat you and Jesus too." He stop.

So that's how come I asked My Man Bovanne to dance. He ain't my man mind you, just a nice ole gent from the block that we all know cause he fixes things and the kids like him. Or used to fore Black Power got hold their minds and mess em around till they can't be civil to ole folks. So we at this benefit for my niece's cousin who's runnin for somethin with this Black party somethin or other behind her. And I press up close to dance with Bovanne who blind and I'm hummin and he hummin, chest to chest like talkin. Not jammin my breasts into the man. Wasn't bout tits. Was bout vibrations. And he dug it and asked me what color dress I had on and how my hair was fixed and how I was doin without a man, not nosy but nice-like, and who was at this affair and was the canapés dainty-stingy or healthy enough to get hold of proper. Comfy and cheery is what I'm tryin to get across. Touch talkin like the heel of the hand on the tambourine or on a drum.

But right away Joe Lee come up on us and frown for dancin so close to the man. My own son who knows what kind of warm I am about; and don't grown men call me long distance and in the middle of the night for a little Mama comfort? But he frown. Which ain't right since Bovanne can't see and defend himself. Just a nice old man who fixes toasters and busted irons and bicycles and things and changes the lock on my door when my men friends get messy. Nice man. Which is not why they invited him. Grass roots you see. Me and Sister Taylor and the woman who does heads at Mamies and the man from the barber shop, we all there on account of we grass roots. And I ain't never been souther than Brooklyn Battery and no more country than the window box on my fire escape. And just yesterday my kids tellin me to take them countrified rags off my head and be cool. And now can't get Black enough to suit em. So everybody passin sayin My Man Bovanne. Big deal, keep steppin and don't even stop a minute to get the man a drink or one of them cute sandwiches or tell him what's goin on. And him standin there with a smile ready case someone do speak he want to be ready. So that's how come I pull him on the dance floor and we dance squeezin past the tables and chairs and all them coats and people standin round up in each other face talkin bout this and that but got no use for this blind man who mostly fixed skates and scooters for all these folks when they was just kids. So I'm pressed up close and we touch talkin with the hum. And here come my daughter cuttin her eye at me like she do when she tell me about my "apolitical" self like I got hoof and mouf disease and there ain't no hope at all. And I don't pay her no mind and just look up in Bovanne shadow face and tell him his stomach like a drum and he laugh. Laugh real loud. And here come my youngest, Task, with a tap on my elbow like he the third-grade monitor and I'm cuttin up on the line to assembly.

"I was just talkin on the drums," I explained when they hauled me into the kitchen. I figured drums was my best defense. They can get ready for drums what with all this heritage business. And Bovanne stomach just like that drum Task give me when he come back from Africa. You just touch it and it hum thizzm, thizzm. So I stuck to the drum story. "Just drummin that's all."

"Mama, what are you talkin about?"

"She had too much to drink," say Elo to Task cause she don't hardly say nuthin to me direct no more since that ugly argument about my wigs.

"Look here Mama," say Task, the gentle one. "We just tryin to pull your coat. You were makin a spectacle of yourself out there dancing like that."

"Dancin like what?"

Task run a hand over his left ear like his father for the world and his father before that.

"Like a bitch in heat," say Elo.

"Well uhh, I was goin to say like one of them sex-starved ladies gettin on in years and not too discriminating. Know what I mean?"

I don't answer cause I'll cry. Terrible thing when your own children talk to you like that. Pullin me out the party and hustlin me into some stranger's kitchen in the back of a bar just like the damn police. And ain't like I'm old old. I can still wear me some sleeveless dresses without the meat hangin off my arm. And I keep up with some things through my kids. Who ain't kids no more. To hear them tell it. So I don't say nuthin.

"Dancin with that tom," say Elo to Joe Lee, who leanin on the folks' freezer. "His feet can smell a cracker a mile away and go into their shuffle number post haste. And them eyes. He could be a little considerate and put on some shades. Who wants to look into them blown-out fuses that—"

"Is this what they call the generation gap?" I say.

"Generation gap," spits Elo, like I suggested castor oil and fricassee possum in the milk-shakes or somethin. "That's a white concept for a white phenomenon. There's no generation gap among Black people. We are a col—"

"Yeh, well never mind," says Joe Lee. "The point is Mama . . . well, it's pride. You embarrass yourself and us too dancin like that."

"I wasn't shame." Then nobody say nuthin. Them standin there in they pretty clothes with drinks in they hands and gangin up on me, and me in the third-degree chair and nary a olive to my name. Felt just like the police got hold to me.

"First of all," Task say, holding up his hand and tickin off the offenses, "the dress. Now that dress is too short, Mama, and too low-cut for a woman your age. And Tamu's going to make a speech tonight to kick off the campaign and will be introducin you and expecting you to organize the council of elders—"

"Me? Didn nobody ask me nuthin. You mean Nisi? She change her name?"

"Well, Norton was supposed to tell you about it. Nisi wants to introduce you and then encourage the older folks ass. And people'll say, 'Ain't that the horny bitch that was to form a Council of the Elders to act as an advisory—' "

"And you going to be standing there with your boobs out and that wig on your head and that hem up to your grindin with the blind dude?"

"Elo, be cool a minute," say Task, gettin to the next finger. "And then there's the drinkin. Mama, you know you can't drink cause next thing you know you be laughin loud and carryin on," and he grab another finger for the loudness. "And then there's the dancin. You been tattooed on the man for four records straight and slow draggin even on the fast numbers. How you think that look for a woman your age?"

"What's my age?"

"What?"

"I'm axin you all a simple question. You keep talkin bout what's proper for a woman my age. How old am I anyhow?" And Joe Lee slams his eyes shut and squinches up his face to figure. And Task run a hand over his ear and stare into his glass like the ice cubes goin calculate for him. And Elo just starin at the top of my head like she goin rip the wig off any minute now.

"Is your hair braided up under that thing? If so, why don't you take it off? You always did do a neat cornroll."

"Uh huh," cause I'm thinkin how she couldn't undo her hair fast enough talking bout cornroll so countrified. None of which was the subject. "How old, I say?"

"Sixtee-one or—"

"You a damn lie Joe Lee Peoples."

"And that's another thing," say Task on the fingers.

"You know what you can all kiss," I said, gettin up and brushin the wrinkles out my lap.

"Oh, Mama," Elo say, puttin a hand on my shoulder like she hasn't done since she left home and the hand landin light and not sure it supposed to be there. Which hurt me to my heart. Cause this was the child in our happiness fore Mr. Peoples die. And I carried that child strapped to my chest till she was nearly two. We was close is what I'm tryin to tell you. Cause it was more me in the child than the others. And even after Task it was the girlchild I covered in the night and wept over for no reason at all less it was she was a chub-chub like me and not very pretty, but a warm child. And how did things get to this, that she can't put a sure hand on me and say Mama we love you and care about you and you entitled to enjoy yourself cause you a good woman?

"And then there's Reverend Trent," say Task, glancin from left to right like they hatchin a plot and just now lettin me in on it. "You were suppose to be talking with him tonight, Mama, about giving us his basement for campaign headquarters and—"

"Didn nobody tell me nuthin. If grass roots mean you kept in the dark I can't use it. I really can't. And Reven Trent a fool anyway the way he tore into the widow man up there on Edgecomb cause he wouldn't take in three of them foster children and the woman not even comfy in the ground yet and the man's mind messed up and—"

"Look here," say Task. "What we need is a family conference so we can get all this stuff cleared up and laid out on the table. In the meantime I think we better get back into the other room and tend to business. And in the meantime, Mama, see if you can't get to Reverend Trent and—"

"You want me to belly rub with the Reven, that it?"

"Oh damn," Elo say and go through the swingin door.

"We'll talk about all this at dinner. How's tomorrow night, Joe Lee?" While Joe Lee being self-important I'm wonderin who's doin the cookin and how come no body ax me if I'm free and do I get a corsage and things like that. Then Joe nod that it's O.K. and he go through the swingin door and just a little hubbub come through from the other room. Then Task smile his smile, lookin just like his daddy, and he leave. And it just me in this stranger's kitchen, which was a mess I wouldn't never let my kitchen look like. Poison you just to look at the pots. Then the door swing the other way and it's My Man Bovanne standin there sayin Miss Hazel but lookin at the deep fry and then at the steam table, and most surprised when I come up on him from the other direction and take him on out of there. Pass the folks pushin up towards the stage where Nisi and some other people settin and ready to talk, and folks gettin to the last of the sandwiches and the booze fore they settle down in one spot and listen serious. And I'm thinkin bout tellin Bovanne what a lovely long dress Nisi got on and the earrings and her hair piled up in a cone and the people bout to hear how we all gettin screwed and gotta form our own party and everybody there listenin and lookin. But instead I just haul the man on out of there, and Joe Lee and his wife look at me like I'm terrible, but they ain't said boo to the man yet. Cause he blind and old and don't nobody there need him since they grown up and don't need they skates fixed no more.

"Where we goin, Miss Hazel?" Him knowin all the time.

"First we gonna buy you some dark sunglasses. Then you comin with me to the supermarket so I can pick up tomorrow's dinner, which is goin to be a grand thing proper and you invited. Then we goin to my house."

"That be fine. I surely would like to rest my feet." Bein cute, but you got to let men play out they little show, blind or not. So he chat on bout how tired he is and how he appreciate me takin him in hand this way. And I'm thinkin I'll have him change the lock on my door first thing. Then I'll give the man a nice warm bath with jasmine leaves in the water and a little Epsom salt on the sponge to do his back. And then a good rubdown with rose water and olive oil. Then a cup of lemon tea with a taste in it. And a little talcum, some of that fancy stuff Nisi mother sent over last Christmas. And then a massage, a good face massage round the forehead which is the worryin part. Cause you gots to take care of the older folks. And let them know they still needed to run the mimeo machine and keep the spark plugs clean and fix the mailboxes for folks who might help us get the breakfast program goin, and the school for the little kids and the campaign and all. Cause old folks is the nation. That what Nisi was sayin and I mean to do my part.

"I imagine you are a very pretty woman, Miss Hazel."

"I surely am," I say just like the hussy my daughter always say I was.

CUTTER

At the same moment Jorge recognized the voice, the caller started his story. It usually went like this: he had just completed a rape, he was still in the victim's house or apartment, and he had dialed Helpline because he wanted to get caught—he'd read a story in the paper about a crisis line tracing a rapist's call. Hadn't they started a trace?

In fact, Jorge had done just that. He'd stood behind his desk, and waving to Roberta, he pointed at the phone number beneath the clock—police trace—and she called it in. Once started, it could take anywhere from ten minutes to half an hour. When they had the number, the police would call back. Many of their traces had ended with a cop picking up the by-now silent phone, telling the agency they were taking someone to the emergency room, or that the paramedics were administering CPR—or whatever it might be.

The caller was silent, then said, "Jorge, got it going yet?" Jorge hated having to play along with this guy. He had the feeling the caller thought of him as someone he had captured, a kind of prisoner or hostage. Keeping his voice calm, he said, "Is this Buddy?"

"Yeah, sure, you know it is."

"Buddy, if you really want to be caught, why don't you give me your phone number and I'll be glad to send the police? Or, just turn yourself in. If you've hurt someone, that will keep you from hurting again. If you need help, we'll see you get help." Jorge picked up a plexiglass cube filled with viscous goo. He tipped it slowly.

"Can't you trace my number, man? Hey, I know you can do it when the chips are really down. When someone's bleeding or nodding off. What's the problem?"

"That's what I want to know, what's the problem? We're a suicide and crisis intervention agency; we help people who need help. Why are you wasting our time with games?"

"Games?"

"What do you want, Buddy?"

"I want you to find me." He said, "I was sure no one can." Something about that last statement wasn't right. The tenses. Jorge noted the phrase on his pad. He looked over at Roberta, who sat with her hand on the phone. They were the only ones in the office now. They looked at the clock. Three or four minutes since the start of the call. Jorge said, "You've just raped someone?"

"She's right here."

"Can you put her on?" You never knew. Maybe he'd be dumb enough to do it. Maybe the request would convolute into a challenge Buddy couldn't resist, and she'd blurt her address. Wishful thinking?

There was something muffled. A hand perhaps muting the mouthpiece. Buddy's voice came back on. "She won't talk."

"Why not?"

"She says she's scared."

Jorge decided to kick things up a notch and push it. "Well, then, after you leave, can you tell her to report the rape?"

There was a long pause and Buddy said, "She can't do that. She's too scared. She knows I'll come back."

Jorge said, "You're a nice guy. Who are you?"

Buddy didn't answer. In a standoff, they drifted into small talk. Jorge slowly tipped the plexiglass cube, checked the clock. Over ten minutes now. Across the room, Roberta waited for the police call-back.

"What's her name? Your victim?" Jorge pushed. You never knew what a caller would give you.

Buddy said, "I don't know. I didn't ask her. I do what I want, I always know no one could touch me." There it was again. Something funny in that sentence. Always know. Past tense. Present tense. "How come someone like me can get away with this, mi hijo? Hey, almost fifteen minutes for you guys. If I was bleeding, if I was full of pills and nodding off here, wouldn't you be able to connect?"

"Are you bleeding? Are you full of pills?"

"I'm waiting here for you, mi hijo. Why can't you find me?"

Trying to control his feelings of helplessness and anger, Jorge said, "Well, it's not my fault, Buddy, you and I are doing pretty well tonight but the police are so slow. Is that my fault?"

Buddy laughed. "No, mi hijo, you've done okay. I've got to go now. Give some of your other callers a chance."

"Buddy . . ."

The phone went dead. Jorge dropped the receiver on the desk, flung the plexiglass cube into the wastebasket. He looked at Roberta and shook his head.

Roberta said, "Good try. I thought you'd get him. The cops have been so slow lately." She glanced at the clock. "You kept him on fourteen minutes tonight. Last time, it was, what?"

"Eleven minutes."

"He's got something going with you, Jorge. I had three hangups earlier. It must have been Buddy looking for you to answer. And he's staying on longer each time. Next time he's going to stay on too long, they'll connect on the trace, we'll get him."

Jorge shook his head. Christ, who was he? What did he want? Jorge checked his notes, went to the files and pulled his other cards. *Buddy. Duane.* Tonight's call was consistent with his other rape stories. He'd been phoning on and off for almost a month; sometimes he said he was at his own home and was worried about a gay co-worker who kept calling. For this story, he used the name Duane, but Jorge knew it was the same caller and on his reports wrote in the names *Buddy/Duane* on each card.

Of course, there was no way to confirm whether these stories were fact or fiction, and Jorge rarely read the newspapers with the idea of confirming anything a caller might have said or done—suicides, crimes, family violence, obituaries. His first couple of years with the agency he had tried that, but it tended to make him a little crazy, and he'd stopped. Still he hadn't come across any articles about victims reporting or describing a rapist who hung around and made phone calls to a crisis hotline challenging them to catch him. Yet rape victims didn't always report rapes. And tonight, Buddy had said the woman wouldn't talk or give her name because she was afraid he'd come back—reason enough to remain silent.

Jorge looked over his notes. There was that odd thing about the tenses. The mix of past and present. And then, too, tonight, Buddy had called him *mi hijo,* my son. That was new. Jorge was the bilingual speaker for the agency, but he still didn't know what to make of this. It could be part of the ruse. Either the guy was very clever or very crazy or both.

And what did the caller really want? Jorge wasn't sure, but Roberta was right. Buddy's calls had been getting longer; one of these times Jorge was going to keep him talking until they could run a trace. That's what the caller wanted, wasn't it? To be caught?

Jorge looked around the office—the white fluorescent lights, the desks with their phones and glowing computer screens. There was Mondragon's old desk in the corner. Phil Mondragon. The weird thing, the hard thing for Jorge was that as he talked to the caller, he kept seeing Mondragon's face. His curly black hair, white skin, his dark brown eyes. He heard Phil in the caller's nervous energy, the taunting contempt. In fact, the very first time he'd heard Buddy's voice—before he'd told his rape story or gone into his history as Duane, Jorge had said, "Phil?" And the caller hadn't replied for a long moment.

Mondragon, Jorge knew, was capable of pulling something like this off. He was familiar with the agency and social services system. And if anyone had the voices, it was Mondragon. In his time at the agency, he had come to be referred to as *The Voice*. And when he'd been in one of his many personas as a counselor, he was great. Quiet, tender, yet firm and immovable with a codependent woman on her third go-around. Tough with a drunken, bullying ex-con looking to be convinced to get back on his medication, yet fighting it. In quiet times between calls, he'd do voices and characters: James Mason; Montgomery Clift; Muhammad Ali; Roseanne Barr; a perfect Betty Davis; an insidious Richard the Third courting Lady Anne, which he'd played in Drama School; a reprise of his raging Ned Weeks, from community theater's *The Normal Heart*.

But Phil had lost it. First, he'd quit the agency—they'd given him a party on what was to be his last shift and the end of his old life—to take a small part in a movie in L.A. The movie's financing had collapsed and after kicking around L.A. for ten months, he decided to come back and regroup. He'd returned to his girl's house in the middle of a sweltering afternoon, and just before ringing the doorbell, he'd heard sounds of love-making and done an about-face. He'd picked up his old job at Helpline, but had been unable to keep a sarcasm and taunting contempt out of his voice. Part of it, Jorge thought, was that Mondragon was so good and facile with voices and in seducing people into believing he sympathized with their situations, that he had come to feel an enormous contempt for himself and, subsequently, the callers.

One night Mondragon shook Jorge and made a believer out of him. Jorge had taken a convoluted phone call from a first-time caller who had identified herself only as Miranda H. Four marriages, fourth one breaking up. Husbands always untrustworthy and unfaithful. Molested by her father. A drinking problem. Two suicide attempts. Well, they weren't really attempts, but she'd mixed alcohol and sleeping pills and come to in the ER with her stomach being pumped both times. She was drinking now. He could hear ice cubes clinking in her glass and her speech starting to slur. She refused every attempted referral Jorge made for counseling. What, she said, was the use? She'd tried them all. He'd been unable to get her to give him her number and was thinking of starting a trace when she'd made an elegiac statement about life being a one-way journey down a lilac-scented path to death and hung up.

Jorge put his line on hold and went to the bathroom. As he'd returned, Mondragon, reading the paper at his desk, glanced up at Jorge. "Yo, brother, you looking whipped. Qué pasa, amigo-dude?"

Jorge mentioned the long call, Miranda H. Mondragon nodded sympathetically. Hey, did she keep talking about a big yellow dog—Biff?—with weak hindquarters, five hundred dollars on surgery for its prolapsed rectum? Jorge said, "That's the one. Have you talked with her before? She said she was a first-time caller."

Mondragon shrugged, "Nope, never talked to her," and then, picking up his paper, Mondragon slurred in her voice, "No matter what anyone says or does, I know life is just a pointless, lilac-scented slouch toward endless death. I'll probably see all four of my husbands there. If there's nothing you can say or do to change that fact, I don't see what we have to talk about."

The exact words of Miranda H. Jorge stared at Mondragon's raised newspaper. Biff with the prolapsed rectum. Mondragon, he realized, had placed the call from one of the back offices. They had often tested each other with little telephone games. But nothing like this. This was something else, a quantum leap, a tour de force. Mondragon had whipped him. Jorge hadn't had a clue.

But Mondragon had gone too far, even for Mondragon. After giving him repeated warnings, Jean, their supervisor, ran a check, calling and playing the part of a woman who wanted to leave her husband but was afraid she'd hurt his feelings so badly he'd kill himself and didn't know what to do. Mondragon had given her nothing but sarcasm, suggested she can the bum, be better off without him, and get a vibrator with six speeds. Not to mention that their standard opening, *Helpline,* had been a stuttering Porky Pig. HhhhhhELP LlllIINE.

Jean came out of the back offices and said, "That's all, Phil. I'll take over your phone as of right now—you can pick up two weeks' severance pay this Friday. I suggest you see a counselor yourself. You know the agencies, but take this." She handed him a note with several referrals. "Get help."

Now that he was fired, he suddenly seemed sorry and desperate, "Hey, I knew you were the caller, Jean . . . that's why I played it the way I did. I knew it was you."

She shook her head. "You didn't have a clue who it was when you answered the phone stuttering like Porky Pig. If I had been a caller and had heard that . . ."

Jorge watched Mondragon. With a tired, silly shrug, palms turned up, and a cartoon character's roll of his eyes, Mondragon smiled—a perfect little shit-eating grin—and stuttered in a Speedy Gonzalez accent, "Ttttthhhat's aallll, folks. Ttttthhhat's aallll, Phil." As he passed, he glared at Jorge, yet his eyes were blind with a moist fury; he kicked over a chair and slammed the door. Jorge was amazed by the outburst.

Hey, Jorge thought, as he fished the plexiglass cube out of the waste-basket and placed it back on the desk, Mondragon was definitely capable of pulling off the Buddy ruse. He checked over his scramble of notes, took out a card, but put his phone on hold. Christ, this place had really been bugging him lately. Was it just his mood, or had the agency come to overshadow almost every aspect of his life? There'd been the bad timing of the other night; *that* had been the agency, too.

He looked at a poster scotch-taped to the door. Across the top, it said: Miguel Angelo Rivera. Below, a fine-lined drawing, a length of tapered calf in a fishnet stocking, an impossibly high stilleto heel coming down on a smoking cigarette butt. At the bottom: Hotel Santa Cruz. Club Easy, June 28, 9 and 12 P.M. Which had been last week. Miguel, he just now realized, had been on his mind since that night, when Jorge had to rush off from the Club without a word. He'd felt uneasy since.

Miguel. Ten years ago, when Jorge was a young social worker running a group for disturbed children at Las Familias, Miguel had just been taken from his parents. His stepfather had been molesting him and his sister for years. Finally, a teacher who'd been observing the boy—his withdrawn and depressed behavior, his bruises—called Child Protective Services.

At eleven, Miguel Angelo was a beautiful boy, slim, with golden skin, blue-green eyes which tipped up at the corners, high cheekbones, full lips, and glossy, straight black hair which fell to his shoulders. In the group, he remained silent and withdrawn. Then, without warning or apparent provocation, he would weep, howl, pull his hair, tremble, and scratch his cheeks. Jorge would talk to him softly, and sometimes Miguel would let Jorge hold his hand, hug and console him.

In time, Jorge had taken Miguel to the movies and bowling and brought him home to his parents' for dinner several nights a week. Jorge wanted Miguel to be with adults, a mother and father, who could be trusted. He wanted Miguel to be with a Hispanic family. Jorge had not always been Hispanic or Chicano. For a long time, he'd seen himself as the world saw him: a spic, a beaner, a greaser. He'd been beaten and humiliated by his grade-school teachers when he'd lapse into Spanish from English. As a teenager, he'd been furious, reckless. He still had a tattoo from those high-school days, a stemmed rose entwined with a dagger dripping blood and rose petals on his chest. In the shower, an Anglo linebacker had placed his finger on Jorge's chest. "What's this, verga,[1] it takes a tough man to make a tender chicken, some shit like that?"

1. Cock (i.e., penis).

And they'd fought. One night, without provocation, his car had been pulled over by a cop. As he'd stepped out, the white cop had brought his gun down on his head and split his scalp open. Wherever he turned, there was trouble. It had been a Hispanic woman, a chicana, a social worker, who taught him who he was and why he was angry and how to value and accept himself. He understood Miguel. Jorge had retained a special attachment to him.

After a couple of years of hearings, pretrial motions, and delays, Miguel, as a thirteen-year-old, had testified against his stepfather in trial, and it had been his testimony and that of his sister which sent him to prison. Afterward, Miguel seemed to regress, and Jorge understood that Miguel, though relieved, felt that he had betrayed his stepfather. At times, Jorge even thought that Miguel yearned for the man, despite what he'd done.

By now, he was turning from a boy into an adolescent, *beautiful* being the only word to describe him. Whenever Jorge ran into him, he could see an enormous torment within Miguel's face. His voice had dropped to barely a whisper. He'd gone to the community college, studied art one semester, and then, painfully cut off from everyone, he'd disappeared.

For a while, there had been no word of him and then Jorge heard that Miguel Angelo Rivera was down in Douglas on the Arizona-Sonora border, and that he did a stage show in a gay bar there called Serafino's; he dressed and sang as a woman and word was that he was beautiful and that he was knocking them dead. Jorge had no idea what to think, and last week, after more than two years, Miguel had come back to town, and Jorge had gone down to the Club Easy to see for himself what had happened to Miguel.

Club Easy was on the first floor of the old and dilapidated Hotel Santa Cruz. Inside, Jorge eased into a thick darkness. He sensed, then slowly made out a large crowd sitting with faces turned up to a raised stage where some-one—Linda Ronstadt?—sang "Love Me Tender."

Jorge didn't know what he'd been expecting, but in the white lights, there was a beautiful, slender woman: long legs in sheer black stockings, high black heels, a black leather mini skirt, a short-sleeved white silk blouse. Then, the face, the high cheek-bones, the blue-green eyes accented by bluish eye shadow, and the lips, the incredible, beautiful full lips, in glossy red lipstick. Though somewhere in him Jorge knew this must be Miguel, before he could check himself, he felt a leap of desire. Then, confusion and self-reproach. People stood around him all the way to the bar, and in the blacked-out room, with everyone motionless, each person's face turned up to Miguel Angelo Rivera lip-synching "Love Me Tender," it was as if everyone were dreaming this same dream.

Slowly, he started working his way forward through the crowd. Even as he got closer, Jorge could see that Miguel Angelo had none of the giveaway signs of the drag queen—large hands or prominent jaw. From time to time, he would stop and look from Miguel Angelo to the faces of the audience. Here, a row of women, silent, watched him. There, a couple, and beyond them, two men, arms around each other's waists. They looked silently into him, as if searching for a line of current where male met female.

Jorge had almost reached the stage when Miguel, peering out into the dark, spotted him. For a moment, he leaned forward and sang to him, and then, never breaking his persona, he pointed a polished nail toward the bar, and Jorge nodded, yes, he'd meet him there.

But before Miguel had been able to finish the show, Jorge's beeper had gone off—he was the Spanish speaker on call that night—and he'd gone out to take a two-hour long suicide call. He'd never made it back. He had no idea what Miguel had thought, his rushing out of there like that. After more than two years of being gone, had he taken it as a rejection of his appearing in drag? Uncertain how to reach Miguel Angelo, he'd called the next afternoon and left a message for him at the Club Easy—Miguel, sorry, called away on an emergency, I'll be back in touch. You were great. Jorge.

And he'd been meaning to see Miguel. But each day, something had come up. This, he realized as he looked at the poster—the fishnet stocking, the stiletto heel—was what had really been making him so edgy all week. Not Buddy or Duane or anything else that was going on at Helpline. Not really.

He circled back to his desk and reread his notes: rape call. Under caller, he wrote *Buddy,* and within moments, he felt himself being drawn back into obsessing about Buddy. At a recent staff meeting, each counselor had submitted a list of possible callers who might be Buddy—callers who had been overly threatening and contentious. By the time they'd finished, there were at least fifteen names. Several counselors, including Jorge, had submitted Dawn's name. Dawn was a very troubling possibility. Besides Mondragon, Jorge thought Dawn was the most likely caller. At times, he thought, she was the only real possibility.

Dawn had been molested by her grandfather, father, and uncles from the time she was two, and had also been used in satanic rituals. At fourteen, stressed by intense nightmares and flashbacks, Dawn had blossomed multiple personalities. She referred to them as the kids, and she had named them for Jorge, the way a mother would introduce children to a visitor, with affection, consternation, tenderness, exasperation, and, in her case, fear; there were the twins, Jody and Jan, they were ten and very sweet; there was the sluttish, angry teenager, Arlene, who had gotten in so much trouble cutting high school, getting arrested for drunken driving, and shoplifting; there was Jimmy Joe, a thuggish 19-year-old hood who took girls for rides in the desert, slapped them around, raped them. Jimmy Joe was rough and unpredictable. Dawn named eleven kids.

Jorge had only heard about Jimmy Joe from Dawn, but never actually heard his voice come out of her; could Jimmy Joe be the rapist? Dawn would call and say, I had flashbacks all afternoon and some of the kids came out. She'd say she couldn't stand it anymore, talk about killing herself. After several calls, it occurred to Jorge that if Dawn had multiple personalities, then who was Dawn? She said, "Dawn is someone I put together from watching the kids on the *Brady Bunch,* looking at posters of Farrah Fawcett—I have posters of her all over my room—and talking to shrinks. Dawn is the one who tries to take care of the kids."

Dawn's name had come up on almost half the staff's list of possible identities for Buddy—Dawn's Jimmy Joe as Buddy and Duane. As no one knew how to handle it, a wait-and-see attitude was adopted. When the meeting broke up, Jean cautioned everyone. No matter what each counselor thought, the caller—Buddy/Duane—couldn't be dismissed; this was the hard part. There was a very good chance that the caller was exactly who he said he was— a rapist—and that the calls were authentic. She acknowledged this held the agency hostage to the caller, but they'd just have to do the best they could until they got a break. Oddly to Jorge, Mondragon's name had not surfaced, and Jorge kept his suspicions to himself for the time being.

Jorge finished logging the night's calls and straightened his desk. Resolutely, he placed the plexiglass cube in a drawer. He walked to the window to check the parking lot for Jill, his replacement, who took the midnight to eight shift. Now it was ten of twelve. Jorge began to pace. He really wanted to get out of here and away from all this. Tonight, he was going to make it down to Club Easy and try to reconnect with Miguel. He felt a strange disquiet.

The show had just finished and people at the dark bar were talking about Miguel—how incredible, imagine legs like that on a man, they're better than mine; the amazing color of his eyes, the way he moved, his lips. Listening to the comments, Jorge worked his beer in circles. Someone in a white T-shirt and faded blue jeans slipped onto the stool beside him, and it was a moment before he realized it was Miguel with his long hair pulled tightly back into a pony tail. Except for nail polish, all traces of the make-up, lipstick and eye shadow, were gone, and no one recognized or noticed him.

Jokingly, Jorge said, "Hey, querido. Or," he added, "should I say, querida?"

Miguel smiled. Jorge said, "You were fantastic." He meant it. "Hey, sorry about last week, the way I just disappeared, but I got a call right before the end of the show." He tugged the beeper on his belt, Miguel looked down. "I'm the Spanish speaker for the agency, so you know, I had to run out to a phone. A two-hour suicide call." He shook his head. "Anyway, you got my note?"

"What note?"

"I was afraid of that. I left a note with the bartender. You know, I wanted to get back to see you sooner, but I've been jammed." As he said it, he looked at Miguel's red fingernails on the bar and wondered if he'd really been that busy.

Unable to pick up any kind of ease or rhythm, they spoke haltingly. Finally, Jorge thought to ask him about the border. Serafino's, where it had started. In a quiet voice, Miguel told how he'd gone there to get out of town; he'd started as a busboy. Anything was fine, he just wanted to make a break. After a few weeks, bored, he'd been playing with the mike late one afternoon, the place nearly empty—a few people at the bar, the waitresses setting up. He'd been pretending to sing to the jukebox. The waitresses laughed and encouraged him. Someone played Linda Ronstadt's "Ohh Baby Baby." He'd closed his eyes, forgotten everyone, drifted off, just flowed into the music. Halfway through the song, he'd looked out. Everyone had gravitated toward the tables and stood motionless, watching him. Within a few days, there was lipstick from a waitress, eye shadow, then the skirt, the heels, and stockings. Each just seemed to be there, inevitable, and he had not resisted.

Miguel's voice was barely audible, and now that he was off stage, his brilliance had receded into a distance, and Jorge almost felt a barrier in its place. Whose barrier, he wasn't sure. Maybe Miguel's. Maybe his, Jorge's. Miguel slid his fingertips up and down the neck of the bottle, drew circles in the moisture of the bar, his long red nails coming to rest near Jorge's hand, then moving away. The silence lengthened, and then Jorge, uncertain where to go next, asked Miguel if he could sing, if he'd ever tried—and Miguel said softly, "Oh, no, that doesn't matter. I have no voice. I can't even carry a tune." He'd shrugged as if nothing could be more self-evident, or beside the point, and Jorge, feeling stupid, nodded, of course it didn't.

Again the silence grew longer, and again Jorge felt that distance. Then, Miguel stood and, looking into the back bar mirror, remained beside his stool. "Gotta go. You can reach me here. See you later." It sounded more like a question and Jorge said, "Of course. I'll come back. We'll get together. Sorry again about the other night." Did Miguel believe him, that he hadn't been able to stick around, that he'd really had to take a suicide call? Jorge could only hope so. As Miguel reached the end of the bar, Jorge saw him as he might be in twenty years, a slight, shy man on the verge of middle age, and he couldn't help but wonder what it would be like to grow old as a drag queen. They nodded at each other and waved.

Jorge turned over and fought back the covers. He lay motionless, took several deep breaths, but the voices followed him like sonar. Buddy. Dawn. Mondragon. Mondragon as Miranda H. He heard Dawn saying in a small voice, "The kids came out today."

He reached over in the dark, turned on his radio, and searched for something without words, jazz. He settled back, followed the swift flight of a guitar, began to drift. Faraway, someone appeared out of a circle of light. He drifted. He heard someone crying and felt an ache of tenderness. He turned on his side and walked into a hot, dry wind of voices. The kids? The kids came out. Somewhere on a fault line in the night, he slow-danced feverishly with a beautiful woman in a white T-shirt and tight jeans.

June was gone and a week of July. Day after day, the desert sky was cloudless. Just after noon the sun drifted to a stop and, becalmed, hung overhead; the streets and alleys went from three- to two-dimensional in the white light, and everything dried up in the sun. Towering over the city, the mountains too, dried brown, looked as if they had been air-brushed onto a silvery blue distance. In the second week in July, an arsonist torched the mountain woods, and in high westerly winds the woods burned out of control. They burned out of control for days. Evenings, people came home from work to find deer and javelinas, foxes and snakes, coyotes and flocks of birds, drinking from their backyard swimming pools in the foothills. Nights, the dense blackness of the mountains blazed with thousands of beautiful, liquidly shimmering fires, as if the stars had come down out of the sky, and each star was burning on the mountain. A fine ash sifted over the city.

The fire triggered something in people, and day and night Helpline was flooded with callers. The chronics called and obsessed through old problems. They forgot or refused to take their medication and, hallucinatory, ranted into the phone. The incidence of domestic violence doubled and tripled, and Helpline sent women and children to battered women's shelters and told women how and where to get restraining orders. There were serious suicide attempts and Helpline dispatched the police. One night Buddy called with another rape victim at his feet and taunted Jorge to find him and stayed on seventeen minutes, but he couldn't be traced and Jorge called and berated a bored dispatcher at the police department who said she'd file a report.

Another night, Duane called about the gay co-worker who was phoning him at home, and Jorge pretended he didn't know it was Buddy's other voice, tried to trace him, and failed. Part of him said, as he hung up the phone, don't I know this guy? He became motionless in his swivel chair as a voice within jolted him: yes, you do, it's Miguel Angelo. Though Jorge couldn't say how or why, he was suddenly sure. Then he felt the thick, feverish dream of the other night envelop him, slow-dancing with a beautiful woman in a white

T-shirt and tight jeans. That, too, was Miguel Angelo. What, was he starting to lose it completely? He felt his certainty give way.

Mondragon? If it was Mondragon, hey, maybe he didn't want to recognize it. Jorge liked Mondragon. He really didn't want to think Mondragon could be doing something like this. And doing it to him. And if he identified Mondragon, well, what then? What was he supposed to do? Follow through on the trace, send the cops, have Mondragon charged by the agency? Jorge didn't know, but if things kept up, maybe it was coming to that.

A few minutes later someone with a soft, husky voice called in and wanted to know if the people on TV, you know, the ones in the cop shows, bled real blood when they were shot or stabbed, and Jorge, after a long pause—genuine schizo caller, outpatient who needed a shot of Haldol, or just a bored summer-school student?—said, yes, they bled real blood, always real blood, the caller asked, who cleans it up, Jorge said he didn't know, but he'd check it out, before he could say more, he heard the dial tone. He pulled a card to him. Caller. Jorge wrote, unknown . . . he hesitated. Male? Female? Something in that voice. An alarm went off in him, loud and clear, and he went to the files, pulled out the great steel drawers, dropped to his knees, and began to dig in the S's.

He found the file under: Samantha/Sam. There were at least forty cards held together with a heavy clip, cards in a dozen different staff members' handwriting. Caller: Sam, Amber . . . Jean had crossed out each name and written in *Samantha* or *Absolutely Samantha*. Christ, how had he—how had they, the staff, and particularly Jean and himself—overlooked Samantha/Sam as Buddy/Duane? It had been almost a year since her last call, but still, what an oversight! That soft, husky voice.

Jorge leafed the cards. Many were in his handwriting. God, he had forgotten. She had started out calling as Samantha—hey, call me Sam, okay? A runaway teenager with a guy named Nicky just out of a correctional institution, they were trying to make it to Hawaii. . . . He flipped through the cards: Amber. Tiffany. All girls on the run with good/bad boyfriends. Jean had figured out they were the same caller. Then, amazingly, there was Howard, whose wife had taken their three kids and left him; he was going crazy. And Dell, with his soft Southern accent. So polite. Yes, sir, no, ma'am. Dell usually called at two in the morning while waiting for his girl to come home. She was out with another man, yes, sir. Again, both Jean and Jorge had finally grown suspicious, figured out Howard and Dell were the same caller, and then Jean also figured it out—that soft, husky voice—was Samantha. Even after the staff had been warned, Samantha went on hooking counselors for months. Howard. Dell. Amber. Perhaps her pièce de résistance had been Amorita. Amorita was a seven-year-old girl who was home alone. Her daddy was dying of cancer in the hospital. Her mommy worked. Staff workers read to her night after night. *The Velveteen Rabbit, The Cat in the Hat, The Black Stallion.* It had been months before Jean identified her as Samantha.

Jorge stood with the file. How had every single person in the agency overlooked this? Okay, the caller had been quiescent for a year, but still someone should have thought of Samantha. These callers were like weird strains of aerobically borne viruses or molds triggered out of dormancy by who knew what, electromagnetic activity, X-rays from deep space, who knew? He wrote Jean a note: Buddy/Duane, our rape caller? He clipped it to Samantha's file and put it in Jean's box. Then, as he sat back down at his desk, his sense of certainty went out of him. What if Sam and Amber and Howard and Amorita were Buddy? They still had to catch him.

One night Jorge received a succession of calls which pushed him over the edge. The first, toward the last hour of his shift, had been from an unknown woman. The voice was so soft he could barely hear it, and he had thought of Samantha and Mondragon's Miranda H. He went ahead with the usual questions to ground the caller and bring her out. What's going on tonight? What'd you do today? Gradually, he got the woman to speak up, though he could still barely make her out. It was like this when they'd been crying, or when they were paralyzed by depression.

She said she hadn't gone out today, she'd been too depressed. She didn't have many friends. She stayed by herself. She had no close relationships, she lived alone. Within a few minutes, Jorge suddenly knew that she was going to turn out to be a cutter. Cutters, he had noticed, seemed to have similar histories: they were almost always young women who had been sexually abused; they had extremely low self-esteem and suffered numbing depression, like this caller. Softly and gently, Jorge asked questions into her paralyzed silence. No, she had not called the agency before. She didn't feel like giving a first name. Okay, that was fine.

Convinced she was a cutter, Jorge decided to head for it and started to set her up. She sounded very depressed. Was she in counseling? Sort of—she went to a group. What group? AMAC. Had he heard of it? Yes, Adults Molested As Children. And was it helping? Not really. Was she feeling suicidal tonight? Yes. Did she have a method at her disposal? Yes. What was that? Razor. The word hung. Razor. They were there. He listened into the phone. The silence grew longer. He had been doing it all for her, but now he waited. She had to make the next move. He watched the second hand go around on the clock.

The minute hand jumped twice before she said softly, "I have this strange urge to cut myself." Jorge nodded. He'd seen the arms of cutters, the thin tracings and maps left by razor blades. For some it was a kind of foreplay to wrist slashing. For others, cutting was release enough, an end in itself. Jorge said, "Have you cut yourself before?"

"No. I'm fighting it," she said in a near whisper, "but I'm feeling very alone."

"I understand," Jorge said. He knew that often it was just the sound of a human voice that could make a difference, and so he stayed on, searching for questions to ask her, trying to get her to talk. Finally, after a long silent impasse, he said, "If you think you're going to cut yourself, will you call us back before you do anything?"

"I'll try," she said in a halting voice, "Will you be there?"

He'd glanced at the clock. He was going off soon. "Not much longer, but there is always someone here."

"But *you* won't be there?"

"Not tonight."

The caller was silent. After a moment, Jorge heard her start to cry. As she had been unwilling to give her name, he could only make a kind of undefined sound into the phone. She hung up. Stunned, Jorge listened to the dial tone, then let out an exhausted sigh. There was something about the way she'd said *you*—*you* won't—which made him think of Mondragon's saying, "All we're doing is acting. We're pretending we're here for people, but we're not. It's a con job." Now Mondragon seemed right. Jorge knew he was exhausted. He put his phone on hold, went into a small back office, and turning off the lights, he stretched out on the floor and lay in the dark.

When he returned, blinking into the glare of the office lights, the moment he released the hold button, the phone rang. Picking up, he recognized Buddy. Or was it Samantha? He waved at Marilyn and pointed at the trace number. They'd gotten no more than two minutes into the call, when something in him snapped at the sound of the taunting voice; he'd been keeping it from himself, but there was no longer any doubt, and he stood suddenly at his desk. "Goddamnit, Mondragon, why the fuck are you doing this to me? Chinga tu madre! Hijo de puta!"[1]

He banged down the receiver. Marilyn and Roberta looked at him, then each other. He slammed out of the room and down the long dark hall of the office building, punching the walls. It was the first time ever in his career as a counselor at Helpline—four years—that anyone had pulled him out of his counselor's persona. Worse, somewhere in him, he was still just a furious seventeen-year-old pachuca with a rose and dagger on his chest.

---

1. "Go fuck your mother! Son of a whore!"

Shaking his head, he walked the length of the hall several times, then took off early, and went for a long drive, finally coming to a stop facing the Hotel Santa Cruz. He left the engine running and stared at the hotel. Inside, in the Club Easy, Miguel Angelo wore a tight mini skirt and black silk stockings and lip-synched to Linda Ronstadt, Whitney Houston, and Janet Jackson in a circle of white lights. He saw Miguel's glossy red lips. His blue-green eyes. He saw Miguel's red fingernails drawing circles on the bar, his fingertips moving up and down slowly on the neck of the bottle, felt a wave of uneasiness roll through his stomach. He stared at the hotel. Something inside told him this was what was making him so edgy, not Buddy—hell, the agency had never really gotten to him before. He was divorced and between girlfriends, but turning queer? He liked women. He knew he liked women, not men dressed as women. He was sure of that. He revved the engine, slammed it into drive, and drove.

The next afternoon, Jorge had little trouble finding Mondragon's bungalow at the end of a narrow dirt road, and standing outside his garden gate, hand on the latch, he hesitated. The front of the house was surrounded by a six-foot high fence made of salvaged wood and corrugated iron, but which created, nonetheless, a pleasingly ordered pattern. Jorge peered through a crack and spotted Mondragon standing in the garden; he was partially hidden by roof-high sunflowers. He wore nothing but a black belt tied around his waist and a jockstrap, and sweating, he moved in a slowly undulating wave: tai chi. Jorge worked the latch, called out, and stepped inside. A neatly manicured dirt path curved toward the front door, and waist-high mounds of dirt were covered with flowers—marigolds, zinnias, verbena, and lantana—all giving off a pungent odor in the midday sun.

Without stopping his movement, Mondragon rotated toward Jorge and went into a slight crouch, his hands raised. Only a gringo like this could be doing tai chi or whatever it was gringos did in the desert sun in July. Mondragon's curly black hair had grown out, he was unshaven, and there was something crazed and contemptuous in his brown eyes which made Jorge uneasy.

Mondragon said softly, "Qué pasa, amigo-dude?"

"I'm okay. How've you been, Phil?"

"Just how you see."

Jorge wasn't sure how he saw. Mondragon stopped moving and stood motionless among the towering sunflowers, sweat dripping from his chin and streaming down his chest. Damp with sweat and dry-mouthed, Jorge decided small talk wouldn't work. He said, "Phil, I know what you think of the agency—Jean, the way she fired you, all of it. And I know you had some trouble leading up to it. L.A. Your girl. I understand. A lot of the time I feel like

you do about the agency. You were right about some things—the easy seduction, the way we're all maybe playing a part we can't deliver on, the way
it's a kind of act." Jorge surprised himself and tried to shut up.

Mondragon stood still. Without turning to look, he let a hand inch away
until it found a sunflower stalk.

Jorge went on. "And so, yeah, calling us, putting on an act, challenging
us, I understand, Phil. It's the perfect reply. But listen, man, whatever you
think of the agency, please stop calling us now. Buddy, Miranda H . . ." He
trailed off. "Are you calling us?"

Phil curled his fingers gently around the thick green stalk. He said very
simply, "Why would I call you?" Jorge watched him closely and thought Mondragon was masterful in his ingenuousness.

"I don't know. But if you are calling, please stop." Mondragon smiled, a
gentle, pitying, slightly contemptuous smile. "Phil, if and when the agency
does catch you, they'll press charges." Phil shook his head. "But the real danger here is someone's going to get lost in the shuffle and die in the confusion
this thing is making."

Mondragon remained smiling at him. Jorge turned and walked back
down the path. As he reached the gate, Mondragon called him. "Amigo-
dude?"

"What?"

"Would you like a glass of water?"

Jorge hesitated. Brilliant. The sly guile, the contempt. Mondragon.
Jorge shook his head no. Mondragon was unreadable, and now he realized
that no matter what Mondragon had said, he wouldn't have believed him. As
he closed the gate, he looked back once more. Mondragon, in his black belt
and jockstrap, and holding the sunflower stalk, was smiling and looking up
at the sun.

Several days later there was an emotional staff meeting. Jorge's explosive
hang-up on Buddy was raised, and Jorge shook his head in disbelief that
Roberta and Marilyn would rat him off. Unbelievable. Though Jean said no
one was more sympathetic than she, the agency could not afford to deal with
callers that way. And it still hadn't been established that Buddy was a hoax.
Incidentally, that kind of uncontrolled response was just the payoff someone
like Buddy was working for. Someone said to Jorge, "You're holding back
anger. Talk about it." After a long silence, Jorge said, "Fuck you. How's that?"

In that deteriorating atmosphere, Jean went over possible callers. She
thanked Jorge for the suggestion about Samantha/Sam/Howard/Dell and said
that she thought Samantha had to be number one on their list of candidates.
When the name was mentioned, everyone murmured. Christ almighty, how

had everyone forgotten about Samantha? Well, she hadn't called in over a year . . . yeah, but, still. Never mind. They would start checking her out, but as of now, it remained tough because as far as anyone knew, she had never had a social worker, never taken any referrals. She would be tough. Again, Dawn's name was brought up. Jean had recently spoken with Dawn and thought she was in a difficult, suicidal phase. The kids were coming out all the time now. Arlene. Jimmy Joe. Dawn was very afraid of Jimmy Joe, who was a dangerous and unstable personality. Jimmy Joe *was* a rapist.

Now Jorge thought of mentioning Mondragon, but just couldn't bring himself to do it. His old authority problems? Wasn't he keeping something from himself so he wouldn't have to dime Phil? Christ, he knew it was Mondragon. So what? Be like these gringa counselors, rat him off? Better to let Mondragon keep calling. Catch him or not, whatever. Another voice, cold and out of nowhere, said, or am I going crazy and can't tell what's what because I'm turning queer? And that one made his stomach roll over. The meeting broke up with nothing resolved. Jorge stood and walked out quickly, pushing past staff members.

Jorge made sure the catch on the window was in place and leaned on the windowsill. Covering the late afternoon sun, an ashen wall rose in the west. Dust. A while later, the wind bent the palms and eucalypti, the sky went black, and when Jorge leaned on the sill again, a fine layer of dust coated his hands. Then it was hot and still, and slowly the stars came out. Jorge took a call and after a few moments recognized the voice of the woman, the cutter. She seemed very far away and because Jorge was tired and could barely make her out, he momentarily imagined her buried somewhere in that wall of dust. She was very depressed. She had a razor. Had she used it? She didn't answer. Maybe this would be a good time to tell me your first name? After a long silence, she hung up. Jorge noted the time, took a deep breath, and went to the coke machine.

When he returned, there was a hang-up, and then Jorge took a call and recognized Buddy's voice. He snapped his fingers at Marilyn, who started the trace. Buddy didn't mention Jorge's explosion of the other night. Nor did he begin in his usual taunting way by asking if Jorge had started the trace. Instead, talking almost gently to Jorge, mi hijo, he seemed to be going in and out of a past and a meandering present, and suddenly, Jorge knew that this guy wasn't Samantha or Mondragon, this guy must be for real. He talked about how hard it had been in prison, mi hijo, how much he had missed his children, how he had never meant to hurt them, that no one was supposed to get hurt, but he couldn't help himself, wasn't it that way, too, with the way the government had put Indians on the reservation, mi hijo? Jorge listened. Did he know this guy from somewhere? Or was he going crazy himself? And what about Cortez? Jorge lost him completely with Cortez. I'll tell you about Cortez. Much of the rambling Jorge couldn't follow, but almost afraid to breathe, he just kept murmuring, yes, yes, yes, I see, I understand, all of the time thinking of Mondragon's saying how it was all just an act, Jorge understood nothing. He watched the minute hand going around, twelve minutes, fifteen minutes, eighteen minutes, Marilyn's phone rang, she wrote quickly, she held her hand overhead in a fist, a number and address, she called 9 1 1, sent the cops. Jorge went on listening. After a few minutes, Buddy said talking so much was making him thirsty, he was going to get a drink, he'd be right back, he had more to tell Jorge.

Buddy put the phone down and then it was silent, and Jorge paced behind his desk, listening into the receiver. The phone remained silent for a long time. Ten, fifteen minutes. Then, someone, breathless, picked up the phone, and Jorge's heart started to pound. "This is Sergeant Vega here . . . who is this? Who is this?"

"Helpline. Jorge of Helpline. I'm still on. We started the trace and sent you." Jorge explained quickly about Buddy, the rapist, the calls. "Who's down there?"

"Just the woman. The guy, whoever he is, he's gone. There's blood everywhere. We're taking the woman to the ER."

"Which ER?"

"Kino."

Jorge hung up, circled the office, took a hug from Marilyn, and then said, "Can you cover for me? I've got to go." In his car, he sat numb and then started driving. He drove south. In the hot stillness, undulating white clouds choked the silvery streetlights, and Jorge, stopped at a red light, could see they were huge winged grasshoppers swarming in from the desert. He watched a cloud shaping and reshaping itself. In his four years at Helpline, he realized he'd never seen a caller's face. This latest victim knew something. Jorge didn't know exactly what he wanted. He couldn't stop seeing Mondragon's face. He realized the summer, the heat, the weeks of taking calls from Buddy and Duane and Dawn and dozens of others, maybe he'd lost it more than a little. He drove south.

In the emergency room, people waited—mothers and fathers with crying children, a weeping woman, a man who lay on his side groaning. A huge, fat white woman was brought in by cops who had arrested her in a bar brawl; they couldn't take her to jail until she sobered up. Restrained, she cursed and abused everyone, momentarily broke away from the cops, filled the corridor with threats.

At the end of the hall, there was an alcove, and Jorge saw more cops and a woman's back. One cop stood by the woman and another was talking to the nurse a few steps away. Jorge could see they were about to take her inside, and that she was covered with blood. She turned as Jorge approached, and Jorge saw Miguel Angelo in his skirt and black stockings.

Miguel looked at Jorge and said in the small, not quite comprehending voice of the small boy he remembered, "Where've you been?"

Jorge looked at Miguel's face and then he saw the many faces moving beneath the make-up, the tormented boy, the boy who had sent his stepfather to prison; he saw the nondescript, middle-aged man he'd momentarily seen in the Club Easy, whom he now recognized as Buddy, the stepfather who had held his son hostage night after night; and, as Miguel held out his hand—the beautiful painted long nails, the bloody tracks of the razor up and down his arms—Jorge recognized his unknown female, his cutter, the woman Miguel had become.

Miguel said, "I'm alone. Where've you been?"

Jorge stretched out his hand into Miguel's vast, uncrossable distance. "I'm here, mi hijo.[1] I've always been here." Jorge took Miguel's slim hand which was thick with blood. From down the hall, they could hear the fat woman cursing and the cops trying to restrain her.

---

1. My son.

T. Coraghessan Boyle

I DATED JANE AUSTEN

Her hands were cold. She held them out for me as I stepped into the parlor. "Mr. Boyle," announced the maid, and Jane was rising to greet me, her cold white hands like an offering. I took them, said my good evenings, and nodded at each of the pairs of eyes ranged round the room. There were brothers, smallish and large of head, whose names I didn't quite catch; there was her father, the Reverend, and her sister, the spinster. They stared at me like sharks on the verge of a feeding frenzy. I was wearing my pink boots, 'Great Disasters' T-shirt and my Tiki medallion. My shoulders slumped under the scrutiny. My wit evaporated.

"Have a seat, son," said the Reverend, and I backed onto a settee between two brothers. Jane retreated to an armchair on the far side of the room. Cassandra, the spinster, plucked up her knitting. One of the brothers sighed. I could see it coming, with the certainty and illogic of an aboriginal courtship rite: a round of polite chit-chat.

The Reverend cleared his throat. "So what do you think of Mrs. Radcliffe's new book?"

I balanced a glass of sherry on my knee. The Reverend, Cassandra and the brothers revolved tiny spoons around the rims of teacups. Jane nibbled at a croissant and focused her huge unblinking eyes on the side of my face. One of the brothers had just made a devastating witticism at the expense of the *Lyrical Ballads* and was still tittering over it. Somewhere cats were purring and clocks ticking. I glanced at my watch: only seventeen minutes since I'd stepped in the door.

I stood. "Well Reverend," I said, "I think it's time Jane and I hit the road."

He looked up at the doomed Hindenburg blazing across my chest and smacked his lips. "But you've only just arrived."

There really wasn't much room for Cassandra in the Alfa Romeo, but the Reverend and his troop of sons insisted that she come along. She hefted her skirts, wedged herself into the rear compartment and flared her parasol, while Jane pulled a white cap down over her curls and attempted a joke about Phaetons and the winds of Aeolus. The Reverend stood at the curb and watched my fingers as I helped Jane fasten her seatbelt, and then we were off with a crunch of gravel and a billow of exhaust.

The film was Italian, in black and white, full of social acuity and steamy sex. I sat between the two sisters with a bucket of buttered popcorn. Jane's lips were parted and her eyes glowed. I offered her some popcorn. "I do not think that I care for any just now, thank you," she said. Cassandra sat stiff and erect, tireless and silent, like a mileage marker beside a country lane. She was not interested in popcorn either.

The story concerned the seduction of a long-legged village girl by a mustachioed adventurer who afterward refuses to marry her on the grounds that she is impure. The girl, swollen with child, bursts in upon the nuptials of her seducer and the daughter of a wealthy merchant, and demands her due. She is turned out into the street. But late that night, as the newlyweds thrash about in the bridal bed—

It was at this point that Jane took hold of my arm and whispered that she wanted to leave. What could I do? I fumbled for her wrap, people hissed at us, great nude thighs slashed across the screen, and we headed for the glowing EXIT sign.

I proposed a club. "Oh do let's walk!" Jane said. "The air is so frightfully delicious after that close, odious theatre—don't you think?" Pigeons flapped and cooed. A panhandler leaned against the fender of a car and drooled into the gutter. I took Jane's arm. Cassandra took mine.

At *The Mooncalf* we had our wrists stamped with luminescent ink and then found a table near the dance floor. The waitress' fingernails were green daggers. She wore a butch haircut and three-inch heels. Jane wanted punch, Cassandra tea. I ordered three margaritas.

The band was recreating the fall of the Third Reich amid clouds of green smoke and flashing lights. We gazed out at the dancers in their jumpsuits and platform shoes as they bumped bums, heads and genitals in time to the music. I thought of Catherine Morland at Bath and decided to ask Jane for a dance. I leaned across the table. "Want to dance?" I shouted.

"Beg your pardon?" Jane said, leaning over her margarita.

"Dance," I shouted, miming the action of holding her in my arms.

"No, I'm very sorry," she said. "I'm afraid not."

Cassandra tapped my arm. "I'd love to," she giggled.

Jane removed her cap and fingered out her curls as Cassandra and I got up from the table. She grinned and waved as we receded into the crowd. Over the heads of the dancers I watched her sniff suspiciously at her drink and then sit back to ogle the crowd with her black satiric eyes.

Then I turned to Cassandra. She curtsied, grabbed me in a fox trot sort of way and began to promenade round the floor. For so small a woman (her nose kept poking at the moribund Titanic listing across my lower ribcage), I was amazed at her energy. We pranced through the hustlers and bumpers like kiddies round a Maypole. I was even beginning to enjoy myself when I glanced over at our table and saw that a man in fierce black sideburns and mustache had joined Jane. He was dressed in a ruffled shirt, antique tie and coattails that hung to the floor as he sat. At that moment a fellow terpsichorean flung his partner into the air, caught her by wrist and ankle and twirled her like a toreador's cape. When I looked up again Jane was sitting alone, her eyes fixed on mine through the welter of heads.

The band concluded with a crunching metallic shriek and Cassandra and I made our way back to the table. "Who was that?" I asked Jane.

"Who was whom?"

"That mustachioed murderer's apprentice you were sitting with."

"Oh," she said. "Him."

I realized that Cassandra was still clutching my hand.

"Just an acquaintance."

As we pulled into the drive at Steventon, I observed a horse tethered to one of the palings. The horse lifted its tail, then dropped it. Jane seemed suddenly animated. She made a clucking sound and called to the horse by name. The horse flicked its ears. I asked her if she liked horses. "Hm?" she said, already looking off toward the silhouettes that played across the parlor curtains. "Oh yes, yes. Very much so," she said, and then she released the seatbelt, flung back the door and tripped up the stairs into the house. I killed the engine and stepped out into the dark drive. Crickets sawed their legs together in the bushes. Cassandra held out her hand.

Cassandra led me into the parlor where I was startled to see the mustachioed ne'er-do-well from *The Mooncalf.* He held a teacup in his hand. His boots shone as if they'd been razor-stropped. He was talking with Jane.

"Well, well," said the Reverend, stepping out of the shadows. "Enjoy yourselves?"

"Oh, immensely, father," said Cassandra.

Jane was grinning at me again. "Mr. Boyle," she said. "Have you met Mr. Crawford?" The brothers, with their fine bones and disproportionate heads, gathered round. Crawford's sideburns reached nearly to the line of his jaw. His mustache was smooth and black. I held out my hand. He shifted the teacup and gave me a firm handshake. "Delighted," he said.

We found seats (Crawford shoved in next to Jane on the love seat; I wound up on the settee between Cassandra and a brother in naval uniform), and the maid served tea and cakes. Something was wrong—of that I was sure. The brothers were not their usual witty selves, the Reverend floundered in the midst of a critique of Coleridge's cult of artifice, Cassandra dropped a stitch. In the corner, Crawford was holding a whispered colloquy with Jane. Her cheeks, which tended toward the flaccid, were now positively bloated, and flushed with color. It was then that it came to me. "Crawford," I said, getting to my feet. "*Henry* Crawford?"

He sprang up like a gunfighter summoned to the OK Corral. "That's right," he leered. His eyes were deep and cold as crevasses. He looked pretty formidable—until I realized that he couldn't have been more than five-three or -four, give or take an inch for his heels.

Suddenly I had hold of his elbow. The Tiki medallion trembled at my throat. "I'd like a word with you outside," I said. "In the garden."

The brothers were on their feet. The Reverend spilled his tea. Crawford jerked his arm out of my grasp and stalked through the door that gave onto the garden. Nightsounds grated in my ears, the brothers murmured at my back, and Jane, as I pulled the door closed, grinned at me as if I'd just told the joke of the century.

Crawford was waiting for me in the ragged shadows of the trees, turned to face me like a bayed animal. I felt a surge of power. I wanted to call him a son of a bitch, but, in keeping with the times, I settled for cad. "You cad," I said, shoving him back a step, "how dare you come sniffing around her after what you did to Maria Bertram in *Mansfield Park?* It's people like you—corrupt, arbitrary, egocentric—that foment all the lust and heartbreak of the world and challenge the very possibility of happy endings."

"Hah!" he said. Then he stepped forward and the moon fell across his face. His eyes were like the birth of evil. In his hand, a riding glove. He slapped my face with it. "Tomorrow morning, at dawn," he hissed. "Beneath the bridge."

"Okay, wiseguy," I said, "okay," but I could feel the Titanic sinking into my belt.

A moment later the night was filled with the clatter of hoofs.

I was greeted by silence in the parlor. They stared at me, sated, as I stepped through the door. Except for Cassandra, who mooned at me from behind her knitting, and Jane, who was bent over a notebook, scribbling away like a court recorder. The Reverend cleared his throat and Jane looked up. She scratched off another line or two and then rose to show me out. She led me through the parlor and down the hall to the front entrance. We paused at the door.

"I've had a memorable evening," she said, and then glanced back to where Cassandra had appeared at the parlor door. "Do come again." And then she held out her hands.

Her hands were cold.

Ian Frazier

DATING YOUR MOM

In today's fast-moving, transient, rootless society, where people meet and make love and part without ever really touching, the relationship every guy already has with his own mother is too valuable to ignore. Here is a grown, experienced, loving woman—one you do not have to go to a party or a singles bar to meet, one you do not have to go to great lengths to get to know. There are hundreds of times when you and your mother are thrown together naturally, without the tension that usually accompanies courtship—just the two of you, alone. All you need is a little presence of mind to take advantage of these situations. Say your mom is driving you downtown in the car to buy you a new pair of slacks. First, find a nice station on the car radio, one that she likes. Get into the pleasant lull of freeway driving—tires humming along the pavement, air-conditioner on max. Then turn to look at her across the front seat and say something like, "You know, you've really kept your shape, Mom, and don't think I haven't noticed." Or suppose she comes into your room to bring you some clean socks. Take her by the wrist, pull her close, and say, "Mom, you're the most fascinating woman I've ever met." Probably she'll tell you to cut out the foolishness, but I can guarantee you one thing: she will never tell your dad. Possibly she would find it hard to say, "Dear, Piper just made a pass at me," or possibly she is secretly flattered, but, whatever the reason, she will keep it to herself until the day comes when she is no longer ashamed to tell the world of your love.

Dating your mother seriously might seem difficult at first, but once you try it I'll bet you'll be surprised at how easy it is. Facing up to your intention is the main thing: you have to want it bad enough. One problem is that lots of people get hung up on feelings of guilt about their dad. They think, Oh, here's this kindly old guy who taught me how to hunt and whittle and dyna-mite fish—I can't let him go on into his twilight years alone. Well, there are two reasons you can dismiss those thoughts from your mind. First, *every* woman, I don't care who she is, prefers her son to her husband. That is a simple fact; ask any woman who has a son, and she'll admit it. And why shouldn't she prefer someone who is so much like herself, who represents nine months of special concern and love and intense physical closeness—someone whom she actually created? As more women begin to express the need to have something all their own in the world, more women are going to start being honest about this preference. When you and your mom begin going together, you will simply become part of a natural and inevitable historical trend.

Second, you must remember this about your dad: you have your mother, he has his! Let him go put the moves on his own mother and stop messing with yours. If his mother is dead or too old to be much fun anymore, that's not your fault, is it? It's not your fault that he didn't realize his mom for the woman she was, before it was too late. Probably he's going to try a lot of emotional blackmail on you just because you had a good idea and he never did. Don't buy it. Comfort yourself with the thought that your dad belongs to the last generation of guys who will let their moms slip away from them like that.

Once your dad is out of the picture—once he has taken up fly-tying, joined the Single Again Club, moved to Russia, whatever—and your mom has been wooed and won, if you're anything like me you're going to start having so much fun that the good times you had with your mother when you were little will seem tame by comparison. For a while, Mom and I went along living a contented, quiet life, just happy to be with each other. But after several months we started getting into some different things, like the big motorized stroller. The thrill I felt the first time Mom steered me down the street! On the tray, in addition to my Big Jim doll and the wire with the colored wooden beads, I have my desk blotter, my typewriter, an in-out basket, and my name plate. I get a lot of work done, plus I get a great chance to people-watch. Then there's my big, adult-sized highchair, where I sit in the evening as Mom and I watch the news and discuss current events, while I paddle in my food and throw my dishes on the floor. When Mom reaches to wipe off my chin and I take her hand, and we fall to the floor in a heap—me, Mom, highchair, and all—well, those are the best times, those are the very best times.

It is true that occasionally I find myself longing for even more—for things I know I cannot have, like the feel of a firm, strong, gentle hand at the small of my back lifting me out of bed into the air, or someone who could walk me around and burp me after I've watched all the bowl games and had about nine beers. Ideally, I would like a mom about nineteen or twenty feet tall, and although I considered for a while asking my mom to start working out with weights and drinking Nutrament, I finally figured, Why put her through it? After all, she is not only my woman, she is my best friend. I have to take her as she is, and the way she is is plenty good enough for me.

AREN'T YOU HAPPY FOR ME?

"William Coombs, with two *o*'s," Melanie Ballinger told her father over long distance. "Pronounced just like the thing you comb your hair with. Say it."

Ballinger repeated the name.

"Say the whole name."

"I've got it, sweetheart. Why am I saying it?"

"Dad, I'm bringing him home with me. We're getting *married*."

For a moment, he couldn't speak.

"Dad? Did you hear me?"

"I'm here," he said.

"Well?"

Again, he couldn't say anything.

"Dad?"

"Yes," he said. "That's—that's some news."

"That's all you can say?"

"Well, I mean—Melanie—this is sort of quick, isn't it?" he said.

"Not that quick. How long did you and Mom wait?"

"I don't remember. Are you measuring yourself by that?"

"You waited six months, and you do too remember. And this is five months. And we're not measuring anything. William and I have known each other longer than five months, but we've been together—you know, as a couple—five months. And I'm almost twenty-three, which is two years older than Mom was. And don't tell me it was different when *you* guys did it."

"No," he heard himself say. "It's pretty much the same, I imagine."

"Well?" she said.

"Well," Ballinger said. "I'm—I'm very happy for you."

"You don't sound happy."

"I'm happy. I can't wait to meet him."

"Really? Promise? You're not just saying that?"

"It's good news, darling. I mean I'm surprised, of course. It'll take a little getting used to. The—the suddenness of it and everything. I mean, your mother and I didn't even know you were seeing anyone. But no, I'm—I'm glad. I can't wait to meet the young man."

"Well, and now there's something *else* you have to know."

"I'm ready," John Ballinger said. He was standing in the kitchen of the house she hadn't seen yet, and outside the window his wife, Mary, was weeding in the garden, wearing a red scarf and a white muslin blouse and jeans, looking young—looking, even, happy, though for a long while there had been between them, in fact, very little happiness.

"Well, this one's kind of hard," his daughter said over the thousand miles of wire. "Maybe we should talk about it later."

"No, I'm sure I can take whatever it is," he said.

The truth was that he had news of his own to tell. Almost a week ago, he and Mary had agreed on a separation. Some time for them both to sort things out. They had decided not to say anything about it to Melanie until she arrived. But now Melanie had said that she was bringing someone with her.

She was hemming and hawing on the other end of the line: "I don't know, see, Daddy, I—God. I can't find the way to say it, really."

He waited. She was in Chicago, where they had sent her to school more than four years ago, and where after her graduation she had stayed, having landed a job with an independent newspaper in the city. In March, Ballinger and Mary had moved to this small house in the middle of Charlottesville, hoping that a change of scene might help things. It hadn't; they were falling apart after all these years.

"Dad," Melanie said, sounding helpless.

"Honey, I'm listening."

"Okay, look," she said. "Will you promise you won't react?"

"How can I promise a thing like that, Melanie?"

"You're going to react, then. I wish you could just promise me you wouldn't."

"Darling," he said, "I've got something to tell you, too. Promise me *you* won't react."

She said "Promise" in that way the young have of being absolutely certain what their feelings will be in some future circumstance.

"So," he said. "Now, tell me whatever it is." And a thought struck through him like a shock. "Melanie, you're not—you're not pregnant, are you?"

She said, "How did you *know*?"

He felt something sharp move under his heart. "Oh, Lord. Seriously?"

"Jeez," she said. "Wow. That's really amazing."

"You're—*pregnant.*"

"Right. My God. You're positively clairvoyant, Dad."

"I really don't think it's a matter of any clairvoyance, Melanie, from the way you were talking. Are you—is it sure?"

"Of course it's sure. But—well, that isn't the really hard thing. Maybe I should just wait."

"Wait," he said. "Wait for what?"

"Until you get used to everything else."

He said nothing. She was fretting on the other end, sighing and starting to speak and then stopping herself.

"I don't know," she said finally, and abruptly he thought she was talking to someone in the room with her.

"Honey, do you want me to put your mother on?"

"No, Daddy. I wanted to talk to you about this first. I think we should get this over with."

"Get this over with? Melanie, what're we talking about here? Maybe I should put your mother on." He thought he might try a joke. "After all," he added, "I've never been pregnant."

"It's not about being pregnant. You *guessed* that."

He held the phone tight against his ear. Through the window, he saw his wife stand and stretch, massaging the small of her back with one gloved hand. *Oh, Mary.*

"Are you ready?" his daughter said.

"Wait," he said. "Wait a minute. Should I be sitting down? I'm sitting down." He pulled a chair from the table and settled into it. He could hear her breathing on the other end of the line, or perhaps it was the static wind he so often heard when talking on these new phones. "Okay," he said, feeling his throat begin to close. "Tell me."

"William's somewhat older than I am," she said. "There." She sounded as though she might hyperventilate.

He left a pause. "That's it?"

"Well, it's how much."

"Okay."

She seemed to be trying to collect herself. She breathed, paused. "This is even tougher than I thought it was going to be."

"You mean you're going to tell me something harder than the fact that you're pregnant?"

She was silent.

"Melanie?"

"I didn't expect you to be this way about it," she said.

"Honey, please just tell me the rest of it."

"Well, what did you mean by that, anyway?"

"Melanie, *you said* this would be hard."

Silence.

"Tell me, sweetie. Please?"

"I'm going to." She took a breath. "Dad, William's sixty—he's—he's sixty—sixty-three years old."

Ballinger stood. Out in the garden his wife had got to her knees again, pulling crabgrass out of the bed of tulips. It was a sunny near-twilight, and all along the shady street people were working in their little orderly spaces of grass and flowers.

"Did you hear me, Daddy? It's perfectly all right, too, because he's really a *young* sixty-three, and *very* strong and healthy, and look at George Burns."

"George Burns," Ballinger said. "George—George Burns? Melanie, I don't understand."

"Come on, Daddy, stop it."

"No, what're you telling me?" His mind was blank.

"I said William is sixty-three."

"William who?"

"Dad. My fiancé."

"Wait, Melanie. You're saying your fiancé, the man you're going to marry, *he's* sixty-three?"

"A young sixty-three," she said.

"Melanie. Sixty-three?"

"Dad."

"You didn't say six feet three?"

She was silent.

"Melanie?"

"Yes."

"Honey, this is a joke, right? You're playing a joke on me."

"It is not a—it's not that. God," she said. "I don't believe this."

"You don't believe—" he began. "You don't believe—"

"Dad," she said. "I told you—" Again, she seemed to be talking to someone else in the room with her. Her voice trailed off.

"Melanie," he said. "Talk into the phone."

"I know it's hard," she told him. "I know it's asking you to take a lot in."

"Well, no," Ballinger said, feeling something shift inside, a quickening in his blood. "It's—it's a little more than that, Melanie, isn't it? I mean it's not a weather report, for God's sake."

"I should've known," she said.

"Forgive me for it," he said, "but I have to ask you something."

"It's all right, Daddy," she said as though reciting it for him. "I know what I'm doing. I'm not really rushing into anything—"

He interrupted her. "Well, good God, somebody rushed into something, right?"

"Daddy."

"Is that what you call *him*? No, *I'm* Daddy. You have to call him *Grand-daddy*."

"That is *not* funny," she said.

"I wasn't being funny, Melanie. And anyway, that wasn't my question." He took a breath. "Please forgive this, but I have to know."

"There's nothing you really *have* to know, Daddy. I'm an adult. I'm telling you out of family courtesy."

"I understand that. Family courtesy exactly. Exactly, Melanie, that's a good phrase. Would you please tell me, out of family courtesy, if the baby is his."

"Yes." Her voice was small now, coming from a long way off.

"I am sorry for the question, but I have to put all this together. I mean you're asking me to take in a whole lot here, you know?"

"I said I understood how you feel."

"I don't think so. I don't think you quite understand how I feel."

"All right," she said. "I don't understand how you feel. But I think I knew how you'd react."

For a few seconds, there was just the low, sea sound of long distance.

"Melanie, have you done any of the math on this?"

"I should've bet money," she said in the tone of a person who has been proven right about something.

"Well, but Jesus," Ballinger said. "I mean he's older than *I* am, kid. He's—he's a *lot* older than I am." The number of years seemed to dawn on him as he spoke; it filled him with a strange, heart-shaking heat. "Honey, nineteen years. When he was my age, I was only two years older than you are now."

"I don't see what that has to do with anything," she said.

"Melanie, I'll be forty-five *all the way* in December. I'm a *young* forty-four."

"I know when your birthday is, Dad."

"Well, good God, this guy's nineteen years older than your own father."

She said, "I've grasped the numbers. Maybe you should go ahead and put Mom on."

"Melanie, you couldn't pick somebody a little closer to my age? Some snot-nosed forty-year-old?"

"Stop it," she said. "Please, Daddy. I know what I'm doing."

"Do you know how old he's going to be when your baby is ten? Do you? Have you given that any thought at all?"

She was silent.

He said, "How many children are you hoping to have?"

"I'm not thinking about that. Any of that. This is now, and I don't care about anything else."

He sat down in his kitchen and tried to think of something else to say. Outside the window, his wife, with no notion of what she was about to be hit with, looked through the patterns of shade in the blinds and, seeing him, waved. It was friendly, and even so, all their difficulty was in it. Ballinger waved back. "Melanie," he said, "do you mind telling me just where you happened to meet William? I mean how do you meet a person forty years older than you are. Was there a senior citizen–student mixer at the college?"

"Stop it, Daddy."

"No, I really want to know. If I'd just picked this up and read it in the newspaper, I think I'd want to know. I'd probably call the newspaper and see what I could find out."

"Put Mom on," she said.

"Just tell me how you met. You can do that, can't you?"

"Jesus Christ," she said, then paused.

Ballinger waited.

"He's a teacher, like you and Mom, only college. He was my literature teacher. He's a professor of literature. He knows everything that was ever written, and he's the most brilliant man I've ever known. You have no idea how fascinating it is to talk with him."

"Yes, and I guess you understand that over the years that's what you're going to be doing a *lot* of with him, Melanie. A lot of talking."

"I am carrying the proof that disproves *you*," she said.

He couldn't resist saying, "Did *he* teach you to talk like that?"

"I'm gonna hang up."

"You promised you'd listen to something *I* had to tell *you*."

"Okay," she said crisply. "I'm listening."

He could imagine her tapping the toe of one foot on the floor: the impatience of someone awaiting an explanation. He thought a moment. "He's a professor?"

"That's not what you wanted to tell me."

"But you said he's a professor."

"Yes, I said that."

"Don't be mad at me, Melanie. Give me a few minutes to get used to the idea. Jesus. Is he a professor emeritus?"

"If that means distinguished, yes. But I know what you're—"

"No, Melanie. It means *retired*. You went to college."

She said nothing.

"I'm sorry. But for God's sake, it's a legitimate question."

"It's a stupid, mean-spirited thing to ask." He could tell from her voice that she was fighting back tears.

"Is he there with you now?"

"Yes," she said, sniffling.

"Oh, Jesus Christ."

"Daddy, why are you being this way?"

"Do you think maybe we could've had this talk alone? What's he, listening on the other line?"

"No."

"Well, thank God for that."

"I'm going to hang up now."

"No, please don't hang up. Please let's just be calm and talk about this. We have some things to talk about here."

She sniffled, blew her nose. Someone held the phone for her. There was a muffled something in the line, and then she was there again. "Go ahead," she said.

"Is he still in the room with you?"

"Yes." Her voice was defiant.

"Where?"

"Oh, for God's sake," she said.

"I'm sorry, I feel the need to know. Is he sitting down?"

"I *want* him here, Daddy. We both want to be here," she said.

"And he's going to marry you."

"Yes," she said impatiently.

"Do you think I could talk to him?"

She said something he couldn't hear, and then there were several seconds of some sort of discussion, in whispers. Finally she said, "Do you promise not to yell at him?"

"Melanie, he wants me to promise not to *yell* at him?"

"Will you promise?"

"Good God."

"Promise," she said. "Or I'll hang up."

"All right. I promise. I promise not to yell at him."

There was another small scuffing sound, and a man's voice came through the line. "Hello, sir." It was, as far as Ballinger could tell, an ordinary voice, slightly lower than baritone. He thought of cigarettes. "I realize this is a difficult—"

"Do you smoke?" Ballinger interrupted him.

"No, sir."

"All right. Go on."

"Well, I want you to know I understand how you feel."

"Melanie says she does, too," Ballinger said. "I mean I'm certain you both *think* you do."

"It was my idea that Melanie call you about this."

"Oh, really. That speaks well of you. You probably knew I'd find this a little difficult to absorb and that's why you waited until Melanie was pregnant, for Christ's sake."

The other man gave forth a small sigh of exasperation.

"So you're a professor of literature."

"Yes, sir."

"Oh, you needn't 'sir' me. After all, I mean I *am* the goddam kid here."

"There's no need for sarcasm, sir."

"Oh, I wasn't being sarcastic. That was a literal statement of this situation that obtains right here as we're speaking. And, really, Mr. . . . It's Coombs, right?"

"Yes, sir."

"Coombs, like the thing you comb your hair with."

The other man was quiet.

"Just how long do you think it'll take me to get used to this? You think you might get into your seventies before I get used to this? And how long do you think it'll take my wife who's twenty-one years younger than you are to get used to this?"

Silence.

"You're too old for my *wife,* for Christ's sake."

Nothing.

"What's your first name again?"

The other man spoke through another sigh. "Perhaps we should just ring off."

"Ring off. Jesus. Ring off? Did you actually say 'ring off'? What're you, a goddam limey or something?"

"I am an American. I fought in Korea."

"Not World War One?"

The other man did not answer.

"How many other marriages have you had?" Ballinger asked him.

"That's a valid question. I'm glad you—"

"Thank you for the scholarly observation, *sir.* But I'm not sitting in a class. How many did you say?"

"If you'd give me a chance, I'd tell you."

Balllinger said nothing.

"Two, sir. I've had two marriages."

"Divorces?"

"I have been widowed twice."

"And—oh, I get it. You're trying to make sure that that never happens to you again."

"This is not going well at all, and I'm afraid I—I—" The other man stammered, then stopped.

"How did you expect it to go?" Ballinger demanded.

"Cruelty is not what I'd expected. I'll tell you that."

"You thought I'd be glad my daughter is going to be getting social security before I do."

The other was silent.

"Do you have any other children?" Ballinger asked.

"Yes, I happen to have three." There was a stiffness, an overweening tone, in the voice now.

"And how old are they, if I might ask."

"Yes, you may."

Ballinger waited. His wife walked in from outside, carrying some cuttings. She poured water in a glass vase and stood at the counter arranging the flowers, her back to him. The other man had stopped talking. "I'm sorry," Ballinger said. "My wife just walked in here and I didn't catch what you said. Could you just tell me if any of them are anywhere near my daughter's age?"

"I told you, my youngest boy is thirty-eight."

"And you realize that if *he* wanted to marry my daughter I'd be upset, the age difference there being what it is." Ballinger's wife moved to his side, drying her hands on a paper towel, her face full of puzzlement and worry.

"I told you, Mr. Ballinger, that I understood how you feel. The point is, we have a pregnant woman here and we both love her."

"No," Ballinger said. "That's not the point. The point is that you, sir, are not much more than a goddam statutory rapist. That's the point." His wife took his shoulder. He looked at her and shook his head.

"What?" she whispered. "Is Melanie all right?"

"Well, this isn't accomplishing anything," the voice on the other end of the line was saying.

"Just a minute," Ballinger said. "Let me ask you something else. Really now. What's the policy at that goddam university concerning teachers screwing their students?"

"Oh, my God," his wife said as the voice on the line huffed and seemed to gargle.

"I'm serious," Ballinger said.

"Melanie was not my student when we became involved."

"Is that what you call it? Involved?"

"Let me talk to Melanie," Ballinger's wife said.

"Listen," he told her. "Be quiet."

Melanie was back on the line. "Daddy? Daddy?"

"I'm here," Ballinger said, holding the phone from his wife's attempt to take it from him.

"Daddy, we're getting married and there's nothing you can do about it. Do you understand?"

"Melanie," he said, and it seemed that from somewhere far inside himself he heard that he had begun shouting at her. "Jee-zus good Christ. Your fiancé was almost *my* age *now* the day you were *born*. What the hell, kid. Are you crazy? Are you out of your mind?"

His wife was actually pushing against him to take the phone, and so he gave it to her. And stood there while she tried to talk.

"Melanie," she said. "Honey, listen—"

"Hang up," Ballinger said. "Christ. Hang it up."

"Please. Will you go in the other room and let me talk to her?"

"Tell her I've got friends. All these nice men in their forties. She can marry any one of my friends—they're babies. Forties—cradle fodder. Jesus, any one of them. Tell her."

"Jack, stop it." Then she put the phone against her chest. "Did you tell her anything about us?"

He paused. "That—no."

She turned from him. "Melanie, honey. What is this? Tell me, please."

He left her there, walked through the living room to the hall and back around to the kitchen. He was all nervous energy, crazy with it, pacing. Mary stood very still, listening, nodding slightly, holding the phone tight with both hands, her shoulders hunched as if she were out in cold weather.

"Mary," he said.

Nothing.

He went into their bedroom and closed the door. The light coming through the windows was soft gold, and the room was deepening with shadows. He moved to the bed and sat down, and in a moment he noticed that he had begun a low sort of murmuring. He took a breath and tried to be still. From the other room, his wife's voice came to him. "Yes, I quite agree with you. But I'm just unable to put this . . ."

The voice trailed off. He waited. A few minutes later, she came to the door and knocked on it lightly, then opened it and looked in.

"What," he said.

"They're serious." She stood there in the doorway.

"Come here," he said.

She stepped to his side and eased herself down, and he moved to accommodate her. He put his arm around her, and then, because it was awkward, clearly an embarrassment to her, took it away. Neither of them could speak for a time. Everything they had been through during the course of deciding about each other seemed concentrated now. Ballinger breathed his wife's presence, the odor of earth and flowers, the outdoors.

"God," she said. "I'm positively numb. I don't know what to think."

"Let's have another baby," he said suddenly. "Melanie's baby will need a younger aunt or uncle."

Mary sighed a little forlorn laugh, then was silent.

"Did you tell her about us?" he asked.

"No," she said. "I didn't get the chance. And I don't know that I could have."

"I don't suppose it's going to matter much to her."

"Oh, don't say that. You can't mean that."

The telephone on the bedstand rang, and startled them both. He reached for it, held the handset toward her.

"Hello," she said. Then: "Oh. Hi. Yes, well, here." She gave it back to him.

"Hello," he said.

Melanie's voice, tearful and angry: "You had something you said you had to tell *me*." She sobbed, then coughed. "Well?"

"It was nothing, honey. I don't even remember—"

"Well, I want you to know I would've been better than you were, Daddy, no matter how hard it was. I would've kept myself from reacting."

"Yes," he said. "I'm sure you would have."

"I'm going to hang up. And I guess I'll let you know later if we're coming at all. If it wasn't for Mom, we wouldn't be."

"We'll talk," he told her. "We'll work on it. Honey, you both have to give us a little time."

"There's nothing to work on as far as William and I are concerned."

"Of course there are things to work on. Every marriage—" His voice had caught. He took a breath. "In every marriage there are things to work on."

"I know what I know," she said.

"Well," said Ballinger. "That's—that's as it should be at your age, darling."

"Goodbye," she said. "I can't say any more."

"I understand," Ballinger said. When the line clicked, he held the handset in his lap for a moment. Mary was sitting there at his side, perfectly still.

"Well," he said. "I couldn't tell her." He put the handset back in its cradle. "God. A sixty-three-year-old son-in-law."

"It's happened before." She put her hand on his shoulder, then took it away. "I'm so frightened for her. But she says it's what she wants."

"Hell, Mary. You know what this is. The son of a bitch was her goddam teacher."

"Listen to you—what are you saying about her? Listen to what you're saying about her. That's our daughter you're talking about. You might at least try to give her the credit of assuming that she's aware of what she's doing."

They said nothing for a few moments.

"Who knows," Ballinger's wife said. "Maybe they'll be happy for a time."

He'd heard the note of sorrow in her voice, and thought he knew what she was thinking; then he was certain that he knew. He sat there remembering, like Mary, their early happiness, that ease and simplicity, and briefly he was in another house, other rooms, and he saw the toddler that Melanie had been, trailing through slanting light in a brown hallway, draped in gowns she had fashioned from her mother's clothes. He did not know why that particular image should have come to him out of the flow of years, but for a fierce minute it was uncannily near him in the breathing silence; it went over him like a palpable something on his skin, then was gone. The ache which remained stopped him for a moment. He looked at his wife, but she had averted her eyes, her hands running absently over the faded denim cloth of her lap. Finally she stood. "Well," she sighed, going away. "Work to do."

"Mary?" he said, low; but she hadn't heard him. She was already out the doorway and into the hall, moving toward the kitchen. He reached over and turned the lamp on by the bed, and then lay down. It was so quiet here. Dark was coming to the windows. On the wall there were pictures; shadows, shapes, silently clamoring for his gaze. He shut his eyes, listened to the small sounds she made in the kitchen, arranging her flowers, running the tap. *Mary,* he had said. But he could not imagine what he might have found to say if his voice had reached her.

Jamaica Kincaid

MY MOTHER

Immediately on wishing my mother dead and seeing the pain it caused her, I was sorry and cried so many tears that all the earth around me was drenched. Standing before my mother, I begged her forgiveness, and I begged so earnestly that she took pity on me, kissing my face and placing my head on her bosom to rest. Placing her arms around me, she drew my head closer and closer to her bosom, until finally I suffocated. I lay on her bosom, breathless, for a time uncountable, until one day, for a reason she has kept to herself, she shook me out and stood me under a tree and I started to breathe again. I cast a sharp glance at her and said to myself, "So." Instantly I grew my own bosoms, small mounds at first, leaving a small, soft place between them, where, if ever necessary, I could rest my own head. Between my mother and me now were the tears I had cried, and I gathered up some stones and banked them in so that they formed a small pond. The water in the pond was thick and black and poisonous, so that only unnamable invertebrates could live in it. My mother and I now watched each other carefully, always making sure to shower the other with words and deeds of love and affection.

＊　＊　＊

I was sitting on my mother's bed trying to get a good look at myself. It was a large bed and it stood in the middle of a large, completely dark room. The room was completely dark because all the windows had been boarded up and all the crevices stuffed with black cloth. My mother lit some candles and the room burst into a pink-like, yellow-like glow. Looming over us, much larger than ourselves, were our shadows. We sat mesmerized because our shadows had made a place between themselves, as if they were making room for someone else. Nothing filled up the space between them, and the shadow of my mother sighed. The shadow of my mother danced around the room to a tune that my own shadow sang, and then they stopped. All along, our shadows had grown thick and thin, long and short, had fallen at every angle, as if they were controlled by the light of day. Suddenly my mother got up and blew out the candles and our shadows vanished. I continued to sit on the bed, trying to get a good look at myself.

※ ※ ※

My mother removed her clothes and covered thoroughly her skin with a thick gold-colored oil, which had recently been rendered in a hot pan from the livers of reptiles with pouched throats. She grew plates of metal-colored scales on her back, and light, when it collided with this surface, would shatter and collapse into tiny points. Her teeth now arranged themselves into rows that reached all the way back to her long white throat. She uncoiled her hair from her head and then removed her hair altogether. Taking her head into her large palms, she flattened it so that her eyes, which were by now ablaze, sat on top of her head and spun like two revolving balls. Then, making two lines on the soles of each foot, she divided her feet into crossroads. Silently, she had instructed me to follow her example, and now I too traveled along on my white underbelly, my tongue darting and flickering in the hot air. "Look," said my mother.

※ ※ ※

My mother and I were standing on the seabed side by side, my arms laced loosely around her waist, my head resting securely on her shoulder, as if I needed the support. To make sure she believed in my frailness, I sighed occasionally—long soft sighs, the kind of sigh she had long ago taught me could evoke sympathy. In fact, how I really felt was invincible. I was no longer a child but I was not yet a woman. My skin had just blackened and cracked and fallen away and my new impregnable carapace had taken full hold. My nose had flattened; my hair curled in and stood out straight from my head simultaneously; my many rows of teeth in their retractable trays were in place. My mother and I wordlessly made an arrangement—I sent out my beautiful sighs, she received them; I leaned ever more heavily on her for support, she offered her shoulder, which shortly grew to the size of a thick plank. A long time passed, at the end of which I had hoped to see my mother permanently cemented to the seabed. My mother reached out to pass a hand over my head, a pacifying gesture, but I laughed and, with great agility, stepped aside. I let out a horrible roar, then a self-pitying whine. I had grown big, but my mother was bigger, and that would always be so. We walked to the Garden of Fruits and there ate to our hearts' satisfaction. We departed through the southwesterly gate, leaving as always, in our trail, small colonies of worms.

▩ ▩ ▩

With my mother, I crossed, unwillingly, the valley. We saw a lamb grazing and when it heard our footsteps it paused and looked up at us. The lamb looked cross and miserable. I said to my mother, "The lamb is cross and miserable. So would I be, too, if I had to live in a climate not suited to my nature." My mother and I now entered the cave. It was the dark and cold cave. I felt something growing under my feet and I bent down to eat it. I stayed that way for years, bent over eating whatever I found growing under my feet. Eventually, I grew a special lens that would allow me to see in the darkest of darkness; eventually, I grew a special coat that kept me warm in the coldest of coldness. One day I saw my mother sitting on a rock. She said, "What a strange expression you have on your face. So cross, so miserable, as if you were living in a climate not suited to your nature." Laughing, she vanished. I dug a deep, deep hole. I built a beautiful house, a floorless house, over the deep, deep hole. I put in lattice windows, most favored of windows by my mother, so perfect for looking out at people passing by without her being observed. I painted the house itself yellow, the windows green, colors I knew would please her. Standing just outside the door, I asked her to inspect the house. I said, "Take a look. Tell me if it's to your satisfaction." Laughing out of the corner of a mouth I could not see, she stepped inside. I stood just outside the door, listening carefully, hoping to hear her land with a thud at the bottom of the deep, deep hole. Instead, she walked up and down in every direction, even pounding her heel on the air. Coming outside to greet me, she said, "It is an excellent house. I would be honored to live in it," and then vanished. I filled up the hole and burnt the house to the ground.

▩ ▩ ▩

My mother has grown to an enormous height. I have grown to an enormous height also, but my mother's height is three times mine. Sometimes I cannot see from her breasts on up, so lost is she in the atmosphere. One day, seeing her sitting on the seashore, her hand reaching out in the deep to caress the belly of a striped fish as he swam through a place where two seas met, I glowed red with anger. For a while then I lived alone on the island where there were eight full moons and I adorned the face of each moon with expressions I had seen on my mother's face. All the expressions favored me. I soon grew tired of living in this way and returned to my mother's side. I remained, though glowing red with anger, and my mother and I built houses on opposite banks of the dead pond. The dead pond lay between us; in it, only small invertebrates with poisonous lances lived. My mother behaved toward them as if she had suddenly found herself in the same room with relatives we had long since risen above. I cherished their presence and gave them names. Still I missed my mother's close company and cried constantly for her, but at the end of each day when I saw her return to her house, incredible and great deeds in her wake, each of them singing loudly her praises, I glowed and glowed again, red with anger. Eventually, I wore myself out and sank into a deep, deep sleep, the only dreamless sleep I have ever had.

One day my mother packed my things in a grip and, taking me by the hand, walked me to the jetty, placed me on board a boat, in care of the captain. My mother, while caressing my chin and cheeks, said some words of comfort to me because we had never been apart before. She kissed me on the forehead and turned and walked away. I cried so much my chest heaved up and down, my whole body shook at the sight of her back turned toward me, as if I had never seen her back turned toward me before. I started to make plans to get off the boat, but when I saw that the boat was encased in a large green bottle, as if it were about to decorate a mantelpiece, I fell asleep, until I reached my destination, the new island. When the boat stopped, I got off and I saw a woman with feet exactly like mine, especially around the arch of the instep. Even though the face was completely different from what I was used to, I recognized this woman as my mother. We greeted each other at first with great caution and politeness, but as we walked along, our steps became one, and as we talked, our voices became one voice, and we were in complete union in every other way. What peace came over me then, for I could not see where she left off and I began, or where I left off and she began.

My mother and I walk through the rooms of her house. Every crack in the floor holds a significant event: here, an apparently healthy young man suddenly dropped dead; here a young woman defied her father and, while riding her bicycle to the forbidden lovers' meeting place, fell down a precipice, remaining a cripple for the rest of a very long life. My mother and I find this a beautiful house. The rooms are large and empty, opening on to each other, waiting for people and things to fill them up. Our white muslin skirts billow up around our ankles, our hair hangs straight down our backs as our arms hang straight at our sides. I fit perfectly in the crook of my mother's arm, on the curve of her back, in the hollow of her stomach. We eat from the same bowl, drink from the same cup; when we sleep, our heads rest on the same pillow. As we walk through the rooms, we merge and separate, merge and separate; soon we shall enter the final stage of our evolution.

■ ■ ■

The fishermen are coming in from sea; their catch is bountiful, my mother has seen to that. As the waves plop, plop against each other, the fishermen are happy that the sea is calm. My mother points out the fishermen to me, their contentment is a source of my contentment. I am sitting in my mother's enormous lap. Sometimes I sit on a mat she has made for me from her hair. The lime trees are weighed down with limes—I have already perfumed myself with their blossoms. A hummingbird has nested on my stomach, a sign of my fertileness. My mother and I live in a bower made from flowers whose petals are imperishable. There is the silvery blue of the sea, crisscrossed with sharp darts of light, there is the warm rain falling on the clumps of castor bush, there is the small lamb bounding across the pasture, there is the soft ground welcoming the soles of my pink feet. It is in this way my mother and I have lived for a long time now.

Abby Frucht

FRUIT OF THE MONTH

I went strawberry picking with June in her pickup truck ten years ago, in May. Late May, in Virginia. June came early, before Jack got home from work, so we left without him. I left a note on the door. When I get back, said the note, I'll make us some strawberry daiquiris and we'll sit together on the porch and drink them all night long, listening to mosquitos. The nature of my notes to him was always, and still is, piquant, because he likes them that way. He is a sentimental man; he keeps my letters in a shoebox tied with string. In the dark interior of the box the ink doesn't fade, nor does the paper deteriorate. Every couple of years he replaces the string, which turns gray from being so often tied and untied.

June said she knew a place where we could get the strawberries free. I said, Illegally, you mean? and she said, Well, yes. If we took the freeway east a couple of miles and then turned off on a dirt road we would come to the edge of a commercial farm surrounded by barbed wire that had been rolled up the way they rolled it in the army during a war, but further on, just where the dirt road ended near a creek, there was a tree you could climb. By climbing this tree and shimmying out along one of its branches you would scale the barbed wire, dropping down just on the other side of it into the strawberry fields. June wore her hair very long at the time, blond and fine with a touch of a ripple, like the stuff you peel off corn ears. Even now, if I am shucking corn, I think of this. How I looked up from the strawberry patch, from my knees where I had landed, and saw June scaling the barbed wire after me, her long bare legs straddling the tree branch, her hair covering her face. It was a hot afternoon, and the scent of greenery was sharp in the air, and I have never forgotten it. We squatted together between the steaming furrows of earth, pinching the berries and eating some. If they don't come off at once in your hand, June said, leave them on the stems to ripen for next time.

We dropped the berries into a book satchel she was wearing on a strap over her shoulder, and after a while the khaki canvas, bulging with fruit, was stained pink. Our fingers were pink, and our knees, and the edges of our mouths. In the distance, across the shimmering acres of strawberry leaves, like water in the sun, we could make out the wide-brimmed hats of the legitimate berry pickers, and beyond them the low flat white building where the bushels were weighed and paid for, and where the cars were parked. Children played and shouted along the perimeter of the farm, and people gathered on the hoods of their cars to talk and sunbathe. We stayed low and quiet, hoping we wouldn't be seen.

I tired quickly. My legs and lower back ached, and my neck and arms stiffened. I blamed my fatigue on the heat and on my period, which had started that morning. I felt heavy and bloated and entirely out of whack. My head hurt. Finally I lay back on my elbows and told June to go right on picking without me; I was perfectly happy simply to be there. I think I fell asleep. Time passed. The sun got low. The crowd thinned out. When I opened my eyes the first thing I saw was a ladybug that had landed on my stomach. It was opening and closing its small spotted wings in a rhythmic way. One two. One two. I thought of the nursery rhyme, and then immediately of Jack, who would be waiting for me, probably standing near an open window with a tall iced glass of water, sipping and watching the road. His lips would be cool, and his eyes troubled. He keeps his anger inside, in what I've begun to call Hot Storage, and allows it to surface only in the face of a more worldly injustice. And by then it has boiled and sweetened and grown thick. Several days after I went strawberry picking he threw our hairbrush at Ronald Reagan, who was president at the time. Reagan was on the news. He was saying he supported the E and the R but not the A of the Equal Rights Amendment, and Jack got mad and threw our brush at the television screen, breaking it. The brush, I mean. I reattached the handle with duct tape, and we still use it.

When the ladybug had flown off I sat up and saw June straddling the branch again and munching on a strawberry. She grinned down at me. I was still exhausted and my only inclination was to lie back down and sleep some more, but I pulled myself up, and let June pull me up into the tree. She had scratched her leg on the barbed wire; there was a thin trickle of blood. We made our way across the tree and back down into the pickup. June turned the radio on. The song was See You in September. June leaned over and took my head in her hands and kissed me, first on the eyes, then full on the mouth. I was surprised. I responded. Then she said, There, I've been wanting to do that, and she drove me home.

I told Jack about this later, over our daiquiris. He was on his third, but I was still toying with my first, because I still felt weak and knew if I drank much more I would get sick. Also, I knew I would be driving out to Norfolk early the next morning to go sailing with June on her brother's boat. Her brother was wealthy and out of town. I told Jack that June's brother's boat was small, big enough only for two. I considered this to be a white lie. I told him also about the kiss, saying how shocked I had been. Jack was entirely silent. He stirred his drink, and watched the moths that were beating against the light bulb, and lifted, by arching his foot, a tennis ball that had rolled out from under his chair. That tennis ball has always been a mystery; neither one of us plays and we've never figured out how it got there. He would straighten his leg, the ball wedged in the arch of his foot, then spread his toes apart and let it fall. He did this over and over until it bounced out of reach. Then he put his drink down on the cement, but gently, so there wasn't a sound, and went inside. I followed, the screen door banging behind me. He filled a teacup with strawberries, sprinkled it with sugar, and carried it upstairs. He put the teacup on the night table. I began to undress him and we showered. Jack said, Your fingers are pink. That was all he said. We toweled ourselves dry and lay down in bed, our arms slung across each other's necks. I watched him sleep, as June had watched me. Jack has remained entirely silent in fact, about all of this, for years.

The drive out to Norfolk was long and agitating, twenty-five miles on the highway stuck behind some drunken slob in a Winnebago. He had opened the back door and stood with one foot on the fender, in a stained tee shirt and shorts, guzzling beer, then tossing the empty cans out onto the highway. All this at fifty-five miles per hour. The beer cans soared crazily in the hot morning light, then veered and bounced off on the shoulder abreast of my car. I was afraid to pass him—What if he fell off?—and I never did get close enough to read the license plate. I slowed to forty, till the Winnebago was a speck in the distance, then sped up till I was close enough to have to slow down again. I hated that man. Eventually I lost him, thank god, and got on my way, but the Hampton Bridge was jammed with traffic, everybody headed for the beach. So it was nearly ten o'clock when I pulled into Norfolk, along a road that skirted the harbor, past the convention center and into the slums where June lived. I had never been there before, and will tell you right now that I never went back. The narrow street was pocked with craters. June's apartment building made me think of the Triangle Shirtwaist Factory, broad and tall, wood frame with row upon row of small windows, some of them broken, the ancient panes warped. I parked across the street, in a lot strewn with rubbish and whiskey bottles, behind a church that looked firebombed. June's truck was there. I hurried across in my clogs and running shorts. I felt like a child in a war zone. The door was locked. A second door was also locked, so I sat down on the hot gritty stoop and waited to be let in. In the ten minutes that passed I thought about getting back into my car and driving home, but the harbor, several blocks up on the other side of the road, was just visible, dotted with sails. Besides, I was hungry. June had promised me breakfast. Strawberry pancakes and coffee, she'd said. Finally a man with a cat in his arms came shuffling up the steps and pulled out a key.

Inside was a wide hallway and three sets of steps, one more dilapidated than the last. I chose the steps with the working light bulb. June lived on the third floor, down a hall lined with green doors and covered with old gray shiny linoleum. The linoleum had buckled, and as I walked along, it made all sorts of obscene noises under my feet. I wondered how June could live in such a place. I hadn't known her very long, having met her through a friend, and that she lived in such a seedy spot excited me. Then, when I knocked and there was no response, I thought perhaps she had mistakenly given me the wrong address, the address of a friend or relative she had been thinking of. I jiggled the door knob. It turned, and the door opened but was blocked after several inches by a chain bolt. I peered inside. The room was in disarray. Books everywhere, and clothes, and a folding table stacked with cardboard boxes, and underneath the table a heap of shoes, including what looked like a snowshoe. There was the sickening odor of propane gas, and another of what I guessed was a kitty litter that hadn't been changed. The gas worried me. I began to knock more vigorously, and even took off my clog and started banging on the door with the wooden sole. Someone in the apartment across the hall opened his door and looked out.

"Are you one of June's friends?" he said. His tone was vaguely sarcastic.

"I guess so," I said.

"She should be out in a minute," he said. "Just keep banging."

At last the chain was unhitched, and there was June, wrapped in a blanket, her beautiful hair fanning over her shoulders. Her face was bleary with sleep but her eyes were wide open. She seemed surprised to see me, as if she had never asked me to come, or, really, as if she had never seen me before in her life.

"Come in," she said.

"I'm sorry I'm late," I said, realizing at once how ridiculous that was. I followed her in, and she stood in the center of the messy room and stared around at the clutter as if looking for someplace to put me. She cleared some books from a chair and sat down in it herself. A door clicked open from a room in the back. "Just a minute," June called, and the door clicked shut. She yawned, and pulled a bare arm out from under the blanket, and found a cigarette on the table and lit it. It was the first time I saw her with a cigarette. Her hand, I noticed, was perfectly steady. She stared at me and let out a stream of smoke. "I think I need to get a little more sleep," she began. "I was up all night. Don't go. There's food . . ." She gestured toward the kitchen. "I'll be up in a while. Not long. I still want to go sailing."

"So do I," I lied. I didn't know if I was angry or hurt or both. Anyway I tried not to show it. She smiled at me weakly and left. For a while I examined the room but there was too much to look at, piles of books and papers, odds and ends, and on the top shelf of the bookcase, sitting all in a row and out of my reach, a bunch of old stuffed animals. On the walls were some charcoal drawings of June, but the likenesses weren't that good and the shading amateur. I had been wrong about the kitty litter. There was a dog mess, on a sheaf of newspaper spread out in one corner of the kitchen. It was a small dog. A Pekinese. I found her asleep in a bread basket on a low shelf of the open cupboard. I lifted her up and carried her over to the window and we stood there and looked out at the back of a building exactly like the one we were in. Staring across at its windows, I expected to see the two of us looking back at ourselves. I held the dog close to my breast, like an infant. She pressed her nose against the pane and left a small moist dot on the glass. The window, I saw, was covered with these spots. After a time she started squirming and I lowered her back into her basket.

I opened the refrigerator. There were two ceramic bowls piled high with strawberries, and a glass jar filled with brown water. I unscrewed the lid and sniffed, apprehensive about what I might find. Spiced tea. I poured myself a glass and sat on the floor in the main room with a bowl of strawberries cradled in my lap, pinching the tops off and popping them into my mouth one after another. I dropped the green leafy tops back into the bowl. I can't tell you how lonely I felt. I was sitting in a square of sunlight, and when it shifted I inched along with it. Someone was moaning at the back of the house, and gasping. It was impossible to know whether the person who was moaning was the same one who was gasping. Then the telephone rang. It was right at my feet but I didn't pick it up. I let it ring. It rang twelve times. The gasping and moaning continued. My mouth began to sting, from the cold tartness of the berries, but I kept on eating. I held each berry whole in my mouth, sucking the juices out, then pressing it up against the roof of my mouth and crushing it under my tongue. My stomach made wet sloshing noises like a washing machine. I picked up the phone and dialed home, wanting suddenly more than anything to talk with Jack, to tell him what a lousy time I was having and that I wished I hadn't come and that I hoped he would forgive me.

"Forgive you for what?" Jack said.

I didn't know how to respond to that. I sat there in silence. The moaning had ceased but the dog was whimpering. Somehow, I had shut the cupboard door and locked it inside. I got up, carrying the phone, and went into the kitchen to free it. With my free hand I stroked the dog's head, tracing the shape of its broad bony skull with my fingers.

"What's that?" said Jack.

"A dog," I said.

"What do you have in your mouth?"

"A strawberry."

"When are you coming home?"

"I don't know," I said. "Tonight. It's a long drive for nothing."

"Mmmm." Jack said. He would be pressing his lips together, turning them under and holding them shut with his teeth. How familiar he was. He is a gentle man; I have never known another man who does that with his teeth.

"I'll have to be going," I said. "This is costing June a lot of money."

"Mmmm," Jack said. He hung up first. He always guesses when I am waiting for him to hang up, and he never makes me wait too long.

June's lover was tall and olive-skinned and had a mustache almost as thick as a man's. She might have taken some pills. She walked with a swagger, in a bleached denim jacket and jeans and square-toed boots, and she had a mole on her face, in precisely the spot where Marilyn Monroe had one. The effect was freakish. Her name was Faye. I thought to myself, Swarthy Faye. Faye the Pirate. Captain Faye and the Sharks. I saw her as the lead singer in a rock band, dressed in cloak and dagger on a darkened stage in a low-ceilinged room, breathing a song. Her voice would be deep and airy like the sound a bottle makes when you blow into it. I can't remember her voice, now. I don't know that I heard it even once. She stayed close to June, like a bodyguard, and gave her looks fraught with meaning that I could not decipher.

June seemed confused. I think she had expected me to leave while they were still in bed, at the same time hoping I would stay. I was determined to go sailing. Otherwise, I told myself, why would I have come? She still looked tired, and she had wrapped her hair in a madras scarf so you couldn't see it. She was smoking again. Faye kept the cigarettes in the breast pocket of her jacket, and every time June wanted a smoke she had to reach in and get one.

"You had a telephone call," I said, in a voice that was too cheerful. I worked as a receptionist at a hotel in town, and that was my receptionist voice.

"Who was it?" asked June, startled.

"No one," I said. "I mean I didn't answer it."

"Thank god," June said. Faye smiled, only barely, and at no one in particular. We drank instant coffee black, because the fake cream was stuck like a rock in the bottom of the jar. June bent a spoon, trying to get it out. We all laughed when she held up the bent spoon, then stopped abruptly when it clattered in the sink. There was no mention of a breakfast more substantial than strawberries and coffee. By then, anyway, it was lunchtime. Sun streaming through the windows. June's arms golden in the sunlight. I was wondering whether, had June and I been alone, we would have made pancakes. All at once I remembered the time years ago when, as a teenager, I spent my first night with a boy, on a mattress in the closet of an empty house on some church grounds. In the morning we went to the house of a friend, a motherly girl in an apron, who cooked a batch of pancakes and left the kitchen while we ate them. Thinking of this, I couldn't recall the boy's name. The sole image I had was of his Adam's apple bobbing up and down above my face, the forlorn, boyish shape of the bone with the skin stretched whitely over it. I remembered I told him his balls looked like plums, and how shocked he looked when I said it.

The noon hour stretched on. Then June stood up suddenly and announced it was time to go sailing. We walked the few blocks to the harbor, June chatting on and off about how rich her brother was. His boat was moored at a dock crowded with other boats. There were hordes of people, tying and untying ropes, having just come in or else preparing to go out into the bay, and some who just lounged around in bathing suits as if they had no intention of going anywhere. I have never familiarized myself with the mechanics of sailing, and sat on the deck, holding my clogs in my lap while June and Faye passed ropes back and forth and hooked and unhooked things. June disappeared below for a minute, and reappeared with three chilled beers that she passed around. Faye popped the tab off and tossed it right into the water, where it floated. I glanced at June, who shrugged sheepishly, and for a moment there was only the two of us, in the boat that was creaking and bobbing. She made a point of sitting near me while applying some tanning lotion. She had stripped down to her swim suit. When there was too much lotion left over on her hands she rubbed it into my neck. Her hands were warm. The scent of coconuts rose around us. I didn't know what to do. Faye stared out at the harbor past a string of boats, drinking her beer very fast. Then, when she was finished, she crushed the can with her boot and threw it with perfect aim into the mouth of a trash can on the dock, disappointing me. June clapped, and Faye came over to join her, and they started the motor and we were off.

It was slow going. The harbor was jammed. I was struck by the camaraderie of boaters; there was much waving and shouting back and forth. Every few yards we had to stop and sit still while the hot smell of gasoline seared the air. I cringed each time Faye lit June's cigarette, half expecting a blast. Faye wouldn't look at me but June smiled each time the sun dipped behind a cloud. There were clouds suddenly, loose black clumps in patches on the hard blue sky, throwing intermittent shadows on the water. You could see, if you looked way into the distance into the bay itself, how the strung sails brightened and then vanished and then brightened again as they traveled through light and darkness.

"Jack would have liked this," I said.

"You should have brought him along," said June.

"You should have told me to," I said. Faye took June's hand and placed her own long-boned hand on top of it. They nuzzled and sighed.

At the lip of the bay the coast guard stopped us. There was a man with a megaphone. A storm was approaching. The clouds had clumped overhead and there was thunder far off. The air had grown thick, and electric. A few tendrils of hair had escaped from June's scarf; they glowed like filaments. Goose bumps appeared on our arms, but there was nothing to be frightened of as long as we turned back. I was relieved. The ocean looked crazy. We hadn't even put up our sails. The city was still in sunlight, but we knew it wouldn't last. We shared another beer, not bothering to speak above the churn of the motors. Docked, we covered the boat with a tarpaulin and walked home as the rain started falling. I have never seen such large drops of rain, like grapes. June caught some in her mouth, and then Faye took her jacket off and lifted it over our heads. More than once I stepped out of my clogs and they waited for me without turning around. We all smelled by the time we got home. Salt and sweat. The apartment was stifling and so dark we were blinded. June sniffed. "I've got to change that newspaper," she said. "Poor Phyllis." Then she turned to me and touched me very lightly on the wrist. "Faye and I are taking a shower," she said.

I kissed Phyllis goodbye and grabbed a handful of strawberries and left. For a while I sat in the car and waited for the rain to let up, and chewed slowly to ward off my hunger. For days, I felt, I had been eating nothing else, like someone lost in a forest. I just wanted to get home. I didn't know why I had come. I didn't want to know. On the highway I took a wrong turn. They had to turn me around at a toll booth, stopping traffic so I could cut across the lanes. The man in the booth had a strawberry nose. "Thanks," I said, "I would have ended up in Florida," but I don't think he heard me.

Jack wasn't home when I got there. He had been busy; the bed was stacked with laundry. The windows were open, and the floor was streaked with rain. Summer where we live is the season of mildew, and I could smell it on the towel as I wiped the perspiration from my face. I was tired, too tired to undress. I fell among the fresh-washed clothes and slept.

Later that night, Jack came home. He smelled like soap. I have never asked him where he was and he has never told me. At the time I was too sick to care. My throat and tongue were parched, and my limbs ached dully. He helped me out of my clothes, and fed me water and aspirin. He dampened a washcloth and held it briefly to my face, which he told me was swollen. My lips felt swollen and tasted of brine. I refused to eat. Jack brought me hot cups of broth, which cooled before I touched them.

"What could it be?" he said, on the second day, when I was feeling a little better. I was sitting up in bed, just sitting, still dazed, doing nothing.

"Strawberries," I said. "That has to be it. Look at this rash. What else could it be?"

"Mmmm," Jack said. He was brushing my hair, a lock at a time. His strokes were even and gentle. That was when we turned the television on, and Ronald Reagan said what he said, and Jack threw the brush and hit him in the face and broke it. It fell to the floor in two pieces. I don't remember the rest of the news, if there was any. We just sat very close. I think I told him about the man in the Winnebago, just then remembering him. Then we both went to sleep. Ten years have gone by, and it is suddenly the season, and believe me when I say I haven't touched another strawberry since.

DAMBALLAH

Orion let the dead, gray cloth slide down his legs and stepped into the river. He picked his way over slippery stones till he stood calf deep. Dropping to one knee he splashed his groin, then scooped river to his chest, both hands scrubbing with quick, kneading spirals. When he stood again, he stared at the distant gray clouds. A hint of rain in the chill morning air, a faint, clean presence rising from the far side of the hills. The promise of rain coming to him as all things seemed to come these past few months, not through eyes or ears or nose but entering his black skin as if each pore had learned to feel and speak.

He watched the clear water race and ripple and pucker. Where the sun cut through the pine trees and slanted into the water he could see the bottom, see black stones, speckled stones, shining stones whose light came from within. Above a stump at the far edge of the river, clouds of insects hovered. The water was darker there, slower, appeared to stand in deep pools where tangles of root, bush and weed hung over the bank. Orion thought of the eldest priest chalking a design on the floor of the sacred *obi*. Drawing the watery door no living hands could push open, the crossroads where the spirits passed between worlds. His skin was becoming like that in-between place the priest scratched in the dust. When he walked the cane rows and dirt paths of the plantation he could feel the air of this strange land wearing out his skin, rubbing it thinner and thinner until one day his skin would not be thick enough to separate what was inside from everything outside. Some days his skin whispered he was dying. But he was not afraid. The voices and faces of his fathers bursting through would not drown him. They would sweep him away, carry him home again.

In his village across the sea were men who hunted and fished with their voices. Men who could talk the fish up from their shadowy dwellings and into the woven baskets slung over the fishermen's shoulders. Orion knew the fish in this cold river had forgotten him, that they were darting in and out of his legs. If the whites had not stolen him, he would have learned the fishing magic. The proper words, the proper tones to please the fish. But here in this blood-soaked land everything was different. Though he felt their slick bodies and saw the sudden dimples in the water where they were feeding, he understood that he would never speak the language of these fish. No more than he would ever speak again the words of the white people who had decided to kill him.

The boy was there again hiding behind the trees. He could be the one. This boy born so far from home. This boy who knew nothing but what the whites told him. This boy could learn the story and tell it again. Time was short but he could be the one.

"That Ryan, he a crazy nigger. One them wild African niggers act like he fresh off the boat. Kind you stay away from less you lookin for trouble." Aunt Lissy had stopped popping string beans and frowned into the boy's face. The pause in the steady drumming of beans into the iron pot, the way she scrunched up her face to look mean like one of the Master's pit bulls told him she had finished speaking on the subject and wished to hear no more about it from him. When the long green pods began to shuttle through her fingers again, it sounded like she was cracking her knuckles, and he expected something black to drop into the huge pot.

"Fixin to rain good. Heard them frogs last night just a singing at the clouds. Frog and all his brothers calling down the thunder. Don't rain soon them fields dry up and blow away." The boy thought of the men trudging each morning to the fields. Some were brown, some yellow, some had red in their skins and some white as the Master Ryan black, but Aunt Lissy blacker. Fat, shiny blue-black like a crow's wing.

"Sure nuff crazy." Old woman always talking. Talking and telling silly stories. The boy wanted to hear something besides an old woman's mouth. He had heard about frogs and bears and rabbits too many times. He was almost grown now, almost ready to leave in the mornings with the men. What would they talk about? Would Orion's voice be like the hollers the boy heard early in the mornings when the men still sleepy and the sky still dark and you couldn't really see nobody but knew they were there when them cries and hollers came rising through the mist.

Pine needles crackled with each step he took, and the boy knew old Ryan knew somebody spying on him. Old nigger guess who it was, too. But if Ryan knew, Ryan didn't care. Just waded out in that water like he the only man in the world. Like maybe wasn't no world. Just him and that quiet place in the middle of the river. Must be fishing out there, some funny old African kind of fishing. Nobody never saw him touch victuals Master set out and he had to be eating something, even if he was half crazy, so the nigger must be fishing for his breakfast. Standing there like a stick in the water till the fish forgot him and he could snatch one from the water with his beaky fingers.

A skinny-legged, black waterbird in the purring river. The boy stopped chewing his stick of cane, let the sweet juice blend with his spit, a warm syrup then whose taste he prolonged by not swallowing, but letting it coat his tongue and the insides of his mouth, waiting patiently like the figure in the water waited, as the sweet taste seeped away. All the cane juice had trickled down his throat before he saw Orion move. After the stillness, the illusion that the man was a tree rooted in the rocks at the riverbed, when motion came, it was too swift to follow. Not so much a matter of seeing Orion move as it was feeling the man's eyes inside him, hooking him before he could crouch lower in the weeds. Orion's eyes on him and through him boring a hole in his chest and thrusting into that space one word *Damballah*. Then the hooded eyes were gone.

On a spoon you see the shape of a face is an egg. Or two eggs because you can change the shape from long oval to moons pinched together at the middle seam or any shape egg if you tilt and push the spoon closer or farther away. Nothing to think about. You go with Mistress to the chest in the root cellar. She guides you with a candle and you make a pouch of soft cloth and carefully lay in each spoon and careful it don't jangle as up and out of the darkness following her rustling dresses and petticoats up the earthen steps each one topped by a plank which squirms as you mount it. You are following the taper she holds and the strange smell she trails and leaves in rooms. Then shut up in a room all day with nothing to think about. With rags and pieces of silver. Slowly you rub away the tarnished spots; it is like finding something which surprises you though you knew all the time it was there. Spoons lying on the strip of indigo: perfect, gleaming fish you have coaxed from the black water.

Damballah was the word. Said it to Aunt Lissy and she went upside his head, harder than she had ever slapped him. Felt like crumpling right there in the dust of the yard it hurt so bad but he bit his lip and didn't cry out, held his ground and said the word again and again silently to himself, pretending nothing but a bug on his burning cheek and twitched and sent it flying. Damballah. Be strong as he needed to be. Nothing touch him if he don't want. Before long they'd cut him from the herd of pickaninnies. No more chasing flies from the table, no more silver spoons to get shiny, no fat, old woman telling him what to do. He'd go to the fields each morning with the men.

Holler like they did before the sun rose to burn off the mist. Work like they did from can to caint. From first crack of light to dusk when the puddles of shadow deepened and spread so you couldn't see your hands or feet or the sharp tools hacking at the cane.

He was already taller than the others, a stork among the chicks scurrying behind Aunt Lissy. Soon he'd rise with the conch horn and do a man's share so he had let the fire rage on half his face and thought of the nothing always there to think of. In the spoon, his face long and thin as a finger. He looked for the print of Lissy's black hand on his cheek, but the image would not stay still. Dancing like his face reflected in the river. Damballah. "Don't you ever, you hear me, ever let me hear that heathen talk no more. You hear me, boy? You talk Merican, boy." Lissy's voice like chicken cackle. And his head a barn packed with animal noise and animal smell. His own head but he had to sneak round in it. Too many others crowded in there with him. His head so crowded and noisy lots of time don't hear his own voice with all them braying and cackling.

Orion squatted the way the boy had seen the other old men collapse on their haunches and go still as a stump. Their bony knees poking up and their backsides resting on their ankles. Looked like they could sit that way all day, legs folded under them like wings. Orion drew a cross in the dust. Damballah. When Orion passed his hands over the cross the air seemed to shimmer like it does above a flame or like it does when the sun so hot you can see waves of heat rising off the fields. Orion talked to the emptiness he shaped with his long black fingers. His eyes were closed. Orion wasn't speaking but sounds came from inside him the boy had never heard before, strange words, clicks, whistles and grunts. A singsong moan that rose and fell and floated like the old man's busy hands above the cross. Damballah like a drum beat in the chant. Damballah a place the boy could enter, a familiar sound he began to anticipate, a sound outside of him which slowly forced its way inside, a sound measuring his heartbeat then one with the pumping surge of his blood.

The boy heard part of what Lissy saying to Primus in the cooking shed: "Ryan he yell that heathen word right in the middle of Jim talking bout Sweet Jesus the Son of God. Jump up like he snake bit and scream that word so everybody hushed, even the white folks what came to hear Jim preach. Simple Ryan standing there at the back of the chapel like a knot poked out on somebody's forehead. Lookin like a nigger caught wid his hand in the chicken coop. Screeching like some crazy hoot owl while Preacher Jim praying the word of the Lord. They gon kill that simple nigger one day."

Dear Sir:

The nigger Orion which I purchased of you in good faith sight unseen on your promise that he was of sound constitution "a full grown and able-bodied house servant who can read, write, do sums and cipher" to recite the exact words of your letter dated April 17, 1852, has proved to be a burden, a deficit to the economy of my plantation rather than the asset I fully believed I was receiving when I agreed to pay the price you asked. Of the vaunted intelligence so rare in his kind, I have seen nothing. Not an English word has passed through his mouth since he arrived. Of his docility and tractability I have seen only the willingness with which he bares his leatherish back to receive the stripes constant misconduct earn him. He is a creature whose brutish habits would shame me were he quartered in my kennels. I find it odd that I should write at such length about any nigger, but seldom have I been so struck by the disparity between promise and performance. As I have accrued nothing but expense and inconvenience as a result of his presence, I think it only just that you return the full amount I paid for this flawed *piece of the Indies.*

You know me as an honest and fair man and my regard for those same qualities in you prompts me to write this letter. I am not a harsh master, I concern myself with the spiritual as well as the temporal needs of my slaves. My nigger Jim is renowned in this county as a preacher. Many say I am foolish, that the words of scripture are wasted on these savage blacks. I fear you have sent me a living argument to support the critics of my Christianizing project. Among other absences of truly human qualities I have observed in this Orion is the utter lack of a soul.

She said it time for Orion to die. Broke half the overseer's bones knocking him off his horse this morning and everybody thought Ryan done run away sure but Mistress come upon the crazy nigger at suppertime on the big house porch naked as the day he born and he just sat there staring into her eyes till Mistress screamed and run away. Aunt Lissy said Ryan ain't studying no women, ain't gone near to woman since he been here and she say his ain't the first black butt Mistress done seen all them nearly grown boys walkin round summer in the onliest shirt Master give me barely come down to they knees and niggers man nor woman don't get drawers the first. Mistress and Master both seen plenty. Wasn't what she saw scared her less she see the ghost leaving out Ryan's body.

The ghost wouldn't steam out the top of Orion's head. The boy remembered the sweaty men come in from the fields at dusk when the nights start to cool early, remembered them with the drinking gourds in they hands scooping up water from the wooden barrel he filled, how they throw they heads back and the water trickles from the sides of they mouth and down they chin and they let it roll on down they chests, and the smoky steam curling off they shoulders. Orion's spirit would not rise up like that but wiggle out his skin and swim off up the river.

The boy knew many kinds of ghosts and learned the ways you get round their tricks. Some spirits almost good company and he filled the nothing with jingles and whistles and took roundabout paths and sang to them when he walked up on a crossroads and yoo-hooed at doors. No way you fool the haunts if a spell conjured strong on you, no way to miss a beating if it your day to get beat, but the ghosts had everything in they hands, even the white folks in they hands. You know they there, you know they floating up in the air watching and counting and remembering them strokes Ole Master laying cross your back.

They dragged Orion across the yard. He didn't buck or kick, but it seemed as if the four men carrying him were struggling with a giant stone rather than a black bag of bones. His ashy nigger weight swung between the two pairs of white men like a lazy hammock but the faces of the men all red and twisted. They huffed and puffed and sweated through they clothes carrying Ryan's bones to the barn. The dry spell had layered the yard with a coat of dust. Little squalls of yellow spurted from under the men's boots. Trudging steps heavy as if each man carried seven Orions on his shoulders. Four grown men struggling with one string of black flesh. The boy had never seen so many white folks dealing with one nigger. Aunt Lissy had said it time to die and the boy wondered what Ryan's ghost would think dropping onto the dust surrounded by the scowling faces of the Master and his overseers.

One scream that night. Like a bull when they cut off his maleness. Couldn't tell who it was. A bull screaming once that night and torches burning in the barn and Master and the men coming out and no Ryan.

Mistress crying behind a locked door and Master messing with Patty down the quarters.

In the morning light the barn swelling and rising and teetering in the yellow dust, moving the way you could catch the ghost of something in a spoon and play with it, bending it, twisting it. That goldish wash on everybody's bare shins. Nobody talking. No cries nor hollers from the fields. The boy watched till his eyes hurt, waiting for a moment when he could slip unseen into the shivering barn. On his hands and knees hiding under a wagon, then edging sideways through the loose boards and wedge of space where the weathered door hung crooked on its hinge.

The interior of the barn lay in shadows. Once beyond the sliver of light coming in at the cracked door the boy stood still till his eyes adjusted to the darkness. First he could pick out the stacks of hay, the rough partitions dividing the animals. The smells, the choking heat there like always, but rising above these familiar sensations the buzz of flies, unnaturally loud, as if the barn breathing and each breath shook the wooden walls. Then the boy's eyes followed the sound to an open space at the center of the far wall. A black shape there. Orion there, floating in his own blood. The boy ran at the blanket of flies. When he stomped, some of the flies buzzed up from the carcass. Others too drunk on the shimmering blood ignored him except to join the ones hovering above the body in a sudden droning peal of annoyance. He could keep the flies stirring but they always returned from the recesses of the high ceiling, the dark corners of the building, to gather in a cloud above the body. The boy looked for something to throw. Heard his breath, heavy and threatening like the sound of the flies. He sank to the dirt floor, sitting cross-legged where he had stood. He moved only once, ten slow paces away from Orion and back again, near enough to be sure, to see again how the head had been cleaved from the rest of the body, to see how the ax and tongs, branding iron and other tools were scattered around the corpse, to see how one man's hat and another's shirt, a letter that must have come from someone's pocket lay about in a helter-skelter way as if the men had suddenly bolted before they had finished with Orion.

Forgive him, Father. I tried to the end of my patience to restore his lost soul. I made a mighty effort to bring him to the Ark of Salvation but he had walked in darkness too long. He mocked Your Grace. He denied Your Word. Have mercy on him and forgive his heathen ways as you forgive the soulless beasts of the fields and birds of the air.

She say Master still down slave row. She say everybody fraid to go down and get him. Everybody fraid to open the barn door. Overseer half dead and the Mistress still crying in her locked room and that barn starting to stink already with crazy Ryan and nobody gon get him.

And the boy knew his legs were moving and he knew they would carry him where they needed to go and he knew the legs belonged to him but he could not feel them, he had been sitting too long thinking on nothing for too long and he felt the sweat running on his body but his mind off somewhere cool and quiet and hard and he knew the space between his body and mind could not be crossed by anything, knew you mize well try to stick the head back on Ryan as try to cross that space. So he took what he needed out of the barn, unfolding, getting his gangly crane's legs together under him and shouldered open the creaking double doors and walked through the flame in the center where he had to go.

Damballah said it be a long way a ghost be going and Jordan chilly and wide and a new ghost take his time getting his wings together. Long way to go so you can sit and listen till the ghost ready to go on home. The boy wiped his wet hands on his knees and drew the cross and said the word and settled down and listened to Orion tell the stories again. Orion talked and he listened and couldn't stop listening till he saw Orion's eyes rise up through the back of the severed skull and lips rise up through the skull and the wings of the ghost measure out the rhythm of one last word.

Late afternoon and the river slept dark at its edges like it did in the mornings. The boy threw the head as far as he could and he knew the fish would hear it and swim to it and welcome it. He knew they had been waiting. He knew the ripples would touch him when he entered.

X AND O

So I'm going Whaaa-t! I already missed my period by four days! And he goes like Naw, you're just . . . you're not. Are you? So go get checked out. Where? I dunno. The Public Health Department? And then, Are you knocked up, really? Well, I mean, its not that big a deal, is it? You messed up. No sweat. Only he's talking West Texas, Waaal, and real slow and all that, not like in California where I came from. Waaal, what did they tell you at the health department? Did you see one of themmm—counselors? I go Yeah. They get your name: O. Your age: 16. They don't tell you to do it or not do it. But they ask, like, "Can you support the baby?" Stuff like that.

And I tell him, it's all set up if I want it—. And then I go—I have to do something! I can't have it! I—we—can't have it! I'm saying this to X. And he goes Yeah, I know. And I go Yeah, you're right.

So we're all of a sudden in a panic to get it done. I want to do it today. I don't want another night of thinking about it, nightmares and all. Of course, they can't do it that quick. I sneak out of the house and telephone this clinic and make the appointment for Thursday, and feel better. Next day I cancel it without telling him. I can't. I can't. It's too terrible. It's a person, tiny as it is. It's on the way, coming at me in nightmares. But coming, for sure.

Jeeze, he was furious, you know, when he found out I canceled. He goes Why didn't we talk about it because by God he's involved too and it's his decision too. So I go You really don't care. I screamed about him having his fun and now look, and just get rid of it, huh—it doesn't mean nothing. Act like its a nothing! I'm a nothing! And like that. I mean, I sort of flipped out because I never have screamed at him and he had to close my mouth with his hand and throw me on the floor at his apartment. And I didn't care. Maybe that would make it come.

So then we got crazy and really tried to miscarry it. I went to a park by myself and jogged until I couldn't go any more. I hung upside down on the monkey bars, did push-ups and sit-ups. He knew a girl who had a vibrator—I don't know how he knew this girl had this thing. I was too shook up to think about it, and he wanted to go borrow it from her and try this—dumb, just like a guy. But I go No, what will she think? It wouldn't work anyway. Nothing worked. No way was it going to let go.

And I was still kind of wanting it anyway, it was kind of a nice feeling having it inside of me. It was ours.

But it was like three things kept crashing through all my thoughts. The three things hadn't ever been connected before and now they were like jammed into one. Sex, pregnancy, abortion. Sex gets you pregnant and then you either have it or do away with it. Sex-pregnancy-abortion. It was like beating into my head in my nightmares and all day in school. I . . . it didn't help in the girls' bathroom either—I mean, I would go in there, like to barf, but I never could, and would sit and strain hoping it would break loose, and there were three stalls and fuck on the walls of each one—no matter what one you went in—fuck-fuck-fuck. Three stalls, three fucks.

I would sit and remember him throwing French fries in the air and catching them in his mouth. I worked about two months in a place called French Fry City, it wasn't just fries but burgers and stuff and he got lots of practice waiting for me to get off. And the easy way he slid in behind the wheel all in one move.

And we used to smooch at stop lights. Like tight together in the front seat of this supercab pickup he had. You could tell his pickup anywhere in town. He worked at a sparkle shop and he had done it all over in purple and gold metal flake, chrome mag wheels, chrome 10-inch drop bumper, headache rack, and running boards. It looked like a boat. What else? Yeah, a chrome rollbar and a light-bar with four lights, two amber, two white; and a shotgun rack. Not another one like it, and besides that, he had this bumper sticker "Ask me if I give a shit." That was him. That truck was him and he was that truck.

He was wanting to get a lift kit and convert it to a monster, but he went Yeah, he would use that money if we needed it to get it done, and borrow on his paycheck. And I had a little birthday money in the bank. It looked like he was beginning to not want us to get married. Not now, not ever. Ever. Ever and never. Forever and never. Those words ran around in my head, too. Words like Elsa Scott, our English teacher used. We used to get a really big yak out of her.

. . . Mr. Superslung. My girlfriend warned me he could kill you with his eyes. Watch you bleed. Like, he was drop-dead gorgeous. He still is. Really. But all that is gone. It was stupid anyway. It seems like it never happened.

So anyway . . . Oh. I guess I wasn't sleeping, I wasn't eating except nachos and Cokes. I would barely make it until I could get to a pay phone and call him. Then we wouldn't say anything. There would just be long silences and, Well, what are we going to do, and like that, and he would get jumpy and go Well I have to go now, back to work.

But anyway, we decided to go ahead and do it. Did I say that yet? That was the last thing we decided, anyway. Yeah, I go, you're right.

I just went "home" sick from school one morning and he drove me to the clinic.

It was a weird scene. It wasn't like any experience I ever had (my girl-friend, the one who warned me about X, said the same thing, she had one too); and God willing I will never have it again, but like she said we were up against it and there wasn't any other way out.

Tell my mom? She had me. My grandmother had her.

It was a normal looking place, like an office; shrubs and little trees, those kind of trees in office parks that never get any bigger. There were these Jesus freaks standing around in a bunch. Don't pay them no mind he goes when he helped me down out of the supercab and he took my arm, like rough, and gave them the finger.

Then, Oh God, he got a big goop of pink bubble gum from the parking lot stuck on the heel of his boot. We had to stop while he scraped it off with his pocket knife. It didn't want to come off. He had to scrape and scrape. God, Oh God. Here now, hell, don't pitch a fit in the street. It got all over his knife. He had to clean his knife on the curb. C'mon baby. You're gonna be glad after it's over.

He wasn't even there after it was over. At the beginning of it I had my sheet telling all about it; X paid the fee; I signed three forms; he had to go in the waiting room; it was soft colors, dusty rose and soft blue, and beige; it was kind of rich-looking, with magazines and all, but it was like fakey. They gave me blood and urine tests; a pelvic—flat on your back with your feet in these stirrup-things, he was asking like did I have any favorite rock stars—with his fingers feeling for something. Then we went to get counseled and she asked if we had any problems with our decision and nobody said anything; she did all the talking, telling all of what they were going to do, more than I wanted to know; taking care of yourself afterwards; using contraceptives. They must have a hard time not acting bored, there were so many lined up, exact same stuff over and over. That's all they did in there. Then you put on the gown and the paper shoes and then a counselor goes in with you and holds your hand if you want; all the while they were playing this soft rock, and now in the operating room or whatever they call it, when you go in you notice it sud-denly has burst out louder to cover screaming or whatever; but I had made up my mind I wasn't going to freak out and I didn't. I just held the lady's hand tight and tried to shut out that frigging music.

He wasn't even there when I got through. It was the most alone I have ever been. He had a reason I found out later but I was really pissed and, you know, crying, when he wasn't there. He spun up in his brother's car like twenty minutes later. He started telling me all this stuff about moving the pickup. He was worrying about his pickup and that the Jesus freaks might damage it and all. How he moved it to the alley first, and then went back and drove it home and had to find his brother and borrow his brother's car, and I was hurting like hell and pissed off and then he said How'd it go? And I wanted to kill him or die myself.

No. I wanted it back. I go Give it back to me! I want it back!—It's funny, it's just like when I was nine my grandmother died, you know, the exact same thing, I screamed and yelled the same thing, I want her back! I want her back! They had to take me to her house, I made them take me to see for myself she wasn't there. And, same exact thing, I was empty inside and the whole earth seemed like a grave, and I burst out crying, and walked back and forth.

No, I was hobbling slow back and forth it hurt so bad and he stopped me from doing that and put me in his brother's car and took me to the apartment to rest until school was out and then I had to go home like nothing happened. Really. My brother was zapping zits in the bathroom when I got there and I couldn't get him out. Then I finally did and I changed the pad and went to bed for sixteen hours and I go, Just a bad period, to my mom. I got a big picture of telling my mom Gee, Mom, guess what?—My friend couldn't tell her mom, either. I mean, your *mom*. She had you.

I always had nightmares all through this, every night I got a nightmare. Then one night I dreamed it came back and it was real, I mean a real baby for sure and it smiled at me and . . . like—it wasn't a girl or a boy, it was just baby—I can't explain, it was like love showing itself to me. Like, it's okay, you know?

And he went That don't make any sense. It's in your mind. It was a goop of jelly. And I went Yeah, you're right.

I still get crazy, especially since we have split up. I still feel like a nothing. But I don't get any more nightmares.

Helena Maria Viramontes

THE MOTHS

I was fourteen years old when Abuelita[1] requested my help. And it seemed
only fair. Abuelita had pulled me through the rages of scarlet fever by placing, removing and replacing potato slices on the temples of my forehead; she
had seen me through several whippings, an arm broken by a dare jump off
Tío Enrique's toolshed, puberty, and my first lie. Really, I told Amá, it was
only fair.

Not that I was her favorite granddaughter or anything special. I wasn't
even pretty or nice like my older sisters and I just couldn't do the girl things
they could do. My hands were too big to handle the fineries of crocheting or
embroidery and I always pricked my fingers or knotted my colored threads
time and time again while my sisters laughed and called me bull hands with
their cute waterlike voices. So I began keeping a piece of jagged brick in my
sock to bash my sisters or anyone who called me bull hands. Once, while we
all sat in the bedroom, I hit Teresa on the forehead, right above her eyebrow
and she ran to Amá with her mouth open, her hand over her eye while blood
seeped between her fingers. I was used to the whippings by then.

I wasn't respectful either. I even went so far as to doubt the power of
Abuelita's slices, the slices she said absorbed my fever. "You're still alive,
aren't you?" Abuelita snapped back, her pasty gray eye beaming at me and
burning holes in my suspicions. Regretful that I had let secret questions drop
out of my mouth, I couldn't look into her eyes. My hands began to fan out,
grow like a liar's nose until they hung by my side like low weights. Abuelita
made a balm out of dried moth wings and Vicks and rubbed my hands, shaped
them back to size and it was the strangest feeling. Like bones melting. Like

1. Grandma (Spanish); other Spanish words for relatives mentioned in the story are *Tío*, Uncle, *Amá*,
Mother, and *Apá*, Dad.

sun shining through the darkness of your eyelids. I didn't mind helping Abuelita after that, so Amá would always send me over to her.

In the early afternoon Amá would push her hair back, hand me my sweater and shoes, and tell me to go to Mama Luna's. This was to avoid another fight and another whipping, I knew. I would deliver one last direct shot on Marisela's arm and jump out of our house, the slam of the screen door burying her cries of anger, and I'd gladly go help Abuelita plant her wild lilies or jasmine or heliotrope or cilantro or hierbabuena in red Hills Brothers coffee cans. Abuelita would wait for me at the top step of her porch holding a hammer and nail and empty coffee cans. And although we hardly spoke, hardly looked at each other as we worked over root transplants, I always felt her gray eye on me. It made me feel, in a strange sort of way, safe and guarded and not alone. Like God was supposed to make you feel.

On Abuelita's porch, I would puncture holes in the bottom of the coffee cans with a nail and a precise hit of a hammer. This completed, my job was to fill them with red clay mud from beneath her rose bushes, packing it softly, then making a perfect hole, four fingers round, to nest a sprouting avocado pit, or the spidery sweet potatoes that Abuelita rooted in mayonnaise jars with toothpicks and daily water, or prickly chayotes[2] that produced vines that twisted and wound all over her porch pillars, crawling to the roof, up and over the roof, and down the other side, making her small brick house look like it was cradled within the vines that grew pear-shaped squashes ready for the pick, ready to be steamed with onions and cheese and butter. The roots would burst out of the rusted coffee cans and search for a place to connect. I would then feed the seedlings with water.

But this was a different kind of help, Amá said, because Abuelita was dying. Looking into her gray eye, then into her brown one, the doctor said it was just a matter of days. And so it seemed only fair that these hands she had melted and formed found use in rubbing her caving body with alcohol and marihuana, rubbing her arms and legs, turning her face to the window so that she could watch the Bird of Paradise blooming or smell the scent of clove in the air. I toweled her face frequently and held her hand for hours. Her gray wiry hair hung over the mattress. Since I could remember, she'd kept her long hair in braids. Her mouth was vacant and when she slept, her eyelids never closed all the way. Up close, you could see her gray eye beaming out the window, staring hard as if to remember everything. I never kissed her. I left the window open when I went to the market.

Across the street from Jay's Market there was a chapel. I never knew its denomination, but I went in just the same to search for candles. I sat down

2. Squashlike fruit.

on one of the pews because there were none. After I cleaned my fingernails, I looked up at the high ceiling. I had forgotten the vastness of these places, the coolness of the marble pillars and the frozen statues with blank eyes. I was alone. I knew why I had never returned.

That was one of Apá's biggest complaints. He would pound his hands on the table, rocking the sugar dish or spilling a cup of coffee and scream that if I didn't go to mass every Sunday to save my goddamn sinning soul, then I had no reason to go out of the house, period. Punto final.[3] He would grab my arm and dig his nails into me to make sure I understood the importance of catechism. Did he make himself clear? Then he strategically directed his anger at Amá for her lousy ways of bringing up daughters, being disrespectful and unbelieving, and my older sisters would pull me aside and tell me if I didn't get to mass right this minute, they were all going to kick the holy shit out of me. Why am I so selfish? Can't you see what it's doing to Amá, you idiot? So I would wash my feet and stuff them in my black Easter shoes that shone with Vaseline, grab a missal and veil, and wave good-bye to Amá.

I would walk slowly down Lorena to First to Evergreen, counting the cracks on the cement. On Evergreen I would turn left and walk to Abuelita's. I liked her porch because it was shielded by the vines of the chayotes and I could get a good look at the people and car traffic on Evergreen without them knowing. I would jump up the porch steps, knock on the screen door as I wiped my feet and call Abuelita? mi Abuelita? As I opened the door and stuck my head in, I would catch the gagging scent of toasting chile on the placa.[4] When I entered the sala,[5] she would greet me from the kitchen, wringing her hands in her apron. I'd sit at the corner of the table to keep from being in her way. The chiles made my eyes water. Am I crying? No, Mama Luna, I'm sure not crying. I don't like going to mass, but my eyes watered anyway, the tears dropping on the tablecloth like candle wax. Abuelita lifted the burnt chiles from the fire and sprinkled water on them until the skins began to separate. Placing them in front of me, she turned to check the menudo.[6] I peeled the skins off and put the flimsy, limp looking green and yellow chiles in the molcajete[7] and began to crush and crush and twist and crush the heart out of the tomato, the clove of garlic, the stupid chiles that made me cry, crushed them until they turned into liquid under my bull hand. With a wooden spoon, I scraped hard to destroy the guilt, and my tears were gone. I put the bowl of chile next to a vase filled with freshly cut roses. Abuelita touched my hand

3. Period.
4. Round cast-iron griddle.
5. Living room.
6. Tripe soup.
7. Mixing vessel, mortar.

and pointed to the bowl of menudo that steamed in front of me. I spooned some chile into the menudo and rolled a corn tortilla thin with the palms of my hands. As I ate, a fine Sunday breeze entered the kitchen and a rose petal calmly feathered down to the table.

I left the chapel without blessing myself and walked to Jay's. Most of the time Jay didn't have much of anything. The tomatoes were always soft and the cans of Campbell soups had rusted spots on them. There was dust on the tops of cereal boxes. I picked up what I needed: rubbing alcohol, five cans of chicken broth, a big bottle of Pine Sol. At first Jay got mad because I thought I had forgotten the money. But it was there all the time, in my back pocket.

When I returned from the market, I heard Amá crying in Abuelita's kitchen. She looked up at me with puffy eyes. I placed the bags of groceries on the table and began putting the cans of soup away. Amá sobbed quietly. I never kissed her. After a while, I patted her on the back for comfort. Finally: "¿Y mi Amá?"[8] she asked in a whisper, then choked again and cried into her apron.

Abuelita fell off the bed twice yesterday, I said, knowing that I shouldn't have said it and wondering why I wanted to say it because it only made Amá cry harder. I guess I became angry and just so tired of the quarrels and beatings and unanswered prayers and my hands just there hanging helplessly by my side. Amá looked at me again, confused, angry, and her eyes were filled with sorrow. I went outside and sat on the porch swing and watched the people pass. I sat there until she left. I dozed off repeating the words to myself like rosary prayers: when do you stop giving when do you start giving when do you . . . and when my hands fell from my lap, I awoke to catch them. The sun was setting, an orange glow, and I knew Abuelita was hungry.

There comes a time when the sun is defiant. Just about the time when moods change, inevitable seasons of a day, transitions from one color to another, that hour or minute or second when the sun is finally defeated, finally sinks into the realization that it cannot with all its power to heal or burn, exist forever, there comes an illumination where the sun and earth meet, a final burst of burning red orange fury reminding us that although endings are inevitable, they are necessary for rebirths, and when that time came, just when I switched on the light in the kitchen to open Abuelita's can of soup, it was probably then that she died.

The room smelled of Pine Sol and vomit and Abuelita had defecated the remains of her cancerous stomach. She had turned to the window and tried to speak, but her mouth remained open and speechless. I heard you, Abuelita, I said, stroking her cheek, I heard you. I opened the windows of the house

8. And my Mother?

and let the soup simmer and overboil on the stove. I turned the stove off and poured the soup down the sink. From the cabinet I got a tin basin, filled it with lukewarm water and carried it carefully to the room. I went to the linen closet and took out some modest bleached white towels. With the sacredness of a priest preparing his vestments, I unfolded the towels one by one on my shoulders. I removed the sheets and blankets from her bed and peeled off her thick flannel nightgown. I toweled her puzzled face, stretching out the wrinkles, removing the coils of her neck, toweled her shoulders and breasts. Then I changed the water. I returned to towel the creases of her stretch-marked stomach, her sporadic vaginal hairs, and her sagging thighs. I removed the lint from between her toes and noticed a mapped birthmark on the fold of her buttock. The scars on her back which were as thin as the life lines on the palms of her hands made me realize how little I really knew of Abuelita. I covered her with a thin blanket and went into the bathroom. I washed my hands, and turned on the tub faucets and watched the water pour into the tub with vitality and steam. When it was full, I turned off the water and undressed. Then, I went to get Abuelita.

She was not as heavy as I thought and when I carried her in my arms, her body fell into a V, and yet my legs were tired, shaky, and I felt as if the distance between the bedroom and bathroom was miles and years away. Amá, where are you?

I stepped into the bathtub one leg first, then the other. I bent my knees slowly to descend into the water slowly so I wouldn't scald her skin. There, there, Abuelita, I said, cradling her, smoothing her as we descended, I heard you. Her hair fell back and spread across the water like eagle's wings. The water in the tub overflowed and poured onto the tile of the floor. Then the moths came. Small, gray ones that came from her soul and out through her mouth fluttering to light, circling the single dull light bulb of the bathroom. Dying is lonely and I wanted to go to where the moths were, stay with her and plant chayotes whose vines would crawl up her fingers and into the clouds; I wanted to rest my head on her chest with her stroking my hair, telling me about the moths that lay within the soul and slowly eat the spirit up; I wanted to return to the waters of the womb with her so that we would never be alone again. I wanted. I wanted my Amá. I removed a few strands of hair from Abuelita's face and held her small light head within the hollow of my neck. The bathroom was filled with moths, and for the first time in a long time I cried, rocking us, crying for her, for me, for Amá, the sobs emerging from the depths of anguish, the misery of feeling half born, sobbing until finally the sobs rippled into circles and circles of sadness and relief. There, there, I said to Abuelita, rocking us gently, there, there.

Edward P. Jones

YOUNG LIONS

He stood naked before the open refrigerator in the darkened kitchen, downing the last of the milk in a half-gallon carton. Carol, once again, had taped a note to the carton. Caesar Matthews did not have to read it to know that it told him she loved him with all her heart, or that she would miss him all that day. She used to pin such notes to her pillow before she went off in the morning, leaving him still asleep. But in the night, when she brushed her hair as she prepared for bed, she would find the notes still pinned to the pillow, undisturbed and so perhaps unread. So now she taped them to milk cartons, for he could not begin his day without drinking milk, or she taped them to his gold key ring, or pinned them to the zippers of the expensive pants she knew he would wear that day. In more than two years, the wording on the notes had not changed very much. Sometimes, when he thought of it, he would fold the paper with the words and place it on the kitchen table between the salt and pepper shakers, to let her know he had come upon it before he ventured out.

This morning, after he had finished the last of the milk, without reading the words, he tossed the carton in a high arc across the room into the trash can. He pulled up the window shade and let in the morning light. He was anxious to be out in the streets; there was nothing like an empty apartment to bring down the soul.

The night before, for the fourth time in a week, he had dreamed about the retarded woman. Sherman would have told him such dreams were a good sign. Caesar was left now with only fragments of the dreams, the splintered memory that he had been roaming about in some foreign land, and the retarded woman had been standing among tall trees in that land. She never seemed to be hiding, as she should have been, but appeared to wave to him. He could not remember anything after she waved. He did remember with certainty that in all the dreams the woman was known to him not as being retarded but as being feeble-minded, which was the phrase his father had always used.

He was still naked when the telephone rang, standing at the bathroom door wondering if he wanted a shower. "These are the times," Carol would have joked, "when we miss our mothers most."

Manny, on the telephone, asked if he wanted to tend bar that evening and make some change. "I was about to hop over your place," Caesar said. He never liked Manny Soto calling his apartment, for Manny always whispered on the phone and made each word he spoke sound obscene. "He talk that way cause he's a fence and every other bad thing in the world," Sherman had said once. "He think people are listenin to everything he says, and maybe by whisperin, they'll hear a little less."

"Coincidences. Coincidences. Heh, heh," Manny said. "Good minds think a lot, they say. I was just checking to be sure, heh, heh, to see if you might be available, heh, heh." The inappropriate laughing was also why he didn't like Manny calling.

"But listen: You heard what Sherman is doing now, heh, heh, heh?" Manny said. This time he obviously felt the whole thing was funny, and he asked Caesar again.

Caesar told him no, that he had last seen Sherman in Howard Hospital. "Two, three months ago," he said.

"Well, since you last saw him, he's gone up in the world. Or gone down, whichever the case may be, heh, heh." He hung up without another word.

While dressing, Caesar found another note pinned to the collar of his shirt. He read it, crumbled it for effect, and propped it against a picture they had had taken together at a Southeast club. He would remind Carol of all the notes when he told her about the retarded woman. "Dancing with me don't end that way," were the first words she had ever spoken to him. "Try me and see." He had gone to Manny's place with Sherman Wheeler and Sherman's old lady, Sandra Wallington, and, after a good bit of coaxing by Sandra, he had asked a woman sitting alone two tables away to dance. He and the woman had slow-dragged through one record, then another, and as the woman ground her body into his, she would bite and tug at his earlobe with her lips. When the second record ended, she unwound herself and went back without a word to her table. There was now a man at her table, and the man stood and pulled the woman's chair away from the table for her. The man and the woman sat down. The woman's back was to Caesar, who stood dumbly looking at the back of her neck and at the man. The man stood again, and he looked at Caesar with the patience of someone who had nothing better to do. "No one," the man said finally, "gets more than two dances free." He sat again and Caesar, after a few moments, found his way back to Sherman and Sandra.

"Dancing with me don't end that way." He had been about to sit when Carol tugged at his shirt sleeve. He allowed her to lead him away to the dance floor. "Try me and see."

He decided that morning on the desert-brown leather jacket, a present from Carol for his twenty-second birthday two years ago. It was October, and in that month and in November before the days turned colder heading into December, he enjoyed wearing the jacket, enjoyed the opulent sound of leather with each move he made. He checked the jacket's pockets to make certain he had his address book. There was not much in the book—a few names and telephone numbers of people he knew from Manny's. But there were also the addresses and phone numbers of the three women—their names coded to read like male friends in case Carol saw them—he would go to when he and Carol argued, or when he simply wanted to spend the night with a woman whose body, whose responses, he could not easily anticipate.

He put the Beretta in one of the jacket's pockets. The moment he touched it the memory of the times he had used it came back to him. He liked remembering. The last time had been eight months ago when they crossed into Maryland and he shot the 7-Eleven clerk in the face. A few miles from the store, back in D.C., Caesar was still laughing about how the man's face had drained of blood as the gun came toward his face. A month before that he had placed the pistol beside the head of a man he and Sherman had caught far up New Hampshire Avenue near the Silver Spring line. The man had looked insulted to be robbed, and Caesar, dangling the man's watch before his eyes, had pulled the trigger to scare him into the proper frame of mind. "I wasn't gonna take this cheap-ass thing," Caesar said about the watch, "but you just ain't got the proper attitude." The bullet had nicked the man's ear, and so it didn't count the way a blast in the face counted. The nice thing about the retarded woman was that he wouldn't even have to take the pistol out of his pocket.

Sherman Wheeler had rarely carried a gun. "My daddy got his toe shot off tryin to quick-draw one a those things," he said once. "Sides, my mind is the only gun I need." Then he had made his hand into a gun, placed it against his temple, and pretended to pull a trigger. He hadn't liked Caesar carrying a gun, and in their first months together he pulled rank and told him to leave the guns at home when they weren't needed, but Caesar would sneak them out anyway. From the beginning, with the first cheap piece he had stolen during a burglary at a home in Arlington, Caesar had liked carrying a gun. And now, having to work alone without Sherman, he would not step outside the apartment without one.

II

In the vestibule of Manny's Haven at Georgia Avenue and Ingraham Street, there was an impressive collection of Polaroid pictures displayed behind a locked glass case. In most of the dozens of photographs, Manny, always wearing a Hawaiian shirt, stood in the center, his arms around Washington politicians, two-bit celebrities, customers for whom he had a special affection, or wild-eyed, out-of-town relatives. At the very bottom of the display, in two and a half rows, there were also photographs of men who had, as Manny put it, "made irredeemable fools of themselves in my house," as he called his bar. Most of these men, usually too drunk even to remember where they were, had refused to leave the bar when told, and Manny had had the bouncers toss them out. But throwing them out was never enough, and he would also have the bouncers beat them on the sidewalk. "Take his picture! Take his goddamn picture!" became his euphemism to the bouncers for throwing a man out and putting a hurting on him. The majority of the men were photographed leaning against the front of the bar just below the neon sign that blinked Manny's Haven. They were alone in their pictures with their bloodied faces, except, now and again, for the hand of some unseen bouncer that kept the fellow from falling over.

Manny was reading the *Post* aloud at a table near the bar when Caesar arrived that morning. Manny was alone, which didn't make Caesar happy. The whole place was dark, except for the tiny lamp on the table. Manny did not look up at first when Caesar sat down across from him and said, "Mornin."

Manny finished the page and put the newspaper aside, took off his glasses and rubbed his closed eyes with his knuckles. "Young Blood," he said, squinting. "Ain't seen you in a month of Sundays. Thought you mighta gone away on vacation." Manny dressed the way a very small child would without the help of an adult. "I always expect to look under the table and find him with his shoes on the wrong feet," Sherman had said once, "with knots and shit in the shoelaces, insteada little bows." Manny had hundreds of Hawaiian shirts, including some very expensive ones dating back to the 1920s and 1930s. He wore one every day of the year. This morning he had on a particularly loud silk and rayon thing with palm trees that looked not like trees but tiny green explosions. He was quite a thin man, and all his shirts hung loosely on him, the way they would hang on wire hangers.

"I'll need you for tonight and two three more nights this week," Manny said. "You got time for that?"

Caesar nodded. Bartending would tide him over until things were finished with the retarded woman. He could hear the rumblings of the men in the basement, sorting and cataloging the stolen stuff Manny had bought from thieves. Manny would send all of it on to an apartment on Florida Avenue where people came shopping to buy it for a little more than what Manny paid for it.

"What's this about you not hearing about Sherman?" Manny said. "Thought you two was closer than dick and his two nuts."

"We was once," Caesar said. Manny blinked, waiting for more. He undoubtedly knew everything already, but Caesar knew that having to tell him was the price of doing business with him. Besides, there was nothing to betray. He told Manny what little Sherman had told him in the hospital the last time he saw him: Sherman had ODed at the home of a woman who catered to a small group of people with "functional habits," people who could work and carry on their lives without the rest of the world knowing they needed special recreation in their off hours. A person could go to one of Regina's houses on M Street and relax in one of her small rooms, and after a few hours of traveling, get up and go home.

"I know this woman," Manny said. "Regina Carstairs. Oh, such a fine house in the Gold Coast. I went to her place for a function once, raising money for the mayor. The house where no junkie is allowed. But I didn't enjoy myself because she had somebody watch me all the time like I was going to steal something." Manny indicated with his fingers that he wanted more.

There's not much more, Caesar said. Sherman had traveled out on a far limb one night with just a one-way ticket. Regina thought he was dead or neardead and had people dump him in a tree box on a street blocks and blocks from her house. ("Another satisfied customer," Manny interjected. "One million and counting.") Caesar did not tell Manny that in the hospital he and Sandra, Sherman's woman, had argued, with Sandra accusing him of dumping Sherman at death's door. He had looked to Sherman for support, but in the end Sherman had raised the arm without the IV and begged Caesar to go. "I'll call you," Sherman had said.

"I got some pictures here you might be interested in, heh, heh," Manny said. "Got some nice pictures. Oh, do I got the nice pictures. Bet a million you didn't know he was on that heroin shit, did you?"

Caesar said no.

"Well, I did. It's hard to tell with some fools, but I knew." He was leaning back in his chair, his arms crossed. He was thin enough for Caesar to see the edges of the chair on either side of him. "That's the thing with that heroin shit. You see, with your average crackhead, they're climbing the walls and everything. You ask them the time and they're ready to kill you cause you ain't got your own watch. But with heroin, you ask them the time, and they're ready to give you the watch. And Sherman was the mellowest man I knew." He leaned forward. "You wanna see my pictures, heh, heh? The proof from our man Polaroid that our man from Sixteenth Street has come up in the world."

Caesar was curious, but he did not want to see. It was as if someone had asked if he wanted to see pictures of his naked father. "We can take him," Caesar had said once about Manny. "We can take him. Come in wearin masks and shit. We can clean his ass out and live like kings." "And then where we gonna live?" Sherman had said. "Even if we got a million dollars from him, where in the fuckin world would we live? Stop bein such a hothead all the time, man. Manny still payin people back for some small thing they probably did to him when he was five years old."

"Come on," Manny said. "Peek on the wild side." In fall and winter, Manny's Hawaiian shirts had two pockets, and he took a set of photographs out of the left pocket.

The pictures were of a security guard standing with folded arms between two paintings in what was clearly a museum. The man seemed to stand with an air of importance and authority, but the more Caesar studied the first pictures the more he saw that the man would never be anything more than a guard whose job was simply to stand between two paintings. The man's expression changed but slightly in the series of photographs, but in the last one, as if he was finally aware that he was the photographer's real subject, he was turning his head away and the camera caught only a blur. The guard, in a dark blue uniform, wore a dark blue hat with a shiny shield in the front, and though the hat was pulled down low over his forehead, Caesar could see that the mouth and chin were Sherman's. "My father gave me my eyes and nose, but I got my mouth and chin from my old lady." Sherman had been on his own since he was ten, but he always spoke of his parents as if he had had a full life with them.

"They were taken in the Smithsonian," Manny was saying. "Not the one with that big elephant—that's my favorite—but the art museum, the one with the paintings. When I heard he was working there, I just had to see it. So I had this guy and his whore that owed me a favor: Act like tourists and go down there and pretend they were Bamas in town to see the pictures, heh, heh." Manny tapped his forehead. "Smart. Real smart."

Caesar got up. "I gotta be movin. Be back at seven, okay?"

"Seven's fine," Manny said, kissing the pictures and putting them back in his pocket. "Any later and you'll be late."

III

He felt suddenly exhausted and afraid and considered returning to the apartment, but Carol was not there and an empty place brought down the soul. Then he thought of the retarded woman and things brightened a bit. He took a bus downtown to see the woman for what would be the last time before Friday.

He had been following her for all of two months, since a week or so after he saw Sherman in the hospital. He had first come upon her waiting for the bus with three of her housemates. They were all adults, all at least thirty years old, but they talked as if they were new to the world and excited about being in it. The two men talked very loudly, as if they were not afraid to share whatever they were saying. Caesar figured from the beginning that the larger of the two women was the weakest, would be the easiest to pick off.

He had stood a few feet from them, pretending he too was waiting for the bus. Days later he learned that the retarded woman lived only two blocks from the bus stop in a house with perhaps six other retarded people of various ages and with a woman in her fifties. He figured the older woman was there to look after the seven. Except for the older woman, he learned, all of them worked, or at least did something that took them out of the house each morning. The retarded woman he was interested in worked in a French restaurant on Connecticut Avenue near Lafayette Park.

And so for two months he had secretly placed himself in her life, doing all the scoping out, the drudgery that had once been left up to Sherman. "You'd fuck it up," Sherman had said once. "I know you." "Have some faith in me," Caesar would laugh. "Have a little faith." "I know you, mothafucka."

Week after week, Caesar had followed the retarded woman as she made her way to work, sitting in the back of the bus so he could see when she got off. At K Street, she always walked the block and a half to the restaurant. He hung around near the restaurant, sometimes for the entire day, learning her schedule. He often saw her sweeping up the alley in the back where the employees entered and where deliveries were made. About two thirty or so most afternoons, after they had probably eaten lunch, the retarded woman and a much older woman would walk to Lafayette Park and stay for up to thirty minutes. After they went back to work, he would not see the girl again until about five, when she left work and took the bus home.

On Saturdays, she came to work at noon and stayed until eight or nine in the evening. But it was only the Fridays that concerned him now. For on Fridays, each Friday evening, she left work and walked up Connecticut Avenue to Dupont Circle, where she deposited her paycheck at American Security. He would stand beside her on most Fridays over those months as she took forever to fill out the deposit slip, making first one mistake, then another, then dropping the crossed-out slips into the wastebasket beside the table. After she got on line, he would pick up every slip she had dropped. Then he would stand behind her until she had completed things with the teller.

It was a little before two when he got to the restaurant. The retarded woman and her friend soon came out to Connecticut, heading for Lafayette Park. Not quite two thirty, but close enough to the times of other days not to worry. As the women often did, they walked holding hands. They wore green uniforms and though they seemed to polish their white shoes every day, he had noticed that they were scuffed plenty by midday. He knew their first and last names, he knew where the old woman lived, having followed her home one evening, he knew the retarded woman's favorite candy, he even knew the station the old woman had her radio tuned to.

"I can see me sometime holdin my own little baby," the retarded woman said after they sat down on a bench facing the White House, "rockin her and feedin her and doin such." The sun was warm, and Caesar sat on the grass Indian-style a few feet behind the women. He opened a newspaper he had taken from a trash can, but he watched the tourists taking photographs and the government people eating their lunches.

"Thought everything would work with Fred and me," the retarded woman said. "He like the job they got him. Me and him would sit on the stoop, makin plans bout our future."

Caesar knew about her Fred, but he had never learned if he was one of those loud talkers he had seen in the first weeks at the bus stop.

"People call us the lovebirds," the retarded woman said. " 'Look at em. Look at them lovebirds.' "

The old woman was eating orange pieces from a small plastic bag, and now and again, when the breeze shifted, the smell of oranges came to Caesar. He watched a black family come up to a very old white man at the Lafayette statue. The father gave his camera to the white man and then stood in front of the statue beside his wife and behind his three children. The oldest boy closed his eyes and would not open them again until it was all done. The old man took the family's picture, and when the mother raised one finger, the old man advanced the film and snapped again.

"Then he commence to change. He talk back to Miss Prentiss," the retarded woman was saying. "His job call Miss Prentiss and said he all the time late. Wouldn't do what they told him."

"Anna, he musta told you what was the matter," the old woman said.

"No, ma'am, Miss Elsie," the retarded woman said. "He never did. Yesday I got home, a car came with two men and they took him back to Laurel." Caesar watched as the father read what was on the side of the statue and then the father looked up at the man on the horse, shading his eyes. His little girl did the same.

The black family crossed Pennsylvania Avenue, and the father gave the oldest boy the camera so he could take pictures of the White House. Then they went down to the corner and joined the line going in.

Caesar was only half listening; there was no more that would help on Friday. The problem would be Carol. He put the newspaper aside and lay down, closing his eyes. He would not follow them back to work. On another day not long ago, he had waited for the retarded woman across the street in front of the copier business until she got off from work. He had followed her to the bus stop. She was overweight, and he saw that walking was not easy for her in the heat. For the first time since he had been following her, she was not wearing her uniform. She had on a blue skirt and a pink blouse, which she wore outside the skirt. She had on tiny, gold-plated earrings a person might not notice until he was within a foot or so of her, and that was how close he was when he walked past her. She smelled of garlic and, beneath that, of a soap that reminded him of the halls in the hospital where his mother had died.

It was a crime, Sherman had said, to fall asleep anywhere but in a safe place, and so he was up and off a few minutes after the women left. He felt he wanted to see Sherman and left the park at the corner of Pennsylvania and 16th, heading in the direction where he thought the museum was. In both his lives, he had never come down to the world below Constitution Avenue, except for those times when relatives came from out of town. His mother and father would bring everyone down to see the Washington they put on postcards and in the pages of expensive coffee-table books. He knew that his father worked in one of the government buildings, but he didn't know which one. His father was the kind of man who, if he looked out his office window and saw his son, would come down the stairs three at a time and hold him until someone called the police. "Call the law! I have a thief who robbed me! Call the law!"

At 15th and Constitution, among the tourists and office workers, he gave up the idea of seeing Sherman. It would be better to start working on Carol. He could see no problems with Anna, the retarded woman, but retarded or not, she was still a woman and there was a danger of her being skittish. He called Carol at work.

He told her that he loved her, then he told her that he missed her. In his mind, he read the words written on her notes.

"I'm glad you told me," she said. "I was beginning to wonder. You made my day."

He promised to fix her dinner before he went to Manny's and he told her once again that he loved her.

"I wish I could record that," she said, "and play it back any time I wanted."

IV

When people found out that Angelo Billings, Caesar's cousin, had in fact stolen the flowers from an I Street florist and taken them to the funeral home, they said he would never again have good luck. Never mind, they said, that he loved

Caesar's mother as much as he loved anyone and that stealing the flowers was his way of showing that love. There were some things God would not tolerate, and stealing flowers for the dead was one of them.

Caesar, though, was moved, and they grew closer after his mother's funeral. Angelo introduced him to Sherman. Angelo, before Caesar gave up on school, would wait for him outside Cardozo High, and they would go to Sherman's two-bedroom apartment on 16th Street, a few blocks up from Malcolm X Park. What fascinated Caesar most about the apartment was the dominance of sound, of noise, as if Sherman were afraid of silence. In every room, there was something playing each second of the day, whether a radio or television or cassette player. In the bathroom, hanging from the shower curtain rod, there was a transistor radio that played around the clock. Sherman lived alone in the apartment, but he had two children by Sandra, who lived elsewhere in the building with the children. Most of the time when Caesar and Angelo visited, they would find Sherman wrapped in his bathrobe sitting on the couch, listening to one of dozens of cassette tapes that Sandra had recorded of the children talking and playing with each other. There were four speakers in the living room that stood three feet high, and he enjoyed playing those cassettes so loud that the noise of the children made it sound like a playground with a hundred children. Now and again, one child would hit the other or say something mean and there would be a fit of crying on the tape. Sherman would jump up and speed the tape past the crying to a place where the talking and playing resumed.

The apartment, despite the noise, became another home for Caesar and he began going there without Angelo after school. Before long, he was leaving home at least two or three days a week and going not to school but straight to Sherman's place, where he'd drop his books at the door beside the two-foot-high porcelain bulldog and make a place for himself in front of the television. In the beginning, he was able to get back home in the evening before his father arrived from work. But as the months wore away to winter, to spring, he was getting home later and later.

One night in April, Sherman dropped him off about three in the morning, and Caesar stood on the sidewalk for a long while looking up at his house. For the first time, all the lights in the house were off. When he opened the front door, his father was standing before him in the darkened hall.

"I'm just slaving away my life to raise up another Angelo," his father hissed, turning on the hall light. "A goddamn no-account." As soon as his hand was off the light switch, he slapped Caesar, knocking him back against the front door. Before Caesar could recover, his father had grabbed him by the shirt with one hand, opened the door with the other, and threw him out on the sidewalk.

"I gave you more chances than you deserved," his father said and closed the inner and outer doors to the house. Caesar, still sprawled on the ground, saw the hall light go out. Seconds later, he saw the light in the upstairs front bedroom, his father's room, go on, and a moment later, that light went out.

He got to his feet and looked up and down French Street. The new leaves rattled as if something were shaking the trees, and the sound unnerved him. He brushed off his clothes, not because of dirt or debris, but because right then he did not know what else to do. Under the street lamp, he looked at the watch Sherman had given him the week before, and it occurred to him that he had never before been awake at that hour in the morning. A cool wind sauntered up the street and chilled him, unnerving him even more, and he suppressed the urge to cry.

He considered pounding on the door, calling his father as loudly as he could and then running away. But he stood quiet. For all of his life, he had been Lemuel Matthews's son, and even now, standing in the dark outside the walls of his father's house, he was still his son and he knew he could not be a bad boy at such a place at such a time in the morning.

He saw the brighter lights at the half smoke joint at the 9th Street corner and he went toward those lights. The place was closed, but he used the outdoor telephone to call Sherman. Sandra answered, and after he had told her what happened, she told him to stay put, that Sherman would be back down to pick him up. While he waited, he called his father's house several times, stepping out of the telephone booth with the receiver as he listened to the ringing. He looked up tree-lined French Street, but there was not enough light to distinguish his house from all the others.

It was true what people said about Angelo's bad luck. He robbed the Riggs Bank on 15th Street in early May, using a gun he had rented for twenty-five dollars a day and a Safeway shopping bag. He was so curious about how much he had gotten away with that as he ran down M Street, he looked in the shopping bag, and at that moment the money, booby-trapped with a red dye packet, exploded in his face. He dropped the bag, cursing the bank teller, but he continued running, trying for the next several blocks to wipe the dye from his face and hands with the shirt he had taken off.

Sherman had thought that Angelo, eager, cocksure, had potential as a partner, but soon after the government people put Angelo away, he began to consider Caesar, who was now staying with him. Caesar knew Sherman didn't have a real job, but he didn't learn until he had been with him two months what he did for a living. He was not particularly surprised or disappointed. Caesar was seventeen, and for the first time in his life, he was living his days without the cocoon of family, and beyond that cocoon, he was learning, anything was possible.

"The first thing we do," Sherman said one day, "is get all your shit from your daddy's place. You gotta have an identity. Get you out in the world so you can stop all that mopin."

The next morning they drove down to the house on French Street and waited in the car until Caesar was certain his father had left for work and his brother and sister had gone to school. Caesar opened the front door with his key. He was surprised his father had not changed the lock, but Sherman was not surprised. "What's there to be afraid of from his own little boy?" Sherman said. Caesar stepped into the hall. Had his father suddenly appeared before him, it would have seemed the most natural thing. Indeed, he expected him, and when he stepped into the living room, he expected his father to be there as well. Sherman, silent, followed as Caesar went through the rooms on the first floor. Caesar touched nearly everything along the way—a lace piece made by his grandmother that was on the back of the easy chair in the living room; a drawing of the house signed and dated by his sister taped to the refrigerator; the kitchen curtains he had helped his mother put up. In a corner of the kitchen counter he found wrapped in a rubber band the letters he had been sending to his father; only the first one had been opened.

"Let's get your stuff," Sherman said after a bit. "Enough of this."

They went upstairs, and in the closet of his father's bedroom, Sherman found a small metal box, broke its tiny lock with his hand, and leisurely went through the papers in the box, putting aside Caesar's birth certificate and the Social Security card he had gotten the year before in hopes of finding an after-school job. Caesar watched.

"You want your mom's death certificate?" Sherman said, reaching the end of the papers in the box.

"No." He turned away and went to his sister's room, where he touched the heads of the three stuffed animals sitting on the pillows of her bed. In the room he had shared with his brother, he took as many of his clothes as he could carry, his hands shaking each time he picked up an item.

In the hall, Sherman was waiting at the head of the stairs. He took some of the clothes from Caesar. "He had a little money in the box, some cash and some gold pieces," Sherman said. "And I found a stack of pictures in a drawer. I got a few of em, mostly some with you in em. Must be your mother, too. I got a lot of em. You might want em later on when you start to forget."

Caesar nodded. In a few minutes they were on 11th Street, heading back uptown. He knew what his father would look like when he realized he had been robbed: the fist pounding the air, that pulsating vein at the left side of his head. For months and months after that, he could conjure up the image whenever he wanted and replay it. That night, they went to Manny's and Carol

YOUNG LIONS • 645

said what she said about dancing with her not ending that way, about trying her and seeing. She took him home that night, and when he woke up the next morning, she was lying on her side watching him. She leaned over and kissed his forehead. "It's all right," she said, "I already went and brushed my teeth." Aside from the ones in Sherman's magazines, she was the first naked woman he had ever seen. She kissed his ear. "There's a toothbrush in there with your name on it," she said. "And I bet I spelled your name right."

Two weeks after Caesar and Sherman went into Caesar's father's house, Sherman took him out for the first time, to burglarize a home in Chevy Chase. Sherman peed on the sofa in the recreation room, having taken a quick dislike to a large painting behind the sofa of a man in a tennis outfit whom he took to be the owner. The next night, in a light rain, they followed a light-skinned, well-dressed fellow from a bar on Capitol Hill to his car parked a block away. The man had tottered the whole distance, not bothering to open the umbrella he was carrying. "Not a sound," Caesar said, placing the pistol at the man's head just as he stuck his key in the car door. "Not a sound. No words. Not one word." Sherman went through the man's pockets, took his wallet and then his watch. "Please, please," the man kept saying, his arms extended high into the air. The man was balding and the hair he had left was combed perfectly to either side of a bald path that went back to the middle of his head. With the light of the street lamps, the robbers could see the beads of rain on the bald path and on his eyeglasses. "Next time," Caesar said as they stepped away from the man, "buy your shit in a liquor store and take it home to drink."

V

On the way home from following Anna that last time, Caesar bought white carnations for Carol and the ingredients for a shrimp creole dinner. He had dinner prepared when she came home, and after they had eaten, with her head swirling just a bit from the wine, he made love to her because he did not know what kind of mood he would be in when he returned from Manny's that night.

Later, as he told her about the retarded woman, he rested his hand on her bare stomach. He could feel her tensing up with each word. He massaged her stomach, then he took her belly button between two fingers and rubbed it gently.

"Don't ask me to do any of that," she said. "Don't bring me into any of that." As long as she believed it did not involve another woman, she had never wanted to know what he and Sherman did. But now she felt all of the not-wanting-to-know had come due and she pulled the sheet up to her neck against the cold.

"There's nothin to it," Caesar said. "In an out. Before you know it, we'll be back home, Carol. I promise."

"Stop. I'm not like you. I don't want to hurt anybody."

"It's just the money," he said, getting up. He began to dress.

"Don't go just yet," she said. She was naked and she got out of bed and put her arms around him. The cold came in the window and she shivered.

"I don't ask a whole fuckin lot of you," he said, "and when I do, you act like this." He left the room and she called to him as she put on her robe. He was out of the apartment before she got in the living room. He took the stairs two at a time, and she continued calling him as she leaned over the banister.

That was Monday. He did not go back home all that week. Manny told him on Friday that he was tired of Carol calling the bar. "Talk to her," Manny said. "Do something to shut that pussy up."

"Come home," Carol said when he finally called her Saturday afternoon. "Come home."

"You forgot what I asked you to do?" he said.

"No, I didn't forget," she said. "Come home."

"Then what do you have ta say bout what I asked?"

She said, "Yes. Yes. C, I can't hurt anybody. I just can't."

"Who said anything about somebody gettin hurt? Nobody'll get hurt. I already told you."

"Come home," she said.

The final days of that October were pleasant, but as the sun set, it grew cooler. There had been rain a few evenings, and when there was no rain, a wind came up that chilled as much as the rain. Caesar wore the tan Burberry Carol had bought for him. And as he sat in Dupont Circle Park watching Carol standing before American Security, there was still enough sunlight left for him to see Anna, a block or so away, make her way with the crowd up Connecticut Avenue.

Carol did not look over at him, and as she paced, she would occasionally pull from her purse the picture of a boy about three years old, study it as if trying to memorize the boy's features, and then return the picture to her purse. Caesar had taken it from Manny's wall of Polaroids, but no one at the bar, not even Manny, could remember who the child was. Carol, however, believed that Caesar knew the boy, and when Caesar laughed, she had flung the picture at him. It had taken him most of the rest of Thursday evening to calm her, convince her that, as his father would have said, he didn't know the boy from Adam.

Still, he could tell from the way she looked at the photograph that everything he had said and done that Thursday was wearing off. Carol finally looked over at him. When Anna was but several yards from her, Caesar pointed at Anna and Carol walked to her. She took Anna by the arm and gently pulled her from the flow of the crowd. "Always say nice, soothin things," he had told Carol. "Talk to her like you were longtime sisters or somethin."

The lights in the park and along the streets came on. Anna's back was to him, but he could see Carol's face. She appeared calm and this surprised him. "The makins of a pro," Sherman would have said. The boy in the picture, dressed in green swimming trunks with his back to some ocean, could well be a grown man by now, or he could be in his grave, Caesar thought, but today, on that street, his mother was saying he needed five thousand dollars for an operation or he would die as sure as anything. "Always make it seem like the choice is hers—whether he lives or whether he dies." Anna took the picture and she looked at it, holding it but a few inches from her face.

Just the way Anna was standing told him that of the million things in the world she could do, she would do the one thing he wanted. And knowing this made up for not being with Sherman. It made up for that old woman who had cut his hand two weeks before when he ran by and tried to grab her money from her coat pocket.

Anna gave back the picture. Satisfied, he took his eyes from the women and watched the passersby heading home. Somewhere, Sherman was about to do the same. He could see Sherman closing a giant museum door so people could not see his roomful of paintings. "No more. No more for the day." It did not hurt as much to think of him now. He looked back at the women in time to see them enter the bank.

When they came out, they crossed the street, and Caesar thought it a nice touch that Carol took Anna by the arm as they crossed. Anna sat on a bench across from Peoples, and for a minute or so more, Carol talked to her. Anna nodded. Everything now should be the closeout, he thought, and he felt she was taking too long. He waited until Carol walked by him and crossed the street, heading down Massachusetts Avenue. When he caught up with her, he took her by the elbow and she pulled away.

"You did good," he said, putting his arm around her. "You did real good. How much did you get?"

"Can't you wait?" she said. "Can't you even wait!" They crossed 18th Street. "Do we have to go into all this out here like this?"

"It's all right, Carol," he said. "She back there. Nothin can happen now."

Midway down the block, he reached for her purse, but again she pulled away from him.

"Stop! Jesus!" She quickened her pace.

He stopped momentarily. "What's wrong with you?"

At Massachusetts and 17th, he managed to lead her into the tiny park. The place was empty except for a bum who was sleeping on a bench several yards away from them. "What the fuck's wrong with you?" He took the purse.

"Don't!" she said, taking it back. "For God sakes, don't!"

He slapped her and grabbed for the bag with the other hand. It opened and everything inside fell out. Seeing the money fall to the ground, he slapped her again, and she began to cry. Her nose bled, and her bottom lip was split in two places, and it bled as well. The bum had awakened, and seeing the woman get slapped, he asked, "What is it there with you two peoples?"

Caesar dropped the purse, and Carol knelt down and began putting things back in it. He pulled her to her feet. "What the hell's wrong with you?"

"Leave me alone. Just leave me alone."

She knelt and he pulled her up again. "I said leave me alone." He slapped her. He could now see the distance between them growing, and seeing that distance and knowing he no longer had the power to close it, he slapped her once more. The blow sent her back a few feet. She said ohh several times, but everything sounded to him like no. She put her hand to her face and trembled.

"Hey there, fella," the bum said. "We gentlemens don't—"

"You want me to come over there and kick your ass?"

The bum was silent. He knew these young lions. He eased himself off the bench and rolled under it. Better to face the rats and the filth than face a young lion in his wrath.

"Carol, get the stuff and let's go home."

She watched him. Stepping up to her, he took out the Beretta and held it to her cheek. "Did you hear what I said?" There was no surprise in her face, and there was no fear. He realized that if he beat her with the pistol, that, too, would not surprise her. And had he shot her, in the face or through the heart, she would not have been surprised at that either. He pocketed the gun and stepped back.

She walked around him and was crying softly as she gathered up the money and her belongings. It had begun to rain and she shook each thing before putting it in the bag. When she was done, she stood and looked at him. Then, as if there was all the time in the world, she walked slowly out of the park, heading down Massachusetts. He watched her until she disappeared among the lights of Dupont Circle, and then he turned away.

There was something in the air, but he could not make out what it was. He walked out of the park. He kept looking behind him, expecting something or someone, but he was alone on the street and he saw nothing but the swirling of dead leaves. He continued looking behind him as he made his way up 17th Street. He took out the address book, but found he could not read the names or the numbers under the feeble street lights. He hurried, hoping for a telephone booth where the light would be brighter. He began to run, and as he ran, he kept trying to read the names and numbers, but the rain was now turning them to blurs. He did not know what was in the air. He only knew that tonight would not be a night to be without shelter.

GRAVITY

Theo had a choice between a drug that would save his sight and a drug that would keep him alive, so he chose not to go blind. He stopped the pills and started the injections—these required the implantation of an unpleasant and painful catheter just above his heart—and within a few days the clouds in his eyes started to clear up, he could see again. He remembered going into New York City to a show with his mother, when he was twelve and didn't want to admit he needed glasses. "Can you read that?" she'd shouted, pointing to a Broadway marquee, and when he'd squinted, making out only one or two letters, she'd taken off her own glasses—harlequins with tiny rhinestones in the corners—and shoved them onto his face. The world came into focus, and he gasped, astonished at the precision around the edges of things, the legibility, the hard, sharp, colorful landscape. Sylvia had to squint through *Fiddler on the Roof* that day, but for Theo, his face masked by his mother's huge glasses, everything was as bright and vivid as a comic book. Even though people stared at him, and muttered things, Sylvia didn't care, he could *see*.

Because he was dying again, Theo moved back to his mother's house in New Jersey. The DHPG injections she took in stride—she'd seen her own mother through *her* dying, after all. Four times a day, with the equanimity of a nurse, she cleaned out the plastic tube implanted in his chest, inserted a sterilized hypodermic and slowly dripped the bag of sight-giving liquid into his veins. They endured this procedure silently, Sylvia sitting on the side of the hospital bed she'd rented for the duration of Theo's stay—his life, he sometimes thought—watching reruns of *I Love Lucy* or the news, while he tried not to think about the hard piece of pipe stuck into him, even though it was a constant reminder of how wide and unswimmable the gulf was becoming between him and the ever-receding shoreline of the well. And Sylvia was intricately cheerful. Each day she urged him to go out with her somewhere—

650

to the library, or the little museum with the dinosaur replicas he'd been fond of as a child—and when his thinness and the cane drew stares, she'd maneuver him around the people who were staring, determined to shield him from whatever they might say or do. It had been the same that afternoon so many years ago, when she'd pushed him through a lobbyful of curious and laughing faces, determined that nothing should interfere with the spectacle of his seeing. What a pair they must have made, a boy in ugly glasses and a mother daring the world to say a word about it!

This warm, breezy afternoon in May they were shopping for revenge. "Your cousin Howard's engagement party is next month," Sylvia explained in the car. "A very nice girl from Livingston. I met her a few weeks ago, and really, she's a superior person."

"I'm glad," Theo said. "Congratulate Howie for me."

"Do you think you'll be up to going to the party?"

"I'm not sure. Would it be okay for me just to give him a gift?"

"You already have. A lovely silver tray, if I say so myself. The thank-you note's in the living room."

"Mom," Theo said, "why do you always have to—"

Sylvia honked her horn at a truck making an illegal left turn. "Better they should get something than no present at all, is what I say," she said. "But now, the problem is, *I* have to give Howie something, to be from me, and it better be good. It better be very, very good."

"Why?"

"Don't you remember that cheap little nothing Bibi gave you for your graduation? It was disgusting."

"I can't remember what she gave me."

"Of course you can't. It was a tacky pen-and-pencil set. Not even a real leather box. So naturally, it stands to reason that I have to get something truly spectacular for Howard's engagement. Something that will make Bibi blanch. Anyway, I think I've found just the thing, but I need your advice."

"Advice? Well, when my old roommate Nick got married, I gave him a garlic press. It cost five dollars and reflected exactly how much I felt, at that moment, our friendship was worth."

Sylvia laughed. "Clever. But my idea is much more brilliant, because it makes it possible for me to get back at Bibi *and* give Howard the nice gift he and his girl deserve." She smiled, clearly pleased with herself. "Ah, you live and learn."

"You live," Theo said.

Sylvia blinked. "Well, look, here we are." She pulled the car into a handicapped-parking place on Morris Avenue and got out to help Theo, but he was already hoisting himself up out of his seat, using the door handle for leverage. "I can manage myself," he said with some irritation. Sylvia stepped back.

"Clearly one advantage to all this for you," Theo said, balancing on his cane, "is that it's suddenly so much easier to get a parking place."

"Oh Theo, please," Sylvia said. "Look, here's where we're going."

She leaned him into a gift shop filled with porcelain statuettes of Snow White and all seven of the dwarves, music boxes which, when you opened them, played "The Shadow of Your Smile," complicated-smelling potpourris in purple wallpapered boxes, and stuffed snakes you were supposed to push up against drafty windows and doors.

"Mrs. Greenman," said an expansive, gray-haired man in a cream-colored cardigan sweater. "Look who's here, Archie, it's Mrs. Greenman."

Another man, this one thinner and balding, but dressed in an identical cardigan, peered out from the back of the shop. "Hello there!" he said, smiling. He looked at Theo, and his expression changed.

"Mr. Sherman, Mr. Baker. This is my son, Theo."

"Hello," Mr. Sherman and Mr. Baker said. They didn't offer to shake hands.

"Are you here for that item we discussed last week?" Mr. Sherman asked.

"Yes," Sylvia said. "I want advice from my son here." She walked over to a large ridged crystal bowl, a very fifties sort of bowl, stalwart and square-jawed. "What do you think? Beautiful, isn't it?"

"Mom, to tell the truth, I think it's kind of ugly."

"Four hundred and twenty-five dollars," Sylvia said admiringly. "You have to feel it."

Then she picked up the big bowl and tossed it to Theo, like a football.

The gentlemen in the cardigan sweaters gasped and did not exhale. When Theo caught it, it sank his hands. His cane rattled as it hit the floor.

"That's heavy," Sylvia said, observing with satisfaction how the bowl had weighted Theo's arms down. "And where crystal is concerned, heavy is impressive."

She took the bowl back from him and carried it to the counter. Mr. Sherman was mopping his brow. Theo looked at the floor, still surprised not to see shards of glass around his feet.

Since no one else seemed to be volunteering, he bent over and picked up the cane.

"Four hundred and fifty-nine, with tax," Mr. Sherman said, his voice still a bit shaky, and a look of relish came over Sylvia's face as she pulled out her checkbook to pay. Behind the counter, Theo could see Mr. Baker put his hand on his forehead and cast his eyes to the ceiling.

It seemed Sylvia had been looking a long time for something like this, something heavy enough to leave an impression, yet so fragile it could make you sorry.

They headed back out to the car.

"Where can we go now?" Sylvia asked, as she got in. "There must be someplace else to go."

"Home," Theo said. "It's almost time for my medicine."

"Really? Oh. All right." She pulled on her seat belt, inserted the car key in the ignition and sat there.

For just a moment, but perceptibly, her face broke. She squeezed her eyes shut so tight the blue shadow on the lids cracked.

Almost as quickly she was back to normal again, and they were driving. "It's getting hotter," Sylvia said. "Shall I put on the air?"

"Sure," Theo said. He was thinking about the bowl, or more specifically, about how surprising its weight had been, pulling his hands down. For a while now he'd been worried about his mother, worried about what damage his illness might secretly be doing to her that of course she would never admit. On the surface things seemed all right. She still broiled herself a skinned chicken breast for dinner every night, still swam a mile and a half a day, still kept used teabags wrapped in foil in the refrigerator. Yet she had also, at about three o'-clock one morning, woken him up to tell him she was going to the twenty-four-hour supermarket, and was there anything he wanted. Then there was the gift shop: She had literally pitched that bowl toward him, pitched it like a ball, and as that great gleam of flight and potential regret came sailing his direction, it had occurred to him that she was trusting his two feeble hands, out of the whole world, to keep it from shattering. What was she trying to test? Was it his newly regained vision? Was it the assurance that he was there, alive, that he hadn't yet slipped past all her caring, a little lost boy in rhinestone-studded glasses? There are certain things you've already done before you even think how to do them—a child pulled from in front of a car, for instance, or the bowl, which Theo was holding before he could even begin to calculate its brief trajectory. It had pulled his arms down, and from that apish posture he'd looked at his mother, who smiled broadly, as if, in the war between heaviness and shattering, he'd just helped her win some small but sustaining victory.

JUST DON'T
TOUCH ANYTHING

from Rule of the Bone

You'll probably think I'm making a lot of this up just to make me sound better than I really am or smarter or even luckier but I'm not. Besides, a lot of the things that've happened to me in my life so far which I'll get to pretty soon'll make me sound evil or just plain dumb or the tragic victim of circumstances. Which I know doesn't exactly prove I'm telling the truth but if I wanted to make myself look better than I am or smarter or the master of my own fate so to speak I could. The fact is the truth is more interesting than anything I could make up and that's why I'm telling it in the first place.

Anyhow my life got interesting you might say the summer I turned fourteen and was heavy into weed but I didn't have any money to buy it with so I started looking around the house all the time for things I could sell but there wasn't much. My mother who was still like my best friend then and my stepfather Ken had this decent house that my mother'd got in the divorce from my real father about ten years ago and about that she just says she got a mortgage not a house and about him she doesn't say much at all although my grandmother does. My mom and Ken both had these cheesy jobs and didn't own anything you could rob at least not without them noticing right away it was gone. Ken worked as a maintenance man out at the airbase which is like being a janitor only he said he was a building services technician and my mom was a bookkeeper at the clinic which is also a nothing job looking at a computer screen all day and punching numbers into it.

It actually started with me roaming around the house after school looking for something that wasn't boring, porn books or videos maybe, or condoms. Anything. Plus who knows, they might have their own little stash of weed. My mom and especially Ken were seriously into alcohol then but maybe they aren't as uptight as they seem, I'm thinking. Anything is possible. The house was small, four rooms and a bathroom, a mobile home on cinderblocks like a regular house only without a basement or garage and no attic and I'd lived there with my mom and my real dad from the time I was three until he left which happened when I was five and after that with my mom and Ken who legally adopted me and became my stepfather up until now, so I knew the place like I knew the inside of my mouth.

I thought I'd poked through every drawer and looked into every closet and searched under every bed and piece of furniture in the place. I'd even pulled out all these old Reader's Digest novels that Ken had found out at the base and brought home to read someday but mainly just to look good in the livingroom and flipped them open one by one looking for one of those secret compartments that you can cut into the pages with a razor and hide things. Nothing. Nothing new, I mean. Except for some old photograph albums of my grandmother's that my mom had that I found in a box on the top shelf of the linen closet. My mom'd showed them to me a few years ago and I'd forgotten probably because they were mostly pictures of people I didn't know like my mom's cousins and aunts and uncles but when I saw them again this time I remembered once looking for pictures of my father from when he was still alive and well and living here in Au Sable and finding only one of him. It was of him and my mom and his car and I'd studied it like it was a secret message because it was the only picture of him I'd ever seen. You'd've thought Grandma at least would've kept a few other snaps but no.

There was though this stack of letters tied with a ribbon in the same box as the albums that my father'd written to my mom for a few months after he left us. I'd never read them before and they turned out pretty interesting. The way it sounded my father was defending himself against my mom's accusations that he'd left us for this female named Rosalie who my mom said had been his girlfriend for years but he was claiming that Rosalie'd only been a normal friend of his at work and so on. He had good handwriting, neat and all the letters slanted the same way. Rosalie didn't matter to him anymore, he said. She never had. He said he wanted to come back. I almost felt sorry for him. Except I didn't believe him.

Plus I didn't need the letters my mom'd written to him in order to know her side of the story because even though I was only a little kid when this all happened I've got memories. If he was such a great guy and all how come he split on us and never sent any money or even tried to be in touch with his own son. My grandmother said just don't think about him anymore, he's probably living it up in some foreign country in the Caribbean or in jail for drugs. She goes, You don't *have* a father, Chappie. Forget him. She was tough, my grandmother, and I used to try and be like her when it came to thinking about my real father. I don't think she knew my mom'd saved my dad's letters. I bet my stepfather didn't know either.

Anyhow this one afternoon I came home from school early because I'd cut the last two periods which was just as well since I didn't have my homework anyhow and both teachers were the kind who boot you out of the class if you come in empty-handed, like it's a punishment that'll make you do better next time. I rummaged around in the fridge and made a bologna and cheese sandwich and drank one of my stepfather's beers and went into the livingroom and watched MTV for a while and played with the cat Willie who got spooked and took off when I accidentally flipped him on his head.

Then I started making my rounds. I really wanted some weed. It had been a couple of days since I'd been high and whenever I went that long I'd get jumpy and restless and kind of irritated at the world, feeling like everything and everyone was out to get me and I was no good and a failure at life which was basically true. A little smoke though and all that irritation and nervousness and my wicked low self-esteem immediately went away. They say weed makes you paranoid but for me it was the opposite.

I'd about given up on finding something in the house that I could rob—a personal possession that could be hocked like the TV or the VCR or the stereo would be instantly noticed when it was gone and all the rest of their stuff was boring household goods that you couldn't sell anyhow like electric blankets and a waffle iron and a clock radio. My mom didn't have any jewels that were worth anything except her wedding ring from my stepfather which she made a big deal out of but it looked like a Wal-Mart's ring to me and besides she always had it on. They didn't even have any decent CDs, all their music was seventies stuff, disco fever and easy listening and suchlike, on cassettes. The only kind of robbing I thought was possible was big time like stealing my stepfather's van while he was asleep for example and I wasn't ready for that.

I was taking one more look into their bedroom closet, down on my hands and knees and groping past my mother's shoes into the darkness when I came to what I'd thought last time was just some folded blankets. But when I felt into the blankets I realized there was something large and hard inside. I pulled out the whole thing and unwrapped what turned out to be these two black briefcases that I'd never seen before.

I sat cross-legged on the floor and put the first briefcase on my lap thinking it was probably locked until it snapped open which surprised me but then the real surprise came when I lifted the lid and saw a .22 automatic rifle broken down into three parts just lying there with a rod and cleaning kit and a box of shells. It wasn't hard to fit the parts together, it even had a scope like an assassin's rifle and pretty soon I was into a Lee Harvey Oswald trip standing by the bedroom window and brushing the curtain away with the tip of the barrel and aiming through the scope at stuff on the street going Pow! Pow!

I blasted a couple of dogs and blew away the mailman and nailed the drivers of cars going by for a while.

Then I remembered the other briefcase and went back to the closet and sat down and opened it. Inside are all these Baggies, thirty or forty of them filled with coins, mostly old quarters and Indian head nickels and even some weird-looking pennies with dates from way back in the early 1900s. Excellent discovery. I figure the rifle must belong to Ken and he stashes it in this briefcase on account of my mom always saying she's scared of guns and the coins too, I'm thinking, because if they were my mom's I would've known it since she pretty much told me everything in those days. Besides she wasn't the hobby type. Ken though was definitely the kind of guy who would have a cool gun and never show it to me or even tell me about it, plus he collected things like exotic beer cans and souvenir coffee mugs from the various theme parks they'd gone to and put them out on shelves where anyone could see although he was always telling me not to touch them because I never left things the way they were which is basically true.

I took the rifle apart and put it back in the briefcase and then I took a couple of coins from each of about six Baggies so he wouldn't know any were missing if he happened to check. Afterwards I wrapped the briefcases back in the blanket and put the bundle behind my mother's shoes in the closet where it had come from.

I had maybe twenty coins, small change, nothing bigger than a quarter and I took them to the pawnshop on Water Street near the old tannery where I knew some kids had hocked stuff they'd stolen from their parents, jewels and watches and so on. The old guy in there didn't say a word or even look at me when I spread the coins out on his counter and asked him how much he'd give me. He was this big fat guy with thick glasses and huge sweat circles under his arms and he scooped up the coins and took them in back where he had an office and a few minutes later he comes out and says eighty dollars which really blew my mind.

Sounds fine to me, man, I told him and he paid me in twenties and I went out already high just thinking about all the skunk I could get for eighty bucks.

I had this very good friend Russ whose mom'd kicked him out in the spring and he and a couple of older guys who were like headbangers and bikers were living in an apartment over the Video Den downtown. Russ was sixteen and had quit school and had this part-time job at the Video Den so that's where I went when I wanted to hang out and get high or just chill until I had to go home. Russ was okay but most people meaning my parents thought he was a loser because he was into heavy metal and all that and did a lot of drugs. At the time he wanted me to get a tattoo because he had one and thought they were cool which they were but I knew what my mom'd say if I came home with a tattoo. I was already driving her and Ken crazy with my lousy grades in school and having to go to summer school now and getting a mohawk haircut and nose rings and being a general pain in the royal ass around the house as Ken liked to say and not helping out enough and I could tell Ken especially was really getting sick of me. I didn't need any more trouble than I already had.

It's amazing how fast good weed goes when you've got the money to buy it with especially when you've got some friends to smoke it with like I had Russ and these older dudes who lived with him. They were what you'd call bikers not Hell's Angels and some of them didn't even have bikes but were the same violent type so they were hard to refuse when they'd come in and see me and Russ rolling joints on the kitchen table. In only a few days my stash was gone and I had to go back to the briefcase in the closet for some more coins. I'd always put the rifle together while I was there and stand at the window hitting imaginary targets coming along the sidewalk or just sit on the floor going Blam! into the darkness of the closet.

It was getting toward the end of summer school and I knew I was going to flunk at least two out of the three courses that I needed to pass just to get out of eighth grade which was going to make my mom crazy and deeply piss off my stepdad who already had his own secret reasons for disliking me but I don't want to talk about that right now, so I was smoking a lot of skunk, more even than usual and was cutting most of my classes and hanging out at Russ's place. Russ and the biker guys were my only friends then really. My stepfather'd developed this new habit of referring to me as *him* and never talking directly to me or even looking at me except when he thought I didn't notice or when he was drunk. He'd like say to my mother, Ask *him* where he's going tonight. Tell *him* to take out the goddam trash. Ask *him* how come he goes around with torn clothes and wearing earrings in his ears like a goddam girl and in his nose for chrissake, he'd say with me watching TV right there in front of him.

As far as he was concerned I was her son now not his even though he'd adopted me when I was eight after they got married and he moved in with us. When I was a real little kid he was an okay stepfather with some significant exceptions you might say, but when I got to be a teenager he sort of pulled out of the family unit and did a lot more heavy drinking which now my mom was into blaming me for. I didn't care if he didn't like me anymore, fine by me but I didn't want her making it into all my fault. Some of it was his.

I went back to the coin collection in the closet a lot that summer always taking only a few coins at a time from six or seven different Baggies and I was starting to figure out which ones were worth the most like the dimes with the lady on it and the Indian head nickels and I'd just take those and mostly not bother with the others. Sometimes the guy at the pawnshop would give me fifty bucks, sometimes I'd get over a hundred. One day he says to me, Where'd you get these coins, kid? and I go into this sad story about my grandmother dying and leaving them to me and I could only sell a few of them at a time because it was all I had of hers and didn't want to let the whole collection go.

I don't know if he believed me but he never asked me about them again and just kept shelling out the bucks which I kept turning into weed. I was a good customer by now and had moved up from buying it off of the couple of older kids who were dealing at school and out at the mall to this Spanish guy named Hector in Plattsburgh who hung around Chi-Boom's which was a kind of club down on Water Street. I bought so much skunk Hector thought I was dealing and a couple of times when I had extra I actually did sell a few bags to friends of Russ's roommates but basically it was me and Russ doing most of it, and the bikers.

Then one night I came home around midnight from Russ's place. I still rode around then on one of those knobby-tired dirt bikes which my mother'd given me a couple of Christmases ago. It was like my trademark, that bike, the way some kids do with their skateboards and I had this habit of taking it into the house at night and parking it in the front hall. Only this one time when I come up the steps carrying my bike the door like opens in front of me and it's my stepfather standing there with my mom right behind him with her face all red from crying. I can see he's deeply pissed and maybe drunk and I naturally think he's been whaling on her which he's been known to do so I shove my bike right into his stomach and the handlebars hit him in the face and knock off his glasses and suddenly everybody is screaming, me included. My stepfather yanks the bike out of my hands and throws it back down the steps and this makes me go crazy and I start calling him all the worst names I can think of like faggot and fucking asshole while he's grabbing me by my arms and pulling me inside the house and telling me to shut the fuck up because of the neighbors and my mother is yelling at me like I'm the one who was whaling on her and tossing kids' bikes around and not her own husband for chrissake.

Finally the door's closed and we're all panting and staring at each other and he says, Get into the livingroom, Chappie, and sit down. We have some news for you, mister, he says, and that's when I remember the coins.

On the coffeetable is the briefcase and it's closed and for a second I think it's the one with the rifle but no, when my stepfather flips it open I see right away it's the one with the coins and I realize for the first time that there aren't very many of them left. It was kind of a shock. None of the plastic bags had more than a few coins inside and some of the bags were completely empty although I didn't remember emptying any and leaving them in the briefcase but it definitely looked like that's what I had done. Dumb. My mom sat down on the couch and looked at the open briefcase like it was a coffin with a body in it and Ken said for me to sit in the chair which I did while he stood between me and the table and crossed his arms like some kind of cop. He had his glasses back on and was calmed down a little but was still steamed I knew from me hitting him with the bike.

I felt like a pathetic jerk sitting there looking at those few remaining coins. I remembered how I'd felt the first time I opened the briefcase and saw inside an endless supply of weed like it was the goose that laid the golden egg. My mom started crying then like she does when I really fuck up and I made a move to get up and comfort her by apologizing like I usually do but Ken told me just to sit there and shut the fuck up even though I hadn't said anything yet.

Chappie, this is the worst thing you've ever done! my mom said and she started sobbing harder. Willie the cat tried to get on her lap but she pushed him away hard and he got down and left the room.

Ken said he didn't give a shit anymore what I robbed from other people or how much dope I bought, that was my problem not his and he'd given up on me anyhow but when I stole from my own mother that's where he drew the line especially when I stole something irreplaceable like those coins. He said I was goddamned lucky I hadn't taken his rifle because he definitely would have called in the cops. Let them handle it. He was sick of feeding and housing and clothing a freeloader and a thief and a drug addict and as far as he was concerned if it was up to him he'd boot me out of the house this very minute except my mother wouldn't let him.

I said to him, I thought they were *your* coins, and he reached out and slapped me real hard on the side of my head.

They were your *mother's!* he said real sarcastic and she went sort of crazy then, screaming about how the coins had been *her* mother's and she'd given them to her years ago along with other precious and sentimental items and someday the coins were going to be mine and really valuable but now I'd gone and stolen them and sold them and spent all the money on drugs so she'd never be able to pass them on to me. Never.

They were only coins, I said which was stupid but I didn't know what else to say and I was feeling really dumb anyhow and lowdown so why not say something that sounded like I felt. They weren't worth much anyhow, I said and my stepfather whacked me on the head again right on the ear this time tearing out an earring which really hurt. But it was like the sight of my blood got to him because then he belted me a couple more times, harder each time until my mother finally hollered for him to stop.

He did and when he went out into the kitchen and got a beer I stood up and still shaking I said real loud, I'm leaving this place!

Neither of them tried to stop me or even said where do you think you're going so I walked out the door and slammed it as hard as I could and picked up my bike where he'd thrown it and went straight over to Russ's who let me sleep on a ratty old couch that was in the livingroom.

The next morning as soon as I knew my mom and Ken would be at work I went over to the house for my clothes and stuff. I took a few towels and a blanket from the linen closet and some shampoo from the bathroom and shoved everything into two pillowcases. I was just about to leave when I remembered the few remaining coins and said to myself why not try and find them and take what's left since they're supposed to be mine someday anyhow. I was feeling hard and cold like a criminal mentality was creeping into me, and it was funny to me that I'd gone and made up the story about my grandmother to the pawnshop guy and then it'd turned out to be almost true.

I put my stuff down by the front door and took a beer from the fridge and popped it and walked back to my mom's and Ken's bedroom. I knew that as the saying goes a friend in weed is a friend indeed and if I was going to crash at Russ's I'd better have some smoke to pass around until I got a job or something.

It didn't seem likely they'd put the coins back in the closet but it was worth a look and sure enough when I reached into the darkness there were the two briefcases wrapped in the blanket the same as the day I found them. Ken and my mom must've thought that after last night I'd be too scared to go back there again but it was like I'd gone too far by now to be scared of anything anymore. The first briefcase had what was left of the coins, maybe fifty or sixty of them in a half-dozen bags which I took. I opened the second case and put the rifle together as usual and loaded it this time just to see how you did it since it was probably my last chance.

I was standing by the window aiming through the scope at a little kid on a tricycle across the street when I heard the bedroom door behind me creak like someone was coming in from the hallway. When I spun around it was Willie the cat jumping onto my mother's bed. I must've been freaked because I aimed the rifle at him and pulled the trigger but nothing happened. Old Willie came down the bed and sniffed the end of the barrel and looked like he was ready to lick it. I pulled the trigger again but still nothing happened and then I realized that the safety was on and the trigger was locked.

I started to look for the safety but just as I found it Willie jumped down off the bed and disappeared into the closet which was lucky for him because as soon as he was out of sight I suddenly saw myself standing there with the gun in my hand and I could see what I'd been trying to do to him and I started to cry then, from my stomach up to my chest and into my head until I was standing there sobbing with my stepfather's stupid rifle in my hand and the last remaining bags of my grandmother's coins on the floor and the black briefcases open beside them. Nothing seemed to matter anymore because everything I touched turned bad so I just started firing. Blam, blam, blam! Mostly I shot at my mom's and stepfather's bed until the rifle was empty.

Then I came out of it like I'd been in a hypnotic trance. I stopped crying and put the rifle on the bed and got down on my hands and knees and tried to get Willie to come out of the closet but he was too scared. I was talking to him like he was my mom saying, I'm sorry I'm sorry I'm sorry, real fast and high-pitched like when I was a little kid and similar stuff happened.

But no way that cat was going to trust me now. Way back there in the dark end of the closet scared out of his mind, he looked like I felt so I figured the best thing I could do was leave him alone. I picked up the coins and walked down the hall.

I hauled my stuff over to Russ's place and stayed there until the last of the coins and the weed ran out and Russ said the older guys didn't want me hanging around anymore. Hector let me have a couple of bags on credit so I could start dealing on my own and then the older guys said I could have the couch in the livingroom at least for the rest of the summer if I kept them in weed and since I was a dealer now that's what I did.

Sometimes that first summer and during the fall too I thought about going back and trying to make peace with my mom and my stepfather even and offering to pay her back for the coins as soon as I got a job but I knew I could never pay her back because it wasn't the money. Those old coins of my grandmother's, they were like my inheritance. Besides my mom was scared of Ken and wanted to keep him happy and since for certain reasons that only I knew about he was relieved that I was finally out of sight and out of mind so to speak, there was no way now she'd let me come home again. So I didn't even try.

Gish Jen

IN THE AMERICAN SOCIETY

1. HIS OWN SOCIETY

When my father took over the pancake house, it was to send my little sister Mona and me to college. We were only in junior high at the time, but my father believed in getting a jump on things. "Those Americans always saying it," he told us. "Smart guys thinking in advance." My mother elaborated, explaining that businesses took bringing up, like children. They could take years to get going, she said, years.

In this case, though, we got rich right away. At two months we were breaking even, and at four, those same hotcakes that could barely withstand the weight of butter and syrup were supporting our family with ease. My mother bought a station wagon with air conditioning, my father an oversized, red vinyl recliner for the back room; and as time went on and the business continued to thrive, my father started to talk about his grandfather and the village he had reigned over in China—things my father had never talked about when he worked for other people. He told us about the bags of rice his family would give out to the poor at New Year's, and about the people who came to beg, on their hands and knees, for his grandfather to intercede for the more wayward of their relatives. "Like that Godfather in the movie," he would tell us as, his feet up, he distributed paychecks. Sometimes an employee would get two green envelopes instead of one, which meant that Jimmy needed a tooth pulled, say, or that Tiffany's husband was in the clinker again.

"It's nothing, nothing," he would insist, sinking back into his chair. "Who else is going to take care of you people?"

My mother would mostly just sigh about it. "Your father thinks this is China," she would say, and then she would go back to her mending. Once in a while, though, when my father had given away a particularly large sum, she would exclaim, outraged, "But this here is the U-S-of-A!"—this apparently

663

having been what she used to tell immigrant stock boys when they came in late.

She didn't work at the supermarket anymore; but she had made it to the rank of manager before she left, and this had given her not only new words and phrases, but new ideas about herself, and about America, and about what was what in general. She had opinions, now, on how downtown should be zoned; she could pump her own gas and check her own oil; and for all she used to chide Mona and me for being "copycats," she herself was now interested in espadrilles, and wallpaper, and most recently, the town country club.

"So join already," said Mona, flicking a fly off her knee.

My mother enumerated the problems as she sliced up a quarter round of watermelon: there was the cost. There was the waiting list. There was the fact that no one in our family played either tennis or golf.

"So what?" said Mona.

"It would be waste," said my mother.

"Me and Callie can swim in the pool."

"Plus you need that recommendation letter from a member."

"Come *on,*" said Mona. "Annie's mom'd write you a letter in a *sec.*"

My mother's knife glinted in the early summer sun. I spread some more newspaper on the picnic table.

"Plus you have to eat there twice a month. You know what that means." My mother cut another, enormous slice of fruit.

"No, I *don't* know what that means," said Mona.

"It means Dad would have to wear a jacket, dummy," I said.

"Oh! Oh! Oh!" said Mona, clasping her hand to her breast. "Oh! Oh! Oh! Oh! Oh!"

We all laughed: my father had no use for nice clothes, and would wear only ten-year-old shirts, with grease-spotted pants, to show how little he cared what anyone thought.

"Your father doesn't believe in joining the American society," said my mother. "He wants to have his own society."

"So go to dinner without him." Mona shot her seeds out in long arcs over the lawn. "Who cares what he thinks?"

But of course we all did care, and knew my mother could not simply up and do as she pleased. For in my father's mind, a family owed its head a degree of loyalty that left no room for dissent. To embrace what he embraced was to love; and to embrace something else was to betray him.

He demanded a similar sort of loyalty of his workers, whom he treated more like servants than employees. Not in the beginning, of course. In the beginning all he wanted was for them to keep on doing what they used to do, and to that end he concentrated mostly on leaving them alone. As the months passed, though, he expected more and more of them, with the result that for all his largesse, he began to have trouble keeping help. The cooks and busboys complained that he asked them to fix radiators and trim hedges, not only at the restaurant, but at our house; the waitresses that he sent them on errands and made them chauffeur him around. Our head waitress, Gertrude, claimed that he once even asked her to scratch his back.

"It's not just the blacks don't believe in slavery," she said when she quit.

My father never quite registered her complaint, though, nor those of the others who left. Even after Eleanor quit, then Tiffany, then Gerald, and Jimmy, and even his best cook, Eureka Andy, for whom he had bought new glasses, he remained mostly convinced that the fault lay with them.

"All they understand is that assembly line," he lamented. "Robots, they are. They want to be robots."

There *were* occasions when the clear running truth seemed to eddy, when he would pinch the vinyl of his chair up into little peaks and wonder if he were doing things right. But with time he would always smooth the peaks back down; and when business started to slide in the spring, he kept on like a horse in his ways.

By the summer our dishboy was overwhelmed with scraping. It was no longer just the hashbrowns that people were leaving for trash, and the service was as bad as the food. The waitresses served up French pancakes instead of German, apple juice instead of orange, spilt things on laps, on coats. On the Fourth of July some greenhorn sent an entire side of fries slaloming down a lady's *massif centrale*. Meanwhile in the back room, my father labored through articles on the economy.

"What is housing starts?" he puzzled. "What is GNP?"

Mona and I did what we could, filling in as busgirls and bookkeepers and, one afternoon, stuffing the comments box that hung by the cashier's desk. That was Mona's idea. We rustled up a variety of pens and pencils, checked boxes for an hour, smeared the cards up with coffee and grease, and waited. It took a few days for my father to notice that the box was full, and he didn't say anything about it for a few days more. Finally, though, he started to complain of fatigue; and then he began to complain that the staff was not what it could be. We encouraged him in this—pointing out, for instance, how many dishes got chipped—but in the end all that happened was that, for the first time since we took over the restaurant, my father got it into his head to fire someone. Skip, a skinny busboy who was saving up for a sports car, said nothing as my father mumbled on about the price of dishes. My father's hands shook as he wrote out the severance check; and he spent the rest of the day napping in his chair once it was over.

As it was going on midsummer, Skip wasn't easy to replace. We hung a sign in the window and advertised in the paper, but no one called the first week, and the person who called the second didn't show up for his interview. The third week, my father phoned Skip to see if he would come back, but a friend of his had already sold him a Corvette for cheap.

Finally a Chinese guy named Booker turned up. He couldn't have been more than thirty, and was wearing a lighthearted seersucker suit, but he looked as though life had him pinned: his eyes were bloodshot and his chest sunken, and the muscles of his neck seemed to strain with the effort of holding his head up. In a single dry breath he told us that he had never bussed tables but was willing to learn, and that he was on the lam from the deportation authorities.

"I do not want to lie to you," he kept saying. He had come to the United States on a student visa, had run out of money, and was now in a bind. He was loath to go back to Taiwan, as it happened—he looked up at this point, to be sure my father wasn't pro-KMT—but all he had was a phony social security card and a willingness to absorb all blame, should anything untoward come to pass.

"I do not think, anyway, that it is against law to hire me, only to be me," he said, smiling faintly.

Anyone else would have examined him on this, but my father conceived of laws as speed bumps rather than curbs. He wiped the counter with his sleeve, and told Booker to report the next morning.

"I will be good worker," said Booker.

"Good," said my father.

"Anything you want me to do, I will do."

My father nodded.

Booker seemed to sink into himself for a moment. "Thank you," he said finally. "I am appreciate your help. I am very, very appreciate for everything." He reached out to shake my father's hand.

My father looked at him. "Did you eat today?" he asked in Mandarin.

Booker pulled at the hem of his jacket.

"Sit down," said my father. "Please, have a seat."

My father didn't tell my mother about Booker, and my mother didn't tell my father about the country club. She would never have applied, except that Mona, while over at Annie's, had let it drop that our mother wanted to join. Mrs. Lardner came by the very next day.

"Why, I'd be honored and delighted to write you people a letter," she said. Her skirt billowed around her.

"Thank you so much," said my mother. "But it's too much trouble for you, and also my husband is . . ."

"Oh, it's no trouble at all, no trouble at all. I tell you." She leaned forward so that her chest freckles showed. "I know just how it is. It's a secret of course, but you know, my natural father was Jewish. Can you see it? Just look at my skin."

"My husband," said my mother.

"I'd be honored and delighted," said Mrs. Lardner with a little wave of her hands. "Just honored and delighted."

Mona was triumphant. "See, Mom," she said, waltzing around the kitchen when Mrs. Lardner left. "What did I tell you? 'I'm just honored and delighted, just honored and delighted.'" She waved her hands in the air.

"You know, the Chinese have a saying," said my mother. "To do nothing is better than to overdo. You mean well, but you tell me now what will happen."

"I'll talk Dad into it," said Mona, still waltzing. "Or I bet Callie can. He'll do anything Callie says."

"I can try, anyway," I said.

"Did you hear what I said?" said my mother. Mona bumped into the broom closet door. "You're not going to talk anything; you've already made enough trouble." She started on the dishes with a clatter.

Mona poked diffidently at a mop.

I sponged off the counter. "Anyway," I ventured. "I bet our name'll never even come up."

"That's if we're lucky," said my mother.

"There's all these people waiting," I said.

"Good," she said. She started on a pot.

I looked over at Mona, who was still cowering in the broom closet. "In fact, there's some black family's been waiting so long, they're going to sue," I said.

My mother turned off the water. "Where'd you hear that?"

"Patty told me."

She turned the water back on, started to wash a dish, then put it back down and shut the faucet.

"I'm sorry," said Mona.

"Forget it," said my mother. "Just forget it."

Booker turned out to be a model worker, whose boundless gratitude translated into a willingness to do anything. As he also learned quickly, he soon knew not only how to bus, but how to cook, and how to wait table, and how to keep the books. He fixed the walk-in door so that it stayed shut, reupholstered the torn seats in the dining room, and devised a system for tracking inventory. The only stone in the rice was that he tended to be sickly; but, reliable even in illness, he would always send a friend to take his place. In this way we got to know Ronald, Lynn, Dirk, and Cedric, all of whom, like Booker, had problems with their legal status and were anxious to please. They weren't all as capable as Booker, though, with the exception of Cedric, whom my father often hired even when Booker was well. A round wag of a man who called Mona and me *shou hou*—skinny monkeys—he was a professed nonsmoker who was nevertheless always begging drags off of other people's cigarettes. This last habit drove our head cook, Fernando, crazy, especially since, when refused a hit, Cedric would occasionally snitch one. Winking impishly at Mona and me, he would steal up to an ashtray, take a quick puff, and then break out laughing so that the smoke came rolling out of his mouth in a great incriminatory cloud. Fernando accused him of stealing fresh cigarettes too, even whole packs.

"Why else do you think he's weaseling around in the back of the store all the time," he said. His face was blotchy with anger. "The man is a frigging thief."

Other members of the staff supported him in this contention and joined in on an "Operation Identification," which involved numbering and initialing their cigarettes—even though what they seemed to fear for wasn't so much their cigarettes as their jobs. Then one of the cooks quit; and rather than promote someone, my father hired Cedric for the position. Rumors flew that he was taking only half the normal salary, that Alex had been pressured to resign, and that my father was looking for a position with which to placate Booker, who had been bypassed because of his health.

The result was that Fernando categorically refused to work with Cedric. "The only way I'll cook with that piece of slime," he said, shaking his huge tattooed fist, "is if it's his ass frying on the grill."

My father cajoled and cajoled, to no avail, and in the end was simply forced to put them on different schedules.

The next week Fernando got caught stealing a carton of minute steaks. My father would not tell even Mona and me how he knew to be standing by the back door when Fernando was on his way out, but everyone suspected Booker. Everyone but Fernando, that is, who was sure Cedric had been the tip-off. My father held a staff meeting in which he tried to reassure everyone that Alex had left on his own, and that he had no intention of firing anyone. But though he was careful not to mention Fernando, everyone was so amazed that he was being allowed to stay that Fernando was incensed nonetheless.

"Don't you all be putting your bug eyes on me," he said. *"He's* the frigging crook." He grabbed Cedric by the collar.

Cedric raised an eyebrow. "Cook, you mean," he said.

At this Fernando punched Cedric in the mouth; and the words he had just uttered notwithstanding, my father fired him on the spot.

With everything that was happening, Mona and I were ready to be getting out of the restaurant. It was almost time: the days were still stuffy with summer, but our window shade had started flapping in the evening as if gearing up to go out. That year the breezes were full of salt, as they sometimes were when they came in from the East, and they blew anchors and docks through my mind like so many tumbleweeds, filling my dreams with wherries and lobsters and grainy-faced men who squinted, day in and day out, at the sky.

It was time for a change, you could feel it; and yet the pancake house was the same as ever. The day before school started my father came home with bad news.

"Fernando called police," he said, wiping his hand on his pant leg.

My mother naturally wanted to know what police; and so with much coughing and hawing, the long story began, the latest installment of which had the police calling immigration, and immigration sending an investigator. My mother sat stiff as whalebone as my father described how the man summarily refused lunch on the house and how my father had admitted, under pressure, that he knew there were "things" about his workers.

"So now what happens?"

My father didn't know. "Booker and Cedric went with him to the jail," he said. "But me, here I am." He laughed uncomfortably.

The next day my father posted bail for "his boys" and waited apprehensively for something to happen. The day after that he waited again, and the day after that he called our neighbor's law student son, who suggested my father call the immigration department under an alias. My father took his advice; and it was thus that he discovered that Booker was right: it was illegal for aliens to work, but it wasn't to hire them.

In the happy interval that ensued, my father apologized to my mother, who in turn confessed about the country club, for which my father had no choice but to forgive her. Then he turned his attention back to "his boys."

My mother didn't see that there was anything to do.

"I like to talking to the judge," said my father.

"This is not China," said my mother.

"I'm only talking to him. I'm not give him money unless he wants it."

"You're going to land up in jail."

"So what else I should do?" My father threw up his hands. "Those are my boys."

"Your boys!" exploded my mother. "What about your family? What about your wife?"

My father took a long sip of tea. "You know," he said finally. "In the war my father sent our cook to the soldiers to use. He always said it—the province comes before the town, the town comes before the family."

"A restaurant is not a town," said my mother.

My father sipped at his tea again. "You know, when I first come to the United States, I also had to hide-and-seek with those deportation guys. If people did not helping me, I'm not here today."

My mother scrutinized her hem.

After a minute I volunteered that before seeing a judge, he might try a lawyer.

He turned. "Since when did you become so afraid like your mother?"

I started to say that it wasn't a matter of fear, but he cut me off.

"What I need today," he said, "is a son."

My father and I spent the better part of the next day standing in lines at the immigration office. He did not get to speak to a judge, but with much persistence he managed to speak to a judge's clerk, who tried to persuade him that it was not her place to extend him advice. My father, though, shamelessly plied her with compliments and offers of free pancakes until she finally conceded that she personally doubted anything would happen to either Cedric or Booker.

"Especially if they're 'needed workers,' " she said, rubbing at the red marks her glasses left on her nose. She yawned. "Have you thought about sponsoring them to become permanent residents?"

Could he do that? My father was overjoyed. And what if he saw to it right away? Would she perhaps put in a good word with the judge?

She yawned again, her nostrils flaring. "Don't worry," she said. "They'll get a fair hearing."

My father returned jubilant. Booker and Cedric hailed him as their savior, their Buddha incarnate. He was like a father to them, they said; and laughing and clapping, they made him tell the story over and over, sorting over the details like jewels. And how old was the assistant judge? And what did she say?

That evening my father tipped the paperboy a dollar and bought a pot of mums for my mother, who suffered them to be placed on the dining room table. The next night he took us all out to dinner. Then on Saturday, Mona found a letter on my father's chair at the restaurant.

Dear Mr. Chang,

You are the grat boss. But, we do not like to trial, so will running away now. Plese to excus us. People saying the law in America is fears like dragon. Here is only $140.

We hope some day we can pay back the rest bale. You will getting interest, as you diserving, so grat a boss you are. Thank you for every thing. In next life you will be burn in rich family, with no more pancaks.

Yours truley,
Booker + Cedric

In the weeks that followed my father went to the pancake house for crises, but otherwise hung around our house, fiddling idly with the sump pump and boiler in an effort, he said, to get ready for winter. It was as though he had gone into retirement, except that instead of moving South, he had moved to the basement. He even took to showering my mother with little attentions, and to calling her "old girl," and when we finally heard that the club had entertained all the applications it could for the year, he was so sympathetic that he seemed more disappointed than my mother.

2 . IN THE AMERICAN SOCIETY

Mrs. Lardner tempered the bad news with an invitation to a bon voyage "bash" she was throwing for a friend of hers who was going to Greece for six months.

"Do come," she urged. "You'll meet everyone, and then, you know, if things open up in the spring . . ." She waved her hands.

My mother wondered if it would be appropriate to show up at a party for someone they didn't know, but "the honest truth" was that this was an annual affair. "If it's not Greece, it's Antibes," sighed Mrs. Lardner. "We really just do it because his wife left him and his daughter doesn't speak to him, and poor Jeremy just feels so *unloved.*"

She also invited Mona and me to the going on, as *"demi-*guests" to keep Annie out of the champagne. I wasn't too keen on the idea, but before I could say anything, she had already thanked us for so generously agreeing to honor her with our presence.

"A pair of little princesses, you are!" she told us. "A pair of princesses!"

The party was that Sunday. On Saturday, my mother took my father out shopping for a suit. As it was the end of September, she insisted that he buy a worsted rather than a seersucker, even though it was only ten, rather than fifty percent off. My father protested that it was as hot out as ever, which was true— a thick Indian summer had cozied murderously up to us—but to no avail. Summer clothes, said my mother, were not properly worn after Labor Day.

The suit was unfortunately as extravagant in length as it was in price, which posed an additional quandary, since the tailor wouldn't be in until Monday. The salesgirl, though, found a way of tacking it up temporarily.

"Maybe this suit not fit me," fretted my father.

"Just don't take your jacket off," said the salesgirl.

He gave her a tip before they left, but when he got home refused to remove the price tag.

"I like to asking the tailor about the size," he insisted.

"You mean you're going to *wear* it and then return it?" Mona rolled her eyes.

"I didn't say I'm return it," said my father stiffly. "I like to asking the tailor, that's all."

The party started off swimmingly, except that most people were wearing bermudas or wrap skirts. Still, my parents carried on, sharing with great feeling the complaints about the heat. Of course my father tried to eat a cracker full of shallots and burnt himself in an attempt to help Mr. Lardner turn the coals of the barbeque; but on the whole he seemed to be doing all right. Not nearly so well as my mother, though, who had accepted an entire cupful of Mrs. Lardner's magic punch, and seemed indeed to be under some spell. As Mona and Annie skirmished over whether some boy in their class inhaled when he smoked, I watched my mother take off her shoes, laughing and laughing as a man with a beard regaled her with navy stories by the pool. Apparently he had been stationed in the Orient and remembered a few words of Chinese, which made my mother laugh still more. My father excused himself to go to the men's room then drifted back and weighed anchor at the hors d'oeuvres table, while my mother sailed on to a group of women, who tinkled at length over the clarity of her complexion. I dug out a book I had brought.

Just when I'd cracked the spine, though, Mrs. Lardner came by to bewail her shortage of servers. Her caterers were criminals, I agreed; and the next thing I knew I was handing out bits of marine life, making the rounds as amicably as I could.

"Here you go, Dad," I said when I got to the hors d'oeuvres table.

"Everything is fine," he said.

I hesitated to leave him alone; but then the man with the beard zeroed in on him, and though he talked of nothing but my mother, I thought it would be okay to get back to work. Just that moment, though, Jeremy Brothers lurched our way, an empty, albeit corked, wine bottle in hand. He was a slim, well-proportioned man, with a Roman nose and small eyes and a nice manly jaw that he allowed to hang agape.

"Hello," he said drunkenly. "Pleased to meet you."

"Pleased to meeting you," said my father.

"Right," said Jeremy. "Right. Listen. I have this bottle here, this most recalcitrant bottle. You see that it refuses to do my bidding. I bid it open sesame, please, and it does nothing." He pulled the cork out with his teeth, then turned the bottle upside down.

My father nodded.

"Would you have a word with it, please?" said Jeremy. The man with the beard excused himself. "Would you please have a goddamned word with it?"

My father laughed uncomfortably.

"Ah!" Jeremy bowed a little. "Excuse me, excuse me, excuse me. You are not my man, not my man at all." He bowed again and started to leave, but then circled back. "Viticulture is not your forte, yes I can see that, see that plainly. But may I trouble you on another matter? Forget the damned bottle." He threw it into the pool, and winked at the people he splashed. "I have another matter. Do you speak Chinese?"

My father said he did not, but Jeremy pulled out a handkerchief with some characters on it anyway, saying that his daughter had sent it from Hong Kong and that he thought the characters might be some secret message.

"Long life," said my father.

"But you haven't looked at it yet."

"I know what it says without looking." My father winked at me.

"You do?"

"Yes, I do."

"You're making fun of me, aren't you?"

"No, no, no," said my father, winking again.

"Who are you anyway?" said Jeremy.

His smile fading, my father shrugged.

"Who are you?"

My father shrugged again.

Jeremy began to roar. "This is my party, *my party*, and I've never seen you before in my life." My father backed up as Jeremy came toward him. *"Who are you? WHO ARE YOU?"*

Just as my father was going to step back into the pool, Mrs. Lardner came running up. Jeremy informed her that there was a man crashing his party.

"Nonsense," said Mrs. Lardner. "This is Ralph Chang, who I invited extra especially so he could meet you." She straightened the collar of Jeremy's peach-colored polo shirt for him.

"Yes, well we've had a chance to chat," said Jeremy.

She whispered in his ear; he mumbled something; she whispered something more.

"I do apologize," he said finally.

My father didn't say anything.

"I do." Jeremy seemed genuinely contrite. "Doubtless you've seen drunks before, haven't you? You must have them in China."

"Okay," said my father.

As Mrs. Lardner glided off, Jeremy clapped his arm over my father's shoulders. "You know, I really am quite sorry, quite sorry."

My father nodded.

"What can I do, how can I make it up to you?"

"No thank you."

"No, tell me, tell me," wheedled Jeremy. "Tickets to casino night?" My father shook his head. "You don't gamble. Dinner at Bartholomew's?" My father shook his head again. "You don't eat." Jeremy scratched his chin. "You know, my wife was like you. Old Annabelle could never let me make things up—never, never, never, never, never."

My father wriggled out from under his arm.

"How about sport clothes? You are rather overdressed, you know, excuse me for saying so. But here." He took off his polo shirt and folded it up. "You can have this with my most profound apologies." He ruffled his chest hairs with his free hand.

"No thank you," said my father.

"No, take it, take it. Accept my apologies." He thrust the shirt into my father's arms. "I'm so very sorry, so very sorry. Please, try it on."

Helplessly holding the shirt, my father searched the crowd for my mother.

"Here, I'll help you off with your coat."

My father froze.

Jeremy reached over and took his jacket off. "Milton's one hundred twenty-five dollars reduced to one hundred twelve-fifty," he read. "What a bargain, what a bargain!"

"Please give it back," pleaded my father. "Please."

"Now for your shirt," ordered Jeremy.

Heads began to turn.

"Take off your shirt."

"I do not take orders like a servant," announced my father.

"Take off your shirt, or I'm going to throw this jacket right into the pool, just right into this little pool here." Jeremy held it over the water.

"Go ahead."

"One hundred twelve-fifty," taunted Jeremy. "One hundred twelve . . ."

My father flung the polo shirt into the water with such force that part of it bounced back up into the air like a fluorescent fountain. Then it settled into a soft heap on top of the water. My mother hurried up.

"You're a sport!" said Jeremy, suddenly breaking into a smile and slapping my father on the back. "You're a sport! I like that. A man with spirit, that's what you are. A man with panache. Allow me to return to you your jacket." He handed it back to my father. "Good value you got on that, good value."

My father hurled the coat into the pool too. "We're leaving," he said grimly. "Leaving!"

"Now, Ralphie," said Mrs. Lardner, bustling up; but my father was already stomping off.

"Get your sister," he told me. To my mother: "Get your shoes."

"That was *great,* Dad," said Mona as we walked down to the car. "You were *stupendous.*"

"Way to show 'em," I said.

"What?" said my father offhandedly.

Although it was only just dusk, we were in a gulch, which made it hard to see anything except the gleam of his white shirt moving up the hill ahead of us.

"It was all my fault," began my mother.

"Forget it," said my father grandly. Then he said, "The only trouble is I left those keys in my jacket pocket."

"Oh *no,*" said Mona.

"Oh no is right," said my mother.

"So we'll walk home," I said.

"But how're we going to get into the *house,*" said Mona.

The noise of the party churned through the silence.

"Someone has to going back," said my father.

"Let's go to the pancake house first," suggested my mother. "We can wait there until the party is finished, and then call Mrs. Lardner."

Having all agreed that that was a good plan, we started walking again.

"God, just think," said Mona. "We're going to have to *dive* for them."

My father stopped a moment. We waited.

"You girls are good swimmers," he said finally. "Not like me."

Then his shirt started moving again, and we trooped up the hill after it, into the dark.

THE PUGILIST
AT REST

Hey Baby got caught writing a letter to his girl when he was supposed to be taking notes on the specs of the M-14 rifle. We were sitting in a stifling hot Quonset hut during the first weeks of boot camp, August 1966, at the Marine Corps Recruit Depot in San Diego. Sergeant Wright snatched the letter out of Hey Baby's hand, and later that night in the squad bay he read the letter to the Marine recruits of Platoon 263, his voice laden with sarcasm. *"Hey, Baby!"* he began, and then as he went into the body of the letter he worked himself into a state of outrage and disgust. It was a letter to *Rosie Rottencrotch,* he said at the end, and what really mattered, what was really at issue and what was of utter importance was not *Rosie Rottencrotch* and her steaming-hot panties but rather the muzzle velocity of the M-14 rifle.

Hey Baby paid for the letter by doing a hundred squat thrusts on the concrete floor of the squad bay, but the main prize he won that night was that he became forever known as Hey Baby to the recruits of Platoon 263—in addition to being a shitbird, a faggot, a turd, a maggot, and other such standard appellations. To top it all off, shortly after the incident, Hey Baby got a Dear John from his girl back in Chicago, of whom Sergeant Wright, myself, and seventy-eight other Marine recruits had come to know just a little.

Hey Baby was not in the Marine Corps for very long. The reason for this was that he started in on my buddy, Jorgeson. Jorgeson was my main man, and Hey Baby started calling him Jorgepussy and began harassing him and pushing him around. He was down on Jorgeson because whenever we were taught some sort of combat maneuver or tactic, Jorgeson would say, under his breath, "You could get *killed* if you try that." Or, "Your ass is *had,* if you do that." You got the feeling that Jorgeson didn't think loving the American flag and defending democratic ideals in Southeast Asia were all that important. He told me that what he really wanted to do was have an artist's loft in the

SoHo district of New York City, wear a beret, eat liver-sausage sandwiches made with stale baguettes, drink Tokay wine, smoke dope, paint pictures, and listen to the wailing, sorrowful songs of that French singer Edith Piaf, otherwise known as "The Little Sparrow."

After the first half hour of boot camp most of the other recruits wanted to get out, too, but they nourished dreams of surfboards, Corvettes, and blond babes. Jorgeson wanted to be a beatnik and hang out with Jack Kerouac and Neal Cassady, slam down burning shots of amber whiskey, and hear Charles Mingus play real cool jazz on the bass fiddle. He wanted to practice Zen Buddhism, throw the I Ching, eat couscous, and study astrology charts. All of this was foreign territory to me. I had grown up in Aurora, Illinois, and had never heard of such things. Jorgeson had a sharp tongue and was so supercilious in his remarks that I didn't know quite how seriously I should take this talk, but I enjoyed his humor and I did believe he had the sensibilities of an artist. It was not some vague yearning. I believed very much that he could become a painter of pictures. At that point he wasn't putting his heart and soul into becoming a Marine. He wasn't a true believer like me.

Some weeks after Hey Baby began hassling Jorgeson, Sergeant Wright gave us his best speech: "You men are going off to war, and it's not a pretty thing," etc. & etc., "and if Luke the Gook knocks down one of your buddies, a fellow-Marine, you are going to risk your life and go in and get that Marine and you are going to bring him out. Not because I said so. No! You are going after that Marine because *you* are a Marine, a member of the most elite fighting force in the world, and that man out there who's gone down is a Marine, and he's your *buddy.* He is your brother! Once you are a Marine, you are *always* a Marine and you will never let another Marine down." Etc. & etc. "You can take a Marine out of the Corps but you can't take the Corps out of a Marine." Etc. & etc. At the time it seemed to me a very good speech, and it stirred me deeply. Sergeant Wright was no candy ass. He was one squared-away dude, and he could call cadence. Man, it puts a lump in my throat when I remember how that man could sing cadence. Apart from Jorgeson, I think all of the recruits in Platoon 263 were proud of Sergeant Wright. He was the real thing, the genuine article. He was a crackerjack Marine.

In the course of training, lots of the recruits dropped out of the original platoon. Some couldn't pass the physical-fitness tests and had to go to a special camp for pussies. This was a particularly shameful shortcoming, the most humiliating apart from bed-wetting. Other recruits would get pneumonia, strep throat, infected foot blisters, or whatever, and lose time that way. Some didn't qualify at the rifle range. One would break a leg. Another would have a nervous breakdown (and this was also deplorable). People dropped out right and left. When the recruit corrected whatever deficiency he had, or when he got better, he would be picked up by another platoon that was in the stage of basic training that he had been in when his training was interrupted. Platoon 263 picked up dozens of recruits in this fashion. If everything went well, however, you got through with the whole business in twelve weeks. That's not a long time, but it seemed like a long time. You did not see a female in all that time. You did not see a newspaper or a television set. You did not eat a candy bar. Another thing was the fact that you had someone on top of you, watching every move you made. When it was time to "shit, shower, and shave," you were given just ten minutes, and had to confront lines and so on to complete the entire affair. Head calls were so infrequent that I spent a lot of time that might otherwise have been neutral or painless in the eye-watering anxiety that I was going to piss my pants. We *ran* to chow, where we were faced with enormous steam vents that spewed out a sickening smell of rancid, super-heated grease. Still, we entered the mess hall with ravenous appetites, ate a huge tray of food in just a few minutes, and then *ran* back to our company area in formation, choking back the burning bile of a meal too big to be eaten so fast. God forbid that you would lose control and vomit.

If all had gone well in the preceding hours, Sergeant Wright would permit us to smoke one cigarette after each meal. Jorgeson had shown me the wisdom of switching from Camels to Pall Malls—they were much longer, packed a pretty good jolt, and when we snapped open our brushed-chrome Zippos, torched up, and inhaled the first few drags, we shared the overmastering pleasure that tobacco can bring if you use it seldom and judiciously. These were always the best moments of the day—brief respites from the tyrannical repression of recruit training. As we got close to the end of it all Jorgeson liked to play a little game. He used to say to me (with fragrant blue smoke curling out of his nostrils), "If someone said, 'I'll give you ten thousand dollars to do all of this again,' what would you say?" "No way, Jack!" He would keep on upping it until he had John Beresford Tipton, the guy from "The Millionaire," offering me a check for a million bucks. "Not for any money," I'd say.

While they were all smoldering under various pressures, the recruits were also getting pretty "salty"—they were beginning to believe. They were beginning to think of themselves as Marines. If you could make it through this, the reasoning went, you wouldn't crack in combat. So I remember that I had tears in my eyes when Sergeant Wright gave us the spiel about how a Marine would charge a machine-gun nest to save his buddies, dive on a hand grenade, do whatever it takes—and yet I was ashamed when Jorgeson caught me wiping them away. All of the recruits were teary except Jorgeson. He had these very clear cobalt-blue eyes. They were so remarkable that they caused you to notice Jorgeson in a crowd. There was unusual beauty in these eyes, and there was an extraordinary power in them. Apart from having a pleasant enough face, Jorgeson was small and unassuming except for these eyes. Anyhow, when he caught me getting sentimental he gave me this look that penetrated to the core of my being. It was the icy look of absolute contempt, and it caused me to doubt myself. I said, "Man! Can't you get into it? For Christ's sake!"

"I'm not like you," he said. "But I am into it, more than you could ever know. I never told you this before, but I am Kal-El, born on the planet Krypton and rocketed to Earth as an infant, moments before my world exploded. Disguised as a mild-mannered Marine, I have resolved to use my powers for the good of mankind. Whenever danger appears on the scene, truth and justice will be served as I slip into the green U.S.M.C. utility uniform and become Earth's greatest hero."

I got highly pissed and didn't talk to him for a couple of days after this. Then, about two weeks before boot camp was over, when we were running out to the parade field for drill with our rifles at port arms, all assholes and elbows, I saw Hey Baby give Jorgeson a nasty shove with his M-14. Hey Baby was a large and fairly tough young man who liked to displace his aggressive impulses on Jorgeson, but he wasn't as big or as tough as I.

Jorgeson nearly fell down as the other recruits scrambled out to the parade field, and Hey Baby gave a short, malicious laugh. I ran past Jorgeson and caught up to Hey Baby; he picked me up in his peripheral vision, but by then it was too late. I set my body so that I could put everything into it, and with one deft stroke I hammered him in the temple with the sharp edge of the steel butt plate of my M-14. It was not exactly a premeditated crime, although I had been laying to get him. My idea before this had simply been to lay my hands on him, but now I had blood in my eye. I was a skilled boxer, and I knew the temple was a vulnerable spot; the human skull is otherwise hard and durable, except at its base. There was a sickening crunch, and Hey Baby dropped into the ice plants along the side of the company street.

The entire platoon was out on the parade field when the house mouse screamed at the assistant D.I., who rushed back to the scene of the crime to find Hey Baby crumpled in a fetal position in the ice plants with blood all over the place. There was blood from the scalp wound as well as a froth of blood emitting from his nostrils and his mouth. Blood was leaking from his right ear. Did I see skull fragments and brain tissue? It seemed that I did. To tell you the truth, I wouldn't have cared in the least if I had killed him, but like most criminals I was very much afraid of getting caught. It suddenly occurred to me that I could be headed for the brig for a long time. My heart was pounding out of my chest. Yet the larger part of me didn't care. Jorgeson was my buddy, and I wasn't going to stand still and let someone fuck him over.

The platoon waited at parade rest while Sergeant Wright came out of the duty hut and took command of the situation. An ambulance was called, and it came almost immediately. A number of corpsmen squatted down alongside the fallen man for what seemed an eternity. Eventually they took Hey Baby off with a fractured skull. It would be the last we ever saw of him. Three evenings later, in the squad bay, the assistant D.I. told us rather ominously that Hey Baby had recovered consciousness. That's all he said. What did *that* mean? I was worried, because Hey Baby had seen me make my move, but, as it turned out, when he came to he had forgotten the incident and all events of the preceding two weeks. Retrograde amnesia. Lucky for me. I also knew that at least three other recruits had seen what I did, but none of them reported me. Every member of the platoon was called in and grilled by a team of hard-ass captains and a light colonel from the Criminal Investigation Detachment. It took a certain amount of balls to lie to them, yet none of my fellow-jarheads reported me. I was well liked and Hey Baby was not. Indeed, many felt that he got exactly what was coming to him.

The other day—Memorial Day, as it happened—I was cleaning some stuff out of the attic when I came upon my old dress-blue uniform. It's a beautiful uniform, easily the most handsome worn by any of the U.S. armed forces. The rich color recalled Jorgeson's eyes for me—not that the color matched, but in the sense that the color of each was so startling. The tunic does not have lapels, of course, but a high collar with red piping and the traditional golden eagle, globe, and anchor insignia on either side of the neck clasp. The tunic buttons are not brassy—although they are in fact made of brass—but are a delicate gold in color, like Florentine gold. On the sleeves of the tunic my staff sergeant's chevrons are gold on red. High on the left breast is a rainbow display of fruit salad representing my various combat citations. Just below these are my marksmanship badges; I shot Expert in rifle as well as pistol.

I opened a sandalwood box and took my various medals out of the large plastic bag I had packed them in to prevent them from tarnishing. The Navy Cross and the two Silver Stars are the best; they are such pretty things they dazzle you. I found a couple of Thai sticks in the sandalwood box as well. I took a whiff of the box and smelled the smells of Saigon—the whores, the dope, the saffron, cloves, jasmine, and patchouli oil. I put the Thai sticks back, recalling the three-day hangover that particular batch of dope had given me more than twenty-three years before. Again I looked at my dress-blue tunic. My most distinctive badge, the crowning glory, and the one of which I am most proud, is the set of Airborne wings. I remember how it was, walking around Oceanside, California—the Airborne wings and the high-and-tight haircut were recognized by all the Marines; they meant you were the crème de la crème, you were a recon Marine.

Recon was all Jorgeson's idea. We had lost touch with each other after boot camp. I was sent to com school in San Diego, where I had to sit in a hot Class A wool uniform all day and learn the Morse code. I deliberately flunked out, and when I was given the perfunctory option for a second shot, I told the colonel, "Hell no, sir. I want to go 003—infantry. I want to be a ground-pounder. I didn't join the service to sit at a desk all day."

I was on a bus to Camp Pendleton three days later, and when I got there I ran into Jorgeson. I had been thinking of him a lot. He was a clerk in head-quarters company. Much to my astonishment, he was fifteen pounds heavier, and had grown two inches, and he told me he was hitting the weight pile every night after running seven miles up and down the foothills of Pendleton in com-bat boots, carrying a rifle and a full field pack. After the usual what's-been-happening? b.s., he got down to business and said, "They need people in Force Recon, what do you think? Headquarters is one boring motherfucker."

I said, "Recon? Paratrooper? You got to be shittin' me! When did you get so gung-ho, man?"

He said, "Hey, you were the one who *bought* the program. Don't fade on me now, goddamm it! Look, we pass the physical fitness test and then they send us to jump school at Benning. If we pass that, we're in. And we'll pass. Those doggies ain't got jack. Semper fi, motherfucker! Let's do it."

There was no more talk of Neal Cassady, Edith Piaf, or the artist's loft in SoHo. I said, "If Sergeant Wright could only see you now!"

We were just three days in country when we got dropped in somewhere up north near the DMZ. It was a routine reconnaissance patrol. It was not sup-posed to be any kind of big deal at all—just acclimation. The morning after our drop we approached a clear field. I recall that it gave me a funny feeling, but I was too new to fully trust my instincts. *Everything* was spooky; I was fresh meat, F.N.G.—a Fucking New Guy.

Before moving into the field, our team leader sent Hanes—a lance cor-poral, a short-timer, with only twelve days left before his rotation was over— across the field as a point man. This was a bad omen and everyone knew it. Hanes had two Purple Hearts. He followed the order with no hesitation and crossed the field without drawing fire. The team leader signaled for us to fan out and told me to circumvent the field and hump through the jungle to in-vestigate a small mound of loose red dirt that I had missed completely but that he had picked up with his trained eye. I remember I kept saying, "Where?" He pointed to a heap of earth about thirty yards along the tree line and about ten feet back in the bushes. Most likely it was an anthill, but you never knew—it could have been an NVA tunnel. "Over there," he hissed. "Goddamn it, do I have to draw pictures for you?"

I moved smartly in the direction of the mound while the rest of the team reconverged to discuss something. As I approached the mound I saw that it was in fact an anthill, and I looked back at the team and saw they were already halfway across the field, moving very fast.

Suddenly there were several loud hollow pops and the cry "Incoming!" Seconds later the first of a half-dozen mortar rounds landed in the loose earth surrounding the anthill. For a millisecond, everything went black. I was blown back and lifted up on a cushion of warm air. At first it was like the thrill of a carnival ride, but it was quickly followed by that stunned, jangly, electric feeling you get when you hit your crazy bone. Like that, but not confined to a small area like the elbow. I felt it shoot through my spine and into all four limbs. A thick plaster of sand and red clay plugged up my nostrils and ears. Grit was blown in between my teeth. If I hadn't been wearing a pair of Ray-Ban aviator shades, I would certainly have been blinded permanently—as it was, my eyes were loaded with grit. (I later discovered that fine red earth was somehow blown in behind the crystal of my pressure-tested Rolex Submariner, underneath my fingernails and toenails, and deep into the pores of my skin.) When I was able to, I pulled out a canteen filled with lemon-lime Kool-Aid and tried to flood my eyes clean. This helped a little, but my eyes still felt like they were on fire. I rinsed them again and blinked furiously.

I rolled over on my stomach in the prone position and leveled my field-issue M-16. A company of screaming NVA soldiers ran into the field, firing as they came—I saw their green tracer rounds blanket the position where the team had quickly congregated to lay out a perimeter, but none of our own red tracers were going out. Several of the Marines had been killed outright by the mortar rounds. Jorgeson was all right, and I saw him cast a nervous glance in my direction. Then he turned to the enemy and began to fire his M-16. I clicked my rifle on to automatic and pulled the trigger, but the gun was loaded with dirt and it wouldn't fire.

Apart from Jorgeson, the only other American putting out any fire was Second Lieutenant Milton, also a fairly new guy, a "cherry," who was down on one knee firing his .45, an exercise in almost complete futility. I assumed that Milton's 16 had jammed, like mine, and watched as AK-47 rounds, having penetrated his flak jacket and then his chest, ripped through the back of his field pack and buzzed into the jungle beyond like a deadly swarm of bees. A few seconds later, I heard the swoosh of an RPG rocket, a dud round that dinged the lieutenant's left shoulder before it flew off in the bush behind him. It took off his whole arm, and for an instant I could see the white bone and ligaments of his shoulder, and then red flesh of muscle tissue, looking very much like fresh prime beef, well marbled and encased in a thin layer of yellowish-white adipose tissue that quickly became saturated with dark-red blood. What a lot of blood there was. Still, Milton continued to fire his .45. When he emptied his clip, I watched him remove a fresh one from his web gear and attempt to load the pistol with one hand. He seemed to fumble with the fresh clip for a long time, until at last he dropped it, along with his .45. The lieutenant's head slowly sagged forward, but he stayed up on one knee with his remaining arm extended out to the enemy, palm upward in the soulful, heartrending gesture of Al Jolson doing a rendition of "Mammy."

A hail of green tracer rounds buzzed past Jorgeson, but he coolly returned fire in short, controlled bursts. The light, tinny pops from his M-16 did not sound very reassuring, but I saw several NVA go down. AK-47 fire kicked up red dust all around Jorgeson's feet. He was basically out in the open, and if ever a man was totally alone it was Jorgeson. He was dead meat and he had to know it. It was very strange that he wasn't hit immediately.

Jorgeson zigged his way over to the body of a large black Marine who carried an M-60 machine gun. Most of the recon Marines carried grease guns or Swedish Ks; an M-60 was too heavy for traveling light and fast, but this Marine had been big and he had been paranoid. I had known him least of anyone in the squad. In three days he had said nothing to me, I suppose because I was F.N.G., and had spooked him. Indeed, now he was dead. That august seeker of truth, Schopenhauer, was correct: *We are like lambs in a field, disporting themselves under the eye of the butcher, who chooses out first one and then another for his prey. So it is that in our good days we are all unconscious of the evil Fate may have presently in store for us—sickness, poverty, mutilation, loss of sight or reason.*

It was difficult to judge how quickly time was moving. Although my senses had been stunned by the concussion of the mortar rounds, they were, however paradoxical this may seem, more acute than ever before. I watched Jorgeson pick up the machine gun and begin to spread an impressive field of fire back at the enemy. *Thuk thuk thuk, thuk thuk thuk, thuk thuk thuk!* I saw several more bodies fall, and began to think that things might turn out all right after all. The NVA dropped for cover, and many of them turned back and headed for the tree line. Jorgeson fired off a couple of bandoliers, and after he stopped to load another, he turned back and looked at me with those blue eyes and a smile like "How am I doing?" Then I heard the steel-cork pop of an M-79 launcher and saw a rocket grenade explode through Jorgeson's upper abdomen, causing him to do something like a back flip. His M-60 machine gun flew straight up into the air. The barrel was glowing red like a hot poker, and continued to fire in a "cook off" until the entire bandolier had run through.

In the meantime I had pulled a cleaning rod out of my pack and worked it through the barrel of my M-16. When I next tried to shoot, the Tonka-toy son of a bitch remained jammed, and at last I frantically broke it down to find the source of the problem. I had a dirty bolt. Fucking dirt everywhere. With numbed fingers I removed the firing pin and worked it over with a toothbrush, dropping it in the red dirt, picking it up, cleaning it, and dropping it again. My fingers felt like Novocain, and while I could see far away, I was unable to see up close. I poured some more Kool-Aid over my eyes. It was impossible for me to get my weapon clean. Lucky for me, ultimately.

Suddenly NVA soldiers were running through the field shoving bayonets into the bodies of the downed Marines. It was not until an NVA trooper kicked Lieutenant Milton out of his tripod position that he finally fell to the ground. Then the soldiers started going through the dead Marines' gear. I was still frantically struggling with my weapon when it began to dawn on me that the enemy had forgotten me in the excitement of the firefight. I wondered what had happened to Hanes and if he had gotten clear. I doubted it, and hopped on my survival radio to call in an air strike when finally a canny NVA trooper did remember me and headed in my direction most ricky-tick.

With a tight grip on the spoon, I pulled the pin on a fragmentation grenade and then unsheathed my K-bar. About this time Jorgeson let off a horrendous shriek—a gut shot is worse than anything. Or did Jorgeson scream to save my life? The NVA moving in my direction turned back to him, studied him for a moment, and then thrust a bayonet into his heart. As badly as my own eyes hurt, I was able to see Jorgeson's eyes—a final flash of glorious azure before they faded into the unfocused and glazed gray of death. I repinned the grenade, got up on my knees, and scrambled away until finally I was on my feet with a useless and incomplete handful of M-16 parts, and I was running as fast and as hard as I have ever run in my life. A pair of Phantom F-4s came in very low with delayed-action high-explosive rounds and napalm. I could feel the almost unbearable heat waves of the latter, volley after volley. I can still feel it and smell it to this day.

Concerning Lance Corporal Hanes: they found him later, fried to a crisp by the napalm, but it was nonetheless ascertained that he had been mutilated while alive. He was like the rest of us—eighteen, nineteen, twenty years old. What did we know of life? Before Vietnam, Hanes didn't think he would ever die. I mean, yes, he knew that in theory he would die, but he *felt* like he was going to live forever. I know that I felt that way. Hanes was down to twelve days and a wake-up. When other Marines saw a short-timer get greased, it devastated their morale. However, when I saw them zip up the body bag on Hanes I became incensed. Why hadn't Milton sent him back to the rear to burn shit or something when he got so short? Twelve days to go and then mutilated. Fucking Milton! Fucking second lieutenant!

Theogenes was the greatest of gladiators. He was a boxer who served under the patronage of a cruel nobleman, a prince who took great delight in bloody spectacles. Although this was several hundred years before the times of those most enlightened of men Socrates, Plato, and Aristotle, and well after the Minoans of Crete, it still remains a high point in the history of Western civilization and culture. It was the approximate time of Homer, the greatest poet who ever lived. Then, as now, violence, suffering, and the cheapness of life were the rule.

The sort of boxing Theogenes practiced was not like modern-day boxing with those kindergarten Queensberry Rules. The two contestants were not permitted the freedom of a ring. Instead, they were strapped to flat stones, facing each other nose-to-nose. When the signal was given, they would begin hammering each other with fists encased in heavy leather thongs. It was a fight to the death. Fourteen hundred and twenty-five times Theogenes was strapped to the stone and fourteen hundred and twenty-five times he emerged a victor.

Perhaps it is Theogenes who is depicted in the famous Roman statue (based on the earlier Greek original) of "The Pugilist at Rest." I keep a grainy black-and-white photograph of it in my room. The statue depicts a muscular athlete approaching his middle age. He has a thick beard and a full head of curly hair. In addition to the telltale broken nose and cauliflower ears of a boxer, the pugilist has the slanted, drooping brows that bespeak torn nerves. Also, the forehead is piled with scar tissue. As may be expected, the pugilist has the musculature of a fighter. His neck and trapezius muscles are well developed. His shoulders are enormous; his chest is thick and flat, without the bulging pectorals of the bodybuilder. His back, oblique, and abdominal muscles are highly pronounced, and he has that greatest asset of the modern boxer—sturdy legs. The arms are large, particularly the forearms, which are reinforced with the leather wrappings of the cestus. It is the body of a small heavyweight—lithe rather than bulky, but by no means lacking in power: a Jack Johnson or a Dempsey, say. If you see the authentic statue at the Terme Museum, in Rome, you will see that the seated boxer is really not much more than a light-heavyweight. People were small in those days. The important thing was that he was perfectly proportioned.

The pugilist is sitting on a rock with his forearms balanced on his thighs. That he is seated and not pacing implies that he has been through all this many times before. It appears that he is conserving his strength. His head is turned as if he were looking over his shoulder—as if someone had just whispered something to him. It is in this that the "art" of the sculpture is conveyed to the viewer. Could it be that someone has just summoned him to the arena? There is a slight look of befuddlement on his face, but there is no trace of fear. There is an air about him that suggests that he is eager to proceed and does not wish to cause anyone any trouble or to create a delay, even though his life will soon be on the line. Besides the deformities on his noble face, there is also the suggestion of weariness and philosophical resignation. *All the world's a stage, and all the men and women merely players.* Exactly! He knew this more than two thousand years before Shakespeare penned the line. How did he come to be at this place in space and time? Would he rather be safely removed to the countryside—an obscure, stinking peasant shoving a plow behind a mule? Would that be better? Or does he revel in his role? Perhaps he once did, but surely not now. Is this the great Theogenes or merely a journeyman fighter, a former slave or criminal bought by one of the many contractors who for months trained the condemned for their brief moment in the arena? I wonder if Marcus Aurelius loved the "Pugilist" as I do, and came to study it and to meditate before it.

I cut and ran from that field in Southeast Asia. I've read that Davy Crockett, hero of the American frontier, was cowering under a bed when Santa Anna and his soldiers stormed into the Alamo. What is the truth? Jack Dempsey used to get so scared before his fights that he sometimes wet his pants. But look what he did to Willard and to Luis Firpo, the Wild Bull of the Pampas! It was something close to homicide. What is courage? What is cowardice? The magnificent Roberto Duran gave us *"No más,"* but who had a greater fighting heart than Duran?

I got over that first scare and saw that I was something quite other than that which I had known myself to be. Hey Baby proved only my warm-up act. There was a reservoir of malice, poison, and vicious sadism in my soul, and it poured forth freely in the jungles and rice paddies of Vietnam. I pulled three tours. I wanted some payback for Jorgeson. I grieved for Lance Corporal Hanes. I grieved for myself and what I had lost. I committed unspeakable crimes and got medals for it.

It was only fair that I got a head injury myself. I never got a scratch in Vietnam, but I got tagged in a boxing smoker at Pendleton. Fought a bad-ass light-heavyweight from artillery. Nobody would fight this guy. He could box. He had all the moves. But mainly he was a puncher—it was said that he could punch with either hand. It was said that his hand speed was superb. I had finished off at least a half rack of Hamm's before I went in with him and started getting hit with head shots I didn't even see coming. They were right. His hand speed *was* superb.

I was twenty-seven years old, smoked two packs a day, was a borderline alcoholic. I shouldn't have fought him—I knew that—but he had been making noise. A very long time before, I had been the middleweight champion of the 1st Marine Division. I had been a so-called war hero. I had been a recon Marine. But now I was a garrison Marine and in no kind of shape.

He put me down almost immediately, and when I got up I was terribly afraid. I was tight and I could not breathe. It felt like he was hitting me in the face with a ball-peen hammer. It felt like he was busting light bulbs in my face. Rather than one opponent, I saw three. I was convinced his gloves were loaded, and a wave of self-pity ran through me.

I began to move. He made a mistake by expending a lot of energy trying to put me away quickly. I had no intention of going down again, and I knew I wouldn't. My buddies were watching, and I had to give them a good show. While I was afraid, I was also exhilarated; I had not felt this alive since Vietnam. I began to score with my left jab, and because of this I was able to withstand his bull charges and divert them. I thought he would throw his bolt, but in the beginning he was tireless. I must have hit him with four hundred left jabs. It got so that I could score at will, with either hand, but he would counter, trap me on the ropes, and pound. He was the better puncher and was truly hurting me, but I was scoring, and as the fight went on the momentum shifted and I took over. I staggered him again and again. The Marines at ringside were screaming for me to put him away, but however much I tried, I could not. Although I could barely stand by the end, I was sorry that the fight was over. Who had won? The referee raised my arm in victory, but I think it was pretty much a draw. Judging a prizefight is a very subjective thing.

About an hour after the bout, when the adrenaline had subsided, I realized I had a terrible headache. It kept getting worse, and I rushed out of the NCO Club, where I had gone with my buddies to get loaded.

I stumbled outside, struggling to breathe, and I headed away from the company area toward Sheepshit Hill, one of the many low brown foothills in the vicinity. Like a dog who wants to die alone, so it was with me. Everything got swirly, and I dropped in the bushes.

I was unconscious for nearly an hour, and for the next two weeks I walked around like I was drunk, with double vision. I had constant headaches and seemed to have grown old overnight. My health was gone.

I became a very timid individual. I became introspective. I wondered what had made me act the way I had acted. Why had I killed my fellowmen in war, without any feeling, remorse, or regret? And when the war was over, why did I continue to drink and swagger around and get into fistfights? Why did I like to dish out pain, and why did I take positive delight in the suffering of others? Was I insane? Was it too much testosterone? Women don't do things like that. The rapacious Will to Power lost its hold on me. Suddenly I began to feel sympathetic to the cares and sufferings of all living creatures. You lose your health and you start thinking this way.

Has man become any better since the times of Theogenes? The world is replete with badness. I'm not talking about that old routine where you drag out the Spanish Inquisition, the Holocaust, Joseph Stalin, the Khmer Rouge, etc. It happens in our own backyard. Twentieth-century America is one of the most materially prosperous nations in history. But take a walk through an American prison, a nursing home, the slums where the homeless live in cardboard boxes, a cancer ward. Go to a Vietnam vets' meeting, or an A.A. meeting, or an Overeaters Anonymous meeting. *How hollow and unreal a thing is life, how deceitful are its pleasures, what horrible aspects it possesses.* Is the world not rather like a hell, as Schopenhauer, that clearheaded seer—who has helped me transform my suffering into an object of understanding—was so quick to point out? They called him a pessimist and dismissed him with a word, but it is peace and self-renewal that I have found in his pages.

About a year after my fight with the guy from artillery I started having seizures. I suffered from a form of left-temporal-lobe seizure which is sometimes called Dostoyevski's epilepsy. It's so rare as to be almost unknown. Freud, himself a neurologist, speculated that Dostoyevski was a hysterical epileptic, and that his fits were unrelated to brain damage—psychogenic in origin. Dostoyevski did not have his first attack until the age of twenty-five, when he was imprisoned in Siberia and received fifty lashes after complaining about the food. Freud figured that after Dostoyevski's mock execution, the four years' imprisonment in Siberia, the tormented childhood, the murder of his tyrannical father, etc. & etc.—he had all the earmarks of hysteria, of grave psychological trauma. And Dostoyevski had displayed the trademark features of the psychomotor epileptic long before his first attack. These days physicians insist there is no such thing as the "epileptic personality." I think they say this because they do not want to add to the burden of the epileptic's suffering with an extra stigma. Privately they do believe in these traits. Dostoyevski was nervous and depressed, a tormented hypochondriac, a compulsive writer obsessed with religious and philosophic themes. He was hyperloquacious, raving, etc. & etc. His gambling addiction is well known. By most accounts he was a sick soul.

 The peculiar and most distinctive thing about his epilepsy was that in the split second before his fit—in the aura, which is in fact officially a part of the attack—Dostoyevski experienced a sense of felicity, of ecstatic well-being unlike anything an ordinary mortal could hope to imagine. It was the experience of satori. Not the nickel-and-dime satori of Abraham Maslow, but the Supreme. He said that he wouldn't trade ten years of life for this feeling, and I, who have had it, too, would have to agree. I can't explain it, I don't understand it—it becomes slippery and elusive when it gets any distance on you—but I have felt this down to the core of my being. Yes, God exists! But then it slides away and I lose it. I become a doubter. Even Dostoyevski, the fervent Christian, makes an almost airtight case against the possibility of the existence of God in the

Grand Inquisitor digression in *The Brothers Karamazov*. It is probably the greatest passage in all of world literature, and it tilts you to the court of the atheist. This is what happens when you approach Him with the intellect.

It is thought that St. Paul had a temporal-lobe fit on the road to Damascus. Paul warns us in First Corinthians that God will confound the intellectuals. It is known that Muhammad composed the Koran after attacks of epilepsy. Black Elk experienced fits before his grand "buffalo" vision. Joan of Arc is thought to have been a left-temporal-lobe epileptic. Each of these in a terrible flash of brain lightning was able to pierce the murky veil of illusion which is spread over all things. Just so did the scales fall from my eyes. It is called the "sacred disease."

But what a price. I rarely leave the house anymore. To avoid falling injuries, I always wear my old boxer's headgear, and I always carry my mouthpiece. Rather more often than the aura where "every common bush is afire with God," I have the typical epileptic aura, which is that of terror and impending doom. If I can keep my head and think of it, and if there is time, I slip the mouthpiece in and thus avoid biting my tongue. I bit it in half once, and when they sewed it back together it swelled enormously, like a huge red-and-black sausage. I was unable to close my mouth for more than two weeks.

The fits are coming more and more. I'm loaded on Depakene, phenobarbital, Tegretol, Dilantin—the whole shit load. A nurse from the V.A. bought a pair of Staffordshire terriers for me and trained them to watch me as I sleep, in case I have a fit and smother facedown in my bedding. What delightful companions these dogs are! One of them, Gloria, is especially intrepid and clever. Inevitably, when I come to I find that the dogs have dragged me into the kitchen, away from blankets and pillows, rugs, and objects that might suffocate me; and that they have turned me on my back. There's Gloria, barking in my face. Isn't this incredible?

My sister brought a neurosurgeon over to my place around Christmas—not some V.A. butcher but a guy from the university hospital. He was a slick dude in a nine-hundred-dollar suit. He came down on me hard, like a used-car salesman. He wants to cauterize a small spot in a nerve bundle in my brain. "It's not a lobotomy, it's a *cingulotomy*," he said.

Reckless, desperate, last-ditch psychosurgery is still pretty much unthinkable in the conservative medical establishment. That's why he made a personal visit to my place. A house call. Drumming up some action to make himself a name. "See that bottle of Thorazine?" he said. "You can throw that poison away," he said. "All that amitriptyline. That's garbage, you can toss that, too." He said, "Tell me something. How can you take all of that shit and still walk?" He said, "You take enough drugs to drop an elephant."

He wants to cut me. He said that the feelings of guilt and worthlessness, and the heaviness of a heart blackened by sin, will go away. "It is *not* a lobotomy," he said.

I don't like the guy. I don't trust him. I'm not convinced, but I can't go on like this. If I am not having a panic attack I am engulfed in tedious, unrelenting depression. I am overcome with a deadening sense of languor; I can't *do* anything. I wanted to give my buddies a good show! What a goddamn fool. I am a goddamn fool!

It has taken me six months to put my thoughts in order, but I wanted to do it in case I am a vegetable after the operation. I know that my buddy Jorgeson was a real American hero. I wish that he had lived to be something else, if not a painter of pictures then even some kind of fuckup with a factory job and four divorces, bankruptcy petitions, in and out of jail. I wish he had been that. I wish he had been *anything* rather than a real American hero. So, then, if I am to feel somewhat *indifferent* to life after the operation, all the better. If not, not.

If I had a more conventional sense of morality I would shitcan those dress blues, and I'd send that Navy Cross to Jorgeson's brother. Jorgeson was the one who won it, who pulled the John Wayne number up there near Khe Sanh and saved my life, although I lied and took the credit for all of those dead NVA. He had created a stunning body count—nothing like Theogenes, but Jorgeson only had something like twelve minutes total in the theater of war.

The high command almost awarded me the Medal of Honor, but of course there were no witnesses to what I claimed I had done, and I had saved no one's life. When I think back on it, my tale probably did not sound as credible as I thought it had at the time. I was only nineteen years old and not all that practiced a liar. I figure if they *had* given me the Medal of Honor, I would have stood in the ring up at Camp Las Pulgas in Pendleton and let that light-heavyweight from artillery fucking kill me.

Now I'm thinking I might call Hey Baby and ask how he's doing. No shit, a couple of neuropsychs—we probably have a lot in common. I could apologize to him. But I learned from my fits that you don't have to do that. Good and evil are only illusions. Still, I cannot help but wonder sometimes if my vision of the Supreme Reality was any more real than the demons visited upon schizophrenics and madmen. Has it all been just a stupid neurochemical event? Is there no God at all? The human heart rebels against this.

If they fuck up the operation, I hope I get to keep my dogs somehow— maybe stay at my sister's place. If they send me to the nuthouse I lose the dogs for sure.

FAMILY

The days were brief and attenuated and the season appeared to be fixed—neither summer nor winter, spring nor fall. A thermal haze of inexpressible sweetness (though bearing tiny bits of grit or mica) had eased into the valley from the industrial regions to the north, and there were nights when the sun set slowly at the western horizon as if sinking through a porous red mass, and there were days when a hard-glaring moon like bone remained fixed in a single position, prominent in the sky. Above the patchwork of excavated land bordering our property—*all* of which had formerly been our property in Grandfather's time: thousands of acres of fertile soil and open grazing land—a curious fibrillating rainbow sometimes appeared, its colors shifting even as you stared, shades of blue, turquoise, iridescent green, russet red, a lovely translucent gold that dissolved to moisture as the thermal breeze stirred, warm and stale as an exhaled breath. And if I'd run excited to tell others of the rainbow, it was likely to have vanished when they came.

"Liar!" my older brothers and sisters said, "—don't promise rainbows when there aren't any!"

Father laid his hand on my head, saying, with a smiling frown, "Don't speak of anything if you aren't certain it will be true for others, not simply for yourself. Do you understand?"

"Yes, Father," I said quietly. Though I did not understand.

This story begins in the time of family celebration—after Father made a great profit selling all but fifteen acres of his inheritance from Grandfather; and he and Mother were like a honeymoon couple, giddy with relief at having escaped the fate of most of our neighbors in the Valley, rancher-rivals of Grandfather's, and their descendants, who had sold off their property before the market began to realize its full potential. ("Full potential" was a term Father often uttered, as if its taste pleased him.) Now these old rivals were without land, and their investments yielded low returns; they'd gone away to live in cities of ever-increasing disorder, where no country people, especially once-aristocratic country people, could endure to live for long. They'd virtually prostituted themselves, Father said, "—and for so little!"

It was a proverb of Grandfather's time that a curse would befall anyone in the Valley who gloated over a neighbor's misfortune but, as Father observed, "It's damned difficult *not* to feel superior, sometimes." And Mother said, kissing him, "Darling—you're absolutely right!"

Our house was made of granite, limestone, and beautiful red-orange brick; the new wing, designed by a famous Japanese architect, was mainly tinted glass, overlooking the Valley, where on good days we could see for many miles and on humid-hazy days we could barely see beyond the fence at the edge of our property. Father, however, preferred the roof of the house: in his white suit (linen in warm weather, light wool in cold), cream-colored fedora cocked back on his head, high-heeled leather-tooled boots, he spent most of his waking hours on the highest peak of the highest roof, observing through high-powered binoculars the astonishing progress of construction in the Valley—for overnight, it seemed, there had appeared roads, expressways, sewers, drainage pipes, "planned communities" with such melodic names as Whispering Glades, Murmuring Oaks, Pheasant Run, Deer Willow, all of them walled to keep out trespassers, and, even more astonishing, immense towers of buildings made of aluminum, and steel, and glass, and bronze, buildings whose magnificent windows winked and glimmered like mirrors, splendid in sunshine like pillars of flame . . . such beauty, where once there'd been mere earth and sky, it caught at your throat like a great bird's talons. "The ways of beauty are as a honeycomb," Father told us mysteriously.

So hypnotized was Father by the transformation of the Valley, he often forgot where he was; failed to come downstairs for meals, or for bed. If Mother, meaning to indulge him, or hurt by his growing indifference to her, did not send a servant to summon him, he was likely to spend an entire night on the roof; in the morning, smiling sheepishly, he would explain that he'd fallen asleep, or, conversely, he'd been troubled by having seen things for which he could not account—shadows the size of longhorns moving ceaselessly beyond our twelve-foot barbed wire fence and inexplicable winking red lights fifty miles away in the foothills. "Optical illusions!" Mother said, "—or the ghosts of old slaughtered livestock, or airplanes. Have you forgotten, darling, you sold thirty acres of land, for an airport at Furnace Creek?" "These lights more resemble fires," Father said stubbornly. "And they're in the foothills, not in the plain."

There came then times of power blackouts, and financial losses, and Father was forced to surrender all but two or three of the servants, but he maintained his rooftop vigil, white-clad, a noble ghostly figure holding binoculars to his eyes, for he perceived himself as a *witness* and believed, if he lived to a ripe old age like Grandfather (who was in his hundredth year when at last he died—of a riding accident), he would be a chronicler of these troubled times, like Thucydides. For, as Father said, "Is there a new world struggling to be born—or only struggle?"

Around this time—because of numerous dislocations in the Valley: the abrupt abandoning of homes, for instance—it happened that packs of dogs began to roam about looking for food, particularly by night, poor starving creatures that became a nuisance and should be, as authorities urged, shot down on sight—these dogs not being feral by birth but former household pets, highly bred beagles, setters, cocker spaniels, terriers, even the larger and coarser type of poodle—and it was the cause of some friction between Mother and Father that, despite his rooftop presence by day and by night, Father nonetheless failed to spy a pack of these dogs dig beneath our fence and make their way to the dairy barn where they tore out the throats—surely this could not have been in silence!—of our remaining six Holsteins, and our last two she-goats, before devouring the poor creatures; nor did Father notice anything unusual the night two homeless derelicts, formerly farmhands of ours, impaled themselves on the electric fence and died agonizing deaths, their bodies found in the morning by Kit, our sixteen-year-old.

Kit, who'd liked the men, said, "—I hope I never see anything like that again in my life!"

It's true that our fence was charged with a powerful electric current, but in full compliance with County Farm and Home Bureau regulations.

Following this, Father journeyed to the state capital with the intention of taking out a sizable loan, and re-establishing, as he called it, old ties with his political friends, or with their younger colleagues; and Mother joined him a few days later for a greatly needed change of scene—"Not that I don't love you all, and the farm, but I need to see other sights for a while!—and I need to be *seen*." Leaving us when they did, under the care of Mrs. Hoyt (our housekeeper) and Cory (our eldest sister), was possibly not a good idea: Mrs. Hoyt was aging rapidly, and Cory, for all the innocence of her marigold eyes and melodic voice, was desperately in love with one of the National Guardsmen who patrolled the Valley in jeeps, authorized to shoot wild dogs, and, when necessary, vandals, arsonists, and squatters who were considered a menace to the public health and well-being. And when Mother returned from the capital, unaccompanied by Father, after what seemed to the family a long absence (two weeks? two months?), it was with shocking news: she and Father were going to separate.

Mother said, "Children, your father and I have decided, after much soul-searching deliberation, that we must dissolve our wedding bond of nearly twenty years." As she spoke Mother's voice wavered like a girl's but fierce little points of light shone in her eyes.

We children were so taken by surprise we could not speak, at first.

Separate! Dissolve! We stood staring and mute; not even Cory, Kit, and Dale, not even Lona who was the most impulsive of us, could find words with which to protest—the younger children began whimpering helplessly, soon joined by the rest. Mother clutched at her hair, saying, "Oh please don't! I can hardly bear the pain as it is!" With some ceremony she then played for us a video of Father's farewell to the family, which drew fresh tears . . . for there, framed astonishingly on our one hundred-inch home theater screen, where we'd never seen his image before, was Father, dressed not in white but in somber colors, his hair in steely bands combed wetly across the dome of his skull, and his eyes puffy, an unnatural sheen to his face as if it had been scoured, hard. He was sitting stiffly erect; his fingers gripped the arms of his chair so tightly the blood had drained from his knuckles; his words came slow, halting, and faint, like the faltering progress of a gut-shot deer across a field. *Dear children, your mother and I . . . after years of marriage . . . of very happy marriage . . . have decided to . . . have decided. . . .* One of the vexatious low-flying helicopters belonging to the National Guard soared past our house, making the screen shudder, but the sound was garbled in any case, as if the tape had been clumsily cut and spliced; Father's beloved face turned liquid and his eyes began to melt vertically, like oily tears; his mouth was distended like a drowning man's. As the tape ended we could discern only sounds, not words, resembling *Help me* or *I am innocent* or *Do not forget me beloved children I AM YOUR FATHER*—and then the screen went dead.

That afternoon Mother introduced us to the man who was to be Father's successor in the household! and to his three children, who were to be our new brothers and sister—we shook hands shyly, in a state of mutual shock, and regarded one another with wide staring wary eyes. Our new father! Our new brothers and sister! So suddenly, and with no warning! Mother explained patiently, yet forcibly, her new husband was no mere *step*father but a true *father*, which meant that we were to address him as "Father" at all times, with respect, and even in our most private innermost thoughts we were to think of him as "Father": for otherwise he would be hurt, and displeased. And moved to discipline us.

So too with Einar and Erastus, our new *brothers* (not *step*brothers), and Fifi, our new *sister* (not *step*sister).

New Father stood before us smiling happily, a man of our old Father's age but heavier and far more robust than that Father, with an unusually large head, the cranium particularly developed, and small shrewd quick-darting eyes beneath brows of bone. He wore a tailored suit with wide shoulders that exaggerated his bulk and sported a red carnation in his lapel; his black shoes, a city man's shoes, shone splendidly, as if phosphorescent. "Hello Father," we murmured shyly, hardly daring to raise our eyes to his, "—Hello Father." The man's jaws were strangely elongated, the lower jaw at least an inch longer than the upper, so that a wet malevolent ridge of teeth was revealed. As so often happened in those days, a single thought passed like lightning among us children, from one to the other to the other, each of us smiling guiltily as it struck us: *Crocodile! Why, here's Crocodile!* Only little Jori burst into frightened tears and New Father surprised us all by stooping to pick her up gently in his arms and comfort her . . . "Hush, hush little girl! Nobody's going to hurt *you!*" and we others could see how the memory of our beloved former Father began to pass from her, like dissolving smoke. Jori was three years old at this time, too young to be held accountable.

New Father's children were tall, big-boned, and solemn, with a faint greenish-peevish cast to their skin, like many city children; the boys had inherited their father's large head and protruding jaws but the girl, Fifi, seventeen years old, was striking in her beauty, with pale blond fluffy hair as lovely as Cory's, and thickly lashed honey-brown eyes in which something mutinous glimmered. That evening, certain of the boys—Dale, Kit, and Hewett— gathered around Fifi to tell her wild tales of the Valley, how we all had to protect ourselves with Winchester rifles and shotguns, from trespassers, and how there was a mysterious resurgence of rats on the farm, as a consequence of excavation in the countryside, and these tales, just a little exaggerated, made the girl shudder and shiver and giggle, leaning toward the boys as if to invite their protection. Ah, Fifi was so pretty! But when Dale hurried off to fetch her a goblet of ice water at her request, she took the goblet from him, lifted it prissily to the light to examine its contents, and asked rudely, "Is this water pure? Is it safe to *drink?*" It was true, our well water had become strangely effervescent, and tasted of rust; after a heavy rainfall there were likely to be tiny red-wriggly things in it, like animated tails; so we had learned not to examine it too closely, just to drink it, and, as our attacks of nausea, diarrhea, dizziness, and amnesia, were only sporadic, we rarely worried but tried instead to be grateful, as Mrs. Hoyt used to urge us, that unlike many of our neighbors we had any drinking water at all. So it was offensive to us to see our new sister Fifi making such a face, handing the goblet back to Dale, and asking haughtily how anyone in his right mind could drink such—*spilth.* Dale said, red-faced, *"How?* This is *how!"* and drank the entire glass in a single thirsty gulp. And he and Fifi stood staring at each other, trembling with passion.

As Cory observed afterward, smiling, yet with a trace of envy or resentment, "It looks as if 'New Sister' has made a conquest!"

"But what will she do," I couldn't help asking, "—if she can't drink our water?"

"She'll drink it," Cory said, with a grim little laugh. "And she'll find it delicious, just like the rest of us."

Which turned out, fairly quickly, to be so.

Poor Cory! Her confinement came in a time of ever-increasing confusion . . . prolonged power failures, a scarcity of all food except canned foods, a scarcity too of ammunition so that the price of shotgun shells doubled and quadrupled; and the massive sky by both day and night was crisscrossed by the contrails of unmarked jet planes (Army or Air Force bombers?) in designs both troubling and beautiful, like the web of a gigantic spider. By this time construction in most parts of the Valley, once so energetic, had been halted; part-completed high-rise buildings punctuated the landscape; some were no more than concrete foundations upon which iron girders had been erected, like exposed bone. How we children loved to explore! The "Mirror Tower" (as we called it: once, it must have had a real, adult name) was a three-hundred-story patchwork of interlocking slots of reflecting glass with a subtle turquoise tint and, where its elegant surface had once mirrored scenes of sparkling natural beauty, there was now a drab scene, or succession of scenes, as on a video screen no one was watching: clouds like soiled cotton batting, smoldering slag heaps, decomposing garbage, predatory thistles and burdocks grown to the height of trees. Traffic, once so congested on the expressways, had dwindled to four or five diesel trucks per day hauling their heavy cargo (rumored to be diseased livestock bound for northern slaughterhouses) and virtually no passenger cars; sometimes, unmarked but official-looking vehicles, like jeeps but much larger than jeeps, passed in lengthy convoys, bound for no one knew where. There were strips of pavement, cloverleafs, that coiled endlessly upon themselves, beginning to be cracked and overgrown by weeds and elevated highways that broke off abruptly in mid-air, thus, as state authorities warned travelers, they were in grave danger, venturing into the countryside, of being attacked by roaming gangs—but the rumor was, as Father insisted, the most dangerous gangs were rogue Guardsmen who wore their uniforms inside out and gas masks strapped over their faces, preying upon the very citizens they were sworn to protect! None of the adults left our family compound without being armed and of course we younger children were forbidden to leave at all—when we did, it was by stealth.

All schools, private and public, had been shut down indefinitely.

"One long holiday!" as Hewett said.

The most beautiful and luxurious of the model communities, which we called "The Wheel" (its original name was Paradise Hollow), had suffered some kind of financial collapse, so that its well-to-do tenants were forced to emigrate back to the cities from which they'd emigrated to the Valley only about eighteen months before. (We called the complex "The Wheel" because its condominiums, office buildings, shops, schools, hospitals, and crematoria were arranged in spokes radiating outward from a single axis and were ingeniously protected at their twenty-mile circumference not by a visible wall, which the Japanese architect who'd designed it had declared a vulgar and outmoded concept, but by a force field of electricity of lethal voltage.) Though the airport at Furnace Creek was officially closed we sometimes saw, late at night, small aircraft including helicopters taking off and landing there; were wakened by the insectlike whining of their engines, and their winking red lights; and one night when the sun remained motionless at the horizon for several hours and visibility was poor, as if we were in a dust storm yet a dust storm without wind, a ten-seater airplane crashed in a slag heap that had once been a grazing pasture for our cows, and some of the older boys went by stealth to investigate . . . returning with sober, stricken faces, refusing to tell us, their sisters, what they had seen except to say, "Never mind! Don't ask!" Fifteen miles away in the western foothills were mysterious encampments, said to be unauthorized settlements of city dwellers who had fled their cities at the time of the "urban collapse" (as it was called), as well as former ranch families, and various wanderers and evicted persons, criminals, the mentally ill, and victims and suspected carriers of contagious diseases . . . all of these considered "outlaw parties" subject to severe treatment by the National Guardsmen, for the region was now under martial law, and only within family compounds maintained by state-registered property owners and heads of families were civil rights, to a degree, still operative. Eagerly, we scanned the Valley for signs of life, passing among us a pair of heavy binoculars, unknown to Father and Mother—like forbidden treasure these binoculars were, though their original owner was forgotten. (Cory believed that this person, a man, had lived with us before Father's time, and had been good to us, and kind. But no one, not even Cory, could remember his name, nor even what he'd looked like.)

Cory's baby was born the very week of the funerals of two of the younger children, who had died, poor things, of a violent dysentery, and of Uncle Darrah, who'd died of shotgun wounds while driving his pickup truck along a familiar road in the Valley; but this coincidence, Mother and Father assured us, was only that—a coincidence, and not an omen. Mother led us one by one into the drafty attic room set aside for Cory and her baby and we stared in amazement at the puppy-sized, florid-faced, screaming, yet so wonderfully alive creature . . . with its large soft-looking head, its wizened angry features, its smooth, poreless skin. How had Cory, one of us, accomplished *this!* Sisters and brothers alike, we were in awe of her, and a little fearful.

Mother's reaction was most surprising. She seemed furious with Cory, saying that the attic room was good enough for Cory's "outlaw child," sometimes she spoke of Cory's "bastard child"—though quick to acknowledge, in all fairness, the poor infant's parentage was no fault of its own. But it was "fit punishment," Mother said, that Cory's breasts ached when she nursed her baby, and that her milk was threaded with pus and blood . . . "fit punishment for shameful sluttish behavior." Yet the family's luck held, for only two days after the birth Kit and Erastus came back from a nocturnal hunting expedition with a dairy cow: a healthy, fat-bellied, placid creature with black-and-white-marbled markings similar to those of our favorite cow, who had died long ago. This sweet-natured cow, named Daisy, provided the family with fresh, delicious, seemingly pure milk, thus saving Cory's bastard-infant's life, as Mother said spitefully—"Well, the way of Providence *is* a honeycomb!"

Those weeks, Mother was obsessed with learning the identity of Cory's baby's father—Cory's "secret lover," as Mother referred to him. Cory, of course, refused to say—even to her sisters. She may have been wounded that the baby's father had failed to come forward to claim his child, or her; poor Cory, once the prettiest of the girls, now disfigured with skin rashes like fish scales over most of her body, and a puffy, bloated appearance, and eyes red from perpetual weeping. Mother herself was frequently ill with a similar flaming rash, a protracted respiratory infection, intestinal upsets, bone-aches, and amnesia; like everyone in the family except, oddly, Father, she was plagued with ticks—the smallest species of deer tick that could burrow secretly into the skin, releasing an analgesic spittle to numb the skin, thus able to do its damage, sucking blood contentedly for weeks until, after weeks, it might drop off with a *ping!* to the floor, black, shiny, now the size of a watermelon seed, swollen with blood. What loathsome things!—Mother developed a true horror of them, for they seemed drawn to her, especially to her white, wild-matted hair.

By imperceptible degrees Mother had shrunk to a height of less than five feet, very unlike the statuesque beauty of old photographs, with that head of white hair and pebble-colored eyes as keen and suspicious as ever, and a voice so brassy and penetrating it had the power to paralyze any of us where we stood . . . even the eldest of her sons, Kit, Hewett, Dale, tall bearded men who carried firearms even inside the compound, were intimidated by Mother and, like Cory, were inclined to submit to her authority. When Mother interrogated Cory, *"Who* is your lover? Why are you so ashamed of him? Did

you find him in the drainage pipe, or in the slag heap?—in the compost?" Cory
bit her lip and said quietly, "Even if I see his face sometimes, Mother, in my
sleep, I can't recall his name. Or who he was, or is. Or claimed to be."

Yet Mother continued, risking Father's displeasure, for she began to
question *all males* with whom she came into contact, not excluding Cory's
own blood-relations—cousins, uncles, even brothers!—even those ravaged
men and boys who made their homes, so to speak, beyond the compound, as
she'd said jeeringly, in the drainage pipe, in the slag heap, in the compost.
(These men and boys were not official residents on our property but were
enlisted by the family in times of crisis and emergency.) But no one confessed—no one acknowledged Cory's baby as his. And one day when Cory
lay upstairs in the attic with a fever, and I was caring for the baby, excitedly
feeding it from a bottle in the kitchen, Mother entered with a look of such
determination I felt a sudden fear for the baby, hugging it to my chest, and
Mother said, "Give me the bastard, girl," and I said weakly, "No Mother, don't
make me," and Mother said, "Are you disobeying me, girl? *Give me the bastard,*"
and I said, backing away, daringly, yet determined too, "No Mother, Cory's
baby belongs to Cory, and to all of us, and it isn't a bastard." Mother advanced
upon me, furious; her pebble-colored eyes now rimmed with white; her fingers—what talons they'd become, long, skinny, clawed!—outstretched. Yet
I saw that in the very midst of her passion she was forgetting what she intended
to do, and that this might save Cory's baby from harm.

(For often in those days when the family had little to eat except worm-
riddled apples from the old orchard, and stunted blackened potatoes, and such
game, or wildlife, that the men and boys could shoot, and such canned goods
as they could acquire, we often, all of us, young as well as old, forgot what
we were doing in the very act of doing it; plucking bloody feathers from a
quail, for instance, and stopping vague and dreamy wondering what on earth
am I doing? here? at the sink? *is* this a sink? what is this limp little body? this
instrument—a knife?—in my hands? and naturally in the midst of speaking
we might forget the words we meant to speak, for instance *water, rainbow, grief,
love, filth, Father, deer-tick, God, milk, sky* . . . and Father who'd become brooding with the onset of age worried constantly that we, his family, might one
day soon lose all sense of ourselves as a family should we forget, in the same
instant, all of us together, the sacred word *family*.)

And indeed, there in the kitchen, reaching for Cory's baby with her
talonlike fingers, Mother was forgetting. And indeed, within the space of a
half minute, she had forgotten. Staring at the defenseless living thing, the quivering, still-hungry creature in my arms, with its soft flat shallow face of utter
innocence, its tiny recessed eyes, its mere holes for nostrils, its small pursed
mouth set like a manta ray's in its shallow face, Mother could not, simply could
not, summon back the word *baby*, or *infant*, nor even the cruel *Cory's bastard,*

always on her lips. And at that moment there was a commotion outside by the compound gate, an outburst of gunfire, familiar enough yet always jarring when unexpected, and Mother hurried out to investigate. And Cory's baby returned to sucking hungrily and contentedly at the bottle's frayed rubber nipple, and all was safe for now.

But Cory, my dear sister, died a few days later.

Lona discovered her in her place of exile in the attic, in her bed, eyes opened wide and pale mouth contorted, the bedclothes soaked in blood . . . and when in horror Lona drew the sheet away she saw that Cory's breasts had been partly hacked away, or maybe devoured?—and her chest cavity exposed; she must have been attacked in the night by rats and was too weak or too terrified to scream for help. Yet her baby was sleeping placidly in its crib beside the bed, miraculously untouched . . . sunk in its characteristic sleep to that profound level at which organic matter seems about to revert to the inorganic, to perfect peace. For some reason the household rats with their glittering amaranthine eyes and stiff hairless tails and unpredictable appetites had spared it!—or had missed it altogether!

Lona snatched the baby up out of its crib and ran downstairs screaming for help; and so fierce was she in possession she would not give up the baby to anyone, saying, dazed, sobbing, yet in a way gloating, "This is my baby. This is Lona's baby now." Until Father, with his penchant for logic, rebuked her: "Girl, it is the family's baby now."

And Fifi too had a baby—beautiful blond Fifi; or, rather, the poor girl writhed and screamed in agony for a day and a night before giving birth to a perfectly formed but tiny baby weighing only two pounds that lived only a half hour. How we wept, how we pitied our sister!—in the weeks that followed nothing would give her solace, even the smallest measure of solace, except our musical evenings, at which she excelled. For if Dale tried to touch her, to comfort her, she shrank from him in repugnance; nor would she allow Father, or any male, to come near. One night she crawled into my bed and hugged me in her icy bone-thin arms. "What I love best," she whispered, "—is the black waves that splash over us, endlessly, at night,—do you know those waves, sister? and do you love them as I do?" And my heart was so swollen with feeling I could not reply, as I wished to, "Oh *yes.*"

Indeed, suddenly the family had taken up music. In the evenings by kerosene lamp. In the predawn hours, roused from our beds by aircraft overhead, or the barking of wild dogs, or the thermal winds. We played such musical instruments as fell into our hands discovered here and there in the house, or by way of strangers at our gate eager to barter anything they owned for food.

Kit took up the violin shyly at first and then with growing confidence and joy for, it seemed, he had musical talent—practicing for hours on the beautiful though scarified antique violin that had once belonged to Grandfather, or Great-grandfather (so we surmised: an old portrait depicted a child of about ten posed with the identical violin tucked under his chin); Jori and Vega took up the piccolo, which they shared; Hewett the drums, Dale the cymbals, Einar the oboe, Fifi the piano . . . and the rest of us sang, sang our hearts out.

We sang after Mother's funeral and we sang that week a hot feculent wind blew across the Valley bearing the odor of decomposing flesh and we sang (though often coughing and choking, from the smoke) when fires raged out of control in the dry woodland areas to the east, an insidious wind then too blowing upon our barricaded compound and handsome house atop a high hill, a wind intent upon seeking us out, it seemed, carrying sparks to our sanctuary, our place of privilege, destroying us in fire as others both human and beast were being destroyed . . . and how else for us to endure such odors, such sights, such sounds, than to take up our instruments and play them as loudly as possible, and sing as loudly as possible, and sing and sing and sing until our throats were raw, how else?

Yet, the following week became a time of joy and feasting, since Daisy the cow was dying in any case and might as well be quickly slaughtered, when Father, surprising us all, brought his new wife home to meet us: New Mother we called her, or Young Mother, or Pretty Mother, and Old Mother, that fierce stooped wild-eyed old woman was soon forgotten, even the mystery of her death soon forgotten (for had she like Cory died of household rats? or had she, like poor Erastus, died of a burst appendix? had she drowned somehow in the cistern, had she died of thirst and malnutrition locked away in the attic, had she died of a respiratory infection, of toothache, of heartbreak, of her own rage, or of age, or of Father's strong fingers closing around her neck . . . or had she not "died" at all but passed quietly into oblivion, as the black waves splashed over her, and Young Mother stepped forward smiling happily to take her place).

Young Mother was so pretty!—plump, and round-faced, her complexion rich and ruddy, her breasts like large balloons filled to bursting with warm liquid, and she gave off a hot intoxicating smell of nutmeg, and tiny flames leapt from her when, in a luxury of sighing, yawning, and stretching, she lifted the heavy mass of red-russet hair that hung between her shoulder blades and fixed upon us her smiling-dark gaze. "Mother!" we cried, even the eldest of us, "— oh Mother!" hoping would she hug us, would she kiss and hug us, fold us in those plump strong arms, cuddle our faces against those breasts, each of us, all of us, weeping, in her arms, those arms, oh Mother, *there*.

Lona's baby was not maturing as it was believed babies should normally mature, nor had it been named since we could not determine whether it was male or female, or somehow both, or neither; and this household problem,

Young Mother addressed herself to at once. No matter Lona's desperate love of the baby, Young Mother was "practicalminded" as she said: for why else had Father brought her to this family but to take charge, to reform it, to give *hope?* She could not comprehend, she said, laughing incredulously, how and why an extra mouth, a useless mouth, perhaps even a dangerous mouth, could be tolerated at such a time of near-famine, in violation of certain government edicts as she understood them. "Drastic remedies in drastic times," Young Mother was fond of saying. Lona said, pleading, "I'll give it my food, Mother—I'll protect it with my life!" And Young Mother simply repeated, smiling so broadly her eyes were narrowed almost to slits, "Drastic remedies in drastic times!"

There were those of us who loved Lona's baby, for it *was* flesh of our flesh, it *was* part of our family; yet there were others, mainly the men and boys, who seemed nervous in its presence, keeping a wary distance when it crawled into a room to nudge its large bald head or pursed mouth against a foot, an ankle, a leg. Though it had not matured in the normal fashion, Lona's baby weighed now about thirty pounds; but it was soft as a slug is soft; or an oyster, with an oyster's general shape—apparently boneless; the hue of unbaked bread dough, and hairless. As its small eyes lacked an iris, being entirely white, it must have been blind; its nose was but a rudimentary pair of nostrils, holes in the center of its face; its fishlike mouth was deceptive in that it seemed to possess its own intelligence, being ideally formed, not for human speech, but for seizing, sucking, and chewing. Though it had at best only a cartilaginous skeleton it did boast two fully formed rows of tiny needle-sharp teeth, which it was not shy of using, particularly when ravenous for food; and it was often ravenous. At such times it groped its way around the house, silent, by instinct, sniffing and quivering, and if by chance it was drawn by the heat of your blood to your bed it would burrow beneath the covers, and nudge, and nuzzle, and begin like a nursing infant to suck virtually any part of the body though preferring of course a female's breasts . . . and if not stopped in time it would start to bite, chew, *eat* . . . in all the brute innocence of appetite. So some of us surmised, though Lona angrily denied it, that the baby's first mother (a sister of ours whose name we had forgotten) had not died of rat bites after all but of having been attacked in the night and partly devoured by her own baby.

(In this, Lona was duplicitous. She took care never to undress in Mother's presence for fear Mother's sharp eye would discover the numerous wounds on her breasts, belly, and thighs.)

As the family had a time-honored custom of debating issues in a democratic manner—for instance should we pay the exorbitant price a cow or a she-goat now commanded on the open market, or should the boys be given permission to acquire one of these beasts however they could, for instance should we try to feed the starving men, women, and children who gathered outside our fence, even if it was food too contaminated for the family's consumption—so naturally the issue of Lona's baby was taken up too and soon threatened to split the family into two warring sides. Mother argued persuasively, almost tearfully, that the baby was "worthless, repulsive, and might one day be dangerous,"—not guessing that it had already proved dangerous; and Lona argued persuasively, and tearfully, that "Lona's baby," as she called it, was a living human being, a member of the family, one of *us*. Mother said hotly, "It is not one of *us,* girl, if by *us* you mean a family that includes *me,*" and Lona said, daringly, "It is one of *us* because it predates any family that includes *you*— 'Mother.' "

So they argued; and others joined in; and emotions ran high. It was strange how some of us changed our minds several times, now swayed by Mother's reasoning, and now by Lona's; now by Father who spoke on behalf of Mother, or by Hewett who spoke on behalf of Lona. Was it weeks, or was it months, that the debate raged?—and subsided, and raged again?—and Mother dared not put her power to the vote for fear that Lona's brothers and sisters would side with Lona out of loyalty if not love for the baby. And Father acknowledged reluctantly that however any of us felt about the baby it *was* our flesh and blood and embodied the Mystery of Life: ". . . its soul bounded by its skull, and its destiny no more problematic than the sinewy tubes that connect its mouth and its anus. Who are we to judge!"

Yet Mother had her way, as slyboots Mother was always to have her way . . . one March morning soliciting the help of several of us, who were sworn to secrecy and delighted to be her handmaidens, in a simple scheme: Lona being asleep in the attic, Mother led the baby out of the house by holding a piece of bread soaked in chicken blood in front of its nostrils, led it crawling across the hard-packed wintry earth, to the old hay barn, and, inside, led it to a dark corner where we helped her lift it and lower it carefully into an aged rain barrel empty except for a wriggling mass of half-grown rats, that squealed in great excitement at being disturbed, and at the smell of the blood-soaked bread which Mother dropped with the baby. We then nailed a cover in place; and, as Mother said, her skin warmly flushed and her breath coming fast, "There, girls—it is entirely out of our hands."

And then one day it was spring. And Kit, grinning, led a she-goat proudly into the kitchen, her bags primed with milk, swollen pink dugs leaking milk! How grateful we all were, those of us who were with child especially, after the privations of so long a winter, or winters, during which time certain words have all but faded from our memories, for instance *she-goat,* and *milk,* and as we realized *rainbow,* for the rainbow too re-appeared, one morning, shimmering and translucent across the Valley, a phenomenon as of the quivering of millions of butterflies' iridescent wings. In the fire-scorched plain there grew a virtual sea of fresh green shoots and in the sky enormous dimpled clouds and that night we gathered around Fifi at the piano to play our instruments and to sing. Father had passed away but Mother had remarried: a husky bronze-skinned horseman whose white teeth flashed in his beard, and whose rowdy pinches meant love and good cheer, not meanness. We were so happy we debated turning the calendar ahead to the New Year. We were so happy we debated abolishing the calendar entirely and declaring this the First Day of Year One, and beginning Time anew.

The Practice of Writing–
The Writing Workshop

It is easy to work when the soul is at play.

—*Emily Dickinson*

Writing workshops have become enormously popular in the United States in the past several decades, for a number of very good reasons. There is no atmosphere quite so intense, so exciting and occasionally dramatic as a writing workshop when discussion is sharp and imaginative, and when the work being critiqued is of a sufficient quality. Like play readings, without which even an experienced playwright can't comprehend the effect of his or her work on a "live" audience, writing workshops allow the apprentice-writer access to readers otherwise faceless, anonymous, unknown. And there is an element of surprise and playfulness in many writing workshops that can be immensely stimulating to all involved.

"Creative" writing simply means original, imaginative writing in contrast to functional, nonfiction writing; in fact, all good writing, even the reportorial and technical, can be "creative." Writers are individuals born with a love for language, for communicating—"telling." The forms of telling are many, but the impulse is a simple one: the desire to bring into the world something that did not previously exist, stamped with the individual's perspective and personal style. Writing workshops are for writers what art classes, acting classes, music lessons are for other kinds of performers: such workshops can't imbue participants with "talent" but they are invaluable for developing and honing what talent already exists. For writing, like life, is not only an art, but a craft.

In the workshop, I define my role as that of an ideal editor, not a "teacher" in the conventional sense of that word. I am not a rejecting editor, not a censorious or severely critical or interfering editor, but one who defines herself primarily as a friend of the text and a friend of the writer—"Exactly in that order," as I tell students. The other writers in the workshop take on, for the duration of the workshop, roles as editors, too: it's our task to work meticulously with the material given us for that session, and to contribute all that we possibly can to improving it. The mythic/playful premise of my workshops is that we are the editorial staff of a first-rate literary magazine; we are all being paid generously high salaries to bring out the very best issue of the magazine we can, given our material, and so we should take our responsibilities seriously. The writer—unlike real writers in real life—is privileged to overhear our commentary. Sometimes we turn to the writer to ask questions, but not often; the most practical procedure is for the writer to sit quietly and listen, and at the end of the discussion speak or ask questions of the "editors."

Sometimes, I ask a writer to read part of his or her work aloud. Hearing the "voice" of the text can be enormously valuable to both writers and readers. And criticism is always constructive. ("Negative" criticism, the kind that wounds and demoralizes not only the object of the criticism but others who witness it, has never seemed to me to be of any value at all.)

As I've indicated above, writing workshops, like formal courses in music instruction, art, dance, and theater, focus upon the work-in-progress of individuals, with accompanying readings that have been selected, like the prose pieces in this anthology, to aid the writer in his or her practice. There is no mystique about the "writing workshop"—no one tries to teach anyone to write, for writing skills are already assumed. (At Princeton University, where I've taught since 1978, admission to workshops is by application only; workshops are no larger than ten students, and meet for approximately two hours once a week. Further instruction may be given in individual conferences, as required.)

Workshops are arranged so that writers have ample time to read one another's work beforehand, take notes on it, and prepare to offer thoughtful criticism; workshops are in fact excellent training for editors-to-be. Each member of the workshop should expect to contribute, and criticism should be of two distinct types, both enormously important for the writer to hear:

impressionistic
• did the reader *like* the story?
• was the story read with genuine interest?
• would the reader wish to read more work by this writer?

editorial
• are there grammatical errors, misspellings, awkward language, metaphors that don't work, repetitions, confusing passages?

- are there parts of the story that retard the movement to no significant purpose?
- is the opening the very best opening, or might the story open more effectively with another scene?
- is the ending the very best ending?
- is it both a surprise and inevitable?
- can the story be trimmed?
- is this its most effective order of scenes, or might it be more dramatically rearranged?
- is the title the very best title?
- are there other, alternate titles the writer considered?
- are there scenes in earlier drafts that have been left out?
- are the characters' names carefully chosen?
- does the story achieve closure?
- does the story read smoothly?

"Optional assignments" are sometimes beneficial in writing workshops, particularly for younger students; so is the keeping of a journal or diary. At the start of the workshop, writers may be asked if they have anything to read of a brief, informal nature: a selection from a journal, a quick character sketch, snatches of overheard dialogue.

Here are some of the "optional assignments" I have given in my workshops:

- Having read Virginia Woolf's "Moments of Being," write of a "moment of being" in your own life in a page or two.

- "An unsolved mystery is a thorn in the heart." This is the opening line of a short prose piece you are going to write, meditating upon an "unsolved mystery" in your own life.

- You are going to write a letter to someone whom you have hurt, betrayed, disappointed in some way. Your letter seeks to explain your behavior, which has been a source of mystery and guilt to you, too. You may want to alter the exact terms of the equation: what "really" happened may be significantly changed, like the identity of the person or persons involved. But you will be writing about an authentic emotional episode.

- You will describe, as minutely as possible, a significant place, conveying, by means of language, the emotion generated by this place in your imagination.

- Overheard dialogue, unedited.
  Overheard dialogue, edited.

- You have been commissioned to "interview" an older relative, asking questions, eliciting answers, and then, in presenting the speaker's voice, removing yourself entirely.

- Your challenge is to present a self-portrait by way of an image. Describe yourself in metaphorical terms yet as accurately as possible.

- You recall an event that, in retrospect, significantly changed your life. Employing the prism of a mature consciousness imposed upon a less mature consciousness, in the mode of James Joyce's "The Sisters," dramatize this event.

- You are to take a prose piece of yours and shift its perspective. If it's first-person, you will recast it from a third-person perspective; if third-person or omniscient, from a first-person perspective.

- A very brief play, two voices in dialogue. One voice stimulates and generates the other voice; they seem actually to be "speaking" of their own volition. (This sketch is sometimes fully realized as the core of a story.)

- A vivid, sharply focused description of a person, at the end of which the person comes alive, speaks, and acts.

- Observed "outer" events, as a reporter might see them.
  The minutely analyzed "inner" reality of these events.

- A brief plot that passes through several characters' consciousnesses, residing in none. "Plot" as "character."

- A follow-up on a "character sketch" after some months or years. How your original assessment was prescient, or mistaken. The phenomenon of "time" in human relations.

- Choose a writer whose style you admire, and write "in style of." *Not* parody.

- A miniature narrative consisting of a single sentence.

- A journal entry transposed into fictional terms. The "I"-observations given to another person, not yourself.

- A brief dramatic monologue in the voice of someone very different from you. Different sex, race, age, sensibility.

- A re-vision of a myth, fairy tale, legend in a contemporary setting.

- A concept-generated story, in which "idea" is predominant. Human agents might be designated as merely initials, incidental factors in an impersonal equation.

Of all human activities, writing seriously, writing intensely, is surely among the most solitary. The concentration required for the creation of original work can be exhausting, though it's hoped the results will be exhilarating, too. In the end, we can depend only upon our own judgment and self-definition, guided by our intuition in writing as in our lives. Yet, in our apprentice years, the advantages of the writing workshop are many: we have a circle of like-minded colleagues, who can understand our ideals and frustrations as no one else can; we have helpful, often astute and enthusiastic critics; we have readers, and friends.

Jonathan Ames (b. 1964)

Born in New Jersey, Ames is now a resident of New York City. His first novel, composed of related short stories, is *I Pass Like Night*, from which "A Portrait of a Father" is taken.

Margaret Atwood (b. 1939)

Born in Canada, and a longtime resident of Toronto, Atwood is an internationally renowned author of numerous novels and story collections, including *Surfacing, The Handmaid's Tale, The Robber Bride,* and *Alias Grace* (novels), and *Dancing Girls, Bluebird's Egg,* and *Wilderness Tips* (stories). Atwood is also a celebrated poet; her early collection, *The Circle Game,* won the Canadian Governor General's Award for Poetry in 1966.

Toni Cade Bambara (1939–1996)

Born in New York City, Bambara was a novelist, short story writer, civil rights activist, and teacher whose primary subject was the African American community. Her major titles are *Gorilla, My Love* and *The Sea Birds Are Still Alive,* both collections of stories, and *The Salt Eaters,* a novel.

Russell Banks (b. 1940)

Born in Newton, Massachusetts, and raised in New Hampshire, Banks now divides his residence between Keene Valley in the Adirondacks and Princeton, New Jersey, where he teaches at the university. He is known for his powerfully rendered works of prose fiction, among them the novels *Continental Drift, Affliction, The Sweet Hereafter,* and *The Rule of the Bone,* from which the excerpt in this anthology is taken.

Donald Barthelme (1931–1989)

Born in Philadelphia, raised in Houston, Texas, and a longtime resident of New York City, the spiritual setting for his numerous fabulist tales and prose pieces, Barthelme is known primarily for the short story collections *Come Back, Dr. Caligari; Unspeakable Practices, Unnatural Acts; City Life;* and *Guilty Pleasures,* and the novels *Snow White* and *The Dead Father.*

Richard Bausch (b. 1952)

Born in Fairfax, Virginia, and a longtime resident of that city, Bausch teaches at George Mason University. His novels include *Violence, The Last Good Time,* and the recent *Good Evening Mr. & Mrs. America,* and *All the Ships at Sea;* his highly acclaimed short stories have been collected in *The Fireman's Wife* and *Ten Stories.*

Ruth Behar (b. 1956)

Born in Havana, Cuba, Behar teaches anthropology at the University of Michigan at Ann Arbor and is the author of *Translated Woman: Crossing the Border with Esperanza's Story* and *The Vulnerable Observer: Anthropology That Breaks Your Heart.* She has edited *Bridges to Cuba* and coedited *Women Writing Culture.*

Madison Smartt Bell (b. 1957)

A resident of Maryland, Bell teaches writing at Goucher College. His titles include the novels *The Year of Silence, Doctor Sleep,* the widely acclaimed *All Souls' Rising,* and most recently *Ten Indians;* his short story collections are *Zero db* (from which "Naked Lady" is taken) and *Barking Man.*

Pinckney Benedict (b. 1964)

Born and raised in Lewisburg, West Virginia, the setting for most of his fiction, Benedict now lives in Holland, Michigan, where he teaches at Hope College. He has published one novel, *Dogs of God,* and two story collections, *Town Smokes* and *The Wrecking Yard.*

Jorge Luis Borges (1899–1986)

A poet, short story writer, and essayist born in Buenos Aires, Borges has long been associated with experimental "fictions" of a highly original, mock-philosophical, and elegantly analytical nature. His major work includes *Ficciones, The Aleph and Other Stories, Dreamtigers, The Book of Imaginary Beings,* and the speculative *Other Inquisitions.*

Tadeusz Borowski (1922–1951)

Borowski was a Polish fiction writer and poet who was incarcerated in the German concentration camps at Auschwitz and Dachau during 1943–45 and who later committed suicide in Warsaw, not yet thirty years old. His collections of prose pieces are *Farewell to Maria* and *A World of Stone,* from which the thematically related stories were selected for an English edition of his work entitled *This Way for the Gas, Ladies and Gentlemen.*

T. Coraghessan Boyle (b. 1948)

Born and raised in Peekskill, New York, now a resident of Montecito, California, Boyle is much acclaimed for his popular, highly original works of fiction, which include the story collections *Descent of Man* and *Greasy Lake* and the novels *East Is East, The Road to Wellville,* and *The Tortilla Curtain.*

Italo Calvino (1923–1985)

Calvino was an Italian journalist, short story writer, and novelist born in Santiago de las Vegas, Cuba, whose most influential titles are his imaginative fantasies *Cosmicomics, Invisible Cities* (from which the stories in this anthology are taken), and *If on a Winter's Night a Traveler.*

Peter Carey (b. 1943)
Born in Australia and now a resident of New York City, Carey is a distinctive stylist known for his idiosyncratic fictions. Among his novels are *Bliss* and *Oscar and Lucinda;* his story collections include *The Fat Man in History* and *War Crimes.*

Angela Carter (1940–1992)
Carter was an English-born experimental writer and fantasist whose highly influential "re-visions" of traditional fairy tales are collected in *The Bloody Chamber.* Other major titles are *Black Venus, American Ghosts, Old World Wonders,* and the posthumously assembled *Burning Your Boats.*

Raymond Carver (1938–1988)
Born in Oregon and raised in Yakima, Washington, Carver is widely acclaimed as one of the most accomplished of postwar American short story writers and is often described as an heir of Hemingway and Sherwood Anderson. Among his major titles are *Will You Please Be Quiet, Please?, What We Talk About When We Talk About Love, Cathedral,* and *Where I'm Calling From,* published the year he died. He is less known but much admired as a poet as well—see the collection *Ultramarine* and the posthumously published *A New Walk to the River.*

John Cheever (1912–1981)
Born in Quincy, Massachusetts, Cheever was an inspired fantasist-chronicler of postwar middle-class Caucasian New England mores. His novels include *The Wapshot Chronicle, Bullet Park,* and *Falconer,* but he is most admired for his distinctive short stories, which are collected in *The Enormous Radio, The Housebreaker of Shady Hill, The World of Apples,* and *The Stories of John Cheever.*

Anton Chekhov (1860–1904)
Chekhov was a renowned Russian dramatist and fiction writer whose plays (among them *Uncle Vanya, The Three Sisters,* and *The Cherry Orchard*) helped redefine modern theater, as his numerous short stories, collected in thirteen volumes, helped redefine modern fiction.

Carlos Cumpián (b. 1900)
A veteran Chicano writer, Cumpián is publisher of MARCH/Abrazo Poetry Press (based in Chicago) and author of the poetry collections *Coyote Sun* and *Latino Rainbow.*

Jon Davis (b. 1952)
Currently residing in New Mexico, Davis is the author of the poetry collection *Dangerous Amusements.*

Lydia Davis (b. 1947)
Born in Northampton, Massachusetts, Davis currently lives in upstate New York. A translator and short story writer of inspired experimental works that are usually minimalist in execution, Davis has published a novel, *The End of the Story,* and two collections of short fiction, *Story and Other Stories* and *Break It Down,* from which "Cockroaches in Autumn" is taken.

James Dickey (1923–1997)

Born in Atlanta, Georgia, and a longtime resident of Columbia, South Carolina, Dickey is known for both his controversial novels (including *Deliverance,* which he adapted as a screenplay) and his exuberant lyric-narrative poetry. His major volumes are *Into the Stone, Drowning with Others, Helmets, Buckdancer's Choice, The Zodiac,* and *The Strength of Fields.* At the time of his death, he was Poet-in-Residence at the University of South Carolina.

Annie Dillard (b. 1945)

Born in Pennsylvania and educated at Hollins College, Dillard is a lyric-philosophical stylist known for both her prose and her poetry. Among her acclaimed titles are *Pilgrim at Tinker Creek, An American Childhood* (a personal memoir), *Tickets for a Prayer Wheel* (poetry), and *The Living* (a novel).

E. L. Doctorow (b. 1931)

Born in New York City, the setting for a number of his vividly realized novels, Doctorow is a highly original writer known for his exploration of popular American genres. Among his major titles are *The Book of Daniel, Ragtime, Loon Lake, World's Fair,* and *Billy Bathgate;* his stories are collected in *Lives of the Poets.*

Stuart Dybek (b. 1942)

Born and raised in Chicago, the setting of his most characteristic work, Dybek is the author of two highly regarded story collections, *Childhood and Other Neighborhoods* and *The Coast of Chicago.* He is now a resident of Kalamazoo, Michigan, where he teaches at Western Michigan University.

Harlan Ellison (b. 1934)

A longtime resident of Los Angeles, Ellison is prolific and renowned in the field of science and horror fiction, in which he has published hundreds of short stories. Among his collections are *Approaching Oblivion, Deathbird Stories, Angry Candy,* and *The Essential Ellison.*

William Faulkner (1897–1962)

Faulkner was a novelist and short story writer best known for his work set in the mythical Yoknapatawpha County, a fictional analogue to the region surrounding his birthplace of Oxford, Mississippi. Among Faulkner's major titles are *The Sound and the Fury; As I Lay Dying; Light in August; Absalom, Absalom!;* and *The Hamlet.* Faulkner has been equally honored for his numerous short stories, which have been reprinted in his *Collected Stories.* He won the Nobel Prize for Literature in 1949.

M. F. K. Fisher (1908–1992)

Born in Michigan, raised in California, and a longtime resident of France, Fisher originated an entirely new genre—the "food essay." She has been widely celebrated for her distinctive style in such books as *The Gastronomical Me, Among Friends,* and *Sister Age.*

Richard Ford (b. 1944)

Ford is a novelist and short story writer born in Jackson, Mississippi. His single volume of short stories is the much-acclaimed *Rock Springs;* his novels include *The Sportswriter* and its sequel *Independence Day.* Ford currently divides his time among New Orleans, Louisiana, and rural Montana.

Ian Frazier (b. 1951)
Born in Cleveland, Ohio, and now a resident of Brooklyn, New York, Frazier is much admired for his satiric-comic prose pieces, which are included in such volumes as *Nobody Better, Better Than Nobody,* and *Dating Your Mom.*

Robert Frost (1874–1963)
Though born in San Francisco, Frost has been long associated with rural New England, which provided the setting and inspiration for most of his poetry. A pioneer in the use of American speech and "ordinary" life elevated to the level of tragic art, Frost authored many collections of poems, including *North of Boston, West-Running Brook,* and *In the Clearing;* the standard edition of his work is *The Poetry of Robert Frost.*

Abby Frucht (b. 1957)
Currently a resident of Wisconsin, Frucht is the author of the novels *Snap, Licorice, Are You Mine?* and *Life Before Death.* Her short stories have been collected in *Fruit of the Month,* which won the Iowa Short Fiction Award.

Erika Funkhouser (b. 1949)
Among her titles are *Natural Affinities* and *Sure Shot,* from which the selection in this anthology is taken.

Mikal Gilmore (b. 1951)
Born in Portland, Oregon, and now a resident of Los Angeles, Mikal Gilmore is the younger brother of Gary Gilmore, a convicted murderer whose role in his own execution by firing squad in Utah in 1971 drew international notoriety. Gilmore is now a pop culture critic for *Rolling Stone* and other magazines and author of the family memoir *Shot in the Heart,* from which "The Dream" is taken.

Nadine Gordimer (b. 1923)
This South African novelist, essayist, and short story writer won the Nobel Prize for Literature in 1991. Gordimer's themes are nearly always socially determined; she was a long and impassioned foe of South African apartheid. Her major titles are the novels *The Conservationist, Burger's Daughter,* and *July's People,* and the story collections *Not for Publication* and *A Soldier's Embrace.*

Daniel Halpern (b. 1945)
Halpern is a poet, editor, and publisher (of the distinguished literary magazine *Antaeus* and the Ecco Press) whose work has been collected into several volumes of poetry, including *Seasonal Rights, Tango,* and *Foreign Neon.* His *Selected Poems* appeared in 1994.

Joy Harjo (b. 1951)
A member of the Muscogee tribe of Oklahoma, and now a resident of New Mexico, Harjo is the author of *In Mad Love and War, She Had Some Horses,* and, her most recent collection, *The Woman Who Fell from the Sky.*

Jana Harris (b. 1947)
Born in San Francisco, and a longtime resident of the foothills of the Cascade Mountains near Seattle, Washington, Harris is the author of several books of poetry, including *The*

Sourlands and *Oh How Can I Keep On Singing: Voices of Pioneer Women,* from which the poems in this anthology are taken; her novel is *Alaska.*

Nathaniel Hawthorne (1804–1864)
Hawthorne was born in Salem, Massachusetts, the descendant of Puritans and the great-grandson of a judge involved in the notorious Salem witch trials. Long revered for his novels *The Scarlet Letter* and *The House of the Seven Gables* and for his numerous short stories, Hawthorne presents himself in a wholly different idiom in his relatively unknown, posthumously published journals, to which the title *American Notebooks* has been given.

Ernest Hemingway (1899–1961)
Hemingway was born in Oak Park, Illinois, but was a longtime American expatriate. The author of numerous highly acclaimed novels such as *The Sun Also Rises, A Farewell to Arms,* and *For Whom the Bell Tolls,* Hemingway was perhaps even more distinguished as a writer of short stories. His classics include "The Snows of Kilimanjaro," "The Short Happy Life of Francis Macomber," and "Big Two-Hearted River," among others from his first collection *In Our Time* (1925). He was awarded the Nobel Prize for Literature in 1954.

William Heyen (b. 1940)
Born in Long Island, New York, and a longtime resident of Brockport, New York, Heyen is primarily known as a poet of Whitmanesque dimensions and lyricism in such books as *Depth of Field, Noise in the Trees, The Swastika Poems, The Chestnut Rain, The Host,* and, most recent, *Crazy Horse in Stillness.*

Homer (9th or 8th century B.C.?)
Virtually nothing is known about Homer, the presumed author of the two great epic poems of ancient Greece, *The Iliad* and *The Odyssey,* though he is among the most widely read and profoundly influential of all world poets.

Zora Neale Hurston (1891–1960)
Hurston was born in Eatonville, Florida—the first incorporated, self-governing, all-black town in the United States. Hurston was an anthropologist, novelist, short story writer, and essayist whose major titles are the novels *Jonah's Gourd Vine* and *Their Eyes Were Watching God,* the folklore collections *Mules and Men* and *Talk My Horse,* and the autobiography *Dust Tracks on the Road.* Among her posthumous publications are *I Love Myself When I Am Laughing . . . And Then Again When I Am Looking Mean* and *Impressive: A Zora Neale Hurston Reader.*

Gish Jen (b. 1955)
Born in New York City and now living in Cambridge, Massachusetts, Jen is an astute, seriocomic writer whose novels are *Typical American* and *Mona in the Promised Land.*

Edward P. Jones (b. 1950)
Born and raised in Washington, D.C., Jones is a member of the faculty at George Mason University and a visiting instructor at Princeton University. *Lost in the City,* an award-winning collection of stories, from which "Young Lions" is taken, is his first book.

Thom Jones (b. 1945)
A former marine and amateur boxer, Jones is the author of the much-praised collections *The Pugilist at Rest* and *Cold Snap*. He teaches at the University of Iowa.

James Joyce (1882–1941)
Born in Dublin, and long an exile in Europe, Joyce was one of the great revolutionaries of twentieth-century modernist prose. Like Chekhov, Joyce has been immensely influential as a writer of short fiction. His titles are *Dubliners* (a collection of related stories all set in Dublin) and the novels *A Portrait of the Artist as a Young Man, Ulysses,* and *Finnegans Wake.*

Franz Kafka (1832–1924)
Kafka was born in Prague, Czechoslovakia, and is considered one of the most influential European writers of the twentieth century. Distinguished by his mordant, surreal fictions, Kafka died before most of his work was published. Among his major titles are the novels *The Trial* and *The Castle* and the short stories "The Metamorphosis," "In the Penal Colony," and "A Hunger Artist."

Jack Kerouac (1922–1969)
Born in Lowell, Massachusetts, and for much of his life an itinerant traveler, Kerouac was the most celebrated (and notorious) writer of the American "Beat Generation." His major titles are *On the Road, The Dharma Bums, Big Sur,* and *Desolation Angels.*

Stephen King (b. 1947)
Born and raised in Maine, where he has long been a resident, King is the author under his own name and under the pseudonym Richard Bachman of many short stories and novels. His major titles include *Carrie, The Shining, The Stand, Pet Sematary, The Green Mile, Desperation,* and *The Regulators*. His short fiction has been collected in *Night Shift, Different Seasons, Skeleton Crew,* and *Nightmares & Dreamscapes.*

Maxine Hong Kingston (b. 1940)
Kingston was born in Stockton, California, and is a longtime resident of Berkeley. A memoirist, novelist, and fantasist, Kingston has authored such highly influential works as *The Woman Warrior: Memoirs of a Girlhood Among Ghosts, China Men,* and the novel *Tripmaster Monkey: His Fake Book.*

Jamaica Kincaid (b. 1949)
Kincaid was born Elaine Potter Richardson in St. John's, Antigua, in the British West Indies, and is now a resident of Bennington, Vermont. She is known for her distinctive prose voice in such works of fiction as *At the Bottom of the River* (from which "My Mother" is taken), *Annie John, Lucy,* and *The Autobiography of My Mother.*

Phyllis Koestenbaum (b. 1930)
Born in Brooklyn, New York, Koestenbaum is a poet, teacher, and scholar associated with the Institute for Research on Women and Gender at Stanford University. Among her books of poetry are *14 Criminal Sonnets.*

Maxine Kumin (b. 1925)

Kumin was born in Philadelphia, but has long been associated with rural northern New Hampshire, the setting for many of her poems and short stories. Her highly regarded poetry collections include *Up Country: Poems of New England, The Retrieval System,* and *The Long Approach;* her most recent book is *Women, Animals, and Vegetables,* a collection of stories and essays.

D. H. Lawrence (1885–1930)

Born in Nottinghamshire, England, David Herbert Lawrence was a novelist, short story writer, poet, critic, and world traveler whose most characteristic work is set in England and is rendered in a vivid, dramatic style. Among his major titles are the novels *Sons and Lovers, The Rainbow, Women in Love,* and *Lady Chatterley's Lover. The Complete Short Stories of D. H. Lawrence* are collected in three volumes.

David Leavitt (b. 1961)

Born in Pittsburgh, Pennsylvania, raised in Palo Alto, California, and now a resident of Florence, Italy, Leavitt is regarded as one of the most talented writers of his generation. He is the author of short fiction collected in *Family Dancing* and *A Place I've Never Been* and of the novels *Equal Affections* and *While England Sleeps.*

Li-Young Lee (b. 1957)

Born in Jakarta, Indonesia, to Chinese parents, Lee emigrated to the United States as a young child. He is now a resident of Chicago. His poetry collections are *Rose* and *The City in Which I Love You,* and his first book of prose is the personal memoir *The Winged Seed: A Remembrance.*

Alan Lightman (b. 1948)

Lightman, a resident of Cambridge, Massachusetts, teaches physics and writing at MIT. His first book of fiction is *Einstein's Dreams,* from which the selections in this text have been taken.

H. P. Lovecraft (1890–1937)

Born in Providence, Rhode Island, and obsessed with a mythapoetic "ancient" New England landscape in which he set most of his fantastic tales, Lovecraft is generally regarded as the twentieth-century heir of Edgar Allan Poe. Among his most famous titles are "The Dunwich Horror," "At the Mountains of Madness," "The Shadow Over Innsmouth," and "The Rats in the Walls," included in this anthology.

Emily Mann (b. 1952)

Born in Northampton, Massachusetts, raised in Chicago, and now a resident of Princeton, New Jersey, where she is artistic director of the McCarter Theatre, Mann writes "documentary" plays—intensely realized poetic dramas—including *Still Life, Execution of Justice, Greensboro: A Requiem,* and *Having Our Say.*

Katherine Mansfield (1888–1923)

New Zealand-born, Mansfield was a well-known London literary figure by her early twenties. Exclusively a short story writer in the Chekhovian vein, she is best known for *Bliss and Other Stories* and *The Garden Party and Other Stories,* both published in the early 1920s.

Jane Martin (b. 19??)
"Jane Martin" is a pseudonym for a playwright believed to be a resident of Kentucky who for many years has been associated with the Actors Theatre of Louisville. Martin's best-known play is *Talking With,* from which the monologue "Twirler" is taken.

Carson McCullers (1917–1967)
Born in Columbus, Georgia, McCullers was a poetic chronicler of the South. Her first novel, *The Heart Is a Lonely Hunter,* brought her immediate success; other acclaimed titles are *The Member of the Wedding, Reflections in a Golden Eye,* and *The Ballad of the Sad Cafe,* a novella that was later dramatized by Edward Albee.

Lorrie Moore (b. 1957)
Moore currently resides in Madison, Wisconsin. Her idiosyncratic, wittily melancholic short stories have been collected in *Self-Help* and *Like Life,* and she has published two novels, *Anagrams* and *Who Will Run the Frog Hospital?*

Alberto Moravia (1907–1990)
Moravia was a Roman-born writer acclaimed for his portrayal of postwar Italian society. A virtuoso composer of the short story, Moravia was a bestselling novelist and a journalist as well. His novels include *Time of Indifference, The Woman of Rome, The Conformist* (which was made into a prizewinning film), and *Two Women;* his story collections include *Roman Tales* and *The Voice of the Sea.*

Jewel Mogan (b. 1936)
Born in Plaquemine, Louisiana, the setting for many of her stories, Mogan now lives in Lubbock, Texas. Her volume of stories is the prizewinning *Beyond Telling.*

Bharati Mukherjee (b. 1940)
Born in Calcutta, India, Mukherjee emigrated to the United States in 1961. She has lived in Canada and now resides in Berkeley, California, where she teaches at the University of California. Stimulated to write by the "exuberance of imagination," Mukherjee is the author of, among other titles, the highly regarded story collections *Darkness* and *The Middleman* and the novels *Wife* and *Jasmine.*

Joyce Carol Oates (b. 1938)
Born in Lockport, New York, Oates is a longtime resident of Princeton, New Jersey, where she teaches at Princeton University. She is the author of numerous books, including the novels *them, What I Lived For, Zombie,* and *We Were the Mulvaneys,* and the short story collections *Where Are You Going, Where Have You Been?, Heat,* and *Will You Always Love Me?*

Flannery O'Connor (1925–1964)
Born in Savannah, Georgia, and a longtime resident of the country town of Milledgeville, Georgia, which provided the basis for the setting of much of her mordant, blackly comic fiction, O'Connor has been widely praised as an original stylist with a vision both satiric and religious. Her total oeuvre consists of the short novels *Wise Blood* and *The Violent Bear*

It Away, prose pieces *Mystery and Manners,* and the posthumously published *Collected Stories* (1971).

Alicia Ostriker (b. 1937)

Born in New York City and a longtime resident of Princeton, New Jersey, Ostriker is a professor of English and creative writing at Rutgers University. She is the author of a number of poetry collections, including *The Imaginary Lover* and *The Crack in Everything,* and such revisionist critical studies as *The Nakedness of the Fathers,* from which "The Cave" is taken.

Ovid (43 B.C.–17 C.E.)

Ovid was a Roman poet most honored for his *The Art of Love* and *The Metamorphoses.* Technically brilliant and imaginatively adventuresome, Ovid has been immensely influential in the West throughout the centuries. He died in exile at Tomis, a port on the extreme edge of the Roman Empire, banished by the emperor Augustus for obscure reasons.

Ron Padgett (b. 1942)

Padgett was born in Tulsa, Oklahoma, and is now a resident of New York City. Among his titles are *The Big Something* and *Blood Work: Selected Prose.*

Grace Paley (b. 1922)

Paley was born and still lives in New York City, the setting for virtually all of her stories. She is known for her seriocomic conversational style and the seeming effortlessness of her narration. Her major titles are *The Little Disturbances of Man, Enormous Changes at the Last Minute,* and *Later the Same Day.*

Robert Phillips (b. 1938)

Born in Delaware, for many years a resident of New York State, and now a resident of Houston, Texas, Phillips is the author of several works of poetry, including *Personal Accounts, Running on Empty,* and *Breakdown Lane.*

C. E. Poverman (b. 1944)

Born in New Haven, Connecticut, much-traveled in his youth, and now residing in Tucson, Arizona, where he teaches in the writing program at the University of Arizona, Poverman is known primarily for *Susan, Solomon's Daughter, My Father in Dreams,* and *On the Edge,* novels; and *Skin,* a story collection.

Jean Rhys (1894?–1979)

Born and raised in Dominica in the West Indies and a longtime British resident, Rhys chronicled a particular sort of lyric female despair in such striking novels as *Good Morning, Midnight* and *Wide Sargasso Sea.* The relatively few short stories that she wrote were collected in *The Left Bank, Tigers Are Better-Looking,* and *Sleep It Off, Lady.*

Bruno Schulz (1892–1942)

A high-school teacher in Drogobych, a small town in southern Poland, Schulz was a writer of subtle distortions, as imaginative as Kafka though his work is less imbued with nightmare. His fiction is composed entirely of short stories. *Cinnamon Shops* (retitled *The Street of Crocodiles* in its American edition) appeared in 1934; *Sanatorium Under the Sign of the Hourglass,* from which "Father's Last Escape" is taken, was published in 1937.

Anne Sexton (1928–1974)

Born in Newton, Massachusetts, and a longtime resident of New England, Sexton was acclaimed and in some quarters denounced for her boldly confessional poetry. She is the author of, among other titles, *To Bedlam and Part Way Back, All My Pretty Ones, Transformations* (from which "Snow White and the Seven Dwarfs" is taken), and the posthumous *The Awful Rowing Toward God.* Her work has been collected in *The Complete Poems* and her letters in *Anne Sexton: A Portrait in Letters.*

Gary Soto (b. 1952)

Soto was born in south Fresno, California—the meticulously observed setting of many of his poems of barrio life. He now teaches at the University of California, Berkeley, and is one of the most widely read and admired of Chicano poets. Among Soto's numerous titles are *The Elements of San Joaquin, Living Up the Street, Who Will Know Us?, Pieces of the Heart,* and *New and Selected Poems.*

Elizabeth Tallent (b. 1954)

Born in Washington, D.C., and now a resident of New Mexico, Tallent is known primarily for her elegantly written short stories, collected in *In Constant Flight* and *Time with Children.* She is also the author of the novel *Museum Pieces.*

James Tate (b. 1943)

Born and raised in Kansas City, Missouri, Tate is the author of a number of poetry collections, including *Distance from Loved Ones.* His *Selected Poems* won the 1991 Pulitzer Prize for Poetry and the Poetry Society of America's William Carlos Williams Award.

Robert Taylor, Jr. (b. 1941)

Taylor was born in Oklahoma and now lives in Lewisburg, Pennsylvania, where he teaches at Bucknell University. Among his published books are *Lost Sister* and *Lady of Spain.*

Dylan Thomas (1914–1953)

The work of this widely celebrated Welsh poet and prose writer is characterized by stylistic exuberance, technical proficiency, and occasional obscurity. The quintessential twentieth-century romantic poet, Thomas was doomed to excess; his drinking and overspending were legendary. Among his finest works are the poetry collections *Death and Entrances* and *In Country Sleep;* the prose titles *The Map of Love, A Prospect of the Sea,* and *Portrait of the Artist as a Young Dog;* and the verse play *Under Milk Wood.*

Henry David Thoreau (1817–1862)

Born in Concord, Massachusetts, Thoreau was a poet, essayist, and naturalist best known for his sojourn at Walden Pond, during which he lived, in practical terms, the esoteric tenets of Transcendentalism. His great works are *Walden* and the essay "Civil Disobedience," yet the massive *Journal,* unpublished during his lifetime, contains passages of surpassing beauty and perception.

Chase Twichell (b. 1950)

Born in New England, Twichell divides her time between Keene Valley in the Adirondacks and Princeton, New Jersey. She is the author of, among other poetry titles, *The Odds, Perdido,* and *The Ghost of Eden.*

John Updike (b. 1932)

Updike was born in Shillington, Pennsylvania, in a rural area in which his most power-fully rendered fiction is set. Well known as a novelist (*Couples, In the Beauty of the Lilies,* and the cycle of novels about "Rabbit" Angstrom), and equally skilled as a writer of short stories *(Pigeon Feathers, Museums and Women, Problems,* and most recently *The Afterlife),* he is one of the virtuoso stylists of our time.

Helena María Viramontes (b. 1954)

Born in East Los Angeles, now living and teaching in Irvine, California, Viramontes is the author of the prizewinning *The Moths and Other Stories* and coeditor of *Chicana Creativity and Criticism: Charting New Frontiers in American Literature.*

Tom Wayman (b. 1945)

Wayman was born in Ontario, Canada, but has spent most of his adult life in British Columbia. One of Canada's most admired poets, his major titles are *Money and Rain: Tom Wayman Live!, The Face of Jack Munro, Introducing Tom Wayman,* and *I'll Be Right Back: Poems 1980–1996.*

John Edgar Wideman (b. 1941)

Born in Pittsburgh, Pennsylvania, the "Homewood" setting for most of his stories, and now living in Amherst, Massachusetts, Wideman is an experimental stylist concerned with the moral and spiritual condition of the African American community. His major titles include *Sent For You Yesterday, Reuben, Philadelphia Fire, The Cattle Killing,* and *Damballah* (from which the story in this anthology is taken). His prizewinning memoirs are *Brothers and Keepers* and *Fatheralong.*

C. K. Williams (b. 1936)

Williams was born in Newark, New Jersey, and is now a resident of Princeton, New Jersey (where he teaches at Princeton University), and Paris, France. He is a poet, translator, and essayist among whose outstanding volumes of poetry are *Tar, A Dream of Mind,* and *The Vigil.* A collection of his *Selected Poems* was published in 1994.

William Carlos Williams (1883–1963)

Born in Rutherford, New Jersey, Williams was a practicing physician as well as an iconoclastic writer during most of his long life. Among his many monumental works is the poetry collection *Spring and All* and the poem-cycle *Paterson* as well as a number of highly distinctive short stories narrated in a vernacular voice. His stories are gathered in *The Collected Stories of William Carlos Williams* (formerly entitled *The Farmer's Daughters*).

August Wilson (b. 1945)

Wilson was born in Pittsburgh, the setting for much of his work. One of the most celebrated of contemporary American playwrights, Wilson is the author of a cycle of plays that chronicle black American life through the decades of the twentieth century. He won the Pulitzer Prize for two of the plays from that series: *Fences* (set in the 1950s) and *The Piano Lesson* (set in the 1930s). His most recent installment is *Seven Guitars.*

Tobias Wolff (b. 1945)

Born in Birmingham, Alabama, raised in Washington State, and now a resident of Palo Alto, California, where he teaches in the writing program at Stanford University, Wolff is much honored for his sharply realized, dramatic short stories, which are collected in such volumes as *In the Garden of the North American Martyrs, Back in the World,* and *The Night in Question.* His memoirs are *This Boy's Life* and *Pharoah's Army.*

Virginia Woolf (1882–1941)

Born in London, Woolf was associated with the literary circle known popularly as Bloomsbury. A highly original stylist of the inner life in her fiction (*Mrs. Dalloway, To the Lighthouse, The Waves,* and *Between the Acts,* among other novels), she was vivid, direct, and frequently searing in her letters and diaries, all of which have been published to much critical acclaim.

James Wright (1927–1980)

Wright, born in Martins Ferry, Ohio, was a Pulitzer Prize–winning poet and translator whose most influential work includes the poetry collections *Saint Judas, The Branch Will Not Break, Shall We Gather at the River, To a Blossoming Pear Tree,* and the posthumously published *The Shape of Light.* His *Above the River: The Complete Poems* was published in 1990.

Richard Wright (1908–1960)

Born in extreme poverty in Mississippi, Wright lived most of his adult life in exile from his native South. Wright was one of the most gifted and astute of black cultural critics, as well as a brilliant novelist *(Native Son)* and memorist. His story collection *Eight Men* appeared posthumously in 1961.